The Grove Press Reader, 1951–2001

The Grove Press Reader,
1951–2001

Edited and with an Introduction

by S. E. Gontarski

Grove Press
New York

Published simultaneously in Canada
Printed in the United States of America

FIRST EDITION

Editor's note: The dates of publication refer to the date of publication by Grove Press, and not necessarily
to the date of original publication. A list of dates of original publication appears on page 419.

Library of Congress Cataloging-in-Publication Data
The Grove Press reader. 1951-2001/edited by S. E. Gontarski

   p.   cm.

  ISBN 0-8021-3780-6

  1. Literature—Collections.   I. Gontarski, S. E.   II. Grove Press.

PN6014 .G75 2001

808.8'004–dc21   00-049051

Design by Laura Hough

Grove Press
841 Broadway
New York, NY 10003

01 02 03 04   10 9 8 7 6 5 4 3 2 1

FOR BARNEY,

The spirit of Grove

Contents

꽃

The *1970s and 1980s*

The *1990s*

S. E. GONTARSKI

༺༻

Introduction:
The Life and Times of Grove Press

Q: Do you have a publishing philosophy—does Grove Press have a specific purpose other than to publish quality work?

A: There's a purpose, but the only way you could discern the purpose is by looking at the books we publish.
          —Barney Rosset to interviewer John Oakes (1981)

At the Knickerbocker Grill, directly across from the site of the original Cedar Bar on the corner of 9th Street and University Place, Barney Rosset, still alert and energetic at seventy-eight, sips a second lunchtime martini and waves a free arm, saying, "It all happened within five blocks of here." The peripatetic Rosset began publishing in 1951 in his brownstone apartment at 59 West 9th Street, then moved to a succession of Greenwich Village locations.[1] The "it" of Rosset's comment includes not only Grove Press, the failing company he bought in 1951 for $3,000 and built into the era's most explosive and influential publishing house, but more broadly much of that cultural, political, and sexual upheaval we loosely call "the sixties."

Rosset and Grove sat at the eye of that destabilizing storm. In fact, they generated much of its energy and turbulence as this small, unknown reprint house developed into, for nearly three decades, the most aggressive, innovative, audacious, reckless, and finally self-destructive publishing concern in the United States. Grove would enjoy its most dramatic national impact between 1959, when Rosset published the most infamous literary work of his day, D. H. Lawrence's *Lady Chatterley's Lover,* in its first unexpurgated, commercial edition, to the end of the 1970s, when the romantic pursuit of personal liberty waned

---

1. From 59 West 9th Street Grove moved to 795 Broadway; 64 University Place; 80 University Place; 52 East 11th Street (where the Evergreen Theater and the Black Circle Bar were located); 214 Mercer Street; East 11th Street once again; and finally to the near-fortress at 196 West Houston Street.

and America began a process of sexual and political resublimation. Grove could still be provocative well into the 1980s, however, even as material wealth grew to become the measure of worth and value. In the second act of the Grove drama, Rosset would have no role, and Grove would struggle for direction and definition through the late '80s until it merged with Atlantic Monthly Press in 1993. For all his enthusiasm, audacity, vision, and moral courage, Rosset could never quite develop a sustainable long-term business plan for the press, could neither foresee nor adequately respond to the postsixties political realignments, could not, in fact, guide the press beyond its adolescent phase. By the mid-1980s the debts of a floundering Grove were such that a sale or merger was inevitable if the press was to remain an independent publisher of high-quality manuscripts.

For the previous three decades, however, readers had sought out and bought books because they were Grove Press books, and Grove books were, from 1951 to 1986, Rosset books, the publications reflecting his personality, tastes, impulses, and dogged will. From the first, publishing was for Rosset less an economic enterprise than a crusade. As early as March 30, 1953, only a year after he gained full control of Grove, *Newsweek* featured the publisher in its industry profile, "Advance-Garde Advance," and reported Rosset's publishing philosophy: "He has no intention of making each [book] pay its own way." That spirit would guide Grove through the next three decades. Nat Sobel, for instance, who came to Grove in 1960 as assistant sales manager, recalls telling Rosset, "You know, I can't sell poetry. How come we're doing this? I can't sell it. And Barney said, 'I don't expect you to sell it.' 'Why are we doing it then?' I asked. And he said, 'I've taken a lot out of publishing, and this is my way of putting something back in.'" That was an unconventional way to run a commercial publishing venture, but Grove's signature was its unconventionality, from publishing Roger Casement's *Black Diaries*[2] and Lawrence's *Lady Chatterley* in 1959, to Henry Miller's *Tropic of Cancer* in 1961 and William Burroughs's *Naked Lunch* in 1962, to the secret sabotage manual the CIA distributed in Nicaragua under the title *The Freedom Fighter's*

2. *The Black Diaries* have been the source of much controversy ever since Peter Singleton-Gates brought them to French publisher Maurice Girodias, who edited the papers with Singleton-Gates and published them in an edition of 1,500 copies under his Olympia Press imprint in Paris in 1959. The authenticity of these diaries has been the source of considerable speculation, most recently in the "Home News" section of *The New York Times* (March 24, 1994), where Alan Hamilton writes, "Historians have argued for years over the authenticity of parts of the diaries, which appear to show that one of the great heroes of Irish nationalism, hanged in Pentonville as a traitor in 1916, was a promiscuous homosexual" (7).

Manual, complete with instructions for building a "bomba incendiaria ('coctel Molotof')," as late as 1985. These were books about which Rosset was passionate, often as much for their political as for their literary impact. Rosset understood early on that sex was a political issue, and that censorship, in any of its guises, was simply a means of social and political control, and so he put all his energy and resources into combating it. Gilbert Sorrentino, a Grove editor from 1965 to 1970, attributes much of Grove's unprecedented success to Rosset's character. "Grove flourished," he said, "because it considered the tastes and prejudices and opinions of—*not* some amorphous audience whose desires had to be satisfied—[but] its editors. And above all Barney's tastes and opinions. Barney even liked the porno stuff; for instance, *Harriet Marwood, Governess* was a book Barney selected to be published because *he* admired it. This was a very unusual way to run a publishing house . . . that which appealed to Barney was published by Grove." In the mid-'60s, for example, Rosset, quixotically, published a Russian-language edition of *Tropic of Cancer* and thought for a time of having it smuggled into the Soviet Union. He was convinced that Miller could liberate a sexually repressed Soviet Union and thereby promote political reform.[3]

The entire editorial machinery of Grove would be halted mid-project on occasion and redirected to Rosset's current passion—whatever it happened to be. In 1966 he grew preoccupied with the massive *My Secret Life,* and he wanted to publish it ahead of any possible competitor since it was, by virtue of its subject matter, not subject to copyright. He hoped to build on the success of the equally massive *My Life and Loves* by Frank Harris, the five volumes of which Grove published in 1963. In Grove's early years the source of much of its most provocative material was Maurice Girodias of the Olympia Press in Paris. Girodias had brought the Casement *Diaries, My Life and Loves,* and *The Story of O* to Rosset's attention. He also had close ties with Henry Miller, and he was instrumental in Rosset's signing a reluctant Miller to an American contract for the *Tropics.* With *My Secret Life* Rosset had a provocative book of his own, a book which, like *My Life and Loves,* he considered the equivalent of *Lady Chatterley's Lover,* and so he wanted to rush it into print. "The job was copyedited in about a week," notes Sorrentino, "galleys took about another week to be delivered, proofs were ready in about another week, and I think we had the finished books less than a month later. It was really a crash job. We did some others as fast, but none in which the social mores of the time, leavened by the desire for profit, came into direct

3. As he was on other issues, Rosset seemed to have been some thirty years ahead of history on this one.

conflict with the house's [other] projects." The Grove edition appeared in a complete, two-volume boxed set of 2,359 pages, with an introduction by G. Legman, and it was soon followed by an "Abridged but Unexpurgated" Evergreen Black Cat paperback that carried a *Book Week* blurb: "The anonymous autobiography of a wealthy Victorian who lived for sex alone." For Rosset, the notorious book was less a credible autobiography than a sexography, a specimen of mannered Victorian erotica, with each episode escalating in candor and overtness to play on the reader's desire.

Amid the genteel world of New York publishing in the 1950s and 1960s, Rosset was the rogue who personalized publishing, made it an extension of his will, psyche, and libido. Guided by his political instincts, Rosset understood long before the phrase became fashionable that "the personal was political." If on occasion his tastes appeared eccentric, his decisions whimsical, he nonetheless pursued them to the point of obsession. As Kent Carroll, who with fellow Grove alumnus Herman Graf went on to found Carroll and Graf, quipped, Rosset has "a whim of steel."

Much of what appeared to be whim, however, was calculated enthusiasm nurtured deep in Rosset's soul, lifelong political values shaped as early as the seventh grade. That "whim of steel" led Rosset to revitalize American publishing in the '50s and '60s and to profoundly alter America's reading habits. Books indeed change minds, change lives, change history, but first they need a readership—they need to be published—and in the ethos of 1950s America publication of almost anything outside local community standards presented insuperable obstacles. The results of Rosset's audacity, persistence, and at times recklessness are summed up by long-time editor Jason Epstein, "He's altered the climate of publishing to *everybody's advantage*." Grove author Hubert Selby, Jr. concurred: "Certainly everybody from my generation is indebted to Barney. It's hard to believe that it was not so long ago that D. H. Lawrence was banned in this country." And Grove's senior editor, Fred Jordan, summarized Rosset's achievement thus: "Beyond changing the law it is also probably fair to say [that] every writer writing today is to some extent changed by the knowledge that entire areas of human experience which had been taboo for writers of other generations are, *if he or she wishes to explore them*, freely available." In November of 1988, three years after he sold and was then dismissed from the publishing firm he brought to national prominence, Barney Rosset received the PEN American Center's Publisher Citation, "for distinction and continuous service to international letters, to the freedom and dignity of writers, and to the free transmission of the printed word across the barriers of poverty, ignorance, censorship and repression."

Within a Budding Grove

In 1951 Barnet Rosset, Jr. was a twenty-nine-year-old undergraduate at the New School for Social Research when he bought from John Balcomb and Robert Phelps the name and assets of a small, foundering, two-year-old publishing house. While many in America enjoyed the postwar economic prosperity and while race relations had improved, at least in the military, during the war, much in American life at the end of the Truman years seemed mired in an earlier century. The racial law of the land remained *Plessy v. Ferguson;* the Warren Court's unanimous ruling on the much-delayed *Brown v. Board of Education* was three years away, although Oliver Brown had already filed what would be a landmark suit by 1951. Racial barriers showed cracks, however, as white teenagers began buying what were then dubbed "race records," a variety of jazz termed rhythm and blues. Soon white performers appropriated that raw energy and called it rock 'n' roll.

An equally undisciplined, antiliterary energy began to emerge with Jack Kerouac's *The Town and the City,* published in 1950 to almost universal neglect. Soon after, Kerouac took to the road again, gathering material that would find its way into the novel *On the Road* (1957), which helped shape the sensibility of America's postwar generation. Allen Ginsberg's "barbaric yawp" against American materialism and self-satisfaction, "Howl," debuted at San Francisco's Gallery Six in October of 1955. It was published shortly thereafter in Lawrence Ferlinghetti's new Pocket Poets Series and was quickly prosecuted for obscenity. Most of the readings at Gallery Six were performed to jazz accompaniment, not to the regularities of swing but to the disjunctive rhythms of bebop and free jazz. The new beat reverberated in the visual arts as well, as New York "action" painters depicted unmediated libido, raw subconscious energy on canvas.

Official American morality may still have been defined by the Comstock Laws (which denied the U.S. mails to anything deemed obscene or pornographic, like *Lady Chatterley*), but Professor Alfred Kinsey of Indiana University had already published the first of his "Kinsey Reports," *Sexual Behavior in the Human Male,* in 1948, to suggest that sanctioned sexuality was not always the guiding principle in American bedrooms. Kinsey's *Sexual Behavior in the Human Female* followed in 1953 with even more startling findings. Gregory Goodwin Pincus had begun trials with newly synthesized progesterone to impede ovulation in rabbits by 1951. In the fall of 1953 a twenty-seven-year-old Hugh Hefner bought the rights to Tom Kelley's photographs of Marilyn Monroe for $500 through a classified ad and used them to launch what was to be called *Stag Party* but became *Playboy*. The era of commodifying and merchandizing sex had begun as Goody Pincus's rabbits were transformed into Hef's bunnies.

Meanwhile, in Paris a Rumanian immigrant trying to learn English through a rudimentary language book found the experience so absurd that he wrote a strange, disjointed play about it. The comedy opened at a left-bank pocket theater in 1951. Half a century later Eugène Ionesco's *La Cantatrice Chauve* (*The Bald Soprano*) is still playing at the Huchette theater, along with his *La Leçon* (*The Lesson*). Just up the hill in Montparnasse, Suzanne Descheveaux-Dumesnil, future wife of Irish immigrant Samuel Beckett, circulated two plays among producers. By January of 1949, Beckett had completed *Eleuthéria* and a new French play, *En attendant Godot* (*Waiting for Godot*), written "as a relaxation to get away from the awful prose I was writing at the time," *Molloy* and *Malone meurt* (*Malone Dies*) in particular. Mme. Descheveaux-Dumesnil met with little success until she saw a production of August Strindberg's *Ghost Sonata* performed at the Gaité Montparnasse in the early spring of 1950. The play, staged by Roger Blin, a disciple of Antonin Artaud's, had impressed her, and she dropped the typescripts at the box office for him. Blin was interested in the plays, and he liked *Waiting for Godot*, even though he frankly did not understand it. Funding problems delayed the opening and forced Blin to stage the smaller and cheaper *Godot* first. With its production in January of 1953, a new era in theater history would begin.

Thus, all the pieces for a profound upheaval, a national redirection if not redefinition—in literature, morality, and race relations—were in place by 1951 when Rosset bought a publishing house that had stalled after reprinting three neglected masterworks—Herman Melville's *The Confidence-Man* (1949), *The Verse in English of Richard Crashaw* (1950), and the *Selected Writings of the Ingenious Mrs. Aphra Behn* (1950). Grove's fourth book, and Rosset's first, was a variorum edition of another neglected oddity, Matthew G. Lewis's *The Monk* (1952), and with it the Rosset era at Grove Press began. Shortly thereafter he reprinted Henry James's *The Golden Bowl* (then out of print) at the suggestion of his first wife, the painter Joan Mitchell, and in 1953 he issued selections from the writings of the Marquis de Sade with Simone de Beauvoir's influential essay "Must We Burn Sade?" which had originally appeared in *Les Temps Modernes* in December 1951 and January 1952.

By the end of the '50s Grove had moved quickly to bring to national prominence the art and artists of the disillusioned counterculture, provocative and even pugnacious material that appealed to Rosset's sensibility: the San Francisco and New York poets; the New York "action" painters; the French Surrealists and 'Pataphysicians; the German Expressionists; the dramatists of the Absurd and the *romanciers* of the *Nouveau roman*. Under Rosset Grove focused attention on and developed such nascent fields as black, ethnic, and third-world literatures, publishing critical books on and anthologies of Japanese and Chinese literature barely a decade after the Second World War and during the Korean conflict.[4] Grove published books on the politics of the New Left, on the alternate or counter psychology of Transactional Analysis, on the international art film, and musically on jazz, the African-American avant-garde. (Rosset had little personal interest in the emerging rock 'n' roll.)

Although Rosset had been a member of the Communist Party briefly in his youth, the press itself developed no particular program or ideology of its own beyond a broad-based avant-gardism, a general postwar dissatisfaction with the status quo, a militant antiauthoritarianism, empathy for the oppressed, and an unwavering commitment to complete freedom of expression in speech, print, and, finally, film. It had a Left-leaning ideology, an Americanized version of Marxism, and sympathy with the labor movement, but Rosset's socialism and political activism were always leavened with an entrepreneurial spirit. His father had been, after all, president and director of the Metropolitan Trust Company in Chicago, and it was Rosset's trust fund and then his inheritance that funded the early years of Grove. With such solid financial backing Grove was able to publish the vast reservoir of unpublished and repressed material of several generations, paying little attention to profit and loss. As Kent Carroll notes:

> There is an argument that says in the mid-'50s Barney, by taste and instinct, tapped into something remarkable. There was all this literature that had been written in Europe from the 1930s—Henry Miller—up until the early 1950s—Beckett—that hadn't been published in the U.S. for a range of reasons. The most obvious one is that it was considered obscene or, in some cases, politically subversive. It also appeared that it wasn't to the American taste, that in a nation that read the *Saturday Evening Post* there wasn't any audience for Jean Genet. And once Barney began to exploit that body of work it turned out to be the mother lode.

Gilbert Sorrentino, who had cut his editorial teeth line-editing *The Autobiography of Malcolm X* with his Grove mentor Harry Braverman, agrees.

---

4. Rosset published Donald Keene's *Japanese Literature: An Introduction for Western Readers* early in 1955 and *Anthology of Japanese Literature from the Earliest Era to the Mid-Nineteenth Century*, also in 1955. The latter was a UNESCO project.

It should be made clear . . . that the genius of the house lay not so much in discovering writers, but in making itself receptive to writers who had already been writing for a small and very *au courant* audience. Grove, to put it very bluntly, had plenty of money, was presided over by Barney Rosset, a man of singular and often eccentric tastes and enthusiasms, and was run by editors who always had the chance to push for the most unlikely projects. Grove, in an odd way, at least for the five years I worked there [1965–70], was a trade publisher with the spirit of a little magazine or small press. Put it this way: Grove actively sought materials which most other publishers would run from in panic, and then Rosset had the means whereby to acquire, publish, and distribute them.

By the spring of 1953, partly at the suggestion of Wallace Fowlie, his professor at the New School for Social Research, as well as Sylvia Beach, among others, Rosset moved to publish the new playwrights writing in French, Jean Genet, Eugène Ionesco, and Samuel Beckett, authors whose work would soon become synonymous—in the United States, at any rate—with Grove Press. With them Grove's championing of the new drama began. And Grove's commitment to new European theater, which included publishing Artaud's polemic, *The Theater and Its Double*, would help transform American theater as well. That spring Rosset began negotiations with Beckett, who, in a letter of June 25, 1953, suggested not only his own uncompromising position toward his work but set the tone for Grove's battles against censorship for the next two decades.

With regard to my work in general, I hope you realize what you are letting yourself in for. I do not mean the heart of the matter, which is unlikely to disturb anybody, but certain obscenities of form which may not have struck you in French as they will in English, and which frankly (it is better that you should know this before we get going) I am not at all disposed to mitigate. I do not of course realize what is possible in America from this point of view and what is not. Certainly as far as I know such passages, faithfully translated, would not be tolerated in England. I think you might do well to talk to Fowlie about this.

Duly warned, indeed exhilarated by Beckett's warning, Rosset persevered not only with the "obscenities of form" in Beckett's work but pushed on to publish and distribute through the mail the unexpurgated *Lady Chatterley's Lover*, which even Sylvia Beach of Shakespeare and Company, publisher of James Joyce's *Ulysses*, had rejected.

Despite his reputation for impulsive decision making, Rosset knew as early as 1954 that he would publish *Lady Chatterley's Lover* at all cost, and he began by dispatching critic and novelist Mark Schorer, professor of English at the University of California, Berkeley, to Taos, New Mexico, to discuss publication prospects with Lawrence's widow, Frieda Lawrence-Ravagli, and to examine the final manuscript of the novel. In a letter to Rosset of December 4, 1954, shortly before she died, Frieda Lawrence-Ravagli sanctioned the publication of the unexpurgated *Lady Chatterley's Lover*. Rosset prepared the way by first publishing Schorer's essay "On *Lady Chatterley*" in the inaugural issue of Grove's literary magazine, *Evergreen Review*, in 1957. He then used the essay as an "Introduction" to the novel in May of 1959. The legal battle won, Rosset published the entire thirty-page ruling by Judge Frederick van Pelt Bryan against the U.S. Postal Service and in favor of Grove Press in *Evergreen Review* No. 9 (summer 1959).

When he bought Grove Press, Rosset had no publishing background beyond an adolescent compulsion to scratch the "G" out of the Grosset & Dunlap colophon of his schoolbooks. He did, however, have an acute political sensitivity shaped in part by books like Edgar Snow's *Red Star over China* and André Malraux's *Man's Fate*. In 1947 Rosset had moved to New York to begin his first postwar commercial enterprise, a film production company called Target Films. Its sole release was *Strange Victory* (1949), a full-length documentary dissecting race relations in postwar America. The didactic film argued "that the four freedoms for which World War II was fought should be the reward of all and not the few before we find ourselves in the same trap in which Europe found itself before the war." As the film's narration notes, World War II was a "strange victory with the ideas of the loser still active in the land of the winner." The documentary was well received critically and won first prize at the Karlovy-Vary Film Festival, but it attracted few viewers when it was released to a self-satisfied America in 1949. The social conscience that Rosset brought to his documentary, however, would soon infuse his publishing house.

If Grove's publishing philosophy was amorphous in the 1950s, it coalesced by the end of the decade and was expressed directly and cogently in a remarkable interview Rosset conducted with Italian publisher Giangiacomo Feltrinelli for New York radio station WNET in 1959. Rosset stood on the brink of what would be his first publishing triumph, and he interviewed another fresh, young publisher who had just scored a publishing coup by acquiring international publishing rights to Boris Pasternak's novel *Dr. Zhivago* just before it was banned by the Soviet government. Rosset soon brought the conversation around to an issue very much on his mind as well: censorship. Feltrinelli generally agreed with Rosset's anticensorship position, but he reserved a role for government in restricting "expressions which have no artistic value but only thrive on obscenity." Rosset bristled, "Do you feel that there are people qualified to state whether something ceases to have artistic merit and crosses over that line into the area of obscenity?" Rosset pressed Feltrinelli, "What damage do you feel that the publication of so-called obscene literature would do to the population? I ask this rather loaded question, Mr. Feltrinelli, because I personally feel that in a free society there are a number of risks that one must take in order to have that [freedom]. One of them I feel is that there must be complete freedom of expression." Feltrinelli agreed but retreated from Rosset's absolutism, calling for restriction "if this publication goes over the limit." Rosset hammered his point yet again: "Mr. Feltrinelli, I would like to interject here that I feel that personally there hasn't been a word written or uttered that shouldn't be published." If overt political commitment or ideology existed at Grove, it was to such unfettered freedom of expression in all its diversity and perversity.

The Evergreen Review

One of Rosset's salient management skills has been his ability to recognize editorial talent, to find key personnel at just the right time. Shortly after acquiring the press, for instance, Rosset enrolled in a night class on publishing at Columbia University offered by Saxe Commins of Random House. There he met Don Allen, who became Grove's first employee, though he stayed on only briefly at first. When Allen returned, he had worked freelance with Arabel J. Porter on *New World Writing* for New American Library and on *Modern Writing*, published by *Partisan Review,* and he wanted Rosset to develop something similar at Grove, that is, to produce a high-quality journal of new writing to appear periodically, but in the form of a paperback. The result was *Evergreen Review* No. 1, which appeared in 1957. Named after Grove's growing line of trade paperbacks, the first *Evergreen Review* carried its own Evergreen number, E-59, and represented a synthesis of the interests of its editors. Allen had been reading Henri Michaux's *Miserable Miracle,* an account of the author's experiments with mescaline, and he followed the poets of the "Berkeley Renaissance" of 1947–49, and then of the San Francisco Beat writers who succeeded them. Rosset steered the magazine toward more topical and political issues than those found in either *New World Writing* or *Modern Writing,* and his own interest in photography and film was reflected throughout *Evergreen*'s history. Rosset had been publishing postwar, avant-garde writers since 1953, and *Evergreen Review* No. 1 contained a short story by one of Grove's major discoveries, Samuel Beckett, titled "Dante and the Lobster," which revived interest in his collection of stories, banned in Ireland in 1934, *More Pricks Than Kicks*.

Evergreen Review No. 2 was even more stunning, a special issue on the "San Francisco Scene." Rosset and Allen relied heavily on Kenneth Rexroth for its selections, and Rexroth turned for advice to Allen Ginsberg. Devoted to West Coast Beat writers, it focused on emerging voices, including Ginsberg's own "Howl," reprinted from Ferlinghetti's Pocket Poet's Series, No. 4 (but excluding the fourth and most offensive section), and an excerpt from Henry Miller's *Big Sur and the Good Life*, which Rosset was even then using to prepare for Grove's most audacious publication, *Tropic of Cancer*. *Evergreen Review* quickly became the vanguard of Grove's anticensorship crusade, concluding its first year by publishing "Horn on *Howl*" in No. 4, in which Ferlinghetti reported on Judge Clayton Horn's ruling that Ginsberg's *Howl* was not obscene. The seizure, trial, and subsequent publicity turned *Howl* into a best-seller for the fledgling City Lights Books. The lesson was not lost on Rosset.

By the spring of 1959 Don Allen had established himself on the West Coast and was losing interest in actively co-editing *Evergreen Review*. Soon after Rosset hired Richard Seaver, who would become managing editor of *Evergreen* with No. 9 (summer 1959) and one of Grove's most distinctive editors. Seaver had gone to Paris in 1951 to study at Sorbonne. There he became associated with a group of expatriates, including Christopher Logue, Alexander Trocchi, Baird Bryant, Patrick Bowles, Austryn Wainhouse, and Wainhouse's wife Muffie, who had published one volume of a literary journal called *Merlin*.[5] Seaver had recently discovered two postwar French novels by Samuel Beckett, *Molloy* and *Malone meurt*, in the window of the French publisher Les Editions de Minuit as he passed to and from his makeshift residence on the rue de Sabot. Seaver found the novels so exhilarating he quickly wrote an essay, "Samuel Beckett: An Introduction," for the second number of *Merlin* (summer 1952). That began a close association between Beckett and Seaver. The group that Beckett called the "*Merlin* juveniles" soon formed an association with Maurice Girodias of Olympia Press to finance the magazine and a series of Merlin books, beginning with Samuel Beckett's then unpublished *Watt*. By 1956 the association of Collection Merlin, Olympia Press, and Grove Press jointly brought out the English edition of *Molloy*, which had been translated by Patrick Bowles in collaboration with Beckett. Seaver had also done some major translations for Girodias, including (with Austryn Wainhouse) two collections of work by the

5. For fuller details of Seaver's Paris years and his connection to *Merlin* see his "Introduction" to *"I can't go on, I'll go on": A Selection from Samuel Beckett's Work* (New York: Grove Press, 1974), ix–xlviii, and Christopher Logue, *Prince Charming: A Memoir* (London: Faber and Faber Ltd., 1999).

Marquis de Sade, *Justine, Philosophy in the Bedroom, and other Writings* and *The 120 Days of Sodom and Other Writings,* and most notably perhaps (in collaboration with the author) two of Beckett's early stories, "The Expelled" and "The End." Seaver thus became the ideal choice to succeed Don Allen at the *Evergreen Review,* and went on to become one of Grove's most influential editors by solidifying Grove's French connection.

Seaver's first issue as managing editor opened with Henry Miller's eloquent "Defense of the Freedom to Read," an essay in the form of a letter to his Norwegian attorney, Trygve Hirsch, to assist in defense of his novel *Sexus* against charges in Oslo that it was obscene writing. "Statement in Support of the Freedom to Read" then became a Grove-led petition that was published as the cover to *Evergreen Review* No. 25 (July–August 1962), in the midst of the *Tropic of Cancer* litigation. The last of the quarto-formatted issues, No. 31, included excerpts from works that would become emblems of the age, Richard Brautigan's *Trout Fishing in America* and Pauline Réage's *Story of O,* for example, but it carried another letter on censorship, "Written Address to the Italian Judge" (May 1963), in which Jack Kerouac defended his novel *The Subterraneans*—published in the United States by Grove and in Italy by Feltrinelli Editore—against charges of obscenity.

With No. 32 (April–May 1964) *Evergreen* became a glossy, visually oriented commercial magazine. Advertising increased but much of it was politically driven—advertising as editorial commentary—a form of capitalism in the service of the revolution that Rosset seems to have devised. *Evergreen* continued its commitment to experimental writing with William Burroughs's neo-Dadaist "Cut-Ups Self-Explained," but the issue paved the way for Grove's move into film by testing the censorship standard for visual art with a portfolio of double-exposed nudes by American photographer Emil J. Cadoo. The photos exposed *Evergreen* to criminal prosecution as well. On June 12, 1964, detectives from the Nassau County Vice Squad raided the printing plant on Long Island and carried off 21,000 unbound copies of *Evergreen* No. 32. Rosset retaliated, published another Cadoo nude in No. 33, and explained the police seizure in a short note called "About *Evergreen Review* No. 32." But No. 33 was also seized; this time the offending item was a poem by Judith Malina (codirector, with Julian Beck, of the Living Theatre), "last performance at the living theatre invective." The poem concluded, "I suggest an overthrow of all governments by love. / I suggest direct action: / Ergo: Fuck the USA." No. 34 contained yet another Cadoo photograph as well as the sort of works that were becoming *Evergreen*'s signature: Susan Sontag's now famous "Against Interpretation," Samuel Beckett's *Play,* and Hubert Selby's "The Queen Is Dead," the last anticipating Grove's publication of Selby's controversial *Last Exit to*

Brooklyn. By 1967, then, Lawrence, Miller, Burroughs, and Selby had been published and defended, and the police actions against *Evergreen* Nos. 32 and 33 overturned; thus *Evergreen* had much to celebrate as it ended its first decade. Grove Press marked the milestone by publishing the encyclopedia-sized, 800-page *Evergreen Review Reader: A Ten-year Anthology of America's Leading Literary Magazine* in 1968. Two years later the magazine would again be under siege; a year after that it would disappear—along with the era it had championed.

Publishing Guerrillas, Guerrilla Publishing

The shift in *Evergreen* to a more commercial format reflected a Rosset preoccupation, first in print, then in theater and film, to move radical politics—which for him included explicit sexuality—onto a broader, more populist stage. His principal vehicle was the house magazine *Evergreen*, which had grown from a circulation of 7,500 as a literary quarterly in 1957, to 125,000 as a glossy monthly in February 1968, and would peak at just over 200,000 in 1970, just before its demise. Many a critic would decry the change. The shift from print-driven quarto to slick, glossy monthly, however, reflected the spirit of its time. If one of the longest-lasting effects of the sixties was the erosion of elite, high culture and the celebration of popular arts, a sort of artistic democratization, that ideological change was reflected in and abetted by what was now called simply *Evergreen*. In 1968 Grove launched an advertising campaign in the New York City subways with a series of startling posters promoting *Evergreen*. One of the most political of the images featured Paul Davis's portrait of Cuban revolutionary Che Guevara with the caption, "The spirit of Che lives in the new *Evergreen*." The campaign would be the pinnacle of Rosset's editorial manipulation of advertising, and with it Grove would merchandise political revolution on an unprecedented scale. The poster version of the Guevara cover would become an icon of the age as Grove encouraged one and all to "Join the Underground."

Following the news of Guevara's death in October of 1967 came the additional revelation that at the time of his death he carried on his person diaries for the Bolivian campaign of 1966 and 1967. Amid the international scramble to acquire their publication rights, Rosset, who was already aggressively publishing material supporting the Cuban revolution, began his own covert action to acquire the diaries. He held a series of clandestine, late-night meetings with members of the Cuban Mission to the United Nations at a New York restaurant, and received the name of a contact in La Paz, one General Torres. On

March 27, 1968, from his preferred venue, a bar on Third Avenue, Rosset tele-phoned a friend and sometime Grove employee, Joe Liss, a radio, television, and film writer, and dispatched him to Bolivia the next day with $8,500 in cash sewn into his clothing to secure the diaries.

Liss learned, however, that, like booty, the diaries had been dispersed among several Bolivian generals. He negotiated for six pages from a pair of Bolivian journalists, Luis J. Gonzáles and Gustavo A. Sánchez Salazar, who were writing a book on Guevara's adventures in Bolivia. Liss then wired Rosset that acquisition of the diaries had stalled. With the delay, Rosset himself en-tered the hunt. Along with editor Fred Jordan, he flew to La Paz, then on to Cochabamba to meet Gonzáles and Salazar. There he negotiated for thirty more pages of the diaries and for the González/Salazar book, for which he offered an astonishing $27,000 advance, $2,000 cash on the spot.

Rosset did not have enough of the diary to publish a book but he pre-pared to publish the thirty-six pages he did have in *Evergreen,* adding an index of "Who's Who in Che's Diary," drawings by Argentine artist Carlos Bustos of the Cuban agents working in Bolivia, and photographs of Guevara, most dra-matically one "taken in Vallegrande on October 9 [1967] shortly after he was killed in the village of Higuera." *Evergreen* No. 57 (August 1968) appeared con-currently, and was designed to compete with a special number of *Ramparts* magazine devoted entirely to the diaries and the book version published by Bantam Books.[6] The González/Salazar book, *The Great Rebel: Che Guevara in Bolivia,* appeared from Grove Press as a hardback (GP-542) and an Ever-green Black Cat mass-market paperback (B-277) in 1969. A portion of it called "Tania: Che's Woman in Bolivia" also appeared in *Evergreen* No. 60.

Although it avoided legal consequences of unauthorized publication of the Guevara excerpts (the *Ramparts* and Bantam versions were published with the consent of Che's widow and the imprimatur of the Cuban government), Grove became the lightning rod for the political reaction. On the eve of Grove's

6. Both *Ramparts* and *Evergreen* had been competing to publish Guevara's work earlier that year, as well. In its January 1968 issue *Ramparts* published an excerpt from *Venceremos: The Speeches and Writings of Ernesto Che Guevara,* edited by John Gerassi. *Ramparts* announced the publisher as Macmillan for March of 1968, but the volume was finally published by Simon & Schuster that same year. This early *Ramparts* piece already used images of a dead Che in "Vallegrande" as its cover and as a motif throughout the excerpt, but the photograph is not identified as that of a dead Che. *Evergreen* published Guevara's earlier diary entries, "Where it All Began: The Landing in Cuba," in its February 1968 issue, No. 51, an excerpt from what was first announced as *The Cuban Revolu-tionary War* but was published under the title *Reminiscences of the Cuban Revolution,* trans. by Victoria Ortiz, by Monthly Review Press and distributed by Grove Press, Black Cat edition B-177.

publication of the diaries, a small band of anti-Castro Cubans (supported or at least encouraged, Rosset has always contended, by the CIA) responded to Grove's celebration of "Guevara's Romantic Marxism" in *Evergreen* No. 51 (February 1968), to the anticipated publication of the Bolivian diaries, and to Grove's support of the Castro revolution in general with direct action. First, a series of threats was made against *Evergreen*, of which the FBI was fully aware, Rosset contends, but Grove was offered no police protection. Then in the early morning of July 26, 1968, days before *Evergreen* No. 57 was to appear, a fragmentation grenade was launched through a window on the 11th Street side of Grove's University Place editorial offices.

Credit for the attack was claimed by the Movimento Nacional de Coalicion Cubano, or M.N.C.C., and it was timed to coincide with and so to discredit a Cuban national holiday, celebration of the fifteenth anniversary of Castro's July 26 rebellion against Batista. Twelve hours after the explosion, Grove received a bomb threat and evacuated its editorial offices of fifty-five staff members. Such threats, coupled with mysterious fires and repeated false alarms, became part of editorial life at Grove over the next several years, and they disrupted Grove's editorial process considerably. What the bombing and subsequent harassment did not disrupt was Rosset's commitment to publishing the works of Cuban revolutionaries. He allowed the excerpts from the Bolivian diaries to appear as scheduled in the next *Evergreen* despite continued threats.

Working at Grove Press in the 1960s became hazardous as threats appeared periodically from various disaffected or disenfranchised revolutionaries and reactionaries. In 1968 Valerie Solanis, whose *S.C.U.M. (Society for Cutting Up Men) Manifesto* Grove had under consideration, targeted Rosset directly. She was reported lurking outside Grove's offices on several occasions with an ice pick awaiting Rosset's appearance. Claudia Menza, an editorial assistant at Grove then serving as Rosset's personal assistant, recalls warning him: "You can't go out to lunch because Valerie Solanis is downstairs with an ice pick, and she's going to try to kill you. . . . And Barney said to me, 'Dear! if I ran away from everybody who was going to kill me with an ice pick or some other thing, I'd never go to lunch at all. I'm going at one o'clock.'" He did, without incident. Several days later, however, Solanis found Andy Warhol at his Union Square "Factory" and shot him.

We Are Furious (Yellow)

At its economic peak, Grove Press became the target of a series of economic and political attacks from an unexpected quarter, the political Left. A pair of concurrent disruptions—a union action and a rising feminist reaction to what was then still called the "free speech movement" or, alternately, the "sexual revolution"—would prove near fatal as Grove's six-million-dollar 1969 revenues seemed to attract unwanted attention.[7]

The Publishing Employees Organizing Committee of the Fur, Leather, and Machinists Workers Joint Board (AFL-CIO) moved to unionize Grove's editorial staff (the warehouse workers were already unionized). On April 8, 1970, several of Grove's editorial staff attended a union rally and took out union cards. Shortly thereafter Grove discharged nine of them, union activist and militant feminist Robin Morgan among them. On April 13, Morgan retaliated with a group of eight women by occupying the publisher's sixth-floor executive offices and by shifting the terms of the conflict, now charging the press with "crimes against women." The protesters made a series of far-reaching demands but very few dealt with traditional union concerns like salaries and benefits. On the contrary, their demands were decidedly political and finally punitive: that Grove establish twenty-four-hour free child care for its employees, that profits from the best-selling *Autobiography of Malcolm X* be diverted to the black community, and that profits from Grove's erotica go to "women who are the special victims of this propaganda," particularly in the form of a defense fund for prostitutes. The group claimed that Grove "earned millions off the basic theme of humiliating, degrading, and dehumanizing women through sado-masochistic literature, pornographic films, and oppressive and exploitative practices against its own female employees." The protesters mocked Grove's recent economic triumph *I Am Curious (Yellow,* 1969) in film by wearing buttons that proclaimed, "We Are Furious (Yellow)."

What for some had been a decade-long struggle for personal freedom and sexual liberation had been for others simply another form of exploitation and expropriation, this time against women and their bodies. Under the general slogan "Freedom for Everyone or Freedom for No One," the protesters issued a manifesto that struck at the heart of Grove Press as a company, as a capitalist venture, and mocked the company's leftist politics. The group's goal seemed to be nothing short of the destruction of a press around which much of the social revolution they represented coalesced, and their manifesto singled out Rosset in particular for attack:

---

7. In 1967 Grove began moving aggressively into film, opening its own Evergreen Theater at the West 11th Street facility. Rosset was trying to do for film what he had done for print by importing films with overt and direct sexual content. Plunging headlong if somewhat recklessly into the film business, by 1969 Grove's film library had grown to some 400 documentaries, shorts, and feature-length films.

No more business as usual for Grove Press and *Evergreen* Magazine!

No more using of women's bodies as filth-objects (both black and white) to sell a phony radicalism-for-profit to the middle-American-white-male!

No more using of women's bodies to rip off enormous profits for a few wealthy capitalist dirty old straight white men, such as Barney Rosset!

No more using of women as shit workers to produce material that degrades them; no more underpaid, demeaning, degrading work for anyone!

No more scapegoating of women for daring to demand the rights and respect that are—for any human being—inalienable!

No more wearing of a radical mask by these exploiters to cover the sexist leer, the racist smirk, the boss-man's frown!

No more union busting by rich-man Rosset!
> Fact: One woman worker was denied the health insurance coverage for her child that is automatically given to male workers who have children. The sole reason: she was a woman!

No more mansions on Long Island for boss-man Rosset and his executive yes-men flunkies, segregated mansions built with extortionist profits from selling *The Autobiography of Malcolm X*, a best-seller—and not one black welfare mother a penny better off after millions of copies made Rosset rich!

No more Latin American executive junkets for the rich men who sell the books of Che, Bosch, Debray to get rich while the Latin cities they visit are choked with hungry babies!

No more peddling of Grove movies that offer nudity as "sexual liberation" but present women as "hung-up" and men as "liberated," and that force women to act out their bestialized oppression while the whole world is watching, making Rosset rich!

No more financing of male-left radicals in cushy lifestyles by selling their hypocritical radicalism to *Evergreen* for lots of money—a magazine that with *Playboy* is one of the heaviest anti-women propaganda machines in the country.

No more male radicals who can ignore the oppression of women—as sex objects, as workers, as union organizers, as feminists, as radicals, as revolutionaries, as socialists—and continue to reap profits based on the degradation of women!!!

No more, no more, no more. Shut it down. Close it up. We want reparations!

In one of the many ironies that pervaded this confrontation, after having the women arrested for defacing Grove's property, Grove's attorneys fought to have the protesters released and all charges dropped even as the protesters were claiming to have done considerably more damage than they did. Grove prosecuting attorneys were, in short, arguing for acquittal while the protesters' defense attorneys were arguing for maximum punishment. The era of image politics was thus well under way. But even as the union was decisively defeated by a vote of Grove employees, the issues raised during the twin confrontations would prove to be mortally divisive for Grove. Writers like Julius Lester, whose *Look Out, Whitey, Black Power's Gonna Get Your Mama* Grove published as a Black Cat paperback in 1969, responded to the racial implications of the protest and sided with the protesters in a letter to Rosset of April 14, 1970:

> If the charges against the women are not dropped and their demands [not] met, I am left with little choice but to see that no future books of mine are published by Grove Press, that no further articles of mine appear in *Evergreen Review* and that my name no longer be listed in *Evergreen* as a Contributing Editor.

Lester stayed on long enough, however, to have his say in *Evergreen*. In No. 82 (September 1970) he published "Women—The Male Fantasy," in which he outlined what would become almost a handbook for the victim culture of the 1980s.

The political fissure at Grove quickly widened. James Forman, author of *Sammy Young, Jr.* (1969) also joined the union rally on April 16. In an open letter to Fred Jordan in *Evergreen* No. 80 (July 1970), Carl Oglesby, editor of *The New Left Reader* (1969) and one of the "male radicals" writing for *Evergreen*, resigned, siding with the protesters. The following month (*Evergreen* No. 81), again in an open letter citing "political integrity," contributing editor Jack Newfield followed suit, noting, "I think Carl [Oglesby] is essentially correct about the way *Evergreen* portrays women." For Fred Jordan, who answered Oglesby's letter directly in *Evergreen* No. 80, the issue was neither gender bias nor worker exploitation but censorship, the attempt to shut down and silence Grove and *Evergreen*. Jordan chided Oglesby for avoiding that issue: "Can't you understand that censorship must be fought with every means at your disposal no matter where the threat comes from? . . . Robin's demands for censorship were indistinguishable from those of the lunatic Right who have advocated the suppression of Grove and *Evergreen* for years."

By 1970, then, Grove Press was caught in a seismic political shift that would perhaps become fully evident only in retrospect—the break of the women's movement from the values and finally the politics of the New Left. Grove Press represented the tail end of an avant-garde tradition that held in contempt any aesthetic convention, any social value, any political ideology that interfered with the freedom of the artist and, indeed, of the individual. That was the position Rosset had made clear to Giangiacomo Feltrinelli in 1959. By 1970, however, the lack of an ethical dimension to the free-speech revolution had become painfully apparent; that is, although the *texts* that Grove was publishing had changed little since its inception, the *context* had, and literature is a cultural product inseparable from its context. The political shift in 1970 that split Grove's constituency and devastated *Evergreen*'s subscriptions was then exacerbated by a series of financial crises. What had seemed an endless supply of revenue from the film *I Am Curious (Yellow)* had all but ceased by the end of 1970, and concurrently the New York real estate market, into which Grove had invested much of its excess capital, most of it into the massive Mercer Street office complex, had collapsed.[8]

---

8. The renovation of the six-story Mercer Street building with full basement, central air-conditioning, and two new elevators (one for the exclusive use of Rosset and his senior editors)—32,000 square feet of usable space—was completed in 1970, just as the New York City real estate market deflated. The stunning renovation, which cost nearly $2 million, was designed by architects Heery & Heery and the results won the 1970 Interior Design Award in a competition sponsored by *Architectural Record*. But the architectural masterpiece turned into a financial nightmare. The value of the building was declining as it was being renovated. In 1970 the cost of building and renovation was approximately $800,000 more than its current appraised valuation of $1,320,000. By December 31, 1971, Grove Press's liabilities exceeded its assets by nearly $5 million. In a desperate attempt to avoid bankruptcy and facing a depressed real estate market, Grove Press sold on June 19, 1972, its Mercer Street building and its contents, as well as the additional land and buildings adjacent to it (purchased in 1969 and 1970 for $202,873), for approximately $550,000 (after expenses of sale). A total of $2,259,164 in building, land, improvements, furnishings, and equipment sold for barely $100,000 above the mortgage debt. In another attempt to stave off bankruptcy Grove sold its Evergreen Book Club to improve cash flow. In the latter part of 1971 Grove suspended publication of its monthly periodical *Evergreen Review*. In 1972 Grove tried to revive *Evergreen* as a quarterly, but only a single issue was published in 1972 and only two (both in paperback format) in 1973, the first a special issue on *Last Tango in Paris* and the second a general issue, which included the entire text of Samuel Beckett's *The Lost Ones*. The single issue in 1972 generated $70,756 and the two issues in 1973 generated $103,805.

Rosset's own summary of Grove's decline has focused almost exclusively on the political, however. The issues were detailed in a poignant letter of January 9, 1975 to *New York Times* investigative reporter Seymour Hersh. Rosset had reason to believe that Hersh would be sympathetic to Grove's plight and so receptive to its entreaty. He and his staff outlined Grove's political history and sent it to Hersh over Fred Jordan's signature, trying to interest Hersh in an investigation of a CIA connection in the decline of the press:

a. Grove Press and the magazine it published, *Evergreen Review,* were among the first in the United States to take a determined stand against the war in Vietnam.

b. Grove Press published many of the original texts of such Third World authors as Frantz Fanon and Regis Debray which became handbooks for the anti-colonialist movement in Asia, South America, and Africa, and had an incalculable effect on the Black movement as well as the radical movement in the United States.

c. Grove Press was the publisher of many of the rebellious voices of the Black movement in the United States, including Malcolm X, Imamu Amiri Baraka (LeRoi Jones), and others.

d. Grove Press and *Evergreen Review* were among the first to publish reports of the CIA involvement in the military operations in Bolivia against Che Guevara, and Grove Press was among the first to publish the writings of Che Guevara in the United States . . .

e. Grove Press published, among others, an exposé of the U.S. involvement in the overthrow of Juan Bosch in the Dominican Republic, by Juan Bosch himself [*Pentagonism: A Substitute for Imperialism* (1968) (GP 504)], which was a serious attack on the power of the Pentagon and its interference in the affairs of Latin American countries.

f. *Evergreen Review* was one of the most outspoken critics of the Government's prosecution of the Chicago Seven and one of its reports on the tampering by the Government with the Chicago Seven jury became a cornerstone in the appeal of the sentence which was finally overturned.

g. Grove Press and *Evergreen Review* were among the first to publish the writings of Fidel Castro in the United States, and to report on the accomplishments of the revolution in Cuba.

h. Grove Press was the publisher of Soviet spy Kim Philby's memoirs, *My Silent War* [1968], which, as you have reported, first exposed the role of Jim Angleton in the CIA.

For whatever reasons, Hersh chose not to follow up on Jordan's letter, and so Grove continued its own investigation into what Rosset has always believed to be a government conspiracy against the press. Six months later, some of Rosset's suspicions were officially confirmed. On June 6, 1975, the Rockefeller Commission released its report on the illegal domestic activities of the CIA, and it singled out Grove Press as one of the CIA's targets: "An extreme example of the extent to which collection [of information] could go once a file was opened is contained in the Grove Press, Inc. file. The file apparently was opened because the company had published a book by Kim Philby, the British intelligence officer who turned out to be a Soviet agent. The name of Grove Press was thus listed as having intelligence interest, and the CHAOS analysts [the name of the Special Operations Group within the CIA that investigated 'foreign contacts with American dissidents'] collected all available information on the company," according to the report (p. 144).[9]

Almost immediately Rosset filed a million-dollar lawsuit against the "Central Intelligence Agency, George Bush, William E. Colby, James Schlesinger, Richard Helms, John A. McCone, William F. Raborn, Jr., James J. Angleton, Raymond Rocca, William J. Hood, Newton S. Miller, Thomas Karamessines, Richard Ober, John Doe, Richard Roe, Jane Doe and other unknown employees of the Central Intelligence Agency and other Agencies of the Federal Government" to secure additional information. Rosset claimed that what little information the CIA released was "sanitized." In its press release Grove charged that "the reason the Agency is withholding disclosure of its files on Grove Press is because such revelation would prove CIA actions which had been 'improper, unlawful, and criminal.'" The suit forced release under the Freedom of Information Act of masses of documents—censored, of course—which demonstrated that Grove's activities were closely *monitored*, but charges and suspicions that the CIA *interfered* directly and overtly with the operations of Grove have never been substantiated, even after Grove's own thorough and costly investigation. What is undeniable, however, is that the conjunction of events documented in Grove's letter to Hersh, in the Rockefeller Commission report, in its own internal investigation, and in its civil suit against the CIA irreparably damaged the press.

9. The report, commissioned by President Gerald R. Ford and chaired by Vice President Nelson A. Rockefeller, was formally titled *Report to the President by the Commission on CIA Activities Within the United States*. It was published by the U.S. Government Printing Office, stock number 041-015-00074-8.

Good-bye to All That

By 1980 the future of Grove as an independent publisher of quality books looked dim. Its constituency had splintered amid the politics of the '70s. The backlog of unpublished and formerly restricted material that Grove fought to publish in the 1960s and 1970s was essentially depleted; what remained was now available to all publishers, and so Grove was forced to compete with other houses for manuscripts at a time when it was severely undercapitalized. Yet it occasionally uncovered a neglected manuscript. In 1980, for example, Kent Carroll came upon John Kennedy Toole's much-rejected comic masterpiece, *A Confederacy of Dunces,* as it was about to be published by the Louisiana State University Press, and he bought the world English paperback rights for Grove for $2,000. But such triumphs were too few to sustain the foundering press through the 1980s.

Grove continued to lose money, and so Rosset began to search for buyers, and in 1985 he sold Grove to oil heiress Ann Getty and British publisher George Weidenfeld for some $2 million in an effort to revitalize the flagging company. Part of the motive for the sale was to support Grove's revival of *Evergreen,* a trial issue of which, No. 98, appeared in 1984 with new work by writers who, like Samuel Beckett, had become Grove legends.

The terms of the sale seemed to allow Rosset to retain editorial control for some five years, but soon after the sale the anticorporate Rosset was dismissed, the *Evergreen* revival abandoned. Rosset filed suit over his dismissal, but the terms of the settlement were finally so unfavorable to him that he had to sign a disclaimer indemnifying his attorney. For one, to prevent his taking any Grove authors with him when he left, Rosset was barred from contact with Grove authors until 1990. In a letter to Melvin L. Wulf of Bedlock, Levine and Hoffman dated July 15, 1986, Rosset accepted such terms and ended his suit with these words: "I have listened carefully to your advice and I have rejected it for reasons of my own. I believe your criticism of the settlement agreement is sound and that everything you say about it is right. However, for my own personal reasons, I choose to sign it." Rosset's perceptions of his dismissal and his explanation of what he called "personal reasons" for accepting the settlement (that is, beyond his immediate need for the settlement cash) were summarized in an unsent letter he drafted to Ann Getty. He seemed unaware of any difficulties with the new owners, and his dismissal took him by surprise: "I do not remember having any disagreement with you, or for that matter any serious one with George [Weidenfeld]." The conflict finally left Rosset "exhausted, traumatized, grief stricken—you name it. But, oddly, there was little anger on my part. Nor has there ever been. And now, my feelings about Grove Press and its personnel are very friendly."

The Grove Press Rosset sold to Getty and Weidenfeld in 1985 had fallen precipitately from its peak. In fact, Grove was already in steady financial decline by May of 1970, when it had tried to build on the success of its major film release *I Am Curious (Yellow)* with a sequel, *I Am Curious (Blue)*. In a letter to shareholders for the 1970 "Grove Press Annual Report" Rosset admitted that the sequel was released "without approaching the success of the earlier film." Revenue from *I Am Curious (Yellow)* itself had plummeted from $6,100,000 in 1969 (although by year's end $375,000 had been spent defending the film, a legal battle that Grove finally lost) to $1,600,000 in 1970 and $100,000 in 1971. By 1970 Grove Press had reported a loss (after extraordinary charges) of $2,302,445. According to its 1972 annual report, Grove absorbed some $447,000 worth of unrecoverable advances from authors and filmmakers, "including advances for works not completed." Its publicly traded common stock, which was offered at $7.00 per share in 1967, had peaked at $36.50 per share in 1969 but had fallen to $2.63 per share in 1970 and $.06 per share in 1973 when trading was suspended.

Once Rosset had been dismissed, Fred Jordan, who had recently returned to Grove, was appointed temporarily to lead the post-Rosset company, and he was at first, naturally enough, optimistic about the future. "The new owners have been able to provide the [financial] support which has led to a true renaissance," he was quoted as saying. That had been exactly Rosset's hope when he sold Grove in 1985, but the "true renaissance" never occurred, with or without Rosset. Jordan himself was fully aware of the difficulties facing a new Grove in the altered social climate of the mid-1980s. "The kind of writers for which Grove provided a home in the sixties because they were outside the establishment are now being published by all the 'respectable' houses," he noted, "so that we must compete with everyone else for their books. So in a sense we have a price [to pay] for our success. The new ownership with its resources makes that possible." If the debts that the new owners inherited along with Grove's powerful backlist were substantial, the strategies for recovery seemed only to drive the company further into debt.

With a rejection of Rosset, moreover, the new owners rejected some of Grove's heritage as well, at least its seedier side. They abandoned the profitable Victorian Library of erotica (much of which Rosset subsequently used to start Blue Moon Books in 1987), and Grove/Weidenfeld began the process of competing for new authors at a time of rapidly escalating advances. By the mid-'80s, however, publishing had become an author's market, a climate exactly the opposite of that in which Rosset began. The largest advance that Grove had paid to Nobel Prize winner Samuel Beckett was $2,500. During this period advances even at Grove reached the high six figures.

By 1989–90 the Grove/Weidenfeld imprint had published some significant new authors (Penelope Lively and Bharati Mukherjee among them), but it had yet to produce the sort of book that could turn a company around financially. Ann Getty's financial advisers began urging divestiture. Rosset immediately tried to repurchase Grove a second time. In 1986, just after his dismissal, he had offered Getty and Weidenfeld a reported $4.5 million to buy Grove back, but that offer was spurned. When Grove was put on the market in 1990, Rosset, with a consortium of publishers, several of whom were former Grove editors turned publishers (Kent Carroll and Herman Graf of Carroll and Graf, Neil Ortenberg of Thunder's Mouth Press, Glenn Young of Applause Theatre Book Publishers, and John Oakes and Dan Simon of Four Walls Eight Windows), offered some $11.5 million for the press he sold five years earlier for $2 million—again to no avail. Then, as quickly as the press was put on the market (and as potential buyers began to withdraw), Getty halted the sale and pledged that Grove would remain "an independent publishing house dedicated to publishing quality works" (*New York Times*, May 9, 1990). Production was halved from seventy to some thirty-five titles, and a downsized Grove began to limp along. By February of 1993, however, a merger was announced with Atlantic Monthly Press; Grove would now be led by Atlantic Monthly's former senior editor and current publisher, Morgan Entrekin. Financing for the merger was arranged by Joan Bingham, founder and publisher of the *Washington Weekly*, who would become vice president and an active acquisitions editor at Grove/Atlantic.

Grove/Atlantic

As early as 1990 Kent Carroll, one of the former Grove editors then trying to buy back Grove with Rosset, suggested that if Grove were to merge a likely partner would be Atlantic Monthly Press, which has its own long and distinguished history. Founded in 1917 as an affiliate of the magazine, that is, some thirty-five years before Grove Press, Atlantic Monthly Press quickly developed an independent profile as its books won more than sixteen Pulitzer Prizes and National Book Awards over the next sixteen years. It was publishing best-selling, award-winning titles like *Mutiny on the Bounty, Good-bye, Mr. Chips, Drums Along the Mohawk, Ship of Fools, Fire in the Lake, The Soul of the New Machine,* and *Blue Highways*. In 1985 the press was spun off from the magazine, and a year later Carl Navarre purchased it and set about making it an independent house.

Morgan Entrekin bought the company in August of 1991, but it came without its previous strong backlist, which stayed with Little, Brown when

Atlantic Monthly severed all ties with its parent company in 1989. Atlantic was, however, quickly developing a strong frontlist with authors like Patricia Highsmith, J. P. Donleavy, Bruce Jay Friedman, P. J. O'Rourke, Richard Ford, Raymond Carver, Jeanette Winterson, Tobias Wolff, Rian Malan, and Ron Chernow, author of the National Book Award–winning *The House of Morgan*. What Atlantic lacked, however, was a backlist, and so, as Carroll had suggested, the two companies seemed complementary—Atlantic Monthly's frontlist to Grove's backlist (which included four Grove-nurtured Nobel Prize winners). In Entrekin's words, the union was "a perfect fit."

Immediately after the merger, Entrekin announced austerity measures. He would cut "overhead to the bone" in order to return Grove to profitability. The most painful decisions were those involving personnel, but, as Entrekin noted, "[Grove Press] was staffed like a Random House or a Doubleday." In individual interviews he personally dismissed almost all of Grove's thirty or so employees, retaining or rehiring a handful to smooth the transition and maintain a tradition, most notably Eric Price and Judith Hottensen, who became mainstays of the merged company. Others were rehired as needed, as part-time or freelance editors to complete projects in progress. Entrekin's strategy with his new company was exactly the one he used to stabilize Atlantic Monthly Press, a feat that brought high praise from industry analysts. D. T. Max, for one, writing in the weekly *Variety,* noted, "Entrekin has successfully run [Atlantic Monthly Press] since 1991 without backlist, reference, children's or textbook income, an unprecedented highwire act in modern publishing" (February 22, 1993). With the purchase of Grove, Entrekin was back on the highwire, but this time with a net, Grove's backlist. The trimmer Grove/Atlantic would publish some fifty titles per year combined and market them aggressively.

The 1993 merger was not without its skeptics, however. Norton chairman Donald Lamm, for one, seems to have missed the possible symbiosis in the merger when he observed, "If you put two sick people together in a ward, I don't know that they improve faster. Maybe they just communicate their illnesses to each other." And much of Grove's former staff was, not unexpectedly, hostile; Entrekin was out to destroy Grove, they charged, his only interest being to pillage Grove's backlist. To charges that "He's killed Grove," Entrekin responded, "I'm absolutely going to be publishing new Grove books, and I'd be foolish not to because that imprint has value. . . . It would be smarter for me to fold the AtMo name and publish things under Grove."

The problems facing Entrekin in 1993 were finally exactly those that faced Rosset after 1970 and Getty/Weidenfeld in 1985: how to return Grove Press to profitability while maintaining something of the Grove spirit when the age that fostered and nourished it had passed? Entrekin's solution was to return Grove to and keep it focused on its historic strengths. Much of Rosset's economic failure with Grove grew out of what was finally a prescient vision of the future of American publishing. He saw as early as 1963 when he established the Evergreen Theater, Inc., began producing films the following year (Samuel Beckett's *Film* being his one tangible product), and moved Grove Press into film distribution in 1967 that book publishing would become part of media conglomerates. In the near term, however, Rosset's aggressive move into film may finally have been as devastating to Grove as any other single force, especially since, as much of his staff felt, Rosset lost interest in books. That same shift from the word to the image would drive the change to a glossy *Evergreen* in May of 1964, but by 1972 *Evergreen* too had collapsed. Without question copious amounts of energy and resources were diverted in the late '60s and early '70s from what might have been Grove's prime focus, the publication of quality manuscripts, into enterprises that were costlier and so riskier. As Kent Carroll, the editor closest to Grove's move into film, has observed, "The movie part of [Grove] absorbed Barney's time and attention for a while, and Barney insisted that Dick Seaver, Fred Jordan, and other key people get involved in film, so it was like this giant sponge that was soaking up everything, and detracting from the publishing side of the business, and so it had a dual effect. Not only was it a financial drain, but it also shifted the energies and the focus of the company from what Grove did best."

In many respects the merger with Atlantic Monthly Press would allow Grove to return to what it did best and do so on a scale that was manageable. The most persistent question about long-term prospects for the merged press remains, however: How much of the Grove spirit is sustainable in a new era and a new century? *The Grove Press Reader, 1951–2001* provides one response to that question as it outlines the strong continuity between at least the early Rosset Grove and the current Entrekin Grove.

Grove/Atlantic is now publishing Will Self and Dennis Cooper, for instance, writers who are pushing the borders of what is permissible in, and acceptable as, literature. And J. P. Donleavy and Terry Southern, early Olympia Press authors whom Rosset would like to have published, are now Grove/Atlantic authors. Rosset's yardstick for measuring Grove's purpose or philosophy remains a useful measure of Entrekin's Grove/Atlantic. To the question does Grove/Atlantic have a purpose beyond generally publishing quality works, the response remains, "There's a purpose, but the only way you could discern the purpose is by looking at the books we publish." A *Grove Press Reader, 1951–2001*, then, not only celebrates Grove's survival through a turbulent half century but proclaims a triumph, that the best of the spirit of Grove is being cultivated at Grove/Atlantic. With the merger, moreover, Entrekin moved Atlantic Monthly's offices into those of Grove, rather than the other way around, as an acknowledgment of Grove's roots in the neighborhood where, as Rosset said, "it all happened." At 841 Broadway, Grove/Atlantic is not five blocks from the 9th Street brownstone where the Grove legend began and not much farther from Grove Street, after which the original company was named.

For Further Reading

"Barney Rosset: The Art of Publishing II" (an interview with Ken Jordan), *The Paris Review*, 145 (1998): 171–215.

S. E. Gontarski, *Modernism, Censorship, and the Politics of Publishing: The Grove Press Legacy* (Chapel Hill, N.C.: Hanes Foundation, Rare Book Collection / University Library, The University of North Carolina at Chapel Hill, 2000).

Charles Rembar, *The End* of *Obscenity: The Trials* of *"Lady Chatterley," "Tropic of Cancer," and "Fanny Hill"* (New York: Random House, 1968).

The Review of Contemporary Fiction: Grove Press Number, ed. by S. E. Gontarski, vol. 10, no. 3 (Fall 1990).

The 1950s

BARNEY ROSSET INTERVIEWS
GIANGIACOMO FELTRINELLI, WNET RADIO [1959]

❧☙

Doctor Zhivago and Censorship

BARNEY ROSSET: Mr. Feltrinelli, could you tell me, someone who has not been in publishing too long myself, when you started publishing books and what kind of books did you publish in Italy?

FELTRINELLI: We started publishing books in 1955. Apart from some exceptions the books were rather bad books.

BARNEY ROSSET: Why did you come to America at this time?

FELTRINELLI: I came to America because we are now publishing better books. We want to publish still far better books. I thought that direct and personal contact with American publishers was an important step to develop our publishing activity, to get new authors on our list, and to have a direct survey of literary production in America.

BARNEY ROSSET: Are there any writers that you heard about, that made an impression on you and stand out in your mind? Are there three or four writers that would be most likely to be published by you in Italy?

FELTRINELLI: I have not found very many. It's a period of transition. There are a few newcomers who will be big probably in a few years: James Purdy, Jack Kerouac, although he is no youngster anymore. We hope to have a number of these books on our list.

BARNEY ROSSET: You mention the word "Beatnik." I find myself allergic to this word. What do you mean when you say "Beatnik"?

FELTRINELLI: A new generation of hard authors and writers who tell the facts of life as they see it, in a harsh way, telling them in a crude way.

BARNEY ROSSET: Do you think that this is good or bad? Do you think that this is the kind of writing that would appeal to you and to other people in Italy?

FELTRINELLI: I think that there are a number of points about this type of writing. It puts aside all the phony, dulcificated, making life rosy and so on. In every country there are problems and there is good and bad, and the only way to deal with that is to write about it or speak about it in direct terms.

BARNEY: You have been an unusual figure to arrive on the public scene in recent years. It's not often that a publisher of books has created the attention that you have, Mr. Feltrinelli. It's been mainly centered around the publication of Boris Pasternak's book *Doctor Zhivago*. Could you tell us how you came to publish this book?

FELTRINELLI: The novel came to me in the simplest of ways. I had a friend staying in Moscow scouting for me, and telling me what was new.

BARNEY ROSSET: Excuse me. But I find that a very interesting point. How does one have a friend staying in Moscow who is scouting for you? This is something that I feel jealous of and wonder how one has such a thing.

FELTRINELLI: There are a number of young Italian men who study at a university in Moscow for two or three years. One of them before leaving asked me if I was interested in getting regular news about new Russian literature or nonfiction. I said "Yes, naturally." When he was staying there in 1956, he heard about Pasternak's forthcoming novel. I said "OK, go ahead." He contacted the author. They made the necessary agreements for its publication in Italy. The book was still scheduled for publication in the Soviet Union. There was no problem of the ban. This friend of mine brought me the original manuscript. I picked up the manuscript in Berlin. It was typed with his personal corrections and deletions.

BARNEY ROSSET: During this time did you hear anything from Pasternak himself?

FELTRINELLI: I got a number of letters from Pasternak and he seemed interested in its publication in Italy.

BARNEY ROSSET: Here, in this country, we read that at some point along the way, there seemed to be some change take place: either he or other people in the Soviet Union changed their minds.

FELTRINELLI: After being announced as a publication in the fall of '56 in Moscow, there was a change. At first I was asked to delay the publication until October 1957, to which I agreed because my translation wasn't ready. Afterwards the publication (in Russia) was definitely dropped. A number of representatives of Soviet writers, especially Aleksei Surkov, who was the chairman of the Soviet writers union, came to visit me. We discussed the book and he was very critical of the book. He tried to dissuade publication of this book.

BARNEY ROSSET: What did you think of his attempts to dissuade you?

FELTRINELLI: I felt that his political judgments were influenced by a strange political narrow-mindedness, I should say. It had nothing to do with an objective judgment of the book, which I do not consider an anti-Soviet novel or an anti-communist novel. It's a novel about hard times in a country. It's about human beings and their struggle in life. It contains a number of fundamental lessons which apply to every human being in a modern society.

BARNEY ROSSET: Would you have felt differently if it had been an anti-Soviet novel?

FELTRINELLI: The question for me is a question of quality. I don't think that literary art can be judged strictly by political issues and political schemes.

BARNEY ROSSET: I certainly agree with you. But when Surkov felt that the book shouldn't be published because of what he felt to be its anti-Soviet nature, did this cause you to have any new feelings about the Soviet Union itself?

FELTRINELLI: I was surprised that a country forty years after a successful revolution, with the Soviets still in power, that the Soviets should be so preoccupied with such a novel. I thought that it was absolutely ridiculous. Such human experiences can happen practically under any government in any country.

BARNEY ROSSET: Personally, as a publisher, I have always been interested in censorship. This has always been an important problem in the United States. Freedom of the press. We think that you have had some firsthand experiences in this matter since you published *Doctor Zhivago*. Do you think that there should be any censorship either by the church or the state on moral, political, or obscenity grounds? In other words, do you think that there should be any censorship in a free society?

FELTRINELLI: I don't think that in a free society there can be any censorship. What I think is that if somebody undertakes a publication of works that are of books and other forms of expressions which have no artistic value but only strive for obscenity, then they should be brought to court and a discussion made, a debate on the grounds of obscenity and whether they can be prosecuted or not.

BARNEY ROSSET: Do you feel that there are people qualified to state whether something ceases to have artistic merit and crosses over that line into the area of obscenity?

FELTRINELLI: This is a very difficult question and it is nearly as difficult as the first one you put, Mr. Rosset. I don't think one can define who's who, but the fact that only after the actual publication, the author or a publishing house or a newspaper, can be prosecuted allows the gathering or the forming of a general opinion about the subject. Then the discussion is much larger than the one that takes place in the court. Therefore, when public opinion is made on a subject then we can have bad judgment on one case. But public opinion if roused and when roused will slowly influence the legislature and the judges as to what is what.

BARNEY ROSSET: Of course, it's rather a moot point as to whether this public opinion will influence the legislatures and the judges in a good direction. But let's agree that eventually one could decide on what was obscene and what wasn't. What damage do you feel that the publication of so-called obscene litera-ture would do to the population? I ask this rather loaded question, Mr. Feltrinelli, because I personally feel that in a free society, or a reasonable facsimile thereof, there's a number of risks that one must take in order to have that society. One of them, I feel, is that there must be complete freedom of expression.

FELTRINELLI: I quite agree with you, Mr. Rosset. In fact, let me say that I do not conceive that in a free country there should be censorship. What I said and what I stressed was that after publication, if this publication goes over the limit (now it's always difficult to decide what this limit is, I know), then the person responsible for this publication should be prosecuted. In a free society there have always been irresponsible persons who want to cash in and go over the limit. I say no censorship, but after something is published it has to be discussed.

BARNEY ROSSET: There has always been some form of censorship in every soci-ety. As a young boy who grew up under the regime of Mussolini in Italy, Mr. Feltrinelli, what sort of censorship took place during those years?

FELTRINELLI: I was really too young to know much about it. What I knew was that there was censorship on news, on politics, and on books and literature, anything that could be considered critical of the Fascist state.

BARNEY ROSSET: That is certainly something we would all have expected. I'm rather curious to know what were the laws or customs at that time insofar as the publishing of materials which could be considered pornographic or obscene?

FELTRINELLI: I couldn't tell you. When the war started I was fourteen years old and knew nothing about pornography.

BARNEY ROSSET: Today in Italy what type of censorship, if any, exists insofar as the church is concerned or the government, and if any censorship exists today what form does it take? Who says what you cannot print?

FELTRINELLI: Nobody says. There doesn't exist any form of censorship in Italy today. When you publish a book, if the general attorney sees in it anything which is rebellious or pornographic, he may sue the publisher and the author.

BARNEY ROSSET: I think that we have a little confusion here over the meaning of the word "censorship." It appears to me that you're considering censorship as something which is done before the act. In other words, a book or a magazine or a newspaper which is read by some official before it is published and perhaps certain sections are deleted. I think that here (in the United States) we would think that after the book had been published, if the author or publisher or seller of the book or magazine was arrested because he was selling a certain book or magazine, that this would be censorship. How does this happen in Italy if a similar thing happens after publication?

FELTRINELLI: You are exact in the definition of my sense of the word "censorship." What I consider censorship is previous to publication. In Italy, there is nothing previous to publication. There is activity after publication, and this is on different grounds. You will see the "Left" press prosecuted because it attacks somebody and discovers somebody's personal level of businesses, more or less sordid, and then it will be prosecuted on the grounds of creating disturbances. You will find important authors often attacked on the grounds of pornography, but I must say that on the whole the Italian courts do not follow the line of the general attorney, that is, of the prosecution. In all cases that I know of publishers and authors being prosecuted by the general attorney, the court decided against the prosecutor's view.

BARNEY ROSSET: What if the general public felt that the general intent of the publisher was to publish a book which might perhaps have superficial artistic ends, but was really basically meant to be a pornographic, obscene publication— what if the general public came to that decision and what if the courts also came to that decision, and on the basis of this unanimity of feeling the courts confiscated the book? Would you feel that they were doing the right thing?

FELTRINELLI: No. Because life is a continuous development. There are forces which are established today and which will be overcome by new forces tomorrow. I mean the majority may never hold from the minority the possibility of getting to be the majority.

BARNEY ROSSET: A moment ago, though, I thought that you felt that after a book was published that then the public and various forms of public debate would form its own opinion on a book or a magazine and it would arrive at a more or less correct solution. In this century, as somebody, myself, who is about to publish *Lady Chatterley's Lover*. This book has been banned in this country since its inception, since the book was first published in Italy, I might say, in 1928. When attempts have been made to bring it into this country it has been declared obscene by various legal authorities. What am I to think? Am I publishing a book which is obscenity for obscenity's sake because of previous legal decisions? Or am I to go on my own judgment that it is something that I wish to distribute to the public?

FELTRINELLI: I think that you do right when you go on your own judgment. Experiences of men and women are experiences of human beings, and I don't see why, their intimate lives, their love lives, and their sex lives: I don't see why one shouldn't write about them. All these questions are extremely controversial. Nobody has a definite answer. I don't think that you have a definite answer on all these questions. . . .

BARNEY ROSSET: Mr. Feltrinelli, I would like to interject here that I feel that personally there hasn't been a word written or uttered that shouldn't be published, singly or in multiples. I think that is stating my position.

FELTRINELLI: But you are a responsible man who will not use words only to make money in the worst way. I know that it is extremely difficult and extremely controversial where the limit is. I know that when a limit is imposed it usually is used on a larger field and for other purposes than the purposes which it was meant for. This is a big problem: the irresponsibility of some people who have publishing means.

BARNEY ROSSET: One last question. I think that in general we both agree that censorship is a bad thing. You may feel that there are certain instances when censorship is called for. I don't think that there are any such instances. What do you think are the best ways, or are there existing forces in society today, which go to make for a free press?

FELTRINELLI: I don't know if I have an answer for that. I mean freedom, parliament, decentralized government, and decentralization of responsibilities, the possibility of people to meet, to talk, to discuss, to publish their words, is the only real way against censorship. Censorship is in many instances the battle of new forces against old forces. You have this happen in your body all the time. It's a daily fight which will always exist and must be carried on with extreme energy. This is still an unsolved problem of modern advanced countries.

BARNEY ROSSET: Thank you, Signor Feltrinelli. For those of you who might have tuned in late, the man whom we have just interviewed is Signor Feltrinelli, Italian publisher, a very bold and fortunate man. He is the first to publish anywhere in the world the novel *Doctor Zhivago* by the Nobel Prize winner Boris Pasternak, Soviet author. Hope you enjoyed it. This is Barney Rosset. Thanks for listening.

MATTHEW G. LEWIS

❦

FROM *The Monk* [1952]

Scarce had he pronounced the last word, when the effects of the charm were evident. A loud burst of thunder was heard, the prison shook to its very foundations, a blaze of lightning flashed through the cell, and in the next moment, borne upon sulphurous whirlwinds, Lucifer stood before him a second time. But he came not as when at Matilda's summons he borrowed the seraph's form to deceive Ambrosio. He appeared in all that ugliness which since his fall from heaven had been his portion. His blasted limbs still bore marks of the Almighty's thunder. A swarthy darkness spread itself over his gigantic form: his hands and feet were armed with long talons. Fury glared in his eyes, which might have struck the bravest heart with terror. Over his huge shoulders waved two enormous sable wings: and his hair was supplied by living snakes, which twined themselves round his brows with frightful hissings. In one hand he held a roll of parchment, and in the other an iron pen. Still the lightning flashed around him, and the thunder with repeated bursts seemed to announce the dissolution of Nature.

Terrified at an apparition so different from what he had expected, Ambrosio remained gazing upon the fiend, deprived of the power of utterance. The thunder had ceased to roll: universal silence reigned through the dungeon.

"For what am I summoned hither?" said the dæmon, in a voice which *sulphurous fogs had damped to hoarseness.*

At the sound Nature seemed to tremble. A violent earthquake rocked the ground, accompanied by a fresh burst of thunder, louder and more appalling than the first.

Ambrosio was long unable to answer the dæmon's demand.

"I am condemned to die," he said with a faint voice, his blood running cold while he gazed upon his dreadful visitor. "Save me! bear me from hence!"

"Shall the reward of my services be paid me? Dare you embrace my cause? Will you be mine, body and soul? Are you prepared to renounce him who made you, and him who died for you? Answer but 'Yes!' and Lucifer is your slave."

"Will no less price content you? Can nothing satisfy you but my eternal ruin? Spirit, you ask too much. Yet convey me from this dungeon. Be my servant for one hour, and I will be yours for a thousand years. Will not this offer suffice?"

"It will not. I must have your soul: must have it mine, and mine for ever."

"Insatiate dæmon! I will not doom myself to endless torments. I will not give up my hopes of being one day pardoned."

"You will not? On what chimæra rest then your hopes? Short-sighted mortal! Miserable wretch! Are you not guilty? Are you not infamous in the eyes of men and angels? Can such enormous sins be forgiven? Hope you to escape my power? Your fate is already pronounced. The Eternal has abandoned you. Mine you are marked in the book of destiny, and mine you must and shall be."

"Fiend! 'tis false. Infinite is the Almighty's mercy, and the penitent shall meet his forgiveness. My crimes are monstrous, but I will not despair of pardon. Haply, when they have received due chastisement—"

"Chastisement? Was purgatory meant for guilt like yours? Hope you, that your offences shall be bought off by prayers of superstitious dotards and droning monks? Ambrosio! be wise. Mine you must be. You are doomed to flames, but may shun them for the present. Sign this parchment: I will bear you from hence, and you may pass your remaining years in bliss and liberty. Enjoy your existence. Indulge in every pleasure to which appetite may lead you. But from the moment that it quits your body, remember that your soul belongs to me, and that I will not be defrauded of my right."

The monk was silent: but his looks declared that the tempter's words were not thrown away. He reflected on the conditions proposed with horror. On the other hand, he believed himself doomed to perdition, and that, by refusing the dæmon's succour, he only hastened tortures which he never could escape. The fiend saw that his resolution was shaken. He renewed his instances, and endeavoured to fix the abbot's indecision. He described the agonies of death in the most terrific colours; and he worked so powerfully upon Ambrosio's despair and fears, that he prevailed upon him to receive the parchment. He then struck the iron pen which he held into a vein of the monk's left hand. It pierced deep, and was instantly filled with blood: yet Ambrosio felt no pain from the wound. The pen was put into his hand: it trembled. The wretch placed the parchment on the table before him, and prepared to sign it. Suddenly he held his hand: he started away hastily, and threw the pen upon the table.

"What am I doing?" he cried. Then turning to the fiend with a desperate air, "Leave me! begone! I will not sign the parchment."

"Fool!" exclaimed the disappointed dæmon, darting looks so furious as penetrated the friar's soul with horror. "Thus am I trifled with? Go then! Rave in agony, expire in tortures, and then learn the extent of the Eternal's mercy! But beware how you make me again your mock! Call me no more, till resolved to accept my offers. Summon me a second time to dismiss me thus idly, and these talons shall rend you into a thousand pieces. Speak yet again: will you sign the parchment?"

"I will not. Leave me. Away!"

Instantly the thunder was heard to roll horribly: once more the earth trembled with violence: the dungeon resounded with loud shrieks, and the dæmon fled with blasphemy and curses.

At first, the monk rejoiced at having resisted the seducer's arts, and obtained a triumph over mankind's enemy: but as the hour of punishment drew near, his former terrors revived in his heart. Their momentary repose seemed to have given them fresh vigour. The nearer that the time approached, the more did he dread appearing before the throne of God. He shuddered to think how soon he must be plunged into eternity—how soon meet the eyes of his Creator, whom he had so grievously offended. The bell announced midnight. It was the signal for being led to the stake. As he listened to the first stroke, the blood ceased to circulate in the abbot's veins. He heard death and torture murmured in each succeeding sound. He expected to see the archers entering his prison; and as the bell forbore to toll, he seized the magic volume in a fit of despair. He opened it, turned hastily to the seventh page, and, as if fearing to allow himself a moment's thought, ran over the fatal lines with rapidity. Accompanied by his former terrors, Lucifer again stood before the trembler.

"You have summoned me," said the fiend. "Are you determined to be wise? Will you accept my conditions? You know them already. Renounce your claim to salvation, make over to me your soul, and I bear you from this dungeon instantly. Yet is it time. Resolve, or it will be too late. Will you sign the parchment?"

"I must—Fate urges me—I accept your conditions."

"Sign the parchment," replied the dæmon in an exulting tone.

The contract and the bloody pen still lay upon the table. Ambrosio drew near it. He prepared to sign his name. A moment's reflection made him hesitate.

"Hark!" cried the tempter: "they come. Be quick. Sign the parchment, and I bear you from hence this moment."

In effect, the archers were heard approaching, appointed to lead Ambrosio to the stake. The sound encouraged the monk in his resolution.

"What is the import of this writing?" said he.

"It makes your soul over to me for ever, and without reserve."

"What am I to receive in exchange?"

"My protection, and release from this dungeon. Sign it, and this instant I bear you away."

Ambrosio took up the pen. He set it to the parchment. Again his courage failed him. He felt a pang of terror at his heart, and once more threw the pen upon the table.

"Weak and puerile!" cried the exasperated fiend. "Away with this folly! Sign the writing this instant, or I sacrifice you to my rage."

At this moment the bolt of the outward door was drawn back. The prisoner heard the rattling of chains: the heavy bar fell: the archers were on the point of entering. Worked up to phrensy by the urgent danger, shrinking from the approach of death, terrified by the dæmon's threats, and seeing no other means to escape destruction, the wretched monk complied. He signed the fatal contract, and gave it hastily into the evil spirit's hands, whose eyes, as he received the gift, glared with malicious rapture.

"Take it!" said the God-abandoned. "Now then save me! Snatch me from hence!"

"Hold! Do you freely and absolutely renounce your Creator and his Son?"

"I do! I do!"

"Do you make over your soul to me for ever?"

"For ever!"

"Without reserve or subterfuge? without future appeal to the divine mercy?"

The last chain fell from the door of the prison. The key was heard turning in the lock. Already the iron door grated heavily upon its rusty hinges—

"I am yours for ever, and irrevocably!" cried the monk wild with terror: "I abandon all claim to salvation. I own no power but yours. Hark! hark! they come! Oh! save me! bear me away!"

"I have triumphed! You are mine past reprieve, and I fulfil my promise."

While he spoke, the door unclosed. Instantly the dæmon grasped one of Ambrosio's arms, spread his broad pinions, and sprang with him into the air. The roof opened as they soared upwards, and closed again when they had quitted the dungeon.

In the mean while, the gaoler was thrown into the utmost surprise by the disappearance of his prisoner. Though neither he nor the archers were in time to witness the monk's escape, a sulphurous smell prevailing through the prison sufficiently informed them by whose aid he had been liberated. They hastened to make their report to the Grand Inquisitor. The story, how a sorcerer had been carried away by the Devil, was soon noised about Madrid; and for some days the whole city was employed in discussing the subject. Gradually it ceased to be the topic of conversation. Other adventures arose whose novelty engaged universal attention: and Ambrosio was soon forgotten as totally as if he never had existed. While this was passing, the monk, supported by his infernal guide, traversed the air with the rapidity of an arrow; and a few moments placed him upon a precipice's brink, the steepest in Sierra Morena.

Though rescued from the Inquisition, Ambrosio as yet was insensible of the blessings of liberty. The damning contract weighed heavy upon his mind; and the scenes in which he had been a principal actor, had left behind them such impressions as rendered his heart the seat of anarchy and confusion. The objects now before his eyes, and which the full moon sailing through clouds permitted him to examine, were ill calculated to inspire that calm of which he stood so much in need. The disorder of his imagination was increased by the wildness of the surrounding scenery; by the gloomy caverns and steep rocks, rising above each other, and dividing the passing clouds; solitary clusters of trees scattered here and there, among whose thick-twined branches the wind of night sighed hoarsely and mournfully; the shrill cry of mountain eagles, who had built their nests among these lonely deserts; the stunning roar of torrents, as swelled by late rains they rushed violently down tremendous precipices; and the dark waters of a silent sluggish stream, which faintly reflected the moon-beams, and bathed the rock's base on which Ambrosio stood. The abbot cast round him a look of terror. His infernal conductor was still by his side, and eyed him with a look of mingled malice, exultation, and contempt.

"Whither have you brought me?" said the monk at length in an hollow trembling voice: "Why am I placed in this melancholy scene? Bear me from it quickly! Carry me to Matilda!"

The fiend replied not, but continued to gaze upon him in silence. Ambrosio could not sustain his glance; he turned away his eyes, while thus spoke the dæmon:

"I have him then in my power! This model of piety! this being without reproach! this mortal who placed his puny virtues on a level with those of angels. He is mine! irrevocably, eternally mine! Companions of my sufferings! denizens of hell! How grateful will be my present!"

He paused; then addressed himself to the monk—

"Carry you to Matilda?" he continued, repeating Ambrosio's words: "Wretch! you shall soon be with her! You well deserve a place near her, for hell boasts no miscreant more guilty than yourself. Hark, Ambrosio, while I unveil your crimes! You have shed the blood of two innocents; Antonia and Elvira perished by your hand. That Antonia whom you violated, was your sister! that Elvira whom you murdered, gave you birth! Tremble, abandoned hypocrite! inhuman parricide! incestuous ravisher! tremble at the extent of your offences! And you it was who thought yourself proof against temptation, absolved from human frailties, and free from error and vice! Is pride then a virtue? Is inhumanity no fault? Know, vain man! that I long have marked you for my prey: I watched the movements of your heart; I saw that you were virtuous from vanity, not principle, and I seized the fit moment of seduction. I observed your blind idolatry of the Madonna's picture. I bade a subordinate but crafty spirit assume a similar form, and you eagerly yielded to the blandishments of Matilda. Your pride was gratified by her flattery; your lust only needed an opportunity to break forth; you ran into the snare blindly, and scrupled not to commit a crime, which you blamed in another with unfeeling severity. It was I who threw Matilda in your way; it was I who gave you entrance to Antonia's chamber; it was I who caused the dagger to be given you which pierced your sister's bosom; and it was I who warned Elvira in dreams of your designs upon her daughter, and thus, by preventing your profiting by her sleep, compelled you to add rape as well as incest to the catalogue of your crimes. Hear, hear, Ambrosio! Had you resisted me one minute longer, you had saved your body and soul. The guards whom you heard at your prison-door, came to signify your pardon. But I had already triumphed: my plots had already succeeded. Scarcely could I propose crimes so quick as you performed them. You are mine, and Heaven itself cannot rescue you from my power. Hope not that your penitence will make void our contract. Here is your bond signed with your blood; you have given up your claim to mercy, and nothing can restore to you the rights which you have foolishly resigned. Believe you, that your secret thoughts escaped me? No, no, I read them all! You trusted that you should still have time for repentance. I saw your artifice, knew its falsity, and rejoiced in deceiving the deceiver! You are mine beyond reprieve: I burn to possess my right, and alive you quit not these mountains."

During the dæmon's speech, Ambrosio had been stupefied by terror and surprise. This last declaration roused him.

"Not quit these mountains alive?" he exclaimed: "Perfidious, what mean you? Have you forgotten our contract?"

The fiend answered by a malicious laugh:

"Our contract? Have I not performed my part? What more did I promise than to save you from your prison? Have I not done so? Are you not safe from the Inquisition—safe from all but from me? Fool that you were to confide yourself to a devil! Why did you not stipulate for life, and power, and pleasure? Then all would have been granted: now, your reflections come too late. Miscreant, prepare for death; you have not many hours to live!"

On hearing this sentence, dreadful were the feelings of the devoted wretch! He sank upon his knees, and raised his hands towards heaven. The fiend read his intention, and prevented it—

"What?" he cried, darting at him a look of fury: "Dare you still implore the Eternal's mercy? Would you feign penitence, and again act an hypocrite's part? Villain, resign your hopes of pardon. Thus I secure my prey!"

As he said this, darting his talons into the monk's shaven crown, he sprang with him from the rock. The caves and mountains rang with Ambrosio's shrieks. The dæmon continued to soar aloft, till reaching a dreadful height, he released the sufferer. Headlong fell the monk through the airy waste; the sharp point of a rock received him; and he rolled from precipice to precipice, till, bruised and mangled, he rested on the river's banks. Life still existed in his miserable frame: he attempted in vain to raise himself; his broken and dislocated limbs refused to perform their office, nor was he able to quit the spot where he had first fallen. The sun now rose above the horizon; its scorching beams darted full upon the head of the expiring sinner. Myriads of insects were called forth by the warmth; they drank the blood which trickled from Ambrosio's wounds; he had no power to drive them from him, and they fastened upon his sores, darted their stings into his body, covered him with their multitudes, and inflicted on him tortures the most exquisite and insupportable. The eagles of the rock tore his flesh piece-meal, and dug out his eye-balls with their crooked beaks. A burning thirst tormented him; he heard the river's murmur as it rolled beside him, but strove in vain to drag himself towards the sound. Blind, maimed, helpless, and despairing, venting his rage in blasphemy and curses, execrating his existence, yet dreading the arrival of death destined to yield him up to greater torments, six miserable days did the villain languish. On the seventh a violent storm arose: the winds in fury rent up rocks and forests: the sky was now black with clouds, now sheeted with fire: the rain fell in torrents; it swelled the stream; the waves overflowed their banks; they reached the spot where Ambrosio lay, and, when they abated, carried with them into the river the corse of the despairing monk.

SIMONE DE BEAUVOIR

※

"Must We Burn Sade?"

FROM *The Marquis de Sade: An Essay by Simone de Beauvoir with Selections from His Writings* [1953]

Translated from the French by Annette Michelson

When we meet Sade he is already mature, and we do not know how he has become what he is. Ignorance forbids us to account for his tendencies and spontaneous behavior. His emotional nature and the peculiar character of his sexuality are for us data which we can merely note. Because of this unfortunate gap, the truth about Sade will always remain closed to us; any explanation would leave a residue which only the childhood history of Sade might have clarified.

Nevertheless, the limits imposed on our understanding ought not to discourage us, for Sade, as we have said, did not restrict himself to a passive submission to the consequences of his early choices. His chief interest for us lies not in his aberrations, but in the manner in which he assumed responsibility for them. He made of his sexuality an ethic; he expressed this ethic in works of literature. It is by this deliberate act that Sade attains a real originality. The reason for his tastes is obscure, but we can understand how he erected these tastes into principles.

Superficially, Sade, at twenty-three, was like all other young aristocrats of his time; he was cultured, liked the theater and the arts, and was fond of reading. He was dissipated, kept a mistress—la Beauvoisin—and frequented the brothels. He married, without enthusiasm and in conformance to parental wishes, a young girl of the petty aristocracy, Renée-Pélagie de Montreuil, who was, however, rich. That was the beginning of the disaster that was to resound—and recur—throughout his life. Married in May, Sade was arrested in October for excesses committed in a house which he had been frequenting since June. The reasons for arrest were grave enough for Sade to send letters, which went astray, to the governor of the prison, begging him to keep them secret, lest he be hopelessly ruined. This episode suggests that Sade's eroticism had already assumed a disquieting character. This hypothesis is confirmed by the fact that a year later Inspector Marais warned the procuresses to stop giving their girls to the Marquis. But the interest of all this lies not in its value as information, but in the revelation which it constituted for Sade himself. On the verge of his adult life be made the brutal discovery that there was no conciliation possible between his social existence and his private pleasures.

There was nothing of the revolutionary nor even of the rebel about young Sade. He was quite prepared to accept society as it was. At the age of twenty-three he was obedient enough to his father* to accept a wife whom he disliked, and he envisaged no other life than the one to which his heredity destined him. He was to become a husband, father, marquis, captain, lord of the manor, and lieutenant general. He had not the slightest wish to renounce the privileges assured by his rank and his wife's fortune. Nevertheless, these things could not satisfy him. He was offered activities, responsibilities, and honors; nothing, no simple venture interested, amused, or excited him. He wished to be not only a public figure, whose acts are ordained by convention and routine, but a live human being as well. There was only one place where he could assert himself as such, and that was not the bed in which he was received only too submissively by a prudish wife, but in the brothel where he bought the right to unleash his fantasies.

And there was one dream common to most young aristocrats of the time. Scions of a declining class which had once possessed concrete power, but which no longer retained any real hold on the world, they tried to revive symbolically, in the privacy of the bedchamber, the status for which they were nostalgic, that of the lone and sovereign feudal despot. The orgies of the Duke of Carolais, among others, were bloody and famous. Sade, too, thirsted for this illusion of power. "What does one want when one is engaged in the sexual act? That everything about you give you its utter attention, think only of you, care only for you . . . every man wants to be a tyrant when he fornicates." The intoxication of tyranny leads directly to cruelty, for the libertine, in hurting the object that serves him, "tastes all the pleasures which a vigorous individual feels in making full use of his strength; he dominates, he is a tyrant."

Actually, whipping a few girls (for a consideration agreed upon in advance) is rather a petty feat; that Sade sets so much store on it is enough to cast suspicion upon him. We are struck by the fact that beyond the walls of his "little house" it did not occur to him to "make full use of his strength." There is no hint of ambition in him, no spirit of enterprise, no will to power, and I am quite prepared to believe that he was a coward. He does, to be sure, systematically endow his heroes with traits which society regards as flaws, but he paints Blangis with a satisfaction that justifies the assumption that this is a projection of himself, and the

---

*Klossowski is surprised by the fact that Sade bore his father no ill will. But Sade did not instinctively detest authority. He admits the right of the individual to exploit and to abuse his privileges. At first, Sade, who was heir to the family fortune, fought society only on the individual, emotional level, through women: his wife and mother-in-law.

following words have the direct ring of a confession: "A determined child might have frightened this colossus . . . he grew timid and cowardly, and the idea of an equally matched fight, however safe, would have sent him fleeing to the ends of the earth." The fact that Sade was at times capable of extravagant boldness, both out of rashness and generosity, does not invalidate the hypothesis that he was afraid of people and, in a more general way, afraid of the reality of the world.

If he talked so much about his strength of soul, it was not because he really possessed it, but because he longed for it. When faced with adversity, he would whine and get upset and become completely distraught. The fear of want which haunted him constantly was a symptom of a much more generalized anxiety. He mistrusted everything and everybody because he felt himself maladjusted. He was maladjusted. His behavior was disorderly. He accumulated debts; he would fly into a rage for no reason at all, would run away, or would yield at the wrong moment. He fell into every possible trap. He was uninterested in this boring and yet threatening world which had nothing valid to offer him and from which he hardly knew what to ask. He was to seek his truth elsewhere. When he writes that the passion of jealousy "subordinates" and "at the same time unites" all other passions, he gives us an exact description of his own experience. He subordinated his existence to his eroticism because eroticism appeared to him to be the only possible fulfillment of his existence. If he devoted himself to it with such energy, shamelessness, and persistence, he did so because he attached greater importance to the stories he wove around the act of pleasure than to the contingent happenings; he chose the imaginary.

At first Sade probably thought himself safe in the fool's paradise which seemed separated from the world of responsibility by an impenetrable wall. And perhaps, had no scandal broken out, he would have been but a common debauchee, known in special places for rather special tastes. Many libertines of the period indulged with impunity in orgies even worse. But scandal was probably inevitable in Sade's case. There are certain "sexual perverts" to whom the myth of Dr. Jekyll and Mr. Hyde is perfectly applicable. They hope, at first, to be able to gratify their "vices" without compromising their public characters. If they are imaginative enough to visualize themselves, little by little, in a dizziness of pride and shame, they give themselves away—like Charlus, despite his ruses, and even because of them. To what extent was Sade being provocative in his imprudence? There is no way of knowing. He probably wished to emphasize the radical separation between his family life and his private pleasures, and probably, too, the only way he could find satisfaction in this clandestine triumph lay in pushing it to the point where it burst forth into the open. His surprise is that of the child who keeps striking at a vase until it finally breaks. He was playing with fire and still thought himself master, but society was lying in wait. Society wants undisputed possession. It claims each individual unreservedly. It quickly seized upon Sade's secret and classified it as crime.

Sade reacted at first with prayer, humility, and shame. He begged to be allowed to see his wife, accusing himself of having grievously offended her. He begged to confess and open his heart to her. This was not mere hypocrisy. A horrible change had taken place overnight; natural, innocent practices, which had been hitherto merely sources of pleasure, had become punishable acts. The young charmer had changed into a black sheep. He had probably been familiar since childhood—perhaps through his relations with his mother—with the bitter pangs of remorse, but the scandal of 1763 revived them dramatically. Sade had a foreboding that he would henceforth and for the rest of his life be a culprit. For he valued his diversions too highly to think, even for a moment, of giving them up. Instead, he rid himself of shame through defiance. It is significant that his first deliberately scandalous act took place immediately after his imprisonment. La Beauvoisin accompanied him to the château of La Coste and, taking the name of Madame Sade, danced and played before the Provençal nobility, while the Abbé de Sade was forced to stand dumbly by. Society denied Sade illicit freedom; it wanted to socialize eroticism. Inversely, the Marquis' social life was to take place henceforth on an erotic level. Since one cannot, with any peace of mind, separate good from evil and devote one's self to each in turn, one has to assert evil in the face of good, and even as a function of good.

Sade tells us repeatedly that his ultimate attitude has its roots in resentment. "Certain souls seem hard because they are capable of strong feelings, and they are sometimes very distant; their apparent unconcern and cruelty are but ways, known only to themselves, of feeling more strongly than others."* And Dolmancé** attributes his vice to the wickedness of men. "It was their ingratitude which dried up my heart, their treachery which destroyed in me those baleful virtues for which, like you, I may have been born." The fiendish morality which he later established in theoretical form was first a matter of actual experience.

It was through Renée-Pélagie that Sade came to know all the insipidity and boredom of virtue. He lumped them together in the disgust which only a creature of flesh and blood can arouse. But he learned also from Renée, to his delight, that Good, in concrete, fleshly, individual form, can be vanquished in single combat. His wife was not his enemy, but like all the wife-characters she inspired, a choice victim, a willing accomplice. The relationship between Blamont and his wife is probably a fairly precise reflection of Sade's with the

*Aline et Valcour.
**La Philosophie dans le Boudoir.

Marquise. Blamont takes pleasure in caressing his wife at the very moment that he is hatching the blackest plots against her. To inflict enjoyment—Sade understood this 150 years before the psychoanalysts, and his works abound in victims submitted to pleasure before being tortured—can be a tyrannical violence; and the torturer disguised as lover delights to see the credulous lover, swooning with voluptuousness and gratitude, mistake cruelty for tenderness. The joining of such subtle pleasures with the performance of social obligation is doubtless what led Sade to have three children by his wife.

And he had the further satisfaction of seeing virtue become the ally of vice, and its handmaiden. Madame de Sade concealed her husband's delinquencies for years; she bravely engineered his escape from Miolans, fostered the intrigue between her sister and the Marquis, and later, lent her support to the orgies at the château of La Coste. She went even so far as to inculpate herself when, in order to discredit the accusations of Nanon, she hid some silverware in her bags. Sade never displayed the least gratitude. In fact, the notion of gratitude is one at which he keeps blasting away most furiously. But he very obviously felt for her the ambiguous friendship of the despot for what is unconditionally his. Thanks to her, he was able not only to reconcile his role of husband, father, and gentleman with his pleasures, but he established the dazzling superiority of vice over goodness, devotion, fidelity, and decency, and flouted society prodigiously by submitting the institution of marriage and all the conjugal virtues to the caprices of his imagination and senses.

If Renée-Pélagie was Sade's most triumphant success, Madame de Montreuil embodies his failure. She represents the abstract and universal justice which inevitably confronts the individual. It was against her that he most eagerly entreated his wife's support. If he could win his case in the eyes of virtue, the law would lose much of its power, for its most formidable arms were neither prison nor the scaffold, but the venom with which it could infect vulnerable hearts. Renée became perturbed under the influence of her mother. The young canoness grew fearful. A hostile society invaded Sade's household and dampened his pleasures, and he himself yielded to its power. Defamed and dishonored, he began to doubt himself. And that was Madame de Montreuil's supreme crime against him. A guilty man is, first of all, a man accused; it was she who made a criminal of Sade. That is why he never left off ridiculing her, defaming her, and torturing her throughout his writings; he was killing off his own faults in her. There is a possible basis for Klossowski's theory that Sade hated his own mother; the singular character of his sexuality suggests this. But this hatred would never have been inveterate had not Renée's mother made motherhood hateful to him. Indeed, she played such an important and frightful role that it may well be that she was the sole object of his attack. It is certainly she, in any case, whom he savagely submits to the jeers of her own daughter in the last pages of *La Philosophie dans le Boudoir*.

If Sade was finally beaten by his mother-in-law and by the law, he was accomplice to this defeat. Whatever the role of chance and of his own imprudence in the scandal of 1763, there is no doubt that he afterwards sought a heightening of his pleasures in danger. We may therefore say that he desired the very persecutions which he suffered with indignation. Choosing Easter Sunday to decoy the beggar, Rose Keller, into his house at Arcueil meant playing with fire. Beaten, terrorized, inadequately guarded, she ran off, raising a scandal for which Sade paid with two short terms in prison.

During the following three years of exile which, except for a few periods of service, he spent on his property in Provence, he seemed sobered. He played the husband and lord of the manor most conscientiously. He had two children by his wife, received the homage of the community of Saumane, attended to his park, and read and produced plays in his theater, including one of his own. But he was ill-rewarded for this edifying behavior. In 1771, he was imprisoned for debt. Once he was released, his virtuous zeal cooled off. He seduced his young sister-in-law, of whom he seemed, for a while, genuinely fond. She was a canoness, a virgin, and his wife's sister, all of which lent a certain zest to the adventure. Nevertheless, he went to seek still other distractions in Marseille, and in 1772 the "affair of the aphrodisiac candies" took on unexpected and terrifying proportions. While in flight to Italy with his sister-in-law, he and Latour, his valet, were sentenced to death in absentia, and both of them were burned in effigy on the town square of Aix. The canoness took refuge in a French convent, where she spent the rest of her life, and he hid away in Savoy. He was caught and locked up in the château of Miolans, but his wife helped him escape. However, he was henceforth a hunted man. Whether roaming through Italy or shut up in his castle, he knew that he would never be allowed a normal life.

Occasionally, he took his lordly role seriously. A troupe of actors was staying on his property to give *The Cuckold, Whipped and Happy*. Sade, irritated perhaps by the title, ordered that the posters be defaced by the town clerk, as being "disgraceful and a challenge to the freedom of the Church." He expelled from his property a certain Saint-Denis, against whom he had certain grievances, saying, "I have every right to expel all loafers and vagrants from my property." But these acts of authority were not enough to amuse him. He tried to realize the dream which was to haunt his books. In the solitude of the château of La Coste, he set up for himself a harem submissive to his whims. With the aid of the Marquise, he gathered together several handsome valets, a secretary who was illiterate but attractive, a luscious cook, a chambermaid, and two young girls provided by bawds. But La Coste was not the inaccessible fortress of *Les 120 Journées de Sodome;* it was surrounded by society. The maids escaped, the chambermaid left to give birth to a child whose paternity she attributed to Sade, the cook's father came to shoot Sade, and the handsome secretary was sent for by his parents. Only Renée-Pélagie conformed to the character assigned to her by her husband; all the others claimed the right to live their own lives, and Sade was once again made to understand that he could not turn the real world of hard fact into a theater.

This world was not content to thwart his dreams; it repudiated him. Sade fled to Italy, but Madame de Montreuil, who had not forgiven him for having seduced her younger daughter, lay in wait for him. When he got back to France, he ventured into Paris, and she took advantage of the occasion to have him locked up on the 13th of February, 1777, in the château of Vincennes. He was brought to trial and sent back to Aix and took refuge at La Coste, where, under the resigned eye of his wife, he embarked on an idyl with his housekeeper, Mademoiselle Rousset. But by the 7th of November, he was back again at Vincennes, "locked up behind nineteen iron doors, like a wild beast."

And now begins another story. For eleven years—first at Vincennes and then in the Bastille—a man lay dying in captivity, but a writer was being born. The man was quickly broken. Reduced to impotence, not knowing how long his imprisonment would last, his mind wandered in delirious speculation. With minute calculations, though without any facts to work on, he tried to figure out how long his sentence would last. He recovered possession of his intellectual powers fairly quickly, as can be seen from his correspondence with Madame de Sade and Mademoiselle Rousset. But the flesh surrendered, and he sought compensation for his sexual starvation in the pleasures of the table. His valet, Carteron, tells us that "he smoked like a chimney" and "ate enough for four men" while in prison. Extreme in everything, as he himself declares, he became wolfish. He had his wife send him huge hampers of food, and he grew increasingly fat. In the midst of complaints, accusations, pleas, supplications, he still amused himself a bit by torturing the Marquise; he claimed to be jealous, accused her of plotting against him, and when she came to visit him, found fault with her clothes and ordered her to dress with extreme austerity. But these diversions were few and pallid. From 1782 on, he demanded of literature alone what life would no longer grant him: excitement, challenge, sincerity, and all the delights of the imagination. And even then, he was "extreme"; he wrote as he ate, in a frenzy. After *Dialogue entre un prêtre et un moribond* came *Les 120 Journées de Sodome, La Novelle Justine, Aline et Valcour.* According to the catalogue of 1788, he had by then written 35 acts for the theater, half a dozen tales, almost all of *Le Portefeuille d'un homme de lettres,* and the list is probably still incomplete.

When Sade was freed, on Good Friday of 1790, he could hope and did hope that a new period lay open before him. His wife asked for a separation. His sons (one was preparing to emigrate and the other was a Knight of Malta) were strangers to him; so was his "good, husky farm wench" of a daughter. Free of his family, he whom the old society had called an outcast was now going to try to adapt himself to the one which had just restored to him his dignity as a citizen. His plays were performed in public; *Oxtiern* was even a great success; he enrolled in the *Section des Piques* and was appointed president; he enthusiastically wrote speeches and drew up petitions. But the idyl with the Revolution did not last long. Sade was fifty years old, had a questionable past and an aristocratic disposition, which his hatred of the aristocracy had not subdued, and he was once again at odds with himself. He was a republican and, in theory, even called for complete socialism and the abolition of property, but insisted on keeping his castle and properties. The world to which he tried to adapt himself was again an all too real world whose brutal resistance wounded him. And it was a world governed by those universal laws which he regarded as abstract, false, and unjust. When society justified murder in their name, Sade withdrew in horror.

SAMUEL BECKETT AND BARNEY ROSSET

❧

Letters [1953–1955]

June 18, 1953

Dear Mr. Beckett,

It is about time that I write a letter to you—now that agents, publishers, friends, etc., have all acted as go-betweens. A copy of our catalogue has already been mailed to you, so you will be able to see what kind of publisher you have been latched onto. I hope that you won't be too disappointed.

We are very happy to have the contract back from Minuit, and believe me, we will do what we can to make your work known in this country.

The first order of the day would appear to be the translation. I have just sent off a letter to Alex Trocchi telling him that the difficulties did not seem as ominous from here as they evidently do from there to him at least.

If you would accept my first choice as translator the whole thing would be easily settled. That choice of course being you. That already apparently is a satisfactory condition insofar as the play is concerned. The agent here tells me that you have agreed to our proposal, and he is drawing up a simple letter contract now which we will mail to you tomorrow.

I explained to Trocchi at great length, and probably with great density, why I thought it better for Merlin not to publish the first act in advance of book publication. It seems to me that a whole act hardly comes under the heading of an "excerpt" and might really serve to take a little of the edge off of the book publication. I suggested instead that they publish excerpts from the novels whenever pieces are ready, and join me in putting the play out as a book as soon as conveniently possible. I hope that you will join me in this idea. *En Attendant Godot* should burst upon us as an entity in my opinion.

As for the translation of the novels, I am waiting first, to hear from you, what you advise, and whether or not you will tackle them yourself. If your decision is no, and I do hope that it won't be, we can discuss between us the likely people to do it. An interesting thing has happened here in that regard. A young man, Belgian by birth, who moved to this country some seven years ago, seems to me to be quite a talented writer. He originally wrote in French, but in the last few years he has turned to English, and I find no stiltedness or other problems in his use of our language. Beyond that, he is a great admirer of your work, and he immediately set to work to do a translation of Godot when someone told him I might publish it here. Now that you are doing it yourself there is not much future for his work, but I thought if you were willing I would show you what he did, and it might indicate to you whether or not he might be capable of doing the novels. If you look at this job please do not hesitate to give us your real opinion, one way or the other. His unsolicited effort is the only thing that has been done toward translation from here, so my mind is completely open—excepting that I think you should do it.

Sylvia Beach is certainly the one you must blame for your future appearance on the Grove Press list. I went to see her with your work on my mind, and after she talked of you . . . [scratched out] . . . I immediately decided that what the Grove Press needed most in the world was Samuel Beckett. I told her that, and then she suggested that I make a specific offer. I certainly had not thought of that up to the very moment she took out a piece of paper and pencil and prepared to write down the terms.

A second person was also very important. He is Wallace Fowlie. At my request he read the play and the two novels with great care and came back with the urgent plea for me to take on your work. Fowlie is also on your list. His new translation of Rimbaud's *Illuminations,* and a long study of them, is just now coming out. If you would like it, or any other book on the Grove List, please ask for them and they are yours. To go back to Fowlie has spent many years in France, has written books on Mallarmé, a second on Rimbaud, his autobiography (*Pantomimes*), a book on surrealism, two volumes of poetry written in French, and so on. He does not usually speak in superlatives, but about your work he did, and that weighed a good deal with me. Then of course, I do happen to be the editor and owner of this publishing company, and I like your work too.

Chatto and Windus have not one single copy available of your book on Proust. If you ever come across one I would much appreciate it if you would let me borrow it. Proust is my particular passion and I would so much like to know what you have, or had, to say about him. Bernard Frechtman and Annette Michelson, who tell me they do not know you, live in Paris at 28 rue des Abbesses, Paris [18th (*sic*)]. They are close friends of the Grove Press, and both have done translations for us from the French. I am not suggesting them as translators, but Bernie knows I am going to do your work and he has written telling me that he is a very deep admirer of yours, and that *Godot* is the most exciting and important piece of theater to appear in many years. They are nice people and I do hope that you meet them. I now remember that Bernie also strongly urged that I get you to do your own translations.

This would seem to be an already indecently long letter, so I will close. If you would give me your own address we might be able to communicate directly in the future.

Sincerely,
(signed)
Barney Rosset

6 Rue des Favorites   June 25, 1953
Paris 15 me

Dear Mr Rosset

Thank you for your letter of June 18th. Above my private address, confidentially. For serious matters write to me here, for business to Lindon, Ed. de Minuit, please.

Re translations. I shall send you to-day or to-morrow my first version of *Godot*. This text is also in the hands of Mr Harold L. Oram, 8 West 40th Street, New York, who has our authority to treat for the performance rights up till I think November 1st. This translation has been rushed, so that Mr Oram may have something to work on as soon as possible, but I do not think the final version will differ from it very much. I should like to know what date roughly you have in view for publication. Before or after performance in USA (highly doubtful) does not much matter, I think. Here the book [scribbled out] appeared before, and sold after, performance.

With regard to the novels my position is that I should greatly prefer not to undertake the job myself, while having the right to [scribbled out] revise whatever translation is made. But I know from experience how much more difficult it is to revise a bad translation than to do the thing oneself. That is why I should like to see a few brief specimens of translation before coming to a decision. Trocchi has kindly undertaken to produce three specimens of the first 10 pages of *Molloy* and *Malone*. If your Belgian (whose beginning of *Godot* it would interest me to see) could do a few pages of *Molloy*, I should be very glad too. My idea was that it would be easier to collaborate with a translator living here. In any case it is a job for a professional writer and one prepared to write in his own way within the limits of mine, if that makes any sense, and beyond them too, when necessary. I translated myself some years ago two very brief fragments for Georges Duthuit's *Transition*. If I can get hold of the number in which they appeared I shall send it to you.

I understand very well your point of view when you question the propriety of the publication in *Merlin* of Act 1 of *Godot* and I have no doubt that Trocchi will appreciate it too.

My own copy of my *Proust* has disappeared and I really do not know where to suggest your looking for one. It is a very youthful work, but perhaps not entirely beside the point. Its premises are less feeble than its conclusions.

With regard to my work in general, I hope you realize what you are letting yourself in for. I do not mean the heart of the matter, which is unlikely to disturb anybody, but certain obscenities of form which may not have struck you in French as they will in English, and which frankly (it is better that you should know this before we get going) I am not at all disposed to mitigate. I do not of course realize what is possible in [scribbled out] America from this point of view and what is not. Certainly as far as I know such passages, faithfully translated, would not be tolerated in England. I think you might do well to talk to Fowlie about this.

Sylvia Beach said very nice things about the Grove Press and that you might be over here in the late summer. I hope you will.

Thank you for your interesting catalogue. I shall certainly ask you for some of your books at a later stage.

Thanking you for taking this chance with my work and wishing us a fair wind, I am

Yours sincerely
Samuel Beckett

July 13, 1953

Dear Mr. Beckett:

It was nice to receive your letter of June 25 and then your letter of July 5.

First, I must tell you that I have not received your translation of *Godot*. I am most anxious to see it. I would like to plan on publication of the play for 1954, either in the first or second half of the year, depending entirely upon completion date of the translation. I would think the ideal thing would be to coincide publication with performance, but that is ideal only and I would not think it wise to indefinitely postpone publication while waiting for the performance.

I made an appointment to see Mr. Oram, whom I met briefly some time ago, next Tuesday and we will discuss the whole matter. I was not aware of the fact that Mr. Oram was involved with the theatre and I am still somewhat wondering about it but perhaps I will know more after I have lunch with him. He told me that he was an intimate friend of yours and, of course, I was surprised to hear this.

As to the translation of the novels, I am naturally disappointed to hear that you prefer not to undertake translation of the novels yourself. I can well see your point, however, and it would seem a little sad to attempt to take off that much time to go back over your own book but I hope that you will change your mind. I note that *Murphy* was published in England by Routledge and it does not seem completely out of the question that they would be willing to again publish your books. I will send on to you the first few pages of *Godot* translated by my acquaintance here and I believe he will also undertake to do a few pages of *Molloy*. I would appreciate it very much if I could also see specimens given to you by Trocchi provided they are acceptable, or nearly acceptable to you; otherwise there would not be much point in sending them on to me. Of course it would be easier to collaborate with a translator living in France but, on the other hand, correspondence would not seem to be an insurmountable problem.

As to the obscenities within books, my suggestion is that we do not worry about that until it becomes necessary. Sometimes things like that have a way of solving themselves.

I do hope you locate a copy of *Transition* with the fragments translated by yourself.

I do plan on going to Europe in the fall, and I will certainly look forward to meeting you then.

Yours sincerely,
Barney Rosset

6 Rue des Favorites   July 28th 1953
Paris 15 me

Dear Mr. Rosset

Herewith the specimen translation I told you about, as revised by me. I find it satisfactory. If you do too, will you get in touch with the translator, Patrick Bowles, 5 Cité Vaneau, Paris 7 me. It is going to be a slow job and we are both anxious to get on with it. All that is required now is your approbation and that the question of the translator's fee should be settled to the satisfaction of Bowles and yourself.

Yours sincerely,
(signed)
Samuel Beckett

7/31/53

Dear Mr. Beckett,

Your translation of *Godot* did finally arrive, and also I received a copy from Oram. I like it very much, and it seems to me that you have done a fine job. The long speech by Lucky is particularly good and the whole play reads extremely well.

If I were to make any criticism it would be that one can tell that the translation was done by a person more used to "English" speech than American. Thus the use of words such as bloody—and a few others—might lead the audience to think the play was originally done by an Englishman in English. This is a small point, but in a few places the neutralization of the speech away from the specifically English flavor might have the result of enhancing the French origins for an American reader. Beyond that technical point I have little to say, excepting that I am now extremely desirous of seeing the play on a stage—in any language.

I am sending on the fragment of *Godot* translated by the man here. You will have to decide from that if his work interests you. I personally think that he did a rather good job, but if you much prefer the person you have found then by all means send me the sample you have. I read the fragments by you in *Transition* and again I must say that I liked them very much—leading to the continuance of my belief that you would be the best possible translator. I really do not see how anybody else can get the sound quality, to name one thing, but I am willing to be convinced.

By all means, the translation should be done with only those modifications required by the change from one language to another. If an insurmountable obstacle is to appear, let it first appear.

I will look forward to hearing about progress towards a translation.

Yours sincerely,
(signed)
Barney Rosset

August 4, 1953

Dear Mr. Beckett,

I am putting aside *Watt*, which I received this morning, to write this letter. Fifty pages poured over me and I will inundate myself again as soon as possible. One irritation did jut out at me and that is the lack of good proofreading in the pages I went through. I do hope that the misspellings, inverted letters, etc., are dealt with before the printing is done. To find one word deliberately distorted and the next botched by the type-setter can spoil the tone so easily. Also it is a shame that the type-face used is so scrubby and ugly. Good writing can also look well without losing any of its intrinsic value—or so it would seem to me.

After the sample of *Godot* went back to you, the first part of *Molloy* arrived and I was most favorably impressed with it. I remember Bowles' story in the second issue of *Merlin* and it does seem that he has real sympathy for your writing. If you feel satisfied, and find it convenient to work with him, then my opinion would be to tell you to go ahead. Short of your doing the work yourself the best would be able to really guide someone else along—and that situation you seem to have found.

Again a mention of words. Those such as *skivvy* and *cutty* are unknown here, and when used they give the writing a most definite British stamp. That is perfectly all fight [sic] if it is the effect you desire. If you are desirous of a little more vagueness as to where the scene is set it would be better to use substitutes which are of common usage both here and in Britain.

Watt came here through the good graces of the Marian Saunders agency. I would think that Merlin might have leaked a copy out to me, but it did get here so I cannot complain too bitterly. My suggestion on *Watt* is that part of the edition bear the imprint of Grove Press on the title page, that the reverse of the title page say Copyright 1953 [illegible] by Samuel Beckett, and we will undertake to copyright it for you in this country. The Grove Press part of the edition, at least, should be printed on good paper and put in a binding up to American standards. The books should be sold to us at cost by Merlin and the profit to you and them (whatever your arrangement with them is) will come out of royalties on which we will make a small advance. This will keep the price of the book at the lowest possible figure and give it a fighting chance to get sold.

I am happy to be reading *Watt* and I hope to see more of *Molloy* soon.

> With best regards,
> (signed)
> Barney Rosset

6 Rue des Favorites   September 1, 1953
Paris 15 me

Dear Mr Rosset

Thank you for your letters of August 4th and July 31st both received yesterday only and also for the translation from *Godot*. It has as you say great merits, but [scribbled out] I think all things considered it is better for Bowles to go on with the job he has so well begun. Will you convey my [scribbled out] thanks to your translator and my congratulations for his excellent version.

I am glad you liked the specimen from *Molloy*. Bowles too will be very glad. I hope the question of his remuneration will soon be settled satisfactorily to you both and that we can get seriously to work on this very difficult job.

Watt I believe is now out, but I have not yet seen it. Standards of book presentation are not the same here as with you and the resources of Merlin are very limited. What matters to me is that this work refused by a score of London publishers in the years following the war is at last between boards. A handsomer edition in America would of course give me great pleasure. I am so hopelessly incompetent in these matters that it is better I should not intervene in your negotiations with Merlin. I am in advance in agreement with whatever arrangement you come to with them.

It is good news that my translation of *Godot* meets with your approval. It was done in great haste [scribbled out] to facilitate the negotiations of Mr Oram and I do not myself regard it as very satisfactory. But I have not yet had the courage to revise it. (The copy made by the services of Mr Oram contains a number of mistakes.) I understand your point about the [scribbled out] Anglicisms and shall be glad to consider whatever suggestions you have to make in this connexion. But the problem involved here is a far-reaching one. Bowles's text as revised by me [scribbled out] is bound to be quite [scribbled out] unamerican in rhythm and atmosphere and the mere substitution here and there of the American for the English term is hardly likely to improve matters, on the contrary. We can of course avoid those words which are incomprehensible to the American reader, such as *skivvy* and *cutty*, and it will be a [scribbled out] help to have them pointed out to us. In *Godot* I tried to retain the French atmosphere as much as possible and you may have noticed [scribbled out] that the use of English and American place-names is confined to Lucky whose [scribbled out] own name might seem to justify them.

Yours sincerely
Samuel Beckett

Ussy-sur-Marne   14-10-53
Seine-et-Marne

Dear Mr Rosset
Sorry not to have seen you both again before your departure. I received your pneu here in the country only last Monday, i.e. the day you were leaving.

You will no doubt have seen Bowles and heard about progress on *Molloy*. I am quite pleased with the result and hope you are too.

I too greatly enjoyed our evening together. May we have another as good in the not too distant future.

My very kind regards to Mrs Rosset.

Yours sincerely
Sam. Beckett

October 19, 1953

Dear Samuel Beckett,

Loly and I were sorry not to see you again, but I think our memories of our last visit will last us a while. Loly finished reading *Malone Meurt* last night and she liked it exceedingly much. Now on to *L'Innommable*.

This morning I was summoned to the office of one Marian Saunders, literary agent, and was told by same that due to me the New York production had not proceeded. Somehow this was because I have a letter contract with you (drawn up and presented to me by the Marian Saunders office I might add) which necessitated my approval of New York production, plus the implication that I might like to be paid something. It seems that Oram feels that he cannot go around getting permission from two people (you and me). I told Saunders that in the first place I thought it ridiculous to say that our contract had deterred Oram, but that if it actually did I would be only too happy to tell him, in writing, that if he obtained your permission to any production, my permission would automatically go along with yours. My only concern would be to be sure that any cuts, changes, or additions to the script were passed upon and approved by you. That seems both fair and reasonably simple. As to payment, I suggest that I get 1% of the proceeds. I also think that to be fair, but if any violent objections are raised I am certainly not going to stop any serious attempt at production. Incidentally, that 1% would in no way affect anything you are to get.

We like the *Molloy* translation *very* much, and we are looking forward very keenly to seeing more. My congratulations to you and Patrick for the good work.

Best,
(signed)
Barney Rosset

6 Rue des Favorites   October 27th 1953
Paris 15 me

My dear Barney
      Thank you for your letter of Oct 19th. If I had known a little earlier I
would have come up for the day to wish you a fair wind. But as it was there was
literally not time.
      I know you will do all you can to help with *Godot* in New York. Your 1%
seems what they call here dérisoire.
      Sorry you weren't at the Babylone last night when I am told the audience
expelled manu militari an indignant female heckler. [scribbled out] "Conasse,
va te coucher." They are playing on to Nov 8, then going on tour, in Germany
mostly.
      Work with Pat Bowles proceeds apace, i.e. about a page an hour. Yester-
day we did the unpleasant Ruth or Edith idyll which I fear may [scratched out]
shake you in English.

> With my kind remembrance to Loly I am,
> Yours very sincerely
> Sam. Beckett

6 Rue des Favorites   20/11/53
Paris 15 me

My dear Loly
      Many thanks for your letter of November 5th. Thank you also for the
two books arrived the other day. I am glad you have decided to bring
[scribbled out] *Godot* in the Spring. As you say there is no point in waiting
for the performance. I am beginning now to revise my translation and
hope to let you have the definitive text next month. As you have probably
heard from Pat Bowles we have now finished translating the first part of
Molloy. I leave it to you [scribbled out] to judge the result, I am beyond
doing so. I don't think it stinks too much of a translation, but it certainly
doesn't take kindly to English. The dernière at the Babylone was last
Sunday week, now the little company is in Germany. No news yet. I
think there is increasing resistance to the play in Germany. I'm just as
glad. Have been up to my eyes all this time in translations and am now in
the country unsuccessfully recovering. *Watt* in French is something
horrible. Have you read *The Catcher in the Rye* by Salinger? Bowles lent it
to me and I liked it very much indeed, more than [scribbled out] anything

for a long time. I'll write again when I'm less tired, less stupid and less gloomy.

Friendly greetings to you both.
Sam. Beckett

6 Rue des Favorites   14/12/53
Paris 15°

Dear Barney and Loly

Sorry for the no to design you seem to like. It was good of you to consult me. Don't think of me as a nietman. The idea is all right. But I think the variety of symbols is a bad mistake. They make a hideous column and destroy the cohesion of the page. And I don't like the suggestion and the attempt to express it a hierarchy of characters. A la rigueur, if you wish, simple capitals, E. for Estragon, V. for Vladimir, etc., since no confusion is possible, and perhaps no heavier in type than those of the text. But I prefer the full name. Their repetition, even when corresponding speech amounts to no more than a syllable, has its function in the sense that it reinforces the repetitive text. The symbols are variety and the whole affair is monotony. Another possibility is to set the names in the middle of the page and text beneath, thus:

[scribbled out]

ESTRAGON
I'd rather he'd dance, it'd be more fun.

POZZO
Not necessarily.

ESTRAGON
Wouldn't it, Didi, be more fun?

VLADIMIR
I'd like well to hear him think.

ESTRAGON
Perhaps he could dance first and think afterwards, if it isn't too much to ask him.

But personally I prefer the Minuit composition. The same is used by Gallimard for Adamov's theatre (1st vol. just out). But if you prefer the simple capitals it will be all right with me.

Could you not possibly postpone setting of galleys until 1st week in January, by which time you will have received the definitive text? I have made a fair number of changes, particularly in Lucky's tirade and a lot of correcting would be avoided if you could delay things for a few weeks.

I was annoyed by NWW's [*New World Writing*] horrible montage. The excerpt is always unsatisfactory, but let it at least be continuous. I don't mind how short it is, or with how little beginning or end, but I refuse to be short-circuited like an ulcerous gut.

Molloy hasn't advanced much further. I am tired and most of the time in the country. But part 2 will go faster. And there does not seem to be any great hurry.

Signed yesterday for London [scribbled out] West End production within
6 months, producer probably Peter Glenville. Oram as you probably know has renounced.

The tour of Babylone *Godot* mostly in Germany (including the Gründgens theatre in Düsseldorf), but also as far as the Milan Piccolo, seems to have been successful. They are opening again here day after to-morrow for a month or 6 weeks, then off on tour again. Marvellous photos, unposed, much superior to the French, were taken in Krefeld during actual performance. One in particular is fantastic (end of Act 1, Vladimir drawing Estragon towards wings, with moon and tree). It *is* the play and would make a remarkable cover for your book. I shall call at the theatre this afternoon before posting this and add address of photographer in case you are interested in purchasing the set.

Best wishes for Xmas and the New Year.

Sam
Samuel Beckett
FOTO DÖNITZ
KREFELD
WINNERTZHOF 20
GERMANY [A]

April 14, 1954

Dear Samuel,
Waiting for Godot seems to be finally ready to come off the press. Quite a wait it has been—in fact so long that we have decided to postpone publication date until next fall. We expect the book to be a handsome one and copies will be dispatched out the instant they arrive—we hope they will gain your blessing.

It has been so long since we have heard from you. What has been happening with the translation . . . I'm almost afraid to ask, but we would like to know.

Very warmest greetings from Loly and myself.

Yours,
Barney Rosset

We are still hoping you pay us a visit one of these days—noted in the *New York Times* that *Godot* will be put on in London . . . Hope it is true.

6 Rue de Favorites
Paris 15me

21-4-54

My dear Barney

Thanks for your letter. Sorry *Godot* is postponed to the autumn. I'm sure I'll be very pleased with the book. The Ed. de Minuit are also doing a reimpression with photos.

We were all set for a London West End performance until the Lord Chamberlain got going. His incriminations are so preposterous that I'm afraid the whole thing is off. He listed 12 passages for omission! The things I had expected and which I was half prepared to amend (reluctantly), but also [scribbled out] passages that are vital to the play (first 15 lines of Lucky's tirade and the passage end of Act II from "But you can't go barefoot" to "and they crucified quick") and impossible either to alter or suppress. However Albery (the theatre director) is trying to arrange things in London. I am to see him this week-end and all is not yet definitely lost. It would be a pity, as there was talk of Alec Guinness for the role of Estragon.

With regard to translation I fear I have been very remiss. The revision of the German *Molloy* finished me. I have not seen or heard from Bowles for a long time. I revised the first few pages of Part II of *Molloy* and that was our last contact. With the delayed appearance of *Godot* I suppose there is no great hurry about *Molloy*. Sometimes I feel the only alternative is [scribbled out] to wash my hands of it entirely or to do it entirely myself.

Received *New World Writing* with Niall Montgomery. Witty specificiation.

Hope indeed I shall be in the States some day if only in order to take advantage of your hospitality. Am buried in the Ile de France at the moment and find it no better or worse than anything else.

Shall let you know how the London affair works out.

With best wishes to you both,

Yours ever

Sam Beckett

December 13, 1955

Dear Samuel,

Enclosed is the latest Grove Press Catalogue. Next season will see you moved back to the front with *Malone* after a little respite on page 10. Also see pages 20 and 26.

Now I am being reassured from all sides—cable from Curtis Brown and so forth. Today Myerberg called me and that is what provokes this letter. He is all amicability and charm, but no photograph is forthcoming until at least the end of the month, which of course is ridiculous if the book is to be ready for any part of the production. So I am going ahead with the old jacket, as is. No copy—just photo front and back. It did seem strange to me however and I do hope everything is all right.

Then I asked if you were coming, and he said you wanted to come, but it seems there was a problem of money to pay your way. This astounded me in view of what I had been told previously and also in view of the fact that Myerberg asked me to write to you, offering you a free trip, etc. He also said, in what now seems scrabbled in my mind—that the whole production would cost only about $15,000.00 to $25,000.00 (very very low for a production these days) and that most of the money was his. I asked him why nobody ever asked me for the money, if it was in short supply, and he said he would send over the papers showing how the production is set up. He said that all costs might be paid for by the time the production got to Broadway. That would be wonderful for everybody. Anyway, the whole thing was sort of circuitous—although I hope all for the better—BUT do you really want to come, and is there now a problem of expenses being paid, or did Myerberg interject that for the first time when he spoke to me. Because if that is the situation I certainly think something can be worked out and we should decide how—immediately.

Myerberg says the play is in rehearsal. Hope that is also true.

No word from you since setting up of meeting with Schneider. I would very much like to hear from you—do send word, any word.

Yours

(signed)

Barney Rosset

SAMUEL BECKETT

✂

FROM *Waiting for Godot* [1954]

Translated from the French by the author

POZZO: Stop! (*Lucky stops.*) Back! (*Lucky moves back.*) Stop! (*Lucky stops.*) Turn!
(*Lucky turns towards auditorium.*) Think!
During Lucky's tirade the others react as follows.
1) Vladimir and Estragon all attention, Pozzo dejected and disgusted.
2) Vladimir and Estragon begin to protest, Pozzo's sufferings increase.
3) Vladimir and Estragon attentive again, Pozzo more and more agitated and
groaning.
4) Vladimir and Estragon protest violently. Pozzo jumps up, pulls on the rope.
General outcry. Lucky pulls on the rope, staggers, shouts his text. All three throw
themselves on Lucky who struggles and shouts his text.

LUCKY: Given the existence as uttered forth in the public works of Puncher and
Wattmann of a personal God quaquaquaqua with white beard quaquaquaqua
outside time without extension who from the heights of divine apathia divine
athambia divine aphasia loves us dearly with some exceptions for reasons unknown but time will tell and suffers like the divine Miranda with those who for
reasons unknown but time will tell are plunged in torment plunged in fire whose
fire flames if that continues and who can doubt it will fire the firmament that is
to say blast hell to heaven so blue still and calm so calm with a calm which even
though intermittent is better than nothing but not so fast and considering what is
more that as a result of the labors left unfinished crowned by the Acacacacademy
of Anthropopopometry of Essy-in-Possy of Testew and Cunard it is established
beyond all doubt all other doubt than that which clings to the labors of men that
as a result of the labors unfinished of Testew and Cunard it is established as
hereinafter but not so fast for reasons unknown that as a result of the public
works of Puncher and Wattmann it is established beyond all doubt that in view
of the labors of Fartov and Belcher left unfinished for reasons unknown of
Testew and Cunard left unfinished it is established what many deny that man
in Possy of Testew and Cunard that man in Essy that man in short that man in
brief in spite of the strides of alimentation and defecation wastes and pines wastes
and pines and concurrently simultaneously what is more for reasons unknown

in spite of the strides of physical culture the practice of sports such as tennis
football running cycling swimming flying floating riding gliding conating
camogie skating tennis of all kinds dying flying sports of all sorts autumn
summer winter winter tennis of all kinds hockey of all sorts penicilline and
succedanea in a word I resume flying gliding golf over nine and eighteen holes
tennis of all sorts in a word for reasons unknown in Feckham Peckham Fulham
Clapham namely concurrently simultaneously what is more for reasons unknown but time will tell fades away I resume Fulham Clapham in a word the
dead loss per head since the death of Bishop Berkeley being to the tune of one
inch four ounce per head approximately by and large more or less to the nearest decimal good measure round figures stark naked in the stockinged feet in
Connemara in a word for reasons unknown no matter what matter the facts are
there and considering what is more much more grave that in the light of the
labors lost of Steinweg and Peterman it appears what is more much more grave
that in the light the light the light of the labors lost of Steinweg and Peterman
that in the plains in the mountains by the seas by the rivers running water running fire the air is the same and then the earth namely the air and then the earth
in the great cold the great dark the air and the earth abode of stones in the great
cold alas alas in the year of their Lord six hundred and something the air the
earth the sea the earth abode of stones in the great deeps the great cold on sea
on land and in the air I resume for reasons unknown in spite of the tennis the
facts are there but time will tell I resume alas alas on on in short in fine on on
abode of stones who can doubt it I resume but not so fast I resume the skull
fading fading fading and concurrently simultaneously what is more for reasons
unknown in spite of the tennis on on the beard the flames the tears the stones so
blue so calm alas alas on on the skull the skull the skull the skull in Connemara
in spite of the tennis the labors abandoned left unfinished graver still abode of
stones in a word I resume alas alas abandoned unfinished the skull the skull in
Connemara in spite of the tennis the skull alas the stones Cunard (*mêlée, final
vociferations*) tennis . . . the stones . . . so calm . . . Cunard . . . unfinished . . .

SAMUEL BECKETT

❦

FROM *Molloy* [1955]

Translated from the French by Patrick Bowles in
collaboration with the author

I am in my mother's room. It's I who live there now. I don't know how I got
there. Perhaps in an ambulance, certainly a vehicle of some kind. I was helped.
I'd never have got there alone. There's this man who comes every week. Perhaps I got there thanks to him. He says not. He gives me money and takes away
the pages. So many pages, so much money. Yes, I work now, a little like I used
to, except that I don't know how to work any more. That doesn't matter apparently. What I'd like now is to speak of the things that are left, say my goodbyes,
finish dying. They don't want that. Yes, there is more than one, apparently.
But it's always the same one that comes. You'll do that later, he says. Good.
The truth is I haven't much will left. When he comes for the fresh pages he
brings back the previous week's. They are marked with signs I don't understand. Anyway I don't read them. When I've done nothing he gives me nothing, he scolds me. Yet I don't work for money. For what then? I don't know.
The truth is I don't know much. For example my mother's death. Was she already dead when I came? Or did she only die later? I mean enough to bury. I
don't know. Perhaps they haven't buried her yet. In any case I have her room.
I sleep in her bed. I piss and shit in her pot. I have taken her place. I must re-
semble her more and more. All I need now is a son. Perhaps I have one somewhere. But I think not. He would be old now, nearly as old as myself. It was a
little chambermaid. It wasn't true love. The true love was in another. We'll
come to that. Her name? I've forgotten it again. It seems to me sometimes that
I even knew my son, that I helped him. Then I tell myself it's impossible. It's
impossible I could ever have helped anyone. I've forgotten how to spell too,
and half the words. That doesn't matter apparently. Good. He's a queer one
the one who comes to see me. He comes every Sunday apparently. The other
days he isn't free. He's always thirsty. It was he told me I'd begun all wrong,
that I should have begun differently. He must be right. I began at the beginning, like an old ballocks, can you imagine that? Here's my beginning. Because
they're keeping it apparently. I took a lot of trouble with it. Here it is. It gave
me a lot of trouble. It was the beginning, do you understand? Whereas now
it's nearly the end. Is what I do now any better? I don't know. That's beside the

point. Here's my beginning. It must mean something, or they wouldn't keep it.
Here it is.

This time, then once more I think, then perhaps a last time, then I think
it'll be over, with that world too. Premonition of the last but one but one. All
grows dim. A little more and you'll go blind. It's in the head. It doesn't work
any more, it says, I don't work any more. You go dumb as well and sounds
fade. The threshold scarcely crossed that's how it is. It's the head. It must have
had enough. So that you say, I'll manage this time, then perhaps once more,
then perhaps a last time, then nothing more. You are hard set to formulate this
thought, for it is one, in a sense. Then you try to pay attention, to consider with
attention all those dim things, saying to yourself, laboriously, It's my fault.
Fault? That was the word. But what fault? It's not goodbye, and what magic in
those dim things to which it will be time enough, when next they pass, to say
goodbye. For you must say goodbye, it would be madness not to say goodbye,
when the time comes. If you think of the forms and light of other days it is
without regret. But you seldom think of them, with what would you think of
them? I don't know. People pass too, hard to distinguish from yourself. That
is discouraging. So I saw A and C going slowly towards each other, unconscious of what they were doing. It was on a road remarkably bare, I mean without hedges or ditches or any kind of edge, in the country, for cows were chewing
in enormous fields, lying and standing, in the evening silence. Perhaps I'm in-
venting a little, perhaps embellishing, but on the whole that's the way it was.
They chew, swallow, then after a short pause effortlessly bring up the next
mouthful. A neck muscle stirs and the jaws begin to grind again. But perhaps
I'm remembering things. The road, hard and white, seared the tender pastures,
rose and fell at the whim of hills and hollows. The town was not far. It was two
men, unmistakably, one small and one tall. They had left the town, first one,
then the other, and then the first, weary or remembering a duty, had retraced
his steps. The air was sharp for they wore greatcoats. They looked alike, but
no more than others do. At first a wide space lay between them. They couldn't
have seen each other, even had they raised their heads and looked about, because of this wide space, and then because of the undulating land, which caused
the road to be in waves, not high, but high enough, high enough. But the moment came when together they went down into the same trough and in this
trough finally met. To say they knew each other, no, nothing warrants it. But
perhaps at the sound of their steps, or warned by some obscure instinct, they
raised their heads and observed each other, for a good fifteen paces, before they
stopped, breast to breast. Yes, they did not pass each other by, but halted, face
to face, as in the country, of an evening, on a deserted road, two wayfaring
strangers will, without there being anything extraordinary about it. But they

knew each other perhaps. Now in any case they do, now I think they will know each other, greet each other, even in the depths of the town. They turned towards the sea, which, far in the east, beyond the fields, loomed high in the waning sky, and exchanged a few words. Then each went on his way. Each went on his way, A back towards the town, C on by-ways he seemed hardly to know, or not at all, for he went with uncertain step and often stopped to look about him, like someone trying to fix landmarks in his mind, for one day perhaps he may have to retrace his steps, you never know. The treacherous hills where fearfully he ventured were no doubt only known to him from afar, seen perhaps from his bedroom window or from the summit of a monument which, one black day, having nothing in particular to do and turning to height for solace, he had paid his few coppers to climb, slower and slower, up the winding stones. From there he must have seen it all, the plain, the sea, and then these self-same hills, that some call mountains, indigo in places in the evening light, their serried ranges crowding to the skyline, cloven with hidden valleys that the eye divines from sudden shifts of colour and then from other signs for which there are no words, nor even thoughts. But all are not divined, even from that height, and often where only one escarpment is discerned, and one crest, in reality there are two, two escarpments, two crests, riven by a valley. But now he knows these hills, that is to say he knows them better, and if ever again he sees them from afar it will be I think with other eyes, and not only that but the within, all that inner space one never sees, the brain and heart and other caverns where thought and feeling dance their sabbath, all that too quite differently disposed. He looks old and it is a sorry sight to see him solitary after so many years, so many days and nights unthinkingly given to that rumour rising at birth and even earlier, What shall I do? What shall I do? now low, a murmur, now precise as the headwaiter's And to follow? and often rising to a scream. And in the end, or almost, to be abroad alone, by unknown ways, in the gathering night, with a stick. It was a stout stick, he used it to thrust himself onward, or as a defence, when the time came, against dogs and marauders. Yes, night was gathering, but the man was innocent, greatly innocent, he had nothing to fear, though he went in fear, he had nothing to fear, there was nothing they could do to him, or very little. But he can't have known it. I wouldn't know myself, if I thought about it. Yes, he saw himself threatened, his body threatened, his reason threatened, and perhaps he was, perhaps they were, in spite of his innocence. What business has innocence here? What relation to the innumerable spirits of darkness? It's not clear. It seemed to me he wore a cocked hat. I remember being struck by it, as I wouldn't have been for example by a cap or by a bowler. I watched him recede, overtaken (myself) by his anxiety, at least by an anxiety which was not necessarily his, but of which as it were he partook. Who knows if it wasn't my own anxiety overtaking him. He hadn't seen me. I was perched higher than the road's highest point and flattened what is more against a rock the same colour as myself, that is grey. The rock he probably saw. He gazed around as if to engrave the landmarks on his memory and must have seen the rock in the shadow of which I crouched like Belaqua, or Sordello, I forget. But a man, a fortiori myself, isn't exactly a landmark, because. I mean if by some strange chance he were to pass that way again, after a long lapse of time, vanquished, or to look for some lost thing, or to destroy something, his eyes would search out the rock, not the haphazard in its shadow of that unstable fugitive thing, still living flesh. No, he certainly didn't see me, for the reasons I've given and then because he was in no humour for that, that evening, no humour for the living, but rather for all that doesn't stir, or stirs so slowly that a child would scorn it, let alone an old man. However that may be, I mean whether he saw me or whether he didn't, I repeat I watched him recede, at grips (myself) with the temptation to get up and follow him, perhaps even to catch up with him one day, so as to know him better, be myself less lonely. But in spite of my soul's leap out to him, at the end of its elastic, I saw him only darkly, because of the dark and then because of the terrain, in the folds of which he disappeared from time to time, to re-emerge further on, but most of all I think because of other things calling me and towards which too one after the other my soul was straining, wildly. I mean of course the fields, whitening under the dew, and the animals, ceasing from wandering and settling for the night, and the sea, of which nothing, and the sharpening line of crests, and the sky where without seeing them I felt the first stars tremble, and my hand on my knee and above all the other wayfarer, A or C, I don't remember, going resignedly home. Yes, towards my hand also, which my knee felt tremble and of which my eyes saw the wrist only, the heavily veined back, the pallid rows of knuckles. But that is not, I mean my hand, what I wish to speak of now, everything in due course, but A or C returning to the town he had just left. But after all what was there particularly urban in his aspect? He was bare-headed, wore sand-shoes, smoked a cigar. He moved with a kind of loitering indolence which rightly or wrongly seemed to me expressive. But all that proved nothing, refuted nothing. Perhaps he had come from afar, from the other end of the island even, and was approaching the town for the first time or returning to it after a long absence. A little dog followed him, a pomeranian I think, but I don't think so. I wasn't sure at the time and I'm still not sure, though I've hardly thought about it. The little dog followed wretchedly, after the fashion of pomeranians, stopping, turning in slow circles, giving up and then, a little further on, beginning all over again. Constipation is a sign of good health in pomeranians. At a given moment, preestablished if you like, I don't much mind, the gentleman turned back, took the little creature in his arms, drew the cigar from his lips and buried his face in the orange fleece, for it was a gentleman, that was obvious. Yes, it was an orange pomeranian, the less I think of it the more certain I am. And yet. But would he have come from afar, bare-headed, in sand-shoes, smoking a cigar, followed by a pomeranian? Did he not seem rather to have issued from the ramparts, after a good dinner, to take his dog and himself for a walk, like so many citizens, dreaming and farting, when the weather is fine? But was not perhaps in reality the cigar a cutty, and were not the sand-shoes boots, hobnailed, dust-whitened, and what prevented the dog from being one of those stray dogs that you pick up and take in your arms, from compassion or because you have long been straying with no other company than the endless roads, sands, shingle, bogs and heather, than this nature answerable to another court, than at long intervals the fellow-convict you long to stop, embrace, suck, suckle and whom you pass by, with hostile eyes, for fear of his familiarities? Until the day when, your endurance gone, in this world for you without arms, you catch up in yours the first mangy cur you meet, carry it the time needed for it to love you and you it, then throw it away. Perhaps he had come to that, in spite of appearances. He disappeared, his head on his chest, the smoking object in his hand. Let me try and explain. From things about to disappear I turn away in time. To watch them out of sight, no, I can't do it. It was in this sense he disappeared. Looking away I thought of him, saying, He is dwindling, dwindling. I knew what I meant. I knew I could catch him, lame as I was. I had only to want to. And yet no, for I did want to. To get up, to get down on the road, to set off hobbling in pursuit of him, to hail him, what could be easier? He hears my cries, turns, waits for me. I am up against him, up against the dog, gasping, between my crutches. He is a little frightened of me, a little sorry for me, I disgust him not a little. I am not a pretty sight, I don't smell good. What is it I want? Ah that tone I know, compounded of pity, of fear, of disgust. I want to see the dog, see the man, at close quarters, know what smokes, inspect the shoes, find out other things. He is kind, tells me of this and that and other things, whence he comes, whither he goes. I believe him, I know it's my only chance to—my only chance, I believe all I'm told, I've disbelieved only too much in my long life, now I swallow everything, greedily. What I need now is stories, it took me a long time to know that, and I'm not sure of it. There I am then, informed as to certain things, knowing certain things about him, things I didn't know, things I had craved to know, things I had never thought of. What rigmarole. I am even capable of having learnt what his profession is, I who am so interested in professions. And to think I try my best not to talk about myself. In a moment I shall talk about the cows, about the sky, if I can. There I am then, he leaves me, he's in a hurry. He didn't seem to be in a hurry, he was loitering, I've already said so, but after three min-

utes of me he is in a hurry, he has to hurry. I believe him. And once again I am
I will not say alone, no, that's not like me, but, how shall I say, I don't know,
restored to myself, no, I never left myself, free, yes, I don't know what that
means but it's the word I mean to use, free to do what, to do nothing, to know,
but what, the laws of the mind perhaps, of my mind, that for example water
rises in proportion as it drowns you and that you would do better, at least no
worse, to obliterate texts than to blacken margins, to fill in the holes of words
till all is blank and flat and the whole ghastly business looks like what is, senseless, speechless, issueless misery. So I doubtless did better, at least no worse,
not to stir from my observation post. But instead of observing I had the weakness to return in spirit to the other, the man with the stick. Then the murmurs
began again. To restore silence is the role of objects. I said, Who knows if he
hasn't simply come out to take the air, relax, stretch his legs, cool his brain by
stamping the blood down to his feet, so as to make sure of a good night, a joyous awakening, an enchanted morrow. Was he carrying so much as a scrip?
But the way of walking, the anxious looks, the club, could these be reconciled
with one's conception of what is called a little turn? But the hat, a town hat, an
old-fashioned town hat, which the least gust would carry far away. Unless it
was attached under the chin, by means of a string or an elastic. I took off my
hat and looked at it. It is fastened, it has always been fastened, to my buttonhole, always the same buttonhole, at all seasons by a long lace. I am still alive
then. That may come in useful. The hand that held the hat I thrust as far as
possible from me and moved in an arc, to and fro. As I did so, I watched the lapel
of my greatcoat and saw it open and close. I understand now why I never wore a
flower in my buttonhole, though it was large enough to hold a whole nosegay.
My buttonhole was set aside for my hat. It was my hat that I beflowered. But it is
neither of my hat nor of my greatcoat that I hope to speak at present, it would
be premature. Doubtless I shall speak of them later, when the time comes to
draw up the inventory of my goods and possessions. Unless I lose them between
now and then. But even lost they will have their place, in the inventory of my
possessions. But I am easy in my mind, I shall not lose them. Nor my crutches,
I shall not lose my crutches either. But I shall perhaps one day throw them away.
I must have been on the top, or on the slopes, of some considerable eminence,
for otherwise how could I have seen, so far away, so near at hand, so far beneath, so many things, fixed and moving. But what was an eminence doing in
this land with hardly a ripple? And I, what was I doing there, and why come?
These are things that we shall try and discover. But these are things we must
not take seriously. There is a little of everything, apparently, in nature, and
freaks are common. And I am perhaps confusing several different occasions,
and different times, deep down, and deep down is my dwelling, oh not deepest

down, somewhere between the mud and the scum. And perhaps it was A one day at one place, then C another at another, then a third the rock and I, and so on for the other components, the cows, the sky, the sea, the mountains. I can't believe it. No, I will not lie, I can easily conceive it. No matter, no matter, let us go on, as if all arose from one and the same weariness, on and on heaping up and up, until there is no room, no light, for any more. What is certain is that the man with the stick did not pass by again that night, because I would have heard him, if he had. I don't say I would have seen him, I say I would have beard him. I sleep little and that little by day. Oh not systematically, in my life without end I have dabbled with every kind of sleep, but at the time now coming back to me I took my doze in the daytime and, what is more, in the morning. Let me hear nothing of the moon, in my night there is no moon, and if it happens that I speak of the stars it is by mistake. Now of all the noises that night not one was of those heavy uncertain steps, or of that club with which he sometimes smote the earth until it quaked. How agreeable it is to be confirmed, after a more or less long period of vacillation, in one's first impressions. Perhaps that is what tempers the pangs of death. Not that I was so conclusively, I mean confirmed, in my first impressions with regard to—wait—C. For the wagons and carts which a little before dawn went thundering by, on their way to market with fruit, eggs, butter and perhaps cheese, in one of these perhaps he would have been found, overcome by fatigue or discouragement, perhaps even dead. Or he might have gone back to the town by another way too far away for me to hear its sounds, or by little paths through the fields, crushing the silent grass, pounding the silent ground. And so at last I came out of that distant night, divided between the murmurs of my little world, its dutiful confusions, and those so different (so different?) of all that between two suns abides and passes away. Never once a human voice. But the cows, when the peasants passed, crying in vain to be milked. A and C I never saw again. But perhaps I shall see them again. But shall I be able to recognize them? And am I sure I never saw them again? And what do I mean by seeing and seeing again?

EUGÈNE IONESCO

꒰ꙮ꒱

"The Bald Soprano: The Tragedy of Language"

FROM *Notes and Counter Notes:*

Writings on the Theater [1964]

Translated from the French by Donald Watson

In 1948, before writing my first play, *The Bald Soprano*, I did not want to become a playwright. My only ambition was to learn English. Learning English does not necessarily lead to writing plays. In fact it was because I failed to learn English that I became a dramatist. Nor did I write these plays as a kind of revenge for my failure, although *The Bald Soprano* has been called a satire on the English middle-classes. If I had tried and failed to learn Italian, Russian or Turkish, it would have been quite as easy to say that the play resulting from these vain efforts was a satire on Italian, Russian or Turkish society. I feel I should make myself clear. This is what happened: nine or ten years ago, in order to learn English, I bought an English-French Conversation Manual for Beginners. I set to work. I conscientiously copied out phrases from my manual in order to learn them by heart. Then I found, reading them over attentively, that I was learning not English but some very surprising truths: that there are seven days in the week, for example, which I happened to know before; or that the floor is below us, the ceiling above us, another thing that I may well have known before but had never thought seriously about or had forgotten, and suddenly it seemed to me as stupefying as it was indisputably true. I suppose I must have a fairly philosophical turn of mind to have noticed that these were not just simple English phrases with their French translation which I was copying into my exercise book, but in fact fundamental truths and profound statements.

For all that, I had not yet reached the point of giving English up. And a good thing too, for after these universal truths the author of my manual passed on from the general to the particular; and in order to do so, he expressed himself, doubtless inspired by the Platonic method, in the form of dialogue. In the third lesson two characters were brought together and I still cannot tell whether they were real or invented: Mr. and Mrs. Smith, an English couple. To my great surprise Mrs. Smith informed her husband that they had several children, that they lived in the outskirts of London, that their name was Smith, that Mr. Smith worked in an office, that they had a maid called Mary, who was English too, that for twenty years they had known some friends called Martin, and that their home was a castle because "An Englishman's home is his castle."

Of course, I imagine Mr. Smith must have been somewhat aware of all this; but you can never be sure, some people are so absent-minded; besides, it is good to remind our fellows of things they may be in danger of forgetting or take too much for granted. Apart from these particular eternal truths, there were other temporal truths which became clear: for example, that the Smiths had just dined and that, according to the clock, it was nine o'clock in the evening, English time.

Allow me to draw your attention to the nature of Mrs. Smith's assertions, which are perfectly irrefutable truisms; and also to the positively Cartesian approach of the author of my English Manual, for it was his superlatively systematic pursuit of the truth which was so remarkable. In the fifth lesson the Martins, the Smiths' friends, arrived; the conversation was taken up by all four and more complex truths were built upon these elementary axioms: "The country is more peaceful than big cities," some maintained; "Yes, but cities are more highly populated and there are more shops," replied the others, which is equally true and proves, moreover, that contrasting truths can quite well coexist.

It was at that moment that I saw the light. I no longer wanted merely to improve my knowledge of the English language. If I had persisted in enlarging my English vocabulary, in learning words, simply in order to translate into another language what I could just as well say in French, without paying any attention to the matter contained in these words, in what they reveal, this would have meant falling into the sin of formalism, which those who nowadays direct our thinking so rightly condemn. I had become more ambitious: I wanted to communicate to my contemporaries the essential truths of which the manual of English-French conversation had made me aware. On the other hand the dialogue between the Smiths, the Martins, the Smiths *and* the Martins, was genuinely dramatic, for drama *is* dialogue. So what I had to produce was a play. Therefore I wrote *The Bald Soprano,* which is thus a specifically didactic work for the theatre. And why is this work called *The Bald Soprano* and not *English Made Easy,* which I first thought of calling it, or *The English Hour,* which is the title that occurred to me a little later? It would take too long to explain in full: one of the reasons why *The Bald Soprano* received this title is that no prima donna, with or without hair, appears in the play. This detail should suffice. A whole section of the play is made by stringing together phrases taken from my English Manual; the Smiths and the Martins in the Manual are the Smiths and the Martins in my play, they are the same people, utter the same maxims, and perform the same actions or the same "inactions." In any "didactic drama," it is not our business to be original, to say what we think ourselves: that would be a serious crime against objective truth; we have only, humbly, to pass on the knowledge which has itself been passed to us, the ideas we have been given. How could I have allowed myself to make the slightest change to words expressing in such an edifying manner the ultimate truth? As it was genuinely didactic, my play must on no account be original or demonstrate my own talent!

. . . However, the text of *The Bald Soprano* only started off as a lesson (and a plagiarism). An extraordinary phenomenon took place, I know not how: before my very eyes the text underwent a subtle transformation, against my will. After a time, those inspired yet simple sentences, which I had so painstakingly copied into my schoolboy's exercise book detached themselves from the pages on which they had been written, changed places all by themselves, became garbled and corrupted. Although I had copied them down so carefully, so correctly, one after the other, the lines of dialogue in the manual had got out of hand. It happened to dependable and undeniable truths such as "the floor is below us, the ceiling above us." An affirmation, as categorical as it is sound, such as: the seven days of the week are Monday, Tuesday, Wednesday, Thursday, Friday, Saturday, Sunday, so deteriorated that Mr. Smith, my hero, informed us that the week was composed of three days, which were: Tuesday, Thursday and Tuesday. My characters, my worthy bourgeois, the Martins, husband and wife, were stricken with amnesia: although seeing each other and speaking to each other every day, they no longer recognized each other. Other alarming things happened: the Smiths told us of the death of a certain Bobby Watson, impossible to identify, because they also told us that three-quarters of the inhabitants of the town, men, women, children, cats and ideologists, were all called Bobby Watson. Finally a fifth and unexpected character turned up to cause more trouble between the peaceable couples: the Captain of the Fire Brigade. And he told stories which seemed to be about a young bull that gave birth to an enormous heifer, a mouse that begot a mountain; then the fireman went off so as not to miss a fire that had been foreseen three days before, noted in his diary and due to break out at the other side of the town, while the Smiths and the Martins took up their conversation again. Unfortunately the wise and elementary truths they exchanged, when strung together, had gone mad, the language had become disjointed, the characters distorted; words, now absurd, had been emptied of their content and it all ended with a quarrel the cause of which it was impossible to discover, for my heroes and heroines hurled into one another's faces not lines of dialogue, not even scraps of sentences, not words, but syllables or consonants or vowels! . . .

. . . For me, what had happened was a kind of collapse of reality. The words had turned into sounding shells devoid of meaning; the characters too, of course, had been emptied of psychology and the world appeared to me in an unearthly, perhaps its true, light, beyond understanding and governed by arbitrary laws.

While writing this play (for it had become a kind of play or anti-play, that is to say, a real parody of a play, a comedy of comedies), I had felt genuinely uneasy, sick and dizzy. Every now and then I had to stop working and, wondering what devil could be forcing me on to write, I would go and lie down on the sofa, afraid I might see it sinking into the abyss; and myself with it. When I had finished, I was nevertheless very proud of it. I imagined I had written something like the *Tragedy of language!* . . . When it was acted, I was almost surprised to hear the laughter of the audience, who took it all (and still take it) quite happily, considering it a comedy all right, even a sort of joke. A few avoided this mistake (Jean Pouillon, for example) and recognized a certain malaise. Others realized that I was poking fun at the theatre of Bernstein and his actors: Nicolas Bataille's cast had already realized this, when they had tried to act the play (especially during the first performances) as if it were a melodrama.

Later, serious critics and scholars analyzed the work and interpreted it solely as a criticism of bourgeois society and a parody of boulevard theatre. I have just said that I accept thus interpretation too: but to my mind there is no question of it being a satire of a petit bourgeois mentality that belongs to any particular society. It is above all about a kind of universal petite bourgeoisie, the petit bourgeois being a man of fixed ideas and slogans, a ubiquitous conformist: this conformism is, of course, revealed by the *mechanical language*. The text of *The Bald Soprano,* or the Manual for learning English (or Russian or Portuguese), consisting as it did of ready-made expressions and the most threadbare clichés, revealed to me all that is automatic in the language and behavior of people: "talking for the sake of talking," talking because there is nothing personal to say, the absence of any life within, the mechanical routine of everyday life, man sunk in his social background, no longer able to distinguish himself from it. The Smiths and the Martins no longer know how to talk because they no longer know how to think, they no longer know how to think because they are no longer capable of being moved, they have no passions, they no longer know how to be, they can become anyone or anything, for as they are no longer themselves, in an impersonal world, they can only be someone else, they are interchangeable: Martin can change places with Smith and vice versa, no one would notice the difference. A tragic character does not change, he breaks up; he is himself, he is *real.* Comic characters are people who do not exist.

(The start of a talk given to the French Institute in Italy, 1958.)

EUGÈNE IONESCO

❦

FROM *The Bald Soprano* [1956]

Translated from the French by Donald M. Allen

MR. SMITH: A conscientious doctor must die with his patient if they can't get well together. The captain of a ship goes down with his ship into the briny deep, he does not survive alone.

MRS. SMITH: One cannot compare a patient with a ship.

MR. SMITH: Why not? A ship has its diseases too; moreover, your doctor is as hale as a ship; that's why he should have perished at the same time as his patient, like the captain and his ship.

MRS. SMITH: Ah! I hadn't thought of that . . . Perhaps it is true . . . And then, what conclusion do you draw from this?

MR. SMITH: All doctors are quacks. And all patients too. Only the Royal Navy is honest in England.

MRS. SMITH: But not sailors.

MR. SMITH: Naturally. [*A pause. Still reading his paper:*] Here's a thing I don't understand. In the newspaper they always give the age of deceased persons but never the age of the newly born. That doesn't make sense.

MRS. SMITH: I never thought of that!
[*Another moment of silence. The clock strikes seven times. Silence. The clock strikes three times. Silence. The clock doesn't strike.*]

MR. SMITH [*still reading his paper*]: Tsk, it says here that Bobby Watson died.

MRS. SMITH: My God, the poor man! When did he die?

MR. SMITH: Why do you pretend to be astonished? You know very well that he's been dead these past two years. Surely you remember that we attended his funeral a year and a half ago.

MRS. SMITH: Oh yes, of course I do remember. I remembered it right away, but I don't understand why you yourself were so surprised to see it in the paper.

MR. SMITH: It wasn't in the paper. It's been three years since his death was announced. I remembered it through an association of ideas.

MRS. SMITH: What a pity! He was so well preserved.

MR. SMITH: He was the handsomest corpse in Great Britain. He didn't look his age. Poor Bobby, he'd been dead for four years and he was still warm. A veritable living corpse. And how cheerful he was!

MRS. SMITH: Poor Bobby.

MR. SMITH: Which poor Bobby do you mean?

MRS. SMITH: It is his wife that I mean. She is called Bobby too, Bobby Watson. Since they both had the same name, you could never tell one from the other when you saw them together. It was only after his death that you could really tell which was which. And there are still people today who confuse her with the deceased and offer their condolences to him. Do you know her?

MR. SMITH: I only met her once, by chance, at Bobby's burial.

MRS. SMITH: I've never seen her. Is she pretty?

MR. SMITH: She has regular features and yet one cannot say that she is pretty. She is too big and stout. Her features are not regular but still one can say that she is very pretty. She is a little too small and too thin. She's a voice teacher. [*The clock strikes five times. A long silence.*]

MRS. SMITH: And when do they plan to be married, those two?

MR. SMITH: Next spring, at the latest.

MRS. SMITH: We shall have to go to their wedding, I suppose.

MR. SMITH: We shall have to give them a wedding present. I wonder what?

MRS. SMITH: Why don't we give them one of the seven silver salvers that were given us for our wedding and which have never been of any use to us? [*Silence.*]

MRS. SMITH: How sad for her to be left a widow so young.

MR. SMITH: Fortunately, they had no children.

MRS. SMITH: That was all they needed! Children! Poor woman, how could she have managed!

MR. SMITH: She's still young. She might very well remarry. She looks so well in mourning.

MRS. SMITH: But who would take care of the children? You know very well that they have a boy and a girl. What are their names?

MR. SMITH: Bobby and Bobby like their parents. Bobby Watson's uncle, old Bobby Watson, is a rich man and very fond of the boy. He might very well pay for Bobby's education.

MRS. SMITH: That would be proper. And Bobby Watson's aunt, old Bobby Watson, might very well, in her turn, pay for the education of Bobby Watson, Bobby Watson's daughter. That way Bobby, Bobby Watson's mother, could remarry. Has she anyone in mind?

MR. SMITH: Yes, a cousin of Bobby Watson's.

MRS. SMITH: Who? Bobby Watson?

MR. SMITH: Which Bobby Watson do you mean?

MRS. SMITH: Why, Bobby Watson, the son of old Bobby Watson, the late Bobby Watson's other uncle.

MR. SMITH: No, it's not that one, it's someone else. It's Bobby Watson, the son of old Bobby Watson, the late Bobby Watson's aunt.

MRS. SMITH: Are you referring to Bobby Watson the commercial traveler?

MR. SMITH: All the Bobby Watsons are commercial travelers.

MRS. SMITH: What a difficult trade! However, they do well at it.

MR. SMITH: Yes, when there's no competition.

MRS. SMITH: And when is there no competition?

MR. SMITH: On Tuesdays, Thursdays, and Tuesdays.

MRS. SMITH: Ah! Three days a week? And what does Bobby Watson do on those days?

MR. SMITH: He rests, he sleeps.

MRS. SMITH; But why doesn't he work those three days if there's no competition?

MR. SMITH: I don't know everything. I can't answer all your idiotic questions!

MRS. SMITH [offended]: Oh! Are you trying to humiliate me?

MR. SMITH [all smiles]: You know very well that I'm not.

MRS. SMITH: Men are all alike! You sit there all day long, a cigarette in your mouth, or you powder your nose and rouge your lips, fifty times a day, or else you drink like a fish.

MR. SMITH: But what would you say if you saw men acting like women do, smoking all day long, powdering, rouging their lips, drinking whisky?

MRS. SMITH: It's nothing to me! But if you're only saying that to annoy me . . . I don't care for that kind of joking, you know that very well!
[*She hurls the socks across the stage and shows her teeth. She gets up.**]

MR. SMITH [*also getting up and going toward his wife, tenderly*]: Oh, my little ducky daddles, what a little spitfire you are! You know that I only said it as a joke! [*He takes her by the waist and kisses her.*] What a ridiculous pair of old lovers we are! Come, let's put out the lights and go bye-byes.

MARY [*entering*]: I'm the maid. I have spent a very pleasant afternoon. I've been to the cinema with a man and I've seen a film with some women. After the cinema, we went to drink some brandy and milk and then read the newspaper.

MRS. SMITH: I hope that you've spent a pleasant afternoon, that you went to the cinema with a man and that you drank some brandy and milk.

MR. SMITH: And the newspaper.

MARY: Mr. and Mrs. Martin, your guests, are at the door. They were waiting for me. They didn't dare come in by themselves. They were supposed to have dinner with you this evening.

MRS. SMITH: Oh, yes. We were expecting them. And we were hungry. Since they didn't put in an appearance, we were going to start dinner without them. We've had nothing to eat all day. You should not have gone out!

MARY: But it was you who gave me permission.

MR. SMITH: We didn't do it on purpose.

MARY [*bursts into laughter, then she bursts into tears. Then she smiles*]: I bought me a chamber pot.

MRS. SMITH: My dear Mary, please open the door and ask Mr. and Mrs. Martin to step in. We will change quickly.

---

*In Nicolas Bataille's production, Mrs. Smith did not show her teeth, nor did she throw the socks very far.

[*Mr. and Mrs. Smith exit right. Mary opens the door at the left, by which Mr. and Mrs. Martin enter.*]

MARY: Why have you come so late! You are not very polite. People should be punctual. Do you understand? But sit down there, anyway, and wait now that you're here.
[*She exits. Mr. and Mrs. Martin sit facing each other, without speaking. They smile timidly at each other. The dialogue which follows must be spoken in voices that are drawling, monotonous, a little singsong, without nuances.**]

MR. MARTIN: Excuse me, madam, but it seems to me, unless I'm mistaken, that I've met you somewhere before.

MRS. MARTIN: I, too, sir. It seems to me that I've met you somewhere before.

MR. MARTIN: Was it, by any chance, at Manchester that I caught a glimpse of you, madam?

MRS. MARTIN: That is very possible. I am originally from the city of Manchester. But I do not have a good memory, sir. I cannot say whether it was there that I caught a glimpse of you or not!

MR. MARTIN: Good God, that's curious! I, too, am originally from the city of Manchester, madam!

MRS. MARTIN: That is curious!

MR. MARTIN: Isn't that curious! Only, I, madam, I left the city of Manchester about five weeks ago.

MRS. MARTIN: That is curious! What a bizarre coincidence! I, too, sir, I left the city of Manchester about five weeks ago.

MR. MARTIN: Madam, I took the 8:30 morning train which arrives in London at 4:45.

MRS. MARTIN: That is curious! How very bizarre! And what a coincidence! I took the same train, sir, I too.

MR. MARTIN: Good Lord, how curious! Perhaps then, madam, it was on the train that I saw you?

MRS. MARTIN: It is indeed possible; that is, not unlikely. It is plausible and, after all, why not!—But I don't recall it, sir!

---

*In Nicolas Bataille's production, this dialogue was spoken in a tone and played in a style sincerely tragic.

MR. MARTIN: I traveled second class, madam. There is no second class in England, but I always travel second class.

MRS. MARTIN: That is curious! How very bizarre! And what a coincidence! I, too, sir, I traveled second class.

MR. MARTIN: How curious that is! Perhaps we did meet in second class, my dear lady!

MRS. MARTIN: That is certainly possible, and it is not at all unlikely. But I do not remember very well, my dear sir!

MR. MARTIN: My seat was in coach No. 8, compartment 6, my dear lady.

MRS. MARTIN: How curious that is! My seat was also in coach No. 8, compartment 6, my dear sir!

MR. MARTIN: How curious that is and what a bizarre coincidence! Perhaps we met in compartment 6, my dear lady?

MRS. MARTIN: It is indeed possible, after all! But I do not recall it, my dear sir!

MR. MARTIN: To tell the truth, my dear lady, I do not remember it either, but it is possible that we caught a glimpse of each other there, and as I think of it, it seems to me even very likely.

MRS. MARTIN: Oh! truly, of course, truly, sir!

MR. MARTIN: How curious it is! I had seat No. 3, next to the window, my dear lady.

MRS. MARTIN: Oh, good Lord, how curious and bizarre! I had seat No. 6, next to the window, across from you, my dear sir.

MR. MARTIN: Good God, how curious that is and what a coincidence! We were then seated facing each other, my dear lady! It is there that we must have seen each other!

MRS. MARTIN: How curious it is! It is possible, but I do not recall it, sir!

MR. MARTIN: To tell the truth, my dear lady, I do not remember it either. However, it is very possible that we saw each other on that occasion.

MRS. MARTIN: It is true, but I am not at all sure of it, sir.

MR. MARTIN: Dear madam, were you not the lady who asked me to place her suitcase in the luggage rack and who thanked me and gave me permission to smoke?

MRS. MARTIN: But of course, that must have been I, sir. How curious it is, how curious it is, and what a coincidence!

MR. MARTIN: How curious it is, how bizarre, what a coincidence! And well, well, it was perhaps at that moment that we came to know each other, madam?

MRS. MARTIN: How curious it is and what a coincidence! It is indeed possible, my dear sir! However, I do not believe that I recall it.

MR. MARTIN: Nor do I, madam. [*A moment of silence. The clock strikes twice, then once.*] Since coming to London, I have resided in Bromfield Street, my dear lady.

MRS. MARTIN: How curious that is, how bizarre! I, too, since coming to London, I have resided in Bromfield Street, my dear sir.

MR. MARTIN: How curious that is, well then, well then, perhaps we have seen each other in Bromfield Street, my dear lady.

MRS. MARTIN: How curious that is, how bizarre! It is indeed possible, after all! But I do not recall it, my dear sir.

MR. MARTIN: I reside at No. 19, my dear lady.

MRS. MARTIN: How curious that is. I also reside at No. 19, my dear sir.

MR. MARTIN: Well then, well then, well then, well then, perhaps we have seen each other in that house, dear lady?

MRS. MARTIN: It is indeed possible but I do not recall it, dear sir.

MR. MARTIN: My flat is on the fifth floor, No. 8, my dear lady.

MRS. MARTIN: How curious it is, good Lord, how bizarre! And what a coincidence! I too reside on the fifth floor, in flat No. 8, dear sir!

MR. MARTIN [*musing*]: How curious it is, how curious it is, how curious it is, and what a coincidence! You know, in my bedroom there is a bed, and it is covered with a green eiderdown. This room, with the bed and the green eiderdown, is at the end of the corridor between the w.c. and the bookcase, dear lady!

MRS. MARTIN: What a coincidence, good Lord, what a coincidence! My bedroom, too, has a bed with a green eiderdown and is at the end of the corridor, between the w.c., dear sir, and the bookcase!

MR. MARTIN: How bizarre, curious, strange! Then, madam, we live in the same room and we sleep in the same bed, dear lady. It is perhaps there that we have met!

MRS. MARTIN: How curious it is and what a coincidence! It is indeed possible that we have met there, and perhaps even last night. But I do not recall it, dear sir!

MR. MARTIN: I have a little girl, my little daughter, she lives with me, dear lady. She is two years old, she's blonde, she has a white eye and a red eye, she is very pretty, her name is Alice, dear lady.

MRS. MARTIN: What a bizarre coincidence! I, too, have a little girl. She is two years old, has a white eye and a red eye, she is very pretty, and her name is Alice, too, dear sir!

MR. MARTIN [*in the same drawling, monotonous voice*]: How curious it is and what a coincidence! And bizarre! Perhaps they are the same, dear lady!

MRS. MARTIN: How curious it is! It is indeed possible, dear sir. [*A rather long moment of silence. The clock strikes 29 times.*]

MR. MARTIN [*after having reflected at length, gets up slowly and, unhurriedly, moves toward Mrs. Martin, who, surprised by his solemn air, has also gotten up very quietly. Mr. Martin, in the same flat, monotonous voice, slightly singsong*]: Then, dear lady, I believe that there can be no doubt about it, we have seen each other before and you are my own wife . . . Elizabeth, I have found you again!
[*Mrs. Martin approaches Mr. Martin without haste. They embrace without expression. The clock strikes once, very loud. This striking of the clock must be so loud that it makes the audience jump. The Martins do not hear it.*]

MRS. MARTIN: Donald, it's you, darling!
[*They sit together in the same armchair, their arms around each other, and fall asleep. The clock strikes several more times. Mary, on tiptoe, a finger to her lips, enters quietly and addresses the audience.*]

MARY: Elizabeth and Donald are now too happy to be able to hear me. I can therefore let you in on a secret. Elizabeth is not Elizabeth, Donald is not Donald. And here is the proof: the child that Donald spoke of is not Elizabeth's daughter, they are not the same person. Donald's daughter has one white eye and one red eye like Elizabeth's daughter. Whereas Donald's child has a white right eye and a red left eye, Elizabeth's child has a red right eye and a white left eye! Thus all of Donald's system of deduction collapses when it comes up against this last obstacle, which destroys his whole theory. In spite of the extraordinary coincidences which seem to be definitive proofs, Donald and Elizabeth, not being the parents of the same child, are not Donald and Elizabeth. It is in vain that he thinks he is Donald, it is in vain that she thinks she is Elizabeth. He

believes in vain that she is Elizabeth. She believes in vain that he is Donald—
they are sadly deceived. But who is the true Donald? Who is the true Elizabeth? Who has any interest in prolonging this confusion? I don't know. Let's
not try to know. Let's leave things as they are. [*She takes several steps toward
the door, then returns and says to the audience:*] My real name is Sherlock Holmes.
[*She exits.*]

JACK KEROUAC

꿏

"Written Address to the Italian Judge" [1963]

Re: Attorney General vs. Kerouac

[Jack Kerouac wrote his open letter in defense of *The Subterraneans* before a scheduled trial in Italy, where his novel, published in Milan by Giangiacomo Feltrinelli Editore, has been banned since 1961.]

I wish to address His Honor in my own manner, that is, in a manner untrained in legal learning and court language. Although I have tried to understand the account of the lifelong legal argument between Baron Verulam (Sir Francis Bacon) and Sir Edward Coke, as described in the Eleventh Edition of the Encyclopaedia Britannica, which argument however, I understand, helped to create the basis of English jurisprudence, I could not really make head or tail of the details, not being trained in law study except for occasional idle afternoon library perusals of cases of So-and-So vs. So-and-So involving the collisions of barges et cetera wherein however there is always a perfect settlement based on the available factual evidence.

But I do know this: whatever the decision of the judge may be, "The judge," in the words of Dr. Samuel Johnson addressed to James Boswell, his biographer, "is always right" once the evidence has been weighed and the decision has been made. This is the basis of jurisprudence: "The judge is always right."

I want His Honor to know that I receive no asssistance in this written address to the bench.

First, as to the significance of *The Subterraneans,* you have briefs there, cachets, dossiers of aficionados, papers, all shadowed with social overtones, only of controversial value as evidence.

Second, as to the artistic background of *The Subterraneans:* the form is strictly confessional in accordance with the confessional form of Fyodor Dostoevsky's *Notes from the Underground.* The idea is to tell all about a recently concluded event in all its complexity, at least tell all that can be told without attempting to offend certain basic sensibilities in polite society as well as in a society that accedes to, and more or less votes for, the pacification of instincts such as, say, pacification of the scatological instincts such as, say, the instinct to open your mouth and show what you're eating (as certain cretinous people and maniacs do), or the instinct to publicly describe revolting bodily functions best kept out of sight naturally, or the instinct to deliberately offend the quiet hearts of others in order to get their attention because of vicious jealousy sometimes diagnosed as "frustration." In *The Subterraneans,* when I tell all, I tell within the bounds of institutionalized, modern, reasonably repentant common sense. First I pour out confessions of love, how I first met her, what thoughts and memories were aroused, what I preliminarily attempted, but never in a language that is anything but frankly civil as well as civilized, as well as adultly mondaine, as well as delicately veiled in discussion. There are no descriptions that tend to ruffle the spine towards further provocative or salacious hints, no, it's all there purely stated and then the door is closed to any possible subsequent description which would offend me, the author, as well as anyone else concerned in this delicate matter dealing with delicate matters. I wish to see to it that literature can be complete and yet the door be closed somewhere.

Third, as to the style of *The Subterraneans:* this is the style I've discovered for narrative art, whereby the author stumbles over himself to tell his tale, just as breathlessly as some raconteur rushing in to tell a whole roomful of listeners what has just happened, and once he has told his tale he has no right to go back and delete what the hand hath written, just as the hand that writes upon the wall cannot go back. This decision, rather, this vow I made with regard to the practice of my narrative art frankly, Gentlemen, has its roots in my experience inside the confessionals of a Catholic childhood. It was my belief then that to withhold any reasonably and decently explainable detail from the Father was a sin, although you can be sure that the Father was aware of the difficulties of the delicacy involved. Yet all was well.

I wish the court to review this fact: that the factual evidence in this case is in itself open to interpretation. In the case of a barge ramming a barge, the factual evidence concerns someone at the wheel overlooking a fact of the factor of wind, current, direction, this or that, but none of it is under the shadow of interpretation, because winds, currents, hands in the wheelhouse beg not interpretation.

But in this case, the factual evidence which is the book itself, I beg to remind you, in its entirety and not just in underlined sections for the sake of a prosecutor's brief, is open to interpretation because of the amorphous, chaotic, nay ephemeral nature of narrative art itself. Some like David, some don't, yet David is there (Michelangelo's). Opinions as to the interpretation of the value or non-value of *The Subterraneans* as narrative art, and of *The Subterraneans* as either salacious or non-salacious, are based on opinion merely. I use the word "salacious" instead of the word "obscene" because war, and many other things, are obscene. Obscene is from the Latin *obscaenus,* detestable, unnatural, and from Old English, inauspicious, which can be applied to war, robbery, dishonesty and all sorts of vicious and cruel events, whilst "salacious" is from Latin *salax* or *salacem,* lecherous, and *salire,* to leap, or, leaping lechery. Yet the evidence is there, the book itself. What can a jury do when evidence melts into opinion, and opinion melts into evidence?

In my own opinion, which is mine and mine alone, *The Subterraneans* is an attempt on my part to use spontaneous modern prose to execute the biography of someone else in a given circumstance and time, as completely as possible without offending the humanistic, in any case, human, tastes, of myself or anyone else, for the sake of the entertainment, plus the suffering attention and edification of some reader by the fire of a winter midnight.

In my presentation of the evidence, however, and this is all the evidence there is, I present as exhibit Number One the book itself in its entirety from first sentence to last.

JACK KEROUAC

꧁꧂

FROM *The Subterraneans* [1958]

Once I was young and had so much more orientation and could talk with nervous intelligence about everything and with clarity and without as much literary preambling as this; in other words this is the story of an unself-confident man, at the same time of an egomaniac, naturally, facetious won't do—just to start at the beginning and let the truth seep out, that's what I'll do—. It began on a warm summernight—ah, she was sitting on a fender with Julien Alexander who is . . . let me begin with the history of the subterraneans of San Francisco . . .

Julien Alexander is the angel of the subterraneans, the subterraneans is a name invented by Adam Moorad who is a poet and friend of mine who said "They are hip without being slick, they are intelligent without being corny, they are intellectual as hell and know all about Pound without being pretentious or talking too much about it, they are very quiet, they are very Christlike." Julien certainly is Christlike. I was coming down the street with Larry O'Hara old drinking buddy of mine from all the times in San Francisco in my long and nervous and mad careers I've gotten drunk and in fact cadged drinks off friends with such "genial" regularity nobody really cared to notice or announce that I am developing or was developing, in my youth, such bad freeloading habits though of course they did notice but liked me and as Sam said "Everybody comes to you for your gasoline boy, that's some filling station you got there" or say words to that effect—old Larry O'Hara always nice to me, a crazy Irish young businessman of San Francisco with Balzacian backroom in his bookstore where they'd smoke tea and talk of the old days of the great Basie band or the days of the great Chu Berry—of whom more anon since she got involved with him too as she had to get involved with everyone because of knowing me who am nervous and many leveled and not in the least one-souled—not a piece of my pain has showed yet—or suffering—Angels, bear with me—I'm not even looking at the page but straight ahead into the sadglint of my wallroom and at a Sarah Vaughan Gerry Mulligan Radio KROW show on the desk in the form of a radio, in other words, they were sitting on the fender of a car in front of the Black Mask bar on Montgomery Street, Julien Alexander the Christlike unshaved thin youthful quiet strange almost as you or as Adam might say apocalyptic angel or saint of the subterraneans, certainly star (now), and she, Mardou Fox, whose face when first I saw it in Dante's bar around the corner made me think, "By God, I've got to get involved with that little woman" and maybe too because she was Negro. Also she had the same face that Rita Savage a girlhood girlfriend of my sister's had, and of whom among other things I used to have daydreams of her between my legs while kneeling on the floor of the toilet, I on the seat, with her special cool lips and Indian-like hard high soft cheekbones—same face, but dark, sweet, with little eyes honest glittering and intense she Mardou was leaning saying something extremely earnestly to Ross Wallenstein (Julien's friend) leaning over the table, deep— "I got to get involved with her"—I tried to shoot her the glad eye the sex eye she never had a notion of looking up or seeing—I must explain, I'd just come off a ship in New York, paid off before the trip to Kobe Japan because of trouble with the steward and my inability to be gracious and in fact human and like an ordinary guy while performing my chores as saloon messman (and you must admit now I'm sticking to the facts), a thing typical of me, I would treat the first engineer and the other officers with backwards-falling politeness, it finally drove them angry, they wanted me to say something, maybe gruff, in the morning, while setting their coffee down and instead of which silently on crepefeet I rushed to do their bidding and never cracked a smile or if so a sick one, a superior one, all having to do with that loneliness angel riding on my shoulder as I came down warm Montgomery Street that night and saw Mardou on the fender with Julien, remembering, "O there's the girl I gotta get involved with, I wonder if she's going with any of these boys"— dark, you could barely see her in the dim street—her feet in thongs of sandals of such sexuality-looking greatness I wanted to kiss her, them—having no notion of anything though.

The subterraneans were hanging outside the Mask in the warm night, Julien on the fender, Ross Wallenstein standing up, Roger Beloit the great bop tenorman, Walt Fitzpatrick who was the son of a famous director and had grown up in Hollywood in an atmosphere of Greta Garbo parties at dawn and Chaplin falling in the door drunk, several other girls, Harriet the ex-wife of Ross Wallenstein a kind of blonde with soft expressionless features and wearing a simple almost housewife-in-the-kitchen cotton dress but softly bellysweet to look at—as another confession must be made, as many I must make ere time's sup—I am crudely malely sexual and cannot help myself and have lecherous and so on propensities as almost all my male readers no doubt are the same—confession after confession, I am a Canuck, I could not speak English till I was 5 or 6, at 16 I spoke with a halting accent and was a big blue baby in school though varsity basketball later and if not for that no one would have noticed I could cope in any way with the world (underself-confidence) and would have been put in the madhouse for some kind of inadequacy—

But now let me tell Mardou herself (difficult to make a real confession and show what happened when you're such an egomaniac all you can do is to take off on big paragraphs about minor details about yourself and the big soul details about others go sitting and wailing around)—in any case, therefore, also there was Fritz Nicholas the titular leader of the subterraneans, to whom I said (having met him New Year's Eve in a Nob Hill swank apartment sitting cross-legged like a peyote Indian on a thick rug wearing a kind of clean white Russian shirt and a crazy Isadora Duncan girl with long blue hair on his shoulder smoking pot and talking about Pound and peyote) (thin also Christlike with a faun's look and young and serious and like the father of the group, as say, suddenly you'd see him in the Black Mask sitting there with head thrown back thin dark eyes watching everybody as if in sudden slow astonishment and "Here we are little ones and now what my dears," but also a great dope man, anything in the form of kicks he would want at any time and very intense) I said to him, "Do you know this girl, the dark one?"— "Mardou?"—"That her name? Who she go with?"—"No one in particular just now, this has been an incestuous group in its time," a very strange thing he said to me there, as we walked to his old beat '36 Chevy with no backseat parked across from the bar for the purpose of picking up some tea for the group to get all together, as, I told Larry, "Man, let's get some tea."—"And what for you want all those people?"—"I want to dig them as a group," saying this, too, in front of Nicholas so perhaps he might appreciate my sensitivity being a stranger to the group and yet immediately, etc., perceiving their value—facts, facts, sweet philosophy long deserted me with the juices of other years fled—incestuous—there was another final great figure in the group who was however now this summer not here but in Paris, Jack Steen, very interesting Leslie Howard–like little guy who walked (as Mardou later imitated for me) like a Viennese philosopher with soft arms swinging slight side flow and long slow flowing strides, coming to a stop on corner with imperious soft pose—he too had had to do with Mardou and as I learned later most weirdly—but now my first crumb of information concerning this girl I was SEEKING to get involved with as if not enough trouble already or other old romances hadn't taught me that message of pain, keep asking for it, for like—

Out of the bar were pouring interesting people, the night making a great impression on me, some kind of Truman Capote–haired dark Marlon Brando with a beautiful thin birl or girl in boy slacks with stars in her eyes and hips that seemed so soft when she put her hands in her slacks I could see the change— and dark thin slackpant legs dropping down to little feet, and that face, and with them a guy with another beautiful doll, the guy's name Rob and he's some kind of adventurous Israeli soldier with a British accent whom I suppose you might find in some Riviera bar at 5 A.M. drinking everything in sight alphabetically with a bunch of interesting crazy international-set friends on a spree—Larry O'Hara introducing me to Roger Beloit (I did not believe that this young man with ordinary face in front of me was that great poet I'd revered in my youth, my youth, my youth, that is, 1948, I keep saying my youth)—"This is Roger Beloit?—I'm Bennett Fitzpatrick" (Walt's father) which brought a smile to Roger Beloit's face—Adam Moorad by now having emerged from the night was also there and the night would open—

So we all did go to Larry's and Julien sat on the floor in front of an open newspaper in which was the tea (poor quality L.A. but good enough) and rolled, or "twisted," as Jack Steen, the absent one, had said to me the previous New Year's and that having been my first contact with the subterraneans, he'd asked to roll a stick for me and I'd said really coldly "What for? I roll my own" and immediately the cloud crossed his sensitive little face, etc., and he hated me— and so cut me all the night when he had a chance—but now Julien was on the floor, cross-legged, and himself now twisting for the group and everybody droned the conversations which I certainly won't repeat, except, it was, like, "I'm looking at this book by Percepied—who's Percepied, has he been busted yet?" and such small talk, or, while listening to Stan Kenton talking about the music of tomorrow and we hear a new young tenorman come on, Ricci Comucca, Roger Beloit says, moving back expressive thin purple lips, "This is the music of tomorrow?" and Larry O'Hara telling his usual stock repertoire anecdotes. In the '36 Chevy on the way, Julien, sitting beside me on the floor, had stuck out his hand and said, "My name's Julien Alexander, I have something, I conquered Egypt," and then Mardou stuck her hand out to Adam Moorad and introduced herself, saying, "Mardou Fox," but didn't think of doing it to me which should have been my first inkling of the prophecy of what was to come, so I had to stick my hand at her and say, "Leo Percepied my name" and shake—ah, you always go for the ones who don't really want you—she really wanted Adam Moorad, she had just been rejected coldly and subterra- neanly by Julien—she was interested in thin ascetic strange intellectuals of San Francisco and Berkeley and not in big paranoiac bums of ships and railroads and novels and all that hatefulness which in myself is to myself so evident and so to others too—though and because ten years younger than I seeing none of my virtues which anyway had long been drowned under years of drugtaking and desiring to die, to give up, to give it all up and forget it all, to die in the dark star—it was I stuck out my hand, not she—ah time.

But in eyeing her little charms I only had the foremost one idea that I had to immerse my lonely being ("A big sad lonely man," is what she said to me

one night later, seeing me suddenly in the chair) in the warm bath and salvation of her thighs—the intimacies of young-lovers in a bed, high, facing eye to
eye, breast to breast naked, organ to organ, knee to shivering goose-pimpled
knee, exchanging existential and loveracts for a crack at making it—"making
it" the big expression with her, I can see the little out-pushing teeth through
the little redlips seeing "making it"—the key to pain—she sat in the corner,
by the window, she was being "separated" or "aloof" or "prepared to cut out
from this group" for her own reasons.—In the corner I went, not leaning my
head on her but on the wall and tried silent communication, then quiet words
(as befit party) and North Beach words, "What are you reading?" and for the
first time she opened her mouth and spoke to me communicating a full thought
and my heart didn't exactly sink but wondered when I heard the cultured funny
tones of part Beach, part I. Magnin model, part Berkeley, part Negro highclass,
something, a mixture of *langue* and style of talking and use of words I'd never
heard before except in certain rare girls of course *white* and so strange even
Adam at once noticed and commented with me that night—but definitely the
new bop generation way of speaking, you don't say *I*, you say "ahy" or "Oy"
and long ways, like oft or erstwhile "effeminate" way of speaking so when you
hear it in men at first it has a disagreeable sound and when you hear it in women
it's charming but much too strange, and a sound I had already definitely and
wonderingly heard in the voice of new bop singers like Jerry Winters especially
with Kenton band on the record *Yes Daddy Yes* and maybe in Jeri Southern
too—but my heart sank for the Beach has always hated me, cast me out, over-
looked me, shat on me, from the beginning in 1943 on in—for look, coming
down the street I am some kind of hoodlum and then when they learn I'm not
a hoodlum but some kind of crazy saint they don't like it and moreover they're
afraid I'll suddenly become a hoodlum anyway and slug them and break things
and this I have almost done anyway and in my adolescence did so, as one time
I roamed through North Beach with the Stanford basketball team, specifically
with Red Kelly whose wife (rightly?) died in Redwood City in 1946, the whole
team behind us, the Garetta brothers besides, he pushed a violinist a queer into
a doorway and I pushed another one in, he slugged his, I glared at mine, I was
18, I was a nannybeater and fresh as a daisy too—now, seeing this past in the
scowl and glare and horror and the beat of my brow-pride they wanted nothing to do with me, and so I of course also knew that Mardou had real genuine
distrust and dislike of me as I sat there "trying to (not make IT) but make her"—
unhiplike, brash, smiling, the false hysterical "compulsive" smiling they call
it—me hot—them cool—and also I had on a very noxious unbeachlike shirt,
bought on Broadway in New York when I thought I'd be cutting down the
gangplanks in Kobe, a foolish Crosby Hawaiian shirt with designs, which

malelike and vain after the original honest humilities of my regular self (really) with the smoking of two drags of tea I felt constrained to open an extra button down and so show my tanned, hairy chest—which must have disgusted her— in any case she didn't look, and spoke little and low—and was intent on Julien who was squatting with his back to her—and she listened and murmured the laughter in the general talk—most of the talk being conducted by O'Hara and loudspeaking Roger Beloit and that intelligent adventurous Rob and I, too silent, listening, digging, but in the tea vanity occasionally throwing in "perfect" (I thought) remarks which were "too perfect" but to Adam Moorad who'd known me all the time clear indication of my awe and listening and respect of the group in fact, and to them this new person throwing in remarks intended to sow his hipness—all horrible, and unredeemable.—Although at first, before the puffs, which were passed around Indian style, I had the definite sensation of being able to come close with Mardou and involved and making her that very first night, that is taking off with her alone if only for coffee but with the puffs which made me pray reverently and in serious secrecy for the return of my pre-puff "sanity" I became extremely unself-confident, overtrying, positive she didn't like me, hating the facts—remembering now the first night I met my Nicki Peters love in 1948 in Adam Moorad's pad in (then) the Fillmore, I was standing unconcerned and beerdrinking in the kitchen as ever (and at home working furiously on a huge novel, mad, cracked, confident, young, talented as never since) when she pointed to my profile shadow on the pale green wall and said, "How beautiful your profile is," which so nonplussed me and (like the tea) made me unself-confident, attentive, attempting to "begin to make her," to act in that way which by her almost hypnotic suggestion now led to the first preliminary probings into pride vs. pride and beauty or beatitude or sensitivity *versus* the stupid neurotic nervousness of the phallic type, forever conscious of his phallus, his tower, of women as wells—the truth of the matter being there, but the man unhinged, unrelaxed, and now it is no longer 1948 but 1953 with cool generations and I five years older, or younger, having to make it (or make the women) with a new style and stow the nervousness—in any case, I gave up consciously trying to make Mardou and settled down to a night of digging the great new perplexing group of subterraneans Adam had discovered and named on the Beach.

ANTONIN ARTAUD

※

"The Theater and Cruelty"
FROM *The Theater and Its Double* [1958]
Translated from the French by Mary Caroline Richards

An idea of the theater has been lost. And as long as the theater limits itself to showing us intimate scenes from the lives of a few puppets, transforming the public into Peeping Toms, it is no wonder the elite abandon it and the great public looks to the movies, the music hall, or the circus for violent satisfactions, whose intentions do not deceive them.

At the point of deterioration which our sensibility has reached, it is certain that we need above all a theater that wakes us up: nerves and heart.

The misdeeds of the psychological theater descended from Racine have unaccustomed us to that immediate and violent action which the theater should possess. Movies in their turn, murdering us with second-hand reproductions which, filtered through machines, cannot *unite with* our sensibility, have maintained us for ten years in an ineffectual torpor, in which all our faculties appear to be foundering.

In the anguished, catastrophic period we live in, we feel an urgent need for a theater which events do not exceed, whose resonance is deep within us, dominating the instability of the times.

Our long habit of seeking diversion has made us forget the idea of a serious theater, which, overturning all our preconceptions, inspires us with the fiery magnetism of its images and acts upon us like a spiritual therapeutics whose touch can never be forgotten.

Everything that acts is a cruelty. It is upon this idea of extreme action, pushed beyond all limits, that theater must be rebuilt.

Imbued with the idea that the public thinks first of all with its senses and that to address oneself first to its understanding as the ordinary psychological theater does is absurd, the Theater of Cruelty proposes to resort to a mass spectacle; to seek in the agitation of tremendous masses, convulsed and hurled against each other, a little of that poetry of festivals and crowds when, all too rarely nowadays, the people pour out into the streets.

The theater must give us everything that is in crime, love, war, or madness, if it wants to recover its necessity.

Everyday love, personal ambition, struggles for status, all have value only in proportion to their relation to the terrible lyricism of the Myths to which the great mass of men have assented.

This is why we shall try to concentrate, around famous personages, atrocious crimes, superhuman devotions, a drama which, without resorting to the defunct images of the old Myths, shows that it can extract the forces which struggle within them.

In a word, we believe that there are living forces in what is called poetry and that the image of a crime presented in the requisite theatrical conditions is something infinitely more terrible for the spirit than that same crime when actually committed.

We want to make out of the theater a believable reality which gives the heart and the senses that kind of concrete bite which all true sensation requires. In the same way that our dreams have an effect upon us and reality has an effect upon our dreams, so we believe that the images of thought can be identified with a dream which will be efficacious to the degree that it can be projected with the necessary violence. And the public will believe in the theater's dreams on condition that it take them for true dreams and not for a servile copy or reality; on condition that they allow the public to liberate within itself the magical liberties of dreams which it can only recognize when they are imprinted with terror and cruelty.

Hence this appeal to cruelty and terror, though on a vast scale, whose range probes our entire vitality, confronts us with all our possibilities.

It is in order to attack the spectator's sensibility on all sides that we advocate a revolving spectacle which, instead of making the stage and auditorium two closed worlds, without possible communication, spreads its visual and sonorous outbursts over the entire mass of the spectators.

Also, departing from the sphere of analyzable passions, we intend to make use of the actor's lyric qualities to manifest external forces, and by this means to cause the whole of nature to re-enter the theater in its restored form.

However vast this program may be, it does not exceed the theater itself, which appears to us, all in all, to identify itself with the forces of ancient magic.

Practically speaking, we want to resuscitate an idea of total spectacle by which the theater would recover from the cinema, the music hall, the circus, and from life itself what has always belonged to it. The separation between the analytic theater and the plastic world seems to us a stupidity. One does not separate the mind from the body nor the senses from the intelligence, especially in a domain where the endlessly renewed fatigue of the organs requires intense and sudden shocks to revive our understanding.

Thus, on the one hand, the mass and extent of a spectacle addressed to the entire organism; on the other, an intensive mobilization of objects, gestures, and signs, used in a new spirit. The reduced role given to the understanding leads to an energetic compression of the text; the active role given to obscure poetic emotion necessitates concrete signs. Words say little to the mind; extent and objects speak; new images speak, even new images made with words. But space thundering with images and crammed with sounds speaks too, if one knows how to intersperse from time to time a sufficient extent of space stocked with silence and immobility.

On this principle we envisage producing a spectacle where these means of direct action are used in their totality; a spectacle unafraid of going as far as necessary in the exploration of our nervous sensibility, of which the rhythms, sounds, words, resonances, and twitterings, and their united quality and surprising mixtures, belong to a technique which must not be divulged.

The images in certain paintings by Grünewald or Hieronymus Bosch tell enough about what a spectacle can be in which, as in the brain of some saint, the objects of external nature will appear as temptations.

It is in this spectacle of a temptation from which life has everything to lose and the mind everything to gain that the theater must recover its true signification.

Elsewhere we have given a program which will allow the means of pure staging, found on the spot, to be organized around historic or cosmic themes, familiar to all.

And we insist on the fact that the first spectacle of the Theater of Cruelty will turn upon the preoccupations of the great mass of men, preoccupations much more pressing and disquieting than those of any individual whatsoever.

It is a matter of knowing whether now, in Paris, before the cataclysms which are at our door descend upon us, sufficient means of production, financial or otherwise, can be found to permit such a theater to be brought to life— it is bound to in any case, because it is the future. Or whether a little real blood will be needed, right away, in order to manifest this cruelty.

D. H. LAWRENCE

〷

FROM *Lady Chatterley's Lover* [1959]

Connie was a good deal alone now, fewer people came to Wragby. Clifford no longer wanted them. He had turned against even the cronies. He was queer. He preferred the radio, which he had installed at some expense, with a good deal of success at last. He could sometimes get Madrid or Frankfurt, even there in the uneasy Midlands.

And he would sit alone for hours listening to the loudspeaker bellowing forth. It amazed and stunned Connie. But there he would sit, with a blank entranced expression on his face, like a person losing his mind, and listen, or seem to listen, to the unspeakable thing.

Was he really listening? Or was it a sort of soporific he took, whilst something else worked on underneath in him? Connie did not know. She fled up to her room, or out of doors to the wood. A kind of terror filled her sometimes, a terror of the incipient insanity of the whole civilized species.

But now that Clifford was drifting off to his other weirdness of industrial activity, becoming almost a *creature,* with a hard, efficient shell of an exterior and a pulpy interior, one of the amazing crabs and lobsters of the modern, industrial and financial world, invertebrates of the crustacean order, with shells of steel, like machines, and inner bodies of soft pulp, Connie herself was really completely stranded.

She was not even free, for Clifford must have her there, he seemed to have a nervous terror that she should leave him. The curious pulpy part of him, the emotional and humanly-individual part, depended on her with terror, like a child, almost like an idiot. She must be there, there at Wragby, a Lady Chatterley, his wife. Otherwise he would be lost like an idiot on a moor.

This amazing dependence Connie realized with a sort of horror. She heard him with his pit managers, with the members of his Board, with young scientists, and she was amazed at his shrewd insight into things, his power, his uncanny material power over what is called practical men. He had become a practical man himself, and an amazingly astute and powerful one, a master. Connie attributed it to Mrs. Bolton's influence upon him, just at the crisis in his life.

73

But this astute and practical man was almost an idiot when left alone to his own emotional life. He worshipped Connie, she was his wife, a higher being, and he worshipped her with a queer, craven idolatry, like a savage, a worship based on enormous fear, and even hate of the power of the idol, the dread idol. All he wanted was for Connie to swear, to swear not to leave him, not to give him away.

"Clifford," she said to him—but this was after she had the key to the hut— "would you really like me to have a child one day?"

He looked at her with a furtive apprehension in his rather prominent pale eyes.

"I shouldn't mind, if it made no difference between us," he said.

"No difference to what?" she asked.

"To you and me; to our love for one another. If it's going to affect that, then I'm all against it. Why, I might even one day have a child of my own!"

She looked at him in amazement.

"I mean, it might come back to me one of these days."

She still stared in amazement, and he was uncomfortable.

"So you would not like it if I had a child?" she said.

"I tell you," he replied quickly, like a cornered dog. "I am quite willing, provided it doesn't touch your love for me. If it would touch that, I am dead against it."

Connie could only be silent in cold fear and contempt. Such talk was really the gabbling of an idiot. He no longer knew what he was talking about.

"Oh, it wouldn't make any difference to my feeling for you," she said, with a certain sarcasm.

"There!" he said. "That is the point. In that case I don't mind in the least. I mean it would be awfully nice to have a child running about the house, and feel one was building up a future for it. I should have something to strive for then, and I should know it was your child, shouldn't I, dear? And it would seem just the same as my own. Because it is you who count in these matters. You know that, don't you, dear? I don't enter, I am a cipher. You are the great I-am, as far as life goes. You know that, don't you? I mean, as far as I am concerned. I mean, but for you I am absolutely nothing. I live for your sake and our future. I am nothing to myself."

Connie heard it all with deepening dismay and repulsion. It was one of the ghastly half-truths that poison human existence. What man in his senses would say such things to a woman! But men aren't in their senses. What man with a spark of honor would put this ghastly burden of life-responsibility upon a woman, and leave her there, in the void?

Moreover, in half-an-hour's time, Connie heard Clifford talking to Mrs. Bolton, in a hot, impulsive voice, revealing himself in a sort of passionless passion to the woman, as if she were half mistress, half foster-mother to him. And Mrs. Bolton was carefully dressing him in evening clothes, for there were important business guests in the house.

Connie really sometimes felt she would die at this time. She felt she was being crushed to death by weird lies, and by the amazing cruelty of idiocy. Clifford's strange business efficiency in a way overawed her, and his declaration of private worship put her into a panic. There was nothing between them. She never even touched him nowadays, and he never touched her. He never even took her hand and held it kindly. No, and because they were so utterly out of touch, he tortured her with his declaration of idolatry. It was the cruelty of utter impotence. And she felt her reason would give way, or she would die.

She fled as much as possible to the wood. One afternoon, as she sat brooding, watching the water bubbling coldly in John's Well, the keeper had strode up to her.

"I got you a key made, my Lady!" he said, saluting, and he offered her the key.

"Thank you so much!" she said, startled.

"The hut's not very tidy, if you don't mind," he said. "I cleared it of what I could."

"But I didn't want you to trouble!" she said.

"Oh, it wasn't any trouble. I am setting the hens in about a week. But they won't be scared of you. I s'll have to see to them morning and night, but I shan't bother you any more than I can help."

"But you wouldn't bother me," she pleaded. "I'd rather not go to the hut at all, if I am going to be in the way."

He looked at her with his keen blue eyes. He seemed kindly, but distant. But at least he was sane, and wholesome, if even he looked thin and ill. A cough troubled him.

"You have a cough," she said.

"Nothing—a cold! The last pneumonia left me with a cough, but it's nothing."

He kept distant from her, and would not come any nearer.

She went fairly often to the hut, in the morning or in the afternoon, but he was never there. No doubt he avoided her on purpose. He wanted to keep his own privacy.

He had made the hut tidy, put the little table and chair near the fireplace, left a little pile of kindling arid small logs, and put the tools and traps away as far as possible, effacing himself. Outside, by the clearing, he had built a low little roof of boughs and straw, a shelter for the birds, and under it stood the five coops. And, one day when she came, she found two brown hens sitting alert and fierce in the coops, sitting on pheasants' eggs, and fluffed out so proud and deep in all the heat of the pondering female blood. This almost broke Connie's heart. She, herself, was so forlorn and unused, not a female at all, just a mere thing of terrors.

Then all the five coops were occupied by hens, three brown and a grey and a black. All alike, they clustered themselves down on the eggs in the soft nestling ponderosity of the female urge, the female nature, fluffing out their feathers. And with brilliant eves they watched Connie, as she crouched before them, and they gave short sharp clucks of anger and alarm, but chiefly of female anger at being approached.

Connie found corn in the corn-bin in the hut. She offered it to the hens in her hand. They would not eat it. Only one hen pecked at her hand with a fierce little jab, so Connie was frightened. But she was pining to give them something, the brooding mothers who neither fed themselves nor drank. She brought water in a little tin, and was delighted when one of the hens drank.

Now she came every day to the hens, they were the only things in the world that warmed her heart. Clifford's protestations made her go cold from head to foot. Mrs. Bolton's voice made her go cold, and the sound of the business men who came. An occasional letter from Michaelis affected her with the same sense of chill. She felt she would surely die if it lasted much longer.

Yet it was spring, and the bluebells were coming in the wood, and the leaf-buds on the hazels were opening like the spatter of green rain. How terrible it was that it should be spring, and everything cold-hearted, cold-hearted. Only the hens, fluffed so wonderfully on the eggs, were warm with their hot, brooding female bodies! Connie felt herself living on the brink of fainting all the time.

Then, one day, a lovely sunny day with great tufts of primroses under the hazels, and many violets dotting the paths, she came in the afternoon to the coops and there was one tiny, tiny perky chicken tinily prancing round in front of a coop, and the mother hen clucking in terror. The slim little chick was greyish-brown with dark markings, and it was the most alive little spark of a creature in seven kingdoms at that moment. Connie crouched to watch in a sort of ecstasy. Life, life! Pure, sparky, fearless new life! New life! So tiny and so utterly without fear! Even when it scampered a little scramblingly into the coop again, and disappeared under the hen's feathers in answer to the mother hen's wild alarm-cries, it was not really frightened; it took it as a game, the game of living. For in a moment a tiny sharp head was poking through the gold-brown feathers of the hen, and eyeing the Cosmos.

Connie was fascinated. And at the same time never had she felt so acutely the agony of her own female forlornness. It was becoming unbearable.

She had only one desire now, to go to the clearing in the wood. The rest was a kind of painful dream. But sometimes she was kept all day at Wragby, by her duties as hostess. And then she felt as if she, too, were going blank, just blank and insane.

One evening, guests or no guests, she escaped after tea. It was late, and she fled across the park like one who fears to be called back. The sun was setting rosy as she entered the wood, but she pressed on among the flowers. The light would last long overhead.

She arrived at the clearing, flushed and semi-conscious. The keeper was there, in his shirt-sleeves, just closing up the coops for the night, so the little occupants would be safe. But still one little trio was pattering about on tiny feet, alert drab mites, under the straw shelter, refusing to be called in by the anxious mother.

"I had to come and see the chickens!" she said, panting, glancing shyly at the keeper, almost unaware of him. "Are there any more?"

"Thirty-six so far!" he said. "Not bad!"

He, too, took a curious pleasure in watching the young things come out.

Connie crouched in front of the last coop. The three chicks had run in. But still their cheeky heads came poking sharply through the yellow feathers, then withdrawing, then only one beady little head eyeing forth from the vast mother-body.

"I'd love to touch them," she said, putting her fingers gingerly through the bars of the coop. But the mother-hen pecked at her hand fiercely, and Connie drew back startled and frightened.

"How she pecks at me! She hates me!" she said in a wondering voice. "But I wouldn't hurt them!"

The man standing above her laughed, and crouched down beside her, knees apart, and put his hand with quiet confidence slowly into the coop. The old hen pecked at him, but not so savagely. And slowly, softly, with sure gentle fingers, he felt among the old bird's feathers and drew out a faintly-peeping chick in his closed hand.

"There!" he said, holding out his hand to her. She took the little drab thing between her hands, and there it stood, on its impossible little stalks of legs, its atom of balancing life trembling through its almost weightless feet into Connie's hands. But it lifted its handsome, clean-shaped little head boldly, and looked sharply round, and gave a little "peep."

"So adorable! So cheeky!" she said softly.

The keeper, squatting beside her, was also watching with an amused face the bold little bird in her hands. Suddenly he saw a tear fall on to her wrist.

And he stood up, and stood away, moving to the other coop. For suddenly he was aware of the old flame shooting and leaping up in his loins, that he had hoped was quiescent for ever. He fought against it, turning his back to her. But it leapt, and leapt downward, circling in his knees.

He turned again to look at her. She was kneeling and holding her two hands slowly forward, blindly, so that the chicken should run in to the mother-hen again. And there was something so mute and forlorn in her, compassion flamed in his bowels for her.

Without knowing, he came quickly towards her and crouched beside her again, taking the chick from her hands, because she was afraid of the hen, and putting it back in the coop. At the back of his loins the fire suddenly darted stronger.

He glanced apprehensively at her. Her face was averted, and she was crying blindly, in all the anguish of her generation's forlornness. His heart melted suddenly, like a drop of fire, and he put out his hand and laid his fingers on her knee.

"You shouldn't cry," he said softly.

But then she put her hands over her face and felt that really her heart was broken and nothing mattered any more.

He laid his hand on her shoulder, and softly, gently, it began to travel down the curve of her back, blindly, with a blind stroking motion, to the curve of her crouching loins. And there his hand softly, softly, stroked the curve of her flank, in the blind instinctive caress.

She had found her scrap of handkerchief and was blindly trying to dry her face.

"Shall you come to the hut?" he said, in a quiet, neutral voice.

And closing his hand softly on her upper arm, he drew her up and led her slowly to the hut, not letting go of her till she was inside. Then he cleared aside the chair and table, and took a brown soldier's blanket from the tool-chest, spreading it slowly. She glanced at his face, as she stood motionless.

His face was pale and without expression, like that of a man submitting to fate.

"You lie there," he said softly, and he shut the door, so that it was dark, quite dark.

With a queer obedience, she lay down on the blanket. Then she felt the soft, groping, helplessly desirous hand touching her body, feeling for her face. The hand stroked her face softly, softly, with infinite soothing and assurance, and at last there was the soft touch of a kiss on her cheek.

She lay quite still, in a sort of sleep, in a sort of dream. Then she quivered as she felt his hand groping softly, yet with queer thwarted clumsiness among her clothing. Yet the hand knew, too, how to unclothe her where it wanted. He drew down the thin silk sheath, slowly, carefully, right down and over her feet. Then with a quiver of exquisite pleasure he touched the warm soft body, and touched her navel for a moment in a kiss. And he had to come into her at once, to enter the peace on earth of her soft, quiescent body. It was the moment of pure peace for him, the entry into the body of a woman.

She lay still, in a kind of sleep, always in a kind of sleep. The activity, the orgasm was his, all his; she could strive for herself no more. Even the tightness of his arms round her, even the intense movement of his body, and the springing seed in her, was a kind of sleep, from which she did not begin to rouse till he had finished and lay softly panting against her breast.

Then she wondered, just dimly wondered, why? Why was this necessary? Why had it lifted a great cloud from her and given her peace? Was it real? Was it real?

Her tormented modern-woman's brain still had no rest. Was it real? And she knew, if she gave herself to the man, it was real. But if she kept herself for herself, it was nothing. She was old; millions of years old, she felt. And at last, she could bear the burden of herself no more. She was to be had for the taking. To be had for the taking.

The man lay in a mysterious stillness. What was he feeling? What was he thinking? She did not know. He was a strange man to her, she did not know him. She must only wait, for she did not dare to break his mysterious stillness. He lay there with his arms round her, his body on hers, his wet body touching hers, so close. And completely unknown. Yet not unpeaceful. His very silence was peaceful.

She knew that, when at last he roused and drew away from her. It was like an abandonment. He drew her dress in the darkness down over her knees and stood for a few moments, apparently adjusting his own clothing. Then he quietly opened the door and went out.

She saw a very brilliant little moon shining above the afterglow over the oaks. Quickly she got up and arranged herself; she was tidy. Then she went to the door of the hut.

All the lower wood was in shadow, almost darkness. Yet the sky overhead was crystal. But it shed hardly any light. He came through the lower shadow towards her, his face lifted like a pale blotch.

"Shall we go, then?" he said.

"Where?"

"I'll go with you to the gate."

He arranged things his own way. He locked the door of the hut and came after her.

"You aren't sorry, are you?" he asked, as he went at her side.

"No! No! Are you?" she said.

"For that! No!" he said. Then after a while he added: "But there's the rest of things."

"What rest of things?" she said.

"Sir Clifford. Other folks. All the complications."

"Why complications?" she said, disappointed.

"It's always so. For you as well as for me. There's always complications." He walked on steadily in the dark.

"And are you sorry?" she said.

"In a way!" he replied, looking up at the sky. "I thought I'd done with it all. Now I've begun again."

"Begun what?"

"Life."

"Life!" she echoed, with a queer thrill.

"It's life," he said. "There's no keeping clear. And if you do keep clear you might almost as well die. So if I've got to be broken open again, I have."

She did not quite see it that way, but still . . .

"It's just love," she said cheerfully.

"Whatever that may be," he replied.

They went on through the darkening wood in silence, till they were almost at the gate.

"But you don't hate me, do you?" she said wistfully.

"Nay, nay," he replied. And suddenly he held her fast against his breast again, with the old connecting passion. "Nay, for me it was good, it was good. Was it for you?"

"Yes, for me too," she answered, a little untruthfully, for she had not been conscious of much.

He kissed her softly, softly, with the kisses of warmth.

"If only there weren't so many other people in the world," he said lugubriously.

She laughed. They were at the gate to the park. He opened it for her.

"I won't come any farther," he said.

"No!" And she held out her hand, as if to shake hands. But he took it in both his.

"Shall I come again?" she asked wistfully.

"Yes! Yes!"

She left him and went across the park.

HENRY MILLER

❧❦

Letters to Barney Rosset [1959]

Mr. Barney Rosset   Big Sur, California
The Grove Press,   April 4, 1959
795 Broadway, N.Y.

Dear Mr. Rosset;

Forgive me for not replying sooner to your telegram but we are
leaving for Europe in a few days and I am still struggling to finish a book
(*Nexus*) before leaving and constantly interrupted by visitors.

I presume your offer was prompted by the Foreman case—release of
"Cancer"—recently. I think any attempt to publish these books here is still
premature, but I shall see what my agent, Dr. Hoffman, has to say, and try to
sound out friends who may have a better perspective on the situation than I.
I do know this, that even if the Treasury Department were to lift the ban on
these (and the other) books of mine, which they have not done: the question
of publication and circulation here in America is another matter entirely.
Before any move were made, it would be important to know what might be
the attitude of our Postmaster General.

But there is still another aspect to be considered. By contract I am
obliged to give my publishers, New Directions, first choice on any American
publication. So, until I have had a chance to mull it over carefully, I can say
nothing. I am, however, grateful to you for making the offer. My friend Paul
Jacobs, of the Fund for the Republic, has a fragment of this new book,
Nexus, which he may show you—for possible publication in the Evergreen
Review. This will be another "banned book," but the section in his possession is, I am quite sure, non-censorable. He is at the N.Y. office of the
"Fund" at present, I believe.

With all good wishes, believe me to be

                                              Most sincerely yours,
                                              Henry Miller

Mr. Barney Rosset   Big Sur
The Grove Press,   4/9/59
795 Broadway, N.Y.

Dear Mr. Rosset,

With your last two letters came one from Girodias (delayed in
mails) which made me feel I know you better. Thus far I have heard nothing,
either from my agent in Paris, or the Paris publisher (don't know Filipachi, by
the way), or from James Laughlin, whom I wrote concerning your offer. I'll be
in Paris on the 17th and will see everyone. Will see Laughlin on passing
through N.Y. Would see you too, but have so very little time, will have the
children with me, and will be fagged out—hate planes and all that.

This morning *Lady Chatterley* came—I merely had time to glance
at it. Looks good. And it is, of course, a big step forward. But how slowly
everything proceeds. The "Cancer" will be 25 years old this September.
Soon I'll be dead. I've lived so long without my rightful earnings I'm
used to it now. One has to die first, if you notice, before the ball gets
rolling.

I'll write you again from Paris, when I know more. Meantime once
again—sincere thanks for your sincere desire to do things. My own view is
that it may take another fifty to a hundred years before these banned books
of mine can circulate freely in this country. But I may be wrong.

Oh yes, before I forget . . . Just because you are sincere and coura-
geous, may I bring to your attention three writers whom I long to see
something done for here. Blaise Cendrars, first. (I am mailing you his
latest—*A l'aventure*—which is a collection from various books, and gives
the flavor of the man. Only *Sutter's Gold* (an early work) and some poems
are in translation here. I have a whole chapter on him in "Books in My Life"
(New Directions)—which you might see. He is now paralyzed on one side,
and I fear may die soon.

The second one is Albert Cossery, an Egyptian living in Paris who
writes in French. New Directions gave him up after no luck with two or
three of his books. Viking is now negotiating with him, but I am not at all
sure they will carry through. (If you know Pat Covici there, ask him.)
Cossery's address is—Hôtel de la Louisiane—60, rue de Seine, Paris (6). He
needs help. And I think he is quite unique in his work. I financed the American edition of his first book—short stories—called "Men God Forgot."
(New Directions has a few copies.)

The third man, already published by Knopf (after Viking gave him up)
is Jean Giono, with whom I have long corresponded. There is one book

no one seems to want, and I think it a honey: *Salut pour Melville*. (Thought I had a copy but I guess I gave the last away.) His address is simply—Manosque (Basses Alpes) France.

To come back to Cendrars. If you don't care to publish a "recueil", then have a look at his "Moravagine," which would be a controversial book, somewhat censorable, and a great story. Some one here in America is thinking of doing something about him, but I can't recall now who. Doubt if any of the regular "birds" will—all too fearful, too delicate, too fussy.

You might watch *Time* or *Newsweek* (latter part of April) to see what they report, if anything, on the trial of "Sexus" in Oslo, Norway—before the Supreme Court. If favorable, it might have great repercussions here and elsewhere. This book is banned in France (in *any* language) and in Japan, both in English and Japanese. The Japanese publisher brought out a part of the book—first third—in Japanese, with the censorable passages printed in English. (Have to turn the book around to read the English). Still no go, however.

What I sometimes think is that the way to start the ball rolling is to bring out "Cancer," let's say, with all the censorable words, phrases, sentences, paragraphs deleted. That's what Girodias did with the French version of *Sexus*—giving only a few unexpurgated copies to the reviewers. That brought the authorities down on him pronto.

Enough!

Good wishes.
Henry Miller

P.S. [on page one of original] My address while in Europe will be care of my agent—Dr. Michael A. Hoffmann—77, Blvd. Saint-Michel—Paris (5e).

P.S. [on page two of original] I didn't suggest that excerpt from *Nexus* (for *Evergreen Review*) *because* it was non-censorable. It's one of the best passages in the book—and deals with "writing."

Paris   4/30/59

Dear Mr. Rosset,

No, I don't mind too much if you feel you *must* shorten that fragment from *Nexus*. Here no matter what I offer it's taken and printed as given—no questions. Never quite understand American editorial attitude. But no matter.

Have nothing more to say now about the *Tropics*. But, whether you do it or New Directions, one thing is certain, I will never agree to any cuts or modifications of the text. Not if I were offered ten times as much. For America I will never make any concessions.

However, all this is in the future. I am making no decisions yet.

By now you must have received the other Cendrars' book too—*A l'aventure* (un recueil). I saw Cendrars the other day. We both wept. He is in constant pain, paralyzed, unable to do anything. Heart-rending. You know, I suppose, that some months ago he was given the Legion of Honor by André Malraux. Too late! As usual.

Hope you liked Cossery's "The Lazy Ones." I never read it in translation. Think it may have been castrated. Contains marvelous censorable passages in the original. *He* needs help. It would be something if you could bring him to the American public.

Weather miserable here—can't get warm *indoors*.

Sincerely,
Henry Miller

P.S. If you send check for *Nexus* fragment, send to me at Big Sur. My friend Emil White there handles letters & checks for me.

P.P.S. I have an old Russian friend here—Eugene Pachoutinsky, who saved my life when I was down and out—1930–31—here in Paris. He's just written a book, in French,—un roman-autobiographique—about the days of the Russian Revolution. (He was a "white" Russian.) Has a chapter in it on me—our rencontre—*Cinema Vanves*. There is a copy in N.Y. somewhere—typescript. Would you care to see it? If so, let me know.

HM

The 1960s

RICHARD SEAVER

❧

The 1960s: Within a Budding Grove

Physically, I arrived at Grove Press in the spring of 1959, but, I strongly suspect, I was fated to become a "Grovenik"—as we were affectionately (and sometimes not so affectionately) known in the 1960s—as early as 1952. In the spring of that year, I wrote a piece in the second issue of *Merlin*, the Paris-based literary magazine of which I had recently become an editor, entitled "Samuel Beckett: An Introduction." The year before, between bouts of sowing my wild oats in Paris's wonderfully fertile soil, I had discovered the astonishing work of the then-unknown Irishman whom I knew only as the sometime assistant of James Joyce (an erroneous rumor, though one long perpetrated). In that essay, I boldly proclaimed to the world, with all the wisdom of my twenty-plus years and knowledge of only three novels (*Murphy*, *Watt*, and *Molloy*), one play (*Godot*), and one short story ("The End"), that: "[the work] of Samuel Beckett merits the attention of anyone interested in this century's literature."

Merlin had a circulation of perhaps 2,000—with global sales more or less evenly divided among France (read: Paris), the U.K., and the U.S.—and a subscriber list that, at its peak, numbered perhaps 100. Not unsurprisingly, one of that elite one hundred was Barney Rosset, a young man out of Chicago who had recently bought a virtually moribund New York publishing entity—it had published three books in three years—for the princely sum of $3,000. A few months after the Beckett piece appeared, I received a letter from Rosset saying he was fascinated by my high opinion of Samuel Beckett, adding that he was coming to Paris and would like to meet. We did, all four of us, for both Barney and I were newly married, Barney to his second wife, Loly, a stunning blond German girl, and I to my first (and only), a stunning French brunette, Jeannette. We lunched at a Chinese restaurant and though much of the lunch was taken up with glowing talk of Beckett, I also effused about two other writers we had by then begun publishing in *Merlin*, the Rumanian-born, Paris-based playwright Eugène Ionesco and the novelist and playwright Jean Genet. (As we warmed to each other we quickly learned our political affinities and bugaboos were very much akin.) Barney wanted to meet Beckett; I told him I had met him only twice, that he was very reclusive, but I put him in contact with Beckett's French publisher, Jérôme Lindon, who handled all his foreign rights, and also told him that we—*Merlin*—were bringing out later that year Beckett's last novel written in English, *Watt* (by the 1950s Beckett, having gained virtually no recognition from his writings in English, had turned to writing in French), which I promised to send him.

If we had sat down to lunch cautiously, we parted warmly. In the course of those two or three hours, I had learned that Barney's father was a Chicago banker and that while Barney had earlier aspired to be a filmmaker, he was now committed to publishing.

"How big is Grove now?" I asked him.

"You're looking at roughly half of it," he laughed—and when Barney laughed you could see all the way back to his tonsils. Loly, it turned out, was the Grove sales manager. "That's why I married her," he joked. "I didn't want to lose my sales manager." (As it turned out, he wasn't joking; but that's a whole other story.) Barney assured me that, however small Grove was then, he planned to grow it measurably. As we shook hands, he asked me when I was coming back to the States. I was vague, not trying to be evasive but because I really had no idea.

"When you do," he said—not "if" but "when"—"look me up. And meanwhile, let's keep in touch."

My peripatetic life the next four years—to Europe and the Middle East, South America and the Far East—kept me from seeing Rosset again, but we did exchange letters and I was delighted to read that Grove was publishing not only Beckett but Ionesco and Genet as well. In 1957 when I did get back to New York, I gave him a call. We met a couple of times. I was hoping he'd offer me a job, since by then I had a daughter on the way, but, alas, none was forthcoming. So I took a job with another fledgling publisher, George Braziller. Virtually the week after I started with Braziller, Barney called and offered me a job at Grove. He seemed stricken when I told him where I was, but no more than I. In the next couple of years, Barney and I met occasionally, usually for drinks but two or three times at the Grove offices at 795 Broadway (above Miller's Clothing Store, as Barney would be sure to note with a sly grin), and one day Barney said: "For God's sake, you're wasting your time at Braziller. You should really be at Grove. I can't pay you more than you're earning there, but I can pay just as much."

Three weeks later I walked into the Grove office at 64 University Place, the larger quarters to which Grove had recently moved. The new office was on the second floor of a four-story building that housed, on the ground floor, a Daitch Shopwell supermarket; on the third floor another publisher, Fred

Praeger; and on the fourth floor a third publisher, Sheed & Ward. (Later in the 1960s, people would refer to 64 as the building that housed everything: food [Daitch], sex and leftist politics [Grove], rightist politics [Praeger], and religion [Sheed and Ward].)

From the day I set foot at Grove, I felt at home. During my two years at Braziller I had been called for several job interviews at major, mainstream publishers, but somehow none seemed right for me. Grove was not only publishing the European writers I most admired—mavericks and rebels interested me far more than the tried and true—but also was ferreting out new native talent, especially through its *Evergreen Review,* whose arrival on the scene had neatly coincided with my return to the U.S.

Grove had indeed grown, as Barney had predicted, since the day we had lunched together in Paris six years before. Though much of the growth in the 1950s had been through importing books—and sometimes whole series—from the U.K., the percentage of indigenous publishing was increasing rapidly. More to the point, when I arrived Grove was poised to join battle, knowingly and willfully, with the entire establishment, those repressive forces—benign or malignant—who felt that this country was too immature, or still too Victorian, to deal with the harsh matter of sex, or any politics that went beyond the quadrennial Democrat and Republican conventions.

For years Barney had been planning, and waiting for the opportune moment to publish the first unexpurgated edition of the long-banned D. H. Lawrence masterpiece, *Lady Chatterley's Lover.* During my first days and weeks at Grove, aside from the normal febrile atmosphere that seemed to pervade the place, there was a kind of extra fever pitch as the final preparations for the Lawrence were being made. I think none of us—Don Allen, the senior editor whom Barney had met at a Columbia publishing course they both had attended, or Fred Jordan, another young editor, or even Barney himself—expected the reception of the novel to be easy, but I'm equally sure none of us had any idea how long and arduous and pitched the battle would be. My only contribution to the cause was financial, not editorial: I strongly suggested to Barney that the book, given its nature, could bear a dollar more list price. He agreed, in extremis: the book was on press. So the price was duly raised, and the extra $50,000 ultimately in our coffers did help defray—but only partially—the subsequent legal costs. The book was published in April 1959 and shipped to the stores. The ensuing reviews were broad and favorable, but the censors were quick to move, starting with a deputy police chief in Washington, D.C. On April 30, the book was banned from the mails (the postal authorities were one of the country's dual ad hoc censors in those days; the other, even more ludicrously, was the U.S. Immigration Service, which seemed to delight in seizing "obscene" books from returning overseas travelers). That *Lady Chatterley's Lover* later graced the bestseller lists for months helped the cause, but in truth D. H. Lawrence almost brought Grove Press to its knees. Roughly three months after the *Lady Chatterley* suit was instigated, Federal Judge Frederick van Pelt Bryan, of the Southern District of New York, ruled on July 21, 1959, that the novel was not obscene and could be sold freely and openly. The government, clearly worried about its citizens' purity of mind and body, appealed, and it was not until eight months later that the court of appeals affirmed Bryan's ruling.

Most publishers, after the grueling experience of defending such a book and winning what was, in financial terms at least, a Pyrrhic victory, would doubtless have rested on their laurels. Let someone else take up the cudgels. Not Grove. Waiting in the wings was a whole arsenal of future bombs to be dropped over the next several years, foremost among them Henry Miller's *Tropic of Cancer*—another long-banned work that since the 1930s was freely available in English in France but not in the U.S. or U.K.

In 1961, one year after the *Lady Chatterley* litigation ended, we published Henry Miller's *magnum opus*. Ironically, because Lawrence had knocked out both the Post Office and Customs, and won a federal victory, there was no federal case this time. Instead, every local police chief and district attorney felt free to seize and sue, as indeed they did. At one point, Grove was defending some sixty cases around the country, and its paltry reserves* were strained to the breaking point as lawyers were hired en masse to defend those attacked. Key staff members, from Barney on down, spent more time in court testifying than they did in the office.

Frankly, I don't remember how we managed to survive the *Tropic of Cancer* litigations, but somehow we did and, bruised and battered but still standing, we went on to test a few more waters: William Burroughs's *Naked Lunch*—again available in France from Maurice Girodias's Olympia Press but not in the author's native land; Jean Genet, whose dramatic works Grove had been publishing but whose novels, *The Thief's Journal* and *Our Lady of the Flowers,* had generally been deemed too hot to handle even in France and had been published there by a small but audacious publisher, Arbalète. Finally, in 1949 and '51 respectively, the most prestigious French publisher, Gallimard, screwed its courage to the sticking post and brought out both Genet novels. Armed with

---

*Barney told me many times in later years that rumors of his fortune, like that of Twain's demise, were greatly exaggerated. Further, to put things in perspective, Grove's total volume of business in 1959 was, if memory serves, $350,000. "If only we could get to half a million," Barney said when I took the job in '59, "we'd make money." But as the years rolled by, the barrier to profitability seemed always to be raised just beyond our reach, at least till the mid-1960s.

that house's near-inviolable imprimatur, the Gallic censors, less ardent than the Anglo-Saxon, remained in their corner. But we at Grove had no such illusions about their counterparts here when we released those daring works in the States. In the wings close behind Burroughs were two younger Americans, John Rechy and Hubert Selby, Jr., not to mention, again from the country that produced so much of this censorable material, a mysterious woman, Pauline Réage, whose *Story of O* had since the mid-1950s been the talk and rage of Paris; and, finally, the naughty granddaddy of them all: the infamous, garrulous blasphemer and rebel *extraordinaire*, Donatien-Alphonse-François, a.k.a. the Marquis de Sade.

It would be tempting for those writing of Grove in those years to see a pattern, a well-laid plan, a *strategy*. In fact, remembering that time in the trenches fondly, and even romantically, there was none: one book at a time, one notch of the ratchet tighter, perhaps, but overall strategy—some five- or ten-year plan? Nonsense. The only "strategy" was the choice—and that was indeed calculated—of the order of publication. *Lady Chatterley* was rightly deemed a less difficult book than *Tropic of Cancer*. And, in the event one prevailed legally with the latter—and survived to tell the tale—then *Naked Lunch,* which came flush not only with homosexual sex but also drugs, and without the long history and literary baggage of a Henry Miller, would doubtless prove even more daunting.

Charles Rembar's excellent *The End of Obscenity* details, vividly and accurately, how those battles were fought and, one by one, inch by inch, trench by trench, won over enormous odds. For those of us in those trenches, each day was exciting, exhilarating, rewarding, and exhausting. There were times, too, when it seemed that, to paraphrase Beckett, "We couldn't go on, we must go on." Barney's presumed fortune notwithstanding, the coffers were often dry or close to dry. I remember one day in 1962 Barney, who had disappeared for the morning and most of the afternoon, showed up at four or five o'clock, walked into my office, and announced that he had spent the day trying to get an infusion of capital, without success. So we—the inner circle of Grove that then included not only Fred and myself but Harry Braverman, who went on to become publisher of *Monthly Review Press;* sales manager Nat Sobel; publicity director Morrie Goldfisher; and an ex-union organizer with little book experience but lots of savvy, Jules Geller—decided that if we were to go down we should do so with guns blazing. Not just our one-a-year bomb but three or four, something to remember us by. In the next two to two and a half years we unleashed upon the world (with *Naked Lunch* now safely behind us) no fewer than half a dozen works which, under normal circumstances, we would have published over a five- or six-year period. In quick succession, and not necessarily in that order, came Frank Harris's monumental *My Life and Loves* (with a final chapter by—pseudonymously—my old *Merlin* colleague and Grove author Alex Trocchi), John Rechy's *City of Night,* Jean Genet's *Our Lady of the Flowers* (the original Olympia Press translation being, to use a kindly term, wooden, I was dispatched to Paris for a month to rework it, line by line, with the translator Bernard Frechtman, a job of delicate diplomacy, since Frechtman "owned" the English language rights and did not take kindly to criticism), followed a year later by his *The Thief's Journal,* Selby's *Last Exit to Brooklyn,* and Pauline Réage's *Story of O.*

Instead of heralding our swan song, this compressed publication program was, singly and collectively, so successful that Grove was suddenly back on its feet. All those books turned out to be bestsellers, and, oddly and unexpectedly, none—not even Sade—fell prey to serious assault on the part of the still watchful but increasingly impotent censors. The Grove assault in the 1960s had radically affected the country's values and attitudes, and by the mid-1960s writers were a lot freer to express themselves than ever before. And although it is never safe to say that censorship is dead, it had in that brief period suffered seemingly mortal wounds.

Though these were the most visible works of the Grove '60s, they were only part of the story. The Grove catalog of the period included a wide range of unsensational literary works from around the world, from France (Alain Robbe-Grillet, Marguerite Duras), from Germany (Uwe Johnson, Rolf Hochhuth), from Central and South America (Octavio Paz, Ché Guevara), from Japan (Donald Keene's ground-breaking two-volume anthology of Japanese literature and, late in the decade, Kenzaburo Oë, who, in 1994, would go on to win the Nobel Prize for Literature).

Even more importantly for the future of the house, it had entered into a program of publishing drama—and later film scripts—in book form. Until then, publication of dramatic works in the U.S. in the twentieth century, as I noted a few years ago in a piece on the subject for Cassell's *Companion to Twentieth Century Theatre,* "had been a sometime thing." Publishing drama just didn't pay, mostly because the works, or anthologies, were the fluff of that year's Broadway, destined to disappear as soon as the play in question had finished its run. Grove saw drama as part of literature: starting with Samuel Beckett's *Waiting for Godot* in the 1950s Grove went on to publish Genet and Ionesco from France; Harold Pinter, Tom Stoppard, and Joe Orton from the U.K.; Bertolt Brecht from Germany; Fernando Arrabal from Spain. Though the return was often slow (the modest first printing of *Waiting for Godot,* for example, had still not sold out two years after its publication), Grove rightly sensed that, for plays of lasting merit, there was an enduring market, especially if it could tap the academic market, which it set about doing.

If all the above seems to imply that Grove alone changed the world, let me, to quote my least favorite ex-President, "make myself perfectly clear": it did not. The relative stasis of the 1950s, under gentle Dwight David Eisenhower, had given way at the dawn of a new decade to a bright new leader, "born in this century," who energized the country, including—and perhaps starting with—its youth. In art as well as literature new forces were taking shape: abstract expressionism, pop art, the Beats, the flower children, Woodstock, *Hair*. And in Rosset's native Chicago, another—though far different—kind of rebel had started a magazine, *Playboy*, that was in some ways more shocking and disturbing than Grove's output. Indeed, the times were changing, and looking back, it is hard to conceive of Grove functioning in any other decade of the century in quite the same way. Yet without question, its contribution to change *was* major.

As is often the case, however, he (or she) who makes a revolution has to deal with the consequences. In Grove's case, two major events led to its future woes, which in 1967 were still barely visible, if at all. One was its precipitous move, in 1966, into movies. The culprits were two Grove authors, Phyllis and Eberhad Kraihausen, "sexual consultants" to a number of famous people, including Hollywood stars, who touted to Barney a scandalous Scandanavian film called *I Am Curious, Yellow* that was raising more than eyebrows in its native Sweden. Piqued—and perhaps a little bored with books after his battles of the early '60s—Barney headed for Sweden to view the film for himself. He came back a couple of days later, having purchased American rights for $100,000 (which in today's dollars would of course be a healthy multiple of that figure). In any event, the film appeared with much fanfare and panache, but also with renewed threats of censorship ("You may have won in the book battle, pal, but film's a whole other arena"), which doubtless pleased Barney, who loved both limelight and litigation. The film, which today would seem so tame as to approach utter boredom, showed several scenes of simulated sex—what today would be relegated to soft porn. It took off like a rocket, and money began pouring into the company's coffers at an alarming rate, at least for those of us who know a bit about the economics and financial limitations of book publishing. The good news was that, for those of us who had pinched pennies for years, there was a slight relaxation of the purse strings; the bad news was that, buoyed by that initial success, which in a year doubled or even tripled the company's volume, Barney decided ("Hey, this is easy!") to move deeper into film distribution, especially films from abroad. Only a year or two later, Grove owned the American rights to more foreign films than all the major American movie distributors combined. The only problem was, after filmgoers became less and less curious about *I Am Curious, Yellow,* its receipts rapidly dwindled, and its sequel, *I Am Curious, Blue,** bombed. Grove found itself with all these undistributed films and hardly the wherewithal to subtitle or dub them, much less make prints, release, and market them. So almost as quickly as the windfall had come, it had gone.

Secondly, as inevitably happens, Grove's rapid growth over the previous few years had led it to increase staff and to invest a good deal of its profits in real estate—a sumptuously renovated building at the northeast corner of Bleecker and Mercer Streets, into which one entered through a doorway in the shape of an enormous "G."

"It's right in the heart of NYU," reassured Barney. "Worst case, we can always sell it to the university for a big profit."

As it turned out, "worst case" occurred rather quickly: by 1968, that heady year of rebellion and revolt not only here but in many places around the world, the Grove staff had burgeoned to over a hundred, and, as Dylan predicted, the times they were a-changin'—again. This time Grove was not the perpetrator but the victim: as long as it had been relatively impecunious, it could be let alone, but with the booming book sales, the unexpected film receipts, and its public stock doubling, then doubling again, it suddenly appeared a tempting and easy target. A most unlikely union, the "Fur, Leather, and Machinist Workers," decided to try to unionize Grove. And from an uncommonly unified company with high morale and clear purpose, it became divided overnight, as many, if not most, of the newer employees, who had not been through the Grove wars, sided with the union. For weeks, people huddled in corners, sat down on the job, refused to talk to one another. Strife and dissension replaced unity and camaraderie. In early April 1970, with both production at a standstill and sales declining precipitously, Barney decided to fire nine employees, including several of the "trouble-makers."

Then, on April 13, while Barney was abroad in Denmark, still searching for another *I Am Curious* miracle, a group of nine women, led by former employee and feminist Robin Morgan, invaded the top floor of the Grove offices and barricaded themselves inside. From their precarious aerie, they issued bulletins and ultimatums: threatening to destroy the precious editorial archives, starting with Beckett, they charged us with many crimes, but especially of exploiting women. The very books that had made Grove famous, they maintained, were the most egregious: sex (read: pornography) was degrading to women. Their far-reaching demands were patently ludicrous, but for those who had long

---

*The titles of the cinematic diptych derive from the colors of the Swedish flag.

looked upon Grove as (at best) an irritant in the social contract or (at worst) insidious and dangerous, this was a moment to savor. For, indeed, Grove on this Ides of April was faced with a most serious dilemma: how was this hitherto bastion of freedom, this censor-buster, to handle the situation? To call in the police—those same folk who through the years had invaded bookshops to seize Grove titles—seemed out of the question. But to allow our precious editorial files to be burned or destroyed seemed equally untenable. Apprised of the situation by phone, Barney barked: "Barricaded in our offices? Get them *out* of there." Easier said than done, old boy. From Copenhagen, Barney tried to talk to the women, but they refused his call, saying they'd only deal with me. This was an honor I'd rather have refused. Through the locked door of the sixth-floor entrance, I did my best to reason and convince, to no avail: the response was vituperative and adamant.

Rosset, the Great Liberator of the 1960s, was suddenly, at the dawn of the '70s, the big, bad bogeyman. Meanwhile, news of the invasion had reached the press—presumably by calls made by the nine women occupiers, who had also phoned friends and colleagues in publishing to come to their support. So while inside the building we tried to reason with and persuade the women not to destroy the editorial files, outside on Mercer and Bleecker Street, pickets were rapidly forming. Ultimately, the police were called and the women were carted from the building to the jeers and catcalls of the picketers, who, to their undying shame, included a number of publishing personalities from other houses who had no idea what they were defending or attacking. Wisely, when asked to press charges against the women, Barney chose not to, much to the dismay of the police authorities and the press, both of whom thought they had hooked a big one. Within days, things calmed down, order was more or less restored, but by then the toll taken was just too great. What the combined force of the censors and government authorities—and notably the CIA, which had Grove on its domestic "watch list"—had failed to do, its own employees and the Fur, Leather, and Machinist Workers had royally accomplished: as it moved into the 1970s, the once ebullient, high-profile, tightly knit publisher had finally been brought low. To compound the already dubious, if not impossible, situation, the real estate market in New York collapsed, and the shiny new Bleecker Street headquarters became, almost overnight, a white elephant. New York University, whom we had counted on in times of stress to buy the building for dormitories or classrooms, simply wasn't interested. Apparently NYU had its own financial problems. Thus it was that the remnants of Grove moved back to its small offices on 11th Street between University Place and Broadway, 52 East 11th to be precise, to lick our wounds and, hopefully, try to regroup. But within months I realized that, in these new, severely reduced circumstances, we were far too top heavy. I knew that Barney, whom I looked on as not only a colleague but as a brother, would never fire me. But I also knew he couldn't afford me. So, with enormous sadness and regret, I resigned, leaving behind, I believe, a legacy of good publishing but also a vast storehouse of unforgettable memories, most of them good, some of them great.

"Those were the years, my friends. We thought they'd never end. . . ."

GILBERT SORRENTINO

❦

"The Novelist as Editor: An Interview with S. E. Gontarski"

S. E. GONTARSKI: I think that your transition from the Army to founding and editing *Neon* and then guest editing *Kulchur* is well documented in various essays, but how do we get from *Kulchur* to Grove Press?

GILBERT SORRENTINO: Well, it must have been about, if my memory serves me correctly, it must have been late '63 or early '64. Things were very tough for me and my wife. We just had a new baby. I had a job which was sort of an iffy job, working for a printing house in midtown Manhattan where all the printers are, up in the 40's on the east side around Second Avenue. But it was sort of like a do this do that and do the other thing sort of job. The rationale was that I was going to learn the printing trade, which never really worked out. And then I lost that job because apparently there wasn't enough for me to do, and the fact that there wasn't enough for me to do turned out to be my fault. You know how those things work.

In any event, I lost that job and was really desperate for a job. So, I can't remember how, I got in touch with someone at Grove, I can't remember who it was. It might have been Dick Seaver, but I don't think that I knew Dick Seaver at the time. But I started doing free-lance proofreading at Grove. Apparently my work pleased them: it was careful, I knew how to proofread. Grove, at the time, was giving I guess the standard fee was three-fifty an hour. Somehow I was scuffling and making a few bucks here and a few bucks there. At the time in New York it was possible to live on the kind of money that people hardly believe you when you tell them that you could live on this money. We had a five-room apartment on the lower east side. We paid just under a hundred dollars a month for it. So if you were making, let's say, two hundred dollars a month, you weren't rich, but you were eating and paying your rent. However, this like any free-lance work is so-so. I was doing some free-lance work for a few other publishers by this time as well. So I went to Grove, or called them up, and asked them if there was a way for me to work for them regularly: could I get a job like as an assistant, or an editorial assistant, doing anything? And they asked me to come in, and as I recall I talked to Dick Seaver. Harry Braverman, who at that time was a terrific guy working at Grove. He'd come over from *Monthly Review*, the magazine. An old Marxist, Harry. Socialist with Marxist leanings. And Marilyn Meeker, who was the senior editor at Grove at the time. And we talked for half an hour and they asked me what I could do and I told them what I could do which was proofreading. But I was literate and I thought that I could write some jacket copy for them. They asked me if I ever did any copy editing. I said no, I didn't know anything about it. But they hired me. Ninety dollars a week. But it was a steady ninety bucks a week. You can laugh all you want.

I started in April 1965. I was an editorial assistant helping Harry Braverman. Harry taught me how to copy edit. The first book that I worked on was an anthology of pieces on the Berkeley uprising. I can't remember who edited the book. It was someone involved in the Berkeley uprising. It was an anthology of pieces and Harry gave me the book to copy edit and I didn't know a damn thing about copy editing. Harry said, "Just do what you think you should do." In other words, make all the spelling uniform, make all the punctuation right, that's what copy editing is. I made my mistakes on this book. Harry told me what I'd done wrong. He was a terrific teacher.

And then, the first book that I edited, or learned how to edit, was *The Autobiography of Malcolm X*. I worked with Harry and Alex Haley. Harry gave me my first independent responsibility on that book which was to go to Magnum, and Black Star, and Associated Press to pick out the photographs that would go with the book. So I went through hundreds of photographs to get pictures of Malcolm when he was a boy, when he was a young man, and so on. At that point I then began doing my own work. I began copy editing my own books, and then I wrote flat copy. The first flat copy that I ever wrote for Grove was *The New American Story* which was an anthology of short stories by American writers like Robert Creeley, Hubert Selby, Jr., and others. And so I slowly became an assistant editor and then an editor.

The marvelous thing about Grove was that you learned to do everything on a book. You were the book's everything. Dick Seaver would call you into the office as the managing editor and he'd say, "I have a manuscript for you, and it's going to be on the fall list, so we need it into production in five weeks." And that was it, that was your book. You did everything on that book including working with the book jacket designer, who at the time, Roy Kuhlman was the regular designer. You would talk to Roy Kuhlman about the book, and he would design a jacket according to the conversations you had with him. So you really learned how to do everything at Grove Press. So that's what happened: I started working for them in April 1965, that was that, and I worked for them for five years.

SEG: In what shape was *The Autobiography of Malcolm X* when you got it? Was it finished?

GS: It was in manuscript, in I think a second draft. And Harry would call me in, and I would sit at the desk with Harry, and we would go through the manuscript. Harry was editing, and he would say, "Here, I'm cutting this line out and tell me why I'm cutting that line out." So I looked at it, and I discovered how Harry edited a book, like what he wanted out, what he wanted in. How to keep the author's original intention, how to keep the original language, but how to make the book better. Then, I learned how to do that of course on my own books. It was a rule of thumb, but not always necessarily true, when Grove did a non-fiction book, especially a book that was intended to sell fast, like a pop psychology book, or a self-realization or a self-defeat book, the books were terribly put together because they were written by psychologists, psychiatrists, or doctors who cannot write at all. I mean it is very rare that you can find one who can write. Not only did you have to edit their books heavily, but sometimes you had to, in a sense, rewrite the book. Chapter Three would become the preface. Chapter One would become the appendix. You know, these guys, whatever comes into their minds, they write it down. There's no sense of what they're doing.

However, Grove had such an incredible stable of fiction writers and poets, that there was no editing to do. Like I copy edited Beckett's *Stories and Texts for Nothing:* what copy editing? Beckett's manuscripts are pristine. The way you get them is the way they go to the printers. You just tell the printer how he should arrange the page. So that was how Grove worked. It was a marvelous place to work. You had absolute free rein over the books you were given. Nobody ever bothered you at Grove. They gave you a book, and you did it.

SEG: Did you work closely with Alex Haley?

GS: I met Alex later on, because Harry had been working with him. I had lunch with him a couple of times. We talked together, and I worked with Alex. As I said, mostly that was the book that I learned on.

SEG: Did you also follow the marketing of *The Autobiography of Malcolm X* as well because they really did push that book into new terrain as I recall, to build a sort of classroom structure around it? It's the book with which Grove really developed the field of Black Studies.

GS: That was not my interest. The only thing that I recall being spoken of in the house, and other people in publishing, was Roy Kuhlman's incredible jacket, that white jacket with the black-and-white photograph of Malcolm on the cover. It's much smaller than the jacket; in other words, he didn't let it bleed. A lot of white! The cover and the title, it's really striking. Roy Kuhlman invented the look of the modern dust jacket. Before Roy's dust jackets, the use of white for a dust jacket was never considered, and Roy always used white.

SEG: So what books did you work on? What were your other major books?

GS: I think that one of the most important books was toward the end. The book was never finished, was never finished while I was there because that was when Grove started to have economic problems. The book was ultimately published, but not the way it was supposed to be published, by Seaver-Viking, when Dick was at Viking. It was William S. Burroughs and Brion Gysin's *The Third Mind*, which was published as a standard book, you know, a standard quarto. But it was supposed to be an outsize book with all sorts of different colored pages. It was supposed to have typewritten pages.

SEG: That's the one with the cut-up theories in it?

GS: Yes. It's sort of like a how-to book. That book I worked on for months and months. It never came out. I worked on Clayton Eshleman's translation of *Human Poems* by Cesar Vallejo, a couple of Beckett books, a couple of other Burroughs books, *Soft Machine*, and *The Job*. I worked on Mario Vargas Llosa's *The City and The Dogs*. It was published here as *The Time of the Hero*, which was the title I gave it. It was called *La Ciudad y Los Perros*, and I figured that nobody would understand the title *The City and The Dogs* because "the city" was Lima, and "the dogs" was a nickname given to the cadets at the military school, who are the protagonists of the book. Apparently the term is well known in Lima, but outside Lima I figured that nobody would know what it was. So I decided to call it *The Time of the Hero*. I wrote to either Llosa or his agent about the change of title, and they didn't care.

SEG: Did you work on *Last Exit to Brooklyn*?

GS: *Last Exit* was published before I started working for Grove, but I wrote a piece on *Last Exit;* it was published in *Kulchur* magazine. An essay on *Last Exit*. Actually it was a collection of loose notes that I published as loose notes called "The Art of Hubert Selby." Grove was so worried about that book, that they did everything they could to try to ease it in the market scene. So what they did was they reprinted my essay from *Kulchur,* and they sent a copy of my essay with every copy sent out to reviewers. Cubby, to this day, insists that it was my essay that allowed reviewers to read the book without saying, "This is trash," which may or may not be true. I'm flattered if it is. That's what Grove did, because Grove was trying to legitimize the book. They were trying to make the book more than a sensationalist attempt.

There's an interesting story that Donald Allen may corroborate. It was my understanding that Cubby was really upset about this. He got word from Grove, just after or about the time he signed the contract, that they were nervous about doing the book with "Strike" in it, because Grove did not want to be construed as possibly an anti-labor house. And someone at Grove had read "Strike" as an anti-labor story because the working men in "Strike" are certainly not idealized. And Cubby said, "If you don't want to publish 'Strike,' fuck the whole thing: I don't want the book published." Well, whoever had the objection dropped the objection, of course the book was published with "Strike." I often thought to myself if they hadn't published it with "Strike" it wouldn't be the book that it is because "Strike" is really the core of the book. It holds all the other pieces together. I remember Cubby being really upset because he thought that was the end. He said, "I waited all these years to have this book published, and now I'm going to have to pull it."

SEG: Evidently they are making a movie of that finally.

GS: Oh yes! Cubby was so delighted. He's just delighted.

SEG: You go pretty far back with him?

GS: Since we were boys. Teenagers.

SEG: Oh, is that right? So it's not just since Brooklyn College?

GS: Oh, long before Brooklyn College. Cubby never went to college. I met Cubby in my old neighborhood. I mean we come from the same neighborhood. I guess we met each other at about sixteen.

SEG: And so you stayed friends for the whole time?

GS: Yeah. I don't know *how,* but we did.

SEG: And you started publishing him?

GS: I published his first story, called "Home for Christmas" in *Neon.* That's his first published story. It's an interesting little story. I reread it about a year ago. It has all the earmarks of a Selby story, except with a lot of rough edges. But he was a serious writer. I don't think that I've ever known anyone who really mastered his statement as swiftly as Cubby did, who did extremely intense work. He worked like a dog. He worked like a dog to get said what he wanted to get said. It came so rapidly. The stories started as sketches or ideas that suddenly turned into "Strike" or "The Queen Is Dead." Remarkable stories. As I said in another context, in those days, they were really hot stuff. Good God! Cubby couldn't get those stories published.

SEG: As it turned out, his biggest censorship problems were in England, weren't they?

GS: In England, right, but in the States as well. In one trial, the famous *Provincetown Review* trial, which published "Tra-la-la." *The Provincetown Review* was edited in those days by a guy named Bill Ward; God knows if he's still alive. Seymour Krim was his grey eminence. They published "Tra-la-la" and they pinched some poor bastard up in P town for selling it. Then there was a trial which was a marvelous trial. Cubby didn't go because his attorney said it was better for *The Provincetown Review* if Cubby wasn't there. You know, sort of aloof, whatever. Whatever the strategy was. But Norman Mailer testified for him at the trial, and so did, of all people, Allen Tate. Tate's testimony had something to do with the trial. Cubby was really tickled, his Protestant mind was delighted because Tate said, "It's obvious that this story is deeply Christian in intention, because what it really says in a nutshell is the wages of sin is death."

SEG: Did you have much connection with *The Evergreen Review?*

GS: No. Not really. Although I'd get things in that, I'd get a manuscript of a book, or I'd be looking through stuff that came over the transom, as they say, and I'd see something that could be excerpted for the *Review*. So I'd take it up to Fred Jordan, or send it up to Fred. Or some guy would call up and say, "Do you think that Fred would like to see some of my poems?" I would tell him to send them to me and I'll see what I can do. So it was that kind of situation, but I didn't work with Fred Jordan.

SEG: But you followed the *Review?*

GS: Oh, sure. Absolutely.

SEG: Since you've been in the center of little magazines, publishing during that period, what do you think of the impact of *The Evergreen Review?* Obviously, they had a mass audience unlike a little magazine.

GS: I can't imagine how it did what it did.

DONALD M. ALLEN

☙❧

Preface TO *The New American Poetry,*
1945–1960 [1960]

In the years since the war American poetry has entered upon a singularly rich period. It is a period that has seen published many of the finest achievements of the older generation: William Carlos Williams' *Paterson, The Desert Music and Other Poems,* and *Journey to Love;* Ezra Pound's *The Pisan Cantos, Section: Rock-Drill,* and *Thrones;* H.D.'s later work, culminating in her long poem *Helen in Egypt;* and the recent verse of E. E. Cummings, Marianne Moore, and the late Wallace Stevens. A wide variety of poets of the second generation, who emerged in the thirties and forties, have achieved their maturity in this period: Elizabeth Bishop, Edwin Denby, Robert Lowell, Kenneth Rexroth, and Louis Zukofsky, to name only a few very diverse talents. And we can now see that a strong third generation, long awaited but only slowly recognized, has at last emerged.

These new younger poets have written a large body of work, but most of what has been published so far has appeared only in a few little magazines, as broadsheets, pamphlets, and limited editions, or circulated in manuscript; a larger amount of it has reached its growing audience through poetry readings. As it has emerged in Berkeley and San Francisco, Boston, Black Mountain, and New York City, it has shown one common characteristic: a total rejection of all those qualities typical of academic verse. Following the practice and precepts of Ezra Pound and William Carlos Williams, it has built on their achievements and gone on to evolve new conceptions of the poem. These poets have already created their own tradition, their own press, and their public. They are our avant-garde, the true continuers of the modern movement in American poetry. Through their work many are closely allied to modern jazz and abstract expressionist painting, today recognized throughout the world to be America's greatest achievements in contemporary culture. This anthology makes the same claim for the new American poetry, now becoming the dominant movement in the second phase of our twentieth-century literature and already exerting strong influence abroad.

In order to give the reader some sense of the history of the period and the primary alignment of the writers, I have adopted the unusual device of divid-

ing the poets into five large groups, though these divisions are somewhat arbitrary and cannot be taken as rigid categories. Within each of the five sections
the poets are ranked by year of birth, and their poems by year of composition
as a means of showing the range and variety and sequence of development in
an individual writer's work.

The first group includes those poets who were originally closely identified with the two important magazines of the period, *Origin* and *Black Mountain Review,* which first published their mature work. Charles Olson, Robert
Duncan, and Robert Creeley were on the staff of Black Mountain College in
the early fifties, and Edward Dorn, Joel Oppenheimer, and Jonathan Williams
studied there. Paul Blackburn, Paul Carroll, Larry Eigner, and Denise Levertov
published work in both magazines but had no connection with the college.

While both publication and instruction at Black Mountain College align
Robert Duncan with the first group, he actually emerged in 1947–1949 as a leading poet of the second group, the San Francisco Renaissance, where he was
originally associated with Brother Antoninus, Robin Blaser, Jack Spicer, and
others in Berkeley, and with James Broughton and Madeline Gleason in San
Francisco. Helen Adam, chiefly through her superb readings, has helped establish the ballad made new as an important trend in the poetry of the Bay Area;
and Lawrence Ferlinghetti, through his readings with jazz bands and his record-
ings, has re-created a popular oral poetry we have not had since Vachel Lind-
say. Bruce Boyd, Kirby Doyle, Richard Duerden, and Philip Lamantia are all
natives of the San Francisco area, while Ebbe Borregaard came from Long Island and Lew Welch from the Northwest.

The Beat Generation, the third group, was originally associated with New
York, but they first attracted national attention in San Francisco in 1956 when
Allen Ginsberg, Jack Kerouac, and Gregory Corso joined Gary Snyder, Philip
Whalen, and others in public readings. Three significant publications of 1956–
1957 aligned their work with that of many writers of the first, second, and fifth
groups: *Art II / Moby I, Black Mountain Review* No. 7, and the "San Francisco Scene" issue of *Evergreen Review.*

John Ashbery, Kenneth Koch, and Frank O'Hara, of the fourth group,
the New York Poets, first met at Harvard, where they were associated with the
Poets' Theatre. They migrated to New York in the early fifties, where they met
Edward Field, Barbara Guest, and James Schuyler, and worked with the Living Theatre and the Artists' Theatre.

The fifth group has no geographical definition; it includes younger poets
who have been associated with and in some cases influenced by the leading
writers of the preceding groups, but who have evolved their own original styles
and new conceptions of poetry. Philip Whalen and Gary Snyder grew up in

the Northwest and became close friends at Reed College, before moving to San Francisco. Both Stuart Perkoff and Michael McClure came to the West Coast from the Midwest, Perkoff to settle in Venice West and McClure in San Francisco, where Ron Loewinsohn and David Meltzer have also moved in recent years. John Wieners studied at Black Mountain College and founded *Measure* in his home town of Boston. Edward Marshall, another New England poet, was first published in *Black Mountain Review;* he makes his home in New York. Gilbert Sorrentino lives in Brooklyn, where he edits *Neon,* and LeRoi Jones in New York, where he edits *Yūgen.*

Occasionally arbitrary and for the most part more historical than actual, these groups can be justified finally only as a means to give the reader some sense of milieu and to make the anthology more a readable book and less still another collection of "anthology pieces." The statements on poetics, the biographical notes, and the bibliography are aids to a more exact understanding of literary history.

Charles Olson's "Projective Verse" essay and his letter to Elaine Feinstein present the dominant new double concept: "composition by field" and the poet's "stance toward reality"; and Robert Creeley's two essays give further definition in this area. Robert Duncan and Denise Levertov define positions which differ sharply from Lawrence Ferlinghetti's or Allen Ginsberg's. James Schuyler describes the ambiance of the New York poets, and Philip Whalen, Gary Snyder, Michael McClure, John Wieners, and LeRoi Jones send back reports from the fronts on which they are engaged. These statements are interim reports by the poets; they lead directly back to the poems, to the actual work of the period, waiting to be read and studied for what it alone can reveal.

The preparation of this anthology presented a series of formidable problems. As I have said, only a fraction of the work has been published, and that for the most part in fugitive pamphlets and little magazines. The field is almost completely uncharted; there is, not very surprisingly, very little first-rate criticism of any of the new poetry, and that little has been written by the poets themselves. Consequently, I have had to go directly to the poets for manuscripts and counsel, and I am heavily indebted to each of them for invaluable aid. Charles Olson, Robert Creeley, Frank O'Hara, and Allen Ginsberg have given me throughout the solid support and encouragement without which I should not have been able to complete this project. I owe almost as large a debt to Robin Blaser, LeRoi Jones, and James Schuyler for much needed and deeply appreciated advice and assistance.

ALEXANDER TROCCHI

☙❧

FROM *Cain's Book* [1960]

"Go away," I said to the dog.

A growl came from somewhere near his palpitating underside.—Why, I thought, do I have to put up with this? The dog was just part of it, the last straw; when Tom relaxed and stopped bugging you . . . only on horse . . . the dog came in as an understudy.

In the junkie world there are many such last straws. One finds oneself of necessity giving the other man more latitude. There is no one whom Fay hasn't burned. But she continues to see everyone from time to time, when a man is desperate. Junkies in New York are often desperate. To be a junkie is to live in a madhouse. Laws, police forces, armies, mobs of indignant citizenry crying mad dog. We are perhaps the weakest minority which ever existed; forced into poverty, filth, squalor, without even the protection of a legitimate ghetto. There was never a wandering Jew who wandered farther than a junkie, without hope. Always moving. Eventually one must go where the junk is and one is never certain where the junk is, never sure that where the junk is is not the anteroom of the penitentiary. A Jew can stand up and say: "Yes, I am a Jew and these are my persecutors." There is always a possibility of effective resistance because there were always some gentiles who were not profoundly shocked when a Jew said: "It is not necessarily bad to be a Jew." Such tardy hope as is held out to junkies is that one day they will be regarded not as criminals but as "sick." When the A.M.A. wins the peonage will be less harsh, but the junkie, like the peon, will still have to buy at the commissary.

Thus there is a confederacy amongst users, loose, hysterical, traitorous, unstable, a tolerance that comes from the knowledge that it is very possible to arrive at the point where it is necessary to lie and cheat and steal, even from the friend who gave one one's last fix.

Tom loves his dog. He wrestles with it. It is for him the only being who doesn't present a threat. If it ever turns on him he can always kill it. It was the dog that decided me at one time that I couldn't live with him. It is an angry extension of himself, a weapon.

Except when we are under heroin our relationship is tense and unpredict-able. It is only when I have fixed that I can forgive Tom everything, even the painful slowness, the hothouse movements of his fixing before me. Tom always fixes before me. He doesn't insist upon this. He simply observes a common ritual which I have always refused to observe.

Sometimes we make swift covert journeys at night through the backstreets of Harlem to cop. Tom has good contacts in Harlem and he likes to take me along. If you are a member of any underground in a hostile city it's good for one's morale. In the moonlight as we descend the dark stairs which lead down-wards through a certain park I wait for him to say: "I go first."

I know that he will give me several moments in which to stake the prior claim and I doubt whether he's ever been convinced that I won't do so, even though I've said to him again and again that I don't give a damn who goes first once we're safely locked up in whatever pad and told him he gave me a pain in the ass when he carried on like that. I've waited for a long time for Tom to say: "You go first, Joe," but he never has and I doubt if he ever will. I have asked him why the ritual is so important to him. His answer is the usual one. "You never know when the Man will bust in. If they come, I want to have the shit in me." But that's not good enough. It's not always necessary to be a mouse, even if you're a junkie in New York. This kind of promiscuous creation of tension in a situation which is God knows far too intense already makes me very angry.

Unless I am in physical pain it is immaterial to me who goes first. Tom pretends it isn't that way for him. He's lying. The urgency doesn't exist. To pretend that it does is to prostrate oneself hysterically before a malicious fic-tion. It is quite unlike the hysteria experienced by all of us in the day to day danger of our situation . . . (coming down the stairs at two o'clock in the morn-ing on to the deserted subway platform at 125th Street, followed, it seems, by two unidentified men . . . don't panic . . . looking at us now from the other end of the platform . . . if they come within ten yards get rid of it). It is a submis-sion to the very ignorance that has led to the branding of the junkie as a social menace.

"Dog," I said, "you're a mad dog. I know how you play. If I take that bone away from you you'll get real mad and bite. Who taught you to bite, dog? You know what happens in this world to dogs that bite?"

I don't know what it was that first attracted me to Tom unless it was that I felt him to be attracted to me. We just met, scored, and passed a few days together turning on. Most of my friends, especially those who don't use heroin, disliked him from the beginning, and I have often found myself rushing emotionally and intellectually to his defence. At times, after we had fixed and blown some pot, with a sleek thrust of my own soul, a thrust of empathy, I used to find myself identifying with him. I seldom do it now because Tom bores me nowadays, but I did so, often. But gradually I came to realize that he didn't think like I did, that he took my rationalizations too seriously or not seriously enough.

For example, he still talks about kicking, and at the same time he denies that he is hooked, and yet he has agreed with me again and again that if you simply put heroin down you are avoiding the issue. It isn't the horse, for all the melodramatic talk about withdrawal symptoms. It is the pale rider.

When Tom says: "I'm gonna kick," I say: "Bullshit." He becomes hurt and sullen. He feels I am deserting him. And I suppose I am.

He says he kicked before, the time he went to Lexington.

"Sure, and when you got back here you went straight up to Harlem and copped. A man doesn't kick, Tom. When he thinks in terms of kicking he's hooked. There are degrees of addiction, and the physical part has nothing to do with it. The physical bit comes soon and I suppose that then technically you're hooked. But with the right drugs you can kick that in a few days. The degrees of addiction that matter are psychological, like intellectually how long have you been a vegetable? Are you riding the horse or what? The trouble with you, Tom, is that you really put shit down. You use it most of the time, you dig it, but all the time you're putting it down, talking about kicking. It's not the shit that's got you hooked. You shelve the problem when you think in those terms. You talk all the time about copping and kicking. Talk about copping. Don't talk about kicking. Get high and relax. There are doctors, painters, lawyers on dope, and they can still function. The American people is on alcohol, and that's much more deadly. An alcoholic can't function. You've got to get up off your ass and stop believing their propaganda, Tom. It's too much when the junkies themselves believe it. They tell you it's the shit and most of the ignorant bastards believe it themselves. It's a nice tangible cause for juvenile delinquency. And it lets most people out because they're alcoholics. There's an available pool of wasted-looking bastards to stand trial as the corrupters of their children. It provides the police with something to do, and as junkies and potheads are relatively easy to apprehend because they have to take so many chances to get hold of their drugs, a heroic police can make spectacular arrests, lawyers can do a brisk business, judges can make speeches, the big pedlars can make a fortune, the tabloids can sell millions of copies. John Citizen can sit back feeling exonerated and watch evil get its deserts. That's the junk scene, man. Everyone gets something out of it except the junkie. If he's lucky he can creep round the corner and get a fix. But it wasn't the junk that made him creep. You've got to sing that from the rooftops!"

I have talked to him for hours. But in the end he always comes back to saying he's going to kick. That's because he hasn't really got much choice. He has no money. To get money he has to kick and there's a fat chance of his kicking without money. Still, it bugs me when he goes on talking about kicking.

"I'm gonna kick."

"Man, you'll never kick." Sometimes I don't even say it.

"You bastard, I will."

"O.K. then, you'll kick."

"Sure I will. You think I can go on like this?"

"You did before."

"That's different. I was hung up then. I'll get the place fixed up good. You help me, Joe. If we only had some bread."

"How much rent do you owe?"

"Not much, a few months."

"How many months?"

"Must be about eight."

"You've been goofing for eight months? You owe $320 back rent."

"I'm gonna see him and say I'll pay it off, twenty a week."

"Where are you going to get twenty a week?"

"I can get a job. I'll start kicking tomorrow. I can kick it in three days. I haven't got a real habit. I'll get dollies. I know a stud who knows where to get them cheap. I'll stay off shit. I won't touch the damn stuff."

"Don't talk like an alcoholic."

But it's like telling a man inflicted with infantile paralysis to run a hundred yards. Without the stuff Tom's face takes on a strained expression; as the effect of the last fix wears off all grace dies within him. He becomes a dead thing. For him, ordinary consciousness is like a slow desert at the centre of his being; his emptiness is suffocating. He tries to drink, to think of women, to remain interested, but his expression becomes shifty. The one vital coil in him is the bitter knowledge that he can choose to fix again. I have watched him. At the beginning he's over-confident. He laughs too much. But soon he falls silent and hovers restlessly at the edge of a conversation, as though he were waiting for the void of the drugless present to be miraculously filled. (—*What would you do all day if you didn't have to look for a fix?*) He is like a child dying of boredom, waiting for promised relief, until his expression becomes sullen. Then, when his face takes on a disdainful expression, I know he has decided to go and look for a fix.

"You going to split, Tom?"

"Yeah, you comin'?"

I have gone with him sometimes.

"Look, you've still got some dollies, Tom."

"I finished them."

"Christ, already? O.K. I've got some goofballs and we can get a bottle of cough syrup. You can drink that."

"That stuff's no good."

"It'll cool you."

Two o'clock in the morning. Sitting in Jim Moore's drinking coffee slowly. A few haggard men. A drunk woman trying to get someone to go home with her.

"I'm going home, Tom."

"Where?"

"Bank Street. I'm going to try and get some sleep."

"Look, let me come with you. If I stay around here I'll meet someone and get turned on."

"I thought that's what we were sitting here for."

"No, Joe, it'll be O.K. tomorrow. It'll be three days."

"O.K. Come on then."

We get into the narrow bed and turn off the light. We lie awake for a while in the dark. I say: "Look, Tom, you'll be O.K."

"I think I can sleep."

I feel his arm move round me. I am suddenly very glad he is there.

I used to wonder if we would make love. Sometimes I felt we were on the brink of it. I think it occurred to both of us during those nights Tom slept with me in my single bed on Bank Street, his long brown arm round my body. There hasn't been much of what is ordinarily understood as sexuality in our relationship. The effect of heroin is to remove all physical urgency from the thought of sex. But on those nights we hadn't taken any heroin. We had drunk, turned on pot, taken whatever pills were available, and there were moments when our naked flesh touched and we were at the edge of some kind of release. If either of us had moved the other would probably have followed.

I can see Tom smiling as he comes in, his lips drawn back, showing his long teeth. He is wearing a chamois cap in the style of the English gentleman, a well-cut green pullover, drainpipe trousers, and a pair of oversized, beat-up ankle-boots. Over all he wears a brown leather coat of past days' motorists. When he turns on he walks and stands vaguely like an ape, bent at the knees, bent at the crotch, bent at the midriff, long arms dangling in front. Sometimes he carries an umbrella.

His first glance is at me, smiling across at me with his dark, beautiful eyes. And then, "Down boy! Down! Down, I tell yah! Christ, yah bad bitch!" The dog, its legs rigid, is dragged by the collar across the wooden floor and forced outside the main part of the loft. Tom closes the door quickly behind it, turns to me and grins again.

"You wanna get straight?"

He unbuckles his leather coat, hangs it carefully on a hanger, his cap on a hook, and unwraps the beautifully designed pale green scarf from his shoulders.

When I come with the water he is already pouring the powder from the transparent envelope into the spoon.

"I go first," he says.

I don't answer. I am watching how he lifts the water from the tumbler into the eye-dropper. I am wondering whether he is going to be quick or slow.

His nose is two inches above the spoon as he drops the water from the eye-dropper on to the powder. He holds the spoon near his eyes as he applies matches to it. He sets the spoon back on the table, bubbling.

He is doing all right.

Siphoning up the liquid again, applying the needle with its collar (a strip from the end of a dollar bill) to the neck of the dropper, twisting it on, resting the shot momentarily at the edge of the table while he ties up with the leather belt on his right arm . . . but I am already beyond all that. I am not watching and he is not playing for a public . . . if he is I shan't notice because I am not watching . . . we are both of us, I believe, relating each and separately to the heroin before us. He is stroking the arm he is about to puncture just above a blackish vein and I am already moving to cook up my own fix in the spoon. By the time I have it prepared he is already loosening the belt. And now he presses the bulb. It doesn't take long. It might have taken much longer.

As I take my own fix I am looking at all the needle-marks. They follow the length of the vein down the arm. Since the Man looks for marks I am trying to keep them dispersed, to keep them as impermanent as possible. Some junkies use a woman's cosmetic to mask their marks; it is simpler to stick to one vein until it collapses. They do so and make up their arms, just where the elbow bends, like a woman makes up her face. Shooting in places where the vein is more submerged has over a period of time made quite a mess of my arm. As I fix I am aware of Tom, slightly to one side of me, standing, his left hand lying on the table for balance, smiling idyllically. I wash out the eye-dropper and sit down on the bed. I begin to scratch.

An hour later Tom says: "Man, that's good shit," and he drapes himself at the other end of the bed. The dog barks in the next room.

"Don't let the bastard in," I say.

ALAIN ROBBE-GRILLET

※※

FROM *In the Labyrinth* [1960]

Translated from the French by Richard Howard

The picture, in its varnished wood frame, represents a tavern scene. It is a nine-teenth-century etching, or a good reproduction of one. A large number of people fills the taproom: a crowd of drinkers sitting or standing and, on the far left, the innkeeper standing on a slightly raised platform behind his counter.

The innkeeper is a fat, bald man wearing an apron. He leans forward, both hands resting on the counter's edge, over several half-full glasses that have been set there, his massive shoulders turned toward a small group of burghers in frock coats who appear to be engaged in an animated discussion; standing in various attitudes, many are making expansive gestures that sometimes involve their whole bodies and are doubtless extremely expressive.

To their right—that is, in the center of the print—several groups of drink-ers are sitting at tables irregularly arranged—or rather, crammed—in a space too small to hold them all comfortably. These men too are making extravagant gestures and their faces are violently contorted, but their movements, like their expressions, are suspended and set, which makes their meaning uncertain too; particularly since the words being shouted on all sides seem to have been ab-sorbed by a thick layer of glass. Some men, in the intensity of their feelings, have half risen from their chairs or their benches and are pointing above the intervening heads toward a more remote interlocutor. Everywhere hands are raised, mouths open, heads turn; fists are clenched, pounded on tables or bran-dished in mid-air.

At the far right a group of men, almost all in work clothes like those sit-ting at the tables, have their backs to the latter and are crowding around some poster or picture tacked on the wall. A little in front of them, between their backs and the first row of drinkers facing in the other direction, a boy is sitting on the floor among all these legs with their shapeless trousers, all these clumsy boots stamping about and trying to move toward his left; on the other side he is par-tially protected by the bench. The child is drawn facing straight ahead. He is sitting with his legs folded under him, his arms clasped around a large box some-thing like a shoebox. No one is paying any attention to him. Perhaps he was knocked down in the confusion. As a matter of fact, in the foreground, not far from where he is sitting, a chair has been overturned and is still lying on the floor.

Somewhat apart, as though separated from the crowd surrounding them by an unoccupied zone—narrow, of course, but nevertheless wide enough for their isolation to be noticeable, in any case wide enough to call attention to them though they are in the background—three soldiers are sitting around a smaller table, the second from the rear on the right, their motionlessness and their rigidity in violent contrast with the civilians who fill the room. The soldiers are looking straight ahead, their hands resting on the checkered tablecloth; there are no glasses in front of them. They are the only men whose heads are not bare, for they are wearing low-peaked police caps. Behind them, at the extreme rear, the last seated drinkers are mingled with others standing, forming a jumbled mass; besides, the drawing here is vaguer too. Under the print, in the white margin, someone has written a title: "The Defeat of Reichenfels."

On closer examination, the isolation of the three soldiers seems to result less from the narrow space between them and the crowd than from the direction of the glances around them. All the figures in the background look as if they were passing—or trying to pass, for the space is cramped—behind them to reach the left side of the picture, where there is probably a door (though this hypothetical exit cannot be seen in the picture because of a row of coat racks loaded with hats and coats); every head is looking straight ahead (that is, toward the coat racks), an occasional exception turning to speak to someone who has remained in the rear. Everyone in the crowd gathered on the right is looking toward the right wall. The drinkers at the tables are represented in natural poses, turning toward the center of each group or else toward one neighbor or another. As for the burghers in front of the counter, they too are completely absorbed in their own conversation, and the innkeeper leans toward them without paying any attention to the rest of his customers. Among the various groups circulate a number of persons not yet settled, but obviously soon about to adopt one of several probable attitudes: either examining the poster, sitting down at one of the tables, or else going out behind the coat racks; a moment's scrutiny is enough to reveal that each has already determined what he is going to do next; here as among the groups, no face, no movement betrays hesitation, perplexity, inner vacillation or contradiction. The three soldiers, on the contrary, seem forsaken. They are not talking to each other; they are not looking at anything in particular: neither glasses, nor poster, nor their neighbors. They have nothing to do. No one looks at them and they themselves have nothing to look at. The position of their faces—one full front, the other in profile, the last in a three-quarters view—indicates no common subject of attention. Besides, the first man—the only one whose features are completely visible—betrays no expression whatever, merely a fixed, vacant stare.

The contrast between the three soldiers and the crowd is further accentuated by a precision of line, a clarity in rendering, much more evident in their case than in that of other individuals the same distance from the viewer. The artist has shown them with as much concern for detail and almost as much sharpness of outline as if they were sitting in the foreground. But the composition is so involved that this is not apparent at first glance. Particularly the face shown full front has been portrayed with a wealth of detail that seems quite out of proportion to the indifference it expresses. No specific thought can be attributed to it: it is merely a tired face, rather thin and narrowed further by several days' growth of beard. This thinness, these shadows that accentuate the features without, on the other hand, indicating the slightest individual characteristic nevertheless emphasize the brilliance of the wide-open eyes.

The military overcoat is buttoned up to the neck, where the regimental number is embroidered on a folded tab of the same material. The cap is set straight on the head, covering the hair, which is cut extremely short, judging from its appearance at the temples. The man is sitting up straight, his hands lying flat on the table that is covered with a red-and-white-checkered cloth.

He has finished his drink some time ago. He doesn't look as if the notion of leaving had occurred to him. Yet around him the café's last customers have vanished. The light is dim now: the proprietor turned out most of the lamps before leaving the room himself.

The soldier, eyes wide, continues to stare into the half-darkness a few yards in front of him, where the child is standing, motionless too, his arms stiff alongside his body. But it is as if the soldier didn't see the child—or anything else. He looks as if he had fallen asleep from exhaustion, sitting close to the table, his eyes wide open.

It is the child who speaks first. He says, "Are you asleep?" He has spoken almost in a whisper, as if he were afraid to waken the sleeper. The latter has not stirred. After a few seconds the child repeats his question a trifle louder, "Are you asleep?" and he adds, in the same expressionless, slightly singsong tone of voice, "You can't sleep here, you know."

The soldier has not stirred. The child might suppose he is alone in the room, merely pretending to have a conversation with someone who doesn't exist, or else with a doll, a toy unable to answer. Under these conditions it is certainly no use speaking louder; the voice in fact is that of a child telling himself a story.

But the voice is broken off, as if unable to struggle further against the silence which has prevailed again. The child, too, may have fallen asleep.

"No . . . Yes . . . I know," the soldier says.

Neither one has moved. The child is still standing in the half-darkness, his arms at his sides. He has not even seen the man's lips moving as he sits at the table under the one light bulb still lit in the room; the head has not moved at all, the eyes have not even blinked, and the mouth is still closed.

"Your father . . ." the soldier begins. Then be stops. But this time the lips have stirred a little.

"He's not my father," the child says.

And he turns his head toward the door with its black rectangle of window glass in the upper half.

It is snowing outside. Tiny flakes have begun falling again on the already white road. The wind has risen and is blowing them horizontally, so that the soldier has to keep his head down, a little further down, as he walks, pressing the hand shielding his eyes still harder against his forehead, leaving visible only a few square inches of thin, crunching snow that is already trampled down hard. Reaching a crossroads, the soldier hesitates and looks around for the plaques that should indicate the names of these streets. But it is useless, for there are no blue-enamel plaques here, or else they are set too high and the night is too dark; besides, the tiny, thick flakes quickly blind him when he tries to look up. Then too, a street name would hardly furnish him much in the way of helpful information: he doesn't know this city anyway.

He hesitates for another moment, looks ahead again, then back at the road he has just taken, with its row of street lamps whose circles of light, closer and closer together and less and less bright, soon disappear in the darkness. Then he turns right, onto the cross street which is also deserted, lined with the same kind of apartment houses and the same row of street lamps, quite far apart but set at regular intervals, their dim circles of light revealing the oblique snowfall as he passes each one.

The white flakes, falling thick and fast, suddenly change direction; vertical for a few seconds, they suddenly become almost horizontal. Then they are immobilized for an instant and begin, with a sudden gust of wind, to blow at virtually the same angle in the opposite direction, which they abandon after two or three seconds with no more transition than before, to return to their original orientation, making new, almost horizontal, parallel lines that cross the circle of light from left to right toward the unlighted windows.

In the window recesses the snow has formed an uneven layer, very shallow on the sill but deeper toward the back, making on the right side an already considerable drift, which fills the corner and reaches as high as the pane. All the ground-floor windows, one after the other, show exactly the same amount of snow which has drifted toward the right in the same way.

At the next crossroads, under the corner street lamp, a child is standing. He is partially hidden by the cast-iron post whose conical base conceals the lower part of his body altogether. He is watching the soldier approach. He does not seem bothered by the storm or by the snow that whitens some of his black cape and his beret. He is a boy of about ten, his expression serious. He turns his head as the soldier comes toward him, following him with his eyes as he reaches the lamp post, then passes it. Since the soldier is not walking fast, the child has time to examine him carefully from head to foot: the unshaven cheeks, the apparent fatigue, the dirty and ragged overcoat, the sleeves without braid on them, the wet package under his left arm, both hands thrust deep in his pockets, the hurriedly wrapped, irregular leggings, the wide gash down the back of the right boot, at least six inches long and so deep it looks as if it pierces the leather; yet the boot is not split and the damaged area has merely been smeared with black wax, which now gives it the same dark-gray color as the adjoining surfaces that are still intact.

The man has stopped. Without moving the rest of his body, he has turned his head around toward the child looking at him, already some three steps away, already crisscrossed by many white lines.

A moment later the soldier slowly pivots around and makes a movement toward the street lamp. The boy steps back, against the cast-iron post; at the same time he draws tight the bottom of his cape, holding the cloth from inside without showing his hands. The man has stopped. Now that the gusts of snow are no longer striking him directly in the face, he can hold his head up without too much discomfort.

"Don't be afraid," he says.

He steps toward the child and repeats a little louder, "Don't be afraid."

The child does not answer. Without seeming to feel the thickset flakes that scarcely make him squint, he continues staring at the soldier directly in front of him. The latter begins:

"Do you know where . . ."

But goes no further. The question he was going to ask is not the right one. A gust of wind blows the snow into his face again. He takes his right hand out of his overcoat pocket and shields his eyes with it. He has no glove, his hand is red and dirty. When the gust is over he puts his hand back in his pocket.

"Where does this road go?"

The boy still says nothing. His eyes have left the soldier to look toward the end of the street in the direction the man has indicated with a nod of his head; he sees only the succession of street lamps, closer and closer together, less and less bright, which vanish into the darkness.

"What's the matter, are you afraid I'll eat you?"

"No," the child says. "I'm not afraid."

"Well then, tell me where this road goes."

"I don't know," the child says.

And he raises his eyes toward this ill-dressed, unshaven soldier who doesn't even know where he's going. Then, without warning, he makes a sudden turn, skillfully avoids the base of the lamp post and begins to run as fast as he can along the row of apartment houses, in the opposite direction from the way the soldier came. In a few seconds he has disappeared.

At the next street lamp he appears again for several seconds; he is still running just as fast; his cape billows out behind him. He reappears at each lamp post, once, twice, then no more.

The soldier turns back and continues on his way. Again the snow strikes him directly in the face.

He puts the package under his right arm to try to shield his face with his left hand, for the wind blows more continuously from this side. But he soon gives this up and quickly puts the hand, numb with cold, back in his overcoat pocket. Now he merely turns his head away to get less snow in his eyes, leaning toward the unlighted windows where the white drift continues to accumulate in the right-hand corner of the recess.

Yet this boy with the serious expression is the same boy who led him to the café run by the man who is not his father. And there was a similar scene under the same kind of lamp post, at an identical crossroads. Perhaps it was snowing a little less heavily. The flakes were thicker, heavier, slower. But the boy answered with just as much reticence, holding his black cape tight around his knees. He had the same serious expression and seemed to be just as untroubled by the snow. He hesitated just as long at each question before giving an answer which furnished his interlocutor no information. Where did the street go? A long silent stare toward the presumed end of the street, then the calm voice:

"To the boulevard."

"And this one?"

The boy slowly turns his eyes in the direction the man has just indicated with a nod of his head. His features reveal no difficulty remembering, no uncertainty when he repeats in the same expressionless tone:

"To the boulevard."

"The same one?"

Again there is silence, and the snow falling more and more slowly, heavily.

"Yes," the boy says. Then, after a pause, "No." And finally, with a sudden violence, "It's the boulevard!"

"And is it far?" the soldier asks again.

The child is still looking at the series of street lamps, closer and closer together, less and less bright, which here too vanish into the darkness.

"Yes," he says, his voice calm again and sounding as if it came from far away.

The soldier waits another minute to make sure there will not be another "no." But the boy is already running along the row of apartment houses, down the track of trampled snow the soldier followed in the opposite direction a few minutes earlier. When the running boy crosses a circle of light, his black cape billowing out behind him can be seen for a few seconds, once, twice, three times, smaller and vaguer at each reappearance, until there is nothing but a confused whirl of snow.

Yet it is certainly the same boy who walks ahead of the soldier when the latter comes to the café. Before crossing the doorstep, the child shakes his black cape and takes off his beret, which he knocks twice against the door jamb in order to brush off the bits of ice which have formed in the folds of the cloth. The soldier must have met him several times, while walking in circles through the maze of identical streets. He has never come to any boulevard, any broader road planted with trees or differing in any way at all from the other streets he has taken. Finally the child had spoken a few names, the few street names he knew, which were obviously of no use at all.

Now he is knocking his beret against the door jamb in front of which they both have stopped. The interior is brightly lit. A ruffled curtain of white, translucent material covers the lower part of the window set in the upper part of the door. But for a man of normal height it is easy to see the entire interior: the counter to the left, the tables in the middle, on the right a wall covered with posters of various sizes. There are few drinkers at this late hour: two workmen sitting at one of the tables and a man more carefully dressed standing near the zinc-topped counter over which the proprietor is leaning. The latter is a man of massive stature, whose size is even more noticeable in relation to his customer because of the slightly raised platform he is standing on. Both men have turned their heads toward the door where the boy has just knocked his beret against the jamb.

But they see only the soldier's face above the curtain. And the child, turning the door knob with one hand, again knocks his beret, this time against the door itself, which is already some distance from the jamb. The proprietor's eyes have already left the soldier's pale face that is still silhouetted against the darkness, cut off at chin level by the curtain, and are lowered on the gap widening between door and jamb in order to let in the child.

As soon as he is inside, the latter turns around and gestures to the soldier to follow him. This time everyone stares at the newcomer: the proprietor behind his counter, the man standing in front of it, the two workmen sitting at a table. One of the latter, whose back was to the door, has pivoted on his chair without letting go his glass that is half full of red wine and set in the middle of the checkered tablecloth. The other glass, close beside the first, is also encircled by a large hand which completely conceals the probable contents. To the left, a ring of reddish liquid indicates another place where the same glass had been set down before.

Later, it is the soldier himself who is sitting in front of a similar glass, half full of the same dark-colored wine. On the red-and-white-checkered cloth the glass has left several circular marks, but almost all are incomplete, showing a series of more or less closed arcs, occasionally overlapping, almost dry in some places, in others still shiny with the last drops of liquid leaving a film over the blacker deposit already formed, while elsewhere the rings are blurred by being set too close together, or even half obliterated, perhaps, by a quick dab of a rag.

MARGUERITE DURAS

FROM *Moderato Cantabile* [1960]

Translated from the French by Richard Seaver

"Will you please read what's written above the score?" the lady asked.

"Moderato cantabile," said the child.

The lady punctuated his reply by striking the keyboard with a pencil. The child remained motionless, his head turned towards his score.

"And what does moderato cantabile mean?"

"I don't know."

A woman, seated ten feet away, gave a sigh.

"Are you quite sure you don't know what moderato cantabile means?" the lady repeated.

The child did not reply. The lady stifled an exasperated groan, and again struck the keyboard with her pencil. The child remained unblinking. The lady turned.

"Madame Desbaresdes, you have a very stubborn little boy."

Anne Desbaresdes sighed again.

"You don't have to tell me," she said.

The child, motionless, his eyes lowered, was the only one to remember that dusk had just exploded. It made him shiver.

"I told you the last time, I told you the time before that, I've told you a hundred times; are you sure you don't know what it means?"

The child decided not to answer. The lady looked again at the object before her, her rage mounting.

"Here we go again," said Anne Desbaresdes under her breath.

"The trouble is," the lady went on, "the trouble is you don't want to say it."

Anne Desbaresdes also looked again at this child, from head to toe, but in a different way from the lady.

"You're going to say it this minute," the lady shouted.

The child showed no surprise. He still didn't reply. Then the lady struck the keyboard a third time, so hard that the pencil broke. Right next to the child's hands. His hands were round and milky, still scarcely formed. They were clenched and unmoving.

"He's a difficult child," Anne Desbaresdes offered timidly.

The child turned his head towards the voice, quickly towards his mother, to make sure of her existence, then resumed his pose as an object, facing the score. His hands remained clenched.

"I don't care whether he's difficult or not, Madame Desbaresdes," said the lady. "Difficult or not, he has to do as he's told, or suffer the consequences."

In the ensuing silence the sound of the sea came in through the open window. And with it the muffled noise of the town on this spring afternoon.

"For the last time. Are you sure you don't know what it means?"

A motorboat was framed in the open window. The child, facing his score, hardly moved—only his mother noticed it—as the motorboat passed through his blood. The low purr of the motor could be heard throughout the town. There were only a few pleasure craft. The whole sky was tinted pink by the last rays of the sun. Outside, on the docks, other children stopped and looked.

"Are you really sure, for the last time now, are you sure you don't know what it means?"

Again, the motorboat passed by.

The lady was taken aback by such stubbornness. Her anger abated, and she so despaired at being so unimportant to this child who, by a single gesture, she could have made to answer her, that she was suddenly aware of the sterility of her own existence.

"What a profession, what a profession," she lamented.

Anne Desbaresdes made no comment, but tilted her head slightly as if, perhaps, agreeing.

The motorboat had finally passed from the frame of the open window. The sound of the sea arose, boundless, in the child's silence.

"Moderato?"

The child opened his fist, moved it, and lightly scratched his calf. His gesture was unconstrained, and perhaps the lady admitted its innocence.

"I don't know," he said, after he had finished scratching himself.

The color of the sunset suddenly became so magnificent that it changed the gold of the child's hair.

"It's easy," the woman said a bit more calmly.

She blew her nose.

"What a child," Anne Desbaresdes said happily, "really, what a child! How in the world did I happen to have such an obstinate . . ."

The lady decided that such pride deserved no comment.

"It means," she said to the child, as though admiring defeat, "for the hundredth time, it means moderately and melodiously."

"Moderately and melodiously," the child said mechanically.

The lady turned around.

"Really. I mean *really*."

"Yes, it's terrible," Anne Desbaresdes said, laughing, "stubborn as a goat. It's terrible."

"Begin again," the lady said.

The child did not begin again.

"I said begin again."

The child still did not move. The sound of the sea again filled the silence of his stubbornness. The pink sky exploded in a final burst of color.

"I don't want to learn how to play the piano," the child said.

In the street downstairs a woman screamed, a long, drawn-out scream so shrill it overwhelmed the sound of the sea. Then it stopped abruptly.

"What was that?" the child shouted.

"Something happened," the lady said.

The sound of the sea moved in again. The pink sky began to fade.

"No," said Anne Desbaresdes, "it's nothing."

She got up and went to the piano.

"You're so nervous," the lady said, looking at both of them with a disapproving air.

Anne Desbaresdes took her child by the shoulders, shook him, and almost shouted:

"You've got to learn the piano, you've got to."

The child was also trembling, for the same reason, because he was afraid.

"I don't like the piano," he murmured.

Scattered shouts followed the first, confirming an already established fact, henceforth reassuring. So the lesson went on.

"You've got to," Anne Desbaresdes insisted.

The lady shook her head, disapproving such tenderness. Dusk began to sweep over the sea. And the sky slowly darkened, except for the red in the west, till that faded as well.

"Why?" the child asked.

"Because music, my love . . ."

The child took his time, trying to understand, did not understand, but admitted it.

"All right. But who screamed?"

"I'm waiting," said the lady.

He began to play. The music rose above the murmur of a crowd that was beginning to gather on the dock beneath the window.

"There now, there you are," Anne Desbaresdes said happily, "you see."

"When he wants to," the lady said.

The child finished the sonatina. The noise from the street grew more insistent, invading the room.

"What's going on?" the child asked again.

"Play it again," the lady replied. "And don't forget: moderato cantabile. Think of a lullaby."

"I never sing him songs," Anne Desbaresdes said. "Tonight he's going to ask me for one, and he'll ask me so sweetly I won't be able to refuse."

The lady didn't want to listen. The child began to play Diabelli's sonatina again.

"B flat," the lady said sharply, "you always forget."

The growing clamor of voices of both sexes rose from the dock. Everyone seemed to be saying the same thing, but it was impossible to distinguish the words. The sonatina went innocently along, but this time, in the middle of it, the lady could take no more.

"Stop."

The child stopped. The lady turned to Anne Desbaresdes.

"I'm sure something serious has happened."

They all went to the window. To their left, some twenty yards from the building, a crowd had already gathered on the dock in front of the café door. From the neighboring streets people were running up to join the crowd. Everyone was looking into the café.

"I'm afraid this part of town . . ." the lady said.

She turned and took the boy's arm. "Start again, one last time, where you left off."

"What's happened?"

"Your sonatina."

The child played. He played it at the same tempo as before, and as the end of the lesson approached he gave it the nuances she wanted, moderato cantabile.

"It upsets me when he does as he's told like that," Anne Desbaresdes said. "I guess I don't know what I want. It's a cross I have to bear."

The child went on playing well.

"What a way to bring him up, Madame Desbaresdes," the lady said almost happily.

Then the child stopped.

"Why are you stopping?"

"I thought . . ."

He began playing the sonatina again. The noise of the crowd grew increasingly loud, becoming so powerful, even at that height, that it drowned out the music.

"Don't forget that B flat in the key," the lady said, "otherwise it would be perfect."

Once again the music crescendoed to its final chord. And the hour was up. The lady announced that the lesson was finished for today.

"You'll have plenty of trouble with that one, I don't mind telling you," she said.

"I already do. He worries me to death."

Anne Desbaresdes bowed her head, her eyes closed in the painful smile of endless childbirth. Below, a welter of shouts and orders proved the consummation of an unknown incident.

"Tomorrow we'll know it perfectly," the lady said.

The child ran to the window.

"Some cars are coming," he said.

The crowd blocked both sides of the café entrance, and was still growing, but the influx from the neighboring streets had lessened. Still, it was much larger than one might have suspected. The people moved aside and made a path for a black van to get through. Three men got out and went into the café.

"Police," someone said.

Anne Desbaresdes asked what had happened.

"Someone's been killed. A woman."

She left her child in front of Mademoiselle Giraud's door, joined the body of the crowd, and made her way forward till she reached the front row of silent people looking through the open windows. At the far end of the café, in the semi-darkness of the back room, a woman was lying motionless on the floor. A man was crouched over her, clutching her shoulders, and saying quietly:

"Darling. My darling."

He turned and looked at the crowd; they saw his eyes, which were expressionless, except for the stricken, indelible, inward look of his desire. The patronne stood calmly near the van and waited.

"I tried to call you three times."

"Poor woman," someone said.

"Why?" Anne Desbaresdes asked.

"No one knows."

In his delirium the man threw himself on the inert body. An inspector took him by the arm and pulled him up. He did not resist. It seemed that all dignity had left him forever. He looked absently at the inspector. The inspector let go of him, took a notebook and pencil from his pocket, asked for the man's identity, and waited.

"It's no use. I won't say anything now," the man said.

The inspector didn't press the matter, and went over to join his colleagues who were questioning the patronne at the last table in the back room.

The man sat down beside the dead woman, stroked her hair and smiled at her. A young man with a camera around his neck dashed up to the café door and took a picture of the man sitting there smiling. By the glare of the flash bulb the crowd could see that the woman was still young, and that blood was coming from her mouth in thin trickles, and that there was blood on the man's face where he had kissed her. In the crowd, someone said:

"It's horrible," and turned away.

The man lay down again beside his wife's body, but only for a moment. Then, as if he were tired, he got up again.

"Don't let him get away," the patronne shouted.

But the man had only got up in order to find a better position, closer to the body. He lay there, seemingly resolute and calm, holding her tightly in his arms, his face pressed to hers, in the blood flowing from her mouth.

But the inspectors had finished taking the patronne's testimony and slowly, in single file, walked over to him, an identical air of utter boredom on their faces.

The child, sitting obediently on Mademoiselle Giraud's front steps, had almost forgotten. He was humming the Diabelli sonatina.

"It was nothing," Anne Desbaresdes said. "Now we must go home."

The child followed her. More policemen arrived—too late, for no reason. As they passed the café the man came out, flanked by the inspectors. The crowd parted silently to let him through.

"He's not the one who screamed," the child said. "He didn't scream."

"No, it wasn't he. Don't look."

"Why did she. . . ?"

"I don't know."

The man walked meekly to the van. Then, when he reached it, he shook off the inspectors, and, without a word, ran quickly back towards the café. But just as he got there the lights went out. He stopped dead, again followed the inspectors to the van, and got inside. Then, perhaps, he was crying, but it was already too dark to see anything but his trembling, blood-stained face. If he was crying, it was too dark to see his tears.

"Really," Anne Desbaresdes said as they reached the Boulevard de la Mer, "you might remember it once and for all. Moderato means moderately slow, and cantabile means melodiously. It's easy."

"Statement in Support of the Freedom to Read" [1962]

We, the undersigned, strongly endorse Judge Samuel B. Epstein's defense of the freedom to read in his historic decision in the *Tropic of Cancer* case in Chicago. Judge Epstein, by stating that the "right to free utterance becomes a useless privilege when the freedom to read is restricted or denied," has put the issue of police censorship squarely before the public. In recent months, policemen, encouraged by certain minority pressure groups, have succeeded in forcing their own narrow-minded literary tastes upon many communities.

We believe with Judge Epstein that neither the police nor the courts should be allowed to dictate the reading matter of a free people. The issue is not whether *Tropic of Cancer* is a masterpiece of American literature; rather, it is whether an author of Henry Miller's artistic integrity is entitled to the protections afforded by the Constitution of the United States.

This is an issue of immediate and serious concern to every citizen who holds dear the traditions of our democracy, and who abhors the intrusion of official censorship into the vital area of artistic and literary expression. It is an issue to which we are especially sensitive.

Judge Epstein's ruling against book banning has reaffirmed the right of a free people to decide for itself what it may or may not read. Beyond that, it sounds a clear warning to all of us to guard the principles upon which our country was built.

We urge all who, along with Judge Epstein, resent police censorship in the area of literature and the arts to make their voices heard in their own communities and to defeat any attempts at repression before they are allowed to erode our most precious freedoms.

Herbert M. Alexander
Pocket Books, Inc.
Gay Wilson Allen
Aaron Asher
Meridian Books, Inc.

Harry Ashmore
Encyclopedia Britannica
Herbert S. Bailey, Jr.
Princeton University Press

F. Sherman Baker
St. Martin's Press, Inc.
James Baldwin
Betty Ballantine
Ballantine Books, Inc.
Ian Ballantine
Ballantine Books, Inc.
William Barrett
Sheila Barry
Taplinger Publishing Co., Inc.
Jacques Barzun
Howard K. Bauernfeind
J. B. Lippincott Co.
Saul Bellow
Eric Bentley
Paul Bixler
Antioch Review
Louise Bogan
Charles G. Bolte
The Viking Press, Inc.
Edward E. Booher
McGraw-Hill Book Co.
Keith Botsford
The Noble Savage
Walter I. Bradbury
Harper & Brothers
Ned Bradford
Little, Brown & Co.
George Braziller
George Braziller, Inc.
Germaine Bree
Harvey Breit
John Malcolm Brinnin
George P. Brockway
W. W. Norton & Co. Inc.
Donald W. Brown
Penguin Books, Inc.
Eugene Burdick
Charles R. Byrne
Macfadden-Bartell Corp.

Herb Caen
San Francisco Chronicle
Erskine Caldwell
Angus Cameron
Alfred A. Knopf, Inc.
Truman Capote
Mark Carroll
Harvard University Press
John Ciardi
Ross Claiborne
Dell Publishing Co., Inc.
Harold Clurman
Arthur A. Cohen
Holt, Rinehart & Winston, Inc.
Evan S. Connell
Contact
John Cournos
Pascal Covici
The Viking Press, Inc.
Thomas A. Dardis
Berkley Publishing Corp.
Edward Darling
Beacon Press
Peter H. Davison
Atlantic Monthly Press
Edward Degrazia
Edward C. Delafield, Jr.
Crown Publishers
Patrick Dennis
John Dos Passos
Grant Dugdale
The World Publishing Co.
James W. Ellison
Holt, Rinehart & Winston, Inc.
Richard Ellmann
Jason Epstein
Random House
John Ervin, Jr.
University of Minnesota Press

Clifton Fadiman
John Farrar
Farrar, Straus & Cudahy, Inc.
Lawrence Ferlinghetti
City Lights Books
Philip S. Foner
Citadel Press
Jerome Fried
The World Publishing Co.
John G. Fuller
Saturday Review
Bernard Geis
Bernard Geis Associates
Maxwell Geismar
Jack Gelber
Emanuel Geltman
Horizon Press, Inc.
Arnold Gingrich
Esquire
K. S. Giniger
Hawthorne Books, Inc.
Herbert Gold
Harry Golden
John L. Goldwater
Belmont Books
Mitchell Goodman
Horizon Press, Inc.
Robert Gottlieb
Simon & Schuster, Inc.
Louis C. Greene
R. R. Bowker Co.
Howard Greenfeld
The Orion Press, Inc.
Horace Gregory
John Howard Griffin
Richard L. Grossman
Simon & Schuster, Inc.
William B. Harvey
New York University Press

A. L. Hart, Jr.
The Macmillan Co.
Hiram Haydn
Atheneum Publishers
Hugh M. Hefner
Playboy
Charles A. S. Heinle
Chilton Co. Book Division
Joseph Heller
Lillian Hellman
Cecil Hemley
The Noonday Press
John Hersey
Henry B. Hibbard
Barnes & Noble, Inc.
Granville Hicks
Lawrence Hill
Hill & Wang, Inc.
William Hogan
San Francisco Chronicle
Tay Hohoff
J. B. Lippincott Co.
John Clellon Holmes
Sidney Hook
Irving Howe
Dissent
B. W. Huebsch
The Viking Press, Inc.
Richard Huett
Dell Publishing Co., Inc.
J. Lawrence Hughes
William Morrow & Co., Inc.
Aldous Huxley
Harold E. Ingle
The Johns Hopkins Press
Sidney R. Jacobs
Alfred A. Knopf, Inc.
James M. Jacobson
Pocket Books, Inc.

James Jones

Fred Jordan

Grove Press, Inc.

Mackinlay Kantor

Jeremiah Kaplan

The Crowell-Collier Publishing Co.

Alfred Kazin

Jack Kerouac

Chester Kerr

Yale University Press

Robert Kirsch

Los Angeles Times

Donald S. Klopfer

Random House

Conrad Knickerbocker

Kansas City Star

Kenneth Koch

Herman Kogan

Chicago Sun-Times

Louis Kronenberger

Eric Larrabee

American Heritage

James Laughlin

New Directions

John T. Lawrence

William Morrow & Co., Inc.

Seymour Lawrence

Atlantic Monthly Press

Max Lerner

Freeman Lewis

Pocket Books, Inc.

R. W. B. Lewis

Denver Lindley

The Viking Press, Inc.

Robert Lowell

Storer B. Lunt

W. W. Norton & Co. Inc.

Kenneth McCormick

Doubleday & Co., Inc.

Carson McCullers

Robert M. Macgregor

New Directions

Carey McWilliams

The Nation

Robie Macauley

Kenyon Review

Ian Mackenzie

St. Martin's Press, Inc.

Norman Mailer

Bernard Malamud

Marya Mannes

Daniel Melcher

R. R. Bowker Co.

Frederic G. Melcher

R. R. Bowker Co.

Thorpe Menn

Kansas City Star

Daniel Mich

Look

Arthur Miller

M. Hughes Miller

The Bobbs-Merrill Co., Inc.

Gilbert Millstein

New York Times

Eric Moon

Library Journal

Marianne Moore

Frederick Morgan

Hudson Review

Alice Morris

Harper's Bazaar

Truman Nelson

Hoke Norris

Chicago Sun-Times

Theodore O'Leary

Kansas City Star

Hyung Woong Pak

Chicago Review

Norman Holmes Pearson
Arthur Pell
Liveright Publishing Corp.
Bernard B. Perry
Indiana University Press
Robert Phelps
George Braziller, Inc.
William Phillips
Partisan Review
Samuel H. Post
Belmont Books
Lawrence Clarke Powell
Ben Raeburn
Horizon Press, Inc.
Henry Rago
Poetry
Kennett L. Rawson
David McKay Co., Inc.
Theodor Reik
Elmer Rice
Anders Richter
University of Chicago Press
Harold Robbins
Henry Robbins
Alfred A. Knopf, Inc.
Paul H. Rohmann
Antioch Review
Barney Rosset
Grove Press, Inc.
Philip Roth
William H. Ryan
Angel Island Publications
Howard W. Sams
The Bobbs-Merrill Co., Inc.
Mark Schorer
Webster Schott
Kansas City Star
M. Lincoln Schuster
Simon & Schuster, Inc.

Lew Schwartz
Abelard-Schuman, Ltd.
Peter Schwed
Simon & Schuster, Inc.
William R. Scott
William R. Scott, Inc.
Edwin Seaver
George Braziller, Inc.
Richard Seaver
Grove Press, Inc.
Leon E. Seltzer
Stanford University Press
Rod Serling
Karl Shapiro
Leonard Shatzkin
The Crowell-Collier Publishing Co.
Irwin Shaw
William L. Shirer
James H. Silberman
The Dial Press, Inc.
Henry W. Simon
Simon & Schuster, Inc.
Morris Sorkin
Citadel Press
George Stevens
J. B. Lippincott Co.
Irving Stone
Harold Strauss
Alfred A. Knopf, Inc.
Lyle Stuart
Lyle Stuart
William Styron
Aaron Sussman
Sussman & Sugar, Inc.
Alan Swallow
Alan Swallow, Publisher
Richard Taplinger
Taplinger Publishing Co., Inc.

Frank Taylor
The Racine Press
Evan W. Thomas
Harper & Brothers
Lionel Trilling
Mark Van Doren
Dan Wakefield
Arthur W. Wang
Hill & Wang
Robert Penn Warren
Edwin Watkins
University of Michigan Press
Howard Sayre Weaver
Yale University Press

Richard Wilbur
John C. Willey
William Morrow & Co., Inc.
Edmund Wilson
Thomas J. Wilson
Harvard University Press
Donald Wollheim
Ace Books, Inc.
W. A. Wood
University of Chicago Press
Philip Wylie
Thomas Yoseloff
Thomas Yoseloff, Inc.
Marya Zaturenska

BARNEY ROSSET ON *TROPIC OF CANCER*

FROM *The Paris Review* [1997]

I first went to college at Swarthmore, and that's where I discovered Henry Miller. *They* didn't discover him—he certainly wasn't being taught in English class. I read *Tropic of Cancer,* which I bought at Steloff's Gotham Book Mart on Forty-seventh Street. Who told me about it, I don't know, but I liked it enormously and I wrote my freshman English paper about both it and *The Air Conditioned Nightmare.* My paper was anti-United States—it was all about what a lousy country we live in. My professor said, "Perhaps the jaundice is in the eye of the beholder," meaning my eyes and Miller's. He gave me a B minus.

At Swarthmore I got to hate Quakers. Detest them. They were anti-Semitic at Swarthmore, and there were no blacks, not one. They had fraternities! I say it with venom because I hated the idea. I was most certainly not going to join a fraternity—and nobody asked me. I really got disgusted by the whole place and was desperately unhappy. After I read *Tropic of Cancer,* I left—decided to go to Mexico. Because the book had influenced me so much, I left in the middle of the term. But I ran out of money. I never got to Mexico; I got as far as Florida and I came back. Four weeks had gone by. They had reported me missing to the United States government. My family didn't know where I was. I came back, sort of sadly. At Swarthmore if you missed two classes you automatically flunked. So I went to the dean. He said, "Well, nobody's ever done this before"—there was no precedent for it—"so let's pretend it never happened!" But you know what, I was not happy. It did not make me like him. It didn't change my mind a bit.

That paper, by the way, helped me a great deal years later. At the Chicago trial over *Tropic of Cancer* the prosecutor said, "You don't care about Henry Miller, you're only publishing him for the money." So I took this paper, written in 1940, out of my pocket and started reading it. It made a big point.

The post office didn't come after us, unfortunately. You can't force them to. After *Lady Chatterley,* they never got involved in obscenity suits again. They learned their lesson, I think.

But if the post office doesn't arrest you, there are still many other possibilities for arrest. The local police can go into a store and say, "Take this book off the shelves," and arrest the bookseller. In Brooklyn they came after *me*, the publisher, and charged me with conspiracy. They claimed that Henry Miller and I conspired to have him write *Tropic of Cancer*—that I commissioned him to write it *in Brooklyn* in 1933! That was a mistake, right? I would have been ten years old, and anyway he wrote the book in Paris. It was insane. Then John Ciardi wrote a two-page editorial in the *Saturday Review* blasting the government, absolutely ridiculing the district attorney. In the course of blasting them, he told the history of the book, and that really helped us. I was brought before a grand jury. It was a big room. The jury looked like nice people. The district attorney got up and said, "I understand that the children of these people on the grand jury are able to buy *Tropic of Cancer* at their local newsstand." I said, "Well, that's very good. And if their children bought that book and read it all the way through, then those parents should be congratulated!" The district attorney just got laughed out of there by the grand jury. All the cops in America had settled on page 7 or something as *the* page that made the book arrestable. It's the page where the woman is shitting five franc pieces out of her cunt, and there are wild chickens running around—the DA asked me to read it aloud. I did, and that's when the jury *really* started laughing. And then *he* started laughing. And so they dropped it. The grand jury would not indict me. That was only one of hundreds of cases, all over the country, in *every* state—literally.

ANAÏS NIN

❧

Preface TO *Tropic of Cancer* [1961]

Here is a book which, if such a thing were possible, might restore our appetite for the fundamental realities. The predominant note will seem one of bitterness, and bitterness there is, to the full. But there is also a wild extravagance, a mad gaiety, a verve, a gusto, at times almost a delirium. A continual oscillation between extremes, with bare stretches that taste like brass and leave the full flavor of emptiness. It is beyond optimism or pessimism. The author has given us the last frisson. Pain has no more secret recesses.

In a world grown paralyzed with introspection and constipated by delicate mental meals this brutal exposure of the substantial body comes as a vitalizing current of blood. The violence and obscenity are left unadulterated, as manifestation of the mystery and pain which ever accompanies the act of creation.

The restorative value of experience, prime source of wisdom and creation, is reasserted. There remain waste areas of unfinished thought and action, a bundle of shreds and fibers with which the overcritical may strangle themselves. Referring to his *Wilhelm Meister* Goethe once said: "People seek a central point: that is hard, and not even right. I should think a rich, manifold life, brought close to our eyes, would be enough without any express tendency; which, after all, is only for the intellect."

The book is sustained on its own axis by the pure flux and rotation of events. Just as there is no central point, so also there is no question of heroism or of struggle since there is no question of will, but only an obedience to flow.

The gross caricatures are perhaps more vital, "more true to life," than the full portraits of the conventional novel for the reason that the individual today has no centrality and produces not the slightest illusion of wholeness. The characters are integrated to the false, cultural void in which we are drowning; thus is produced the illusion of chaos, to face which requires the ultimate courage.

The humiliations and defeats, given with a primitive honesty, end not in frustration, despair, or futility, but in hunger, an ecstatic, devouring hunger— *for more life*. The poetic is discovered by stripping away the vestiture of art; by descending to what might be styled "a pre-artistic level," the durable skeleton of form which is hidden in the phenomena of disintegration reappears to be transfigured again in the ever-changing flesh of emotion. The scars are burned away—the scars left by the obstetricians of culture. Here is an artist who re-establishes the potency of illusion by gaping at the open wounds, by courting the stern, psychological reality which man seeks to avoid through recourse to the oblique symbolism of art. Here the symbols are laid bare, presented almost as naively and unblushingly by this overcivilized individual as by the well-rooted savage.

It is no false primitivism which gives rise to this savage lyricism. It is not a retrogressive tendency, but a swing forward into unbeaten areas. To regard a naked book such as this with the same critical eye that is turned upon even such diverse types as Lawrence, Breton, Joyce, and Céline is a mistake. Rather let us try to look at it with the eyes of a Patagonian for whom all that is sacred and taboo in our world is meaningless. For the adventure which has brought the author to the spiritual ends of the earth is the history of every artist who, in order to express himself, must traverse the intangible gridirons of his imaginary world. The air pockets, the alkali wastes, the crumbling monuments, the putrescent cadavers, the crazy jig and maggot dance, all this forms a grand fresco of our epoch, done with shattering phrases and loud, strident hammer strokes.

If there is here revealed a capacity to shock, to startle the lifeless ones from their profound slumber, let us congratulate ourselves; for the tragedy of our world is precisely that nothing any longer is capable of rousing it from its lethargy. No more violent dreams, no refreshment, no awakening. In the anaesthesia produced by self-knowledge, life is passing, art is passing, slipping from us: we are drifting with time and our fight is with shadows. We need a blood transfusion.

And it is blood and flesh which are here given us. Drink, food, laughter, desire, passion, curiosity, the simple realities which nourish the roots of our highest and vaguest creations. The superstructure is lopped away. This book brings with it a wind that blows down the dead and hollow trees whose roots are withered and lost in the barren soil of our times. This book goes to the roots and digs under, digs for subterranean springs.

(1934)

HENRY MILLER

❦

FROM *Tropic of Cancer* [1961]

I am living at the Villa Borghese. There is not a crumb of dirt anywhere, nor a chair misplaced. We are all alone here and we are dead.

Last night Boris discovered that he was lousy. I had to shave his armpits and even then the itching did not stop. How can one get lousy in a beautiful place like this? But no matter. We might never have known each other so intimately, Boris and I, had it not been for the lice.

Boris has just given me a summary of his views. He is a weather prophet. The weather will continue bad, he says. There will be more calamities, more death, more despair. Not the slightest indication of a change anywhere. The cancer of time is eating us away. Our heroes have killed themselves, or are killing themselves. The hero, then, is not Time, but Timelessness. We must get in step, a lock step, toward the prison of death. There is no escape. The weather will not change.

It is now the fall of my second year in Paris. I was sent here for a reason I have not yet been able to fathom.

I have no money, no resources, no hopes. I am the happiest man alive. A year ago, six months ago, I thought that I was an artist. I no longer think about it, I *am*. Everything that was literature has fallen from me. There are no more books to be written, thank God.

This then? This is not a book. This is libel, slander, defamation of character. This is not a book, in the ordinary sense of the word. No, this is a prolonged insult, a gob of spit in the face of Art, a kick in the pants to God, Man, Destiny, Time, Love, Beauty . . . what you will. I am going to sing for you, a little off key perhaps, but I will sing. I will sing while you croak, I will dance over your dirty corpse. . . .

To sing you must first open your mouth. You must have a pair of lungs, and a little knowledge of music. It is not necessary to have an accordion, or a guitar. The essential thing is to *want* to sing. This then is a song. I am singing.

* * *

It is to you, Tania, that I am singing. I wish that I could sing better, more melodiously, but then perhaps you would never have consented to listen to me. You have heard the others sing and they have left you cold. They sang too beautifully, or not beautifully enough.

It is the twenty-somethingth of October. I no longer keep track of the date. Would you say—my dream of the 14th November last? There are intervals, but they are between dreams, and there is no consciousness of them left. The world around me is dissolving, leaving here and there spots of time. The world is a cancer eating itself away. . . . I am thinking that when the great silence descends upon all and everywhere music will at last triumph. When into the womb of time everything is again withdrawn chaos will be restored and chaos is the score upon which reality is written. You, Tania, are my chaos. It is why I sing. It is not even I, it is the world dying, shedding the skin of time. I am still alive, kicking in your womb, a reality to write upon.

Dozing off. The physiology of love. The whale with his six-foot penis, in repose. The bat—*penis libre*. Animals with a bone in the penis. Hence, *a bone on*. . . . "Happily," says Gourmont, "the bony structure is lost in man." Happily? Yes, happily. Think of the human race walking around with a bone on. The kangaroo has a double penis—one for weekdays and one for holidays. Dozing. A letter from a female asking if I have found a title for my book. Title? To be sure: "Lovely Lesbians."

Your anecdotal life! A phrase of M. Borowski's. It is on Wednesdays that I have lunch with Borowski. His wife, who is a dried-up cow, officiates. She is studying English now—her favorite word is "filthy." You can see immediately what a pain in the ass the Borowskis are. But wait. . . .

Borowski wears corduroy suits and plays the accordion. An invincible combination, especially when you consider that he is not a bad artist. He puts on that he is a Pole, but he is not, of course. He is a Jew, Borowski, and his father was a philatelist. In fact, almost all Montparnasse is Jewish, or half-Jewish, which is worse. There's Carl and Paula, and Cronstadt and Boris, and Tania and Sylvester, and Moldorf and Lucille. All except Fillmore. Henry Jordan Oswald turned out to be a Jew also. Louis Nichols is a Jew. Even Van Norden and Chérie are Jewish. Frances Blake is a Jew, or a Jewess. Titus is a Jew. The Jews then are snowing me under. I am writing this for my friend Carl whose father is a Jew. All this is important to understand.

Of them all the loveliest Jew is Tania, and for her sake I too would become a Jew. Why not? I already speak like a Jew. And I am as ugly as a Jew. Besides, who hates the Jews more than the Jew?

Twilight hour. Indian blue, water of glass, trees glistening and liquescent. The rails fall away into the canal at Jaurès. The long caterpillar with lacquered sides dips like a roller coaster. It is not Paris. It is not Coney Island. It is a crepuscular melange of all the cities of Europe and Central America. The railroad yards below me, the tracks black, webby, not ordered by the engineer but cataclysmic in design, like those gaunt fissures in the polar ice which the camera registers in degrees of black.

Food is one of the things I enjoy tremendously. And in this beautiful Villa Borghese there is scarcely ever any evidence of food. It is positively appalling at times. I have asked Boris time and again to order bread for breakfast, but he always forgets. He goes out for breakfast, it seems. And when he comes back he is picking his teeth and there is a little egg hanging from his goatee. He eats in the restaurant out of consideration for me. He says it hurts to eat a big meal and have me watch him.

I like Van Norden but I do not share his opinion of himself. I do not agree, for instance, that he is a philosopher, or a thinker. He is cunt-struck, that's all. And he will never be a writer. Nor will Sylvester ever be a writer, though his name blaze in 50,000-candle-power red lights. The only writers about me for whom I have any respect, at present, are Carl and Boris. They are possessed. They glow inwardly with a white flame. They are mad and tone deaf. They are sufferers.

Moldorf, on the other hand, who suffers too in his peculiar way, is not mad. Moldorf is word drunk. He has no veins or blood vessels, no heart or kidneys. He is a portable trunk filled with innumerable drawers and in the drawers are labels written out in white ink, brown ink, red ink, blue ink, vermilion, saffron, mauve, sienna, apricot, turquoise, onyx, Anjou, herring, Corona, verdigris, gorgonzola. . . .

I have moved the typewriter into the next room where I can see myself in the mirror as I write.

Tania is like Irène. She expects fat letters. But there is another Tania, a Tania like a big seed, who scatters pollen everywhere—or, let us say, a little bit of Tolstoy, a stable scene in which the fetus is dug up. Tania is a fever, too—*les voies urinaires,* Café de la Liberté, Place des Vosges, bright neckties on the Boulevard Montparnasse, dark bathrooms, Poto Sec, Abdullah cigarettes, the adagio sonata *Pathétique,* aural amplificators, anecdotal seances, burnt sienna breasts, heavy garters, what time is it, golden pheasants stuffed with chestnuts, taffeta fingers, vaporish twilights turning to ilex, acromegaly, cancer and delirium, warm veils, poker chips, carpets of blood and soft thighs. Tania says so that every one may hear: "I love him!" And while Boris scalds himself with whisky she says: "Sit down here! O Boris . . . *Russia* . . . what'll I do? I'm bursting with it!"

At night when I look at Boris' goatee lying on the pillow I get hysterical. O Tania, where now is that warm cunt of yours, those fat, heavy garters, those soft, bulging thighs? There is a bone in my prick six inches long. I will ream out every wrinkle in your cunt, Tania, big with seed. I will send you home to your Sylvester with an ache in your belly and your womb turned inside out. Your Sylvester! Yes, he knows how to build a fire, but I know how to inflame a cunt. I shoot hot bolts into you, Tania, I make your ovaries incandescent. Your Sylvester is a little jealous now? He feels something, does he? He feels the remnants of my big prick. I have set the shores a little wider, I have ironed out the wrinkles. After me you can take on stallions, bulls, rams, drakes, St. Bernards. You can stuff toads, bats, lizards up your rectum. You can shit arpeggios if you like, or string a zither across your navel. I am fucking you, Tania, so that you'll stay fucked. And if you are afraid of being fucked publicly I will fuck you privately. I will tear off a few hairs from your cunt and paste them on Boris' chin. I will bite into your clitoris and spit out two franc pieces. . . .

OCTAVIO PAZ

❦

FROM *The Labyrinth of Solitude* [1961]

Translated from the Spanish by Lysander Kemp

The solitary Mexican loves fiestas and public gatherings. Any occasion for getting together will serve, any pretext to stop the flow of time and commemorate men and events with festivals and ceremonies. We are a ritual people, and this characteristic enriches both our imaginations and our sensibilities, which are equally sharp and alert. The art of the fiesta has been debased almost everywhere else, but not in Mexico. There are few places in the world where it is possible to take part in a spectacle like our great religious fiestas with their violent primary colors, their bizarre costumes and dances, their fireworks and ceremonies, and their inexhaustible welter of surprises: the fruit, candy, toys and other objects sold on these days in the plazas and open-air markets.

Our calendar is crowded with fiestas. There are certain days when the whole country, from the most remote villages to the largest cities, prays, shouts, feasts, gets drunk and kills, in honor of the Virgin of Guadalupe or Benito Juárez. Each year on the fifteenth of September, at eleven o'clock at night, we celebrate the fiesta of the *Grito*[1] in all the plazas of the Republic, and the excited crowds actually shout for a whole hour . . . the better, perhaps, to remain silent for the rest of the year. During the days before and after the twelfth of December,[2] time comes to a full stop, and instead of pushing us toward a deceptive tomorrow that is always beyond our reach, offers us a complete and perfect today of dancing and revelry, of communion with the most ancient and secret Mexico. Time is no longer succession, and becomes what it originally was and is: the present, in which past and future are reconciled.

But the fiestas which the Church and State provide for the country as a whole are not enough. The life of every city and village is ruled by a patron saint whose blessing is celebrated with devout regularity. Neighborhoods and trades also have their annual fiestas, their ceremonies and fairs. And each one

[1]Padre Hidalgo's call-to-arms against Spain, 1810.—*Tr.*
[2]Fiesta of the Virgin of Guadalupe.—*Tr.*

of us—atheist, Catholic, or merely indifferent—has his own saint's day, which he observes every year. It is impossible to calculate how many fiestas we have and how much time and money we spend on them. I remember asking the mayor of a village near Mitla, several years ago, "What is the income of the village government?" "About 3,000 pesos a year. We are very poor. But the Governor and the Federal Government always help us to meet our expenses." "And how are the 3,000 pesos spent?" "Mostly on fiestas, señor. We are a small village, but we have two patron saints."

This reply is not surprising. Our poverty can be measured by the frequency and luxuriousness of our holidays. Wealthy countries have very few: there is neither the time nor the desire for them, and they are not necessary. The people have other things to do, and when they amuse themselves they do so in small groups. The modern masses are agglomerations of solitary individuals. On great occasions in Paris or New York, when the populace gathers in the squares or stadiums, the absence of people, in the sense of *a* people, is remarkable: there are couples and small groups, but they never form a living community in which the individual is at once dissolved and redeemed. But how could a poor Mexican live without the two or three annual fiestas that make up for his poverty and misery? Fiestas are our only luxury. They replace, and are perhaps better than, the theater and vacations, Anglo-Saxon weekends and cocktail parties, the bourgeois reception, the Mediterranean café.

In all of these ceremonies—national or local, trade or family—the Mexican opens out. They all give him a chance to reveal himself and to converse with God, country, friends or relations. During these days the silent Mexican whistles, shouts, sings, shoots off fireworks, discharges his pistol into the air. He discharges his soul. And his shout, like the rockets we love so much, ascends to the heavens, explodes into green, red, blue, and white lights, and falls dizzily to earth with a trail of golden sparks. This is the night when friends who have not exchanged more than the prescribed courtesies for months get drunk together, trade confidences, weep over the same troubles, discover that they are brothers, and sometimes, to prove it, kill each other. The night is full of songs and loud cries. The lover wakes up his sweetheart with an orchestra. There are jokes and conversations from balcony to balcony, sidewalk to sidewalk. Nobody talks quietly. Hats fly in the air. Laughter and curses ring like silver pesos. Guitars are brought out. Now and then, it is true, the happiness ends badly, in quarrels, insults, pistol shots, stabbings. But these too are part of the fiesta, for the Mexican does not seek amusement: he seeks to escape from himself, to leap over the wall of solitude that confines him during the rest of the year. All are possessed by violence and frenzy. Their souls explode like the colors and voices and emotions. Do they forget themselves and show their true faces? Nobody knows. The important thing is to go out, open a way, get drunk on noise, people, colors. Mexico is celebrating a fiesta. And this fiesta, shot through with lightning and delirium, is the brilliant reverse to our silence and apathy, our reticence and gloom.

According to the interpretation of French sociologists, the fiesta is an excess, an expense. By means of this squandering the community protects itself against the envy of the gods or of men. Sacrifices and offerings placate or buy off the gods and the patron saints. Wasting money and expending energy affirms the community's wealth in both. This luxury is a proof of health, a show of abundance and power. Or a magic trap. For squandering is an effort to attract abundance by contagion. Money calls to money. When life is thrown away it increases; the orgy, which is sexual expenditure, is also a ceremony of regeneration; waste gives strength. New Year celebrations, in every culture, signify something beyond the mere observance of a date on the calendar. The day is a pause: time is stopped, is actually annihilated. The rites that celebrate its death are intended to provoke its rebirth, because they mark not only the end of an old year but also the beginning of a new. Everything attracts its opposite. The fiesta's function, then, is more utilitarian than we think: waste attracts or promotes wealth, and is an investment like any other, except that the returns on it cannot be measured or counted. What is sought is potency, life, health. In this sense the fiesta, like the gift and the offering, is one of the most ancient of economic forms.

This interpretation has always seemed to me to be incomplete. The fiesta is by nature sacred, literally or figuratively, and above all it is the advent of the unusual. It is governed by its own special rules, that set it apart from other days, and it has a logic, an ethic and even an economy that are often in conflict with everyday norms. It all occurs in an enchanted world: time is transformed to a mythical past or a total present; space, the scene of the fiesta, is turned into a gaily decorated world of its own; and the persons taking part cast off all human or social rank and become, for the moment, living images. And everything takes place as if it were not so, as if it were a dream. But whatever happens, our actions have a greater lightness, a different gravity. They take on other meanings and with them we contract new obligations. We throw down our burdens of time and reason.

In certain fiestas the very notion of order disappears. Chaos comes back and license rules. Anything is permitted: the customary hierarchies vanish, along with all social, sex, caste, and trade distinctions. Men disguise themselves as women, gentlemen as slaves, the poor as the rich. The army, the clergy, and the law are ridiculed. Obligatory sacrilege, ritual profanation is committed. Love becomes promiscuity. Sometimes the fiesta becomes a Black Mass. Regulations, habits and customs are violated. Respectable people put away the dignified expressions and conservative clothes that isolate them, dress up in gaudy colors, hide behind a mask, and escape from themselves.

Therefore the fiesta is not only an excess, a ritual squandering of the goods painfully accumulated during the rest of the year; it is also a revolt, a sudden immersion in the formless, in pure being. By means of the fiesta society frees itself from the norms it has established. It ridicules its gods, its principles, and its laws: it denies its own self.

The fiesta is a revolution in the most literal sense of the word. In the confusion that it generates, society is dissolved, is drowned, insofar as it is an organism ruled according to certain laws and principles. But it drowns in itself, in its own original chaos or liberty. Everything is united: good and evil, day and night, the sacred and the profane. Everything merges, loses shape and individuality and returns to the primordial mass. The fiesta is a cosmic experiment, an experiment in disorder, reuniting contradictory elements and principles in order to bring about a renascence of life. Ritual death promotes a rebirth; vomiting increases the appetite; the orgy, sterile in itself, renews the fertility of the mother or of the earth. The fiesta is a return to a remote and undifferentiated state, prenatal or presocial. It is a return that is also a beginning, in accordance with the dialectic that is inherent in social processes.

The group emerges purified and strengthened from this plunge into chaos. It has immersed itself in its own origins, in the womb from which it came. To express it in another way, the fiesta denies society as an organic system of differentiated forms and principles, but affirms it as a source of creative energy. It is a true "re-creation," the opposite of the "recreation" characterizing modern vacations, which do not entail any rites or ceremonies whatever and are as individualistic and sterile as the world that invented them.

Society communes with itself during the fiesta. Its members return to original chaos and freedom. Social structures break down and new relationships, unexpected rules, capricious hierarchies are created. In the general disorder everybody forgets himself and enters into otherwise forbidden situations and places. The bounds between audience and actors, officials and servants, are erased. Everybody takes part in the fiesta, everybody is caught up in its whirlwind. Whatever its mood, its character, its meaning, the fiesta is participation, and this trait distinguishes it from all other ceremonies and social phenomena. Lay or religious, orgy or saturnalia, the fiesta is a social act based on the full participation of all its celebrants.

Thanks to the fiesta the Mexican opens out, participates, communes with his fellows and with the values that give meaning to his religious or political existence. And it is significant that a country as sorrowful as ours should have so many and such joyous fiestas. Their frequency, their brilliance and excitement, the enthusiasm with which we take part, all suggest that without them we would explode. They free us, if only momentarily, from the thwarted impulses, the inflammable desires that we carry within us. But the Mexican fiesta is not merely a return to an original state of formless and normless liberty; the Mexican is not seeking to return, but to escape from himself, to exceed himself. Our fiestas are explosions. Life and death, joy and sorrow, music and mere noise are united, not to re-create or recognize themselves, but to swallow each other up. There is nothing so joyous as a Mexican fiesta, but there is also nothing so sorrowful. Fiesta night is also a night of mourning.

If we hide within ourselves in our daily lives, we discharge ourselves in the whirlwind of the fiesta. It is more than an opening out: we rend ourselves open. Everything—music, love, friendship—ends in tumult and violence. The frenzy of our festivals shows the extent to which our solitude closes us off from communication with the world. We are familiar with delirium, with songs and shouts, with the monologue . . . but not with the dialogue. Our fiestas, like our confidences, our loves, our attempts to reorder our society, are violent breaks with the old or the established. Each time we try to express ourselves we have to break with ourselves. And the fiesta is only one example, perhaps the most typical, of this violent break. It is not difficult to name others, equally revealing: our games, which are always a going to extremes, often mortal; our profligate spending, the reverse of our timid investments and business enterprises; our confessions. The somber Mexican, closed up in himself, suddenly explodes, tears open his breast and reveals himself, though not without a certain complacency, and not without a stopping place in the shameful or terrible mazes of his intimacy. We are not frank, but our sincerity can reach extremes that horrify a European. The explosive, dramatic, sometimes even suicidal manner in which we strip ourselves, surrender ourselves, is evidence that something inhibits and suffocates us. Something impedes us from being. And since we cannot or dare not confront our own selves, we resort to the fiesta. It fires us into the void; it is a drunken rapture that burns itself out, a pistol shot in the air, a skyrocket.

JORGE LUIS BORGES

"The Babylon Lottery" FROM Ficciones [1962]

Translated from the Spanish by Anthony Kerrigan

Like all men in Babylon I have been a proconsul; like all, a slave; I have also known omnipotence, opprobrium, jail. Look: the index finger of my right hand is missing. Look again: through this rent in my cape you can see a ruddy tatoo on my belly. It is the second symbol, Beth. This letter, on nights of full moon, gives me power over men whose mark is Ghimel; but it also subordinates me to those marked Aleph, who on moonless nights owe obedience to those marked Ghimel. In a cellar at dawn, I have severed the jugular vein of sacred bulls against a black rock. During one lunar year, I have been declared invisible: I shrieked and was not heard, I stole my bread and was not decapitated. I have known what the Greeks did not: uncertainty. In a bronze chamber, faced with the silent handkerchief of a strangler, hope has been faithful to me; in the river of delights, panic has not failed me. Heraclitus of Pontica admiringly relates that Pythagoras recalled having been Pyrrho, and before that Euphorbus, and before that some other mortal. In order to recall analogous vicissitudes I do not need to have recourse to death, nor even to imposture.

I owe this almost atrocious variety to an institution which other republics know nothing about, or which operates among them imperfectly and in secret: the lottery. I have not delved into its history; I do know that the wizards have been unable to come to any agreement; of its powerful designs I know what a man not versed in astrology might know of the moon. I come from a vertiginous country where the lottery forms a principal part of reality: until this very day I have thought about all this as little as I have about the behavior of the indecipherable gods or about the beating of my own heart. Now, far from Babylon and its beloved customs, I think of the lottery with some astonishment and ponder the blasphemous conjectures murmured by men in the shadows at twilight.

My father related that anciently—a matter of centuries; of years?—the lottery in Babylon was a game of plebeian character. He said (I do not know with what degree of truth) that barbers gave rectangular bits of bone or decorated parchment in exchange for copper coins. A drawing of the lottery was held in the middle of the day: the winners received, without further corroboration from chance, silver-minted coins. The procedure, as you see, was elemental.

Naturally, these "lotteries" failed. Their moral virtue was nil. They did not appeal to all the faculties of men: only to their hope. In the face of public indifference, the merchants who established these venal lotteries began to lose money. Someone attempted to introduce a slight reform: the interpolation of a certain small number of adverse outcomes among the favored numbers. By means of this reform, the purchasers of numbered rectangles stood the double chance of winning a sum or of paying a fine often considerable in size. This slight danger—for each thirty favored numbers there would be one adverse number—awoke, as was only natural, the public's interest. The Babylonians gave themselves up to the game. Anyone who did not acquire lots was looked upon as pusillanimous, mean-spirited. In time, this disdain multiplied. The person who did not play was despised, but the losers who paid the fine were also scorned. The Company (thus it began to be known at that time) was forced to take measures to protect the winners, who could not collect their prizes unless nearly the entire amount of the fines was already collected. The Company brought suit against the losers: the judge condemned them to pay the original fine plus costs or to spend a number of days in jail. Every loser chose jail, so as to defraud the Company. It was from this initial bravado of a few men that the all-powerful position of the Company—its ecclesiastical, metaphysical strength—was derived.

A short while later, the reports on the drawings omitted any enumeration of fines and limited themselves to publishing the jail sentences corresponding to each adverse number. This laconism, almost unnoticed at the time, became of capital importance. *It constituted the first appearance in the lottery of non-pecuniary elements.* Its success was great. Pushed to such a measure by the players, the Company found itself forced to increase its adverse numbers.

No one can deny that the people of Babylonia are highly devoted to logic, even to symmetry. It struck them as incoherent that the fortunate numbers should be computed in round figures of money while the unfortunate should be figured in terms of days and nights in jail. Some moralists argued that the possession of money does not determine happiness and that other forms of fortune are perhaps more immediate.

There was another source of restlessness in the lower depths. The members of the sacerdotal college multiplied the stakes and plumbed the vicissitudes of terror and hope; the poor, with reasonable or inevitable envy, saw themselves excluded from this notoriously delicious exhiliration. The just anxiety of all, poor and rich alike, to participate equally in the lottery, inspired an indignant agitation, the memory of which the years have not erased. Certain obstinate souls did not comprehend, or pretended not to comprehend, that a new order had come, a necessary historical stage. . . . A slave stole a crimson ticket, a ticket which earned him the right to have his tongue burned in the next drawing. The criminal code fixed the same penalty for the theft of a ticket. A number of Babylonians argued that he deserved a red-hot poker by virtue of the theft; others, more magnanimous, held that the public executioner should apply the penalty of the lottery, since chance had so determined . . .

Disturbances broke out, there was a lamentable shedding of blood; but the people of Babylon imposed their will at last, over the opposition of the rich. That is: the people fully achieved their magnanimous ends. In the first place, it made the Company accept complete public power. (This unification was necessary, given the vastness and complexity of the new operations.) In the second place, it forced the lottery to be secret, free, and general. The sale of tickets for money was abolished. Once initiated into the mysteries of Bel, every free man automatically participated in the sacred drawings of lots, which were carried out in the labyrinths of the gods every seventy nights and which determined every man's fate until the next exercise. The consequences were incalculable. A happy drawing might motivate his elevation to the council of wizards or his condemnation to the custody of an enemy (notorious or intimate), or to find, in the peaceful shadows of a room, the woman who had begun to disquiet him or whom he had never expected to see again. An adverse drawing might mean mutilation, a varied infamy, death. Sometimes a single event—the tavern killing of C, the mysterious glorification of B—might be the brilliant result of thirty or forty drawings. But it must be recalled that the individuals of the Company were (and are) all-powerful and astute as well. In many cases, the knowledge that certain joys were the simple doing of chance might have detracted from their exellence; to avoid this inconvenience the Company's agents made use of suggestion and magic. Their moves, their management, were secret. In the investigation of people's intimate hopes and intimate terrors, they made use of astrologers and spies. There were certain stone lions, there was a sacred privy called Qaphqa, there were fissures in a dusty aqueduct which, according to general opinion, *led to the Company;* malign or benevolent people deposited accusations in these cracks. These denunciations were incorporated into an alphabetical archive of variable veracity.

Incredibly enough, there were still complaints. The Company, with its habitual discretion, did not reply directly. It preferred to scribble a brief argument—which now figures among sacred scriptures—in the debris of a mask factory. That doctrinal piece of literature observed that the lottery is an interpolation of chance into the order of the world and that to accept errors is not to contradict fate but merely to corroborate it. It also observed that those lions and that sacred recipient, though not unauthorized by the Company (which did not renounce the right to consult them), functioned without official guaranty.

This declaration pacified the public unease. It also produced other effects, not foreseen by the author. It deeply modified the spirit and operations of the Company. (I have little time left to tell what I know; we have been warned that the ship is ready to sail; but I will attempt to explain it.)

Improbable as it may be, no one had until then attempted to set up a general theory of games. A Babylonian is not highly speculative. He reveres the judgments of fate, he hands his life over to them, he places his hopes, his panic terror in them, but it never occurs to him to investigate their labyrinthian laws nor the giratory spheres which disclose them. Nevertheless, the unofficial declaration which I have mentioned inspired many discussions of a juridico-mathematical nature. From one of these discussions was born the following conjecture: if the lottery is an intensification of chance, a periodic infusion of chaos into the cosmos, would it not be desirable for chance to intervene at all stages of the lottery and not merely in the drawing? Is it not ridiculous for chance to dictate the death of someone, while the circumstances of his death—its silent reserve or publicity, the time limit of one hour or one century—should remain immune to hazard? These eminently just scruples finally provoked a considerable reform, whose complexities (intensified by the practice of centuries) are not understood except by a handful of specialists, but which I will attempt to summarize, even if only in a symbolic manner.

Let us imagine a first drawing, which eventuates in a sentence of death against some individual. To carry out the sentence, another drawing is set up, and this drawing proposes (let us say) nine possible executioners. Of these executioners, four can initiate a third drawing which will reveal the name of the actual executioner, two others can replace the adverse order with a fortunate order (the finding of a treasure, let us say), another may exacerbate the death sentence (that is: make it infamous or enrich it with torture), still others may refuse to carry it out. . . .

Such is the symbolic scheme. In reality, *the number of drawings is infinite*. No decision is final, all diverge into others. The ignorant suppose that an infinite number of drawings require an infinite amount of time; in reality, it is quite enough that time be infinitely subdivisible, as is the case in the famous parable of the Tortoise and the Hare. This infinitude harmonizes in an admirable manner with the sinuous numbers of Chance and of the Celestial Archetype of the Lottery adored by the Platonists. . . .

A certain distorted echo of our ritual seems to have resounded along the Tiber: Aelius Lampridius, in his *Life of Antoninus Heliogabalus*, tells of how this emperor wrote down the lot of his guests on seashells, so that one would receive ten pounds of gold and another ten flies, ten dormice, ten bears. It is only right to remark that Heliogabalus was educated in Asia Minor, among the priests of the eponymous god.

There are also impersonal drawings, of undefined purpose: one drawing will decree that a sapphire from Taprobane be thrown into the waters of the Euphrates; another, that a bird be released from a tower roof; another, that a grain of sand be withdrawn (or added) to the innumerable grains on a beach. The consequences, sometimes, are terrifying.

Under the beneficent influence of the Company, our customs have become thoroughly impregnated with chance. The buyer of a dozen amphoras of Damascus wine will not be surprised if one of them contains a talisman or a viper. The scribe who draws up a contract scarcely ever fails to introduce some erroneous datum; I myself, in making this hasty declaration, have falsified or invented some grandeur, some atrocity; perhaps, too, a certain mysterious monotony. . . .

Our historians, the most discerning in the world, have invented a method for correcting chance. It is well known that the operations of this method are (in general) trustworthy; although, naturally, they are not divulged without a measure of deceit. In any case, there is nothing so contaminated with fiction as the history of the Company. . . .

A paleographic document, unearthed in a temple, may well be the work of yesterday's drawing or that of one lasting a century. No book is ever published without some variant in each copy. Scribes take a secret oath to omit, interpolate, vary.

The Company, with divine modesty, eludes all publicity. Its agents, as is only natural, are secret. The orders which it is continually sending out do not differ from those lavishly issued by imposters. Besides, who can ever boast of being a mere imposter? The inebriate who improvises an absurd mandate, the dreamer who suddenly awakes to choke the woman who lies at his side to death, do they not both, perhaps, carry out a secret decision by the Company? This silent functioning, comparable to that of God, gives rise to all manner of conjectures. One of them, for instance, abominably insinuates that the Company is eternal and that it will last until the last night of the world, when the last god annihilates the cosmos. Still another conjecture declares that the Company is omnipotent, but that it exerts its influence only in the most minute matters: in a bird's cry, in the shades of rust and the hues of dust, in the cat naps of dawn. There is one conjecture, spoken from the mouths of masked heresiarchs, to the effect that *the Company has never existed and never will*. A conjecture no less vile argues that it is indifferently inconsequential to affirm or deny the reality of the shadowy corporation, because Babylon is nothing but an infinite game of chance.

"... A Devastating Ridicule of All That Is False ..." [1964]

In life there is that which is funny, and there is that which is politely *supposed* to be funny. Literature, out of a misguided appeal to an imaginary popular taste and the caution of self-distrust, generally follows the latter course, so that the humor found in books is almost always vicarious—meeting certain "traditional" requirements, and producing only the kind of laughter one might expect: rather strained. Burroughs' work is an all-stops-out departure from this practice, and he invariably writes at the very top of his ability.

The element of humor in *Naked Lunch* is one of the book's great moral strengths, whereby the existentialist sense of the *absurd* is taken towards an informal conclusion. It is an absolutely devastating ridicule of all that is false, primitive, and vicious in current American life: the abuses of power, hero worship, aimless violence, materialistic obsession, intolerance, and every form of hypocrisy. No one, for example, has written with such eloquent disgust about capital punishment; throughout *Naked Lunch* recur sequences to portray the unfathomable barbarity of a "civilization" which can countenance this ritual. There is only one way, of course, to ridicule capital punishment—and that is by exaggerating its circumstances, increasing its horror, accentuating the animal irresponsibility of those involved, *insisting* that the monstrous deed be witnessed (and in Technicolor, so to speak) by all concerned. Burroughs is perhaps the first modern writer to seriously attempt this; he is certainly the first to have done so with such startling effectiveness. Social analogy and parallels of this sort abound in *Naked Lunch*, but one must never mistake this author's work for political comment, which, as in all genuine art, is more instinctive than deliberate—for Burroughs is first and foremost a poet. His attunement to contemporary language is probably unequalled in American writing. Anyone with a feeling for English phrase at its most balanced, concise, and arresting cannot fail to see this excellence. For example, in describing the difficulty of obtaining narcotics-prescriptions from wary doctors in the southwestern United States, he writes:

"Itinerant short con and carny hyp men have burned down the croakers of Texas ..."

None of these words are new, but the sudden freshness of using "burned down" (to mean "having exploited beyond further possibility") in this prosaic context indicates his remarkable power of giving life to a dead vernacular.

Or again, where the metaphysical finds expression in slang:

"One day Little Boy Blue starts to slip, and what crawls out would make an ambulance attendant puke . . ."

And, psychological:

"The Mark Inside was coming up on him and that's a rumble nobody can cool . . ."

Imagery of this calibre puts the use of argot on a level considerably beyond merely "having a good ear for the spoken word." Compared to Burroughs' grasp of modern idiom in almost every form of English—and his ability at distillation and ellipsis—the similiar efforts of Ring Lardner, and of Hemingway, appear amateurish and groping.

The role of drugs is of singular importance in Burroughs' work, as it is, indeed, in American life. In no other culture in the history of the world has the use of narcotics, both legal and illicit, become so strange and integral a part of the overall scene. And reviviscent addiction has reached such prevalence and intensity that, in the larger view, it can no longer matter whether it be considered a "crime" or a "sickness"—it is a cultural phenomenon with far more profound implications than either diagnosis suggests.

Burroughs' treatment of narcotics, like his treatment of homosexuality, ranges from that of personal psychology, through the sociological, and finally into pure metaphor. And he is perhaps the first writer to treat either with both humor and humility.

Although *Naked Lunch,* and his second novel, *The Soft Machine,* have not been available (except clandestinely) in either America or England—ostensibly because of the preponderance of "obscene words"—they have had, in their Paris editions, an extremely wide reading among the creatively inclined of both countries. No one writing in English, with the exception of Henry Miller, has done so much towards freeing the reader of the superstitions surrounding the use of certain words and certain attitudes. And it is safe to add that for the new generation of American writers the work of William Burroughs is by far the most seriously influential being done today.

WILLIAM S. BURROUGHS

❧

FROM *Naked Lunch* [1962]

1. *Meeting of International Conference of Technological Psychiatry*

Doctor "Fingers" Schafer, the Lobotomy Kid, rises and turns on the Conferents the cold blue blast of his gaze:

"Gentlemen, the human nervous system can be reduced to a compact and abbreviated spinal column. The brain, front, middle and rear must follow the adenoid, the wisdom tooth, the appendix. . . . I give you my Master Work: *The Complete All American Deanxietized Man*. . . ."

Blast of trumpets: The Man is carried in naked by two Negro Bearers who drop him on the platform with bestial, sneering brutality. . . . The Man wriggles. . . . His flesh turns to viscid, transparent jelly that drifts away in green mist, unveiling a monster black centipede. Waves of unknown stench fill the room, searing the lungs, grabbing the stomach. . . .

Schafer wrings his hands sobbing: "Clarence!! How can you do this to me?? Ingrates!! Every one of them ingrates!!"

The Conferents start back muttering in dismay:

"I'm afraid Schafer has gone a bit too far. . . ."

"I sounded a word of warning. . . ."

"Brilliant chap Schafer . . . but . . ."

"Man will do anything for publicity. . . ."

"Gentlemen, this unspeakable and in every sense illegitimate child of Doctor Schafer's perverted brain must not see the light. . . . Our duty to the human race is clear. . . ."

"Man he done seen the light," said one of the Negro Bearers.

"We must stomp out the Un-American crittah," says a fat, frog-faced Southern doctor who has been drinking corn out of a mason jar. He advances drunkenly, then halts, appalled by the formidable size and menacing aspect of the centipede. . . .

"Fetch gasoline!" he bellows. "We gotta burn the son of a bitch like an uppity Nigra!"

"I'm not sticking my neck out, me," says a cool hip young doctor high on LSD25. . . . "Why a smart D.A. could . . ."

Fadeout. "Order in The Court!"

D.A.: "Gentlemen of the jury, these 'learned gentlemen' claim that the innocent human creature they have so wantonly slain suddenly turned himself into a huge black centipede and it was 'their duty to the human race' to destroy this monster before it could, by any means at its disposal, perpetrate its kind. . . .

"Are we to gulp down this tissue of horse shit? Are we to take these glib lies like a greased and nameless asshole? Where *is* this wondrous centipede?

"'We have destroyed it,' they say smugly. . . . And I would like to remind you, Gentlemen and Hermaphrodites of the Jury, that this Great Beast"— he points to Doctor Schafer—"has, on several previous occasions, appeared in this court charged with the unspeakable crime of brain rape. . . . In plain English"—he pounds the rail of the jury box, his voice rises to a scream—"in plain English, Gentlemen, *forcible lobotomy*. . . ."

The Jury gasps. . . . One dies of a heart attack. . . . Three fall to the floor writhing in orgasms of prurience. . . .

The D.A. points dramatically: "He it is . . . He and no other who has reduced whole provinces of our fair land to a state bordering on the far side of idiocy. . . . He it is who has filled great warehouses with row on row, tier on tier of helpless creatures who must have their every want attended. . . . 'The Drones' he calls them with a cynical leer of pure educated evil. . . . Gentlemen, I say to you that the wanton murder of Clarence Cowie must not go unavenged: This foul crime shrieks like a wounded faggot for justice at least!"

The centipede is rushing about in agitation.

"Man, that mother fucker's hungry," screams one of the Bearers.

"I'm getting out of here, me."

A wave of electric horror sweeps through the Conferents. . . . They storm the exits screaming and clawing. . . .

2. *The County Clerk*

The County Clerk has his office in a huge red brick building known as the Old Court House. Civil cases are, in fact, tried there, the proceeding inexorably dragging out until the contestants die or abandon litigation. This is due to the vast number of records pertaining to absolutely everything, all filed in the wrong place so that no one but the County Clerk and his staff of assistants can find them, and he often spends years in the search. In fact, he is still looking for material relative to a damage suit that was settled out of court in 1910. Large sections of the Old Court House have fallen in ruins, and others are highly dangerous owing to frequent cave-ins. The County Clerk assigns the more dangerous missions to his assistants, many of whom have lost their lives in the service. In 1912 two hundred and seven assistants were trapped in a collapse of the North-by-North-East wing.

When suit is brought against anyone in the Zone, his lawyers connive to have the case transferred to the Old Court House. Once this is done, the plaintiff has lost the case, so the only cases that actually go to trial in the Old Court House are those instigated by eccentrics and paranoids who want "a public hearing," which they rarely get since only the most desperate famine of news will bring a reporter to the Old Court House.

The Old Court House is located in the town of Pigeon Hole outside the urban zone. The inhabitants of this town and the surrounding area of swamps and heavy timber are people of such great stupidity and such barbarous practices that the Administration has seen fit to quarantine them in a reservation surrounded by a radioactive wall of iron bricks. In retaliation the citizens of Pigeon Hole plaster their town with signs: *"Urbanite Don't Let The Sun Set On You Here,"* an unnecessary injunction, since nothing but urgent business would take any urbanite to Pigeon Hole.

Lee's case is urgent. He has to file an immediate affidavit that he is suffering from bubonic plague to avoid eviction from the house he has occupied ten years without paying the rent. He exists in perpetual quarantine. So he packs his suitcase of affidavits and petitions and injunctions and certificates and takes a bus to the Frontier. The Urbanite customs inspector waves him through: "I hope you've got an atom bomb in that suitcase."

Lee swallows a handful of tranquilizing pills and steps into the Pigeon Hole customs shed. The inspectors spend three hours pawing through his papers, consulting dusty books of regulations and duties from which they read incomprehensible and ominous excerpts ending with: "And as such is subject to fine and penalty under act 666." They look at him significantly.

They go through his papers with a magnifying glass.

"Sometimes they slip dirty limericks between the lines."

"Maybe he figures to sell them for toilet paper. Is this crap for your own personal use?"

"Yes."

"He says yes."

"And how do we know that?"

"I gotta affidavit."

"Wise guy. Take off your clothes."

"Yeah. Maybe he got dirty tattoos."

They paw over his body probing his ass for contraband and examine it for evidence of sodomy. They dunk his hair and send the water out to be analyzed. "Maybe he's got dope in his hair."

Finally, they impound his suitcase; and he staggers out of the shed with a fifty pound bale of documents.

A dozen or so Recordites sit on the Old Court House steps of rotten wood. They watch his approach with pale blue eyes, turning their heads slow on wrinkled necks (the wrinkles full of dust) to follow his body up the steps and through the door. Inside, dust hangs in the air like fog, sifting down from the ceiling, rising in clouds from the floor as he walks. He mounts a perilous staircase—condemned in 1929. Once his foot goes through, and the dry splinters tear into the flesh of his leg. The staircase ends in a painter's scaffold, attached with frayed rope and pullies to a beam almost invisible in dusty distance. He pulls himself up cautiously to a ferris wheel cabin. His weight sets in motion hydraulic machinery (sound of running water). The wheel moves smooth and silent to stop by a rusty iron balcony, worn through here and there like an old shoe sole. He walks down a long corridor lined with doors, most of them nailed or boarded shut. In one office, *Near East Exquisitries* on a green brass plaque, the Mugwump is catching termites with his long black tongue. The door of the County Clerk's office is open. The County Clerk sits inside gumming snuff, surrounded by six assistants. Lee stands in the doorway. The County Clerk goes on talking without looking up.

"I run into Ted Spigot the other day . . . a good old boy, too. Not a finer man in the Zone than Ted Spigot. . . . Now it was a Friday I happen to remember because the Old Lady was down with the menstral cramps and I went to Doc Parker's drugstore on Dalton Street, just opposite Ma Green's Ethical Massage Parlor, where Jed's old livery stable used to be. . . . Now, Jed, I'll remember his second name directly, had a cast in the left eye and his wife came from some place out East, Algiers I believe it was, and after Jed died she married up again, and she married one of the Hoot boys, Clem Hoot if my memory serves, a good old boy too, now Hoot was around fifty-four fifty-five year old at the time. . . . So I says to Doc Parker: 'My old lady is down bad with the menstral cramps. Sell me two ounces of paregoric.'

"So Doc says, 'Well, Arch, you gotta sign the book. Name, address and date of purchase. It's the law.'

"So I asked Doc what the day was, and he said, 'Friday the 13th.'

"So I said, 'I guess I already had mine.'

"'Well,' Doc says, 'there was a feller in here this morning. City feller. Dressed kinda flashy. So he's got him a RX for a mason jar of morphine. . . . Kinda funny looking prescription writ out on toilet paper. . . . And I told him straight out: "Mister, I suspect you to be a dope fiend."

"'"I got the ingrowing toe nails, Pop. I'm in agony,"' he says.

"'"Well," I says, "I gotta be careful. But so long as you got a legitimate condition and an RX from a certified bona feedy M.D., I'm honored to serve you."

"'"That croaker's really certified," he say. . . . 'Well, I guess one hand didn't know what the other was doing when I give him a jar of Saniflush by error. . . . So I reckon he's had his too.'

"'Just the thing to clean a man's blood.'

"'You know, that very thing occurred to me. Should be a sight better than sulphur and molasses. . . . Now, Arch, don't think I'm nosey; but a man don't have no secrets from God and his druggist I always say. . . . Is you still humping the Old Gray Mare?'

"'Why, Doc Parker. . . . I'll have you know I'm a family man and an Elder in the First Denominational Non-sextarian Church and I ain't had a piecea hoss ass since we was kids together.'

"'Them was the days, Arch. Remember the time I got the goose grease mixed up with the mustard? Always was a one to grab the wrong jar, feller say. They could have heard you squealing over in Cunt Lick County, just asquealing like a stoat with his stones cut off.'

"'You're in the wrong hole, Doc. It was you took the mustard and me as had to wait till you cooled off.'

"'Wistful thinking, Arch. I read about it one time inna magazin settin' in that green outhouse behind the station. . . . Now what I meant awhile back, Arch, you didn't rightly understand me. . . . I was referring to your wife as the Old Gray Mare. . . . I mean she ain't what she used to be what with all them carbuncles and cataracts and chilblains and haemorrhoids and aftosa.'

"'Yas, Doc, Liz is right sickly. Never was the same after her eleventh miscarriaging. . . . There was something right strange about that. Doc Ferris he told me straight, he said: "Arch, 'tain't fitting you should see that critter." And he gives me a long look made my flesh crawl. . . . Well, you sure said it right, Doc. She ain't what she used to be. In fact, she ain't been able to tell night from day since using them eye drops you sold her last month. . . . But, Doc, you oughtta know I wouldn't be humping Liz, the old cow, meaning no disrespect to the mother of my dead monsters. Not when I got that sweet little ol' fifteen year old thing. . . . You know that yaller girl used to work in Marylou's Hair Straightening and Skin Bleach Parlor over in Nigga town.'

"'Getting that dark chicken meat, Arch? Gettin' that coon pone?'

"'Gettin' it steady, Doc. Gettin' it steady. Well, feller say duty is goosing me. Gotta get back to the old crank case.'

"'I'll bet she needs a grease job worst way.'

"'Doc, she sure is a dry hole. . . . Well, thanks for the paregoric.'

"'And thanks for the trade, Arch. . . . He he he. . . . Say, Archy boy, some night when you get caught short with a rusty load drop around and have a drink of Yohimbiny with me.'

"'I'll do that, Doc, I sure will. It'll be just like old times.'

"So I went on back to my place and heated up some water and mixed up some paregoric and cloves and cinnamon and sassyfrass and give it to Liz, and it eased her some I reckon. Leastwise she let up aggravatin' me. . . . Well, later on I went down to Doc Parker's again to get me a rubber . . . and just as I was leaving I run into Roy Bane, a good ol' boy too. There's not a finer man in this Zone than Roy Bane. . . . So he said to me he says, 'Arch, you see that ol' nigger over there in that vacant lot? Well, sure as shit and taxes, he comes there every night just as regular you can set your watch by him. See him behind them nettles? Every night round about eight thirty he goes over into that lot yonder and pulls himself off with steel wool. . . . Preachin' Nigger, they tell me.'

"So that's how I come to know the hour more or less on Friday the 13th and it couldn't have been more than twenty minutes half an hour after that, I'd took some Spanish Fly in Doc's store and it was jest beginning to work on me down by Grennel Bog on my way to Nigger town. . . . Well the bog makes a bend, used to be nigger shack there. . . . They burned that ol' nigger over in Cunt Lick. Nigger had the aftosa and it left him stone blind. . . . So this white girl down from Texarkana screeches out:

"'Roy, that ol' nigger is looking at me so nasty. Land's sake I feel just dirty all over.'

"'Now, Sweet Thing, don't you fret yourself. Me an' the boys will burn him.'

"'Do it slow, Honey Face. Do it slow. He's give me a sick headache.'

"So they burned the nigger and that ol' boy took his wife and went back up to Texarkana without paying for the gasoline and old Whispering Lou runs the service station couldn't talk about nothing else all Fall: 'These city fellers come down here and burn a nigger and don't even settle up for the gasoline.'

"Well, Chester Hoot tore that nigger shack down and rebuilt it just back of his house up in Bled Valley. Covered up all the windows with black cloth, and what goes on in there ain't fittin' to speak of. . . . Now Chester he's got some right strange ways. . . . Well it was just where the nigger shack used to be, right across from the Old Brooks place floods out every Spring, only it wasn't the Brooks place then . . . belonged to a feller name of Scranton. Now that piece of land was surveyed back in 1919. . . . I reckon you know the man did the job too. . . . Feller name of Hump Clarence used to witch out wells on the side. . . . Good ol' boy too, not a finer man in this Zone than Hump Clarence. . . . Well it was just around about in there I come on Ted Spigot ascrewin a mud puppy."

Lee cleared his throat. The Clerk looked up over his glasses. "Now if you'll take care, young feller, till I finish what I'm asaying, I'll tend to your business."

And he plunged into an anecdote about a nigra got the hydrophobia from a cow.

"So my pappy says to me: 'Finish up your chores, son, and let's go see the mad nigger. . . .' They had that nigger chained to the bed, and he was bawling like a cow. . . . I soon got enough of that ol' nigger. Well, if you all will excuse me I got business in the Privy Council. He he he!"

Lee listened in horror. The County Clerk often spent weeks in the privy living on scorpions and Montgomery Ward catalogues. On several occasions his assistants had forced the door and carried him out in an advanced state of malnutrition. Lee decided to play his last card.

"Mr. Anker," he said, "I'm appealing to you as one Razor Back to another," and he pulled out his Razor Back card, a memo of his lush-rolling youth.

The Clerk looked at the card suspiciously: "You don't look like a bone feed mast-fed Razor Back to me. . . . What you think about the Jeeeeews. . . ?"

"Well, Mr. Anker, you know yourself all a Jew wants to do is doodle a Christian girl. . . . One of these days we'll cut the rest of it off."

"Well, you talk right sensible for a city feller. . . . Find out what he wants and take care of him. . . . He's a good ol' boy."

FRANK HARRIS

❦

FROM *My Life and Loves* [1963]

Memory is the Mother of the Muses, the prototype of the artist. As a rule she selects and relieves out the important, omitting what is accidental or trivial. Now and then, however, she makes mistakes, like all other artists. Nevertheless, I take memory in the main as my guide.

I was born on the 14th of February, 1855, and named James Thomas, after my father's two brothers; my father was in the navy, a lieutenant in command of a revenue cutter or gunboat, and we children saw him only at long intervals.

My earliest recollection is being danced on the foot of my father's brother James, the captain of an Indiaman, who paid us a visit in the south of Kerry when I was about two. I distinctly remember repeating a hymn by heart for him, my mother on the other side of the fireplace, prompting: then I got him to dance me a little more, which was all I wanted. I remember my mother telling him I could read, and his surprise.

The next memory must have been about the same time; I was seated on the floor screaming when my father came in and asked: "What's the matter?"

"It's only Master Jim," replied the nurse crossly; "he's just screaming out of sheer temper, Sir. Look, there's not a tear in his eye."

A year or so later, it must have been, I was proud of walking up and down a long room while my mother rested her hand on my head and called me her walking stick.

Later still I remember coming to her room at night. I whispered to her and then kissed her, but her cheek was cold and she didn't answer, and I woke the house with my shrieking—she was dead. I felt no grief, but something gloomy and terrible in the sudden cessation of the usual household activities.

A couple of days later I saw her coffin carried out, and when the nurse told my sister and me that we would never see our mother again I was surprised merely and wondered why.

My mother died when I was nearly four and soon after we moved to Kingstown near Dublin. I used to get up in the night with my sister Annie, four years my senior, and go foraging for bread and jam or sugar. One morning about daybreak I stole into the nurse's room and saw a man beside her in bed, a man with a red mustache. I drew my sister in and she too saw him. We crept out again without waking them. My only emotion was surprise, but next day the nurse denied me sugar on my bread and butter, and I said: "I'll tell!" I don't know why; I had no inkling then of modern journalism.

"Tell what?" she asked.

"There was a man in your bed last night," I replied.

"Hush, hush!" she said, and gave me the sugar.

After that I found all I had to do was to say "I'll tell!" to get whatever I wanted. My sister even wished to know one day what I had to tell, but I would not say. I distinctly remember my feeling of superiority over her because she had not sense enough to exploit the sugar mine.

When I was between four and five, I was sent with Annie to a girls' boarding school in Kingstown kept by a Mrs. Frost. I was put in the class with the oldest girls on account of my proficiency in arithmetic, and I did my best at it because I wanted to be with them, though I had no conscious reason for my preference. I remember how the nearest girl used to lift me up and put me in my high-chair and how I would hurry over the sums set in compound long division and proportion; for as soon as I had finished, I would drop my pencil on the floor and then turn around and climb down out of my chair, ostensibly to get it, but really to look at the girls' legs. Why? I couldn't have said.

I was at the bottom of the class and the legs got bigger and bigger towards the end of the long table and I preferred to look at the big ones.

As soon as the girl next to me missed me she would move her chair back and call me. I'd pretend to have just found my slate pencil which, I said, had rolled; and she'd lift me back into my high-chair.

One day I noticed a beautiful pair of legs on the other side of the table near the top. There must have been a window behind the girl, for her legs up to the knees were in full light. They filled me with emotion, giving me an indescribable pleasure. They were not the thickest legs, which surprised me. Up to that moment I had thought it was the thickest legs I liked best but now I saw that several girls, three anyway, had bigger legs; but none like hers, so shapely, with such slight ankles and tapering lines. I was enthralled and at the same time a little scared.

I crept back into my chair with one idea in my little head: could I get close to those lovely legs and perhaps touch them—breathless expectancy! I knew I could hit my slate pencil and make it roll up between the files of legs. Next day I did this and crawled right up till I was close to the legs that made my heart beat in my throat and yet gave me a strange delight. I put out my hand to touch them.

Suddenly the thought came that the girl would simply be frightened by my touch and pull her legs back and I should be discovered and—I was frightened.

I returned to my chair to think and soon found the solution. Next day I again crouched before the girl's legs, choking with emotion. I put my pencil near her toes and reached round between her legs with my left hand as if to get it, taking care to touch her calf. She shrieked and drew back her legs, holding my hand tight between them, and cried: "What are you doing there?"

"Getting my pencil," I said humbly. "It rolled."

"There it is," she said, kicking it with her foot.

"Thanks," I replied, overjoyed, for the feel of her soft legs was still on my hand.

"You're a funny little fellow," she said. But I didn't care. I had had my first taste of paradise and the forbidden fruit—authentic heaven!

I have no recollection of her face—it seemed pleasant, that's all I remember. None of the girls made any impression on me but I can still recall the thrill of admiration and pleasure her shapely limbs gave me.

I record this incident at length because it stands alone in my memory and because it shows that sex feeling may manifest itself in early childhood.

One day about 1890 I had Meredith, Walter Pater and Oscar Wilde* dining with me in Park Lane and the time of sex-awakening was discussed. Both Pater and Wilde spoke of it as a sign of puberty. Pater thought it began about thirteen or fourteen and Wilde to my amazement set it as late as sixteen. Meredith alone was inclined to put it earlier.

"It shows sporadically," he said, "and sometimes before puberty."

I recalled the fact that Napoleon tells how he was in love before he was five years old with a schoolmate called Giacominetta, but even Meredith laughed at this and would not believe that any real sex feeling could show itself so early. To prove the point I gave my experience as I have told it here and brought Meredith to pause. "Very interesting," he thought, "but peculiar!"

"In her abnormalities," says Goethe, "nature reveals her secrets." Here is an abnormality, perhaps as such, worth noting.

I hadn't another sensation of sex till nearly six years later when I was eleven, since which time such emotions have been almost incessant.

My exaltation to the oldest class in arithmetic got me into trouble by bringing me into relations with the head-mistress, Mrs. Frost, who was very cross

---

*George Meredith (1828–1909); Harris talks about him at length in vols. I, II. Pater (1839–94). Wilde (1854–1900), of whom Harris has written a fascinating, vastly underrated biography; it is perhaps Harris' best work.

and seemed to think that I should spell as correctly as I did sums. When she found I couldn't, she used to pull my ears and got into the habit of digging her long thumb nail into my ear till it bled. I didn't mind the smart; in fact, I was delighted, for her cruelty brought me the pity of the elder girls who used to wipe my ears with their pocket-handkerchiefs and say that old Frost was a beast and a cat.

One day my father sent for me and I went with a petty officer to his vessel in the harbor. My right ear had bled onto my collar. As soon as my father noticed it and saw the older scars he got angry and took me back to the school and told Mrs. Frost what he thought of her and her punishments.

Immediately afterwards, it seems to me, I was sent to live with my eldest brother Vernon, ten years older than myself, who was in lodgings with friends in Galway while going to college.

There I spent the next five years, which passed leaving a blank. I learned nothing in those years except how to play "tag," "hide and seek," "footer" and "ball." I was merely a healthy, strong little animal without an ache or pain or trace of thought.

Then I remember an interlude at Belfast where Vernon and I lodged with an old Methodist who used to force me to go to church with him and drew on a little black skull-cap during the service, which filled me with shame and made me hate him. There is a period in life when everything peculiar or individual excites dislike and is in itself an offense.

I learned here to "mitch" and lie simply to avoid school and to play, till my brother found I was coughing, and having sent for a doctor, was informed that I had congestion of the lungs; the truth being that I played all day and never came home for dinner, seldom indeed before seven o'clock, when I knew Vernon would be back. I mention this incident because, while confined to the house, I discovered under the old Methodist's bed a set of doctor's books with colored plates of the insides and pudenda of men and women. I devoured all the volumes, and bits of knowledge from them stuck to me for many a year. Curiously enough, the main sex fact was not revealed to me then, but in talks a little later with boys of my own age.

I learned nothing in Belfast but rules of games and athletics. My brother Vernon used to go to a gymnasium every evening and exercise and box. To my astonishment he was not among the best; so while he was boxing I began practicing this and that, drawing myself up till my chin was above the bar, and repeating this till one evening Vernon found I could do it thirty times running: his praise made me proud.

About this time, when I was ten or so, we were all brought together in Carrickfergus. My brothers and sisters then first became living, individual beings to me. Vernon was going to a bank as a clerk and was away all day. Willie, six years older than I was, and Annie, and Chrissie, two years my junior, went to the same day-school, though the girls went to the girls' entrance and had women teachers. Willie and I were in the same class; though he had grown to be taller than Vernon, I could beat him in most of the lessons. There was, however, one important branch of learning in which he was easily the best in the school. The first time I heard him recite *The Battle of Ivry* by Macaulay, I was carried off my feet. He made gestures and his voice altered so naturally that I was lost in admiration.

That evening my sisters and I were together and we talked of Willie's talent. My eldest sister was enthusiastic, which I suppose stirred envy and emulation in me. I got up and imitated him and to my sisters' surprise I knew the whole poem by heart. "Who taught you?" Annie wanted to know, and when she heard that I had learned it just from hearing Willie recite it once, she was astonished and must have told our teacher; for the next afternoon he asked me to follow Willie and told me I was very good. From this time on the reciting class was my chief education. I learned every boy's piece and could imitate them all perfectly, except one red-haired rascal who could recite *The African Chief* better than anyone else, better even than the master. It was pure melodrama but Red-head was a born actor and swept us all away by the realism of his impersonation. Never shall I forget how the boy rendered the words:

> *Look, feast thy greedy eyes on gold,*
> *Long kept for sorest need;*
> *Take it, thou askest sums untold*
> *And say that I am freed.*
>
> *Take it; my wife the long, long day*
> *Weeps by the cocoa-tree,*
> *And my young children leave their play*
> *And ask in vain for me.**

I haven't seen or heard the poem these fifty odd years. It seems tawdry stuff to me now; but the boy's accents were of the very soul of tragedy and I realized clearly that I couldn't recite that poem as well as he did. He was inimitable. Every time his accents and manner altered; now he did these verses wonderfully, at another time those, so that I couldn't ape him; always there was a

---

*An eight-stanza poem by William Cullen Bryant. Harris quotes it accurately.

touch of novelty in his intense realization of the tragedy. Strange to say, it was the only poem he recited at all well.

An examination came and I was the first in the school in arithmetic and first too in elocution. Vernon even praised me, while Willie slapped me and got kicked on the shins for his pains. Vernon separated us and told Willie he should be ashamed of hitting one only half as big as he was. Willie lied promptly, saying I had kicked him first. I disliked Willie, I hardly know why, save that he was a rival in the school life.

After this Annie began to treat me differently and now I seemed to see her as she was and was struck by her funny ways. She wished both Chrissie and myself to call her "Nita"; it was short for Anita, she said, which was the stylish French way of pronouncing Annie. She hated "Annie"—it was "common and vulgar"; I couldn't make out why.

One evening we were together and she had undressed Chrissie for bed, when she opened her own dress and showed us how her breasts had grown while Chrissie's still remained small; and indeed "Nita's" were ever so much larger and prettier and round like apples. Nita let us touch them gently and was evidently very proud of them. She sent Chrissie to bed in the next room while I went on learning a lesson beside her. Nita left the room to get something, I think, when Chrissie called me and I went into the bedroom wondering what she wanted. She wished me to know that her breasts would grow too and be just as pretty as Nita's. "Don't you think so?" she asked, and taking my hand put it on them. And I said, "Yes," for indeed I liked her better than Nita, who was all airs and graces and full of affectations.

Suddenly Nita called me, and Chrissie kissed me whispering: "Don't tell her," and I promised. I always liked Chrissie and Vernon. Chrissie was very clever and pretty, with dark curls and big hazel eyes, and Vernon was a sort of hero and always very kind to me.

I learned nothing from this happening. I had hardly any sex-thrill with either sister, indeed, nothing like so much as I had had five years before, through the girl's legs in Mrs. Frost's school; and I record the incident here chiefly for another reason. One afternoon about 1890, Aubrey Beardsley* and his sister Mabel, a very pretty girl, had been lunching with me in Park Lane. Afterwards we went into the park. I accompanied them as far as Hyde Park Corner. For some reason or other I elaborated the theme that men of thirty

---

*(1872–98). His rise as an illustrator was meteoric; among the books he illustrated were *Morte d'Arthur* and *Salome*, and he helped found the *Yellow Book*, a magazine, in 1894. He, with Wilde, was a leader of the "Decadents" in the 1890's.

or forty usually corrupted young girls, and women of thirty or forty in turn corrupted youths.

"I don't agree with you," Aubrey remarked. "It's usually a fellow's sister who gives him his first lessons in sex. I know it was Mabel here who first taught me."

I was amazed at his outspokenness. Mabel flushed crimson and I hastened to add:

"In childhood girls are far more precocious. But these little lessons are usually too early to matter." He wouldn't have it, but I changed the subject resolutely and Mabel told me some time afterwards that she was very grateful to me for cutting short the discussion. "Aubrey," she said, "loves all sex things and doesn't care what he says or does."

I had seen before that Mabel was pretty. I realized that day when she stooped over a flower that her figure was beautifully slight and round. Aubrey caught my eye at the moment and remarked maliciously, "Mabel was my first model, weren't you, Mabs? I was in love with her figure," he went on judicially. "Her breasts were so high and firm and round that I took her as my ideal." She laughed, blushing a little, and rejoined, "Your figures, Aubrey, are not exactly ideal."

I learned from this little discussion that most men's sisters are just as precocious as mine were and just as likely to act as teachers in matters of sex.

From about this time on the individualities of people began to impress me definitely. Vernon suddenly got an appointment in a bank at Armagh and I went to live with him there, in lodgings. The lodging-house keeper I disliked: she was always trying to make me keep hours and rules, and I was as wild as a homeless dog; but Armagh was wonder city to me. Vernon made me a day-boy at the Royal School: it was my first big school; I learned all the lessons very easily and most of the boys and all the masters were kind to me. The great mall or park-like place in the centre of the town delighted me; I had soon climbed nearly every tree in it, tree climbing and reciting being the two sports in which I excelled.

When we were at Carrickfergus my father had had me on board his vessel and had matched me at climbing the rigging against a cabin boy, and though the sailor was first at the cross-trees, I caught him on the descent by jumping at a rope and letting it slide through my hands, almost at falling speed to the deck. I heard my father tell this afterwards with pleasure to Vernon, which pleased my vanity inordinately and increased, if that were possible, my delight in showing off.

For another reason my vanity had grown beyond measure. At Carrickfergus I had got hold of a book on athletics belonging to Vernon and had there learned that if you went into the water up to your neck and threw yourself boldly forward and tried to swim, you would swim; for the body is lighter than the water and floats.

The next time I went down to bathe with Vernon, instead of going on the beach in the shallow water and wading out, I went with him to the end of the pier. When he dived in, I went down the steps. As soon as he came up to the surface I cried, "Look! I can swim too!" and I boldly threw myself forward and, after a moment's dreadful sinking and spluttering, did in fact swim. When I wanted to get back I had a moment of appalling fear: "Could I turn around?" The next moment I found it quite easy to turn and I was soon safely back on the steps again.

"When did you learn to swim?" asked Vernon, coming out beside me. "This minute," I replied. As he was surprised, I told him I had read it all in his book and made up my mind to venture the very next time I bathed. A little time afterwards I heard him tell this to some of his men friends in Armagh, and they all agreed that it showed extraordinary courage, for I was small for my age and always appeared even younger than I was.

Looking back, I see that many causes combined to strengthen the vanity in me which had already become inordinate and in the future was destined to shape my life and direct its purposes. Here in Armagh everything conspired to foster my besetting sin. I was put among boys of my age, I think in the lower fourth. The form-master, finding that I knew no Latin, showed me a Latin grammar and told me I'd have to learn it as quickly as possible, for the class had already begun to read Caesar. He showed me the first declension *mensa* as the example, and asked me if I could learn it by the next day. I said I would, and as luck would have it, the mathematical master passing at the moment, the form-master told him I was backward and should be in a lower form.

"He's very good indeed at figures," the mathematical master rejoined. "He might be in the Upper Division."

"Really!" exclaimed the form-master. "See what you can do," he said to me. "You may find it possible to catch up. Here's a Caesar too; you may as well take it with you. We have done only two or three pages."

That evening I sat down to the Latin grammar, and in an hour or so had learned all the declensions and nearly all the adjectives and pronouns. Next day I was trembling with hope of praise and if the form-master had encouraged me or said one word of commendation, I might have distinguished myself in the class work, and so changed perhaps my whole life, but the next day he had evidently forgotten all about my backwardness. By dint of hearing the other boys answer I got a smattering of the lessons, enough to get through them without punishment, and soon a good memory brought me among the foremost boys, though I took no interest in learning Latin.

Another incident fed my self-esteem and opened to me the world of books. Vernon often went to a clergyman's who had a pretty daughter, and I too was asked to their evening parties. The daughter found out I could recite and at once it became the custom to get me to recite some poem everywhere we went. Vernon bought me the poems of Macaulay and Walter Scott and I had soon learned them all by heart. I used to declaim them with infinite gusto: at first my gestures were imitations of Willie's: but Vernon taught me to be more natural and I bettered his teaching. No doubt my small stature helped the effect and the Irish love of rhetoric did the rest; but everyone praised me and the showing off made me very vain and—a more important result—the learning of new poems brought me to the reading of novels and books of adventure. I was soon lost in this new world: though I played at school with the other boys, in the evening I never opened a lesson-book. Instead, I devoured Lever and Mayne Reid, Marryat* and Fenimore Cooper with unspeakable delight.

I had one or two fights at school with boys of my own age. I hated fighting, but I was conceited and combative and strong and so got to fisticuffs twice or three times. Each time, as soon as an elder boy saw the scrimmage, he would advise us, after looking on for a round or two, to stop and make friends. The Irish are supposed to love fighting better than eating; but my school days assure me, however, that they are not nearly so combative, or perhaps, I should say, so brutal, as the English.

In one of my fights a boy took my part and we became friends. His name was Howard and we used to go on long walks together. One day I wanted him to meet Strangways, the Vicar's son, who was fourteen but silly, I thought. Howard shook his head: "He wouldn't want to know me," he said. "I am a Roman Catholic." I still remember the feeling of horror his confession called up in me: "A Roman Catholic! Could anyone as nice as Howard be a Catholic?"

I was thunderstruck and this amazement has always illumined for me the abyss of Protestant bigotry, but I wouldn't break with Howard, who was two years older than I and who taught me many things. He taught me to like Fenians, though I hardly knew what the word meant. One day I remember he showed me posted on the court house a notice offering £5000 sterling as reward to anyone who would tell the whereabouts of James Stephen,** the Fenian head-centre. "He's travelling all over Ireland," Howard whispered. "Everybody knows

---

*Charles James Lever (1806–72); Thomas Mayne Reid (1818–83); Frederick Marryat (1792–1848). All were English writers of adventure novels.

**(1825–1901). After being wounded in Ballingarry in 1848, he escaped to France and then to America, where he helped found the Fenian Brotherhood. He returned to Ireland and was forced to flee again in 1865. Allowed to return to Dublin in 1886, he died there.

him," adding with gusto, "but no one would give the head-centre away to the dirty English." I remember thrilling to the mystery and chivalry of the story. From that moment, head-centre was a sacred symbol to me as Howard.

One day we met Strangways and somehow or other began talking of sex. Howard knew all about it and took pleasure in enlightening us both. It was Cecil Howard who first initiated Strangways and me, too, in self-abuse. In spite of my novel reading, I was still at eleven too young to get pleasure from the practice; but I was delighted to know how children were made and a lot of new facts about sex. Strangways had hair about his private parts, as indeed Howard had, also, and when he rubbed himself and the orgasm came, a sticky, milky fluid spirted from Strangway's cock, which Howard told us was the man's seed, which must go right into the woman's womb to make a child.

A week later Strangways astonished us both by telling how he had made up to the nursemaid of his younger sisters and got into her bed at night. The first time she wouldn't let him do anything, it appeared, but, after a night or two, he managed to touch her sex and assured us it was all covered with silky hairs. A little later he told us how she had locked her door and how the next day he had taken off the lock and got into bed with her again. At first she was cross, or pretended to be, he said, but he kept on kissing and begging her, and bit by bit she yielded, and he touched her sex again. "It was a slit," he said. A few nights later, he told us he had put his prick into her and, "Oh! by gum, it was wonderful, wonderful!"

"But how did you do it?" we wanted to know, and he gave us his whole experience.

"Girls love kissing," he said, "and so I kissed and kissed her and put my leg on her, and her hand on my cock and I kept touching her breasts and her cunny (that's what she calls it) and at last I got on her between her legs and she guided my prick into her cunt (God, it was wonderful!) and now I go with her every night and often in the day as well. She likes her cunt touched, but very gently," he added; "she showed me how to do it with one finger like this," and he suited the action to the word.

Strangways in a moment became to us not only a hero but a miracleman; we pretended not to believe him in order to make him tell us the truth and we were almost crazy with breathless desire.

I got him to invite me up to the vicarage and I saw Mary the nurse-girl there, and she seemed to me almost a woman and spoke to him as "Master Will" and he kissed her, though she frowned and said, "Leave off" and "Behave yourself," very angrily; but I felt that her anger was put on to prevent my guessing the truth. I was aflame with desire and when I told Howard, he, too, burned with lust, and took me out for a walk and questioned me all over again, and under a haystack in the country we gave ourselves to a bout of frigging, which for the first time thrilled me with pleasure.

All the time we were playing with ourselves, I kept thinking of Mary's hot slit, as Strangways had described it, and, at length, a real orgasm came and shook me; the imagining had intensified my delight.

Nothing in my life up to that moment was comparable in joy to that story of sexual pleasure as described, and acted for us, by Strangways.

JOHN RECHY

※

Introduction TO *City of Night* [1984]

City of Night began as a letter to a friend in Evanston, Illinois. It was written in El Paso the day following my return to my hometown in Texas after an eternity in New Orleans. That "eternity"—a few weeks—ended on Ash Wednesday, the day after Mardi Gras. The letter began:

> "Do you realize that a year ago in December I left New York and came to El Paso and went to Los Angeles and Pershing Square then went to San Diego and La Jolla in the sun and returned to Los Angeles and went to Laguna Beach to a bar on the sand and San Francisco and came back to Los Angeles and went back to the Orange Gate and returned to Los Angeles and Pershing Square and went to El Paso . . . and stopped in Phoenix one night and went back to Pershing Square and on to San Francisco again, and Monterey and the shadow of James Dean because of the movie, and Carmel where there's a house like a bird, and back to Los Angeles and on to El Paso where I was born, then Dallas with Culture and Houston with A Million Population— and on to New Orleans where the world collapsed, and back, now, to El Paso grasping for God knows what?"

The letter went on to evoke crowded memories of that Mardi Gras season, a culmination of the years I had spent traveling back and forth across the country—carrying all my belongings in an army duffel bag; moving in and out of lives, sometimes glimpsed briefly but always felt intensely. In that Carnival city of old cemeteries and tolling church bells, I slept only when fatigue demanded, carried along by "bennies" and on dissonant waves of voices, music, sad and happy laughter. The sudden quiet of Ash Wednesday, the mourning of Lent, jarred me as if a shout to which I had become accustomed had been throttled. I was awakened by *silence*, a questioning silence I had to flee.

I walked into the Delta Airlines office and told a pretty youngwoman there that I *had* to return to El Paso immediately. Though I had left money with my belongings scattered about the city in the several places where I had been "living," I didn't have enough with me for the fare, and a plane would depart within an hour or so. Out of her purse, the youngwoman gave me the money I lacked, and added more, for the cab. I thanked her and asked her name so I might return the money. "Miss Wingfield," she said in a moment of poetry not included in this novel because it is too "unreal" for fiction.

I thought I had ripped up the letter I had written about that Carnival season; I knew I had not mailed it. A week later I found it, crumpled. I rewrote it, trying to shape its disorder. I titled it "Mardi Gras" and sent it out as a short story to the literary quarterly *Evergreen Review*.

In El Paso, a letter arrived from Don Allen, one of the editors of *Evergreen Review,* in response to my story-letter, "Mardi Gras"; he admired it and indicated it was being strongly considered for publication. Was it, perhaps, a part of a novel? he asked.

I had never intended to write about the world I had found first on Times Square. "Mardi Gras" for me remained a letter. But thinking this might assure publication of the story, I answered, oh, yes, indeed, it was part of a novel and "close to half" finished.

By then, I was back in Los Angeles under the warm colorless sun over ubiquitous palmtrees. But the epiphany of questioning silence which had occurred in New Orleans made me experience the streetworld with a clarity the fierceness of the first journey had not allowed. I could "see"—face—its unique turbulence, unique beauty, and, yes, unique "ugliness."

"Mardi Gras" appeared in Issue No. 6 of the famous quarterly that was publishing Beckett, Sartre, Kerouac, Camus, Robbe-Grillet, Ionesco, Artaud. Don Allen wrote that he would be in Los Angeles on business and looked forward to seeing the finished part of my book.

Instead, I showed him part of the setting of the novel I still had no intention of writing. I took this elegantly attired slender New York editor into one of the most "dangerous" bars of the time ("Ji-Ji's" in this book). Pushers hovered outside like tatered paparazzi greeting the queens. Inside the bar, the toughest "male-hustlers" asserted tough poses among the men who sought them or the queens. Don Allen said he thought perhaps the bar was a bit too crowded. As we drove away, the police raided it.

As sections from the growing book continued to appear in *Evergreen Review,* I began getting encouraging letters from readers, agents, and other writers, including Norman Mailer and James Baldwin. When several editors— at Dial, Random House, others—expressed interest in the book, and there were two offers of an advance, I telephoned Don; I could not conceive of this book's appearing other than through Grove Press. Not only was Barney Rosset, its president, publishing the best of the modern authors—and battling literary censorship—but *Evergreen Review* had created the interest in my writing that others were responding to. As my now-editor, Don came to Los Angeles with a contract and an advance for the book I had begun to call "Storm Heaven and Protest."

But I still didn't write it.

I plunged back into my "streetworld." Hitchhiking I met a man who would become instrumental in my finishing this book. I saw him regularly, but I kept my "literary" identity secret; I had learned early—but not entirely correctly—that being smart on the streets included pretending not to be. Not knowing that I had graduated from college and had already published sections from a novel I had a contract for—but concerned that I might be trapped in one of the many possible deadends of the streets—he offered (we were having breakfast in Malibu, the ocean was azure) to send me to school. I was touched by his unique concern, and when he drove me back to my rented room on Hope Street, I asked him to wait. I went inside and autographed a copy of "The Fabulous Wedding of Miss Destiny" and gave it to him. He looked at it, and then at me, a stranger.

Then I needed to flee the closeness increased, perhaps, by the fusion of my two "identities." Consistent with another pattern, a letter arrived from a man who had read my writing: he would be happy to have me visit him on an island near Chicago. A plane ticket followed. Painfully trying to explain to my good friend who had picked me up hitchhiking that I *had* to leave Los Angeles, I left and spent the summer on a private island. When summer was ending, I migrated to Chicago, quickly finding its own Times Square.

But I was pulled back to Los Angeles. Extending the understanding that makes him, always, deeply cherished and special in my life, my friend who had wanted to put me through school—and whose "voice" is heard in part in the character of Jeremy in this book—now offered to help me out while I went to El Paso to finish—where it had begun—the book I again longed to write.

I returned to my mother's small house and wrote every day on a rented Underwood typewriter. My mother kept the house quiet while I worked. After dinner, I would translate into Spanish and read to her (she never learned English) certain passages I considered appropriate. "You're writing a beautiful book, my son." she told me.

Each chapter went through about twelve drafts, some passages through more than that—often, paradoxically, to create a sense of "spontaneity." The first four paragraphs that open this book were compressed from about twenty pages. The first chapter was written last, the last one came first. Although four years elapsed between the time I began this book—with the unsent letter—and the time it was finished, most of it was written during one intense year in El Paso.

Three titles had been announced with published excerpts: *Storm Heaven and Protest, Hey, World!* and *It Begins in the Wind.* The intertwining chapters that connect the portraits were called "City of Night" from the start. But I did not conceive of that as the book's title. I did consider: *Ash Wednesday, Shrove Tuesday, The Fabulous Wedding of Miss Destiny, Masquerade.* Finally, I decided: *Storm Heaven and Protest.* Then Don Allen—always a superb editor—suggested the obvious: *City of Night.*

The book was finished. That night—and this is one of the most cherished memories of my life—my mother, my oldest brother, Robert, and I were weaving about my mother's living room, bumping into each other, each with great stacks of the almost-700-page typescript, collating it—I had made three or four carbon copies.

The manuscript was mailed. I went to return the rented typewriter, but I couldn't part with it. I bought it; I still have the elegant old Underwood, now comfortably "retired."

Proofs came. As I read, I panicked. In print, it was all "different"—wrong! About a third of the way through, I began changing a word here and there, a phrase, a sentence, a paragraph; then I started back at the beginning. By the time I had gone through the galley proofs, the book was virtually rewritten on the margins and on pasted typewritten inserts. But *now*—I knew—it was "right." I called Don, then in San Francisco, to "prepare" him. He was startled but agreed with the alterations. Despite Don's preparation, others at Grove reacted in surprise at the rewritten galleys. Knowing how expensive the resetting would be, I had offered out of my royalties to pay for it—a contractual provision. But Barney Rosset made no objection to changes, and he refused to charge me. Publication was rescheduled, and the book was reset.

I had no doubt that *City of Night* would be an enormous success. I was right. In a reversed way. I had thought it would sell modestly and that the book would be greeted with critical raves. The opposite occurred, dramatically.

Before the official publication date, my book appeared in the No. 8 slot of *Time*'s national bestseller list. Also before publication, I saw my first review. Even for the dark ages of the early 1960's the title of the review in *The New York Review of Books* was vicious in its overt bigotry. What followed matched its headline. The book climbed quickly to the No. 1 spot on bestseller lists in New York, California. Nationally on all lists it reached third place. In a review featured on its cover, *The New Republic* attempted to surpass the attack of *The New York Review of Books;* it was a draw. The book went into a second, third, fourth, fifth, sixth, seventh printing and remained on the bestseller lists for almost seven months. In its assault of about eight lines, *The New Yorker* made one factual mistake and one grammatical error.

Only the book's subject seemed to be receiving outraged attention; its careful structure, whether successful or not, was virtually ignored. I was being viewed and written about as a hustler who had somehow managed to write, rather than as a writer who was writing intimately about hustling—and many other subjects. That persisting view would affect the critical reception of every one of my following books, and still does, to this day.

JOHN RECHY

꧁

FROM *City of Night* [1963]

MISS DESTINY: The Fabulous Wedding

I

The first time I saw Miss Destiny was of course in Pershing Square, on the cool, almost cold, moist evening of a warm smoggy day.

Im sitting in the park with Chuck the cowboy on the railing facing 5th Street. "Oh oh, here comes Miss Destinee," says Chuck, a cowboy youngman with widehat and boots, very slim of course, of course very slow, with sideburns of course almost to his chin, and a giant tattoo on his arm that says: DEATH BEFORE DISHONOR. "Destinee's last husband jes got busted pushing hard stuff, man," Chuck is going on, "an she is hot for a new one, so watch out, man—but if you ain got a pad, you can always make it at Destinee's— it's like a gone mission, man!"

Indeed, indeed! here comes Miss Destiny! fluttering out of the shadows into the dimlights along the ledges like a giant firefly—flirting, calling out to everyone: "Hello, darling, I love you—I love you too, dear—so very much—ummmm!" Kisses flung recklessly into the wind. . . . "What oh what did Chuck say to you, darling?" to me, coming on breathlessly rushing words. "You must understand right here and now that Chuck still loves me, like all my exhusbands (youre new in town, dear, or I would certainly have seen you before, and do you have a place to stay?—I live on Spring Street and there is a 'Welcome!' mat at the door)—oh, they *nevuh!* can forget me—of course I loved Chuck once too—" (sigh) "—such a butch cowboy, look at him—but havent I loved every new hustler in town?—but oh this restlessness in me!— and are you married, dear?—oh, the lady doth indeed protest Too Much—" (this last addressed to Jenny Lu, still bumping (woe-*uh!*). "I *adore* Married men—as long as they are Faithful to me, you understand, of course—and I must warn you right here and now about Pauline, who is the most evil people in this city and you must stay away from her when she tries to make out with

all kinds of—Ah Beg To Tell You—" ("Whe-woo!" sighed Chuck.) "—
untrue promises as some—people—have—found—out—" looking coldly
at Chuck, then rushing on: "Oh I am, as everyone will tell you, A Very Restless Woman—"

She—he (Miss Destiny is a man)—went on about her—his—restlessness,
her husbands, asking me questions in between, figuring out how Bad I was ("Have
you been 'interviewed' yet by Miss Lorelei?—I mean Officer Morgan, dear—
we call her Miss Lorelei. And dont let her scare you, dear—and Im sure you
wont—why, Miss Lorelei—I mean, Sergeant Morgan—is as much a lady as I
am: I saw her in the mensroom one time, and she ran everybody out—except this
cute young boy—and— . . .")—looking alternately coyly and coldly at Chuck
then me seductively: all of which you will recognize as the queen's technique to
make you feel like such an irresistible so masculine so sexual so swinging stud,
and queens can do it better than most real girls, queens being Uninhibited.

Now Miss Destiny is a youngman possibly 20 but quite as possibly 18 and
very probably 25, with false I.D. like everyone else if she is underage: a slim
young queen with masses and masses of curly red hair (which she fondly calls
her "rair"), oh, and it tumbles gaily over a pale skinny face almost smothering
it at times. Unpredictably occasionally she comes on with crazy Southern sounds
cultivated, you will learn, all the way from northern Pennsylvania.

"Oh my dear!" she exclaims now, fluffing out her "rair," "here I am talking all about my Sex life, and we have not been Properly Introduced! . . . Im
Miss Destiny, dear—and let me hasten to tell you before you hear it wrong from
othuh sources that I am famous even in Los gay Angeles—why, I went to this
straight party in High Drag (and I mean *High*, honey—gown, stockings, os-
trich plumes in my flaming rair), and—"

"An you know who she was dancing with?" Chuck interrupted.

"The Vice, my dear," Miss Destiny said flatly, glowering at Chuck.

"An she was busted, man—for ah mas—mask— . . ."

"Masquerading, dear. . . . But how was I to know the repressed queer was
the vice squad—tell me? . . ." And she goes on breathlessly conjuring up the
Extravagant Scene. . . .

(*Oh shes dancing like Cinderella at the magic ball in this Other World shes
longingly invading, and her prince-charming turns out to be: the vice squad. And oh
Miss Destiny gathers her skirts and tries to run like in the fairytale, but the vice
grabs her roughly and off she goes in a very real coach to the glasshouse, the feathers
trembling now nervously. Miss Destiny insists she is a real woman leave her alone.
(But oh, oh! how can she hide That Thing between his legs which should belong
there only when It is somebody else's?) . . . All lonesome tears and Humiliation,
Miss Destiny ends up in the sex tank: a wayward Cinderella. . . .*)

"Now, honey," she says with real indignation, "I can see them bustin me for Impersonating a man—but a woman!—*really!* . . ." And you will notice that Miss Destiny like all the other swinging queens in the world considers herself every bit a Lady. "But nevuh mind," she went on, "I learned things in the countyfawm I didnt know before—like how to make eyeshadow out of spit and bluejeans—and oh my dear the kites I flew!—I mean to say, no one can say I didnt send my share of invitations out! . . . Of course, I *do* have to go regularly to the county psychiatrist (thats a mind doctor, dears)—to be (would you believe it? this is what they actually told me:) 'cured'! Well! One more session with him, and I'll have *him* on the couch!—but now—" turning her attention to me fullblast, because, you will understand, Miss Destiny scouts at night among the drifting youngmen, and at the same time you can tell shes out to bug Chuck: and when she asked me would I go to the flix with her now ("across the street, where it is Divine but you mustnt be seen there too often," she explains, "because they will think youre free trade— . . ."), Chuck said: "It would not do you no good, Destinee, they will not let you in the men's head."

"*Miss* Destiny, *Mister* Chuck," she corrects him airily.

And went on: "Didn't I tell you all my exhusbands are jealous of me? Chuck lived with me, dear," she explains, "as just about every other studhustler has at one time or another, I must add modestly. But, baby, it was a turbulent marriage (that means very stormy, dear). Why, I just couldnt drag Chuck from the window—he—"

"Oh, man," interrupts Chuck. "Next to Miss Destinee's pad theres this real swell cunt an she walks aroun all day in her brassiere—standin by the window, an she—"

"But I fixed that!" Miss Destiny says triumphantly. "I nailed the damn windowshades so no one can look out at that cunt anymore! . . . Oh!" she sighed, her hand at her forehead, "those days were trying days. Chuck's a good hustler—but hes too lazy even to try to score sometimes. And, honey, my unemployment check went just so far: You see, I took a job just long enough to qualify for unemployment, and then I turned up all madeup and they let me go—and everytime they call me up for a job, why I turn up in drag and they wont have me! . . . But anyway— . . ."

Looking at Chuck and Miss Destiny—as she rushes on now about the Turbulent Times—I know the scene: Chuck the masculine cowboy and Miss Destiny the femme queen: making it from day to park to bar to day like all the others in that ratty world of downtown L.A. which I will make my own: the world of queens and malehustlers and what they thrive on, the queens being technically men but no one thinks of them that way—always "she"—their "husbands" being the masculine vagrants—fleetingly and often out of conve-

nience sharing the queens' pads—never considering theyre involved with another man (the queen), and as long as the hustler goes only with queens—and
with other men only for scoring (which is making or taking sexmoney, getting
a meal, making a pad)—he is himself not considered "queer"—he remains, in
the vocabulary of that world, "trade."

"Yes," Miss Destiny is going on, "those were stormy times with Chuck—
and then, being from cowcountry, God bless him, Chuck believes every Big
story: like when Pauline told him she'd really set him up—"

"Man," Chuck explained, laughing, "Pauline is this queen thats got more
bull than Texas!"

"Can you imagine?" Miss Destiny says to me. "She offered him a Cadillac!
Pauline! Who hasnt even got enough to keep her dragclothes in proper shape! . . .
But nevuhmind, let him be gullible (thats someone who believes untrue stories). And, besides," she says with a toss of her head, "I flipped over Sandy,
a bad new stud. . . . But Chuck's still jealous of me—he knows Im looking
for a new husband—now that poor Sandy (my most recent ex, dear) got
busted, and I know he didnt have any hard narcotics on him like they say he
did—they planted them in his car— . . . Shake that moneymakuh, honey!—"
(this to a spadequeen swishing by) "—and I still love my Sandy—did the best
I could, tried to bail him out, hire a good attuhnee, but it was no good—they
laughed when I said he was my husband. The quality of muhcee is mighty
strained indeed—as the dear Portia said (from Shakespeare, my dears—a very
Great writer who wrote ladies' roles for dragqueens in his time). And it breaks
my heart to think of my poor Sandy in the joint away from women all that
time, him so redhot he might turn queer, but oh no not my Sandy, hes all stud.
If I know him, he'll come out of the joint rich, hustling the guards. . . . And
I tried to be faithful—but the years will be so long—and what can a girl do,
and restless the way I am?—restless and crying muhself to sleep night aftuh
night, missing him—missing him. But my dears, I realize I Will Have To Go
On—he would want it that way. Well, queens have died eaten by the ah
worm of ah love, as the Lovely Cleopatra said—she was The Queen of Ancient Egypt—" (quoting, misquoting Shakespeare—saying it was a lovely
he-roine who said it in the play—taking it for granted—a safe assumption in
her world—that no one will understand her anyway). "Then Miss Thing said
to me (Miss Thing is a fairy perched on my back like some people have a mon-
key or a conscience)," she explained, "well, Miss Thing said to me, 'Miss
Destiny dear, dont be a fool, fix your lovey rair and find you a new husband—
make it permanent this time by really getting Married—and even if you have
to stretch your unemployment, dont allow him to push or hustle' (which
breaks up a marriage)—and Miss Thing said, 'Miss Destiny dear, have a real

wedding this time.' . . . A real wedding," Miss Destiny sighed wistfully. "Like every young girl should have at least once. . . . And when it happens oh it will be the most simpuhlee Fabulous wedding the Westcoast has evuh seen! with oh the most beautiful queens as bridesmaids! and the handsomest studs as ushers! (and you will absolutely have to remove those boots, Chuck)— and *Me!* . . . Me . . . in virgin-white . . . coming down a winding staircase . . . carrying a white bouquet! . . . and my family will be crying for joy. . . . And there will be champagne! cake! a real priest to puhfawm the Ceremony!—" She broke off abruptly, shutting her eyes deliriously as if to visualize the scene better. Then she opened them again, onto the frantic teeming world of Pershing Square. . . .

"They will bust you again for sure if you have that wedding. Miss Destinee," said Chuck gravely.

"It would be worth it," sighed Miss Destiny. "Oh, it would be worth it."

Then we noticed a welldressed man standing a few feet from us in the shadows, staring at us intently until he saw us looking back and he shifted his gaze, began to smoke, looked up furtively again.

Miss Destiny smiled brightly at him, but he didnt smile back at her, and Miss Destiny said obviously he is a queer and so he must want a man. "So darlings, I will leave you to him and him to whomevuh eenie-meenie-miney he wants. But let me tell you, my dear—" me—confidentially "—that when they dress that elegantly around here, why, they will make all kinds of promises and give you oh two bucks," and Chuck said oh no the score was worth at least twenty, and Miss Destiny laughs like Tallulah Bankhead, who is the Idol of all queens, and says in a husky voice, "Dalling, this is not your young inexperienced sistuh you are talkin to, this is your mothuh, who has been a-round. . . . Why, Miss Thing told me about this sweet stud kid going for a dollar!— . . . Ah, well, as my beloved sweet Juliet said, Parting is: such— sweet—sorrow— . . ." And she sighed now, being Juliet, then whispered to me loud enough for Chuck to hear, "There will be other times, my dear— when you are not Working."

And she moved away with peals of queenly laughter, flirting again, fluttering again, flamboyantly swishing, just as she had come on, saying hello to everyone: "Good evening, Miss Saint Moses, dear— . . ." spreading love, throwing kisses, bringing her delicate hands to her face, sighing, "Too Much!" after some goodlooking youngman she digs, glancing back at Chuck and me as the man moved out of the shadows, closer to us, jingling money.

So there goes Miss Destiny leaving Pershing Square, all gayety, all happiness, all laughter.

"I love you too, dear, ummmm, so much. . . ."

2

Those first days in Los Angeles, I was newly dazzled by the world into which my compulsive journey through submerged lives had led me—newly hypnotized by the life of the streets.

I had rented a room in a hotel on Hope Street—on the fringes of that world but still outside of it (in order always to have a place where I could be completely alone when I must be). Thus the duality of my existence was marked by a definite boundary: Pershing Square: east of there when the desire to be with people churned within me; west of there to the hotel when I had to be alone. . . . At times, after having combed the bars, the streets, the park, I would flee as if for protection to that hotel room.

Yet other times I needed people fiercely—needed the anarchy of the streets. . . .

And Main Street in Los Angeles is such an anarchy.

This is clip street, hustle street—frenzied-nightactivity street: the moving back and forth against the walls; smoking, peering anxiously to spot the bulls before they spot you; the rushing in and out of Wally's and Harry's: long crowded malehustling bars.

And here too are the fairyqueens—the queens from Everywhere, America—the queenly exiles looking for new "husbands" restlessly among the vagrant hustlers with no place to stay, and the hustlers will often clip the queens (if there is anything to clip), and the queens will go on looking for their own legendary permanent "Daddies" among the older men who dig the queens' special brand of gone sexplay, seldom finding those permanent connections, and living in Main and Spring Street holes: sometimes making it (employed and unemployed, taking their daddies and being taken by the hustlers)—sometimes hardly, sometimes not at all.

And the malehustlers live with them off and on, making it from bar to lonesome room, bragging about the $50 score with the fruit from Bel Air who has two swimming pools, jack, and said he'd see you again (but if he didnt show, you dont say that), and youre clinching a dime and a nickel for draft beer at Wally's or Harry's or the 1-2-3 or Ji-Ji's so you can go inside and score early, and make it with one of the vagrant young girls to prove to yourself you're still All Right.

And so Main Street is an anarchy where the only rule is Make It! . . . And the only reminders of the world beyond its boundaries are the policewagons that cruise the streets—the cops that pick you at random out of Hooper's all-night coffee shop after 2:00 in the morning. . . . The free jammed ride to the glasshouse for fingerprints . . .

Rock-n-roll sounds fill the rancid air.

This was the world I joined.

A couple of blocks away from Main Street, on Spring—squashed on either side by gray apartment buildings (*walls greasy from days of cheap cooking, cobwebbed lightbulbs feebly hiding in opaque darkness, windowscreens if any smooth as velvet with grime—where queens and hustlers and other exiles hibernate*)—just beyond the hobo cafeteria where panhandlers hang dismally outside in the cruel neonlight (*fugitives from the owlfaces of the Salvation Army fighting Evil with no help from God or the cops; fugitives from Uplifting missionwords and lambstew*)—is the 1-2-3.

Outside, a cluster of pushers gather like nervous caged monkeys, openly offering pills and maryjane thrills, and you see them scurrying antlike to consult with Dad-o, the Negro king of downtown smalltime pushers—and Dad-o, sitting royally at the bar like a heap of very black shiny dough, says yes or no arbitrarily.

And that is the way it is.

"*About Evergreen Review No. 32*"

On June 12, 1964 a Federal Court in Brooklyn put an end to one of the more bizarre episodes of censorship in recent memory. On that day, three judges condemned police seizure of 21,000 copies of *Evergreen Review* No. 32 as "unconstitutional" and ordered their immediate return to the publisher.

The story of *Evergreen*'s suppression began six weeks earlier, on April 24, when Nassau County District Attorney William Cahn, acting on "confidential information," dispatched his Vice Squad raiders into a plant on Long Island where the April-May issue of *Evergreen* was just about to be bound. His detectives lost no time finding the issue "obscene." Without further ado they carried off to a police warehouse all the copies—still mostly unbound—they could find on the premises.

The DA announced to the press he didn't believe he was acting as censor, though he felt duty bound to "prevent Nassau County from becoming a honky-tonk community." He found much to object to in the seized issue, citing among others the poem by Pulitzer Prize winner Karl Shapiro and the chapter from Wayland Young's book *Eros Denied*. But he reserved special disapproval for the portfolio by Emil J. Cadoo, the American photographer living in Paris, whose work has appeared in *Life*, the Paris *Vogue* and other major European magazines, and whose photographs were recently exhibited in Paris at a successful one-man show.

Edward Steichen, director emeritus of photography at the Museum of Modern Art, was one of the many distinguished figures in the world of art and literature who came to the defense of *Evergreen* and Cadoo. There could be no more fitting text to accompany this new Cadoo photograph from his portfolio of nudes done in the double-exposure style than this statement Mr. Steichen made when he learned of *Evergreen*'s seizure.

"I cannot see anything interfering with the publication of these photographs but a flagrant interference with the freedom of the press. There is nothing in the subject matter of these pictures that has not been done by artists in other media, notably in the work of the greatest sculptor of our time, Auguste

Rodin. No valid reason has ever been advanced why the photographer should be denied the privileges accorded to the sculptor or any of the other graphic arts that have represented the human form in the lovers' embrace. These photographs were made by an artist using the camera, and I do not find any trace of vulgarity in them, and they certainly are very far removed from what is ordinarily referred to as pornography. Photography is a medium, when practiced by an artist, that seeks to interpret life. If human beings in the act of making love are indecent then the entire human race stands indicted. As long as the act of lovemaking is in itself not declared illegal and the extermination of the human race presented as a goal of civilization, lovers will continue to make love and babies will be born and it will be interpreted by the artists. I find nothing in these photographs that in the slightest way reflects bad taste, and certainly there is nothing pornographic conveyed. Any action that implies the contrary can only be regarded as an infringement of the freedom of expression accorded to all artists who use the camera as a medium instead of another medium."

JEAN GENET

꙰

FROM *The Thief's Journal* [1964]

Translated from the French by Bernard Frechtman

I give the name violence to a boldness lying idle and enamoured of danger. It can be seen in a look, a walk, a smile, and it is in you that it creates an eddying. It unnerves you. This violence is a calm that disturbs you. One sometimes says: "A guy with class!" Pilorge's delicate features were of an extreme violence. Their delicacy in particular was violent. Violence of the design of Stilitano's only hand, simply lying on the table, still, rendering the repose disturbing and dangerous. I have worked with thieves and pimps whose authority bent me to their will, but few proved to be really bold, whereas the one who was most so—Guy—was without violence. Stilitano, Pilorge and Michaelis were cowards. Java too. Even when at rest, motionless and smiling, there escaped from them through the eyes, the nostrils, the mouth, the palm of the hand, the bulging basket, through that brutal hillock of the calf under the wool or denim, a radiant and somber anger, visible as a haze.

But, almost always, there is nothing to indicate it, save the absence of the usual signs. René's face is charming at first. The downward curve of his nose gives him a roguish look, though the somewhat leaden paleness of his anxious face makes you uneasy. His eyes are hard, his movements calm and sure. In the cans he calmly beats up the queers; he frisks them, robs them; sometimes, as a finishing touch, he kicks them in the kisser with his heel. I don't like him, but his calmness masters me. He operates, in the dead of night, around the urinals, the lawns, the shrubbery, under the trees on the Champs-Elysées, near the stations, at the Porte Maillot, in the Bois de Boulogne (always at night) with a seriousness from which romanticism is excluded. When he comes in, at two or three in the morning, I feel him stocked with adventures. Every part of his body, which is nocturnal, has been involved: his hands, his arms, his legs, the back of his neck. But he, unaware of these marvels, tells me about them in forthright language. From his pockets he takes rings, wedding bands, watches, the evening's loot. He puts them in a big glass which will soon be full. He is not surprised by queers or their ways, which merely facilitate his jobs. When he sits on my bed, my ear snatches at scraps of adventure:

An officer in underwear whose wallet[1] he steals and who, pointing with his forefinger, orders: "Get out!" René-the-wise-guy's answer: "You think you're in the army?" Too hard a punch on an old man's skull. The one who fainted when René, who was all excited, opened a drawer in which there was a supply of phials of morphine. The queer who was broke and whom he made get down on his knees before him. I am attentive to these accounts. My Antwerp life grows stronger, carrying on in a firmer body, in accordance with manly methods. I encourage René, I give him advice, he listens to me. I tell him never to talk first. "Let the guy come up to you, keep him dangling. Act a little surprised when he suggests that you do it. Figure out who to act dumb with."

Every night I get a few scraps of information. My imagination does not get lost in them. My excitement seems to be due to my assuming within me the role of both victim and criminal. Indeed, as a matter of fact, I emit, I project at night the victim and criminal born of me; I bring them together somewhere, and toward morning I am thrilled to learn that the victim came very close to getting the death penalty and the criminal to being sent to the colony or guillotined. Thus my excitement extends as far as that region of myself, which is Guiana.

Without their wishing it, the gestures and destinies of these men are stormy. Their soul endures a violence which it had not desired and which it has domesticated. Those whose usual climate is violence are simple in relation to themselves. Each of the movements which make up this swift and devastating life is simple and straight, as clean as the stroke of a great draftsman—but when these strokes are encountered in movement, then the storm breaks, the lightning that kills them or me. Yet, what is their violence compared to mine, which was to accept theirs, to make it mine, to wish it for myself, to intercept it, to utilize it, to force it upon myself, to know it, to premeditate it, to discern and assume its perils? But what was mine, willed and necessary for my defense, my toughness, my rigor, compared to the violence they underwent like a malediction, risen from an inner fire simultaneously with an outer light which sets them ablaze and illuminates us? We know that their adventures are childish. They themselves are fools. They are ready to kill or be killed over a card game in which an opponent—or they themselves—was cheating. Yet, thanks to such guys, tragedies are possible.

This kind of definition—by so many opposing examples—of violence shows you that I shall not make use of words the better to depict an event or its hero, but so that they may tell you something about myself. In order to under-

1. He says: "I did his wallet."

stand me, the reader's complicity will be necessary. Nevertheless, I shall warn him whenever my lyricism makes me lose my footing.

Stilitano was big and strong. His gait was both supple and heavy, brisk and slow, sinuous; he was nimble. A large part of his power over me—and over the whores of the Barrio Chino—lay in the spittle he passed from one cheek to the other and which he would sometimes draw out in front of his mouth like a veil. "But where does he get that spit," I would ask myself, "where does he bring it up from? Mine will never have the unctuousness or color of his. It will merely be spun glassware, transparent and fragile." It was therefore natural for me to imagine what his penis would be if he smeared it for my benefit with so fine a substance, with that precious cobweb, a tissue which I secretly called the veil of the palace. He wore an old gray cap with a broken visor. When he tossed it on the floor of our room, it suddenly became the carcass of a poor partridge with a clipped wing, but when he put it on, pulling it down a bit over the ear, the opposite edge of the visor rose up to reveal the most glorious of blond locks. Shall I speak of his lovely bright eyes, modestly lowered—yet it could be said of Stilitano: "His bearing is immodest"—over which there closed eyelids and lashes so blond, so luminous and thick, that they brought in not the shade of evening but the shade of evil. After all, what meaning would there be in the sight that staggers me when, in a harbor, I see a sail, little by little, by fits and starts, spreading out and with difficulty rising on the mast of a ship, hesitantly at first, then resolutely, if these movements were not the very symbol of the movements of my love for Stilitano? I met him in Barcelona. He was living among beggars, thieves, fairies and whores. He was handsome, but it remains to be seen whether he owed all that beauty to my fallen state. My clothes were dirty and shabby. I was hungry and cold. This was the most miserable period of my life.

1932. Spain at the time was covered with vermin, its beggars. They went from village to village, to Andalusia because it is warm, to Catalonia because it is rich, but the whole country was favorable to us. I was thus a louse, and conscious of being one. In Barcelona we hung around the Calle Mediodia and the Calle Carmen. We sometimes slept six in a bed without sheets, and at dawn we would go begging in the markets. We would leave the Barrio Chino in a group and scatter over the Parallelo, carrying shopping baskets, for the housewives would give us a leek or turnip rather than a coin. At noon we would return, and with the gleanings we would make our soup. It is the life of vermin that I am going to describe. In Barcelona I saw male couples in which the more loving of the two would say to the other:

"I'll take the basket this morning."

He would take it and leave. One day Salvador gently pulled the basket from my hands and said, "I'm going to beg for you."

It was snowing. He went out into the freezing street, wearing a torn and tattered jacket—the pockets were ripped and hung down—and a shirt stiff with dirt. His face was poor and unhappy, shifty, pale, and filthy, for we dared not wash since it was so cold. Around noon, he returned with the vegetables and a bit of fat. Here I draw attention to one of those lacerations—horrible, for I shall provoke them despite the danger—by which beauty was revealed to me. An immense—and brotherly—love swelled my body and bore me toward Salvador. Leaving the hotel shortly after him, I would see him a way off beseeching the women. I knew the formula, as I had already begged for others and myself: it mixes Christian religion with charity; it merges the poor person with God; it is so humble an emanation from the heart that I think it scents with violet the straight, light breath of the beggar who utters it. All over Spain at the time they were saying:

"Por Dios."

Without hearing him, I would imagine Salvador murmuring it at all the stalls, to all the housewives. I would keep an eye on him as the pimp keeps an eye on his whore, but with such tenderness in my heart! Thus, Spain and my life as a beggar familiarized me with the stateliness of abjection, for it took a great deal of pride (that is, of love) to embellish those filthy, despised creatures. It took a great deal of talent, which came to me little by little. Though I may be unable to describe its mechanism to you, at least I can say that I slowly forced myself to consider that wretched life as a deliberate necessity. Never did I try to make of it something other than what it was, I did not try to adorn it, to mask it, but, on the contrary, I wanted to affirm it in its exact sordidness, and the most sordid signs became for me signs of grandeur.

I was dismayed when, one evening, while searching me after a raid—I am speaking of a scene which preceded the one with which this book begins—the astonished detective took from my pocket, among other things, a tube of vaseline. We dared joke about it since it contained mentholated vaseline. The whole record office, and I too, though painfully, writhed with laughter at the following:

"You take it in the nose?"

"Watch out you don't catch cold. You'd give your guy whooping cough."

I translate but lamely, in the language of a Paris hustler, the malicious irony of the vivid and venomous Spanish phrases. It concerned a tube of vaseline, one of whose ends was partially rolled up. Which amounts to saying that it had been put to use. Amidst the elegant objects taken from the pockets of the men who had been picked up in the raid, it was the very sign of abjection, of that which is concealed with the greatest of care, but yet the sign of a secret grace which was soon to save me from contempt. When I was locked up in a cell, and as soon as I had sufficiently regained my spirits to rise above the misfortune of my arrest, the image of the tube of vaseline never left me. The policemen had shown it to me victoriously, since they could thereby flourish their revenge, their hatred, their contempt. But lo and behold! that dirty, wretched object whose purpose seemed to the world—to that concentrated delegation of the world which is the police and, above all, that particular gathering of Spanish police, smelling of garlic, sweat and oil, but substantial looking, stout of muscle and strong in their moral assurance—utterly vile, became extremely precious to me. Unlike many objects which my tenderness singles out, this one was not at all haloed; it remained on the table a little gray leaden tube of vaseline, broken and livid, whose astonishing discreteness, and its essential correspondence with all the commonplace things in the record office of a prison (the bench, the inkwell, the regulations, the scales, the odor), would, through the general indifference, have distressed me, had not the very content of the tube made me think, by bringing to mind an oil lamp (perhaps because of its unctuous character), of a night light beside a coffin.

In describing it, I re-create the little object, but the following image cuts in: beneath a lamppost, in a street of the city where I am writing, the pallid face of a little old woman, a round, flat little face, like the moon, very pale; I cannot tell whether it was sad or hypocritical. She approached me, told me she was very poor and asked for a little money. The gentleness of that moon-fish face told me at once: the old woman had just got out of prison.

"She's a thief," I said to myself. As I walked away from her, a kind of intense reverie, living deep within me and not at the edge of my mind, led me to think that it was perhaps my mother whom I had just met. I know nothing of her who abandoned me in the cradle, but I hoped it was that old thief who begged at night.

"What if it were she?" I thought as I walked away from the old woman. Oh! if it were, I would cover her with flowers, with gladioluses and roses, and with kisses! I would weep with tenderness over those moon-fish eyes, over that round, foolish face! "And why," I went on, "why weep over it?" It did not take my mind long to replace these customary marks of tenderness by some other gesture, even the vilest and most contemptible, which I empowered to mean as much as the kisses, or the tears, or the flowers.

"I'd be glad to slobber over her," I thought, overflowing with love. (Does the word *glaïeul* [gladiolus] mentioned above bring into play the word *glaviaux* [gobs of spit]?) To slobber over her hair or vomit into her hands. But I would adore that thief who is my mother.

The tube of vaseline, which was intended to grease my prick and those of my lovers, summoned up the face of her who, during a reverie that moved through the dark alleys of the city, was the most cherished of mothers. It had served me in the preparation of so many secret joys, in places worthy of its discrete banality, that it had become the condition of my happiness, as my sperm-spotted handkerchief testified. Lying on the table, it was a banner telling the invisible legions of my triumph over the police. I was in a cell. I knew that all night long my tube of vaseline would be exposed to the scorn—the contrary of a Perpetual Adoration—of a group of strong, handsome, husky policemen. So strong that if the weakest of them barely squeezed his fingers together, there would shoot forth, first with a slight fart, brief and dirty, a ribbon of gum which would continue to emerge in a ridiculous silence. Nevertheless, I was sure that this puny and most humble object would hold its own against them; by its mere presence it would be able to exasperate all the police in the world; it would draw down upon itself contempt, hatred, white and dumb rages. It would perhaps be slightly bantering—like a tragic hero amused at stirring up the wrath of the gods—indestructible, like him, faithful to my happiness, and proud. I would like to hymn it with the newest words in the French language. But I would have also liked to fight for it, to organize massacres in its honor and bedeck a countryside at twilight with red bunting.[2]

The beauty of a moral act depends on the beauty of its expression. To say that it is beautiful is to decide that it will be so. It remains to be proven so. This is the task of images, that is, of the correspondences with the splendors of the physical world. The act is beautiful if it provokes, and in our throat reveals, song. Sometimes the consciousness with which we have pondered a reputedly vile act, the power of expression which must signify it, impel us to song. This means that treachery is beautiful if it makes us sing. To betray thieves would be not only to find myself again in the moral world, I thought, but also to find myself once more in homosexuality. As I grow strong, I am my own god. I dictate. Applied to men, the word beauty indicates to me the harmonious quality of a face and body to which is sometimes added manly grace. Beauty is then accompanied by magnificent, masterly, sovereign gestures. We imagine that they are determined by very special moral attitudes, and by the cultivation of such virtues in ourselves we hope to endow our poor faces and sick bodies with the vigor that our lovers possess naturally. Alas, these virtues, which they themselves never possess, are our weakness.

---

2. I would indeed rather have shed blood than repudiate that silly object.

Now as I write, I muse on my lovers. I would like them to be smeared with my vaseline, with that soft, slightly mentholated substance; I would like their muscles to bathe in that delicate transparence without which the tool of the handsomest is less lovely.

When a limb has been removed, the remaining one is said to grow stronger. I had hoped that the vigor of the arm which Stilitano had lost might be concentrated in his penis. For a long time I imagined a solid member, like a blackjack, capable of the most outrageous impudence, though what first intrigued me was what Stilitano allowed me to know of it: the mere crease, though curiously precise in the left leg, of his blue denim trousers. This detail might have haunted my dreams less had Stilitano not, at odd moments, put his left hand on it, and had he not, like ladies making a curtsey, indicated the crease by delicately pinching the cloth with his nails. I do not think he ever lost his self-possession, but with me he was particularly calm. With a slightly impertinent smile, though quite nonchalantly, he would watch me adore him. I know that he will love me.

HUBERT SELBY, JR.

❦

FROM *Last Exit to Brooklyn* [1964]

"Tralala"

Tralala was 15 the first time she was laid. There was no real passion. Just diversion. She hungout in the Greeks with the other neighborhood kids. Nothin to do. Sit and talk. Listen to the jukebox. Drink coffee. Bum cigarettes. Everything a drag. She said yes. In the park. 3 or 4 couples finding their own tree and grass. Actually she didnt say yes. She said nothing. Tony or Vinnie or whoever it was just continued. They all met later at the exit. They grinned at each other. The guys felt real sharp. The girls walked in front and talked about it. They giggled and alluded. Tralala shrugged her shoulders. Getting laid was getting laid. Why all the bullshit? She went to the park often. She always had her pick. The other girls were as willing, but played games. They liked to tease. And giggle. Tralala didn't fuckaround. Nobody likes a cockteaser. Either you put out or you dont. Thats all. And she had big tits. She was built like a woman. Not like some kid. They preferred her. And even before the first summer was over she played games. Different ones though. She didnt tease the guys. No sense in that. No money either. Some of the girls bugged her and she broke their balls. If a girl liked one of the guys or tried to get him for any reason Tralala cut in. For kicks. The girls hated her. So what. Who needs them. The guys had what she wanted. Especially when they lushed a drunk. Or pulled a job. She always got something out of it. Theyd take her to the movies. Buy cigarettes. Go to a PIZZERIA for a pie. There was no end of drunks. Everybody had money during the war. The waterfront was filled with drunken seamen. And of course the base was filled with doggies. And they were always good for a few bucks at least. Sometimes more. And Tralala always got her share. No tricks. All very simple. The guys had a ball and she got a few bucks. If there was no room to go to there was always the Wolffe Building cellar. Miles and miles of cellar. One screwed and the others played chick. Sometimes for hours. But she got what she wanted. All she had to do was putout. It was kicks too. Sometimes. If not, so what? It made no difference. Lay on your back. Or bend over a garbage can. Better than working. And its kicks. For a while anyway. But time always passes. They grew older. Werent satisfied with the few bucks they got from drunks. Why wait for a drunk to passout. After theyve spent most of their loot. Drop them on their way back to the Armybase. Every night dozens left Willies, a bar across the street from the Greeks. Theyd get them on their way back to the base or the docks. They usually let the doggies go. They didnt have too much. But the seamen were usually loaded. If they were too big or too sober theyd hit them over the head with a brick. If they looked easy one would hold him and the other(s) would lump him. A few times they got one in the lot on 57th street. That was a ball. It was real dark back by the fence. Theyd hit him until their arms were tired. Good kicks. Then a pie and beer. And Tralala. She was always there. As more time passed they acquired valuable experience. They were more selective. And stronger. They didn't need bricks anymore. Theyd make the rounds of the bars and spot some guy with a roll. When he left theyd lush him. Sometimes Tralala would set him up. Walk him to a doorway. Sometimes through the lot. It worked beautifully. They all had new clothes. Tralala dressed well. She wore a clean sweater every few days. They had no trouble. Just stick to the seamen. They come and go and who knows the difference. Who gives a shit. They have more than they need anyway. And whats a few lumps. They might get killed so whats the difference. They stayed away from doggies. Usually. They played it smart and nobody bothered them. But Tralala wanted more than the small share she was getting. It was about time she got something on her own. If she was going to get laid by a couple of guys for a few bucks she figured it would be smarter to get laid by one guy and get it all. All the drunks gave her the eye. And stared at her tits. It would be a slopeout. Just be sure to pick a liveone. Not some bum with a few lousy bucks. None of that shit. She waited, alone, in the Greeks. A doggie came in and ordered coffee and a hamburger. He asked her if she wanted something. Why not. He smiled. He pulled a bill from a thick roll and dropped it on the counter. She pushed her chest out. He told her about his ribbons. And medals. Bronze Star. And a Purpleheart with 2 Oakleaf Clusters. Been overseas 2 years. Going home. He talked and slobbered and she smiled. She hoped he didnt have all ones. She wanted to get him out before anybody else came. They got in a cab and drove to a downtown hotel. He bought a bottle of whiskey and they sat and drank and he talked. She kept filling his glass. He kept talking. About the war. How he was shot up. About home. What he was going to do. About the months in the hospital and all the operations. She kept pouring but he wouldnt pass out. The bastard. He said he just wanted to be near her for a while. Talk to her and have a few drinks. She waited. Cursed him and his goddamn mother. And who gives a shit about your leg gettin all shotup. She had been there over an hour. If hed fucker maybe she could get the money out of his pocket. But he just talked. The hell with it. She hit him over the head with the bottle. She emptied his pockets and left. She took the money out of his wallet and threw the wallet away. She counted it on the subway. 50 bucks. Not bad. Never had this much at once before. Shouldve gotten more though. Listenin to all that bullshit. Yeah. That sonofabitch. I shoulda hitim again. A lousy 50 bucks and hes talkin like a wheel or somethin. She kept 10 and stashed the rest and hurried back to the Greeks. Tony and Al were there and asked her where she was. Alex says ya cutout with a drunken doggie a couple a hours ago. Yeah. Some creep. I thought he was loaded. Didju score? Yeah. How much? 10 bucks. He kept bullshittin how much he had and alls he had was a lousy 10. Yeah? Lets see. She showed them the money. Yasure thats all yagot? Ya wanna search me? Yathink I got somethin stashed up my ass or somethin? We/ll take a look later. Yeah. How about you? Score? We got a few. But you dont have ta worry aboutit. You got enough. She said nothing and shrugged her shoulders. She smiled and offered to buy them coffee. And? Krist. What a bunch of bloodsuckers. OK Hey Alex . . . They were still sitting at the counter when the doggie came in. He was holding a bloodied handkerchief to his head and blood had caked on his wrist and cheek. He grabbed Tralala by the arm and pulled her from the stool. Give me my wallet you goddamn whore. She spit in his face and told him ta go fuckhimself. Al and Tony pushed him against the wall and asked him who he thought he was. Look, I dont know you and you dont know me. I got no call to fight with you boys. All I want is my wallet. I need my ID Card or I cant get back in the Base. You can keep the goddamn money. I dont care. Tralala screamed in his face that he was a no good mothafuckin sonofabitch and then started kicking him, afraid he might say how much she had taken. Ya lousy fuckin hero. Go peddle a couple of medals if yaneed money so fuckin bad. She spit in his face again, no longer afraid he might say something, but mad. Goddamn mad. A lousy 50 bucks and he was cryin. And anyway, he shouldve had more. Ya lousy fuckin creep. She kicked him in the balls. He grabbed her again. He was crying and bent over struggling to breathe from the pain of the kick. If I dont have the pass I cant get in the Base. I have to get back. Theyre going to fly me home tomorrow. I hevent been home for almost 3 years. Ive been all shot up. Please, PLEASE. Just the wallet. Thats all I want. Just the ID Card. PLEASE PLEASE!!! The tears streaked the caked blood and he hung on Tonys and Als grip and Tralala swung at his face, spitting, cursing and kicking. Alex yelled to stop and get out. I dont want trouble in here. Tony grabbed the doggie around the neck and Al shoved the bloodied handkerchief in his mouth and they dragged him outside and into a darkened doorway. He was still crying and begging for his ID Card and trying to tell them he wanted to go home when Tony pulled his head up by his hair and Al punched him a few times in the stomach and then in the face, then held him up while Tony hit him a few times; but they soon stopped, not afraid that the cops might come, but they knew he didnt have any money and they were tired from hitting the seaman they had lushed earlier, so they dropped him and he fell to the ground on his back. Before they left Tralala stomped on his face until both eyes were bleeding and his nose was split and broken then kicked him a few times in the balls. Ya rotten scumbag, then they left and walked slowly to 4th avenue and took a subway to manhattan. Just in case somebody might put up a stink. In a day or two he/ll be shipped out and nobodyll know the difference. Just another fuckin doggie. And anyway he deserved it. They ate in a cafeteria and went to an allnight movie. The next day they got a couple of rooms in a hotel on the east side and stayed in manhattan until the following night. When they went back to the Greeks Alex told them some MPs and a detective were in asking about the guys who beat up a soldier the other night. They said he was in bad shape. Had to operate on him and he may go blind in one eye. Ain't that just too bad. The MPs said if they get ahold of the guys who did it theyd killem. Those fuckin punks. Whad the law say. Nottin. You know. Yeah. Killus! The creeps. We oughtta dumpem on general principles. Tralala laughed. I shoulda pressed charges fa rape. I wont be 18 for a week. He raped me the dirty freaky sonofabitch. They laughed and ordered coffeeand. When they finished Al and Tony figured theyd better make the rounds of a few of the bars and see what was doin. In one of the bars they noticed the bartender slip an envelope in a tin box behind the bar. It looked like a pile of bills on the bottom of the box. They checked the window in the MENS ROOM and the alley behind it then left the bar and went back to the Greeks. They told Tralala what they were going to do and went to a furnished room they had rented over one of the bars on 1st avenue. When the bars closed they took a heavy duty screwdriver and walked to the bar. Tralala stood outside and watched the street while they broke in. It only took a few minutes to force open the window, drop inside, crawl to the bar, pickup the box and climb out the window and drop to the alley. They pried open the box in the alley and started to count. They almost panicked when they finished counting. They had almost 2 thousand dollars. They stared at it for a moment then jammed it into their pockets. Then Tony took a few hundred and put it into another pocket and told Al theyd tell Tratala that that was all they got. They smiled and almost laughed then calmed themselves before leaving the alley and meeting Tralala. They took the box with them and dropped it into a sewer then walked back to the room. When they stepped from the alley Tralala ran over to them asking them how they made out and how much they got and Tony told her to keep quiet that they got a couple a hundred and to play it cool until they got back to the room.

When they got back to the room Al started telling her what a snap it was and how they just climbed in and took the box but Tralala ignored him and kept asking how much they got. Tony took the lump of money from his pocket and they counted it. Not bad eh Tral? 250 clams. Yeah. How about giving me 50 now. What for? You aint going no where now. She shrugged and they went to bed. The next afternoon they went to the Greeks for coffee and two detectives came in and told them to come outside. They searched them, took the money from their pockets and pushed them into their car. The detectives waved the money in front of their faces and shook their heads. Dont you know better than to knock over a bookie drop? Huh? Huh, Huh! Real clever arent you. The detectives laughed and actually felt a professional amazement as they looked at their dumb expressions and realized that they really didnt know who they had robbed. Tony slowly started to come out of the coma and started to protest that they didnt do nothin. One of the detectives slapped his face and told him to shutup. For Christs sake dont give us any of that horseshit. I suppose you just found a couple of grand lying in an empty lot? Tralala screeched, a what? The detectives looked at her briefly then turned back to Tony and Al. You can lush a few drunken seamen now and then and get away with it, but when you start taking money from my pocket youre going too far sonny. What a pair of stupid punks . . . OK sister, beat it. Unless you want to come along for the ride? She automatically backed away from the car, still staring at Tony and Al. The doors slammed shut and they drove away. Tralala went back to the Greeks and sat at the counter cursing Tony and Al and then the bulls for pickinem up before she could get hers. Didnt even spend a penny of it. The goddamn bastards. The rotten stinkin sonsofabitches. Those thievin flatfooted bastards. She sat drinking coffee all afternoon then left and went across the street to Willies. She walked to the end of the bar and started talking with Ruthy, the barmaid, telling her what happened, stopping every few minutes to curse Tony, Al, the bulls and lousy luck. The bar was slowly filling and Ruthy left her every few minutes to pour a drink and when she came back Tralala would repeat the story from the beginning, yelling about the 2 grand and they never even got a chance to spend a penny. With the repeating of the story she forgot about Tony and Al and just cursed the bulls and her luck and an occasional seaman or doggie who passed by and asked her if she wanted a drink or just looked at her. Ruthy kept filling Tralalas glass as soon as she emptied it and told her to forget about it. Thats the breaks. No sense in beatin yahead against the wall about it. Theres plenty more. Maybe not that much, but enough. Tralala snarled, finished her drink and told Ruthy to fill it up. Eventually she absorbed her anger and quieted down and when a young seaman staggered over to her she glanced at him and said yes. Ruthy brought them two drinks and smiled. Tralala watched him take the money out of his pocket and figured it might be worthwhile. She told him there were better places to drink than this crummy dump. Well, lez go baby. He gulped his drink and Tralala left hers on the bar and they left. They got into a cab and the seaman asked her whereto and she said she didnt care, anywhere. OK. Takeus to Times Square. He offered her a cigarette and started telling her about everything. His name was Harry. He came from Idaho. He just got back from Italy. He was going to—she didnt bother smiling but watched him, trying to figure out how soon he would pass out. Sometimes they last allnight. Cant really tell. She relaxed and gave it thought. Cant konkim here. Just have ta wait until he passes out or maybe just ask for some money. The way they throw it around. Just gotta getim in a room alone. If he dont pass out I/ll just rapim with somethin—and you should see what we did to that little ol . . . He talked on and Tralala smoked and the lampposts flicked by and the meter ticked. He stopped talking when the cab stopped in front of the Crossroads. They got out and tried to get in the Crossroads but the bartender looked at the drunken seaman and shook his head no. So they crossed the street and went to another bar. The bar was jammed, but they found a small table in the rear and sat down. They ordered drinks and Tralala sipped hers then pushed her unfinished drink across the table to him when he finished his. He started talking again but the lights and the music slowly affected him and the subject matter was changed and he started telling Tralala what a good lookin girl she was and what a good time he was going to show her; and she told him that she would show him the time of his life and didnt bother to hide a yawn. He beamed and drank faster and Tralala asked him if he would give her some money. She was broke and had to have some money or she/d be locked out of her room. He told her not to worry that hed find a place for her to stay tonight and he winked and Tralala wanted to shove her cigarette in his face, the cheap sonofabitch, but figured she/d better wait and get his money before she did anything. He toyed with her hand and she looked around the bar and noticed an Army Officer staring at her. He had a lot of ribbons just like the one she had rolled and she figured hed have more money than Harry. Officers are usually loaded. She got up from the table telling Harry she was going to the ladies room. The Officer swayed slightly as she walked up to him and smiled. He took her arm and asked her where she was going. Nowhere. O, we cant have a pretty girl like you going nowhere. I have a place thats all empty and a sack of whiskey. Well . . . She told him to wait and went back to the table. Harry was almost asleep and she tried to get the money from his pocket and he started to stir. When his eyes opened she started shaking him, taking her hand out of his pocket, and telling him to wakeup. I thought yawere goin to show me a good time. You bet. He nodded his head and it slowly descended toward the table. Hey Harry, wakeup.

The waiter wants to know if yahave any money. Showem ya money so I wont have to pay. You bet. He slowly took the crumpled mess of bills from his pocket and Tralala grabbed it from his hand and said I toldya he had money. She picked up the cigarettes from the table, put the money in her pocketbook and walked back to the bar. My friend is sleeping so I dont think he/ll mind, but I think we/d better leave. They left the bar and walked to his hotel. Tralala hoped she didnt make a mistake. Harry mightta had more money stashed somewhere. The Officer should have more though and anyway she probably got everything Harry had and she could get more from this jerk if he has any. She looked at him trying to determine how much he could have, but all Officers look the same. Thats the trouble with a goddamn uniform. And then she wondered how much she had gotten from Harry and how long she would have to wait to count it. When they got to his room she went right into the bathroom, smoothed out the bills a little and counted them. 45. Shit. Fuckit. She folded the money, left the bathroom and stuffed the money in a coat pocket. He poured two small drinks and they sat and talked for a few minutes then put the light out. Tralala figured there was no sense in trying anything now so she relaxed and enjoyed herself. They were having a smoke and another drink when he turned and kissed her and told her she had the most beautiful pair of tits he had ever seen. He continued talking for a few minutes, but she didnt pay any attention. She thought about her tits and what he had said and how she could get anybody with her tits and the hell with Willies and those slobs, she/d hang around here for a while and do alright. They put out their cigarettes and for the rest of the night she didnt wonder how much money he had. At breakfast the next morning he tried to remember everything that had happened in the bar, but Harry was only vaguely remembered and he didnt want to ask her. A few times he tried speaking, but when he looked at her he started feeling vaguely guilty. When they had finished eating he lit her cigarette, smiled, and asked her if he could buy her something. A dress or something like that. I mean, well you know . . . Id like to buy you a little present. He tried not to sound maudlin or look sheepish, but he found it hard to say what he felt, now, in the morning, with a slight hangover, and she looked to him pretty and even a little innocent. Primarily he didnt want her to think he was offering to pay her or think he was insulting her by insinuating that she was just another prostitute; but much of his loneliness was gone and he wanted to thank her. You see, I only have a few days leave left before I go back and I thought perhaps we could—that is I thought we could spend some more time together . . . he stammered on apologetically hoping she understood what he was trying to say but the words bounced off her and when she noticed that he had finished talking she said sure. What thefuck. This is much better than wresslin with a drunk and she felt good this morning, much better than yesterday (briefly remembering the bulls and the money they took from her) and he might even give her his money before he went back overseas (what could he do with it) and with her tits she could always makeout and whatthehell, it was the best screwin she ever had . . . They went shopping and and she bought a dress, a couple of sweaters (2 sizes too small), shoes, stockings, a pocketbook and an overnight bag to put her clothes in. She protested slightly when he told her to buy a cosmetic case (not knowing what it was when he handed it to her and she saw no sense in spending money on that when he could as well give her cash), and he enjoyed her modesty in not wanting to spend too much of his money; and he chuckled at her childlike excitement at being in the stores, looking and buying. They took all the packages back to the hotel and Tralala put on her new dress and shoes and they went out to eat and then to a movie. For the next few days they went to movies, restaurants (Tralala trying to make a mental note of the ones where the Officers hungout), a few more stores and back to the hotel. When they woke on the 4th day he told her he had to leave and asked her if she would come with him to the station. She went thinking he might give her his money and she stood awkwardly on the station with him, their bags around them, waiting for him to go on the train and leave. Finally the time came for him to leave and he handed her an envelope and kissed her before boarding the train. She felt the envelope as she lifted her face slightly so he could kiss her. It was thin and she figured it might be a check. She put it in her pocketbook, picked up her bag and went to the waiting room and sat on a bench and opened the envelope. She opened the paper and started reading: Dear Tral: There are many things I would like to say and should have said, but—A letter. A goddamn LETTER. She ripped the envelope apart and turned the letter over a few times. Not a cent. I hope you understand what I mean and am unable to say—she looked at the words—if you do feel as I hope you do Im writing my address at the bottom. I dont know if I/ll live through this war, but—Shit. Not vehemently but factually. She dropped the letter and rode the subway to Brooklyn.

THE MARQUIS DE SADE

❦

FROM *Justine* [1965]

Translated from the French by Richard Seaver and Austryn Wainhouse

Until the recent discovery of Volume I of Sade's miscellaneous works (œuvres diverses), which contains his early occasional prose and verse, as well as his one-act play, Le Philosophe soi-disant, *and an epistolary work,* Voyage de Hollande, *the* Dialogue between a Priest and a Dying Man *was his earliest known work to be dated with certainty. Sade completed it, or completed the notebook which contains it, on July 12, 1782, during the fourth year of his second imprisonment in Vincennes. It is one of the most incisive works of Sade, who is not especially noted for his concision, and is contemporary to* The 120 Days of Sodom, *upon which it is known that he was hard at work that same year. Like* The 120 Days, *the* Dialogue between a Priest and a Dying Man *did not figure in Sade's 1788* Catalogue raisonné, *which was limited to works he wished publicly to acknowledge.*

The Dialogue *did not appear until more than a century after Sade's death. In the course of the nineteenth century, the notebook containing it was sold and resold on a number of occasions at various auctions of autograph manuscripts, and in 1920 Maurice Heine was fortunate enough to be able to purchase it at a sale held on November 6 at Paris' Hôtel Drouot. Six years later he published it with an exhaustive introduction.* Since it is included in a notebook containing primarily rough drafts, notes, and jottings, Lely raises the question as to whether this work was ever polished or reworked to the author's satisfaction. Heine's observation, however, that the manuscript was written in a "firm, legible hand, with few words crossed out" would indicate that Sade may well have been satisfied with its composition. In any event, the work needs no apology.*

What may most astonish the reader about the Dialogue *is the author's failure to acknowledge it. For, compared to much of his other writing, it seems tame*

Dialogue entre un prêtre et un moribond, par Donatien-Alphonse-François, marquis de Sade, publié pour la première fois sur le manuscrit autographe inédit, avec un avant-propos et des notes par Maurice Heine. Paris, Stendhal et Cie., 1926.

indeed, despite the ferocity of its attack on the deity and the clerical establishment. As Heine points out, however, one may tend to give the Age of Reason, from the vantage point of the present century, more than its due. In fact, Sade's position on the subject of religion was far more radical than that of most of his contemporaries, even the most enlightened. When, in the Encyclopedia *of 1751, and under their own signatures, Diderot and d'Alembert can pronounce themselves in the following terms, it is easier to understand Sade's reticence:*

> *Even the more tolerant of men will not deny that the judge has the right to repress those who profess atheism, and even to condemn them to death if there is no other way of freeing society from them. . . . If he can punish those who harm a single person, he doubtless has as much a right to punish those who wrong an entire society by denying that there is a God. . . . Such a man may be considered as an enemy of all men.**

In the light of the above, one reads the Dialogue *with a wider respect for the audacity and uncompromising nature of Sade's mind.*

PRIEST: Come to this the fatal hour when at last from the eyes of deluded man the scales must fall away, and be shown the cruel picture of his errors and his vices—say, my son, do you not repent the host of sins unto which you were led by weakness and human frailty?

DYING MAN: Yes, my friend, I do repent.

PRIEST: Rejoice then in these pangs of remorse, during the brief space remaining to you profit therefrom to obtain Heaven's general absolution for your sins, and be mindful of it, only through the mediation of the Most Holy Sacrament of penance will you be granted it by the Eternal.

DYING MAN: I do not understand you, any more than you have understood me.

PRIEST: Eh?

DYING MAN: I told you that I repented.

PRIEST: I heard you say it.

DYING MAN: Yes, but without understanding it.

PRIEST: My interpretation—

*Ibid.

DYING MAN: Hold. I shall give you mine. By Nature created, created with very keen tastes, with very strong passions; placed on this earth for the sole purpose of yielding to them and satisfying them, and these effects of my creation being naught but necessities directly relating to Nature's fundamental designs or, if you prefer, naught but essential derivatives proceeding from her intentions in my regard, all in accordance with her laws, I repent not having acknowledged her omnipotence as fully as I might have done, I am only sorry for the modest use I made of the faculties (criminal in your view, perfectly ordinary in mine) she gave me to serve her; I did sometimes resist her, I repent it. Misled by your absurd doctrines, with them for arms I mindlessly challenged the desires instilled in me by a much diviner inspiration, and thereof do I repent: I only plucked an occasional flower when I might have gathered an ample harvest of fruit—such are the just grounds for the regrets I have, do me the honor of considering me incapable of harboring any others.

PRIEST: Lo! where your fallacies take you, to what pass are you brought by your sophistries! To created being you ascribe all the Creator's power, and those unlucky penchants which have led you astray, ah! do you not see they are merely the products of corrupted nature, to which you attribute omnipotence?

DYING MAN: Friend—it looks to me as though your dialectic were as false as your thinking. Pray straighten your arguing or else leave me to die in peace. What do you mean by Creator, and what do you mean by corrupted nature?

PRIEST: The Creator is the master of the universe, 'tis He who has wrought everything, everything created, and who maintains it all through the mere fact of His omnipotence.

DYING MAN: An impressive figure indeed. Tell me now why this so very formidable fellow did nevertheless, as you would have it, create a corrupted nature?

PRIEST: What glory would men ever have, had not God left them free will; and in the enjoyment thereof, what merit could come to them, were there not on earth the possibility of doing good and that of avoiding evil?

DYING MAN: And so your god bungled his work deliberately, in order to tempt or test his creature—did he then not know, did he then not doubt what the result would be?

PRIEST: He knew it undoubtedly but, once again, he wished to leave to man the merit of choice.

DYING MAN: And to what purpose, since from the outset he knew the course affairs would take and since, all-mighty as you tell me he is, he had but to make his creature choose as suited him?

PRIEST: Who is there can penetrate God's vast and infinite designs regarding man, and who can grasp all that makes up the universal scheme?

DYING MAN: Anyone who simplifies matters, my friend, anyone, above all, who refrains from multiplying causes in order to confuse effects all the more. What need have you of a second difficulty when you are unable to resolve the first, and once it is possible that Nature may all alone have done what you attribute to your god, why must you go looking for someone to be her overlord? The cause and explanation of what you do not understand may perhaps be the simplest thing in the world. Perfect your physics and you will understand Nature better; refine your reason, banish your prejudices and you'll have no further need of your god.

PRIEST: Wretched man! I took you for no worse than a Socinian—arms I had to combat you. But 'tis clear you are an atheist, and seeing that your heart is shut to the authentic and innumerable proofs we receive every day of our lives of the Creator's existence—I have no more to say to you. There is no restoring the blind to the light.

DYING MAN: Softly, my friend, own that between the two, he who blindfolds himself must surely see less of the light than he who snatches the blindfold away from his eyes. You compose, you construct, you dream, you magnify and complicate; I sift, I simplify. You accumulate errors, pile one atop the other; I combat them all. Which one of us is blind?

PRIEST: Then you do not believe in God at all?

DYING MAN: No. And for one very sound reason: it is perfectly impossible to believe in what one does not understand. Between understanding and faith immediate connections must subsist; understanding is the very lifeblood of faith; where understanding has ceased, faith is dead; and when they who are in such a case proclaim they have faith, they deceive. You yourself, preacher, I defy you to believe in the god you predicate to me—you must fail because you cannot demonstrate him to me, because it is not in you to define him to me, because consequently you do not understand him—because as of the moment you do not understand him, you can no longer furnish me any reasonable argument concerning him, and because, in sum, anything beyond the limits and grasp of the human mind is either illusion or futility; and because your god having to be one or the other of the two, in the first instance I should be mad to believe in him, in the second a fool. My friend, prove to me that matter is inert and I will grant you a creator, prove to me that Nature does not suffice to herself and I'll let you imagine her ruled by a higher force; until then, expect nothing from me, I bow to evidence only, and evidence I perceive only through my senses: my belief goes no farther than they, beyond that point my faith collapses. I believe in the sun because I see it, I conceive it as the focal center of all the inflammable matter in Nature, its periodic movement pleases but does not amaze me. 'Tis a mechanical operation, perhaps as simple as the workings of electricity, but which we are unable to understand. Need I bother more about it? when you have roofed everything over with your god, will I be any the better off? and shall I still not have to make an effort at least as great to understand the artisan as to define his handiwork? By edifying your chimera it is thus no service you have rendered me, you have made me uneasy in my mind but you have not enlightened it, and instead of gratitude I owe you resentment. Your god is a machine you fabricated in your passions' behalf, you manipulated it to their liking; but the day it interfered with mine, I kicked it out of my way, deem it fitting that I did so; and now, at this moment when I sink and my soul stands in need of calm and philosophy, belabor it not with your riddles and your cant, which alarm but will not convince it, which will irritate without improving it; good friends and on the best terms have we ever been, this soul and I, so Nature wished it to be; as it is, so she expressly modeled it, for my soul is the result of the dispositions she formed in me pursuant to her own ends and needs; and as she has an equal need of vices and of virtues, whenever she was pleased to move me to evil, she did so, whenever she wanted a good deed from me, she roused in me the desire to perform one, and even so I did as I was bid. Look nowhere but to her workings for the unique cause of our fickle human behavior, and in her laws hope to find no other springs than her will and her requirements.

PRIEST: And so whatever is in this world, is necessary.

DYING MAN: Exactly.

PRIEST: But if everything is necessary—then the whole is regulated.

DYING MAN: I am not the one to deny it.

PRIEST: And what can regulate the whole save it be an all-powerful and all-knowing hand?

DYING MAN: Say, is it not necessary that gunpowder ignite when you set a spark to it?

PRIEST: Yes.

DYING MAN: And do you find any presence of wisdom in that?

PRIEST: None.

DYING MAN: It is then possible that things necessarily come about without being determined by a superior intelligence, and possible hence that everything derive logically from a primary cause, without there being either reason or wisdom in that primary cause.

PRIEST: What are you aiming at?

DYING MAN: At proving to you that the world and all therein may be what it is and as you see it to be, without any wise and reasoning cause directing it, and that natural effects must have natural causes: natural causes sufficing, there is no need to invent any such unnatural ones as your god who himself, as I have told you already, would require to be explained and who would at the same time be the explanation of nothing; and that once 'tis plain your god is superfluous, he is perfectly useless; that what is useless would greatly appear to be imaginary only, null and therefore nonexistent; thus, to conclude that your god is a fiction I need no other argument than that which furnishes me the certitude of his inutility.

PRIEST: At that rate there is no great need for me to talk to you about religion.

DYING MAN: True, but why not anyhow? Nothing so much amuses me as this sign of the extent to which human beings have been carried away by fanaticism and stupidity; although the prodigious spectacle of folly we are facing here may be horrible, it is always interesting. Answer me honestly, and endeavor to set personal considerations aside: were I weak enough to fall victim to your silly theories concerning the fabulous existence of the being who renders religion necessary, under what form would you advise me to worship him? Would you have me adopt the daydreams of Confucius rather than the absurdities of Brahma, should I kneel before the great snake to which the Blacks pray, invoke the Peruvians' sun or Moses' Lord of Hosts, to which Mohammedan sect should I rally, or which Christian heresy would be preferable in your view? Be careful how you reply.

PRIEST: Can it be doubtful?

DYING MAN: Then 'tis egoistical.

PRIEST: No, my son, 'tis as much out of love for thee as for myself I urge thee to embrace my creed.

DYING MAN: And I wonder how the one or the other of us can have much love for himself, to deign to listen to such degrading nonsense.

PRIEST: But who can be mistaken about the miracles wrought by our Divine Redeemer?

DYING MAN: He who sees in him anything else than the most vulgar of all tricksters and the most arrant of all impostors.

PRIEST: *O God, you hear him and your wrath thunders not forth!*

DYING MAN: No, my friend, all is peace and quiet around us, because your god, be it from impotence or from reason or from whatever you please, is a being whose existence I shall momentarily concede out of condescension for you or, if you prefer, in order to accommodate myself to your sorry little perspective; because this god, I say, were he to exist, as you are mad enough to believe, could not have selected as means to persuade us, anything more ridiculous than those your Jesus incarnates.

PRIEST: What! the prophecies, the miracles, the martyrs—are they not so many proofs?

DYING MAN: How, so long as I abide by the rules of logic, how would you have me accept as proof anything which itself is lacking proof? Before a prophecy could constitute proof I should first have to be completely certain it was ever pronounced; the prophecies history tells us of belong to history and for me they can only have the force of other historical facts, whereof three out of four are exceedingly dubious; if to this I add the strong probability that they have been transmitted to us by not very objective historians, who recorded what they preferred to have us read, I shall be quite within my rights if I am skeptical. And furthermore, who is there to assure me that this prophecy was not made after the fact, that it was not a stratagem of everyday political scheming, like that which predicts a happy reign under a just king, or frost in wintertime? As for your miracles, I am not any readier to be taken in by such rubbish. All rascals have performed them, all fools have believed in them; before I'd be persuaded of the truth of a miracle I would have to be very sure the event so called by you was absolutely contrary to the laws of Nature, for only what is outside of Nature can pass for miraculous; and who is so deeply learned in Nature that he can affirm the precise point where her domain ends, and the precise point where it is infringed upon? Only two things are needed to accredit an alleged miracle, a mountebank and a few simpletons; tush, there's the whole origin of your prodigies; all new adherents to a religious sect have wrought some; and more extraordinary still, all have found imbeciles around to believe them. Your Jesus' feats do not surpass those of Apollonius of Tyana, yet nobody thinks to take the latter for a god; and when we come to your martyrs, assuredly, these are the feeblest of all your arguments. To produce martyrs you need but have enthusiasm on the one hand, resistance on the other; and so long as an opposed cause offers me as many of them as does yours, I shall never be sufficiently authorized to believe one better than another, but rather very much inclined to consider all of them pitiable. Ah my friend! were it true that the god you preach did exist, would he need miracle, martyr, or prophecy to secure recognition? and if, as you declare, the human heart were of his making, would he not have chosen it for the repository of his law? Then would this law, impartial for all mankind because emanating from a just god, then would it be found graved deep and writ clear in all men alike, and from one end of the world to the other; all men, having this delicate and sensitive organ in common, would also re-semble each other through the homage they would render the god whence they had got it; all would adore and serve him in one identical manner, and they would be as incapable of disregarding this god as of resisting the inward im-pulse to worship him. Instead of that, what do I behold throughout this world? As many gods as there are countries; as many different cults as there are differ-ent minds or different imaginations; and this swarm of opinions among which it is physically impossible for me to choose, say now, is this a just god's doing? Fie upon you, preacher, you outrage your god when you present him to me thus; rather let me deny him completely, for if he exists then I outrage him far less by my incredulity than do you through your blasphemies. Return to your senses, preacher, your Jesus is no better than Mohammed, Mohammed no bet-ter than Moses, and the three of them combined no better than Confucius, who did after all have some wise things to say while the others did naught but rave; in general, though, such people are all mere frauds: philosophers laughed at them, the mob believed them, and justice ought to have hanged them.

PRIEST: Alas, justice dealt only too harshly with one of the four.

DYING MAN: If he alone got what he deserved it was he deserved it most richly; seditious, turbulent, calumniating, dishonest, libertine, a clumsy buffoon, and very mischievous; he had the art of overawing common folk and stirring up the rabble; and hence came in line for punishment in a kingdom where the state of affairs was what it was in Jerusalem then. They were very wise indeed to get rid of him, and this perhaps is the one case in which my extremely lenient and also extremely tolerant maxims are able to allow the severity of Themis; I ex-cuse any misbehavior save that which may endanger the government one lives under—kings and their majesties are the only things I respect; and whoever does not love his country and his king were better dead than alive.

PRIEST: But you do surely believe something awaits us after this life, you must at some time or another have sought to pierce the dark shadows enshrouding our mortal fate, and what other theory could have satisfied your anxious spirit, than that of the numberless woes that betide him who has lived wickedly, and an eternity of rewards for him whose life has been good?

DYING MAN: What other, my friend? that of nothingness: it has never held terrors for me, in it I see naught but what is consoling and unpretentious; all the other theories are of pride's composition, this one alone is of reason's. Moreover, 'tis neither dreadful nor absolute, this nothingness. Before my eyes have I not the example of Nature's perpetual generations and regenerations? Nothing perishes in the world, my friend, nothing is lost; man today, worm tomorrow, the day after tomorrow a fly; is it not to keep steadily on existing? And what entitles me to be rewarded for virtues which are in me through no fault of my own, or again punished for crimes wherefor the ultimate responsibility is not mine? how are you to put your alleged god's goodness into tune with this system, and can he have wished to create me in order to reap pleasure from punishing me, and that solely on account of a choice he does not leave me free to determine?

PRIEST: You are free.

DYING MAN: Yes, in terms of your prejudices; but reason puts them to rout, and the theory of human freedom was never devised except to fabricate that of grace, which was to acquire such importance for your reveries. What man on earth, seeing the scaffold a step beyond the crime, would commit it were he free not to commit it? We are the pawns of an irresistible force, and never for an instant is it within our power to do anything but make the best of our lot and forge ahead along the path that has been traced for us. There is not a single virtue which is not necessary to Nature and conversely not a single crime which she does not need and it is in the perfect balance she maintains between the one and the other that her immense science consists; but can we be guilty for adding our weight to this side or that when it is she who tosses us onto the scales? no more so than the hornet who thrusts his dart into your skin.

PRIEST: Then we should not shrink from the worst of all crimes.

DYING MAN: I say nothing of the kind. Let the evil deed be proscribed by law, let justice smite the criminal, that will be deterrent enough; but if by misfortune we do commit it even so, let's not cry over spilled milk; remorse is inefficacious, since it does not stay us from crime, futile since it does not repair it, therefore it is absurd to beat one's breast, more absurd still to dread being punished in another world if we have been lucky to escape it in this. God forbid that this be construed as encouragement to crime, no, we should avoid it as much as we can, but one must learn to shun it through reason and not through false fears which lead to naught and whose effects are so quickly overcome in any moderately steadfast soul. Reason, sir—yes, our reason alone should warn us that harm done our fellows can never bring happiness to us; and our heart, that contributing to their felicity is the greatest joy Nature has accorded us on earth; the entirety of human morals is contained in this one phrase: *Render others as happy as one desires oneself to be,* and never inflict more pain upon them than one would like to receive at their hands. There you are, my friend, those are the only principles we should observe, and you need neither god nor religion to appreciate and subscribe to them, you need only have a good heart. But I feel my strength ebbing away; preacher, put away your prejudices, unbend, be a man, be human, without fear and without hope forget your gods and your religions too: they are none of them good for anything but to set man at odds with man, and the mere name of these horrors has caused greater loss of life on earth than all other wars and all other plagues combined. Renounce the idea of another world; there is none, but do not renounce the pleasure of being happy and of making for happiness in this. Nature offers you no other way of doubling your existence, of extending it.—My friend, lewd pleasures were ever dearer to me than anything else, I have idolized them all my life and my wish has been to end it in their bosom; my end draws near, six women lovelier than the light of day are waiting in the chamber adjoining, I have reserved them for this moment, partake of the feast with me, following my example embrace them instead of the vain sophistries of superstition, under their caresses strive for a little while to forget your hypocritical beliefs.

NOTE

The dying man rang, the women entered; and after he had been a little while in their arms the preacher became one whom Nature has corrupted, all because he had not succeeded in explaining what a corrupt nature is.

HAROLD PINTER

❧

FROM *The Homecoming* [1965]

Lenny comes back into the room, goes to the window and looks out.
He leaves the window and turns on a lamp.
He is holding a small clock.
He sits, places the clock in front of him, lights a cigarette and sits.
Ruth comes in the front door.
She stands still. Lenny turns his head, smiles. She walks slowly into the room.

LENNY: Good evening.

RUTH: Morning, I think.

LENNY: You're right there.

Pause.

My name's Lenny. What's yours?

RUTH: Ruth.

She sits, puts her coat collar around her.

LENNY: Cold?

RUTH: No.

LENNY: It's been a wonderful summer, hasn't it? Remarkable.

Pause.

Would you like something? Refreshment of some kind? An aperitif, anything like that?

RUTH: No, thanks.

LENNY: I'm glad you said that. We haven't got a drink in the house. Mind you, I'd soon get some in, if we had a party or something like that. Some kind of celebration . . . you know.

Pause.

You must be **connected** with my brother in some way. The one who's been abroad.

RUTH: I'm his wife.

LENNY: Eh listen, I wonder if you can advise me. I've been having a bit of a rough time with this clock. The tick's been keeping me up. The trouble is I'm not all that convinced it was the clock. I mean there are lots of things which tick in the night, don't you find that? All sorts of objects, which, in the day, you wouldn't call anything else but commonplace. They give you no trouble. But in the night any given one of a number of them is liable to start letting out a bit of a tick. Whereas you look at these objects in the day and they're just commonplace. They're as quiet as mice during the daytime. So . . . all things being equal . . . this question of me saying it was the clock that woke me up, well, that could very easily prove something of a false hypothesis.

He goes to the sideboard, pours from a jug into a glass, takes the glass to Ruth.

Here you are. I bet you could do with this.

RUTH: What is it?

LENNY: Water.

She takes it, sips, places the glass on a small table by her chair. Lenny watches her.

Isn't it funny? I've got my pyjamas on and you're fully dressed?

He goes to the sideboard and pours another glass of water.

Mind if I have one? Yes, it's funny seeing my old brother again after all these years. It's just the sort of tonic my Dad needs, you know. He'll be chuffed to his bollocks in the morning, when he sees his eldest son. I was surprised myself when I saw Teddy, you know. Old Ted. I thought he was in America.

RUTH: We're on a visit to Europe.

LENNY: What, both of you?

RUTH: Yes.

LENNY: What, you sort of live with him over there, do you?

RUTH: We're married.

LENNY: On a visit to Europe, eh? Seen much of it?

RUTH: We've just come from Italy.

LENNY: Oh, you went to Italy first, did you? And then he brought you over here to meet the family, did he? Well, the old man'll be pleased to see you, I can tell you.

RUTH: Good.

LENNY: What did you say?

RUTH: Good.

Pause.

LENNY: Where'd you go to in Italy?

RUTH: Venice.

LENNY: Not dear old Venice? Eh? That's funny. You know, I've always had a feeling that if I'd been a soldier in the last war—say in the Italian campaign—I'd probably have found myself in Venice. I've always had that feeling. The trouble was I was too young to serve, you see. I was only a child, I was too small, otherwise I've got a pretty shrewd idea I'd probably have gone through Venice. Yes, I'd almost certainly have gone through it with my battalion. Do you mind if I hold your hand?

RUTH: Why?

LENNY: Just a touch.

He stands and goes to her.

Just a tickle.

RUTH: Why?

He looks down at her.

LENNY: I'll tell you why.

Slight pause.

One night, not too long ago, one night down by the docks, I was standing alone under an arch, watching all the men jibbing the boom, out in the harbour, and playing about with the yardarm, when a certain lady came up to me and made me a certain proposal. This lady had been searching for me for days. She'd lost track of my whereabouts. However, the fact was she eventually caught up with me, and when she caught up with me she made me this certain proposal. Well, this proposal wasn't entirely out of order and normally I would have subscribed to it. I mean I would have subscribed to it in the normal course of events. The only trouble was she was falling apart with the pox. So I turned it down. Well, this lady was very insistent and started taking liberties with me down under this arch, liberties which by any criterion I couldn't be expected to tolerate, the facts being what they were, so I clumped her one. It was on my mind at the time to do away with her, you know, to kill her, and the fact is, that as killings go, it would have been a simple matter, nothing to it. Her chauffeur, who had located me for her, he'd popped round the corner to have a drink, which just left this lady and myself, you see, alone, standing underneath this arch, watching all the steamers steaming up, no one about, all quiet on the Western Front, and there she was up against this wall—well, just sliding down the wall, following the blow I'd given her. Well, to sum up, everything was in my favour, for a killing. Don't worry about the chauffeur. The chauffeur would never have spoken. He was an old friend of the family. But . . . in the end I thought . . . Aaah, why go to all the bother . . . you know, getting rid of the corpse and all that, getting yourself into a state of tension. So I just gave her another belt in the nose and a couple of turns of the boot and sort of left it at that.

RUTH: How did you know she was diseased?

LENNY: How did I know?

Pause.

I decided she was.

Silence.

You and my brother are newly-weds, are you?

RUTH: We've been married six years.

LENNY: He's always been my favourite brother, old Teddy. Do you know that? And my goodness we are proud of him here, I can tell you. Doctor of Philosophy and all that . . . leaves quite an impression. Of course, he's a very sensitive man, isn't he? Ted. Very. I've often wished I was as sensitive as he is.

RUTH: Have you?

LENNY: Oh yes. Oh yes, very much so. I mean, I'm not saying I'm not sensitive. I am. I could just be a bit more so, that's all.

RUTH: Could you?

LENNY: Yes, just a bit more so, that's all.

Pause.

I mean, I am very sensitive to atmosphere, but I tend to get desensitized, if you know what I mean, when people make unreasonable demands on me. For instance, last Christmas I decided to do a bit of snow-clearing for the Borough Council, because we had a heavy snow over here that year in Europe. I didn't have to do this snow-clearing—I mean I wasn't financially embarrassed in any way—it just appealed to me, it appealed to something inside me. What I anticipated with a good deal of pleasure was the brisk cold bite in the air in the early morning. And I was right. I had to get my snowboots on and I had to stand on a corner, at about five-thirty in the morning, to wait for the lorry to pick me up, to take me to the allotted area. Bloody freezing. Well, the lorry came, I jumped on the tailboard, headlights on, dipped, and off we went. Got there, shovels up, fags on, and off we went, deep into the December snow, hours before cockcrow. Well, that morning, while I was having my mid-morning cup of tea in a neighbouring cafe, the shovel standing by my chair, an old lady approached me and asked me if I would give her a hand with her iron mangle. Her brother-in-law, she said, had left it for her, but he'd left it in the wrong room, he'd left it in the front room. Well, naturally, she wanted it in the back room. It was a present he'd given her, you see, a mangle, to iron out the washing. But he'd left it in the wrong room, he'd left it in the front room, well that was a silly place to leave it, it couldn't stay there. So I took time off to give her a hand. She only lived up the road. Well, the only trouble was when I got there I couldn't move this mangle. It must have weighed about half a ton. How this brother-in-law got it up there in the first place I can't even begin to envisage. So there I was, doing a bit of shoulders on with the mangle, risking a rupture, and this old lady just standing there, waving me on, not even lifting a little finger to give me a helping hand. So after a few minutes I said to her, now look here, why don't you stuff this iron mangle up your arse? Anyway, I said, they're out of date, you want to get a spin drier. I had a good mind to give her a workover there and then, but as I was feeling jubilant with the snow-clearing I just gave her a short-arm jab to the belly and jumped on a bus outside. Excuse me, shall I take this ashtray out of your way?

RUTH: It's not in my way.

LENNY: It seems to be in the way of your glass. The glass was about to fall. Or the ashtray. I'm rather worried about the carpet. It's not me, it's my father. He's obsessed with order and clarity. He doesn't like mess. So, as I don't believe you're smoking at the moment, I'm sure you won't object if I move the ashtray.

He does so.

And now perhaps I'll relieve you of your glass.

RUTH: I haven't quite finished.

LENNY: You've consumed quite enough, in my opinion.

RUTH: No, I haven't.

LENNY: Quite sufficient, in my own opinion.

RUTH: Not in mine, Leonard.

Pause.

LENNY: Don't call me that, please.

RUTH: Why not?

LENNY: That's the name my mother gave me.

Pause.

Just give me the glass.

RUTH: No.

Pause.

LENNY: I'll take it, then.

RUTH: If you take the glass . . . I'll take you.

Pause.

LENNY: How about me taking the glass without you taking me?

RUTH: Why don't I just take you?

Pause.

LENNY: You're joking.

Pause.

You're in love, anyway, with another man. You've had a secret liaison with another man. His family didn't even know. Then you come here without a word of warning and start to make trouble.

She picks up the glass and lifts it towards him.

RUTH: Have a sip. Go on. Have a sip from my glass.

He is still.

Sit on my lap. Take a long cool sip.

She pats her lap. Pause. She stands, moves to him with the glass.

Put your head back and open your mouth.

LENNY: Take that glass away from me.

RUTH: Lie on the floor. Go on. I'll pour it down your throat.

LENNY: What are you doing, making me some kind of proposal?

She laughs shortly, drains the glass.

RUTH: Oh, I was thirsty.

She smiles at him, puts the glass down, goes into the hall and up the stairs. He follows into the hall and shouts up the stairs.

LENNY: What was that supposed to be? Some kind of proposal?

Silence.
He comes back into the room, goes to his own glass, drains it.

ANONYMOUS

༺✿༻

FROM *My Secret Life* [1966]

A gap in the narrative.—A mistress.—A lucky legacy.—Secret preparations.—A sudden flight.—At Paris.—A dog and a woman.—At a lake-city.—A South American lady.—Mrs. O*b***e.—Glimpses from a bed-room window.—Hairy arm-pits.—Stimulating effects.—Acquaintance made.—The children.— "Play with Mamma like Papa." A water *excursion.—Lewed effects.—Contiguous bed-rooms.—Double doors.—Nights of nakedness.—Her form.—Her sex.—Carnal confessions.—Periodicity of lust.*

I pass over many incidents of a couple of years or more, during which I was well off, had a mistress whom I had seduced, as it is stupidly called, and had children; but it brought me no happiness, and I fled from the connection. All this was never known to the world. My home life at length became so un-bearable, that I at one time thought of realizing all I had, of throwing up all chance of advancement and a promising career which then was before me, and going for ever abroad I knew not where, nor cared. My mother had died, one sister was married, and was not much comfort to me; the other was far off, my brother nowhere. Just then a distant relative left me a largish sum of money, it was scarcely known to any one of my friends, quite unknown at home, and to none until I had spent a good deal of it. I kept the fact to myself till I had put matters in such train that I could get a couple of thousand pounds on account, then qui-etly fitted myself out with clothes. One day I sent home new portmanteaus, and packed up my clothes the same day. "I am going abroad," I said. "When?" "To-night." "Where to? "I don't know,—that is my business." "When do you come back? "Perhaps in a week,—perhaps a year,"—nor did I for a long time. I never wrote to England during that time, excepting to my solicitors and bankers who necessarily knew where I had been at times.

I went first to Paris, where I ran a course of baudy house amusements, saw a big dog fuck a woman who turned her rump towards it as if she were a bitch. The dog licked and smelt her cunt first, and then fucked. He was accus-tomed to the treat. Then I saw a little spaniel lick another French woman's cunt.

She put a little powdered sugar on her clitoris first, and when the dog had licked that off, somehow she made it go on licking, until she spent, or shammed a spend, calling out, "Nini,—cher Nini,—go on Nini,"—in French of course.

I could make a long story out of both of these incidents if it were worth while, but it is not, and only notice that the Newfoundland, whose tongue hung out quite as long as his prick as he was pushing his penis up the French woman's quim, turned suddenly round when it had spent, seemed astonished to find he was not sticking arse to arse with her, and then licked the remains of the sperm off the tip of his prick. It was not a nice sight at all, nor did I ever want to see it again.

There were few large cities of Central Europe I did not see, and think that the best baudy houses in most large cities saw *me*. It was a journey in which my amatory doings were especially with the priestesses of Venus. Beautiful faces and beautiful limbs were sufficient for me, if coupled with ready submission to my wishes. Although I learnt no doubt a great deal, and had my voluptuous tastes cultivated in a high degree, yet they developed none of those outside tastes which ordinarily come with great knowledge and practice in the matters of cunt. I shall only tell the must remarkable fornicating incidents.

I was at the Hotel B*** in a Swiss town by a great lake, had arrived late, and was put into the third story, in a room overlooking a quadrangle. It was hot. I threw up my window when I got out of bed in the morning, and in night-gown looked into the quadrangle, and at the walls and windows of the various bed-rooms opening on to it on three sides. Looking down on my right, and one story below me, I caught sight over the window-curtain of a bed-room, of a female head of long dark hair, and a naked arm brushing it up from behind vigorously. The arm looked the size of a powerful man's, but it was that of a woman. She moved about heedlessly, and soon I saw that she was naked to below her breasts; but I only caught glimpses of that nakedness, for seconds, as she moved backwards and forwards near the window. Then she held up the hair for a minute, and seemed to be contemplating the effect of the arrangement of it, and showed what looked like a nest of hair beneath one armpit. Her flesh looked sallow or brown, and she seemed big and middle-aged. My window was near the angle of the quadrangle, so was hers, on the adjacent side of it. Perhaps from the window where I was, and that above mine only, could be seen all what I saw.

The armpit excited me, and I got lewed, though the glimpses were so few and short. Now I only saw the nape of the neck, and now her back, according to the postures which a woman takes in arranging her hair, and so far as the looking-glass and blinds and my position above let me. Once or so I saw big breasts of a tawny color. Then she looked at her teeth. Then she disappeared, then came forwards again, and I fancied she was naked to the waist. Then I lost sight of her, and again for an instant saw just the top of her naked bum, as if she were stripped, and in stooping down had bent her back towards the window. When she reappeared she was more dressed. She looked up at the sky, approaching the window to do so, caught sight of me, and quickly drew the blind right down.

I went down to breakfast, met some friends, and sitting down to table with them in the large breakfast-room, saw close to me this very lady. I had seen so little of her face that I did not recognize her at first by that; but the darkness of the eye and hair, the fullness of bust, and the brown-tinted skin left me in no doubt. We were introduced to each other. "Mrs. O*b***e, a lady from New Orleans, a great friend of ours,—been travelling with us for some weeks, with her two little children,"—and so on.

I found out from my friends as we smoked our cigars in the gardens after breakfast, that she, with another American lady, and themselves, were going for a long tour, and had been touring for some weeks in Europe. She was the wife of a gentleman who owned plantations, and had gone back to America; intending to rejoin his wife at Paris at Christmas. The lady with the very hairy armpits and her husband were intimate friends of my friends.

I found this party were travelling my road, and I agreed to wait at °°°° as long as they did. We met at meals; I joined in their excursions, and took much notice of her children who got quite fond of me. She seemed to avoid me at first, but in two or three days showed some sympathy. I guessed that my history had been made known to her, and found out at a latter day that it had. "A married man travelling without his wife is dangerous," said she to me one day when we were a merry party. "A married woman without her husband is a danger to me," I replied, and our eyes met, and said more than words.

I objected to my room, and in a few days the hotel-keeper showed me some better rooms. I had then ascertained which hers were, and pointed out the room next to them. "That," said he, "won't do—it's large, and has two beds." "Oh! it's so hot, I want a large room,—show it me." He did. "It's double price." "Never mind,"—and I took it at once. Luck, thought I. Her own room was next, and adjoining it a room in which her two children slept. A half-governess, half-maid who travelled with her, was on another floor,—why I don't know,— perhaps because the next room to the children's was a sitting-room.

My new room had as usual a door communicating with hers. I listened one or two nights and mornings, and heard the slopping of water and rattle of pots, but with difficulty; and nothing sufficiently to stir my imagination or satisfy my curiosity. There were bolts on both sides of the doors, and double doors. I opened mine, and tried if hers was fastened. It was. But I waited my opportunity, intending to try to have her, thinking that a woman who had not had a man for months, and might not for some months more, would be ready for a game of mother and father if she could do so safely.

She was not very beautiful, but was fine, tallish, handsomely formed, with a large bust, and splendid head of hair. Her complexion had the olive tint of some Southerners. One night almost have supposed there was a taint of Negro blood in her, but her features were rather aquiline and good. The face was coldish and stern, the eyes dark and heavy, the only sensuous feature of her face was a full, large-lipped mouth, which was bandy in its expression when she laughed. I guess she was a devil of a temper.

After a day or two I gave up all hope, for she would not understand double entendres, coldly returned my grasp when I shook hands with her, and gave no signs of pleasure in my company, excepting when I was playing with her children. Yet when she looked into my face when laughing; there certainly was something in her eye, which made me think that a pair of balls knocking about her bum would delight her. I used to think much of what a friend of mine, a surgeon in a crack regiment in which I had some friends, used to say, which was this.

"All animals are in rut sometimes, so is a woman, even the coldest of them. It's of no use trying the cold ones, unless they have the tingling in their cunts on them; then they are more mad for it than others, but it doesn't last. If you catch a cold woman just when she is on heat, try her; but how to find out their time, I never knew,—they are damned cunning." So said the surgeon.

I must have caught Mrs. O*b***e on heat I suppose, and it came about soon. We went out for some hours on the lake in a boat. She was timid, and when the boat rocked I held her, squeezed her arm, and my knees went against hers. Another time my thigh was close against hers. I put one of her children on to her lap. The child sat down on my hand, which was between her little bum and her mother's thighs. I kept my hand there, gradually moving it away, creeping it up higher and higher, and gripping the thigh as I moved it towards the belly, but so delicately, as to avoid offence, and I looked her in the face. "Minnie is heavy, isn't she?" I said. "She is getting so," she replied, looking with a full eye at mine.

Now I felt sure from her look, that she knew I was feeling her thigh. I had stirred her voluptuousness. The water got rougher. "I shall be sick," said she. "What! on such a lake!" "Oh! I'm a bad sailor." Placing my arm round her for a minute I pulled her close to me. It became calm, and lovely weather again. The water always upset her, it seemed to stir her up, she said. "I'd like to see you stirred up," said I. Then to avoid remark I changed sides with a lady, and sat opposite to Mrs. O*b***e. We faced each other, looking at each other. I pushed my feet forward, so as to rub my foot against her ankle. She did not remove her foot, but looked at me.

Arrived at *** we dined, and sat afterwards in the garden. It grew dusk, and we separated into groups. I sat by her side, and played with her children. One child said, "Play with me like Papa,—play with Mamma like Papa does." "Shall I play with you like Papa?" said I to Mrs. O*b***e. "I'd rather not," said she. "I'd break an arm to do so," I replied. "Would you?" said she. "Oh! put the children to bed Margaret,"—and the governess with the children and Mrs. O*b***e walked off. I for a minute joined my friends smoking, then cut off by a side-path leading to that through which Mrs. O*b***e would pass. She had just bid the children good night. "I shall come up to see you directly," said she to them,—and to me, "I thought you were going into town." "Yes I think I'll make a night of it,—I'm wild.—I want company." "Fine company it will be, I dare say." "Let me keep you company then." No one was near, I kissed her. She took it very quietly. "Don't now, you'll compromise me." It was now quite dusk. I kissed her again. "I'm dying to sleep with you," I whispered. "You mustn't talk like that,—there now, they will see you,"—then I left her.

I had noticed her habits, and knew that usually she went up to her children soon after they had gone to bed, so I waited at the foot of the stairs. Soon she came. "What, you here?" "Yes, I'm going to bed like you." It was a sultry night, everybody was out of doors, the hotel servants lolling at open windows. No one met us as we went upstairs. "Why that's not your room,—it's next to mine." "Yes it is,—I've been listening to you the last two nights." "Oh! you sly man,—I thought you were sly." "Look what a nice room it is," said I opening the door. There was a dim light in the corridors, none in my room. She looked in, I gave her a gentle squeezing push, and shut the door on us.

"Don't shut the door," said she turning sharply round. I caught and kissed her. "Stop with me, my darling, now you're here,—I'm dying for you,—kiss me, do." "Let me go,—there then,—now let me go,—don't make a noise,—oh! If my governess should hear me, what would she think!" "She is not there." "Sometimes she stays till I go up to the children,—oh! don't now,— you shan't." I had her up against the wall, my arm round her, I was pressing my hand on her belly outside her clothes. She pushed my hand away, I stooped and thrust it up her clothes on to her cunt, and pulling out my prick, pushed her hand on to it. "Let me,—let's do it,—I'm dying for you." "Oh! for God's sake don't, oh! no—now, you'll compromise me,—hish! if she should be listening." For a moment we talked, she quietly struggled, entreating me to desist; but my fingers were well on to her cunt, frigging it. I don't recollect more what she said, but I got her to the side of the bed, pushed her back on it, and thrust my prick up her. "Oh! don't compromise me—don't now." Then she fucked quietly till she gasped out, "Oho—oho," as a torrent of my sperm shot into her cunt.

Excepting from the clear light of the night, which came from the sky through the window in the quadrangle, the room was in darkness. I don't know that my prick ever lingered longer up a woman after fucking and declared that whilst up her, I told how I had seen her brushing her hair, and so on. She said that I should compromise her,—and oh! if she should be with child,—"what will become of me." Feeling the sperm oozing out over my balls, and my prick shrinking, I uncunted. "Oh! what have you made me do, you bad man?" said she sitting upon the side of the bed. "Oh! if they should see me going out of your room,—oh! if she has been listening."

I drew down the blind, and lighted a candle, much against her wish. She sat at the edge of the bed just where she had been fucked, her clothes still partly up. I listened at the door between our two rooms, but heard nothing, then told her again how I had watched her from a top-window, and seen her breasts and armpits. My prick stiffened at my own tale. Sitting down by her side, "Let's do it again my love," I said, and pushed my hand up her clothes. I shall never forget the feel. The whole length of her thighs, as she closed them on my hand felt like a pot of paste. Only a minute's pleasure, and such a mass of sperm! She repulsed me, and stood up.

I stood up too; kissing, coaxing, insisting, she looking at me, I fingering, pulling backwards and forwards the prepuce of my penis. No, she would not. Then I threatened to make a noise, if she would not, and swore I would have her again. She promised to let me if I would let her go to her bed-room first,— she would unlock her side of the two doors, if she could. She was not sure if there was a key,—if not she would open the door on to the corridor, but only at midnight, when the gas was turned out, and few people about. She promised solemnly, and sealed it with a kiss. "Oh! for God's sake be quiet." I opened the door of my bed-room, and saw no one in the lobby. Out she went, and got into her own room unnoticed, Then I opened the door to her room from my side. There were double doors.

She seemed to keep me a long time waiting, though she had scarcely been in her room five minutes. I stripped myself to my shirt, then knocked at the door gently, then louder. A key turned, the door opened. She had only gone in to be sure that the children were in their bed, and the governess not with them. "Oh! I have been so fearful lest she should have been there," she said.

The children were asleep, she had bolted their door. "And now go to bed, and let me also,—there is a dear man, and don't ask anything more of me." "To bed yes, but with you." She begged me not, all in a whisper. My reply was to strip off my shirt, and stand start naked with prick throbbing, and wagging, and nodding with its size, weight, and randiness. "Only once, one more, and then I will be content." "No."

"Then damned if I won't," said I moving towards her. "Hush! my children will hear,—in your room then,"—and she came towards my door. "Oh! nonsense, not with your clothes on,—let us have our full pleasure,—and this hot night too,—take off your things." Little by little she did, and stood in her chemise. I tried all the doors, they were securely fastened, and then I brought her quite into my room. "Leave me alone a minute," she said. But as randy as if I had not left my sperm up her fifteen minutes before, I would not, and pulled her gently toward my bed, tore the clothes off, so as to leave the bottom sheet only on, and got her on to the bed. "Do let me see your cunt." "No,—no,—no." As I pulled up her chemise, down she pushed it. "Oh! no,—I'm sure I shall be with child," said she, "and if I am I'd just best make a hole in the water." Her big breasts were bare, her thighs opened, a grope on the spermy surface, and then fucking began. "Oho!" she sighed out loudly again, as she spent.

Off and on until daybreak we fucked. After the second she gave herself up to pleasure. The randiest slut just out of a three months quodding could not have been hotter or readier for lewed fun with cunt and ballocks. I never had a more randy bed-fellow. She did not even resist the inspection of her cunt, which surprised me a little, considering its condition. Our light burnt out, our games heated us more and more, the room got oppressive. I slipped off her chemise, our naked bodies entwined in all attitudes, and we fucked, and fucked, bathed in sweat, till the sweat and sperm wetted all over the sheet, and we slept. It was broad daylight when we awakened. I was lying sweating with her bum up against my belly, her hair was loose all over her, and the bed. Then we separated and she fled to her room, carrying her chemise with her.

Oh! Lord that sheet!—if ten people had fucked on it, it could not have been more soiled. We consulted how best to hide it from the chamber-maid, and I did exactly the same trick as of former days. Have not all men done it I wonder?

I got a sitz-bath in my room, which was then not a very easy thing to get. I washed in it, wetted all my towels, then took off the sheet, wetted it nearly all over, soiled it, then roughly put it together in a heap, and told the chamber-woman I had used the sheet to dry myself with. She said, "Very well." I don't expect she troubled herself to undo or inspect the wet linen, or thought about the matter.

I went to breakfast at the usual time. "Where is Mrs. O*b***e?" I asked. The governess appeared with the children saying the lady had not slept owing to the heat. She showed up at the table d'hôtel dinner. I avoided her, knowing I should see her soon afterwards, and said I should go and play billiards; but instead, went to my bed-room and read; nursing my concupiscent tool, and imagining coming pleasures.

I heard the children, having opened the door on my side and found that the key of her door was luckily so turned as to leave the key-hole clear. The doors connecting all the rooms were as is often the case in foreign hotels, opposite each other, and I could see across into the children's bed-room. They were putting their night-gowns on in their own room. Then the governess came into her mistress' room and I heard her pissing, but could not see her. To my great amusement, for the slightest acts of a woman in her privacy give me pleasure, she then came forward within range of my peep-hole, and was looking into the pot carefully. Then Mrs. O*b***e came in and the governess left. Mrs. O*b***e went to look at her children and returned, opened our doors, and then we passed another amorous night, taking care to put towels under her bum when grinding. We did not want the sheets to he a witness against us again.

Mrs. O*b***e was not up to the mark, and began to talk that sort of bosh that women do, who are funky of consequences. After a time she warmed, and yielded well to my lubricity. I would see her cunt to begin with. It was a pretty cunt, and not what I had expected, large, fat-lipped, and set in a thicket of black hair, from her bum-hole to her navel; but quite a small slit, with a moderate quantity of hair on her motte, but very thick and crisp. I told her again how I had seen her from the window. The recital seemed to render her randier than either feeling my prick, or my titillation of her quim. The hair in her armpits was thicker, I think, than in any woman I ever had. Her head-hair was superb in its quantity. I made her undo it, and spread it over the bed, and throw up her arms, and show her armpits when I fucked her. She was juicy-cunted, and spent copiously; so did I. The heat was fearful. We fucked stark naked, again.

Later on she told me that she cared about poking but once a month only, and about a week before her courses came on. At other times it annoyed her. Going on the water always upset her stomach, and made her lewed, even if in a boat on a river, and however smooth it was, it upset her that way. At sea it was the same. It made her firstly feel sick, then giddy, then sleepy, but that always two or three hours afterwards, randiness overtook her. After a day or two, the lewedness subsided whether she copulated, or frigged, or not. She told me this as a sort of excuse for having permitted me to spermatize her privates, the night of her excursion on the water with us.

She was curious about my history. I told her I had women at every town I came to. She declared that no other man but I and her husband had ever had her.

IRVING ROSENTHAL

❦

FROM *Sheeper* [1967]

I am locked out of the prose and have been so for days. And the inside of my cock tickles from wearing too tight pants, and knives thrust toward the center of my forehead from behind my eyes, and my asshole itches either with wanting or not wanting to be screwed, and all I can think of is shoe boxes filled with baby bats who don't know how to fly yet, and earthen nests of female earwigs hungrily waiting for their eggs to hatch so they can be mothers, and Huncke about to be busted now that he is bristling with needles again like a porcupine. And though I know I will always find cream to lap up and be gorged with cream like a fat black cat, think of what I have to screen out to go on with the story. And buck the bad grace not to say dereliction of duty of that wrinkled Muse refusing me all help and then dozing off to sleep so frowardly. "It will have to be a construction of your brain alone," she mumbles.

Yet for all my pluck I know I am doomed, for even if I could go on, my fingers can tell only part of the truth—I am under oath—and, besides, decay and dejection poisoned the air I breathed in Trocchi's pad from the first moment I was inside, but at that time I had to see only the good, and so my original vision was discordant and clouded. Even the little true beauty I picked up there, to pop in my mouth and suck on, was mixed with a slow-acting poison to make the eyes opaque and dreamless, and so I wandered through the world with a black notebook I never wrote in, till the Ram broke through the clouds and then the sway of Libra in the heavens swang my heart to beat. No wonder the mind is filled with nicks and nibbles, and in this jumpy and spiritless mood, I take up my pen.

And so Smilowitz and I tumbled out into the night, and a blue needlepoint mist blew into our faces. The street was empty of people but littered with garbage, and we passed a broken bookcase I almost asked Smilowitz to help me lug home, but I gave it up so as not to have gone out falsely. We passed a cat with a piece of raw liver in its mouth furtively searching for a place to eat it. "Blast all cats,"

I said, "for the countless hypodermic needles filled with cat dander serum." Smilowitz stepped into the blue light of a street lamp, took out his wallet, searched through it briefly, and handed me a small printed clipping, watching my face intently as I read it. "Keep it," he said.

> A traveller, coming upon the graveyard of a ruined abbey, saw a procession of cats lowering a small coffin with a crown on it into a grave. Some weeks later he related what he had seen to a friend, and the friend's cat, who had been lying quietly curled up before the fire, on hearing the story sprang up crying out "Now I am king of the cats!"

We continued walking together right up to the door of a ramshackle tenement on Bdellatomy Avenue, where Smilowitz bade me goodnight. As I pushed the door open, a foul draft or rather blast of cockroach odor assaulted me. I made my way upstairs in the dim inner light of a vase, and the first thing I saw when I reached the second floor landing was the legend "Musée Imaginaire" in black Gothic letters, on a shirt cardboard tacked to a door. I could hear no sound from behind that door, either before I knocked or after. I waited a minute and then knocked again, and my knock was answered by a great crash just behind the door, followed by a volley of squeals, as if from women running through rooms. But no one opened the door, and I knocked again.

This time I was answered with loud scrapes and bangs, as if heavy wooden objects were being stacked against the door to barricade it. The transom was glass painted over, for I could see the gleam of a naked light bulb through a tiny spot where the paint had been scratched away. Suddenly that spot went black. An eye was watching me. Then a muffled female voice said, "Who is it?" I said, "Sheeper." Silence. A murmur of consultation. A Scottish-accented voice that must have been Trocchi's said, "Who? Sheeper? Let him in!" More wooden bangs and scrapes as what seemed to be a platform of chairs and tables up to the peephole was dismantled. Finally a latch snapped, a crack of light appeared, and the door swang open smoothly, on a tableau of Trocchi seated in a chair facing the door, squeezing the rubber bulb of a medicine dropper into his arm. He looked up at me, and I saw the pleasure spread on his face like a star. "You are a gracious man," I said.

I am in a market place that suddenly springs to life as the door closes behind me. Everyone is talking at double-time, talking drugs and trading drugs. A fifteen-year-old Porto Rican pusher seems to be auctioning off packets of heroin. A painter with only two teeth left in his mouth works furiously at an easel on which, instead of a canvas, a lady's summer coat has been stretched. He is humming happily and talking to himself as he works. A young girl seated in a chair by the door is sharpening a spike on a matchbook cover (I thought she was filing a fingernail). She looks up into my eyes and asks me what my chemistry is. I am not sure of her meaning until someone nearby says, "Chemistry, chemistry, you know man, your glands." I tell her regretfully that I am queer. The man who translated her question is standing nonchalantly naked with a hard-on I simply can't take my eyes off of.

I manage to shake hands with Trocchi. We rap a bit over the din. I tell him about Allen's note, and he says he is glad I have come, and that I should make myself at home, but that I would have to excuse him for a few minutes as he was in the middle of a lecture when I knocked on the door. He simply turned about-face and walked off.

The floor was completely littered with drawings and manuscripts, and every square inch of every sheet and scrap of paper had been utilized. Manuscript margins were filled with india ink sketches, and handwriting in all colors followed the contours of figure and symbol, giving each graphic form a strange talismanic aureola. All these papers were torn and shoeprinted and formed a thick, uncomfortable carpet. Textures of color, astronomical signs, animal forms, and Greek and Hebrew letters were painted onto the walls themselves, and these designs were partially obscured by numberless abstract paintings taped and tacked to the walls everywhere. Furniture *qua* furniture simply did not exist in the room, but in the carved and painted objects of art strewn carelessly about, one could detect a drawer knob, chair leg, or alabaster lamp base. Propped against the wall were two half-finished paintings on the head and foot boards of a dismantled bed. An old-fashioned icebox had been half-crayoned over into a Persian casque. In the corner of a beautiful batik hanging was the label of a bed sheet company. The texture of broken wood was especially favored, and large wooden splinters that had once made up chairs and tables were painted fastidiously in brilliant parti-colors. Everything functional had been drafted into the service of art, taken apart and reassembled, and many things looked subjected to more than one transformation, as if the lust to create had been so overpowering as to become cannibalistic, or as if each object of art, once created, became as stupid as a lamp or bookend, and had to be destroyed and built anew. The whole room seemed to belong to another world, to whose inhabitants these uncanny furnishings were the beds and chairs of everyday life.

Bits of conversation drifted my way. "I remember the time I couldn't stand the sight of a needle." . . . "A user for twelve years and never been hooked." . . . "I got beat for a fiver today, my last fiver, there must be a panic in this city, and it was people I know man, good people." . . . "Man I used to gross a hundred a

day pushing pot in Needles—and every ounce to friends I turned on myself."
The toothless painter yells out, "It's only a question of time before we're all
busted" and then he laughs insanely. A windowshade flies up. Two girls rush
to the window looking for cops.

Six or seven people stand round a sink in the corner waiting to shoot
up. Only one dropper is functioning. The rest are clogged, leaning in a glass
of water like a few stalks of lily-of-the-valley, on a glass shelf above the sink.
Another glass of water is used to rinse the dropper between fixes, and a third
glass is filled with amphetamine sulfate solution, apparently being used in
wholesale quantity. Why aren't the clogged needles being cleaned? Obviously because everyone enjoys standing around watching each other shoot
up so much. A seventeen-year-old boy in a brilliant white cardigan sweater
grows restless. His hair is black and glossy. There is a long white comb in his
back pocket. His eyes are black and quiet as an angel's. He looks like a student body president. He tilts his head mischievously and asks for a taste. He
means, can he have a fix out of turn. There is a grumble of acquiescence, and
someone hands him a full dropper, saying, "You had two fixes already, go
easy." They watch him tie, and run a pale handsome finger down the vein he
will puncture. How tenderly he handles the needle. How indignantly he refuses someone's offer to shoot him up. And now the needle goes into the
skin—blood—we are breathless. He bolts half the dropper as if he were starving, and then slowly, slowly he boots the last half in, now mixed with blood:
he pulses it in, to extract maximum pleasure, as in fucking. How exquisitely
he shudders. He is paralyzed with pleasure, and his face is a mask of raptur-
ous pain. Here are lusts and pleasures as pure and strong as sexual ones, and
the mechanical act which accompanies them is free of *intercourse* with others
(the voyeurism is gratuitous). All of us have empathic orgasms watching the
boy, you can practically hear us shoot off, one after the other. Someone hungry to fix tells the boy to pull the needle out already, but the boy cannot and
sinks to his knees sweating. The hungry one pulls it out for him, not kindly.
The boy is a kneeling Jesus whom everyone detests and admires. Even Trocchi,
returned, jerks a censorious thumb at him: "He never says anything. He won't
even show us his badge," This is called cop paranoia, and it wanders through
the apartment like anybody else.

The hungry one who shoots up next is a bodybuilder with huge blue
flower tattoos on his arms. He is straight from a health magazine cover and
makes Trocchi standing beside him look even more gaunt and wasted. He has
punctured his skin and is pushing the needle through a vein wall. His face is
screwed up, and the pounds of meat on his arms and back are contracting

clonically. All his huge mammal strength is being used to force the shyest cock in the world into the greediest asshole. Between the big twitches of his muscles there are easier trembles like flowers. Is it a miss? Slowly a red curl of blood rises in the dropper, and we start breathing again. And as he squeezes the rubber bulb, all of us feel the drug hit our brains, in as close empathy with each other's pleasure as with his. I am drowning in forbidden pleasure in an orgy I don't even know how I got into. . . .

IMAMU AMIRI BARAKA (LEROI JONES)

❧

"Uncle Tom's Cabin: Alternate Ending"

FROM *Tales* [1967]

"6½" *was* the answer. But it seemed to irritate Miss Orbach. Maybe not the answer—the figure itself, but the fact it should be there, and in such loose possession.

"OH who is he to know such a thing? That's really improper to set up such liberations. And moreso."

What came into her head next she could hardly understand. A breath of cold. She did shudder, and her fingers clawed at the tiny watch she wore hidden in the lace of the blouse her grandmother had given her when she graduated teachers' college.

Ellen, Eileen, Evelyn . . . Orbach. She could be any of them. Her personality was one of theirs. As specific and as vague. The kindly menace of leading a life in whose balance evil was a constant intrigue but grew uglier and more remote as it grew stronger. She would have loved to do something really dirty. But nothing she had ever heard of was dirty enough. So she contented herself with good, i.e., purity, as a refuge from mediocrity. But being unconscious, or largely remote from her own sources, she would only admit to the possibility of grace. Not God. She would not be trapped into *wanting* even God.

So remorse took her easily. For any reason. A reflection in a shop window, of a man looking in vain for her ankles. (Which she covered with heavy colorless woolen.) A sudden gust of warm damp air around her legs or face. Long dull rains that turned her from her books. Or, as was the case this morning, some completely uncalled-for shaking of her silent doctrinaire routines.

"6½" had wrenched her unwillingly to exactly where she was. Teaching the 5th grade, in a grim industrial complex of northeastern America; about 1942. And how the social doth pain the anchorite.

Nothing made much sense in such a context. People moved around, and disliked each other for no reason. Also, and worse, they said they loved each other, and usually for less reason, Miss Orbach thought. Or would have if she did.

And in this class sat 30 dreary sons and daughters of such circumstance. Specifically, the thriving children of the thriving urban lower middle classes.

Postmen's sons and factory-worker debutantes. Making a great run for America, now prosperity and the war had silenced for a time the intelligent cackle of tradition. Like a huge grey bubbling vat the country, in its apocalyptic version of history and the future, sought now, its equally apocalyptic profile of itself as it had urged swiftly its own death since the Civil War. To promise. Promise. And that to be that all who had ever dared to live here would die when the people and interests who had been its rulers died. The intelligent poor now were being admitted. And with them a great many Negroes . . . who would die when the rest of the dream died not even understanding that they, like Ishmael, should have been the sole survivors. But now they were being tricked. "6½" the boy said. After the fidgeting and awkward silence. One little black boy raised his hand, and looking at the tip of Miss Orbach's nose said 6½. And then he smiled, very embarrassed and very sure of being wrong.

I would have said "No, boy, shut up and sit down. You are wrong. You don't know anything. Get out of here and be very quick. Have you no idea what you're getting involved in? My God . . . you nigger, get out of here and save yourself, while there's time. Now beat it." But those people had already been convinced. Read Booker T. Washington one day, when there's time. What that led to. The 6½'s moved for power . . . and there seemed no other way.

So three elegant Negroes in light grey suits grin and throw me through the window. They are happy and I am sad. It is an ample test of an idea. And besides "6½" is the right answer to the woman's question.

[The psychological and the social. The spiritual and the practical. Keep them together and you profit, maybe, someday, come out on top. Separate them, and you go along the road to the commonest of Hells. The one we westerners love to try to make art out of.]

The woman looked at the little brown boy. He blinked at her, trying again not to smile. She tightened her eyes, but her lips flew open. She tightened her lips, and her eyes blinked like the boy's. She said, "How do you get that answer?" The boy told her. "Well, it's right," she said, and the boy fell limp, straining even harder to look sorry. The Negro in back of the answerer pinched him, and the boy shuddered. A little white girl next to him touched his hand, and he tried to pull his own hand away with his brain.

"Well, that's right, class. That's exactly right. You may sit down now Mr. McGhee."

Later on in the day, after it had started exaggeratedly to rain very hard and very stupidly against the windows and soul of her 5th-grade class, Miss Orbach became convinced that the little boy's eyes were too large. And in fact they did bulge almost grotesquely white and huge against his bony heavy-veined skull. Also, his head was much too large for the rest of the scrawny body.

And he talked too much, and caused too many disturbances. He also stared out the window when Miss Orbach herself would drift off into her sanctuary of light and hygiene even though her voice carried the inanities of arithmetic seemingly without delay. When she came back to the petty social demands of 20th-century humanism the boy would be watching something walk across the playground. OH, it just would not work.

She wrote a note to Miss Janone, the school nurse, and gave it to the boy, McGhee, to take to her. The note read:

"Are the large eyes a sign of ————?"

Little McGhee, of course, could read, and read the note. But he didn't of course understand the last large word which was misspelled anyway. But he tried to memorize the note, repeating to himself over and over again its contents . . . sounding the last long word out in his head, as best he could.

Miss Janone wiped her big nose and sat the boy down, reading the note. She looked at him when she finished, then read the note again, crumpling it on her desk.

She looked in her medical book and found out what Miss Orbach meant. Then she said to the little Negro, Dr. Robard will be here in 5 minutes. He'll look at you. Then she began doing something to her eyes and fingernails.

When the doctor arrived he looked closely at McGhee and said to Miss Janone, "Miss Orbach is confused."

McGhee's mother thought that too. Though by the time little McGhee had gotten home he had forgotten the "long word" at the end of the note.

"Is Miss Orbach the woman who told you to say sangwich instead of sammich," Louise McGhee giggled.

"No, that was Miss Columbe."

"Sangwich, my christ. That's worse than sammich. Though you better not let me hear you saying sammich either . . . like those Davises."

"I don't say sammich, mamma."

"What's the word then?"

"Sandwich."

"That's right. And don't let anyone tell you anything else. Teacher or otherwise. Now I wonder what that word could've been?"

"I donno. It was very long. I forgot it."

Eddie McGhee Sr. didn't have much of an idea what the word could be either. But he had never been to college like his wife. It was one of the most conspicuously dealt with factors of their marriage.

So the next morning Louise McGhee, after calling her office, the Child Welfare Bureau, and telling them she would be a little late, took a trip to the school, which was on the same block as the house where the McGhees lived, to speak to Miss Orbach about the long word which she suspected might be injurious to her son and maybe to Negroes In General. This suspicion had been bolstered a great deal by what Eddie Jr. had told her about Miss Orbach, and also equally by what Eddie Sr. had long maintained about the nature of White People In General. "Oh well," Louise McGhee sighed, "I guess I better straighten this sister out." And that is exactly what she intended.

When the two McGhees reached the Center Street school the next morning Mrs. McGhee took Eddie along with her to the principal's office, where she would request that she be allowed to see Eddie's teacher.

Miss Day, the old, lady principal, would then send Eddie to his class with a note for his teacher, and talk to Louise McGhee, while she was waiting, on general problems of the neighborhood. Miss Day was a very old woman who had despised Calvin Coolidge. She was also, in one sense, exotically liberal. One time she had forbidden old man Seidman to wear his pince-nez anymore, as they looked too snooty. Center Street sold more war stamps than any other grammar school in the area, and had a fairly good track team.

Miss Orbach was going to say something about Eddie McGhee's being late, but he immediately produced Miss Day's note. Then Miss Orbach looked at Eddie again, as she had when she had written her own note the day before.

She made Mary Ann Fantano the monitor and stalked off down the dim halls. The class had a merry time of it when she left, and Eddie won an extra 2 Nabisco graham crackers by kissing Mary Ann while she sat at Miss Orbach's desk.

When Miss Orbach got to the principal's office and pushed open the door she looked directly into Louise McGhee's large brown eyes, and fell deeply and hopelessly in love.

TOM STOPPARD

❦

FROM *Rosencrantz & Guildenstern Are Dead* [1967]

ROS: Incidents! All we get is incidents? Dear God, is it too much to expect a little sustained action?!

And on the word, the Pirates attack. That is to say: Noise and shouts and rushing about. "Pirates."'

Everyone visible goes frantic. Hamlet draws his sword and "rushes downstage. Guil, Ros and Player draw swords and rush upstage. Collision. Hamlet turns back up. They turn back down. Collision. By which time there is general panic right upstage. All four charge upstage with Ros, Guil and Player shouting:

At last!
To arms!
Pirates!
Up there!
Down there!
To my sword's length!
Action!

All four reach the top, see something they don't like, waver, run for their lives downstage:

Hamlet, in the lead, leaps into the left barrel. Player leaps into the right barrel. Ros and Guil leap into the middle barrel. All closing the lids after them.

The lights dim to nothing while the sound of fighting continues. The sound fades to nothing. The lights come up. The middle barrel (Ros and Guil's) is missing.

The lid of the right-hand barrel is raised cautiously, the heads of Ros and Guil appear.

The lid of the other barrel (Hamlet's) is raised. The head of the Player appears. All catch sight of each other and slam down lids.

Pause.

Lids raised cautiously.

ROS (*relief*): They've gone. (*He starts to climb out.*) That was close. I've never thought quicker.

They are all three out of barrels. Guil is wary and nervous. Ros is light-headed. The Player is phlegmatic. They note the missing barrel.

Ros looks round.

ROS: Where's—?

The Player takes off his hat in mourning.

PLAYER: Once more, alone—on our own resources.

GUIL (*worried*): What do you mean? Where is he?

PLAYER: Gone.

GUIL: Gone where?

PLAYER: Yes, we were dead lucky there. If that's the word I'm after.

ROS (*not a pickup*): Dead?

PLAYER: Lucky.

ROS: (*he means*): Is he dead?

PLAYER: Who knows?

GUIL (*rattled*): He's not coming back?

PLAYER: Hardly.

ROS: He's dead then. He's dead as far as we're concerned.

PLAYER: Or we are as far as he is. (*He goes and sits on the floor to one side.*) Not too bad, is it?

GUIL (*rattled*): But he can't—we're supposed to be—we've got a *letter*—we're going to England with a letter for the King—

PLAYER: Yes, that much seems certain. I congratulate you on the unambiguity of your situation.

GUIL: But you don't understand—it contains—we've had our instructions— the whole thing's pointless without him.

PLAYER: Pirates could happen to anyone. Just deliver the letter. They'll send ambassadors from England to explain. . . .

GUIL (*worked up*): Can't you see—the pirates left us home and high—dry and home—drome— (*Furiously.*) The pirates left us high and dry!

PLAYER (*comforting*): There . . .

GUIL (*near tears*): Nothing will be resolved without him. . . .

PLAYER: There . . . !

GUIL: We need Hamlet for our release!

PLAYER: There!

GUIL: What are we supposed to do?

PLAYER: This.

He turns away, lies down if he likes. Ros and Guil apart.

ROS: Saved again.

GUIL: Saved for what?

Ros sighs.

ROS: The sun's going down. (*Pause.*) It'll be night soon. (*Pause.*) If that's west. (*Pause.*) Unless we've—

GUIL (*shouts*): Shut up! I'm sick of it! Do you think conversation is going to help us now?

ROS (*hurt, desperately ingratiating*): I—I bet you all the money I've got the year of my birth doubled is an odd number.

GUIL (*moan*): No-o.

ROS: Your birth!

Guil smashes him down.

GUIL (*broken*): We've travelled too far, and our momentum has taken over; we move idly towards eternity, without possibility of reprieve or hope of explanation.

ROS: Be happy—if you're not even *happy* what's so good about surviving? (*He picks himself up.*) We'll be all right. I suppose we just go on.

GUIL: Go where?

ROS: To England.

GUIL: England! *That's* a dead end. I never believed in it anyway.

ROS: All we've got to do is make our report and that'll be that. Surely.

GUIL: I don't *believe* it—a shore, a harbour, say—and we get off and we stop someone and say—Where's the King?—And he says, Oh, you follow that road there and take the first left and— (*Furiously.*) I don't believe any of it!

ROS: It doesn't sound very plausible.

GUIL: And even if we came face to face, what do we say?

ROS: We say—We've arrived!

GUIL (*kingly*): And who are you?

ROS: We are Guildenstern and Rosencrantz.

GUIL: Which is which?

ROS: Well, I'm—You're—

GUIL: What's it all about?—

ROS: Well, we were bringing Hamlet—but then some pirates—

GUIL: I don't begin to understand. Who are all these people, what's it got to do with me? You turn up out of the blue with some cock and bull story—

ROS (*with letter*): We have a letter—

GUIL (*snatches it, opens it*): A letter—yes—that's true. That's something . . . a letter . . . (*Reads.*) "As England is Denmark's faithful tributary . . . as love between them like the palm might flourish, etcetera . . . that on the knowing of this contents, without delay of any kind, should those bearers, Rosencrantz and Guildenstern, be put to sudden death—"

He double-takes. Ros snatches the letter. Guil snatches it back. Ros snatches it half back. They read it again and look up.

The Player gets to his feet and walks over to his barrel and kicks it and shouts into it.

PLAYER: They've gone? It's all over!

One by one the Players emerge, impossibly, from the barrel, and form a casually menacing circle round Ros and Guil, who are still appalled and mesmerised.

GUIL (*quietly*): Where we went wrong was getting on a boat. We can move, of course, change direction, rattle about, but our movement is contained within a larger one that carries us along as inexorably as the wind and current. . . .

ROS: They had it in for us, didn't they? Right from the beginning. Who'd have thought that we were so important?

GUIL: But why? Was it all for this? Who are we that so much should converge on our little deaths? (*In anguish to the Player:*) Who are *we*?

PLAYER: You are Rosencrantz and Guildenstern. That's enough.

GUIL: No—it is not enough. To be told so little—to such an end—and still, finally, to be denied an explanation—

PLAYER: In our experience, most things end in death.

GUIL (*fear, vengeance, scorn*): Your experience!—*Actors!*

He snatches a dagger from the Player's belt and holds the point at the Player's throat: the Player backs and Guil advances, speaking more quietly.

I'm talking about death—and you've never experienced *that*. And you cannot *act* it. You die a thousand casual deaths—with none of that intensity which squeezes out life . . . and no blood runs cold anywhere. Because even as you die you know that you will come back in a different hat. But no one gets up after *death*—there is no applause—there is only silence and some second-hand clothes, and that's—*death*—

And he pushes the blade in up to the hilt. The Player stands with huge, terrible eyes, clutches at the wound as the blade withdraws: he makes small weeping sounds and falls to his knees, and then right down.

While he is dying, Guil, nervous, high, almost hysterical, wheels on the Tragedians—

If we have a destiny, then so had he—and if this is ours, then that was his— and if there are no explanations for us, then let there be none for him—

The Tragedians watch the Player die: they watch with some interest. The Player finally lies still. A short moment of silence. Then the Tragedians start to applaud with genuine admiration. The Player stands up, brushing himself down.

PLAYER (*modestly*): Oh, come, come, gentlemen—no flattery—it was merely competent—

The Tragedians are still congratulating him. The Player approaches Guil, who stands rooted, holding the dagger.

PLAYER: What did you think? (*Pause.*) You see, it *is* the kind they do believe in—it's what is expected.

He holds his hand out for the dagger. Guil slowly puts the point of the dagger on to the Player's hand, and pushes . . . the blade slides back into the handle. The Player smiles, reclaims the dagger.

For a moment you thought I'd—cheated.

Ros relieves his own tension with loud nervy laughter.

ROS: Oh, very good! *Very* good! Took me in completely—didn't he take you in completely—(*claps his hands*). Encore! Encore!

PLAYER (*activated, arms spread, the professional*): Deaths for all ages and occasions! Deaths by suspension, convulsion, consumption, incision, execution, asphyxiation and malnutrition—! Climactic carnage, by poison and by steel—! Double deaths by duel—! Show!—

Alfred, still in his Queen's costume, dies by poison: the Player, with rapier, kills the "King" and duels with a fourth Tragedian, inflicting and receiving a wound. The two remaining Tragedians, the two "Spies" dressed in the same coats as Ros and Guil, are stabbed, as before. And the light is fading over the deaths which take place right upstage.

(*Dying amid the dying—tragically; romantically.*) So there's an end to that— it's commonplace: light goes with life, and in the winter of your years the dark comes early. . . .

GUIL (*tired, drained, but still an edge of impatience; over the mime*): No . . . no . . . not for *us*, no like that. Dying is not romantic, and death is not a game which will soon be over. . . . Death is not anything . . . death is not . . . It's the absence of presence, nothing more . . . the endless time of never coming back . . . a gap you can't see, and when the wind blows through it, it makes no sound. . . .

The light has gone upstage. Only Guil and Ros are visible as Ros's clapping falters to silence.

Small pause.

ROS: That's it, then, is it?

No answer. He looks out front.

The sun's going down. Or the earth's coming up, as the fashionable theory has it.

Small pause.

Not that it makes any difference.

Pause.

What was it all about? When did it begin?

Pause. No answer.

Couldn't we just stay put? I mean no one is going to come on and drag us off. . . .
They'll just have to wait. We're still young . . . fit . . . we've got years. . . .

Pause. No answer.

(*A cry.*) We've done nothing wrong! We didn't harm anyone. Did we?

GUIL: I can't remember.

Ros pulls himself together.

ROS: All right, then. I don't care. I've had enough. To tell you the truth, I'm
relieved.

And he disappears from view. Guil does not notice.

GUIL: Our names shouted in a certain dawn . . . a message . . . a summons . . .
There must have been a moment, at the beginning, where we could have said—
no. But somehow we missed it. (*He looks round and sees he is alone.*)

Rosen—?
Guil—?

He gathers himself.

Well, we'll know better next time. Now you see me, now you—(*and disappears*).

Immediately the whole stage is lit up, revealing, upstage, arranged in the approximate positions last held by the dead Tragedians, the tableau of court and corpses which is the last scene of Hamlet.

That is: The King, Queen, Laertes and Hamlet all dead. Horatio holds Hamlet. Fortinbras is there.

So are two Ambassadors from England.

AMBASSADOR: The sight is dismal;
and our affairs from England come too late.
The ears are senseless that should give us hearing

to tell him his commandment is fulfilled,
that Rosencrantz and Guildenstern are dead.
Where should we have our thanks?

HORATIO: Not from his mouth,
had it the ability of life to thank you:
He never gave commandment for their death.
But since, so jump upon this bloody question,
you from the Polack wars, and you from England,
are here arrived, give order that these bodies
high on a stage be placed to the view;
and let me speak to the yet unknowing world
how these things came about: so shall you hear
of carnal, bloody and unnatural acts,
of accidental judgments, casual slaughters,
of deaths put on by cunning and forced cause,
and, in this upshot, purposes mistook
fallen on the inventors' heads: all this can I
truly deliver.

But during the above speech, the play fades out, overtaken by dark and music.

CHE GUEVARA

❦

FROM *Bolivian Diaries* [1968]

Translated from the Spanish by Helen R. Lane

Che Guevara's diary has been the cause of great international speculation ever since its capture by the Bolivian military authorities was reported in the press. So far, the Bolivian government has not made public its contents. There have been reports of negotiations between the Bolivian Barrientos regime and international publishing combines for the sale of the diary at sums variously mentioned at between $100,000 and $300,000.

A section of the secret diary has came into *Evergreen*'s possession, along with notebooks and various other documents evidently discovered on the bodies of captured or slain guerrillas. In transcribing all these documents from the photocopies of the handwritten Spanish originals, it became necessary to leave a few gaps where the writing was illegible. These are indicated in the translations published below. Same of the document pages begin or end in the middle of sentences. In order to make them meaningful to the American reader, we have provided the necessary historical explanations and given autobiographical descriptions of the names occurring in the documents.

The diary has also figured prominently in the trial of French writer Régis Debray, author of *Revolution in the Revolution?*, who is now serving a thirty-year jail sentence in Bolivia. Debray himself has said that Che's diary, if published, would prove the charges against him to be spurious. Indeed, it is interesting to note that almost all the documents which have come into *Evergreen*'s possession contain some references to Debray (his code name in the diary is "Danton," but he is also referred to at times as "the Frenchman") or to his fellow-prisoner, Argentine artist Carlos Bustos. In many of the documents the references to Debray were underlined. These sections, then, may well have constituted a prosecution file carefully selected from captured documents to buttress the government's charge that Debray was, in fact, a guerrilla combatant rather than a journalist. The text of these documents proves the flimsy nature of the charge. This would also explain why the Bolivian military authorities refused to make them public.—*Eds.*

Che's Bolivian Campaign

From all appearances guerrilla activities in Bolivia began in the first half of 1966. At this time political experts and veteran fighters of the Cuban Revolution that ended the regime of Fulgencio Batista began to arrive in Bolivia. Mention is generally made of Papi and Ricardo in this connection. The creation of this guerrilla center stems from a direct understanding between Che Guevara and a small pro-Soviet sector of the Bolivian Communist Party (PCB).

As regards the exact date of Che's last arrival in Bolivia, several versions exist: some observers claim that he arrived in July of 1966, others that he arrived in September or October. The truth appears to be that he entered the country at the end of July, remaining only a few days, and then returned for good during the last week in October. He then took upon himself the task of organizing the guerrillas, visiting La Paz, Cochabamba, and Santa Cruz. To be precise, he joined the guerrillas and assumed direct command of them on November 7, in the central camp, or mother-cell, of Ñancahuazú, about eighty-five miles southeast of La Paz. Soon afterward, future guerrillas from Bolivia and from other countries began to be taken in; at the same time a permanent contact network was established between the guerrilla center and the cities most important to the revolutionary movement.

On Sunday, October 8, 1967, the last remaining guerrilla company, composed of seventeen men in all, with Guevara at their head, encountered Company B of the Bolivian Rangers Batallion, commanded by Captain Gary Prado Salmón, a unit belonging to the Eighth Division of the Bolivian army, in Churo ravine.

According to all the information available, Che Guevara was wounded in the first assault wave that took place some time between 10:30 and 11:00 A.M., but was not taken prisoner until 3:00 P.M., being taken by surprise by four soldiers who jumped out of the bushes as he was scaling one side of the ravine, leaning on his companion Willy. At that time Guevara had no more than one wound, in the right calf, with the bullet remaining in his leg; because his rifle had received a blow in the morning's engagement, it was useless and was seized from his hands. In the heat of battle, the soldiers tried to kill their two prisoners on the spot, but Guevara said: "Don't kill us. I am worth more to you alive than dead. I am Che Guevara." The soldiers immediately passed on this piece of news to Captain Prado, who arrived in about fifteen minutes to verify it.

Guevara had a leather pouch hanging from his belt at his right side, another one of cloth at his left side, and a kit-bag over his shoulder. These contained books, memorandum books, poems he himself had written, documents, notebooks with personal observations and descriptions of the behavior of his subordinates, and a few personal effects. His two campaign diaries—bound in red leather, made in Germany and with the dates in German—were found in his kit-bag. One of them corresponded to the year 1966, his notes beginning on November 7 of that year in Ñancahuazú; the other began January 1, 1967. Its last entry, dated the day before, Saturday, October 7, reads: "Eleven months passed for our guerrilla organization with no complications, bucolically, until 12:30, when an old woman with her flock of goats entered the canyon where we were camped, and we had to take her prisoner. The woman gave us no trustworthy information about the soldiers, answering that she didn't know whenever we asked her anything, and saying that she hadn't been around there for some time; the only information she gave out concerned the roads; from what the old woman says, we gather that we are about three miles from Higuera and another three from Jahuey and about 1.2 miles from Pucara. At 17:30, Inti, Aniceto, and Pablito went to the house of the old lady, who has a daughter sick in bed and a sister; they gave her fifty pesos and told them not to say a word, but there is little hope that she will obey, despite her promises."

7. From Guevara's diary. This was the date on which Guevara returned to the central camp at Ñancahuazú after a trip north.

March 20: We left at ten at a good pace. Benigno and El Negro preceded us with a message for Marcos in which he was ordered to take charge of the defense and leave administrative things to Antonio. Joaquin left after having erased the footprints going into the arroyo but with no anxiety. He brings back three barefoot men. At 13 hours when we were making a long halt, Pacho appeared with a message from Marcos. The report gave more detail about the first report by Benigno but it was more complicated now since the guards, numbering sixty, had stationed themselves along the road to Vallegrande and captured one of our messengers from [Moises] Guevara's men, Salustio. They took a mule from us and the jeep was lost. There was no news from Loro who had stayed behind in the post at the little house. We decided nonetheless to go as far as the bear camp, as it is called because one of those animals had been killed there. We sent Miguel and Urbano to prepare food for hungry men and arrived as night was falling. In the camp were Danton, El Pelao, El Chino, as well as Tania, and a group of Bolivians used to bring food in and then withdraw. Rolando has been sent out to organize the withdrawal of everything. There was an atmosphere of defeat everywhere. A little later a Bolivian doctor who has joined the group recently arrived with a message to Rolando in which he was informed that Marcos and Antonio were at the watering place and that he should go be interviewed. I sent him word by the same messenger that a war was won by shooting, and that they should withdraw immediately to the camp and wait for me there. Everything gives the impression of terrible chaos, they don't know what to do.

I had a preliminary talk with El Chino. He is asking for five thousand dollars a month over ten months, and they sent him word from Havana that he should talk things over with me. He also brought a message that Arturo could not decipher because it was very long. I told him that in principle —— in six months. He is thinking of doing it with fifteen men and himself as leader in the zone of Ayacucho with fifteen more after a short delay, and would send them armed as soon as he had trained them for combat. He . . .

9. From Guevara's diary.

March 23: An eventful day in the fight. Pombo wanted to organize a supply expedition farther north to pick up merchandise, but I was opposed until Marcos' situation clears up. A little after eight, Coco arrived on the run with the news that a platoon of the army had fallen into the ambush. The result up to now has been three 60 mm. mortars, sixteen ——, two B2's, three ——, one 30 mm., two radios, boats, etc., seven dead, fourteen prisoners unwounded and four wounded, but we did not manage to capture the provisions. The plan of operation was captured, which consists of advancing along both sides of the Ñancahuazú so as to make contact at a mid-point. We hastily took people over to the other side and I put Marcos and almost all the vanguard at the end of the road being constructed, while the center and part of the rear guard remains for defense and Braulio sets up an ambush at the end of the other road being constructed. We will spend the night this way and see if the famous Rangers arrive tomorrow. A major and a captain taken prisoner talked like parrots.

The message sent with El Chino is being deciphered. It talks about Debré's [sic] trip, the sending of the 60 mm., the requests in the diary, and an explanation of why they don't write to Ivan.

I also have a communication from Sánchez in which he tells about the possibilities of establishing —— at some points.

10. From Guevara's diary. This entry was written two days after the first encounter between guerrillas and the Bolivian armed forces.

March 25: The day went by with nothing new. Leon, Urbano, and Arturo were sent to a lookout spot that overlooks the entrance to the river on both sides. At 12:00 Marcos withdrew from his position in ambush and all the men were con-

centrated at the principal ambush. At 18:30 hours, with almost all the personnel present, I made an analysis of the trip and its significance and exposed the
errors of Marcos, demoting him and naming Miguel leader of the vanguard. At
the same time the lowering in rank of Paco, Pepe, Chingolo, Eusebio, inform-
ing them that they will not eat if they don't work. Their permission to smoke is
being suspended, and their personal things being redistributed among the other
comrades who need them more. I referred to the report of Kolle that he will
come for discussions, and that simultaneously there will be an expulsion of the
members of the youth group present here. What is of interest are deeds; words
that do not match deeds are not important. I announced the search for the cow
and the renewal of the study program.

I talked with Pedro and the doctor, to whom I announced that they were
almost full-fledged guerrilla fighters, and with Apolinar, to whom I gave orders. I criticized Walter for having gone soft during the trip, for his attitude in
combat and for the fear he showed of planes; he did not react well.

We are clearing up details with El Chino and El Pelao and I gave the
Frenchman a long oral report on the situation.

In the course of the meeting this group was given the name of Army for
the National Liberation of Bolivia and a report will be made of the meeting.

11. *From Guevara's diary. The action referred to is the first encounter of the guerrillas with the army, on March 23. Neither
the Bolivian government nor the armed forces gave a report of
this battle, which was the result of an ambush set up by the
guerrillas in Ñancahuazú. Seven soldiers were killed and fourteen
taken prisoner. The prisoners were set free forty-eight hours
later and were allowed to come back the next day for their dead.*

March 27: Today there was an explosion, the news monopolizing every radio
station, producing a multitude of communiqués, including a press conference
by Barrientos. The official version includes one more dead than ours and says
that they were wounded and then shot, and it assigns us fifteen dead and four
prisoners, two of them foreigners, but it also talks about a foreigner who ——
and about the composition of the guerrilla group. It is obvious [that the] de-
serters or the prisoners talked, except that it is not known [exact]ly how much
they said and how they said it. Everything seems to [indicate] that Tania has
been identified; years of good and patient work have thereby been lost. Getting people out is difficult now; I had the impression that Danton didn't find it
at all funny when I told him so. We shall see later.

Benigno, Loro, Julio went out to look for the road to Pirirenda; they are to take two or three days and their instructions are to get to Pirirenda without being seen so as to then make a trip to Gutiérrez. The reconnaissance plane —— some parachutists that the guard reported had fallen in the hunting grounds. Antonio and two others were sent to investigate and try to take prisoners but there was nothing there.

During the night we had a meeting of the staff in which we decided on plans for the days to come. A supply expedition to the little house is to be made tomorrow to pick up corn, then another so as to buy things in Gutiérrez, and finally a little diversionary attack that could be made in the southeast between Pincal and Lagunilla on the vehicles that go through there.

Communiqué No. 1 is being composed, which we will try to get to the journalists in Camiri (1) XVII . . .

12. *From Guevara's diary. It refers to a medical commission sent by the government to bring out bodies of the soldiers killed on March 23. According to the guerrillas, the truce ended on March 26.*

March 28: The radios still isolated with no news about the guerrillas. We are surrounded by two thousand men on one side of this river, and the serum is running out, along with bombardments with napalm; we have ten to fifteen casualties.

I sent Braulio out at the head of nine men to try to find corn. They came back with a string of crazy news: (1) Coco, who had left earlier to bring news, disappears; (2) at 16:00 hours they arrived at the farmhouse; they find that the cave has been searched, but they are spreading out to begin gathering things together when two men from the Red Cross, two doctors, and various unarmed soldiers appear, they are taken prisoner, and it is explained to them that the truce is over, but they are allowed to go on their way; (3) a truck full of soldiers arrives and instead of shooting they tell them to retreat; (4) the soldiers retreat in a disciplined way, and our men accompany the clean-up squad to where the rotten corpses are, but the clean-up men can't carry them and they say that they will come tomorrow to burn them. Two horses of Algarañáz's are confiscated from them and they return, with Antonio, Lucio (?), and Aniceto remaining where the animals can't go. When they went to look for Coco, he turned up; it seems that he'd been asleep.

The Frenchman was too vehement when he stated how useful he could be on the outside.

13. From Guevara's diary. This was Debray and Bustos' first attempt to escape; they got as far as the town of Gutiérrez, about thirty-five miles south of Ñancahuazú.

April 3: The program was completed without a hitch. We went out at 3:30 and marched slowly past the elbow of the shortcut at 6:30 and got to the edge of the farm at 8:30. When we passed by the ambush, only perfectly clean skeletons remained of the bodies of the seven corpses, on which birds of prey had responsibly exercised their function. I sent two men (Urbano and Ñato) to make contact with Rolando, and during the afternoon we went to the Pirabay pass where we slept next to cows and corn.

I spoke with Danton and Carlos, laying out three alternatives for them: following us, going out alone, or going by way of Gutiérrez and from there try their luck as best they could. They said —— tomorrow we'll try our luck.

17. From Guevara's diary.

April 14: A monotonous day. Some things were brought from the refuge for the sick, which gives us food for five days. Cans of milk were searched for in the upper cave, and it was discovered that three cans were inexplicably missing, since —— said UP and no one seems to have had the time to take them out. Milk is one of the things that makes for vices. A mortar and the machine gun were taken out of the special cave in order to reinforce the position until Joaquín comes.

It is not clear how to carry out the operation but it seems best to me to take everybody out and operate a center for the Muyupampa zone and then retreat north. If it were possible, Danton and Carlos would still head for Sucre-Cochabamba, depending on circumstances.

Message No. 2 (D XXI) for the Bolivian people is being written and report No. 4 for Manila which the Frenchman is to take with him.

19. From Guevara's diary. This interview with the authorities of Muyupampa took place the same day that Danton and El Pelao were taken into custody.

April 20: We arrived around one o'clock at the house of Nemesio Caraballo, whom we had met during the night and who had offered us a coffee. The man had gone off, leaving the house locked and the friendship [lasted] only a few minutes. We got together a meal right there, buying corn and squash (called sapallos) from the peons. At about 13:00 hours a truck appeared with a white flag bringing the subprefect, the doctor, and the priest of Muyupampa, this last a German. Inti spoke with them. They came seeking peace but a national-type peace that they offered to be intermediaries for. Inti offered peace for Muyupampa, on the basis of a list of merchandise that they were to bring us before 18:30 hours, which they did not pledge to do because, according to them, the army is in charge of the town, and they asked for the time limit to be extended until 6:00 A.M., which was not granted.

As a sign of their new good will they brought two cartons of cigarettes and the news that as three of them went out they were captured in Muyupampa and two of them were compromised because they had false documents. Things look bad for Carlos; Danton must get out all right.

At 17:30 hours, three AT6's came and subjected us to a small bombardment in the very house where we were cooking. One shell fell fifteen meters away and wounded Ricardo very slightly with a piece of shrapnel. This was the army's reply. The proclamations must be made known so as to totally demoralize the soldiers, who, to judge by those that have been sent, are quite shitty.

We went out at 23:30 hours with two horses, the one that was confiscated and the journalist's, traveling in the direction of Ticucha until 1:30 when we stopped to sleep . . .

25. *From Guevara's diary: resumé of the month of April 1967.*

Resumé of the month [of April]: Things are within the normal although we must lament two severe losses: El Rubio and Rolando—the death of the latter is a severe blow, since I was planning to leave him in charge of the eventual second front. We have had four more actions, all of them with positive results in general and one very good one, the ambush in which El Rubio died.

On another plane: since we are still totally isolated, sickness has undermined the health of some comrades, obliging us to divide forces, which has taken away much of our effectiveness; we have still not been able to make contact with Joaquín. The peasant base continues without making progress although it may be that through planned terror we will succeed in getting the neutrality of some; support will come later. Not a single person has been recruited, and apart from the deaths, El Loro was a casualty at the time of the fighting in Taperillas.

Of the annotated points concerning military strategy it can be confirmed: (a) the controls have not been able to be effective up to now and they cause us deaths, but they allow us to move, on account of their lack of mobility and their weakness; furthermore, since the time of the last ambush against the dogs and the instructor, it is to be presumed that they will be careful about coming into the mountains; (b) the clamor continues but in many places now and when my article is published in Havana there will be no doubt of my presence here. It seems certain that the Americans will intervene strongly here and they are already sending helicopters and apparently Green Berets although they haven't been seen here; (c) the army (at least a company or two) has improved its technique: they surprised us in Taperillas and they were not demoralized in El Mesón; (d) there is no mobilization of the peasants, except for the tasks of securing information which are something of a bother; they are neither quick nor efficient; we can do away with them.

The status of El Chino has been changed and he will be a fighter until the formation of a second or third front.

Danton and Carlos Capac fell victims of their almost desperate anxiety to leave and my lack of energy in stopping them so that communications with Cuba (Danton) were cut off and the plan for action in Argentina (Carlos) can't be used.

To sum it all up, a month in which everything has turned out . . .

27. Apparently a message from Guevara to Castro. "Trio" is the name for the directors of the pro-Soviet wing of the Bolivian Communist Party: Monje, Kolle, and Reyes. People from the youth group are those who took part in guerrilla activities. They were authorized to do so only on their own account, not as representatives of the Party.

May 18—Leche: Danton was carrying a message, and also notations in order to memorize the oral report that I gave him all in code. This is the message: (1) Francisco and Danton arrived, the latter did not know the quantity and left money in La Paz; I intend to give him thirty and keep the rest for him until he ———. He appears to be in poor physical condition and not to have the character to direct a guerrilla group, but this is his business. Danton is supposed to leave but I don't know if he will be able to given the circumstances. (2) The farm was discovered and the army pursued us. We hit first but we are isolated. (3) Ivan is ready to travel but Tania is isolated here, since she came contrary to instructions and was surprised by events. (4) We now have sufficient glucontine, don't send more. (5) There is no news of the trio. I don't trust them either and they expelled the people from the youth group who are with us. (6) I received

everything by radio but it is useless if they don't communicate with La Paz simultaneously; we are isolated for the time being. (7) We still haven't received
messages through Lozano. (8) Farewell letter Danton should be stopped until
further notice. (9) We will try trip to France object organizing base in the south
and rounding up Argentinians; he is also bottled up here. (10) Stop sending
sausages since they took the small valises that were prepared away from us. (11)
Danton will inform you about the second action. (12) Arturo is receiving but
we cannot transmit for the present. (13) Send Francisco's scholarship students
here, inform contact in La Paz will make the first test this zone. (14) Second
front planned, Chapare. I add we have arms for one hundred men more including four 60 [mm.] mortars and ammunition for them, but not a single peasant
has been taken in. We suffered four casualties—Benjamin, Carlos, Bolivians
drowned in accidents; Felix (J. S. G.), and Rolando (S. L.), killed in combat.
The last loss is very important. He was the best man in the guerrilla group.
Marcos relieved of his rank for repeated breaches of discipline; he was allowed
to stay as a combatant. Danton was anxious to leave for Argentina, personal
business matters (among others, he wanted to have a child), and El Pelao
(Fructuoso) was desperate to do so. I divided the forces so as to act quickly,
but there were complications and they were captured. The Englishman is a bona
fide journalist (unless he's from the FBI); we captured [him] and gave him the
task of getting others out; we know nothing of his background, he seemed—.
It was subsequently impossible to join up with Joaquín and we are isolated. I
have twenty-five men and Joaquín seventeen. El Chino decided to stay here to
make his experiment. He is with me.

FRANTZ FANON

꒰꒱

FROM *The Wretched of the Earth* [1968]

Translated from the French by Constance Farrington

The Pitfalls of National Consciousness

History teaches us clearly that the battle against colonialism does not run straight away along the lines of nationalism. For a very long time the native devotes his energies to ending certain definite abuses: forced labor, corporal punishment, inequality of salaries, limitation of political rights, etc. This fight for democracy against the oppression of mankind will slowly leave the confusion of neo-liberal universalism to emerge, sometimes laboriously, as a claim to nationhood. It so happens that the unpreparedness of the educated classes, the lack of practical links between them and the mass of the people, their laziness, and, let it be said, their cowardice at the decisive moment of the struggle will give rise to tragic mishaps.

National consciousness, instead of being the all-embracing crystallization of the innermost hopes of the whole people, instead of being the immediate and most obvious result of the mobilization of the people, will be in any case only an empty shell, a crude and fragile travesty of what it might have been. The faults that we find in it are quite sufficient explanation of the facility with which, when dealing with young and independent nations, the nation is passed over for the race, and the tribe is preferred to the state. These are the cracks in the edifice which show the process of retrogression, that is so harmful and prejudicial to national effort and national unity. We shall see that such retrograde steps with all the weaknesses and serious dangers that they entail are the historical result of the incapacity of the national middle class to rationalize popular action, that is to say their incapacity to see into the reasons for that action.

This traditional weakness, which is almost congenital to the national consciousness of underdeveloped countries, is not solely the result of the mutilation of the colonized people by the colonial regime. It is also the result of the intellectual laziness of the national middle class, of its spiritual penury, and of the profoundly cosmopolitan mold that its mind is set in.

The national middle class which takes over power at the end of the colonial regime is an underdeveloped middle class. It has practically no economic

power, and in any case it is in no way commensurate with the bourgeoisie of
the mother country which it hopes to replace. In its narcissism, the national
middle class is easily convinced that it can advantageously replace the middle
class of the mother country. But that same independence which literally drives
it into a corner will give rise within its ranks to catastrophic reactions, and will
oblige it to send out frenzied appeals for help to the former mother country.
The university and merchant classes which make up the most enlightened section of the new state are in fact characterized by the smallness of their number
and their being concentrated in the capital, and the type of activities in which
they are engaged: business, agriculture, and the liberal professions. Neither
financiers nor industrial magnates are to be found within this national middle
class. The national bourgeoisie of underdeveloped countries is not engaged in
production, nor in invention, nor building, nor labor; it is completely canalized
into activities of the intermediary type. Its innermost vocation seems to be to
keep in the running and to be part of the racket. The psychology of the national
bourgeoisie is that of the businessman, not that of a captain of industry; and it
is only too true that the greed of the settlers and the system of embargoes set
up by colonialism have hardly left them any other choice.

Under the colonial system, a middle class which accumulates capital is an
impossible phenomenon. Now, precisely, it would seem that the historical vocation of an authentic national middle class in an underdeveloped country is to
repudiate its own nature in so far it as it is bourgeois, that is to say in so far as it
is the tool of capitalism, and to make itself the willing slave of that revolutionary capital which is the people.

In an underdeveloped country an authentic national middle class ought
to consider as its bounden duty to betray the calling fate has marked out for it,
and to put itself to school with the people: in other words to put at the people's
disposal the intellectual and technical capital that it has snatched when going
through the colonial universities. But unhappily we shall see that very often the
national middle class does not follow this heroic, positive, fruitful, and just path;
rather, it disappears with its soul set at peace into the shocking ways—shocking because anti-national—of a traditional bourgeoisie, of a bourgeoisie which
is stupidly, contemptibly, cynically bourgeois.

The objective of nationalist parties as from a certain given period is, we
have seen, strictly national. They mobilize the people with slogans of independence, and for the rest leave it to future events. When such parties are questioned on the economic program of the state that they are clamoring for, or on
the nature of the regime which they propose to install, they are incapable of
replying, because, precisely, they are completely ignorant of the economy of
their own country.

This economy has always developed outside the limits of their knowledge. They have nothing more than an approximate, bookish acquaintance with the actual and potential resources of their country's soil and mineral deposits; and therefore they can only speak of these resources on a general and abstract plane. After independence this underdeveloped middle class, reduced in numbers and without capital, which refuses to follow the path of revolution, will fall into deplorable stagnation. It is unable to give free rein to its genius, which formerly it was wont to lament, though rather too glibly, was held in check by colonial domination. The precariousness of its resources and the paucity of its managerial class force it back for years into an artisan economy. From its point of view, which is inevitably a very limited one, a national economy is an economy based on what may be called local products. Long speeches will be made about the artisan class. Since the middle classes find it impossible to set up factories that would be more profit-earning both for themselves and for the country as a whole, they will surround the artisan class with a chauvinistic tenderness in keeping with the new awareness of national dignity, and which moreover will bring them in quite a lot of money. This cult of local products and this incapability to seek out new systems of management will be equally manifested by the bogging down of the national middle class in the methods of agricultural production which were characteristic of the colonial period.

The national economy of the period of independence is not set on a new footing. It is still concerned with the groundnut harvest, with the cocoa crop and the olive yield. In the same way there is no change in the marketing of basic products, and not a single industry is set up in the country. We go on sending out raw materials; we go on being Europe's small farmers, who specialize in unfinished products.

Yet the national middle class constantly demands the nationalization of the economy and of the trading sectors. This is because, from their point of view, nationalization does not mean placing the whole economy at the service of the nation and deciding to satisfy the needs of the nation. For them, nationalization does not mean governing the state with regard to the new social relations whose growth it has been decided to encourage. To them, nationalization quite simply means the transfer into native hands of those unfair advantages which are a legacy of the colonial period.

Since the middle class has neither sufficient material nor intellectual resources (by intellectual resources we mean engineers and technicians), it limits its claims to the taking over of business offices and commercial houses formerly occupied by the settlers. The national bourgeoisie steps into the shoes of the former European settlement: doctors, barristers, traders, commercial travelers, general agents, and transport agents. It considers that the dignity of the country and its own welfare require that it should occupy all these posts. From now on it will insist that all the big foreign companies should pass through its hands, whether these companies wish to keep on their connections with the country, or to open it up. The national middle class discovers its historic mission: that of intermediary.

Seen through its eyes, its mission has nothing to do with transforming the nation; it consists, prosaically, of being the transmission line between the nation and a capitalism, rampant though camouflaged, which today puts on the mask of neo-colonialism. The national bourgeoisie will be quite content with the role of the Western bourgeoisie's business agent, and it will play its part without any complexes in a most dignified manner. But this same lucrative role, this cheap-Jack's function, this meanness of outlook and this absence of all ambition symbolize the incapability of the national middle class to fulfill its historic role of bourgeoisie. Here, the dynamic, pioneer aspect, the character-istics of the inventor and of the discoverer of new worlds which are found in all national bourgeoisies are lamentably absent. In the colonial countries, the spirit of indulgence is dominant at the core of the bourgeoisie; and this is because the national bourgeoisie identifies itself with the Western bourgeoisie, from whom it has learnt its lessons. It follows the Western bourgeoisie along its path of negation and decadence without ever having emulated it in its first stages of exploration and invention, stages which are an acquisition of that Western bourgeoisie whatever the circumstances. In its beginnings, the national bour-geoisie of the colonial countries identifies itself with the decadence of the bour-geoisie of the West. We need not think that it is jumping ahead; it is in fact beginning at the end. It is already senile before it has come to know the petu-lance, the fearlessness, or the will to succeed of youth.

The national bourgeoisie will be greatly helped on its way toward deca-dence by the Western bourgeoisies, who come to it as tourists avid for the exotic, for big game hunting, and for casinos. The national bourgeoisie organizes cen-ters of rest and relaxation and pleasure resorts to meet the wishes of the Western bourgeoisie. Such activity is given the name of tourism, and for the occasion will be built up as a national industry. If proof is needed of the eventual transforma-tion of certain elements of the ex-native bourgeoisie into the organizers of parties for their Western opposite numbers, it is worth while having a look at what has happened in Latin America. The casinos of Havana and of Mexico, the beaches of Rio, the little Brazilian and Mexican girls, the half-breed thirteen-year-olds, the ports of Acapulco and Copacabana—all these are the stigma of this deprava-tion of the national middle class. Because it is bereft of ideas, because it lives to itself and cuts itself off from the people, undermined by its hereditary incapacity to think in terms of all the problems of the nation as seen from the point of view of the whole of that nation, the national middle class will have nothing better to do than to take on the role of manager for Western enterprise, and it will in practice set up its country as the brothel of Europe.

Once again we must keep before us the unfortunate example of certain Latin American republics. The banking magnates, the technocrats, and the big businessmen of the United States have only to step onto a plane and they are wafted into subtropical climes, there for a space of a week or ten days to luxuriate in the delicious depravities which their "reserves" hold for them.

The behavior of the national landed proprietors is practically identical with that of the middle classes of the towns. The big farmers have, as soon as independence is proclaimed, demanded the nationalization of agricultural production. Through manifold scheming practices they manage to make a clean sweep of the farms formerly owned by settlers, thus reinforcing their hold on the district. But they do not try to introduce new agricultural methods, nor to farm more intensively, nor to integrate their farming systems into a genuinely national economy.

In fact, the landed proprietors will insist that the state should give them a hundred times more facilities and privileges than were enjoyed by the foreign settlers in former times. The exploitation of agricultural workers will be intensified and made legitimate. Using two or three slogans, these new colonists will demand an enormous amount of work from the agricultural laborers, in the name of the national effort of course. There will be no modernization of agriculture, no planning for development, and no initiative; for initiative throws these people into a panic since it implies a minimum of risk, and completely upsets the hesitant, prudent, landed bourgeoisie, which gradually slips more and more into the lines laid down by colonialism. In the districts where this is the case, the only efforts made to better things are due to the government; it orders them, encourages them, and finances them. The landed bourgeoisie refuses to take the slightest risk, and remains opposed to any venture and to any hazard. It has no intention of building upon sand; it demands solid investments and quick returns. The enormous profits which it pockets, enormous if we take into account the national revenue, are never reinvested. The money-in-the-stocking mentality is dominant in the psychology of these landed proprietors. Sometimes, especially in the years immediately following independence, the bourgeoisie does not hesitate to invest in foreign banks the profits that it makes out of its native soil. On the other hand large sums are spent on display: on cars, country houses, and on all those things which have been justly described by economists as characterizing an underdeveloped bourgeoisie.

We have said that the native bourgeoisie which comes to power uses its class aggressiveness to corner the positions formerly kept for foreigners. On

the morrow of independence, in fact, it violently attacks colonial personalities:
barristers, traders, landed proprietors, doctors, and higher civil servants. It will
fight to the bitter end against these people "who insult our dignity as a nation."
It waves aloft the notion of the nationalization and Africanization of the ruling
classes. The fact is that such action will become more and more tinged by racism, until the bourgeoisie bluntly puts the problem to the government by saying "We must have these posts." They will not stop their snarling until they
have taken over everyone.

The working class of the towns, the masses of unemployed, the small artisans and craftsmen for their part line up behind this nationalist attitude; but in
all justice let it be said, they only follow in the steps of their bourgeoisie. If the
national bourgeoisie goes into competition with the Europeans, the artisans and
craftsmen start a fight against non-national Africans. In the Ivory Coast, the
anti-Dahoman and anti-Voltaic troubles are in fact racial riots. The Dahoman
and Voltaic peoples, who control the greater part of the petty trade, are, once
independence is declared, the object of hostile manifestations on the part of
the people of the Ivory Coast. From nationalism we have passed to ultra-
nationalism, to chauvinism, and finally to racism. These foreigners are called
on to leave; their shops are burned, their street stalls are wrecked, and in fact
the government of the Ivory Coast commands them to go, thus giving their
nationals satisfaction. In Senegal it is the anti-Soudanese demonstrations which
called forth these words from Mr. Mamadou Dia:

> The truth is that the Senegalese people have only adopted the Mali mys-
> tique through attachment to its leaders. Their adhesion to the Mali has
> no other significance than that of a fresh act of faith in the political
> policy of the latter. The Senegalese territory was no less real, in fact it
> was all the more so in that the presence of the Soudanese in Dakar was
> too obviously manifested for it to be forgotten. It is this fact which
> explains that, far from being regretted, the break-up of the Federation
> has been greeted with relief by the mass of the people and nowhere
> was a hand raised to maintain it.*

While certain sections of the Senegalese people jump at the chance which
is afforded them by their own leaders to get rid of the Soudanese, who hamper
them in commercial matters or in administrative posts, the Congolese, who
stood by hardly daring to believe in the mass exodus of the Belgians, decide to

* Mamadou Dia, *Nations africaines et solidarité mondial*, p. 140.

bring pressure to bear on the Senegalese who have settled in Leopoldville and Elisabethville and to get them to leave.

As we see it, the mechanism is identical in the two sets of circumstances. If the Europeans get in the way of the intellectuals and business bourgeoisie of the young nation, for the mass of the people in the towns competition is represented principally by Africans of another nation. On the Ivory Coast these competitors are the Dahomans; in Ghana they are the Nigerians; in Senegal, they are the Soudanese.

When the bourgeoisie's demands for a ruling class made up exclusively of Negroes or Arabs do not spring from an authentic movement of nationalization but merely correspond to an anxiety to place in the bourgeoisie's hands the power held hitherto by the foreigner, the masses on their level present the same demands, confining however the notion of Negro or Arab within certain territorial limits. Between resounding assertions of the unity of the continent and this behavior of the masses which has its inspiration in their leaders, many different attitudes may be traced. We observe a permanent seesaw between African unity, which fades quicker and quicker into the mists of oblivion, and a heartbreaking return to chauvinism in its most bitter and detestable form.

꩜

FROM *Big Time Buck White* [1969]

JIVE: Ladies and Gentlemen, the meeting is now back on. Big Time Buck White is now open for questions . . . Question time . . .

During the following improvisational question-and-answer period, which was compiled from several performances during the New York run, there are twelve questioners: four plants and eight genuine questioners. Questioner #3 is Whitey, an actor and the only obvious plant. [P = Plant; G = Genuine questioner.]

QUESTIONER #1-P (*white girl*): Over here.

HUNTER: Tap the plate. (*He rushes down.*)

QUESTIONER #1: Mister Buck White, do you like white people?

HUNTER: Did she say what I thought she said?

ALL: WHAT? WHAT THE HELL DID SHE SAY? WHAT?

JIVE: Order! Order . . . Now the lady asked Big Time Buck White a question . . . Big Time Buck White will answer the question.

BIG TIME (*pauses, decides it does not deserve an answer*): *Next* question.

WEASEL: See? You can't trust none of them Whiteys. They all a bunch of Birchers.

RUBBER BAND: That's O.K., Brother, 'cause I *love* to hate.

JIVE: Could we have some more questions?

RUBBER BAND: Dig hatin', Brother.

WEASEL: Dig hate . . . Dig hate.

JIVE: I would like to tell you people a little about the history of Big Time Buck White . . .

BIG TIME: Hey, Jive . . . You got some nice people out there tonight. Yes, you have.

JIVE: Some beauts!

BIG TIME: Let's get back to the questions.

QUESTIONER #2-P (*white man*): Mister Big Buck, does BAD represent itself as being a force in *favor* of Law or *against* it?

BIG TIME: Animals don't have laws, birds don't have laws, bees don't, the only thing in this universe that has laws is man, man he's got his laws. He created laws because man knew that man was a beast. He chewed up maggot-filled dogs and sucked the venom-juice out of reindeer eyeballs. I'm talkin', I'm talkin', I'm talkin' about history, history, fifty thousand years ago, and it seems like today, because today man is filled with useless law. For this is a Great Society that's being born here, free thinkers go to jail, simple souls go to heaven, 'cause laws are obeyed and Lord knows a Whitey obeys laws. He drinks his water from pure white fountains, excremates that good food he eats in lily-white toilets, he even walks the white sidewalks and tells us that Law is a thing he created that teaches him against death. But the walkin' mud of Mississippi is staining those shoes with mud, there's another thing happenin', there's a beauty here that knows before it's told what is right and what is wrong, it knows that your life is the most precious thing you'll ever have and it's your life and your death, and it knows your death is just like what Ray Charles says, when you're dead you die, yes, you die. So crush those timeless laws and useless laws and let man create his own universal form so that men can stand up straight and walk their own little dark areas in life.

JIVE (*cutting in*): O.K. No more laws. Now, next question . . .

RUBBER BAND: Hey Man, the cat's talkin' about Mississippi, Man.

JIVE: Well I want to go somewhere else.

RUBBER BAND: There ain't nothing wrong with talking about a live, uptight, white Baptist, black-hating Mississippi law, you mahogany Eskimo.

JIVE: Shut up, you don't understand nothing, dummy.

HUNTER: Godammit, Jive.

JIVE: I'll close this meeting.

HUNTER: Don't tell a man he don't understand nothin'.

RUBBER BAND: That's right, Man.

JIVE: Ladies and Gentlemen the meeting is now closed. Goodnight.

ALL: Oh no . . . Don't do that . . . Hey, Jive . . .

JIVE: What d'ya think you're doin', then?

BIG TIME (*quietly*): Do we have to show all these people how long we've been ostracized?

WEASEL: OSTRA . . . (*To Honey Man.*) What does he mean by "ostracized"?

JIVE: He means stop playing the part of—uh—John Wayne, you dummy.

WEASEL: John Wayne?

JIVE: That's right, John Wayne.

RUBBER BAND: I ain't no John Wayne, Sucker. What you talkin' about?

BIG TIME: I'm saying that as black men you can do one of two things. Now I don't think I have to say anything more about that.

WEASEL: Good. That's what he says at you Rubber Band. You gotta go around wearing those tight pants like some kind of peacock . . . You got to prove to the whole world that you some kind of a super stud.

RUBBER BAND (*thinks about this*): I *am* Super Stud.

JIVE: Can we have some more questions?

WEASEL: Hey, Jive, nobody goes around callin' me no ostracized.

JIVE: Oh, shut up.

HUNTER (*spying a hand up, heads for audience*): Tap the plate. (*Questioner taps the plate.*)

QUESTIONER #3, WHITEY: Mister Buck White . . .

HUNTER (*checking the plate*): Mister, shut up . . .

WEASEL: Let's see that plate.

HUNTER: (*shows plate to the Organizers*): He did it again. (*To the man in the audience.*) Mister, you owe me four hundred years' back wages! And Sucker, you goin' to pay me my money tonight! (*He starts out to get Whitey.*)

ALL: Hunter, Hunter, go get him, get him, hey, Hunter, get him!

JIVE: (*grabs Hunter*): Come on back here, you. Are you out of your dumb, in-sipid, moronic little mind? You know we don't go beatin' up people anymore, and you know something', you are embarrassing me.

HUNTER: You ought to be.

BIG TIME (*quietly*): It's a shame that throughout history, man, in order to take the next step forward, he has always had to contend with power marches of mice.

HUNTER (*indignant*): *Mice?*

BIG TIME (*simply*): Mice. How many times has this quest for power destroyed the whole process of creativity? That's why a Hitler will make it and a Martin Luther King will get killed.

WEASEL: What you tryin' to say?

HUNTER (*his composure recovered, he speaks to Whitey*): Tap this plate.

WEASEL: Hey, Jive, I'm bringing up another complaint, Man! Nobody goes around callin' me no "mice."

JIVE: Get back there, Weasel.

Weasel moves back into place.

HUNTER: Tap the plate.

WHITEY (*ignores Hunter*): Mister Buck White. How complex . . .

JIVE (*politely*): Oh, Sir, every time you ask Big Time a question, you gotta tap that plate.

RUBBER BAND: Yeah, tap that plate, Mister.

WHITEY (*reluctantly drops a quarter in the plate*): How complex is the black and white situation back there in Watts?

HUNTER: *Sit down!* (*Honey Man chuckles. To Honey Man.*) It ain't funny.

BIG TIME: You see, the black situation in Watts is like the black situation in Harlem and in both cases it is not so much that the black man recognizes that the black man is an inferior man because the black man happens to be a black man. In both cases, it is more that the white man recognizes that the black man recognizes that the black man is an inferior man because he is a black man. Now all of a sudden the white man has gotten busy, and he's trying to tell the black man that he ain't got no reason trying to stay inferior. Well, no matter what happens to that black man, that black man can't turn white. Now that means that long as the white man is busy trying to tell the black man that the black man shouldn't stay inferior, that black man will never believe the white man wants the black man to be anything but inferior.

RUBBER BAND: Sure is complex, ain't it.

HONEY MAN: Worse than that, Rubber Band, worse than that, really.

Jive waits for another question. He points out another questioner.

HUNTER: Tap the plate.

QUESTIONER #4-P (*white teenage boy*): Mister Buck White, when your friend here said this man owes you four hundred years in back wages, you know and I know that that is a lot of bull, because don't give me any of this original sin bit . . . That because I'm white, I owe you four hundred years' back pay . . . I

BIG TIME (*cutting in*): You just listen to me one second here, please. I'm not at your job, kicking the spade out of your hand, you know.

QUESTIONER #4: Now look . . . I'm about seventeen years old, so how can you tell me that I owe you four hundred years of back wages? Say I was just born, now I might have inherited this situation, but don't go blaming me for the other three hundred eighty-three years of it.

BIG TIME: That's a good point, that's a real good point. Now, I wouldn't blame you for nothin' if you were trying to pose as a black man livin' in a black ghetto. But see, you are guilty. It doesn't make any difference whether you feel guilty, it doesn't make any difference whether you individually have castrated the black people or denied them any rights. If you're a white man and you enjoy the fruits of a nation that the black man has essentially built for nothin', you are dead.

JIVE: More questions? (*Sees a hand.*) You, sir.

HUNTER: Tap the plate. (*Hunter sees it is a black man.*) It's a Brother!

RUBBER BAND (*looks over the audience*): Look at the Sister down there with the Brother . . . Shiiiit, Brothers gonna take over Manhattan Island.

WEASEL: Give it soul, Brother.

RUBBER BAND: Tight.

QUESTIONER #5-P (*black man*): You mentioned a few minutes ago about the black man taking away from the whites. You know, the black man, white man thing . . . Could you repeat that a minute . . .

JIVE: Oh, no. That's a Brother all right you dumb Mother . . .

ALL (*shouting at Jive*): Hey, Jive . . . Hey . . . What you doin'? . . .

BIG TIME (*quietly restoring order*): Hey, hey, hey . . . What I'm tryin' to say is there are two sides to that. And one of those sides is not content unless they destroy beauty. They can't look at beauty, they examine it, they got to own it, they got to control it, they got to be the father of it. They treat people like they're children. Like a child that you oppress and criticize until you get to the point where you've done it too much and then you feel guilty about the whole mess, so you buy the little kiddy some toys to play with to make him happy. Now you spend millions of dollars trying to make that little kiddy happy. Well, when that little kiddy who is angry as a kid grows up into a *man* who is angry, well then you really in trouble. And if that anger persists and if that black man understands he don't have to stay, that he can leave, and when he leaves he can take everything with him that he owns, then you better hope that what he owns ain't that house y'all been livin' in so comfortably all these years. What I'm trying to say is that guilt is the feelin' that you get from being a bully, after you've stepped on somebody. Next question.

JIVE: Next question.

HUNTER: Tap the . . . (*Sees it's Whitey again.*) That same sucker! (*Hunter looks at Big Time, who pacifies him with a stern glance. Meekly.*) Sorry, Big Time.

WHITEY: I'm not entirely sure, sir, but you said that a black man could go one of two ways, and I can see a situation today where a lot of white people are afraid that you people won't stop if you get the power that you want . . . that you'll go on and try and dominate everything. Now . . .

HONEY MAN (*breaking in*): DOMINATE! Hey, what the hell are you talkin' about, dominate?

ALL: Yeah . . . What you mean dominate?

WEASEL: Wait a minute, wait a minute. I want to answer this sucker. I'm gonna answer you hard.

BIG TIME (*contemplates a moment*): All right, Weasel, answer the man.

JIVE (*protesting*): Weasel can't answer the man. He's an idiot.

Honey Man and Weasel chuckle at Weasel's victory over Jive.

You better answer him right, you little black sambo.

ALL: Hey . . . don't call him that . . . who you think you are . . . sambo . . .

WEASEL (*moves to center. His big moment. He pauses, confused*): What was that question again?

ALL: Dominate, dominate, DOMINATE!

WEASEL (*to Whitey*): Dominate? Don't you ever learn to talk . . . you're the one who's trying to dominate.

ALL: Yeah . . . that's right . . . yes, sir . . .

BIG TIME (*to Whitey*): It don't seem like the Brothers liked the way you phrased your question. Could you rephrase it?

WHITEY: I don't feel that I was fully understood. Now, Mister Weasel . . .

Audience laughs.

JIVE (*to Whitey, indicating Weasel*): He ain't laughin'.

BIG TIME (*aside*): Weasel, I told you to take that African name yesterday.

WHITEY: Uh . . . Sir? If one goes back to the Civil War, when the North beat the South, and Lincoln allowed the slaves their freedom, and . . .

JIVE (*cutting him off*): Lincoln ALLOWED the slaves their freedom . . . Allowed, right? . . . Did you hear that "allowed"? . . . I want to . . . Damn, it makes me mad, you just think you know so much, don't you, boy? You come in here and you tell *me*, me being black, mind you, that I am allowed something. It doesn't matter if I already own it, hell no. I am black so I am *allowed* something back that was mine to begin with in the first place.

WHITEY: You don't understand . . .

JIVE: Well I understand.

WEASEL: It ain't your country anyway.

WHITEY: Well, I know that.

WEASEL: Who owns it then, who owns it?

WHITEY: Well, it belongs to . . .

WEASEL *and* RUBBER BAND: Who owns it?

WHITEY: Well, it's just that . . .

ALL (*pick up the chant*): Who owns it?

WHITEY: Well, I . . .

ALL: *Who owns it?*

WHITEY (*gives in*): You do.

WEASEL: Damn right I do. Don't come here telling me what to do with my country . . .

KENZABURO OË

❧

FROM *A Personal Matter* [1969]

Translated from the Japanese by John Nathan

Bird, gazing down at the map of Africa that reposed in the showcase with the haughty elegance of a wild deer, stifled a short sigh. The salesgirls paid no attention, their arms and necks goosepimpled where the uniform blouses exposed them. Evening was deepening, and the fever of early summer, like the temperature of a dead giant, had dropped completely from the covering air. People moved as if groping in the dimness of the subconscious for the memory of midday warmth that lingered faintly in the skin: people heaved ambiguous sighs. June—half-past six: by now not a man in the city was sweating. But Bird's wife lay naked on a rubber mat, tightly shutting her eyes like a shot pheasant falling out of the sky, and while she moaned her pain and anxiety and expectation, her body was oozing globes of sweat.

Shuddering, Bird peered at the details of the map. The ocean surrounding Africa was inked in the teary blue of a winter sky at dawn. Longitudes and latitudes were not the mechanical lines of a compass: the bold strokes evoked the artist's unsteadiness and caprice. The continent itself resembled the skull of a man who had hung his head. With doleful, downcast eyes, a man with a huge head was gazing at Australia, land of the koala, the platypus, and the kangaroo. The miniature Africa indicating population distribution in a lower corner of the map was like a dead head beginning to decompose; another, veined with transportation routes, was a skinned head with the capillaries painfully exposed. Both these little Africas suggested unnatural death, raw and violent.

"Shall I take the atlas out of the case?"

"No, don't bother," Bird said. "I'm looking for the Michelin road maps of West Africa and Central and South Africa." The girl bent over a drawer full of Michelin maps and began to rummage busily. "Series number 182 and 185," Bird instructed, evidently an old Africa hand.

The map Bird had been sighing over was a page in a ponderous, leatherbound atlas intended to decorate a coffee table. A few weeks ago he had priced the atlas, and he knew it would cost him five months' salary at the cram-school where he taught. If he included the money he could pick up as a part-time interpreter, he might manage in three months. But Bird had himself and his wife to support, and now the existence on its way into life that minute. Bird was the head of a family!

The salesgirl selected two of the red paperbound maps and placed them on the counter. Her hands were small and soiled, the meagerness of her fingers recalled chameleon legs clinging to a shrub. Bird's eye fell on the Michelin trademark beneath her fingers: the toadlike rubber man rolling a tire down the road made him feel the maps were a silly purchase. But these were maps he would put to an important use.

"Why is the atlas open to the Africa page?" Bird asked wistfully. The salesgirl, somehow wary, didn't answer. Why *was* it always open to the Africa page? Did the manager suppose the map of Africa was the most beautiful page in the book? But Africa was in a process of dizzying change that would quickly outdate any map. And since the corrosion that began with Africa would eat away the entire volume, opening the book to the Africa page amounted to advertising the obsoleteness of the rest. What you needed was a map that could never be outdated because political configurations were settled. Would you choose America, then? North America, that is?

Bird interrupted himself to pay for the maps, then moved down the aisle to the stairs, passing with lowered eyes between a potted tree and a corpulent bronze nude. The nude's bronze belly was smeared with oil from frustrated palms: it glistened wetly like a dog's nose. As a student, Bird himself used to run his fingers across this belly as he passed; today he couldn't find the courage even to look the statue in the face. Bird had glimpsed the doctor and the nurses scrubbing their arms with disinfectant next to the table where his wife had been lying naked. The doctor's arms were matted with hair.

Bird carefully slipped his maps into his jacket pocket and pressed them against his side as he pushed past the crowded magazine counter and headed for the door. These were the first maps he had purchased for actual use in Africa. Uneasily he wondered if the day would ever come when he actually set foot on African soil and gazed through dark sunglasses at the African sky. Or was he losing, this very minute, once and for all, any chance he might have had of setting out for Africa? Was he being forced to say good-by, in spite of himself, to the single and final occasion of dazzling tension in his youth? And what if I am? There's not a thing in hell I can do about it!

Bird angrily pushed through the door and stepped into the early summer evening street. The sidewalk seemed bound in fog: it was the filthiness of the air and the fading evening light. Bird paused to gaze at himself in the wide, darkly shadowed display window. He was aging with the speed of a short-distance runner. Bird, twenty-seven years and four months old. He had been nicknamed "Bird" when he was fifteen, and he had been Bird ever since: the figure awkwardly afloat like a drowned corpse in the inky lake of window glass still resembled a bird. He was small and thin. His friends had begun to put on weight the minute they graduated from college and took a job—even those who stayed lean had fattened up when they got married; but Bird, except for the slight paunch on his belly, remained as skinny as ever. He slouched forward when he walked and bunched his shoulders around his neck; his posture was the same when he was standing still. Like an emaciated old man who once had been an athlete.

It wasn't only that his hunched shoulders were like folded wings, his features in general were birdlike. His tan, sleek nose thrust out of his face like a beak and hooked sharply toward the ground. His eyes gleamed with a hard, dull light the color of glue and almost never displayed emotion, except occasionally to shutter open as though in mild surprise. His thin, hard lips were always stretched tightly across his teeth; the lines from his high cheekbones to his chin described a sharply pointed V. And hair licking at the sky like ruddy tongues of flame. This was a fair description of Bird at fifteen: nothing had changed at twenty. How long would he continue to look like a bird? No choice but living with the same face and posture from fifteen to sixty-five, was he that kind of person? Then the image he was observing in the window glass was a composite of his entire life. Bird shuddered, seized with disgust so palpable it made him want to vomit. What a revelation: exhausted, with a horde of children, old, senile Bird. . . .

Suddenly a woman with a definitely peculiar quality rose out of the dim lake in the window and slowly moved toward Bird. She was a large woman with broad shoulders, so tall that her face topped the reflection of Bird's head in the glass. Feeling as though a monster were stalking him from behind, Bird finally wheeled around. The woman stopped in front of him and peered into his face gravely. Bird stared back. A second later, he saw the hard, pointed urgency in her eyes washing away in the waters of mournful indifference. Though she may not have known its precise nature, the woman had been on the verge of discovering a bond of mutual interest, and had realized abruptly that Bird was not an appropriate partner in the bond. In the same moment, Bird perceived the abnormality in her face which, with its frame of curly, overabundant hair, reminded him of a Fra Angelico angel: he noticed in particular the blond hairs which a razor had missed on her upper lip. The hairs had breached a wall of thick make-up and they were quivering as though distressed.

"Hey!" said the large woman in a resounding male voice. The greeting conveyed consternation at his own rash mistake. It was a charming thing to say.

"Hey!" Bird hurried his face into a smile and returned the greeting in the somewhat hoarse, squawky voice that was another of his birdlike attributes.

The transvestite executed a half-turn on his high heels and walked slowly down the street. For a minute Bird watched him go, then walked away in the other direction. He cut through a narrow alley and cautiously, warily started across a wide street fretted with trolley tracks. Even the hysterical caution which now and then seized Bird with the violence of a spasm evoked a puny bird half-crazed with fear—the nickname was a perfect fit.

That queen saw me watching my reflection in the window as if I were waiting for someone, and he mistook me for a pervert. A humiliating mistake, but inasmuch as the queen had recognized her error the minute Bird had turned around, Bird's honor had been redeemed. Now he was enjoying the humor of the confrontation. *Hey!*—no greeting could have been better suited to the occasion; the queen must have had a good head on his shoulders.

Bird felt a surge of affection for the young man masquerading as a large woman. Would he succeed in turning up a pervert tonight and making him a pigeon? Maybe I should have found the courage to go with him myself.

Bird was still imagining what might have happened had he gone off with the young man to some crazy corner of the city, when he gained the opposite sidewalk and turned into a crowded street of cheap bars and restaurants. We would probably lie around naked, as close as brothers, and talk. I'd be naked too so he wouldn't feel any awkwardness. I might tell him my wife was having a baby tonight, and maybe I'd confess that I've wanted to go to Africa for years, and that my dream of dreams has been to write a chronicle of my adventures when I got back called *Sky Over Africa*. I might even say that going off to Africa alone would become impossible if I got locked up in the cage of a family when the baby came (I've been in the cage ever since my marriage but until now the door has always seemed open; the baby on its way into the world may clang that door shut). I'd talk about all kinds of things, and the queen would take pains to pick up the seeds of everything that's threatening me, one by one he'd gather them in, and certainly he would understand. Because a youth who tries so hard to be faithful to the warp in himself that he ends up searching the street in drag for perverts, a young man like that must have eyes and ears and a heart exquisitely sensitive to the fear that roots in the backlands of the subconscious.

Tomorrow morning we might have shaved together while we listened to the news on the radio, sharing a soap dish. That queen was young but his beard seemed heavy and . . . Bird cut the chain of fantasy and smiled. Spending a night together might be going too far, but at least he should have invited the young man for a drink. Bird was on a street lined with cheap, cozy bars: the crowd sweeping him along was full of drunks. His throat was dry and he wanted a drink, even if he had to have it alone. Pivoting his head swiftly on his long, lean neck, he inspected the bars on both sides of the street. In fact, he had no intention of stopping in any of them. Bird could imagine how his mother-in-law would react if he arrived at the bedside of his wife and newborn child, reeking of whisky. He didn't want his parents-in-law to see him in the grip of alcohol: not again.

Bird's father-in-law lectured at a small private college now, but he had been the chairman of the English department at Bird's university until he had retired. It was thanks not so much to good luck as to his father-in-law's good will that Bird had managed at his age to get a teaching job at a cram-school. He loved the old man, and he was in awe of him. Bird had never encountered an elder with quite his father-in-law's largesse; he didn't want to disappoint him all over again.

Bird married in May when he was twenty-five, and that first summer he stayed drunk for four weeks straight. He suddenly began to drift on a sea of alcohol, a besotted Robinson Crusoe. Neglecting all his obligations as a graduate student, his job, his studies, discarding everything without a thought, Bird sat all day long and until late every night in the darkened kitchen of his apartment, listening to records and drinking whisky. It seemed to him now, looking back on those terrible days, that with the exception of listening to music and drinking and immersing in harsh, drunken sleep, he hadn't engaged in a single living human activity. Four weeks later Bird had revived from an agonizing seven-hundred-hour drunk to discover in himself, wretchedly sober, the desolation of a city ravaged by the fires of war. He was like a mental incompetent with only the slightest chance of recovery, but he had to tame all over again not only the wilderness inside himself, but the wilderness of his relations to the world outside. He withdrew from graduate school and asked his father-in-law to find him a teaching position. Now, two years later, he was waiting for his wife to have their first child. Let him appear at the hospital having sullied his blood with the poisons of alcohol once again and his mother-in-law would flee as if the hounds of hell were at her heels, dragging her daughter and grandchild with her.

Bird himself was wary of the craving, occult but deeply rooted, that he still had for alcohol. Often since those four weeks in whisky hell he had asked himself why he had stayed drunk for seven hundred hours, and never had he arrived at a conclusive answer. So long as his descent into the abyss of whisky remained a riddle, there was a constant danger he might suddenly return.

In one of the books about Africa he read so avidly, Bird had come across this passage: "The drunken revels which explorers invariably remark are still common in the African village today. This suggests that life in this beautiful country is still lacking something fundamental. Basic dissatisfactions are still driving the African villagers to despair and self-abandon." Rereading the passage, which referred to the tiny villages in the Sudan, Bird realized he had been avoiding a consideration of the lacks and dissatisfactions that were lurking in his own life. But they existed, he was certain, so he was careful to deny himself alcohol.

Bird emerged in the square at the back of the honky-tonk district, where the clamor and motion seemed to focus. The clock of lightbulbs on the theater in the center of the square was flashing SEVEN PM—time to ask about his wife. Bird had been telephoning his mother-in-law at the hospital every hour since three that afternoon. He glanced around the square. Plenty of public telephones, but all were occupied. The thought, not so much of his wife in labor as of his mother-in-law's nerves as she hovered over the telephone reserved for in-patients, irritated him. From the moment she had arrived at the hospital with her daughter, the woman had been obsessed with the idea that the staff was try-ing to humiliate her. If only some other patient's relative were on the phone. . . . Lugubriously hopeful, Bird retraced his steps, glancing into bars and coffee houses, Chinese noodle shops, cutlet restaurants, and shoestores. He could al-ways step inside somewhere and phone. But he wanted to avoid a bar if he could, and he had eaten dinner already. Why not buy a powder to settle his stomach?

Bird was looking for a drugstore when an outlandish establishment on a corner stopped him short. On a giant billboard suspended above the door, a cowboy crouched with a pistol flaming. Bird read the legend that flowered on the head of the Indian pinned beneath the cowboy's spurs: GUN CORNER. In-side, beneath paper flags of the United Nations and strips of spiraling green and yellow crepe paper, a crowd much younger than Bird was milling around the many-colored, box-shaped games that filled the store from front to back. Bird, ascertaining through the glass doors rimmed with red and indigo tape that a public telephone was installed in a corner at the rear, stepped into the Gun Corner, passed a Coke machine and a juke box howling rock-n-roll already out of vogue, and started across the muddy wooden floor. It was instantly as if skyrockets were bursting in his ears. Bird toiled across the room as though he were walking in a maze, past pinball machines, dart games, and a miniature forest alive with deer and rabbits and monstrous green toads that moved on a con-veyor belt; as Bird passed, a high-school boy bagged a frog under the admir-ing eyes of his girlfriends and five points clicked into the window on the side of the game. He finally reached the telephone. Dropping a coin into the phone, he dialed the hospital number from memory. In one ear he heard the distant ringing of the phone, the blare of rock-n-roll filled the other, and a noise like ten thousand scuttling crabs: the high teens, rapt over their automated toys, were scuffling the wooden floor with the soft-as-glove-leather soles of their Italian shoes. What would his mother-in-law think of this din? Maybe he should say something about the noise when he excused himself for calling late.

The phone rang four times before his mother-in-law's voice, like his wife's made somewhat younger, answered; Bird immediately asked about his wife, without apologizing for anything.

"Nothing yet. It just won't come; that child is suffering to death and the baby just won't come!"

Wordless, Bird stared for an instant at the numberless antholes in the ebonite receiver. The surface, like a night sky vaulted with black stars, clouded and cleared with each breath he took.

"I'll call back at eight," he said a minute later, then hung up the phone, and sighed.

A drive-a-car game was installed beside the phone, and a boy who looked like a Filipino was seated behind the wheel. Beneath a miniature E-type Jaguar mounted on a cylinder in the center of the board, a painted belt of country scenery revolved continuously, making the car appear to speed forever down a marvelous suburban highway. As the road wound on, obstacles constantly materialized to menace the little car: sheep, cows, girls with children in tow. The player's job was to avoid collisions by cutting the wheel and swiveling the car atop its cylinder. The Filipino was hunched over the wheel in a fury of concentration, deep creases in his short, swarthy brow. On and on he drove, biting his thin lips shut with keen eyeteeth and spraying the air with sibilant saliva, as if convinced that finally the belt would cease to revolve and bring the E-type Jaguar to its destination. But the road unfurled obstacles in front of the little car unendingly. Now and then, when the belt began to slow down, the Filipino would plunge a hand into his pants pocket, grope out a coin, and insert it in the metal eye of the machine. Bird paused where he stood obliquely behind the boy, and watched the game for a while. Soon a sensation of unbearable fatigue crept into his feet. Bird hurried toward the back exit, stepping as though the floor were scorching metal plate. At the back of the gallery, he encountered a pair of truly bizarre machines.

The game on the right was surrounded by a gang of youngsters in identical silk jackets embroidered with gold-and-silver brocade dragons, the Hong Kong souvenir variety designed for American tourists. They were producing loud, unfamiliar noises that sounded like heavy impacts. Bird approached the game on the left, because for the moment it was unguarded. It was a medieval instrument of torture, an Iron Maiden—twentieth-century model. A beautiful, life-sized maiden of steel with mechanical red-and-black stripes was protecting her bare chest with stoutly crossed arms. The player attempted to pull her arms away from her chest for a glimpse of her hidden metal breasts; his grip and pull appeared as numbers in the windows which were the maiden's eyes. Above her head was a chronological table of average grip and pull.

Bird inserted a coin in the slot between the maiden's lips. Then he set about forcing her arms away from her breasts. The steel arms resisted stubbornly: Bird pulled harder. Gradually his face was drawn in to her iron chest. Since her face was painted in what was unmistakably an expression of anguish, Bird had the feeling he was raping the girl. He strained until every muscle in his body began to ache. Suddenly there was a rumbling in her chest as a gear turned, and numbered plaques, the color of watery blood, clicked into her hollow eyes. Bird went limp, panting, and checked his score against the table of averages. It was unclear what the units represented, but Bird had scored 70 points for grip and 75 points for pull. In the column on the table beneath 27, Bird found GRIP: 110— PULL: 110. He scanned the table in disbelief and discovered that his score was average for a man of forty. *Forty!*—the shock dropped straight to his stomach and he brought up a belch. Twenty-seven years and four months old and no more grip nor pull than a man of forty: Bird! But how could it be? On top of everything, he could tell that the tingling in his shoulders and sides would develop into an obstinate muscle ache. Determined to redeem his honor, Bird approached the game on the right. He realized with surprise that he was now in deadly earnest about this game of testing strength.

With the alertness of wild animals whose territory is being invaded, the boys in dragon jackets froze as Bird moved in, and enveloped him with challenging looks. Rattled, but with a fair semblance of carelessness, Bird inspected the machine at the center of their circle. In construction it resembled a gallows in a Western movie, except that a kind of Slavic cavalry helmet was suspended from the spot where a hapless outlaw should have hung. The helmet only partly concealed a sandbag covered in black buckskin. When a coin was inserted in the hole that glared like a cyclops' eye from the center of the helmet, the player could lower the sandbag and the indicator needle reset itself at zero. There was a cartoon of Robot Mouse in the center of the indicator: he was screaming, his yellow mouth open wide, *C'mon Killer! Let's Measure Your Punch!*

When Bird merely eyed the game and made no move in its direction, one of the dragon-jackets stepped forward as if to demonstrate, dropped a coin into the helmet, and pulled the sandbag down. Self-consciously but confident, the youth dropped back a step and, hurling his entire body forward as in a dance, walloped the sandbag. A heavy thud: the rattle of the chain as it crashed against the inside of the helmet. The needle leaped past the numbers on the gauge and quivered meaninglessly. The gang exploded in laughter. The punch had exceeded the capacity of the gauge: the paralyzed mechanism would not reset. The triumphant dragon-jacket aimed a light kick at the sandbag, this time from a karate crouch, and the indicator needle dropped to 500 while the sandbag crawled back into the helmet slowly like an exhausted hermit crab. Again the gang roared.

An unaccountable passion seized Bird. Careful not to wrinkle the maps, he took off his jacket and laid it on a bingo table. Then he dropped into the helmet one of the coins from a pocketful he was carrying for phone calls to the hospital. The boys were watching every move. Bird lowered the sandbag, took one step back, and put up his fists. After he had been expelled from high school, in the days when he was studying for the examination that had qualified him to go to college, Bird had brawled almost every week with other delinquents in his provincial city. He had been feared, and he had been surrounded always by younger admirers. Bird had faith in the power of his punch. And his form would be orthodox, he wouldn't take that kind of ungainly leap. Bird shifted his weight to the balls of his feet, took one light step forward, and smashed the sandbag with a right jab. Had his punch surpassed the limit of 2500 and made a cripple of the gauge? Like hell it had—the needle stood at 300! Doubled over, with his punching fist against his chest, Bird stared for an instant at the gauge in stupefaction. Then hot blood climbed into his face. Behind him the boys in dragon jackets were silent and still. But certainly their attention was concentrated on Bird and on the gauge; the appearance of a man with a punch so numerically meager must have struck them dumb.

Bird, moving as though unaware the gang existed, returned to the helmet, inserted another coin, and pulled the sandbag down. This was no time to worry about correct form: he threw the weight of his entire body behind the punch. His right arm went numb from the elbow to the wrist and the needle stood at a mere 500.

Stooping quickly, Bird picked up his jacket and put it on, facing the bingo table. Then he turned back to the teen-agers, who were observing him in silence. Bird tried for an experienced smile, full of understanding and surprise, for the young champ from the former champion long retired. But the boys merely stared at him with blank, hardened faces, as though they were watching a dog. Bird turned crimson all the way behind his ears, hung his head, and hurried out of the gallery. A great guffawing erupted behind him, full of obviously affected glee.

Dizzy with childish shame, Bird cut across the square and plunged down a dark side street: he had lost the courage to drift with a crowd full of strangers. Whores were positioned along the street, but the rage in Bird's face discouraged them from calling out. Bird turned into an alley where not even whores were lurking, and suddenly he was stopped by a high embankment. He knew by the smell of green leaves in the darkness that summer grass was thick on the slope. On top of the embankment was a train track. Bird peered up and down the track to see whether a train was coming and discovered nothing in the dark. He looked up at the black ink of the sky. The reddish mist hovering above the ground was a reflection of the neon lights in the square. A sudden drop of rain wet Bird's upturned cheek—the grass had been so fragrant because it had been about to rain. Bird lowered his head and, as though for lack of anything else to do, furtively urinated. Before he had finished, he heard chaotic footsteps approaching from behind. By the time he turned around, he was surrounded by the boys in dragon jackets.

With the faint light at their backs, the boys were in heavy shadow, and Bird couldn't make out their expressions. But he remembered their denial of him, thoroughly brutal, that had lurked in their blankness at the Gun Corner. The gang had sighted an existence too feeble, and savage instincts had been roused. Trembling with the need of a violent child to torment a weak playmate, they had raced in pursuit of the pitiful lamb with a punch of 500. Bird was afraid: frantically he searched for a way out. To reach the bright square he would have to rush directly into the gang and break their circle at its strongest point. But with Bird's strength—the grip and pull of a forty-year-old!—that was out of the question: they would easily force him back. To his right was a short alley that dead-ended at a board fence. The narrow alley to his left, between the embankment and a high, wire fence around a factory yard, emerged far on the other side at a busy street. Bird had a chance if he could cover that hundred or so yards without being caught. Resolved, Bird made as if to race for the dead end on his right, wheeled and then charged to the left. But the enemy was expert at this kind of ruse, just as Bird at twenty had been an expert in his own night city. Unfooled, the gang had shifted to the left and regrouped even while Bird was feinting to the right. Bird straightened, and as he hurled himself toward the alley on the left he collided with the black silhouette of a body bent backward like a bow, the same attack the youth had used on the sandbag. No time or room to dodge, Bird took the full force of the worst knock-out punch of his life and fell back onto the embankment. Groaning, he spat saliva and blood. The teen-agers laughed shrilly, as they had laughed when they had paralyzed the punching machine. Then they peered down at Bird silently, enclosing him in an even tighter semicircle. The gang was waiting.

It occurred to Bird that the maps must be getting creased between his body and the ground. And his own child was being born: the thought danced with new poignancy to the frontlines of consciousness. A sudden rage took him, and rough despair. Until now, out of terror and bewilderment, Bird had been contriving only to escape. But he had no intention of running now. If I don't fight now, I'll not only lose the chance to go to Africa forever, my baby will be born into the world solely to lead the worst possible life—it was like the voice of inspiration, and Bird believed.

Raindrops pelted his torn lips. He shook his head, groaned, and slowly rose. The half-circle of teen-agers dropped back invitingly. Then the burliest of the bunch took one confident step forward. Bird let his arms dangle and thrust out his chin, affecting the limp befuddlement of a carnival doll. Taking careful aim, the boy in the jacket lifted one leg high and arched backward like a pitcher going into his windup, then cocked his right arm back as far as it would go and launched forward for the kill. Bird ducked, lowered his head, and drove like a ferocious bull into his attacker's belly. The boy screamed, gagged on vomiting bile, and crumpled silently. Bird jerked his head up and confronted the others. The joy of battle had reawakened in him; it had been years since he had felt it. Bird and the dragon-jackets watched one another without moving, appraising the formidable enemy. Time passed.

Abruptly, one of the boys shouted to the others: "C'mon, let's go! We don't want to fight this guy. He's too fucking old!"

The boys relaxed immediately. Leaving Bird on his guard, they lifted their unconscious comrade and moved away toward the square. Bird was left alone in the rain. A ticklish sense of comedy rose into his throat, and for a minute he laughed silently. There was blood on his jacket, but if he walked in the rain for a while, no one would be able to tell it from water. Bird felt a kind of preliminary peace. Naturally, his chin hurt where the punch had landed, and his arms and back ached; so did his eyes. But he was in high spirits for the first time since his wife's labor had begun. Bird limped down the alley between the embankment and the factory lot. Soon an old-fashioned steam engine spewing fiery cinders came chugging down the track. Passing over Bird's head, the train was a colossal black rhinoceros galloping across an inky sky.

Out on the avenue, as he waited for a cab, Bird probed for a broken tooth with his tongue and spat it into the street.

The 1970s and 1980s

KENT CARROLL

❦

"Grove in the '70s"

One evening, a year before his premature death, I was having dinner in a Greenwich Village restaurant with the satirist Michael O'Donohue. I had known Michael since the end of the 1960s when I first joined Grove Press and he was writing for *Evergreen Review*, most notably the words for the cartoon *Phoebe Zeitgeist*. Michael had gone on to fame and a bit of fortune as one of the original writers for *Saturday Night Live* and, later, the author of hit movie scripts for the likes of his friend and colleague Bill Murray. Michael was one of the great raconteurs; his sensibility had an original edge. (Once at a party at his home on 16th Street he unveiled his latest acquisition: a painting of Desi Arnaz halfway through a sex-change operation.) And so the talk on the occasional evening we spent together was mostly one-way—he talked, I listened—a circumstance with which I was heartily agreeable, as it seemed to me that what he had to say was rather more interesting than most any anecdote or observation I might offer.

On this particular night we spoke of Barney Rosset and Grove Press, not our usual subject. Michael told me of how he had been introduced to Grove and why writing for *Evergreen Review* had been so important for him. In his telling, his adolescent years in upstate New York had not been happy ones. He knew he was different from others his age, largely because he was told so by schoolmates, teachers, and even his family but also because he felt his own otherness. No one else laughed at the things he thought especially funny. People or events that appeared to him to be intriguing or ridiculous were, for family and friends, either taboo or objects of veneration. He told me that during his high school years he became convinced that he was crazy, alone in his off-center view of the world. Then, one day, he came across a copy of *Evergreen Review* and realized that not only was he not alone but that there were smart, talented people out there somewhere, people who also used cutting humor to tell the truth, people who realized that everything was not perfect in that best of all possible places, the USA in the late 1950s and early '60s.

"I lived from issue to issue," he told me. Some of his acquaintances could hardly wait to finish high school so they could get a job and buy a car or go to college and maybe get laid. Michael wanted only to get to New York and see this magical place that seemed able to read his secret thoughts. "*Evergreen Review*," he said, "saved my life."

Michael's response to Grove was not, in my experience, exceptional. Over the past twenty years I have regularly met—even published—a variety of people who, upon discovering I once worked at Grove, were eager to know what it was like: "Did you ever meet Jean Genet or William Burroughs?" No and yes, respectively; my first encounter with the author of *Naked Lunch* was on an afternoon in London in a scene that might have been scripted by Harold Pinter, whom we also published. And, always, the people who asked about Grove insisted on relating, in detail, how its books and the magazine had shaped their lives: the environmental activist who skipped freshman classes on a winter day in Minnesota to finish *The Wretched of the Earth* and the next semester transferred to Berkeley; the playwright recalling the mounting excitement and awakening on seeing his hidden fantasies animated in *City of Night;* the inner-city school teacher who spent his own money to supply his class with copies of *The Autobiography of Malcolm X*. Each keenly remembered a writer who had helped them make sense of who they were meant to be. Only a few books can do this. Grove published many of them.

But that was in the 1960s. The 1970s were a period of decline. When I joined Grove in 1969 the company employed 140 people and had just moved into a lavishly restored office building at the corner of Bleecker and Mercer Streets. Four years later there were fourteen of us working out of Barney's home on West Houston Street, after an interim stopover on East 11th Street in a small building that housed a miniature movie theater and the Black Cat bar, which Barney operated on the financially dubious policy of never charging friends or employees for their drinks.

During the '70s Grove lived on the income generated by its marvelous backlist. There was the occasional new book of note, even the rare, momentary best-seller. But the halcyon days were gone along with the money. Barney's instinct had been to make Grove into what we now would call a multimedia company. And, indeed, instinct it was; his view of the future was always a bit light on planning or details and, later, resources. He wanted a company that could publish a magazine to support its books and discover new writers, and to run a book club that offered publications and avant-garde short films (most in aggressive violation of just about everybody's "community standards") via the mail system so as to circumvent the regular, stodgy channels of distribution. He entered the feature-film business to distribute movies such as Jean-Luc

Godard's *Weekend* and the seminal, if banal, *I Am Curious (Yellow)*. These and other films were, he understood, a natural extension of the publishing operation (a number of them were made by Grove authors such as Marguerite Duras). Maybe Barney was just ahead of his time, as he was when he wrote an essay on *Tropic of Cancer* for a stunned Swarthmore professor in 1940, or when he told the suspicious commander of his film unit in China in 1943 that he'd much rather record the exploits of Mao Tse-tung than those of Chiang Kai-shek.

Barney was not a "visionary." American "visionaries" are usually people who espouse puerile mysticism after having spent too much time under the midday sun in places like Taos, New Mexico. Barney's idea of what America's future could aspire to—racial tolerance, free sexual expression—was based on morality and an acute sense of history. That some of his ideas were not much more than mental curlicues and that some of his behavior was awfully self-centered does not detract from his ethical impulse. America has traveled some distance since the mid-1950s. Today it looks a lot more like what Barney wanted it to be than it resembles the social order championed by those who would have delighted in attending his auto-de-fé. For it was not a "vision"; it was concrete, something one could stake a reputation and private fortune on. Which is what Barney did.

Publishing is an enterprise—more a handicraft than a rational business—where art and commerce collide. Barney understood both elements largely by intuition. But only one grows and prospers primarily by imaginative leaps. An inveterate child of 1930s-style political utopianism, he was a man whose true thoughts and emotions were closer to those of a precocious sixteen-year-old than to those of the charming sophisticate one first met. Barney needed money but disdained what he believed it represented, as when, after his father's death, he sued the state of Illinois to return a prized charter to operate a private bank. (The judge wasn't sure whether to grant his bizarre request or to have him committed.)

In contemporary business terms, Grove never attained the "scale" to successfully realize Rosset's inchoate, if brilliant, strategy. And by the mid-1970s it had neither the staff nor the finances. The early, surprising success of the film division had drained resources from the book division, which had produced the steady, profitable revenues. *Evergreen Review*'s erratic publishing schedule and unpredictable content was disliked by advertisers and abhorred by magazine distributors. (An interview with Yasser Arafat caused almost every copy of one issue to be returned unsold.)

So by the early 1970s the book club had gone the way of the Mercer Street building. *Evergreen Review* was moribund; the film division was manned by two people who rented its library to film societies and college classrooms. There was the occasional new book from stalwarts such as John Rechy (*The Sexual Outlaw*), important new pieces from Samuel Beckett that enhanced his august reputation but did little for Grove's balance sheet, and some unlikely pieces such as the illustrated script tie-in to the movie *American Graffiti,* which sold 300,000 copies, and Judith Exner's *My Story,* bought for one dollar after every reputable New York publisher had rejected her poorly told but important tale of concurrent affairs with President Kennedy and Mafia boss Sam Giancana on the self-righteous grounds that it was a slur on the reputation of JFK.

By this time novels, confessions, polemics, and plays that a decade earlier would have come to Grove by default or natural selection were now being published by large houses that were owned by even larger conglomerates. Grove had opened and changed the culture, and other publishers were harvesting the benefits. Now Grove could no longer afford to sell its own books and so entered into a distribution arrangement with Random House whereby Random would pay Grove a monthly fee that was barely enough to cover Grove's overhead and not nearly sufficient for it to aggressively acquire new titles. Barney believed that Random House made this deal, secured by the contracts on Grove's backlist, in expectation that Grove would go under and Random would inherit a body of titles then, as now, the envy of the New York publishing community. However, considering Grove's declining, even perilous, circumstances, the deal from Random's side was smart business; reasonable and, some thought, generous. Barney chafed under these conditions and expressed his frustration and anger in ways often hard on the patient Random House sales staff, who admired Grove but found meetings with Barney bewildering. As one told me, "He wants to release three new editions of *Story of O,* each with its own cover and all with different prices." Random executives were known to go home and lie down after these meetings.

Barney's resentment of his diminished fortunes and Random House's increasing control of Grove's publishing reached an apex, of sorts, the first day of a winter sales conference held at a luxury beach hotel on the coast of Puerto Rico. Barney and I had flown to San Juan, rented a car, and were on the way to the conference when Barney remembered a building he had visited years before that was a replica, 75 percent of scale, of the bridge deck of the French ocean liner *Normandie.* We found the building in a section of San Juan that had probably never seen good days, and odd it was but clearly recognizable as the ship that had inspired the demented architect. We stopped for a drink. When traveling with Barney, whether a few blocks from Houston Street to Sheridan Square or 3,000 miles to Paris, one always stopped for a drink. Barney's close acquaintance with alcohol and amphetamines was—to put it delicately—a topic of some wonder. A rumor at Grove once had it that a doctor friend had asked Barney if he would donate his body to medical science, first for intensive observation, later to be pickled for posterity.

So stop we did and drink we did, after discovering that the queer building housed a brothel. The women were sweet and congenial and appeared as if they had stayed with a road company of *Gypsy* a dozen years too long. Too soon I had to remind Barney that we needed to leave as we had an hour until the dinner Random House was hosting for us. Barney asked two of the women to accompany us. This was not unexpected behavior and I didn't think much of it until we arrived at the hotel and Barney explained to the women that he wanted both of them to join him at Bob Bernstein's table that evening.

Robert Bernstein, the well-regarded president of Random House, was a famously reserved, even shy, man. Barney's intent was to defy rather than embarrass him, but painful embarrassment all around was my prediction. Barney dismissed my concern. We were saved from ourselves by the sensible women, who realized they too would be made uncomfortable. They refused to attend the dinner but were more than willing to wait in Barney's room until he returned.

As the decade neared its end, Grove's circumstances did not improve. Barney had lost none of his ability to see the world in a creative, if somewhat bent, way that was at once prescient and confusing; he had well understood the meaning of sexual politics a decade before the term was coined, and it was no error that he bought one of the first portable videotape recorders imported into the United States. His plan was to produce a video version of *Evergreen Review*, which we did. But this was before quarter-inch tape and cassettes and by then the money and key people were gone and much of the energy was misplaced.

There were other adventures during that decade: the overnight Air France flight when Barney and I and "Mrs. Baldwin's bug-eyed boy," as Jimmy Baldwin insisted on calling himself, were the only passengers in a 747 first-class section; the brawl with Joan Mitchell (Barney's first wife) and her hangers-on because rats had nibbled one of her paintings, which Barney was meant to be keeping safe; the sex farm in the hills above Topanga Canyon; the night in Paris when Steve McQueen (whom Barney kept confusing with James Garner) tried to buy the movie rights to *Waiting for Godot* and Sam Beckett said no to half a million dollars ("If I wanted it to be a movie I would have written it as a movie"), 10 percent of which would have gone to Grove as his agent; the long, lost weekend . . . but I think I'll save that one for my memoirs.

As I have written elsewhere, one can mount a cogent argument that Barney Rosset was the most important American publisher of the twentieth century. Others published as many books of exceptional quality and some published more Nobel Prize winners. But no other publisher had the cultural and political influence that Barney did. His lawsuits defending *Tropic of Cancer*, *Lady Chatterley's Lover*, *Naked Lunch*, and *I Am Curious (Yellow)* effectively eliminated censorship in the United States. This combination of accomplishments is unmatched and not as honored as it ought to be in this country. For Barney and Grove could only have happened in America, here where we are as ready to borrow from the rest of the world as we are compelled to try and save it. In many important ways Barney embodied the American character. He seized the possibility of the new and the transcendent.

Barney and Grove may once have saved Michael O'Donohue's life. He surely transformed many others, mine included. And that is a life very well spent.

DAVID MAMET

❦

FROM *American Buffalo* [1977]

TEACH: You want to tell me what this thing is?

DON (*Pause*): The thing?

TEACH: Yeah.

Pause.

What is it?

DON: Nothing.

TEACH: No? What is it, jewelry?

DON: No. It's nothing.

TEACH: Oh.

DON: You know?

TEACH: Yeah.

Pause.

Yeah. No. I don't know.

Pause.

Who am I, a *police*man . . . I'm making conversation, huh?

DON: Yeah.

TEACH: Huh?

Pause.

'Cause you know I'm just asking for talk.

DON: Yeah. I know. Yeah, okay.

TEACH: And I can live without this.

DON (*reaches for phone*): Yeah. I know. Hold on. I'll tell you.

TEACH: Tell me if you *want* to, Don.

DON: I want to, Teach.

TEACH: Yeah?

DON: Yeah.

Pause.

TEACH: Well, I'd fucking *hope* so. Am I wrong?

DON: No. No. You're right.

TEACH: I *hope* so.

DON: No, hold on; I gotta make this call.

TEACH: Well, all right. So what is it, jewelry?

DON: No.

TEACH: What?

DON: Coins.

TEACH: (Coins.)

DON: Yeah. Hold on, I gotta make this call.

Don hunts for a card, dials telephone.

(*Into phone*) Hello? This is Donny Dubrow. We were talking the other day. Lookit, sir, if I could get ahold of some of that stuff you were interested in, would you be interested in some of it?

Pause.

Those *things* . . . *Old*, yeah.

Pause.

Various pieces of various types.

Pause.

Tonight. Sometime late. Are they *what* . . . !!?? Yes, but I don't see what kind of a question is that (at the prices we're talking about . . .)

Pause.

No, hey, no, I understand *you* . . .

Pause.

Sometime late.

Pause.

One hundred percent.

Pause.

I feel the same. All right. Good-bye. (*Hangs up.*) Fucking asshole.

TEACH: Guys like that, I like to fuck their wives.

DON: I don't blame you.

TEACH: Fucking *jerk* . . .

DON: (I swear to God . . .)

TEACH: That guy's a collector?

DON: Who?

TEACH: The phone guy.

DON: Yeah.

TEACH: And the other guy?

DON: We spotted?

TEACH: Yeah.

DON: Him, too.

TEACH: So you hit him for his coins.

DON: Yeah.

TEACH: —And you got a buyer in the phone guy.

DON: (Asshole.)

TEACH: The thing is you're not sitting with the shit.

DON: No.

TEACH: The guy's an asshole or he's not, what do you care? It's business.

Pause.

DON: You're right.

TEACH: The guy with the suitcase, he's the mark.

DON: Yeah.

TEACH: How'd you find him?

DON: In here.

TEACH: Came in here, huh?

DON: Yeah.

TEACH: (No shit.)

Pause.

DON: He comes in here one day, like a week ago.

TEACH: For what?

DON: Just browsing. So he's looking in the case, he comes up and with this *buffalo-head* nickel . . .

TEACH: Yeah . . .

DON: From nine*teen*-something. (I don't know. I didn't even know it's there . . .)

TEACH: Uh-huh . . .

DON: . . . and he goes, "How much would that be?"

TEACH: Uh-huh . . .

DON: So I'm about to go, "Two bits," jerk that I am, but something tells me to shut up, so I go, "You tell me."

TEACH: Always good business.

DON: *Oh* yeah.

TEACH: How wrong can you go?

DON: That's what I mean, so then he thinks a minute, and he tells me he'll just *shop* a bit.

TEACH: Uh-huh . . . (*Stares out of window.*)

DON: And so he's *shopping* . . . What?

TEACH: Some cops.

DON: Where?

TEACH: At the corner.

DON: What are they doing?

TEACH: Cruising.

Pause.

DON: They turn the corner?

TEACH: (*waits*): Yeah.

Pause.

DON: . . . And so he's shopping. And he's picking up a beat-up *mirror* . . . an old *kid's* toy . . . a *shaving* mug . . .

TEACH: . . . right . . .

DON: Maybe five, six things, comes to eight bucks. I get 'em and I put 'em in a box and then he tells me he'll go fifty dollars for the nickel.

TEACH: No.

DON: Yeah. So I tell him (get this), "Not a chance."

TEACH: (Took balls.)

DON: (Well, what-the-fuck . . .)

TEACH: (No, I mean it.)

DON: (I took a chance.)

TEACH: (You're goddamn right.)

Pause.

DON (*shrugs*): So I say, "Not a chance," he tells me eighty is his highest offer.

TEACH: (I knew it.)

DON: Wait. So I go, "Ninety-five."

TEACH: Uh-huh.

DON: We settle down on ninety, *takes* the nickel, leaves the box of shit.

TEACH: He pay for it?

DON: The box of shit?

TEACH: Yeah.

DON: No.

Pause.

TEACH: And so what was the nickel?

DON: *I* don't know . . . some rarity.

TEACH: Ninety dollars for a nickel.

DON: Are you kidding, Teach? I bet it's worth five *times* that.

TEACH: Yeah, huh?

DON: Are you kidding me, the guy is going to come in here, he plunks down ninety bucks like nothing. *Shit* yeah.

Pause.

TEACH: Well, what the fuck, it didn't cost you anything.

DON: That's not the point. The next day back he comes and he goes through the whole bit again. He looks at *this,* he looks at *that,* it's a nice *day* . . .

TEACH: Yeah . . .

DON: And he tells me he's the guy was in here yesterday and bought the buffalo off me and do I maybe have some other articles of interest.

TEACH: Yeah.

DON: And so I tell him, "Not offhand." He says that could I get in touch with him, I get some in, so I say "sure," he leaves his card, I'm s'posed to call him anything crops up.

TEACH: Uh-huh.

DON: He comes in here like I'm his fucking doorman.

TEACH: Mmmm.

DON: He takes me off my coin and will I call him if I find another one.

TEACH: Yeah.

DON: Doing me this favor by just coming in my shop.

TEACH: Yeah.

Pause.

Some people never change.

DON: Like he has done me this big favor by just coming in my shop.

TEACH: Uh-huh. (You're going to get him now.)

DON: (You know I am.) So Bob, we kept a lookout on his place, and that's the shot.

TEACH: And who's the chick?

DON: What chick?

TEACH: You're asking Bob about.

DON: Oh yeah. The guy, he's married. I mean (*I* don't know.) We *think* he's married. They got two names on the bell. . . . Anyway, he's living with this chick, *you* know . . .

TEACH: What the hell.

DON: . . . and you should see this chick.

TEACH: Yeah, huh?

DON: She is a knockout. I mean, she is *real* nice-lookin', Teach.

TEACH: (Fuck *him* . . .)

DON: The other day, last Friday like a week ago, Bob runs in, lugs me out to look at 'em, they're going out on bicycles. The ass on this broad, un-be-fucking-lievable in these bicycling shorts sticking up in the air with these short handlebars.

TEACH: (Fuckin' *fruits* . . .)

Pause.

DON: So that's it. We keep an eye on 'em. They both work. . . . (Yesterday he rode his bicycle to work.)

TEACH: He didn't.

DON: Yeah.

TEACH (*snorts*): (With the three-piece suit, huh?)

DON: I didn't see 'em. Bobby saw 'em.

Pause.

And that's the shot. Earl gets me in touch the phone guy, he's this coin collector, and that's it.

TEACH: It fell in your lap.

DON: Yeah.

TEACH: You're going in tonight.

DON: It looks that way.

TEACH: And who's going in?

Pause.

DON: Bobby.

Pause.

He's a good kid, Teach.

TEACH: He's a great kid, Don. You know how I feel about the kid.

Pause.

I *like* him.

DON: He's doing good.

TEACH: I can see that.

Pause.

But I gotta say something here.

DON: What?

TEACH: Only this—and I don't think I'm *getting* at anything—

DON: What?

TEACH (*Pause*): Don't send the kid in.

DON: I shouldn't send Bobby in?

TEACH: No. (Now, just wait a second.) Let's siddown on this. What are we saying here? Loyalty.

Pause.

You know how I am on this. This is great. This is admirable.

DON: What?

TEACH: This loyalty. This is swell. It turns my heart the things that you do for the kid.

DON: What do I do for him, Walt?

TEACH: Things. Things, you know what I mean.

DON: No, I don't do anything for him.

TEACH: In your mind you don't, but the things, I'm saying, that you actually go *do* for him. This is fantastic. All I mean, a guy can be too loyal, Don. Don't be dense on this. What are we saying here? Business.

I mean, the guy's got you're taking his high-speed blender and a Magnavox, you send the kid in. You're talking about a real *job* . . . they don't come in right away and know they been *had* . . .

You're talking maybe a safe, certainly a good lock or two, and you need a guy's looking for valuable shit, he's not going to mess with the stainless steel silverware, huh, or some digital clock.

Pause.

We both know what we're saying here. We both know we're talking about some job needs more than the kid's gonna skin-pop go in there with a *crowbar* . . .

DON: I don't want you mentioning that.

TEACH: It slipped out.

DON: You know how I feel on that.

TEACH: Yes. And I'm sorry, Don. I admire that. All that I'm saying, don't confuse business with pleasure.

DON: But I don't want that talk, only, Teach.

Pause.

You understand?

TEACH: I more than understand, and I apologize.

Pause.

I'm sorry.

DON: That's the only thing.

TEACH: All right. But I tell you. I'm glad I said it.

DON: Why?

TEACH: 'Cause it's best for these things to be out in the open.

DON: But I don't want it in the open.

TEACH: Which is why I apologized.

Pause.

DON: You know the fucking kid's clean. He's trying hard, he's working hard, and you leave him alone.

TEACH: Oh yeah, he's trying *real* hard.

DON: And he's no dummy, Teach.

TEACH: Far from it. All I'm saying, the job is beyond him. Where's the shame in this? This is not jacks, we get up to go home we give everything back. Huh? You want this fucked up?

Pause.

All that I'm saying, there's the least *chance* something might fuck up, you'd get the law down, you would take the shot, and couldn't find the coins *whatever:* If you see the least chance, you cannot afford to take that chance! Don? *I* want to go in there and gut this motherfucker. Don? Where is the shame in this? You take care of him, *fine.* (Now this is loyalty.) But Bobby's got his own best interests, too. And you cannot afford (and simply as a *business* proposition) you cannot afford to take the chance. (*Pause. Teach picks up a strange object.*) What is this?

DON: That?

TEACH: Yes.

DON: It's a thing that they stick in dead pigs keep their legs apart all the blood runs out.

TEACH *nods. Pause.*

TEACH: Mmmm.

Pause.

DON: I set it up with him.

TEACH: "You set it up with him." . . . You set it up and then you told him.

Long pause.

DON: I gave Earl ten percent.

TEACH: Yeah? for what?

DON: The connection.

TEACH: So ten off the top: forty-five, forty-five.

Pause.

DON: And Bobby?

TEACH: A hundred. A hundred fifty . . . we hit big . . . *whatever.*

DON: And *you* what?

TEACH: The *shot.* I *go,* I go *in* . . . I bring the stuff *back* (or wherever . . .)

Pause.

DON: And what do I do?

TEACH: You mind the fort.

Pause.

DON: Here?

TEACH: Well, yeah . . . this is the fort.

Pause.

DON: (You know, this is real classical money we're talking about.)

TEACH: I know it. You think I'm going to fuck with Chump Change?

Pause.

So tell me.

DON: Well, hold on a second. I mean, we're still talking.

TEACH: I'm sorry. I thought we were done talking.

DON: No.

TEACH: Well, then, let's talk some more. You want to bargain? You want to mess with the points?

DON: No. I just want to think for a second.

TEACH: Well, you think, but here's a helpful hint. Fifty percent of some money is better than ninety percent of some broken *toaster* that you're gonna have, you send the kid in. (Which is providing he don't trip the alarm in the *first* place . . .) Don? You don't even know what the *thing* is on this. Where he lives. They got alarms? What *kind* of alarms? What kind of *this* . . . ? And what if (God forbid) the *guy* walks in? Somebody's nervous, whacks him with a table lamp— you wanna get touchy—and you can take your ninety dollars from the nickel shove it up your ass—the good it did you—and you wanna know *why?* (And I'm not *saying* anything . . .) because you didn't take the time to go first-class.

JOHN KENNEDY TOOLE

❧

FROM *A Confederacy of Dunces* [1980]

Patrolman Mancuso enjoyed riding the motorcycle up St. Charles Avenue. At the precinct he had borrowed a large and loud one that was all chromium and baby blue, and at the touch of a switch it could become a pinball machine of flashing, winking, blinking red and white lights. The siren, a cacophony of twelve crazed bobcats, was enough to make suspicious characters within a half-mile radius defecate in panic and rush for cover. Patrolman Mancuso's love for the motorcycle was platonically intense.

The forces of evil generated by the hideous—and apparently impossible to uncover—underground of suspicious characters seemed remote to him this afternoon, though. The ancient oaks of St. Charles Avenue arched over the avenue like a canopy shielding him from the mild winter sun that splashed and sparkled on the chrome of the motorcycle. Although the days had lately been cold and damp, the afternoon had that sudden, surprising warmth that makes New Orleans winters gentle. Patrolman Mancuso appreciated the mildness, for he was wearing only a T-shirt and Bermuda shorts, the sergeant's costume selection for the day. The long red beard that hooked over his ears by means of wires did manage to warm his chest a little; he had snatched the beard from the locker while the sergeant wasn't looking.

Patrolman Mancuso inhaled the moldy scent of the oaks and thought, in a romantic aside, that St. Charles Avenue must be the loveliest place in the world. From time to time he passed the slowly rocking streetcars that seemed to be leisurely moving toward no special destination, following their route through the old mansions on either side of the avenue. Everything looked so calm, so prosperous, so unsuspicious. On his own time he was going up to see that poor Widow Reilly. She had looked so pitiful crying in the middle of that wreck. The least he could do was try to help her.

At Constantinople Street he turned toward the river, sputtering and growling through a declining neighborhood until he reached a block of houses built in the 1880s and 90s, wooden Gothic and Gilded Age relics that dripped carving and scrollwork. Boss Tweed suburban stereotypes separated by alleys so narrow that a yardstick could almost bridge them and fenced in by iron pikes and low walls of crumbling brick. The larger houses had become impromptu apartment buildings, their porches converted into additional rooms. In some of the front yards there were aluminum carports, and bright aluminum awnings had been installed on one or two of the buildings. It was a neighborhood that had degenerated from Victorian to nothing in particular, a block that had moved into the twentieth century carelessly and uncaringly—and with very limited funds.

The address that Patrolman Mancuso was looking for was the tiniest structure on the block, aside from the carports, a Lilliput of the eighties. A frozen banana tree, brown and stricken, languished against the front of the porch, the tree preparing to collapse as the iron fence had done long ago. Near the dead tree there was a slight mound of earth and a leaning Celtic cross cut from plywood. The 1946 Plymouth was parked in the front yard, its bumper pressed against the porch, its taillights blocking the brick sidewalk. But, except for the Plymouth and the weathered cross and the mummified banana tree, the tiny yard was completely bare. There were no shrubs. There was no grass. And no birds sang.

Patrolman Mancuso looked at the Plymouth and saw the deep crease in its roof and the fender, filled with concave circles, that was separated from the body by three or four inches of space. VAN CAMP'S PORK AND BEANS was printed on the piece of cardboard taped across the hole that had been the rear window. Stopping by the grave, he read REX in faded letters on the cross. Then he climbed the worn brick steps and heard through the closed shutters a booming chant.

> Big girls don't cry.
> Big girls don't cry.
> Big girls, they don't cry-yi-yi.
> They don't cry.
> Big girls, they don't cry . . . yi.

While he was waiting for someone to answer the bell, he read the faded sticker on the crystal of the door, "A slip of the lip can sink a ship." Below a WAVE held her finger to lips that had turned tan.

Along the block some people were out on their porches looking at him and the motorcycle. The shutters across the street that slowly flipped up and down to get the proper focus indicated that he also had a considerable unseen audience, for a police motorcycle in the block was an event, especially if its driver wore shorts and a red beard. The block was poor, certainly, but honest. Suddenly self-conscious, Patrolman Mancuso rang the bell again and assumed what he considered his erect, official posture. He gave his audience his Mediterranean profile, but the audience saw only a small and sallow figure whose shorts hung clumsily in the crotch, whose spindly legs looked too naked in comparison to the formal garters and nylon socks that hung near the ankles. The audience remained curious, but unimpressed; a few were not even especially curious, the few who had expected some such vision to visit that miniature house eventually.

Big girls don't cry.
Big girls don't cry.

Patrolman Mancuso knocked savagely at the shutters.

Big girls don't cry.
Big girls don't cry.

"They home," a woman screamed through the shutters of the house next door, an architect's vision of Jay Gould domestic. "Miss Reilly's prolly in the kitchen. Go around the back. What are you, mister? A cop?"

"Patrolman Mancuso. Undercover," he answered sternly.

"Yeah?" There was a moment of silence. "Which one you want, the boy or the mother?"

"The mother."

"Well, that's good. You'd never get a hold of him. He's watching the TV. You hear that? It's driving me nuts. My nerves is shot."

Patrolman Mancuso thanked the woman's voice and walked into the dank alley. In the back yard he found Mrs. Reilly hanging a spotted and yellowed sheet on a line that ran through the bare fig trees.

"Oh, it's you," Mrs. Reilly said after a moment. She had almost started to scream when she saw the man with the red beard appear in her yard. "How you doing, Mr. Mancuso? What them people said?" She stepped cautiously over the broken brick paving in her brown felt moccasins. "Come on in the house and we'll have us a nice cup of coffee."

The kitchen was a large, high-ceilinged room, the largest in the house, and it smelled of coffee and old newspapers. Like every room in the house, it was dark; the greasy wallpaper and brown wooden moldings would have transformed any light into gloom, and from the alley very little light filtered in anyway. Although the interiors of homes did not interest Patrolman Mancuso, still he did notice, as anyone would have, the antique stove with the high oven and the refrigerator with the cylindrical motor on top. Thinking of the electric fryers, gas driers, mechanical mixers and beaters, waffle plates, and motorized rotisseries that seemed to be always whirring, grinding, beating, cooling, hissing, and broiling in the lunar kitchen of his wife, Rita, he wondered what Mrs. Reilly did in this sparse room. Whenever a new appliance was advertised on television, Mrs. Mancuso bought it no matter how obscure its uses were.

"Now tell me what the man said." Mrs. Reilly began boiling a pot of milk on her Edwardian gas stove. "How much I gotta pay? You told him I was a poor widow with a child to support, huh?"

"Yeah, I told him that," Patrolman Mancuso said, sitting erectly in his chair and looking hopefully at the kitchen table covered with oilcloth. "Do you mind if I put my beard on the table? It's kinda hot in here and it's sticking my face."

"Sure, go ahead, babe. Here. Have a nice jelly doughnut. I just bought them fresh this morning over by Magazine Street. Ignatius says to me this morning, 'Momma, I sure feel like a jelly doughnut.' You know? So I went over by the German and bought him two dozen. Look, they got a few left."

She offered Patrolman Mancuso a torn and oily cake box that looked as if it had been subjected to unusual abuse during someone's attempt to take all the doughnuts at once. At the bottom of the box Patrolman Mancuso found two withered pieces of doughnut out of which, judging by their moist edges, the jelly had been sucked.

"Thank you anyway, Miss Reilly. I had me a big lunch."

"Aw, ain't that a shame." She filled two cups half full with thick cold coffee and poured the boiling milk in up to the rim. "Ignatius loves his doughnuts. He says to me, 'Momma, I love my doughnuts.'" Mrs. Reilly slurped a bit at the rim of her cup. "He's out in the parlor right now looking at TV. Every afternoon as right as rain, he looks at that show where them kids dance." In the kitchen the music was somewhat fainter than it had been on the porch. Patrolman Mancuso pictured the green hunting cap bathed in the blue-white glow of the television screen. "He don't like the show at all, but he won't miss it. You oughta hear what he says about them poor kids."

"I spoke with the man this morning," Patrolman Mancuso said, hoping that Mrs. Reilly had exhausted the subject of her son.

"Yeah?" She put three spoons of sugar in her coffee and, holding the spoon in the cup with her thumb so that the handle threatened to puncture her eyeball, she slurped a bit more. "What he said, honey?"

"I told him I investigated the accident and that you just skidded on a wet street."

"That sounds good. So what he said then, babe?"

"He said he don't want to go to court. He wants a settlement now."

"Oh, my God!" Ignatius bellowed from the front of the house. "What an egregious insult to good taste."

"Don't pay him no mind," Mrs. Reilly advised the startled policeman. "He does that all the time he looks at the TV. A 'settlement.' That means he wants some money, huh?"

"He even got a contractor to appraise the damage. Here, this is the estimate."

Mrs. Reilly took the sheet of paper and read the typed column of itemized figures beneath the contractor's letterhead.

"Lord! A thousand and twenty dollars. This is terrible. How I'm gonna pay that?" She dropped the estimate on the oilcloth. "You sure that is right?"

"Yes, ma'am. He's got a lawyer working on it, too. It's all on the up and up."

"Where I'm gonna get a thousand dollars, though? All me and Ignatius got is my poor husband's Social Security and a little two-bit pension, and that don't come to much."

"Do I believe the total perversion that I am witnessing?" Ignatius screamed from the parlor. The music had a frantic, tribal rhythm; a chorus of falsettos sang insinuatingly about loving all night long.

"I'm sorry," Patrolman Mancuso said, almost heartbroken over Mrs. Reilly's financial quandary.

"Aw, it's not your fault, darling," she said glumly. "Maybe I can get a mortgage on the house. We can't do nothing about it, huh?"

"No, ma'am," Patrolman Mancuso answered, listening to some sort of approaching stampede.

"The children on that program should all be gassed," Ignatius said as he strode into the kitchen in his nightshirt. Then he noticed the guest and said coldly, "Oh."

"Ignatius, you know Mr. Mancuso. Say 'Hello.'"

"I do believe that I've seen him about," Ignatius said and looked out the back door.

Patrolman Mancuso was too startled by the monstrous flannel nightshirt to reply to Ignatius's pleasantry.

"Ignatius, honey, the man wants over a thousand dollars for what I did to his building."

"A thousand dollars? He will not get a cent. We shall have him prosecuted immediately. Contact our attorneys, Mother."

"Our attorneys? He's got a estimate from a contractor. Mr. Mancuso here says they's nothing I can do."

"Oh. Well, you shall have to pay him then."

"I could take it to court if you think it's best."

"Drunken driving," Ignatius said calmly. "You haven't a chance."

Mrs. Reilly looked depressed.

"But Ignatius, a thousand twenty dollars."

"I am certain that you can procure some funds," he told her. "Is there any more coffee, or have you given the last to this carnival masker?"

"We can mortgage the house."

"Mortgage the house? Of course we won't."

"What else we gonna do, Ignatius?"

"There are means," Ignatius said absently. "I wish that you wouldn't bother me with this. That program always increases my anxiety anyway." He smelled the milk before putting it into the pot. "I would suggest that you telephone that dairy immediately. This milk is quite aged."

"I can get a thousand dollars over by the Homestead," Mrs. Reilly told the silent patrolman quietly. "The house is good security. I had me a real estate agent offered me seven thousand last year."

"The ironic thing about that program," Ignatius was saying over the stove, keeping one eye peeled so that he could seize the pot as soon as the milk began to boil, "is that it is supposed to be an *exemplum* to the youth of our nation. I would like very much to know what the Founding Fathers would say if they could see these children being debauched to further the cause of Clearasil. However, I always suspected that democracy would come to this." He painstakingly poured the milk into his Shirley Temple mug. "A firm rule must be imposed upon our nation before it destroys itself. The United States needs some theology and geometry, some taste and decency. I suspect that we are teetering on the edge of the abyss."

"Ignatius, I'm gonna have to go by the Homestead tomorrow."

"We shall not deal with those usurers, Mother." Ignatius was feeling around in the cookie jar. "Something will turn up."

"Ignatius, honey, they can put me in jail."

"Ho hum. If you are going to stage one of your hysterical scenes, I shall have to return to the living room. As a matter of fact, I think I will."

He billowed out again in the direction of the music, the shower shoes flapping loudly against the soles of his huge feet.

"What I'm gonna do with a boy like that?" Mrs. Reilly sadly asked Patrolman Mancuso. "He don't care about his poor dear mother. Sometimes I think Ignatius wouldn't mind if they did throw me in jail. He's got a heart of ice, that boy."

"You spoiled him," Patrolman Mancuso said. "A woman's gotta watch she don't spoil her kids."

"How many chirren you got, Mr. Mancuso?"

"Three. Rosalie, Antoinette, and Angelo, Jr."

"Aw, ain't that nice. I bet they sweet, huh? Not like Ignatius." Mrs. Reilly shook her head. "Ignatius was such a precious child. I don't know what made him change. He used to say to me, 'Momma, I love you.' He don't say that no more."

"Aw, don't cry," Patrolman Mancuso said, deeply moved. "I'll make you some more coffee."

"He don't care if they lock me up," Mrs. Reilly sniffed. She opened the oven and took out a bottle of muscatel. "You want some nice wine, Mr. Mancuso?"

"No thanks. Being on the force, I gotta make a impression. I gotta always be on the lookout for people, too."

"You don't mind?" Mrs. Reilly asked rhetorically and took a long drink from the bottle. Patrolman Mancuso began boiling the milk, hovering over the stove in a very domestic manner. "Sometimes I sure get the blues. Life's hard. I worked hard, too. I been good."

"You oughta look on the bright side," Patrolman Mancuso said.

"I guess so," Mrs. Reilly said. "Some people got it harder than me, I guess. Like my poor cousin, wonderful woman. Went to mass every day of her life. She got knocked down by a streetcar over on Magazine Street early one morning while she was on her way to Fisherman's Mass. It was still dark out."

"Personally, I never let myself get low," Patrolman Mancuso lied. "You gotta look up. You know what I mean? I got a dangerous line of work."

"You could get yourself killed."

"Sometimes I don't apprehend nobody all day. Sometimes I apprehend the wrong person."

"Like that old man in front of D. H. Holmes. That's my fault, Mr. Mancuso. I shoulda guessed Ignatius was wrong all along. It's just like him. All the time I'm telling him, 'Ignatius here, put on this nice shirt. Put on this nice sweater I bought you.' But he don't listen. Not that boy. He's got a head like a rock."

"Then sometimes I get problems at home. With three kids, my wife's very nervous."

"Nerves is a terrible thing. Poor Miss Annie, the next-door lady, she's got nerves. Always screaming about Ignatius making noise."

"That's my wife. Sometimes I gotta get outta the house. If I was another kind of man, sometimes I could really go get myself good and drunk. Just between us."

"I gotta have my little drink. It relieves the pressure. You know?"

"What I do is go bowl."

Mrs. Reilly tried to imagine little Patrolman Mancuso with a big bowling ball and said, "You like that, huh?"

"Bowling's wonderful, Miss Reilly. It takes your mind off things."

"Oh, my heavens!" a voice shouted from the parlor. "These girls are doubtless prostitutes already. How can they present horrors like this to the public?"

"I wish I had me a hobby like that."

"You oughta try bowling."

"Ay-yi-yi. I already got arthuritis in my elbow. I'm too old to play around with them balls. I'd wrench my back."

"I got a aunt, sixty-five, a grammaw, and she goes bowling all the time. She's even on a team."

"Some women are like that. Me, I never was much for sports."

"Bowling's more than a sport," Patrolman Mancuso said defensively. "You meet plenty people over by the alley. Nice people. You could make you some friends."

"Yeah, but it's just my luck to drop one of them balls on my toe. I got bum feet already."

"Next time I go by the alley, I'll let you know. I'll bring my aunt. You and me and my aunt, we'll go down by the alley. Okay?"

"Mother, when was this coffee dripped?" Ignatius demanded, flapping into the kitchen again.

"Just about a hour ago. Why?"

"It certainly tastes brackish."

"I thought it was very good," Patrolman Mancuso said. "Just as good as they serve at the French Market. I'm making some more now. You want a cup?"

"Pardon me," Ignatius said. "Mother, are you going to entertain this gentleman all afternoon? I would like to remind you that I am going to the movies tonight and that I am due at the theater promptly at seven so that I can see the cartoon. I would suggest that you begin preparing something to eat."

"I better go," Patrolman Mancuso said.

"Ignatius, you oughta be ashamed," Mrs. Reilly said in an angry voice. "Me and Mr. Mancuso here just having some coffee. You been nasty all afternoon. You don't care where I raise that money. You don't care if they lock me up. You don't care about nothing."

"Am I going to be attacked in my own home before a stranger with a false beard?"

"My heart's broke."

"Oh, really." Ignatius turned on Patrolman Mancuso. "Will you kindly leave? You are inciting my mother."

"Mr. Mancuso's not doing nothing but being nice."

"I better go," Patrolman Mancuso said apologetically.

"I'll get that money," Mrs. Reilly screamed. "I'll sell this house. I'll sell it out from under you, boy. I'll go stay by a old folks' home."

She grabbed an end of the oilcloth and wiped her eyes.

"If you do not leave," Ignatius said to Patrolman Mancuso, who was hooking on his beard, "I shall call the police."

"He *is* the police, stupid."

"This is totally absurd," Ignatius said and flapped away. "I am going to my room."

SAMUEL BECKETT

❦

Ohio Impromptu [1981]

L = *Listener.*
R = *Reader.*
As alike in appearance as possible.
Light on table midstage. Rest of stage in darkness.
Plain white deal table say 8' x 4'.
Two plain armless white deal chairs.
L *seated at table facing front towards end of long side audience right. Bowed head propped on right hand. Face hidden. Left hand on table. Long black coat. Long white hair.*
R *seated at table in profile centre of short side audience right. Bowed head propped on right hand. Left hand on table. Book on table before him open at last pages. Long black coat. Long white hair.*
Black wide-brimmed hat at centre of table.
Fade up.
Ten seconds.
R *turns page.*
Pause.

R: [*Reading.*] Little is left to tell. In a last—

[L *knocks with left hand on table.*]

Little is left to tell.

[*Pause. Knock.*]

In a last attempt to obtain relief he moved from where they had been so long together to a single room on the far bank. From its single window he could see the downstream extremity of the Isle of Swans.

[*Pause.*]

Relief he had hoped would flow from unfamiliarity. Unfamiliar room. Unfamiliar scene. Out to where nothing ever shared. Back to where nothing ever shared. From this he had once half hoped some measure of relief might flow.

[*Pause.*]

Day after day he could be seen slowly pacing the islet. Hour after hour. In his long black coat no matter what the weather and old world Latin Quarter hat. At the tip he would always pause to dwell on the receding stream. How in joyous eddies its two arms conflowed and flowed united on. Then turn and his slow steps retrace.

[*Pause.*]

In his dreams—

[*Knock.*]

Then turn and his slow steps retrace.

[*Pause. Knock.*]

In his dreams he had been warned against this change. Seen the dear face and heard the unspoken words, Stay where we were so long alone together, my shade will comfort you.

[*Pause.*]

Could he not—

[*Knock.*]

Seen the dear face and heard the unspoken words, Stay where we were so long alone together, my shade will comfort you.

[*Pause. Knock.*]

Could he not now turn back? Acknowledge his error and return to where they were once so long alone together. Alone together so much shared. No. What he had done alone could not be undone. Nothing he had ever done alone could ever be undone. By him alone.

[*Pause.*]

In this extremity his old terror of night laid hold on him again. After so long a lapse that as if never been. [*Pause. Looks closer.*] Yes, after so long a lapse that as if never been. Now with redoubled force the fearful symptoms described at length page forty paragraph four. [*Starts to turn back the pages. Checked by L's left hand. Resumes relinquished page.*] White nights now again his portion. As when his heart was young. No sleep no braving sleep till—[*Turns page.*]—dawn of day.

[*Pause.*]

Little is left to tell. One night—

[*Knock.*]

Little is left to tell.

[*Pause. Knock.*]

One night as he sat trembling head in hands from head to foot a man appeared to him and said, I have been sent by—and here he named the dear name—to comfort you. Then drawing a worn volume from the pocket of his long black coat he sat and read till dawn. Then disappeared without a word.

[*Pause.*]

Some time later he appeared again at the same hour with the same volume and this time without preamble sat and read it through again the long night through. Then disappeared without a word.

[*Pause.*]

So from time to time unheralded he would appear to read the sad tale through again and the long night away. Then disappear without a word.

[*Pause.*]

With never a word exchanged they grew to be as one.

[*Pause.*]

Till the night came at last when having closed the book and dawn at hand he did not disappear but sat on without a word.

[*Pause.*]

Finally he said, I have had word from—and here he named the dear name— that I shall not come again. I saw the dear face and heard the unspoken words, No need to go to him again, even were it in your power.

[*Pause.*]

So the sad—

[*Knock.*]

Saw the dear face and heard the unspoken words, No need to go to him again, even were it in your power.

[*Pause. Knock.*]

So the sad tale a last time told they sat on as though turned to stone. Through the single window dawn shed no light. From the street no sound of reawakening. Or was it that buried in who knows what thoughts they paid no heed? To light of day. To sound of reawakening. What thoughts who knows. Thoughts, no, not thoughts. Profounds of mind. Buried in who knows what profounds of mind. Of mindlessness. Whither no light can reach. No sound. So sat on as though turned to stone. The sad tale a last time told.

[*Pause.*]

Nothing is left to tell.

[*Pause.* R *makes to close book.*

Knock. Book half closed.]

Nothing is left to tell.

[*Pause.* R *closes book.*
Knock.
Silence. Five seconds.
Simultaneously they lower their right hands to table, raise their heads and look at each other. Unblinking.
Expressionless.
Ten seconds.
Fade out.]

Robert Coover

❦

FROM *Spanking the Maid* [1982]

She enters, deliberately, gravely, without affectation, circumspect in her mo-
tions (as she's been taught), not stamping too loud, nor dragging her legs after
her, but advancing sedately, discreetly, glancing briefly at the empty rumpled
bed, the cast-off nightclothes. She hesitates. No. Again. She enters. Deliberately and gravely, without affectation, not stamping too loud, nor dragging her
legs after her, not marching as if leading a dance, nor keeping time with her
head and hands, nor staring or turning her head either one way or the other,
but advancing sedately and discreetly through the door, across the polished
floor, past the empty rumpled bed and cast-off nightclothes (not glancing, that's
better), to the tall curtains along the far wall. As she's been taught. Now, with
a humble yet authoritative gesture, she draws the curtains open: Ah! The morning sunlight comes flooding in over the gleaming tiles as though (she thinks)
flung from a bucket. She opens wide the glass doors behind the curtains (there
is such a song of birds all about!) and gazes for a moment into the garden, quite
prepared to let the sweet breath of morning blow in and excite her to the most
generous and efficient accomplishments, but her mind is still locked on that
image, at first pleasing, now troubling, of the light as it spilled into the room:
as from a bucket. . . . She sighs. She enters. With a bucket. She sets the bucket
down, deliberately, gravely, and walks (circumspectly) across the room, over
the polished tiles, past the empty rumpled bed (she doesn't glance at it), to draw
open the tall curtains at the far wall. Buckets of light come flooding in (she is
not thinking about this now) and the room, as she opens wide the glass doors,
is sweetened by the fresh morning air blowing in from the garden. The sun is
fully risen and the pink clouds of dawn are all gone out of the sky (the time
lost: this is what she is thinking about), but the dew is still on every plant in the
garden, and everything looks clean and bright. As will his room when she is
done with it.

He awakes from a dream (something about utility, or futility, and a teacher he
once had who, when he whipped his students, called it his "civil service"), still

wrapped in darkness and hugged close to the sweet breast of the night, but with the new day already hard upon him, just beyond the curtains (he knows, even without looking), waiting for him out there like a brother: to love him or to kill him. He pushes the bedcovers back and sits up groggily to meet its challenge (or promise), pushes his feet into slippers, rubs his face, stretches, wonders what new blunders the maid (where is she?) will commit today. Well. I should at least give her a chance, he admonishes himself with a gaping yawn.

Oh, she knows her business well: to scrub and wax the floors, polish the furniture, make the master's bed soft and easy, lay up his nightclothes, wash, starch, and mend the bedlinens as necessary, air the blankets and clean the bathroom, making certain of ample supplies of fresh towels and washcloths, soap, toilet paper, razor blades and toothpaste—in short, to see that nothing be wanting which he desires or requires to be done, being always diligent in endeavoring to please him, silent when he is angry except to beg his pardon, and ever faithful, honest, submissive, and of good disposition. The trivial round, the common task, she knows as she sets about her morning's duties, will furnish all she needs to ask, room to deny herself, a road (speaking loosely) to bring her daily nearer God. But on that road, on the floor of the bathroom, she finds a damp towel and some pajama bottoms, all puddled together like a cast-off mop-head. Mop-head? She turns and gazes in dismay at the empty bucket by the outer door. Why, she wants to know, tears springing to the corners of her eyes, can't it be easier than this? And so she enters, sets her bucket down with a firm deliberation, leans her mop gravely against the wall. Also a broom, brushes, some old rags, counting things off on her fingers as she deposits them. The curtains have been drawn open and the room is already (as though impatiently) awash with morning sunlight. She crosses the room, past the (no glances) empty rumpled bed, and opens wide the glass doors leading out into the garden, letting in the sweet breath of morning, which she hardly notices. She has resolved this morning—as every morning—to be cheerful and good-natured, such that if any accident should happen to test that resolution, she should not suffer it to put her out of temper with everything besides, but such resolutions are more easily sworn than obeyed. Things are already in such a state! Yet: virtue is made for difficulties, she reminds herself, and grows stronger and brighter for such trials. *"Oh, teach me, my God and King, in all things thee to see, and what I do in any thing, to do it as for thee!"* she sings out to the garden and to the room, feeling her heart lift like a sponge in a bucket. *"A servant with this clause makes drudgery divine: who sweeps a room, as for thy laws, makes that and th'action fine!"* And yes, she can still recover the lost time. She has everything now, the mop and bucket, broom, rags and brushes, her apron pockets are full of polishes, dustcloths and cleaning powders, the cupboards are well stocked with fresh linens, all she really needs now is to keep—but ah! is there, she wonders anxiously, spinning abruptly on her heels as she hears the master relieving himself noisily in the bathroom, any *water* in the bucket—?!

He awakes, squints at his watch in the darkness, grunts (she's late, but just as well, time for a shower), and with only a moment's hesitation, tosses the blankets back, tearing himself free: I'm so old, he thinks, and still every morning is a bloody new birth. Somehow it should be easier than this. He sits up painfully (that divine government!), rubs his face, pushes his feet into slippers, stands, stretches, then strides to the windows at the far wall and throws open the tall curtains, letting the sun in. The room seems almost to explode with the blast of light: he resists, then surrenders to, finally welcomes its amicable violence. He opens wide the glass doors that lead out into the garden and stands there in the sunshine, sucking in deeply the fresh morning air and trying to recall the dream he's just had. Something about a teacher who had once lectured him on humility. Severely. Only now, in the dream, he was himself the teacher and the student was a woman he knew, or thought he knew, and in his lecture "humility" kept getting mixed up somehow with "humor," such that, in effect, he was trying, in all severity, to teach her how to laugh. He's standing there in the sunlight in his slippers and pajama bottoms, remembering the curious strained expression on the woman's face as she tried—desperately, it seemed—to laugh, and wondering why this provoked (in the dream) such a fury in him, when the maid comes in. She gazes impassively a moment (yet humbly, circumspectly) at the gaping fly of his pajamas, then turns away, sets her bucket down against the wall. Her apron strings are loose, there's a hole in one of her black stockings, and she's forgotten her mop again. I'd be a happier man, he acknowledges to himself with a wry sigh, if I could somehow fail to notice these things. "I'll start in the bathroom," she says discreetly. "Sir," he reminds her. "Sir," she says.

And she enters. Deliberately and gravely, as though once and for all, without affectation, somewhat encumbered by the vital paraphernalia of her office, yet radiant with that clear-browed self-assurance achieved only by long and generous devotion to duty. She plants her bucket and brushes beside the door, leans the mop and broom against the wall, then crosses the room to fling open (humbly, authoritatively) the curtains and the garden doors: the fragrant air and sunlight come flooding in, a flood she now feels able to appreciate. The sun is already high in the sky, but the garden is still bejeweled with morning dew and (she remembers to notice) there is such a song of birds all about! What inspiration! She enjoys this part of her work: flushing out the stale darkness of the dead night with such grand (yet circumspect) gestures—it's almost an act of magic! Of course, she takes pleasure in *all* her appointed tasks (she reminds herself), whether it be scrubbing floors or polishing furniture or even scouring out the tub or toilet, for she knows that only in giving herself (as he has told her) can she find herself: true service (he doesn't have to tell her!) is perfect freedom. And so, excited by the song of the birds, the sweet breath of morning, and her own natural eagerness to please, she turns with a glad heart to her favorite task of all: the making of the bed. Indeed, all the rest of her work is embraced by it, for the opening up and airing of the bed is the first of her tasks, the making of it her last. Today, however, when she tosses the covers back, she finds, coiled like a dark snake near the foot, a bloodstained leather belt. She starts back. The sheets, too, are flecked with blood. Shadows seem to creep across the room and the birds fall silent. Perhaps, she thinks, her heart sinking, I'd better go out and come in again. . . .

KATHY ACKER

ℳ

FROM *Blood and Guts in High School* [1984]

Parents Stink

Never having known a mother, her mother had died when Janey was a year old, Janey depended on her father for everything and regarded her father as boyfriend, brother, sister, money, amusement, and father.

Janey Smith was ten years old, living with her father in Merida, the main city in the Yucatan. Janey and Mr. Smith had been planning a big vacation for Janey in New York City in North America. Actually Mr. Smith was trying to get rid of Janey so he could spend all his time with Sally, a twenty-one-year-old starlet who was still refusing to fuck him.

One night Mr. Smith and Sally went out and Janey knew her father and that woman were going to fuck. Janey was also very pretty, but she was kind of weird-looking because one of her eyes was lopsided.

Janey tore up her father's bed and shoved boards against the front door. When Mr. Smith returned home, he asked Janey why she was acting like this.

JANEY: You're going to leave me (*She doesn't know why she's saying this.*)

FATHER (*dumbfounded, but not denying it*): Sally and I just slept together for the first time. How can I know anything?

JANEY (*in amazement. She didn't believe what she had been saying was true. It was only out of petulance*): You ARE going to leave me. Oh no. No. That can't be.

FATHER (*also stunned*): I never thought I was going to leave you. I was just fucking.

JANEY (*not at all calming herself down by listening to what he's saying. He knows her energy rises sharply and crazy when she's scared so he's probably provoking this scene*): You can't leave me. You can't. (*Now in full hysteria.*) I'll . . . (*Realizes she might be flying off the handle and creating the situation. Wants to hear his creation for a minute. Shivers with fear when she asks this.*) Are you madly in love with her?

FATHER (*thinking. Confusion's beginning*): I don't know.

JANEY: I'm not crazy. (*Realizing he's madly in love with the other woman.*) I don't mean to act like this. (*Realizing more and more how madly in love he is. Blurts it out.*) For the last month you've been spending every moment you can with her. That's why you've stopped eating meals with me. That's why you haven't been helping me the way you usually do when I'm sick. You're madly in love with her, aren't you?

FATHER (*ignorant of this huge mess*): We just slept together for the first time tonight.

JANEY: You told me you were just friends like me and Peter (*Janey's stuffed lamb*) and you weren't going to sleep together. It's not like my sleeping around with all these art studs: when you sleep with your best friend, it's really, really heavy.

FATHER: I know, Janey.

JANEY (*she hasn't won that round; she threw betrayal in his face and he didn't totally run away from it*): Are you going to move in with Sally? (*She asks the worst possibility.*)

FATHER (*still in the same sad, hesitant, underlyingly happy because he wants to get away tone*): I don't know.

JANEY (*She can't believe this. Every time she says the worst, it's true*): When will you know? I have to make my plans.

FATHER: We just slept together once. Why don't you just let things lie, Janey, and not push?

JANEY: You tell me you love someone else, you're gonna kick me out, and I shouldn't push. What do you think I am, Johnny? I love you.

FATHER: Just let things be. You're making more of this than it really is.

JANEY (*everything comes flooding out*): I love you. I adore you. When I first met you, it's as if a light turned on for me. You're the first joy I knew. Don't you understand?

FATHER (*silent*).

JANEY: I just can't bear that you're leaving me: it's like a lance cutting my brain in two: it's the worst pain I've ever known. I don't care who you fuck. You know that. I've never acted like this before.

FATHER: I know.

JANEY: I'm just scared you're going to leave me. I know I've been shitty to you: I've fucked around too much; I didn't introduce you to my friends.

FATHER: I'm just having an affair, Janey. I'm going to have this affair.

JANEY (*now the rational one*): But you might leave me.

FATHER (*silent*).

JANEY: OK. (*Getting hold of herself in the midst of total disaster and clenching her teeth.*) I have to wait around until I see how things work out between you and Sally and then I'll know if I'm going to live with you or not. Is that how things stand?

FATHER: I don't know.

JANEY: You don't know! How am I supposed to know?

    That night, for the first time in months, Janey and her father sleep together because Janey can't get to sleep otherwise. Her father's touch is cold, he doesn't want to touch her mostly 'cause he's confused. Janey fucks him even though it hurts her like hell 'cause of her Pelvic Inflammatory Disease.

The following poem is by the Peruvian poet César Vallejo who, born 18 March 1892 (Janey was born 18 April 1964), lived in Paris fifteen years and died there when he was 46:

> *September*
> *This September night, you fled*
> *So good to me . . . up to grief and include!*
> *I don't know myself anything else*
> *But you, YOU don't have to be good.*
>
> *This night alone up to imprisonment no prison*
> *Hermetic and tyrannical, diseased and panic-stricken*
> *I don't know myself anything else*
> *I don't know myself because I am grief-stricken.*
>
> *Only this night is good, YOU*
> *Making me into a whore, no*
> *Emotion possible is distance God gave integral:*
> *Your hateful sweetness I'm clinging to.*
>
> *This September evening, when sown*
> *In live coals, from an auto*
> *Into puddles: not known.*

JANEY (*as her father was leaving the house*): Are you coming back tonight? I don't mean to bug you. (*No longer willing to assert herself.*) I'm just curious.

FATHER: Of course I'll be back.

The moment her father left the house, Janey rushed to the phone and called up his best friend, Bill Russle. Bill had once fucked Janey, but his cock was too big. Janey knew he'd tell her what was happening with Johnny, if Johnny was crazy or not, and if Johnny really wanted to break up with Janey. Janey didn't have to pretend anything with Bill.

JANEY: Right now we're at the edge of a new era in which, for all sorts of reasons, people will have to grapple with all sorts of difficult problems, leaving us no time for the luxury of expressing ourselves artistically. Is Johnny madly in love with Sally?

BILL: No.

JANEY: No? (*Total amazement and hope.*)

BILL: It's something very deep between them, but he's not going to leave you for Sally.

JANEY (*with even more hope*): Then why's he acting this way? I mean: he's talking about *leaving* me.

BILL: Tell me exactly what's been happening, Janey. I want to know for my own reasons. This is very important. Johnny hasn't been treating me like a friend. He won't talk to me anymore.

JANEY: He won't? He feels you're his best friend. (*Making a decision.*) I'll tell you everything. You know I've been very sick.

BILL: I didn't know that. I'm sorry, I won't interrupt anymore.

JANEY: I've been real sick. Usually Johnny helps out when I am, this time he hasn't. About a month ago he told me he was running around with Andrea and Sally. I said, "Oh great," it's great when he has new friends, he's been real lonely, I told him that was great. He said he was obsessed with Sally, a crush, but it wasn't sexual. I didn't care. But he was acting real funny toward me. I've never seen him act like that. The past two months he's treated me like he hates me. I never thought he'd leave me. He's going to leave me.

BILL (*breaking in*): Janey. Can you tell me exactly what happened last night? I have to know everything. (*She tells him.*) What do you think is going on?

JANEY: Either of two . . . I am Johnny. (*Thinks.*) Either of two things. (*Speaks very slowly and clearly.*) First thing: I am Johnny. I'm beginning to have some fame, success, now women want to fuck me. I've never had women want me before. I want everything. I want to go out in the world as far as I can go. Do you understand what I'm talking about?

BILL: Yes. Go on.

JANEY: There are two levels. It's not that I think one's better than the other, you understand, though I do think one is a more mature development than the other. Second level: It's like commitment, You see what you want, but you don't go after every little thing; you try to work it through with the other person. I've had to learn this this past year. I'm willing to work with Johnny.

BILL: I understand what's happening now. Johnny is at a place where he has to try everything.

JANEY: The first level. I agree.

BILL: You've dominated his life since your mother died and now he hates you. He has to hate you because he has to reject you. He has to find out who he is.

JANEY: That would go along with the crisis he was having in his work this year.

BILL: It's an identity crisis.

JANEY: This makes sense. . . . What should I do?

BILL: The thing you can't do is to freak out and lay a heavy trip on him.

JANEY: I've already done that. (*If she could giggle, she would.*)

BILL: You have to realize that you're the one person he hates, you're everything he's trying to get rid of. You have to give him support. If you're going to freak out, call me, but don't show him any emotion. Any emotion he'll hate you even more for.

JANEY: God. You know how I am. Like a vibrating nut.

BILL: Be very very calm. He's going through a hard period, he's very confused, and he needs your support. I'll talk to him and find out more about what's going on. I have to talk to him anyway because I want to find out why he hasn't been friendly to me.

Later that afternoon Mr. Smith came home from work.

JANEY: I'm sorry I got upset last night about Sally. It won't happen again. I think it's great you've got a girlfriend you really care about.

FATHER: I've never felt like this about anyone. It's good for me to know I can feel so strongly.

JANEY: Yes. (*Keeping her cool.*) I just wanted you to know if there's anything I can do for you, I'd like to be your friend. (*Shaking a little.*)

FATHER: Oh, Janey. You know I care for you very deeply. (*That does it: Janey bursts into tears.*) I'm just confused right now. I want to be by myself.

JANEY: You're going to leave me.

FATHER: Just let things be. I've got to go. (*He obviously wants to get out of the room as fast as possible.*)

JANEY: Wait a minute. (*Collecting her emotions and stashing them.*) I didn't mean it. I was going to be calm and supportive like Bill said.

FATHER: What'd Bill say? (*Janey repeats the conversation. Everything comes splurting out now. Janey's not good at holding words back.*) You've completely dominated my life, Janey, for the last nine years and I no longer know who's you and who's me. I have to be alone. You've been alone for a while, you know that need: I have to find out who I am.

JANEY (*her tears dry*): I understand now. I think it's wonderful what you're doing. All year I've been asking you, "What do you want?" and you never knew. It was always me, my voice, I felt like a total nag; I want you to be the man. I can't make all the decisions. I'm going to the United States for a long time so you'll be able to be alone.

FATHER (*amazed she's snapped so quickly and thoroughly from down hysteria to joy*): You're tough, aren't you?

JANEY: I get hysterical when I don't understand. Now everything's OK. I understand.

FATHER: I've got to go out now—there's a party uptown. I'll be back later tonight.

JANEY: You don't have to be back.

FATHER: I'll wake you up, sweetie, when I get back. OK?

JANEY: Then I can crawl in bed and sleep with you?

FATHER: Yes.

DAVID RABE

❦

FROM *Hurlyburly* [1985]

PHIL: Scorn. You feel scorn for me.

EDDIE: No.

PHIL: It's in your eyes.

EDDIE: No. What?

PHIL (*peering into Eddie's eyes*): These dark thoughts, Eddie, I see them reflected in your eyes, they pertain to something other than me, or what?

EDDIE: I'm not having dark thoughts.

PHIL (*backing away*): Beyond the thoughts you're thinking, Eddie.

EDDIE (*he moves to unzip the shaving kit to get out a container of Alka-Seltzer as Phil keeps following him*): No!

PHIL (*still backing away*): Then what the hell are you thinking about? I come for advice and you're off on some other totally unrelated tangent! (*As he spies the suitcase Eddie has been carefully packing.*) Is that the thing here, the goddamn bottom line? I need your attention, and you're off in some fucking daydream? I'm desperate and you are, for crissake, distracted? (*As Eddie has come running forward to save his things.*) Is this friendship, Eddie? Tell me!

EDDIE: Wait a minute.

PHIL: You want a fucking minute? (*Hurling Eddie onto the couch, Phil is on the verge of smashing his fist down on Eddie's face. Recoiling, Eddie covers up.*)

EDDIE: I don't know what you're talking about.

PHIL (*realizing what he is at the edge of doing, Phil pulls back*): Dark thoughts. Your dark thoughts, Eddie. This is not uncommon for people to have them. You were provoked; think nothing of it. But please—this, now—dark thoughts and everything included, this is our friendship. Pay attention to it, it's slipping by.

EDDIE: I wanna! YEAH, but I'm gettin' confused here, Phil. I tol' you—I don't feel good.

PHIL (*seeing the bottle that Eddie didn't pack lying on the side of the couch, he grabs it*): It's chaotic is why you're confused, Eddie. That's why you're confused. Think nothin' of it. I'm confused. (*Opening the bottle, he takes a drink.*) The goddamn situation is like this masked fucking robber come to steal the goods, but we don't even know is he, or isn't he. (*He hands Eddie the open bottle.*) I mean, we got these dark thoughts, I see 'em in you, you don't think you're thinkin' 'em, so we can't even nail that down, how we going to get beyond it? They are the results of your unnoticed inner goings-on or my gigantic paranoia, both of which exist, so the goddamn thing in its entirety is on the basis of what has got to be called a coin toss.

EDDIE: I mean, you come here, you want advice, so I say do this; you say you can't; so I say try something else, but you can't—

PHIL: I'm sorry, Eddie.

EDDIE: I can figure it! You know I can, that's why you came to me. But I feel like you're drillin' little hunks a cottage cheese into my brain. Next thing, you're sayin', it's a goddamn coin toss—it's not a goddamn coin toss!

PHIL: You think I'm being cynical when I say that? Nothing is necessary, Eddie. Not a fucking thing! We're in the hands of something, it could kill us now or later, it don't care. Who is this guy that makes us just—you know—WHAT? (*Seeing the dictionary on the end table, he grabs it, starts leafing pages, looking wildly through it.*) THERE'S A NAME FOR THIS—IT HAPPENS—THERE'S A WORD FOR IT—EVERYBODY KNOWS IT. I CAN'T THINK OF IT. IT'S LIKE A LAW. IT IS A LAW. WHAT'S A LAW? WHAT THE FUCK IS A LAW?! (*He hurls the book onto the floor.*) Cynicism has nothing to do with it, Eddie, I've done my best. The fucking thing is without a clue, except the mess it leaves behind it, the guts and gore. (*Seeing the mess he made, he grabs the suitcase and starts to try to repack it, stuffing things back into it, but he can't. He stops.*) What I'm sayin' is, if my conclusion is contrary to your wishes, at least give me the fucking consideration and respect that you know that at least from my point of view it is based on solid thought and rock-hard evidence that has led me to I have no other choice, so you got no right to fuck with me about it. I want your respect.

EDDIE: You got that, Phil.

PHIL: I do?

EDDIE: Don't you know that?

PHIL: Sometimes I'm out in the rain, I don't even know it's rainin'. (*He paces away.*)

EDDIE: I'm just sayin'—all I'm sayin' is, "Don't have the baby thoughtlessly."

PHIL: Eddie, for godsake, don't terrify me that you have paid no attention! If I was thoughtless would I be here? (*Recoiling, he faces away, sitting on the hassock unable to look at Eddie, who, on the couch, drinks, holding the bottle, pouring drinks into his glass and drinking. Or perhaps, neatly repacks the entire suitcase during this speech.*) I feel like I have pushed thought to the brink where it is just noise and of no more use than a headful of car horns, because the bottom line here that I'm getting at is just this—I got to go back to her. I got to go back to Susie, and if it means havin' a kid, I got to do it. I mean, I have hit a point where I am going round the bend several times a day now, and so far I been on the other side to meet me, but one a these times might be one too many, and what then? I'm a person, Eddie, and I have realized it, who needs like a big-dot-thing, you know— this big-dot-thing around which I can just hang and blab my thoughts and more or less formulate everything as I go, myself included. I mean, I used to spend my days in my car; I didn't know what the fuck I was doin' but it kept me out of trouble until nothin' but blind luck led me to I-am-married, and I could go home. She was my big-dot-thing. Now I'm startin' in my car again, I'm spendin' days on the freeways. Rain or no rain I like the wipers clickin', and all around me the other cars got people in 'em the way I see 'em when they are in cars. These heads, these faces. These boxes of steel with glass and faces inside. I been the last two whole days and nights without seeing another form of human being in his entirety except gas station attendants. The freeways, the cloverleafs got a thing in them some- times it spins me off, I go where I never meant to. There's little back roads and little towns I never heard of them. I start to expect the gas station attendants to know me when I arrive. I get excited that I've been there before. I want them to welcome me. I'm disappointed when they don't.

(*Faintly, the music starts, the music from the beginning, the theme, the harmonica loop from "Unchained Melody."*)

Something that I don't want to be true starts lookin' like it's all that's true only I don't know what it is. No. No. I need my marriage. I come here to tell you. I got to stay married. I'm lost without her.

(*The door to Mickey's room slams as Donna bursts out. Phil, startled, stands up, looking up at her. Eddie is also looking up. She is dressed as she arrived, in her trav- eling clothes. She carries her knapsack and record. She stomps down the stairs to the landing, then faces them.*)

DONNA: You guys have cooked your goose. You can just walk your own dog, and fuck yourselves. These particular tits and ass are taking a hike. (*With the music building, she stomps to the door, opens it, turns, looks at Eddie, who is staring at her, quite ill.*) So this is goodbye. (*She goes out, slamming the door. Eddie and Phil stare after her, unmoving.*)

CURTAIN

BHARATI MUKHERJEE

꽃

"Fathering"

FROM *The Middleman and Other Stories* [1988]

Eng stands just inside our bedroom door, her fidgety fish on the doorknob which Sharon, in a sulk, polished to a gleam yesterday afternoon.

"I'm starved," she says.

I know a sick little girl when I see one. I brought the twins up without much help ten years ago. Eng's got a high fever. Brownish stains stiffen the nap of her terry robe. Sour smells fill the bedroom.

"For God's sake leave us alone," Sharon mutters under the quilt. She turns away from me. We bought the quilt at a garage sale in Rock Springs the Sunday two years ago when she moved in. "Talk to her."

Sharon works on this near-marriage of ours. I'll hand it to her, she really does. I knead her shoulders, and I say, "Easy, easy," though I really hate it when she treats Eng like a deaf-mute. "My girl speaks English, remember?"

Eng can outcuss any freckle-faced kid on the block. Someone in the killing fields must have taught her. Maybe her mama, the honeyest-skinned bar girl with the tiniest feet in Saigon. I was an errand boy with the Combined Military Intelligence. I did the whole war on Dexedrine. Vietnam didn't happen, and I'd put it behind me in marriage and fatherhood and teaching high school. Ten years later came the screw-ups with the marriage, the job, women, the works. Until Eng popped up in my life, I really believed it didn't happen.

"Come here, sweetheart," I beg my daughter. I sidle closer to Sharon, so there'll be room under the quilt for Eng.

"I'm starved," she complains from the doorway. She doesn't budge. The robe and hair are smelling something fierce. She doesn't show any desire to cuddle. She must be sick. She must have thrown up all night. Sharon throws the quilt back. "Then go raid the refrigerator like a normal kid," she snaps.

Once upon a time Sharon used to be a cheerful, accommodating woman. It isn't as if Eng was dumped on us out of the blue. She knew I was tracking my kid. Coming to terms with the past was Sharon's idea. I don't know what happened to *that* Sharon. "For all you know, Jason," she'd said, "the baby died of malaria or something." She said, "Go on, find out and deal with it."

324

She said she could handle being a stepmother—better a fresh chance with some orphan off the streets of Saigon than with my twins from Rochester. My twins are being raised in some organic-farming lesbo commune. Their mother breeds Nubian goats for a living. "Come get in bed with us, baby. Let Dad feel your forehead. You burning up with fever?"

"She isn't hungry, I think she's sick," I tell Sharon, but she's already tugging her sleeping mask back on. "I think she's just letting us know she hurts."

I hold my arms out wide for Eng to run into. If I could, I'd suck the virus right out of her. In the jungle, VC mamas used to do that. Some nights we'd steal right up to a hootch—just a few of us intense sons of bitches on some special mission—and the women would be at their mumbo jumbo. They'd be sticking coins and amulets into napalm burns.

"I'm hungry, Dad." It comes out as a moan. Okay, she doesn't run into my arms, but at least she's come as far in as the foot of our bed. "Dad, let's go down to the kitchen. Just you and me."

I am about to let that pass though I can feel Sharon's body go into weird little jerks and twitches when my baby adds with emphatic viciousness, "Not her, Dad. We don't want her with us in the kitchen."

"She loves you," I protest. Love—not spite—makes Eng so territorial; that's what I want to explain to Sharon. She's a sick, frightened, foreign kid, for Chrissake. "Don't you, Sharon? Sharon's concerned about you."

But Sharon turns over on her stomach. "You know what's wrong with you, Jase? You can't admit you're being manipulated. You can't cut through the 'frightened-foreign-kid' shit."

Eng moves closer. She comes up to the side of my bed, but doesn't touch the hand I'm holding out. She's a fighter.

"I feel fire-hot, Dad. My bones feel pain."

"Sharon?" I want to deserve this woman. "Sharon, I'm so sorry." It isn't anybody's fault. You need uppers to get through peace times, too.

"Dad. Let's go. Chop-chop."

"You're too sick to keep food down, baby. Curl up in here. Just for a bit?"

"I'd throw up, Dad."

"I'll carry you back to your room. I'll read you a story, okay?"

Eng watches me real close as I pull the quilt off. "You got any scars you haven't shown me yet? My mom had a big scar on one leg. Shrapnel. Boom boom. I got scars. See? I got lots of bruises."

I scoop up my poor girl and rush her, terry robe flapping, to her room which Sharon fixed up with white girlish furniture in less complicated days. Waiting for Eng was good. Sharon herself said it was good for our relationship. "Could you bring us some juice and aspirin?" I shout from the hallway.

"Aspirin isn't going to cure Eng," I hear Sharon yell. "I'm going to call Dr. Kearns."

Downstairs I hear Sharon on the phone. She isn't talking flu viruses. She's talking social workers and shrinks. My girl isn't crazy; she's picked up a bug in school as might anyone else.

"The child's arms are covered with bruises," Sharon is saying. "Nothing major. They look like . . . well, they're sort of tiny circles and welts." There's nothing for a while. Then she says, "Christ! no, Jason can't do enough for her! That's not what I'm saying! What's happening to this country? You think we're perverts? What I'm saying is the girl's doing it to herself."

"Who are you talking to?" I ask from the top of the stairs. "What happened to the aspirin?"

I lean as far forward over the railing as I dare so I can see what Sharon's up to. She's getting into her coat and boots. She's having trouble with buttons and snaps. In the bluish light of the foyer's broken chandelier, she looks old, harrowed, depressed. What have I done to her?

"What's going on?" I plead. "You deserting me?"

"Don't be so fucking melodramatic. I'm going to the mall to buy some aspirin."

"How come we don't have any in the house?"

"Why are you always picking on me?"

"Who was that on the phone?"

"So now you want me to account for every call and every trip?" She ties an angry knot into her scarf. But she tells me. "I was talking to Meg Kearns. She says Dr. Kearns has gone hunting for the day."

"Great!"

"She says he has his beeper on him."

I hear the back door stick and Sharon swear. She's having trouble with the latch. "Jiggle it gently," I shout, taking the stairs two at a time. But before I can come down, her Nissan backs out of the parking apron.

Back upstairs I catch Eng in the middle of a dream or delirium. "They got Grandma!" she screams. She goes very rigid in bed. It's a four-poster with canopy and ruffles and stuff that Sharon put on her MasterCard. The twins slept on bunk beds. With the twins it was different, totally different. Dr. Spock can't be point man for Eng, for us.

"She bring me food," Eng's screaming. "She bring me food from the forest. They shoot Grandma! Bastards!"

"Eng?" I don't dare touch her. I don't know how.

"You shoot my grandmother?" She whacks the air with her bony arms. Now I see the bruises, the small welts all along the insides of her arms. Some have to be weeks old, they're that yellow. The twins' scrapes and cuts never turned that ochre. I can't help wondering if maybe Asian skin bruises differently from ours, even though I want to say skin is skin; especially hers is skin like mine.

"I want to be with Grandma. Grandma loves me. I want to be ghost. I don't want to get better."

I read to her. I read to her because good parents are supposed to read to their kids laid up sick in bed. I want to do it right. I want to be a good father. I read from a sci-fi novel that Sharon must have picked up. She works in a camera store in the mall, right next to a B. Dalton. I read three pages out loud, then I read four chapters to myself because Eng's stopped up her ears. Aliens have taken over small towns all over the country. Idaho, Nebraska: no state is safe from aliens.

Some time after two, the phone rings. Since Sharon doesn't answer it on the second ring, I know she isn't back. She carries a cordless phone everywhere around the house. In the movies, when cops have bad news to deliver, they lean on your doorbell; they don't call. Sharon will come back when she's ready. We'll make up. Things will get back to normal.

"Jason?"

I know Dr. Kearns's voice. He saw the twins through the usual immunizations.

"I have Sharon here. She'll need a ride home. Can you drive over?"

"God! What's happened?"

"Nothing to panic about. Nothing physical. She came for a consultation."

"Give me a half-hour. I have to wrap Eng real warm so I can drag her out in this miserable weather."

"Take your time. This way I can take a look at Eng, too."

"What's wrong with Sharon?"

"She's a little exercised about a situation. I gave her a sedative. See you in a half-hour."

I ease delirious Eng out of the overdecorated four-poster, prop her against my body while I wrap a blanket around her. She's a tiny thing, but she feels stiff and heavy, a sleepwalking mummy. Her eyes are dry-bright, strange.

It's a sunny winter day, and the evergreens in the front yard are glossy with frost. I press Eng against my chest as I negotiate the front steps. Where the gutter leaks, the steps feel spongy. The shrubs and bushes my ex-wife planted clog the front path. I've put twenty years into this house. The steps, the path, the house all have a right to fall apart.

I'm thirty-eight. I've let a lot of people down already.

The inside of the van is deadly cold. Mid-January ice mottles the windshield. I lay the bundled-up child on the long seat behind me and wait for the engine to warm up. It feels good with the radio going and the heat coming on. I don't want the ice on the windshield to melt. Eng and I are safest in the van.

In the rear-view mirror, Eng's wrinkled lips begin to move. "Dad, can I have a quarter?"

"May I, kiddo," I joke.

There's all sorts of junk in the pockets of my parka. Buckshot, dimes and quarters for the vending machine, a Blistex.

"What do you need it for, sweetheart?"

Eng's quick. Like the street kids in Saigon who dove for cigarettes and sticks of gum. She's loosened the blanket folds around her. I watch her tuck the quarter inside her wool mitt. She grins. "Thanks, soldier."

At Dr. Kearns's, Sharon is lying unnaturally slack-bodied on the lone vinyl sofa. Her coat's neatly balled up under her neck, like a bolster. Right now she looks amiable, docile. I don't think she exactly recognizes me, although later she'll say she did. All that stuff about Kearns going hunting must have been a lie. Even the stuff about having to buy aspirins in the mall. She was planning all along to get here.

"What's wrong?"

"It's none of my business, Jason, but you and Sharon might try an honest-to-goodness heart-to-heart." Then he makes a sign to me to lay Eng on the examining table. "We don't look so bad," he says to my daughter. Then he excuses himself and goes into a glass-walled cubicle.

Sharon heaves herself into a sitting position of sorts on the sofa. "Everything was fine until she got here. Send her back, Jase. If you love me, send her back." She's slouched so far forward, her pointed, sweatered breasts nearly touch her corduroy pants. She looks helpless, pathetic. I've brought her to this state. Guilt, not love, is what I feel.

I want to comfort Sharon, but my daughter with the wild, grieving pygmy face won't let go of my hand. "She's bad, Dad. Send *her* back."

Dr. Kearns comes out of the cubicle balancing a sample bottle of pills or Caplets on a flattened palm. He has a boxer's tough, squarish hands. "Miraculous stuff, this," he laughs. "But first we'll stick our tongue out and say *ahh*. Come on, open wide."

Eng opens her mouth real wide, then brings her teeth together, hard, on Dr. Kearns's hand. She leaps erect on the examining table, tearing the disposable paper sheet with her toes. Her tiny, funny toes are doing a frantic dance. "Don't let him touch me, Grandma!"

"He's going to make you all better, baby." I can't pull my alien child down, I can't comfort her. The twins had diseases with easy names, diseases we knew what to do with. The thing is, I never felt for them what I feel for her.

"Don't let him touch me, Grandma!" Eng's screaming now. She's hopping on the table and screaming. "Kill him, Grandma! Get me out of here, Grandma!"

"Baby, it's all right."

But she looks through me and the country doctor as though we aren't here, as though we aren't pulling at her to make her lie down.

"Lie back like a good girl," Dr. Kearns commands.

But Eng is listening to other voices. She pulls her mitts off with her teeth, chucks the blanket, the robe, the pajamas to the floor; then, naked, hysterical, she presses the quarter I gave her deep into the soft flesh of her arm. She presses and presses that coin, turning it in nasty half-circles until blood starts to pool under the skin.

"Jason, grab her at the knees. Get her back down on the table."

From the sofa, Sharon moans. "See, I told you the child was crazy. She hates me. She's possessive about Jason."

The doctor comes at us with his syringe. He's sedated Sharon; now he wants to knock out my kid with his cures.

"Get the hell out, you bastard!" Eng yells. "*Vamos!* Bang bang!" She's pointing her arm like a semiautomatic, taking out Sharon, then the doctor. My Rambo. "Old way is good way. Money cure is good cure. When they shoot my grandma, you think pills do her any good? You Yankees, please go home." She looks straight at me. "Scram, Yankee bastard!"

Dr. Kearns has Eng by the wrist now. He has flung the quarter I gave her on the floor. Something incurable is happening to my women.

Then, as in fairy tales, I know what has to be done. "Coming, pardner!" I whisper. "I got no end of coins." I jiggle the change in my pocket. I jerk her away from our enemies. My Saigon kid and me: We're a team. In five minutes we'll be safely away in the cold chariot of our van.

DENNIS COOPER

❧❧

FROM *Closer* [1989]

Philippe

MAKE BELIEVE

Philippe, 43, was so drunk that the bones in his legs seemed to juggle each other. Every step entertained him, though progress was not in the offing. George used to laugh when the older man wobbled like this. To Philippe those were strange little comedies, maybe because they'd grown very infrequent.

He moved from the chair by the telephone to his bookshelf, which he leaned against, one palm outstretched across several spines. They were too slim to read and, at his pressure, receded into the dark at the back of a shelf, where he'd often considered installing a safe.

To keep from falling, he grabbed at the frame of an artwork, which held him upright but skidded sideways on its hidden wire, then tilted up at one end like a sinking steamliner, an image the picture resembled at times, though it was abstract.

"I like this," Philippe said, "because it is not in my way, but it makes the room change because it is not a burden, I think it is called, but is beautiful whatever I see in it. Now I perceive a sinking ship because I am drunk, and that is the best of all I have seen."

He laughed. "When I was in Paris," he thought. He could only remember one person, a boy named Jan who was Belgian and spoke in the strange French some Belgians used. Jan and he couldn't communicate, so they'd undressed. Jan was particularly, if not the best of the . . .

Philippe lost his balance. He clutched at some books, which came loose in his hand, and only managed to keep from collapsing entirely by gripping the arm of the chair with his other hand while waving the hand with the books until his knees could support his weight.

He pulled himself into the chair whose wooden arm had protected him. He looked around the room, which he could barely make out. The boy walked in. He was naked and still kind of damp from the shower. He stared at Philippe for a while, then shrugged and put on his clothes.

When he was dressed, the boy said, "I like you. You're strange, but you're nice." As he said this he gazed at the walls, not at Philippe. "You're from France," he added. Philippe was about to say where in France, but the boy started talking again. "Are you interested in me, because I could make an arrangement?"

Philippe didn't know if he was or not. "Come here," he said. The boy put his hands on his hips and walked over, then bent at the waist so his face was close enough to Philippe's to be studied, not kissed. "Men love me," he said, "because I'm reliable."

Philippe loved his face when it was indifferent, across a bar, but any expression at all hit his features as hard as an earthquake. "I have someone," Philippe said, "but I know a man who will love you." He wrote down Tom's name and phone number.

"When is the best time to call him?" "Tomorrow or anytime," Philippe answered. The boy put the number somewhere on his person. He walked to the door, where Philippe couldn't see. "Oh, I'm Jimmy," he said. "Nice to meet you. Thanks."

Philippe checked his watch, then fell into a half-waking state for an hour, occasionally opening his eyes to double-check the room's tidiness. He needed this. When the buzzer rang he was a fraction more sober, and walked to the door with an obedient, almost refined sweep. "Yes, come in. How are you?" he asked.

George bolted past, found the chair he always used and sat down so hard its supports cracked. "Sorry. I'm, I don't know, fine," he mumbled. He drummed his fists on the arms. "It still hurts, but, you know . . . That's okay." Philippe shut the door, took a seat nearby. "You look tired," he said.

"What?" George asked. Philippe smiled reassuringly. George tried to. "No, I'm just nervous. I can't take acid now because that makes it throb, and I'm not used to being, you know, not stoned." Philippe asked if he wanted a drink. "It throbs," George repeated. His eyes became wooden.

Philippe stroked the boy's messy haircut. The scalp rubbed his palm in thanks. These gestures—the pressure from either side—felt as unusual to Philippe as the language he'd learned to pronounce. He wondered less what he meant by caressing than why he was wondering.

Regaining composure, he asked, "What, I mean how have you been?" George looked relieved. "Oh, I've been kind of better," he said, then went into detail. Philippe could understand George since his English was simple. Still, it had a strange current, circling around and beneath itself.

Philippe tuned in. ". . . My dad gave up, I guess. I think he thought I'd change or something, and he's busy getting over my mom, so as long as I'm there for dinner he doesn't care. It's kind of bad, but he doesn't know where I am now. I try not to worry about it, I mean what Tom did. I know it's my fault. . . ."

George continued, his lips nearly motionless. Philippe smiled when a pause seemed to warrant warmth, knowing that he could agree with whatever George said. The boy longed to speak, and there was "nobody else to speak to," in his words, which was some sort of privilege. Philippe felt removed from these intervals.

"You sound good," Philippe said. George shut his eyes and gripped the chair's arms. "Would you tell me something?" he asked. "See, I have to make a decision. Umm, how do you feel about me? I know you thought I was beautiful, and there's the dead thing you do, but why?"

To Philippe's recollection, George hadn't probed before. Not so much as "What day is it?" He peered at his glass for a moment. "I think you are beautiful," he answered, knowing those words were correct, "and I enjoy what we do." George bit his lip. "You don't love me, right?"

"Yes," Philippe said. "I mean no, but I love what we do." George's head dropped an inch. "I have to think about us," he cringed, "because I'm not sure if we . . . Shit, wait a sec. It'll pass." Philippe smiled, but that seemed inappropriate. He took a drink.

Philippe watched George plod toward the rain-splattered street. Once he tripped over a sprinkler head and fell flat on his face. He struggled up, holding his elbow, and vanished behind a hedge. After a brief intermission, Philippe saw him wandering down the street with his thumb out.

He thought of opening the window to yell, "You are okay, Georges?" If he hadn't come with the boy a half hour ago, he might have splayed on the couch and rerun the best parts of this fall in slow motion. Instead he sealed the blinds, turned, and lowered his eyes to the spot where George usually lay.

The tumble enticed him since it was unreal. It was unreal since he hadn't observed the boy's face as he fell. When Philippe pictured George's expression approaching the ground, he saw pretend pain, the look that would creep over dolls' faces when children left them alone in the dark.

George was hurt, but the specifics could be imagined away. Philippe had repaired them, or given himself that impression, by making believe he'd messed up George himself. This cruelty, however imaginary, fell in line with his wishes. He'd focus his eyes on the new wear and tear and feel very complex.

When he looked at the scars he saw the inside of George, not as cold, gray and empty—as he preferred it to be—but brightly colored and very disorganized. On the negative side, they'd complicated his feelings for death by defining his view of it. On the positive side, they looked like fireworks.

Still, no matter how George had filled up with hieroglyphs, they didn't help Philippe figure things out. Scars merely forced him to stylize his thoughts, until the destruction he saw matched the painstaking beauty he knew in his mind's eye, his tinted lens.

He smiled and went into the kitchen, then dampened a few paper towels. He crouched on the living room rug, collecting the usual stray bits of shit, or, as he'd learned to describe them, "my smelling salts." That was a phrase used by mothers to indicate something that woke people up.

He downed a vodka, his ninth or tenth. When the phone rang he managed to answer it. Tom was calling to talk. He'd just killed someone new. They discussed that, then Tom asked, "How's George holding up?" Philippe considered the question. "Alive," he said.

This led Tom to deliver his typical speech. As Philippe understood it, the points were: (1) Tom realized that he shouldn't have done it, but (2) the worst mistake was in letting George live since (3) the boy knew too much, so (4) . . . Philippe changed the subject.

Philippe lay in bed imagining George's death. He was extremely drunk, his eyes were closed. The world he saw rang with percussion. Skeletons snapped. Blood and entrails exploded on a grand scale, while George, deposited deep in those fireworks, flailed like a tiny, crazed acrobat.

Philippe let himself have preposterous thoughts late at night. Sleepiness didn't discriminate. Death seemed a friend, being so far away. Everything else was a fairy tale. The only difference between, say, a pink unicorn and George's death was the chill off the mind that imagined the latter.

Still, this particular fantasy nagged him. He'd stroll through the streets, eat, bathe, weed his rose garden, and it would gather strength over his head, an insidious halo, as black as dried blood, glittering with the thunder of snapping bones.

It tugged at him like a tornado. He would peer up and see George affixed to its sphere, and the smog made him think of a woodcut he'd seen as a child. It showed every bone in some man's body broken and woven through spokes of a wagon wheel. Hoisted aloft in the Renaissance, they had continued to twirl for Philippe ever since.

This was the grave he'd handpicked for George. It spiraled into the darkness tonight, like a piece of cheap dinnerware covered with jewels, thrown away by a terrified man to re-create the impression of UFOs, or the unknown at least, in the trickier glow of his thoughts.

The UFO reached an ambiguous distance. Philippe changed it into a wound. He was looking inside George's body itself, seeing the tiniest thread of its jumble, the way one might study a theater set if the actual play was impenetrable or performed in a foreign language.

He thought of a huge, torn-up asshole. It belonged to a boy named Ed. That was before George came into the picture. Ed was unbearably cute, until men had worn him away. They'd fastened him to a treadmill that spun until there was nothing around but a vague outline, smeared with blood.

Philippe used to say, "I am going to kill this Ed." He'd meant that. At the moment, he simply pronounced the words, disregarding their meaning, as though he were saying, "Please don't," to the jaws of a lion. A death was beyond his means. He could only squint blearily into its depths, the casual bystander.

When he did, he saw a set of teeth, shiny as jewels, puzzled together and hung from invisible wires. It suggested the bones of a frail human body, and gave off an eerie if elegant glow like a chandelier, though hung so low it blew wildly about in his heated breaths.

He lit a cigarette. The bed was soaked with sweat. When he let his mind drift like this, it beautified every idea he had, but while this rendered them livable, their newfound brilliance left sleep's entrance so shadowy . . . "Quick," he thought, "think straight."

Two years ago Philippe had moved to America. He found its dingiest bars. He paid a series of hustlers to lie very still on his floor and gained a wild reputation. One of his fucks introduced him to someone who then introduced him to someone who'd started a club for men with unusual tastes.

Philippe became the ninth member. They'd meet at the ringleader's house every couple of weeks. Each participant wanted to kill someone cute during sex. None had summoned the strength, so they'd formed a committee to solve the problem of their weakness.

Ed was the evidence. One of the members had found him in some hole. His ass had no muscle tone whatsoever. It billowed out from his back and was always as cold as ice cream. He'd stumble over. They'd act out scenarios using him as a prop, then he'd lurch off.

Philippe found relative peace through this teamwork. It brought certain haunting ideas into focus, particularly shit. It was their major find. It formed a kind of stumbling block, in one's words, between them and their wish. It was, in another's terms, death's mace.

In time, their discussions grew more and more abstract, with references to theological theories and artists' renditions. They lost Philippe, whose grasp of English was basic at best. When even Ed became history, Philippe thought of driving an ambulance.

One night a member asked if he could bring someone in to do a film presentation. The vote was unanimous. The man had a backlog of deaths in the can, as he phrased it. He set up equipment and laid out some background. "The boy you're about to see hitchhiked . . ."

He'd picked up the hitchhiker, coerced him home, got him drunk, numbed his body with Novocain, led him into a basement, started the film rolling, mutilated his ass, asked if he'd like to say any last words, to which the boy had said, "Please don't." Then he'd killed him.

The only sound in the room was the clicking projector. Sometimes the clicks and stabs matched for a few seconds. That made the whole thing seem fake. Then the boy made a very bland face. "Is he dead?" someone asked, "No," the man answered. "Not yet. Watch."

Philippe was astonished. He found himself drifting away, as one tended to do with pornography, or, rather, drifting into the image itself, like a child did when watching cartoons. He'd knelt down a short distance away from them, too shy to join in.

His memory fragmented the rest. Philippe could remember hands scooping out bloody intestines. At what seemed a haphazard point, everyone in the room heard a brief, curt announcement. "Now," it said. Philippe knew that word, but he hadn't realized what it meant at first.

The film ended. It flapped like a bat. People redid their pants. The place felt cold, just a vague square of yellowish light. It shone on their sweaty faces. The man switched it off, flicked a switch on the wall. On came the table lamps.

"What are you feeling, Philippe?" Tired. "Then you should sleep." But I am too tense; I keep thinking. "What kind of thinking?" Well, everything. "Of Georges?" Some. He represents something I have desired for a long time. "How long?" Since before I came to America.

"Why did you come?" I came because in my own country I felt afraid. "Of what?" Everything, but mainly of myself. I was beginning to want what I could not have. "Can you be more clear?" No. When I try, my beliefs or de-

sires come out beautiful. They *are* beautiful to me, but I cannot understand them
in that form.

"You wanted to kill someone?" That is too simple. I thought about killing someone, though I did not know who. My ideas about death are very beautiful, so I wanted to think about killing a beautiful person. "A boy?" Yes. "And
you could not find him there?" I could not find myself there. I was known as
what I am not.

"Who are you?" I am trying to find this out. It is hard. I am driven to do
certain things, and I believe they are helping me, because they seem strong.
"Why Georges?" He makes me feel something. I do not know this answer. "He
has been hurt?" Yes. "By someone you know?" Yes.

"How would you kill Georges?" Very slowly, so I could see everything
in him and know what he has meant to me. "Would you expect to see yourself
in him?" I would expect to see someone who could answer my questions looking at me through him. He would resemble me.

"And Tom?" He is me if I were less alone. "Can you explain that?" He
can kill someone, because he knows who he is. He kills someone to make a
friend, I think. To know someone else. I would kill, if I could do that, to know
myself. We are different, but I understand him.

"Why did you share Georges with Tom?" To compare myself to him.
"Have you learned something?" I have seen small differences, but they are hard
to explain. I think he felt hatred for Georges in his hurry to find a friend. I feel
something like love for Georges, though I do not know why. "Are you weak?"
Yes. "Would you like to change that?" I would not know how.

"Have you made progress?" I am beginning to feel there is no answer for
me. I am too interested in what is beautiful, and when beauty is not somewhere,
I create it. But when something is beautiful it is impossible for me to understand. "How do you mean this?" I mean beauty is powerful. I feel very weak
when I see it, or when I create it. No, I cannot explain.

"Death is beautiful?" It is too beautiful to explain. "But you try." I must.
"Why?" Because I must know what I love, because it is me. "I do not understand." I do not either. "You wish to die?" No, I wish never to die, but to see
myself in death. To know what I am in the answer of death. I am becoming
completely lost. Help.

"I do not know how." You should tell me why I do these things. "But I
cannot, you know this." Yes. "So what will you do now?" I think I must sleep
and try to forget about everything. "Do you think you will do this?" No, but I
must, and I am nearly asleep.

The 1990s

MORGAN ENTREKIN

❧

"Grove in the '90s"

I was first introduced to Grove Press when I was a student in the early 1970s. Most of us can probably remember when we first started reading seriously, discovering authors whose books seized our imaginations and remained imprinted in our memories. I would imagine that most of us didn't notice the imprint on the spines of the books we read at that age—or even at any age, unless we're connected somehow to the publishing industry—and I was no exception.

But there were a few publishers whose colophons became instantly recognizable to me, and which seemed to publish many if not most of the interesting, provocative books to which I was drawn at that time. These were New Directions, Fiction Collective, and, especially, Grove Press. I still recall finding a used paperback copy of *Naked Lunch* and being transfixed by the amazing, revelatory text. From then on I actively looked for titles from Grove Press. Through Grove paperbacks I was introduced to the edgy, groundbreaking work of William S. Burroughs, Jack Kerouac, and Henry Miller; the internationally acclaimed fiction by Jorge Luis Borges, Jean Genet, and Mikhail Bulgakov; the poetry of e. e. cummings and Pablo Neruda, and much more. These books helped to shape me as a person and they ultimately had a great deal to do with my entering the publishing industry.

When I took my first job as an editorial assistant in the late 1970s, I quickly became aware of Grove's reputation within the publishing industry as a whole. While the house had slipped a bit from its colossus-like standing during the 1960s, it remained a model of independent publishing respected by anybody interested in publishing serious literature. Barney Rosset was still in charge of the house then, and as I grew more familiar with the demands of the bottom line, Rosset's uncompromising commitment to his editorial vision grew even more impressive in my eyes.

After acquiring Atlantic Monthly Press and going out on my own as an independent publisher, I would often look to Barney and Grove as a model of sorts. By then he had left his position at Grove, but he remained an archetypal publisher nonetheless, a member of the pantheon inhabited by Alfred Knopf,

Bennett Cerf, Roger Straus, and the other great publishers of the century. I had met Barney a few times, most memorably at the memorial service for Ledig Rowohlt, the great German publisher and a longtime hero of mine. He regaled us with stories of his adventures with Ledig Rowohlt, and his relish in recalling the memories evoked an obvious desire to have fun in the midst of everything. Barney was as committed to enjoying himself as he was to publishing serious books, the rest of the world be damned. His is a contagious enthusiasm, and I continue to find myself inspired by him, the maverick independent publisher bucking trends and publishing books that surprise and stimulate and sometimes even offend—and succeed as a direct result.

Barney's legacy took on a completely different meaning to me when I merged Grove with Atlantic Monthly in 1993, to create the Grove/Atlantic that is today one of the few midsized independent publishers still standing. When I first looked through the Grove catalog and realized what an extraordinary backlist it contained, it was rather a heady feeling to be the publisher of all these great authors who had so inspired me as a student. Since then it has been an enormous pleasure to work closely with the authors and the estates to continue publishing the classics in new editions aimed at new readers. We're also trying to publish new books in the Grove tradition and are committed to publishing poetry, drama, fiction in translation, and important works of history, biography, and narrative journalism. Our efforts on behalf of these new books depend in no small part on the steady stream of income from the backlist that Barney built over his years at the helm of Grove. Many of the books didn't make money at the time, but they have slowly become classics and proven Barney's instincts to be right in the end.

There's also a less tangible, but vastly more powerful benefit to inheriting Barney Rosset's mantle. When I first worked with Barry Hannah to bring his works back into print under the Grove imprint, Barry was delighted to find that his name fell right after Jean Genet, who had long been an icon of his. The booksellers, critics, and writers I met in the early years all offered the warmest wishes for the house's success; they had also been deeply affected by many of the books that Grove published over the years. I suppose it's primarily a sense of participation in a tradition that is much greater than any of us working at the house now or in the past. Perhaps the most powerful example of this sense of participation was the invitation I received to join Kenzaburo Oe for his acceptance of the 1994 Nobel Prize in Literature. The first person I called was Barney. He and his friend Astrid joined Oe's translator John Nathan and his wife, my partner Joan Bingham, and me for the trip to Stockholm. When we were there, Oe reinforced what a privilege it was for me to be taking over the Grove legacy. Oe told me that in the 1960s, a number of publishers had approached him; he had chosen Barney and Grove because of their commitment to fighting the great censorship battles of that era. He implied that Barney's were enormous shoes to fill and warmly wished me the best in doing so.

For almost eight years now we've tried to carry on the tradition that Barney created and to keep the spirit of independent publishing alive. I don't know whether we've succeeded or not, but it's enough for me to stop sometimes and look around my office. My eye usually goes right to the used copy of *Naked Lunch* I found so long ago. It stands right next to a new edition designed and published by the people at the company today. Then I look at the rest of the shelves and see editions of the works I used to admire from what seemed like an unbridgeable distance. They're standing next to other books that we've published over the past eight years, in the same office building that housed Grove when we merged the companies. I look around, it all seems to fit together, and I consider myself extraordinarily lucky to be a part of it.

BANANA YOSHIMOTO

FROM *Kitchen* [1993]

Translated from the Japanese by Megan Backus

The place I like best in this world is the kitchen. No matter where it is, no matter what kind, if it's a kitchen, if it's a place where they make food, it's fine with me. Ideally it should be well broken in. Lots of tea towels, dry and immaculate. White tile catching the light (ting! ting!).

I love even incredibly dirty kitchens to distraction—vegetable droppings all over the floor, so dirty your slippers turn black on the bottom. Strangely, it's better if this kind of kitchen is large. I lean up against the silver door of a towering, giant refrigerator stocked with enough food to get through a winter. When I raise my eyes from the oil-spattered gas burner and the rusty kitchen knife, outside the window stars are glittering, lonely.

Now only the kitchen and I are left. It's just a little nicer than being all alone.

When I'm dead worn out, in a reverie, I often think that when it comes time to die, I want to breathe my last in a kitchen. Whether it's cold and I'm all alone, or somebody's there and it's warm, I'll stare death fearlessly in the eye. If it's a kitchen, I'll think, "How good."

Before the Tanabe family took me in, I spent every night in the kitchen. After my grandmother died, I couldn't sleep. One morning at dawn I trundled out of my room in search of comfort and found that the one place I could sleep was beside the refrigerator.

My parents—my name is Mikage Sakurai—both died when they were young. After that my grandparents brought me up. I was going into junior high when my grandfather died. From then on, it was just my grandmother and me.

When my grandmother died the other day, I was taken by surprise. My family had steadily decreased one by one as the years went by, but when it suddenly dawned on me that I was all alone, everything before my eyes seemed false. The fact that time continued to pass in the usual way in this apartment where I grew up, even though now I was here all alone, amazed me. It was total science fiction. The blackness of the cosmos.

Three days after the funeral I was still in a daze. Steeped in a sadness so great I could barely cry, shuffling softly in gentle drowsiness, I pulled my futon into the deathly silent, gleaming kitchen. Wrapped in a blanket, like Linus, I slept. The hum of the refrigerator kept me from thinking of my loneliness. There, the long night came on in perfect peace, and morning came.

But . . . I just wanted to sleep under the stars.

I wanted to wake up in the morning light.

Aside from that, I just drifted, listless.

However! I couldn't exist like that. Reality is wonderful.

I thought of the money my grandmother had left me—just enough. The place was too big, too expensive, for one person. I had to look for another apartment. There was no way around it. I thumbed through the listings, but when I saw so many places all the same lined up like that, it made my head swim. Moving takes a lot of time and trouble. It takes energy.

I had no strength; my joints ached from sleeping in the kitchen day and night. When I realized how much effort moving would require—I'd have to pull myself together and go look at places. Move my stuff. Get a phone installed—I lay around instead, sleeping, in despair. It was then that a miracle, a godsend, came calling one afternoon. I remember it well.

Dingdong. Suddenly the doorbell rang.

It was a somewhat cloudy spring afternoon. I was intently involved in tying up old magazines with string while glancing at the apartment listings with half an eye but no interest, wondering how I was going to move. Flustered, looking like I'd just gotten out of bed, I ran out and without thinking undid the latch and opened the door. Thank god it wasn't a robber. There stood Yuichi Tanabe.

"Thank you for your help the other day," I said. He was a nice young man, a year younger than me, who had helped out a lot at the funeral. I think he'd said he went to the same university I did. I was taking time off.

"Not at all," he said. "Did you decide on a place to live yet?"

"Not even close." I smiled.

"I see."

"Would you like to come in for some tea?"

"No. I'm on my way somewhere and I'm kind of in a hurry." He grinned. "I just stopped by to ask you something. I was talking to my mother, and we were thinking you ought to come to our house for a while."

"Huh?" I said.

"In any case, why don't you come over tonight around seven? Here's the directions."

"Okay . . ." I said vacantly, taking the slip of paper.

"All right, then, good. Mom and I are both looking forward to your coming." His smile was so bright as he stood in my doorway that I zoomed in for a closeup on his pupils. I couldn't take my eyes off him. I think I heard a spirit call my name.

"Okay," I said. "I'll be there."

Bad as it sounds, it was like I was possessed. His attitude was so totally "cool," though, I felt I could trust him. In the black gloom before my eyes (as it always is in cases of bewitchment), I saw a straight road leading from me to him. He seemed to glow with white light. That was the effect he had on me.

"Okay, see you later," he said, smiling, and left.

Before my grandmother's funeral I had barely known him. On the day itself, when Yuichi Tanabe showed up all of a sudden, I actually wondered if he had been her lover. His hands trembled as he lit the incense; his eyes were swollen from crying. When he saw my grandmother's picture on the altar, again his tears fell like rain. My first thought when I saw that was that my love for my own grandmother was nothing compared to this boy's, whoever he was. He looked that sad.

Then, mopping his face with a handkerchief, he said, "Let me help with something." After that, he helped me a lot.

Yuichi Tanabe . . . I must have been quite confused if I took that long to remember when I'd heard grandmother mention his name.

He was the boy who worked part-time at my grandmother's favorite flower shop. I remembered hearing her say, any number of times, things like, "What a nice boy they have working there. . . . That Tanabe boy . . . today, again. . . ." Grandmother loved cut flowers. Because the ones in our kitchen were not allowed to wilt, she'd go to the flower shop a couple of times a week. When I thought of that, I remembered him walking behind my grandmother, a large potted plant in his arms.

He was a long-limbed young man with pretty features. I didn't know anything more about him, but I might have seen him hard at work in the flower shop. Even after I got to know him a little I still had an impression of aloofness. No matter how nice his manner and expression, he seemed like a loner. I barely knew him, really.

It was raining that hazy spring night. A gentle, warm rain enveloped the neighborhood as I walked with directions in hand.

My apartment building and the one where the Tanabes lived were separated by Chuo Park. As I crossed through, I was inundated with the green smell of the night. I walked, sloshing down the shiny wet path that glittered with the colors of the rainbow.

To be frank, I was only going because they'd asked me. I didn't think about it beyond that. I looked up at the towering apartment building and thought, their apartment on the tenth floor is so high, the view must be beautiful at night. . . .

Getting off the elevator, I was alarmed by the sound of my own footsteps in the hall. I rang the bell, and abruptly, Yuichi opened the door. "Come in."

"Thanks." I stepped inside. The room was truly strange.

First thing, as I looked toward the kitchen, my gaze landed with a thud on the enormous sofa in the living room. Against the backdrop of the large kitchen with its shelves of pots and pans—no table, no carpet, just "it." Covered in beige fabric, it looked like something out of a commercial. An entire family could watch TV on it. A dog too big to keep in Japan could stretch out across it— sideways. It was really a marvelous sofa.

In front of the large window leading onto the terrace was a jungle of plants growing in bowls, planters, and all kinds of pots. Looking around, I saw that the whole house was filled with flowers; there were vases full of spring blooms everywhere.

"My mother says she'll get away from work soon. Take a look around if you'd like. Should I give you the tour? Or pick a room, then I'll know what kind of person you are," said Yuichi, making tea.

"What kind? . . ." I seated myself on the deep, comfy sofa.

"I mean, what you want to know about a house and the people who live there, their tastes. A lot of people would say you learn a lot from the toilet," he said, smiling, unconcerned. He had a very relaxed way of talking.

"The kitchen," I said.

"Well, here it is. Look at whatever you want."

While he made tea, I explored the kitchen. I took everything in: the good quality of the mat on the wood floor and of Yuichi's slippers; a practical minimum of well-worn kitchen things, precisely arranged. A Silverstone frying pan and a delightful German-made vegetable peeler—a peeler to make even the laziest grandmother enjoy slip, slipping those skins off.

Lit by a small fluorescent lamp, all kinds of plates silently awaited their turns; glasses sparkled. It was clear that in spite of the disorder everything was of the finest quality. There were things with special uses, like . . . porcelain bowls, *gratin* dishes, gigantic platters, two beer stems. Somehow it was all very satisfying. I even opened the small refrigerator (Yuichi said it was okay)— everything was neatly organized, nothing just "left."

I looked around, nodding and murmuring approvingly, "Mmm, mmm." It was a good kitchen. I fell in love with it at first sight.

DAGOBERTO GILB

※

"Romero's Shirt"
FROM *The Magic of Blood* [1994]

Juan Romero, a man not unlike many in this country, has had jobs in factories, shops, and stores. He has painted houses, dug ditches, planted trees, hammered, sawed, bolted, snaked pipes, picked cotton and chile and pecans, each and all for wages. Along the way he has married and raised his children and several years ago he finally arranged it so that his money might pay for the house he and his family live in. He is still more than twenty years away from being the owner. It is a modest house even by El Paso standards. The building, in an adobe style, is made of stone which is painted white, though the paint is gradually chipping off or being absorbed by the rock. It has two bedrooms, a den which is used as another, a small dining area, a living room, a kitchen, one bathroom, and a garage which, someday, he plans to turn into another place to live. Although in a development facing a paved street and in a neighborhood, it has the appearance of being on almost half an acre. At the front is a garden of cactus—nopal, ocotillo, and agave—and there are weeds that grow tall with yellow flowers which seed into thorn-hard burrs. The rest is dirt and rocks of various sizes, some of which have been lined up to form a narrow path out of the graded dirt, a walkway to the front porch—where, under a tile and one-by tongue and groove overhang, are a wooden chair and a love seat, covered by an old bedspread, its legless frame on the red cement slab. Once the porch looked onto oak trees. Two of them are dried-out stumps; the remaining one has a limb or two which still can produce leaves, but with so many amputations, its future is irreversible. Romero seldom runs water through a garden hose, though in the back yard some patchy grass can almost seem suburban, at least to him, when he does. Near the corner of his land, in the front, next to the sidewalk, is a juniper shrub, his only bright green plant, and Romero does not want it to yellow and die, so he makes special efforts on its behalf, washing off dust, keeping its leaves neatly pruned and shaped.

These days Romero calls himself a handyman. He does odd jobs, which is exactly how he advertises—"no job too small"— in the throwaway paper. He hangs wallpaper and doors, he paints, lays carpet, does just about any-

thing someone will call and ask him to do. It doesn't earn him much, and
sometimes it's barely enough, but he's his own boss, and he's had so many
bad jobs over those other years, ones no more dependable, he's learned that
this suits him. At one time Romero did want more, and he'd believed that he
could have it simply through work, but no matter what he did his children
still had to be born at the county hospital. Even years later it was there that
his oldest son went for serious medical treatment because Romero couldn't
afford the private hospitals. He tried not to worry about how he earned his
money. In Mexico, where his parents were born and he spent much of his
youth, so many things weren't available, and any work which allowed for food,
clothes, and housing was to be honored—by the standards there, Romero lived
well. Except this wasn't Mexico, and even though there were those who did
worse even here, there were many who did better and had more, and a young
Romero too often felt ashamed by what he saw as his failure. But time passed,
and he got older. As he saw it, he didn't live in poverty, and *here*, he finally
came to realize, was where he was, where he and his family were going to
stay. Life in El Paso was much like the land—hard, but one could make do
with what was offered. Just as his parents had, Romero always thought it was
a beautiful place for a home.

Yet people he knew left—to Houston, Dallas, Los Angeles, San Diego,
Denver, Chicago—and came back for holidays with stories of high wages and
acquisition. And more and more people crossed the river, in rags, taking work,
his work, at any price. Romero constantly had to discipline himself by remembering the past, how his parents lived; he had to teach himself to appreciate what
he did have. His car, for example, he'd kept up since his early twenties. He'd
had it painted three times in that period and he worked on it so devotedly that
even now it was in as good a condition as almost any car could be. For his children he tried to offer more—an assortment of clothes for his daughter, lots of
toys for his sons. He denied his wife nothing, but she was a woman who asked
for little. For himself, it was much less. He owned some work clothes and
T-shirts necessary for his jobs as well as a set of good enough, he thought, shirts
he'd had since before the car. He kept up a nice pair of custom boots, and in a
closet hung a pair of slacks for a wedding or baptism or important mass. He
owned two jackets, a leather one from Mexico and a warm nylon one for cold
work days. And he owned a wool plaid Pendleton shirt, his favorite piece of
clothing, which he'd bought right after the car and before his marriage because
it really was good-looking besides being functional. He wore it anywhere and
everywhere with confidence that its quality would always be both in style and
appropriate.

* * *

The border was less than two miles below Romero's home, and he could see, down the dirt street which ran alongside his property, the desert and mountains of Mexico. The street was one of the few in the city which hadn't yet been paved. Romero liked it that way, despite the run-off problems when heavy rains passed by, as they had the day before this day. A night wind had blown hard behind the rains, and the air was so clean he could easily see buildings in Juárez. It was sunny, but a breeze told him to put on his favorite shirt before he pulled the car up alongside the house and dragged over the garden hose to wash it, which was something he still enjoyed doing as much as anything else. He was organized, had a special bucket, a special sponge, and he used warm water from the kitchen sink. When he started soaping the car he worried about getting his shirt sleeves wet, and once he was moving around he decided a T-shirt would keep him warm enough. So he took off the wool shirt and draped it, conspicuously, over the juniper near him, at the corner of his property. He thought that if he couldn't help but see it, he couldn't forget it, and forgetting something outside was losing it. He lived near a school, and teenagers passed by all the time, and also there was regular foot-traffic—many people walked the sidewalk in front of his house, many who had no work.

After the car was washed, Romero went inside and brought out the car wax. Waxing his car was another thing he still liked to do, especially on a weekday like this one when he was by himself, when no one in his family was home. He could work faster, but he took his time, spreading with a damp cloth, waiting, then wiping off the crust with a dry cloth. The exterior done, he went inside the car and waxed the dash, picked up some trash on the floorboard, cleaned out the glove compartment. Then he went for some pliers he kept in a toolbox in the garage, returned and began to wire up the rear license plate which had lost a nut and bolt and was hanging awkwardly. As he did this, he thought of other things he might do when he finished, like prune the juniper. Except his old shears had broken, and he hadn't found another used pair, because he wouldn't buy them new.

An old man walked up to him carrying a garden rake, a hoe, and some shears. He asked Romero if there was some yard work needing to be done. After spring, tall weeds grew in many yards, but it seemed a dumb question this time of year, particularly since there was obviously so little ever to be done in Romero's yard. But Romero listened to the old man. There were still a few weeds over there, and he could rake the dirt so it'd be even and level, he could clip that shrub, and probably there was something in the back if he were to look. Romero was usually brusque with requests such as these, but he found the old man unique and likeable and he listened and finally asked how much he would want for all those tasks. The old man thought as quickly as he spoke and threw out a number. Ten. Romero repeated the number, questioningly, and the old man backed up, saying well, eight, seven. Romero asked if that was for everything. Yes sir, the old man said, excited that he'd seemed to catch a customer. Romero asked if he would cut the juniper for three dollars. The old man kept his eyes on the evergreen, disappointed for a second, then thought better of it. Okay, okay, he said, but, I've been walking all day, you'll give me lunch? The old man rubbed his striped cotton shirt at his stomach.

Romero liked the old man and agreed to it. He told him how he should follow the shape which was already there, to cut it evenly, to take a few inches off all of it just like a haircut. Then Romero went inside, scrambled enough eggs and chile and cheese for both of them and rolled it all in some tortillas. He brought out a beer.

The old man was clearly grateful, but since his gratitude was keeping the work from getting done—he might talk an hour about his little ranch in Mexico, about his little turkeys and his pig—Romero excused himself and went inside. The old man thanked Romero for the food, and, as soon as he was finished with the beer, went after the work sincerely. With dull shears—he sharpened them, so to speak, against a rock wall—the old man snipped garishly, hopping and jumping around the bush, around and around. It gave Romero such great pleasure to watch that this was all he did from his front window.

The work didn't take long, so, as the old man was raking up the clippings, Romero brought out a five-dollar bill. He felt that the old man's dancing around that bush, in those baggy old checkered pants, was more inspiring than religion, and a couple of extra dollars was a cheap price to see old eyes whiten like a boy's.

The old man was so pleased that he invited Romero to that little ranch of his in Mexico where he was sure they could share some aguardiente, or maybe Romero could buy a turkey from him—they were skinny but they could be fattened—but in any case they could enjoy a bottle of tequila together, with some sweet lemons. The happy old man swore he would come back no matter what, for he could do many things for Romero at his beautiful home. He swore he would return, maybe in a week or two, for surely there was work that needed to be done in the back yard.

Romero wasn't used to feeling so virtuous. He so often was disappointed, so often dwelled on the difficulties of life, that he had become hard, guarding against compassion and generosity. So much so that he'd even become spare with his words, even with his family. His wife whispered to the children that this was because he was tired, and, since it wasn't untrue, he accepted it as the explanation too. It spared him that worry, and from having to discuss why he liked working weekends and taking a day off during the week, like this one.

But now an old man had made Romero wish his family were there with him so he could give as much, *more,* to them too, so he could watch their spin around dances—he'd missed so many—and Romero swore he would take them all into Juárez that night for dinner. He might even convince them to take a day, maybe two, for a drive to his uncle's house in Chihuahua instead, because he'd promised that so many years ago—so long ago they probably thought about somewhere else by now, like San Diego, or Los Angeles. Then he'd take them there! They'd go for a week, spend whatever it took. No expense could be so great, and if happiness was as easy as some tacos and a five-dollar bill, then how stupid it had been of him not to have offered it all this time.

Romero felt so good, felt such relief, he napped on the couch. When he woke up he immediately remembered his shirt, that it was already gone before the old man had even arrived—he remembered they'd walked around the juniper before it was cut. Nevertheless, the possibility that the old man took it wouldn't leave Romero's mind. Since he'd never believed in letting down, giving into someone like that old man, the whole experience became suspect. Maybe it was part of some ruse which ended with the old man taking his shirt, some food, money. This was how Romero thought. Though he held a hope that he'd left it somewhere else, that it was a lapse of memory on his part—he went outside, inside, looked everywhere twice, then one more time after that—his cynicism had flowered, colorful and bitter.

Understand that it was his favorite shirt, that he'd never thought of replacing it and that its loss was all Romero could keep his mind on, though he knew very well it wasn't a son, or a daughter, or a wife, or a mother or father, not a disaster of any kind. It was a simple shirt, in the true value of things not very much to lose. But understand also that Romero was a good man who tried to do what was right and who would harm no one willfully. Understand that Romero was a man who had taught himself to not care, to not want, to not desire for so long that he'd lost many words, avoided many people, kept to himself, alone, almost always, even when his wife gave him his meals. Understand that it was his favorite shirt and though no more than that, for him it was no less. Then understand how he felt like a fool paying that old man who, he considered, might even have taken it, like a fool for feeling so friendly and generous, happy, when the shirt was already gone, like a fool for having all those and these thoughts for the love of a wool shirt, like a fool for not being able to stop thinking them all, but especially the one reminding him that this was what he had always believed in, that loss was what he was most prepared for. And so then you might understand why he began to stare out the window of his home, waiting for someone to walk by absently with it on, for the thief to pass by, careless. He kept a watch out the window as each of his children came in, then his wife. He told them only what had happened and, as always, they left him alone. He stared out that window onto the dirt street, past the ocotillos and nopales and agaves, the junipers and oaks and mulberries in front of other homes of brick or stone, painted or not, past them to the buildings in Juárez, and he watched the horizon darken and the sky light up with the moon and stars, and the land spread with shimmering lights, so bright in the dark blot of night. He heard dogs barking until another might bark farther away, and then another, back and forth like that, the small rectangles and squares of their fences plotted out distinctly in his mind's eye as his lids closed. Then he heard a gust of wind bend around his house, and then came the train, the metal rhythm getting closer until it was as close as it could be, the steel pounding the earth like a beating heart, until it diminished and then faded away and then left the air to silence, to its quiet and dark, so still it was like death, or rest, sleep, until he could hear a grackle, and then another gust of wind, and then finally a car.

He looked in on his daughter still so young, so beautiful, becoming a woman who would leave that bed for another, his sons still boys when they were asleep, who dreamed like men when they were awake, and his wife, still young in his eyes in the morning shadows of their bed.

Romero went outside. The juniper had been cut just as he'd wanted it. He got cold and came back in and went to the bed and blankets his wife kept so clean, so neatly arranged as she slept under them without him, and he lay down beside her.

BARRY HANNAH

❦

"Coming Close to Donna"
FROM *Airships* [1994]

Fistfight on the old cemetery. Both of them want Donna, square off, and Donna and I watch from the Lincoln convertible.

I'm neutral. I wear sharp clothes and everybody thinks I'm a fag, though it's not true. The truth is, I'm not all that crazy about Donna, that's all, and I tend to be sissy of voice. Never had a chance otherwise—raised by a dreadfully vocal old aunt after my parents were killed by vicious homosexuals in Panama City. Further, I am fat. I've got fat ankles going into my suede boots.

I ask her, "Say, what you think about that, Donna? Are you going to be whoever wins's girl friend?"

"Why not? They're both cute," she says.

Her big lips are moist. She starts taking her sweater off. When it comes off, I see she's got great humpers in her bra. There's a nice brown valley of hair between them.

"I can't lose," she says.

Then she takes off her shoes and her skirt. There is extra hair on her thighs near her pantie rim. Out in the cemetery, the guys are knocking the spunk out of each other's cheeks. Bare, Donna's feet are red and not handsome around the toes. She has some serious bunions from her weird shoes, even at eighteen.

My age is twenty. I tried to go to college but couldn't sit in the seats long enough to learn anything. Plus, I hated English composition, where you had to correct your phrases. They cast me out like so much wastepaper. The junior college system in California is tough. So I just went back home. I like to wear smart clothes and walk up and down Sunset Strip. That will show them.

By now, Donna is naked. The boys, Hank and Ken, are still battering each other out in the cemetery. I look away from the brutal fight and from Donna's nakedness. If I were a father, I couldn't conceive of this from my daughter.

"Warm me up, Vince. Do me. Or are you really a fag like they say?"

"Not that much," I say.

I lost my virginity. It was like swimming in a warm, oily room—rather pleasant—but I couldn't finish. I thought about the creases in my outfit.

"Come in me, you fag," says she. "Don't hurt my feelings. I want a fag to come in me."

"Oh, you pornographic witch, I can't," says I.

She stands up, nude as an oyster. We look over at the fight in the cemetery. When she had clothes on, she wasn't much to look at. But naked, she is a vision. She has an urgent body that makes you forget the crooked nose. Her hair is dyed pink, but her organ hair isn't.

We watch Hank and Ken slugging each other. They are her age and both of them are on the swimming team.

Something is wrong. They are too serious. They keep pounding each other in the face past what a human could take.

Donna falls on her knees in the green tufted grass.

She faints. Her body is the color of an egg. She fainted supine, titties and hair upward.

The boys are hitting to kill. They are not fooling around. I go ahead in my smart bell-bottom cuffed trousers. By the time I reach them, they are both on the ground. Their scalps are cold.

They are both dead.

"This is awful. They're *dead,*" I tell Donna, whose eyes are closed.

"What?" says she.

"They killed each other," says I.

"Touch me," she says. "Make me know I'm here."

I thrust my hand to her organ.

"What do we do?" says I.

She goes to the two bodies, and is absorbed in a tender unnatural act over the blue jeans of Hank and Ken. In former days, these boys had sung a pretty fine duet in their rock band.

"I can't make anybody come! I'm no good!" she says.

"Don't be silly," I say. "They're dead. Let's get out of here."

"I can't just get out of here! They were my sweethearts!" she screams. "Do me right now, Vince! It's the only thing that makes sense."

Well, I flung in and tried.

A half year later, I saw her in Hooper's, the pizza parlor. I asked her how it was going. She was gone on heroin. The drug had made her prettier for a while. Her eyes were wise and wide, all black, but she knew nothing except desperation.

"Vince," she said, "if you'd come lay your joint in me, I wouldn't be lost anymore. You're the only one of the old crowd. Screw me and I could get back to my old neighborhood."

I took her into my overcoat, and when I joined her in the street in back of a huge garbage can, she kept asking: "Tell me where it is, the cemetery!"

At the moment, I was high on cocaine from a rich woman's party.

But I drove her—that is, took a taxi—to the cemetery where her lovers were dead. She knelt at the stones for a while. Then I noted she was stripping off. Pretty soon she was naked again.

"Climb me, mount me, fight for me, fuck me!" she screamed.

I picked up a neighboring tombstone with a great effort. It was an old thing, perhaps going back to the nineteenth century. I crushed her head with it. Then I fled right out of there.

Some of us are made to live for a long time. Others for a short time. Donna wanted what she wanted.

I gave it to her.

JERZY KOSINSKI

❦

FROM *The Painted Bird* [1995]

The village lay far from the railroad line and river. Three times a year detachments of German soldiers would arrive to collect the foodstuffs and materials which the peasants were obliged to provide for the army.

I was being kept by a blacksmith who was also the head peasant of the village. He was well respected and esteemed by the villagers. For this reason I was better treated here. However, now and then when they had been drinking the peasants would say that I could only bring misfortune to the community and that the Germans, if they found out about the Gypsy brat, would punish the entire village. But no one dared to say such things directly to the blacksmith's face, and in general I was not bothered. True, the blacksmith liked to slap my face when he was tipsy and I got in his way, but there were no other consequences. The two hired hands preferred to thrash each other rather than me, and the blacksmith's son, who was known in the village for his amorous feats, was almost never on the farm.

Early each morning the blacksmith's wife would give me a glass of hot borscht and a piece of stale bread, which, when soaked in the borscht, gained flavor as rapidly as the borscht lost it. Afterwards I would light the fire in my comet and drive the cattle toward the pasture ahead of the other cowherds.

In the evening the blacksmith's wife said her prayers, he snored against the oven, the hired hands tended the cattle, and the blacksmith's son prowled the village. The blacksmith's wife would give me her husband's jacket to delouse. I would sit in the brightest spot in the room, folding the jacket at various places along the seams and hunting the white, lazily moving blood-filled insects. I would pick them out, put them on the table, and crush them with my fingernail. When the lice were exceptionally numerous the blacksmith's wife would join me at the table and roll a bottle over the lice as soon as I put several of them down. The lice would burst with a crunching sound, their flattened corpses lying in small pools of dark blood. Those that fell onto the dirt floor scurried away in every direction. It was almost impossible to squash them underfoot.

The blacksmith's wife did not let me kill all the lice and bedbugs. Whenever we found a particularly large and vigorous louse, she would carefully catch it and throw it into a cup set aside for this purpose. Usually, when the number of such lice reached a dozen, the wife would take them out and knead them into a dough. To this she added a little human and horse urine, a large amount of manure, a dead spider, and a pinch of cat excrement. This preparation was considered to be the best medicine for a bellyache. When the blacksmith suffered his periodic bellyache, he had to eat several balls of this mixture. This led to vomiting and, as his wife assured him, to the total conquest of the disease, which promptly fled his body. Exhausted by vomiting and trembling like a reed, the blacksmith would lie on the mat at the foot of the oven and pant like a bellows. He would then be given tepid water and honey, which calmed him. But when the pain and fever did not die down, his wife prepared more medicines. She would pulverize horses' bones to fine flour, add a cup of mixed bedbugs and field ants, which would start fighting with each other, mix it all with several hen's eggs, and add a dash of kerosene. The patient had to gulp it all down in one big swallow and was then rewarded with a glass of vodka and a piece of sausage.

From time to time the blacksmith was visited by mysterious mounted guests, who carried rifles and revolvers. They would search the house and then sit down at a table with the blacksmith. In the kitchen the blacksmith's wife and I would prepare bottles of home-brewed vodka, strings of spiced hunter's sausages, cheeses, hard-boiled eggs, and sides of roast pork.

The armed men were partisans. They came to the village very often, without warning. What is more, they fought each other. The blacksmith explained to his wife that the partisans had become divided into factions: the "whites," who wanted to fight both the Germans and the Russians, and the "reds," who wanted to help the Red Army.

Varied rumors circulated in the village. The "whites" wanted also to retain the private ownership of property, leaving the landlords as they were. The "reds," supported by the Soviets, fought for land reform. Each faction demanded increasing assistance from the villages.

The "white" partisans, cooperating with the landlords, took revenge on all who were suspected of helping the "reds." The "reds" favored the poor and penalized the villages for any help they gave to the "whites." They persecuted the families of the rich peasants.

The village was also searched by German troops, who interrogated the peasants about the partisan visits and shot one or two peasants to set an example. In such cases the blacksmith would hide me in the potato cellar while he himself tried to soften the German commanders, promising them punctual deliveries of foodstuffs and extra grain.

Sometimes the partisan factions would attack and kill each other while visiting the village. The village would then become a battlefield; machine guns roared, grenades burst, huts flamed, abandoned cattle and horses bellowed, and half-naked children howled. The peasants hid in cellars embracing their praying women. Half-blind, deaf, toothless old women, babbling prayers and crossing themselves with arthritic hands, walked directly into machine-gun fire, cursing the combatants and appealing to heaven for revenge.

After the battle the village would slowly return to life. But there would be fights among the peasants and boys for the weapons, uniforms, and boots abandoned by the partisans, and also arguments about where to bury the dead and who should dig the graves. Days would pass in argument as the corpses decomposed, sniffed by dogs in the daytime and chewed by rats at night.

I was awakened one night by the blacksmith's wife who urged me to flee. I barely had time to leap out of bed before male voices and rattling weapons could be heard surrounding the hut. I hid in the attic with a sack thrown over my body, clinging to a crack in the planks, through which I could see a large part of the farmyard.

A firm male voice ordered the blacksmith to come out. Two armed partisans dragged the half-naked blacksmith into the yard, where he stood, shivering from cold and hitching up his falling trousers. In a tall cap with star-spangled epaulets on his shoulders, the leader of the band approached the blacksmith and asked him something. I caught a fragment of a sentence: ". . . you helped enemies of the Fatherland."

The blacksmith threw up his hands, swearing in the name of the Son and the Holy Trinity. The first blow felled him. He continued his denials, rising slowly to his feet. One of the men tore out a pole from the fence, swung it through the air and clouted the blacksmith in the face. The blacksmith fell, and the partisans began to kick him all over with their heavy boots. The blacksmith groaned, writhing with pain, but the men did not stop. They leaned over him twisting his ears, stepping on his genitals, breaking his fingers with their heels.

When he ceased to groan and his body sagged, the partisans hauled out the two hired hands, the blacksmith's wife, and his struggling son. They opened wide the doors of the barn and threw the woman and the men across the shaft of a cart in such a way that, with the shaft under their bellies, they hung over it like upset sacks of grain. Then the partisans tore the clothing off their victims and tied their hands to their feet. They rolled up their sleeves and, with steel canes cut from track signal wire, began to beat the squirming bodies.

The crack of the blows rebounded loudly off the taut buttocks while the victims twisted, shrinking and swelling, and howled like a pack of abused dogs. I quivered and sweated with fear.

The blows rained one after another. Only the blacksmith's wife continued to wail, while the partisans exchanged witticisms over her lean, crooked thighs. Since the woman did not stop moaning, they overturned her, face to the sky, her whitening breasts hanging down at both sides. The men struck her heatedly, the rising crescendo of blows slashing the woman's body and belly, now darkened by streams of blood. The bodies on the shaft drooped. The torturers put on their jackets and entered the hut, demolishing the furniture and plundering all in sight.

They entered the attic and found me. They held me up by the neck, turning me around, punching me with their fists, pulling me by the hair. They had immediately assumed I was a Gypsy foundling. They loudly deliberated what to do with me. Then one of them decided I should be delivered up to the German outpost about a dozen miles from the hut. According to him, this would make the commander of the outpost less suspicious of the village, which was already tardy in its compulsory deliveries. Another man agreed, adding rapidly that the whole village might be burned down because of a single Gypsy bastard.

My hands and feet were tied and I was carried outside. The partisans summoned two peasants, to whom they carefully explained something while pointing at me. The peasants listened obediently, with obsequious nods. I was placed on a cart and lashed to a crosstie. The peasants climbed onto the box seat and drove off with me.

The partisans escorted the cart for several miles, swaying freely in their saddles, sharing food from the blacksmith. When we entered the denser part of the forest, they again spoke to the peasants, struck their horses, and vanished in the thicket.

Tired by the sun and by my uncomfortable position, I dozed off into half-sleep. I dreamed I was a squirrel, crouching in a dark tree hole and watching with irony the world below. I suddenly became a grasshopper with long, springy legs, on which I sailed across great tracts of land. Now and then, as if through a fog, I heard the voices of the drivers, the neighing of the horse, and the squeaking of the wheels.

We reached the railroad station at noon and were immediately surrounded by German soldiers in faded uniforms and battered boots. The peasants bowed to them and handed them a note written by the partisans. While a guard went off to call an officer, several soldiers approached the cart and stared at me, exchanging remarks. One of them, a rather elderly man, clearly fatigued by the heat, was wearing spectacles fogged by sweat. He leaned against the cart and watched me closely, with dispassionate, watery-blue eyes. I smiled at him but he did not respond. I looked straight into his eyes and wondered if this would cast an evil spell on him. I thought he might fall sick but, feeling sorry for him, I dropped my gaze.

A young officer emerged from the station building and approached the cart. The soldiers quickly straightened their uniforms and stood at attention. The peasants, not quite sure what to do, tried to imitate the soldiers and also drew themselves up servilely.

The officer tersely said something to one of the soldiers, who came forward from the file, approached me, patted my hair roughly with his hand, looked into my eyes while pulling back my lids, and inspected the scars on my knees and calves. He then made his report to the officer. The officer turned to the elderly bespectacled soldier, issued an order and left.

The soldiers moved away. From the station building a gay tune could be heard. On the tall watchtower with its machine-gun post the guards were adjusting their helmets.

The bespectacled soldier approached me, wordlessly untied the rope with which I had been tied to the cart, looped one end of the rope around his wrist, and with a movement of his hand ordered me to follow him. I glanced back at the two peasants; they were already on the cart, whipping the horse.

We passed the station building. On the way the soldier stopped at a warehouse, where he was handed a small can of gasoline. Then we walked along on the railroad track toward the looming forest.

I was certain that the soldier had orders to shoot me, pour the gasoline over my body and burn it. I had seen this happen many times. I remembered how the partisans had shot a peasant who was accused of being an informer. In that case the victim was ordered to dig a ditch into which his dead body later dropped. I remembered the Germans shooting a wounded partisan who was fleeing into the forest, and the tall flame rising later over his dead body.

I dreaded pain. The shooting would certainly be very painful, and the burning with gasoline even more so. But I could do nothing. The soldier carried a rifle, and the rope tied to my leg was looped over his wrist.

I was barefoot and the crossties, hot from the sun, scorched my feet. I hopped about on the sharp particles of gravel lying between the crossties. I tried several times to walk on the rail, but the rope tied to my leg somehow prevented me from keeping my balance. It was difficult to adjust my small steps to the large, measured stride of the soldier.

He watched me and smiled faintly at my attempt at acrobatics on the rail. The smile was too brief to signify anything; he was going to kill me.

We had already left the station area and now passed the last switchpoint. It was darkening. We drew nearer to the forest and the sun was setting behind the treetops. The soldier halted, put down the gasoline can, and transferred the rifle to his left arm. He sat down on the edge of the track and, heaving a deep sigh, stretched his legs down the embankment. He calmly took off his spectacles, wiped the sweat from his thick brows with his sleeve, and unclipped the small shovel hanging from his belt. He took out a cigarette from his breast pocket and lit it, carefully extinguishing the match.

Silently he watched my attempt to loosen the rope, which was rubbing the skin off my leg. Then he took a small jackknife out of his trouser pocket, opened it, and moving closer held my leg with one hand, and with the other carefully cut the rope. He rolled it up and flung it over the embankment with a sweeping gesture.

I smiled in an attempt to express my gratitude, but he did not smile back. We now sat, he drawing at his cigarette and I observing the bluish smoke drifting upward in loops.

I began to think of the many ways there were of dying. Until now, only two ways had impressed me.

I recalled well the time, in the first days of the war, when a bomb hit a house across the street from my parents' home. Our windows were blown out. We were assaulted by falling walls, the tremor of the shaken earth, the screams of unknown dying people. I saw the brown surfaces of doors, ceilings, walls with the pictures still clinging desperately to them, all falling into the void. Like an avalanche rushing to the street came majestic grand pianos opening and closing their lids in flight, obese, clumsy armchairs, skittering stools and hassocks. They were chased by chandeliers that were falling apart with shrill cries, by polished kitchen pots, kettles, and sparkling aluminum chamber pots. Pages torn out of gutted books fell down, flapping like flocks of scared birds. Bathtubs tore themselves away slowly and deliberately from their pipes, entwining themselves magically in the knots and scrolls of banisters and railings and rain gutters.

As the dust settled, the split house timidly bared its entrails. Limp human bodies lay tossed over the jagged edges of the broken floors and ceilings like rags covering the break. They were just beginning to soak in the red dye. Tiny particles of torn paper, plaster, and paint clung to the sticky red rags like hungry flies. Everything around was still in motion; only the bodies seemed at peace.

Then came the groans and screams of people pinned down by the falling beams, impaled on rods and pipes, partially torn and crushed under chunks of walls. Only one old woman came up from the dark pit. She clutched desperately at bricks and when her toothless mouth opened to speak she was suddenly unable to utter a sound. She was half naked and withered breasts hung from her bony chest. When she reached the end of the crater at the pile of rubble between the pit and the road, she stood up straight for a moment on the ridge. Then she toppled over backwards and disappeared behind the debris.

One could die less spectacularly at the hands of another man. Not long ago, when I lived at Lekh's, two peasants began to fight at a reception. In the middle of the hut they rushed at each other, clutched at each other's throat, and fell on the dirt floor. They bit with their teeth like enraged dogs, tearing off pieces of clothing and flesh. Their horny hands and knees and shoulders and feet seemed to have a life of their own. They jumped about clutching, striking, scratching, twisting in a wild dance. Bare knuckles hit skulls like hammers and bones cracked under stress.

Then the guests, watching calmly in a circle, heard a crushing noise and a hoarse rattle. One of the men stayed on top longer. The other gasped and seemed to be weakening, but still lifted his head and spat in the victor's face. The man on top did not forgive this. He triumphantly blew himself up like a bullfrog and took a wide swing, smashing the other's head in with terrible force. The head did not struggle to rise any more, but seemed to dissolve into a growing pool of blood. The man was dead.

I felt now like the mangy dog that the partisans had killed. They had first stroked his head and scratched him behind the ears. The dog, overwhelmed with joy, yapped with love and gratitude. Then they tossed him a bone. He ran after it, wagging his scruffy tail, scaring the butterflies and trampling flowers. When he seized the bone and proudly lifted it, they shot him.

The soldier hitched up his belt. His movement caught my attention and I stopped thinking for a moment.

Then I tried to calculate the distance to the forest and the time it would take him to pick up his rifle and shoot if I should suddenly escape. The forest was too far; I would die midway on the sandy ridge. At best I might reach the patch of weeds, in which I would still be visible and unable to run fast.

The soldier rose and stretched with a groan. Silence surrounded us. The soft wind blew away the smell of the gasoline and brought back a fragrance of marjoram and fir resin.

He could, of course, shoot me from the back, I thought. People preferred killing a person without looking into his eyes.

The soldier turned toward me and pointing to the forest made a gesture with his hand which seemed to say, "run away, be off!" So the end was coming. I pretended I did not understand and edged toward him. He moved back violently, as if fearing that I might touch him, and angrily pointed to the forest, shielding his eyes with his other hand.

I thought that this was a clever way of tricking me; he was pretending not to look. I stood rooted to the spot. He glanced at me impatiently and said something in his rough tongue. I smiled fawningly at him, but this only exasperated him more. Again he thrust his arm toward the forest. Again I did not move. Then he lay down between the rails, across his rifle, from which he had removed the bolt.

I calculated the distance once more; it seemed to me that this time the risk was small. As I began to move away, the soldier smiled affably. When I reached the edge of the embankment, I glanced back; he was still lying motionless, dozing in the warm sun.

I hastily waved and then leapt like a hare down the embankment straight into the undergrowth of the cool, shady forest. I tore my skin against the ferns as I fled farther and farther until I finally lost my breath and fell down in the moist, soothing moss.

While I lay listening to the sounds of the forest, I heard two shots from the direction of the railroad track. Apparently the soldier was simulating my execution.

Birds awakened and began rustling in the foliage. Right next to me a small lizard leapt out of a root and stared attentively at me. I could have squashed it with a whack of my hand, but I was too tired.

ALINA REYES

꘎꘎

FROM *The Butcher and Other Erotica* [1996]

Translated from the French by David Watson

He smiled, fixing his eyes on mine. This look was the signal. It penetrated behind my pupils, ran all over my body, thrust into my belly. The butcher was about to speak.

'How's my little darling this morning?'

Salivating like a spider spinning his web.

'Did she sleep well? Didn't find the night too long? Didn't miss anything?'

So it began. It was disgusting. And yet so sweet.

'Did you have someone round to take care of your little pussy? You like it, don't you? I can see it in your eyes. I was all alone, I couldn't get to sleep, I was thinking about you a lot, you know . . .'

The butcher completely naked, squeezing his penis in his hand. I felt sticky.

'I'd have preferred it if you were there, of course . . . But you'll come soon, my darling . . . You'll see how I'll take care of you . . . I've got skilful hands, you know . . . and a long tongue, you'll see. I'll lick your cunt like it's never been licked. You can feel it already, can't you? Can you smell the scent of love? Do you like the smell of men when you're about to drink them?'

He was breathing rather than speaking. His words broke against my neck, trickled down my back, over my breasts, my stomach, my thighs. He held me with his small blue eyes, his winning smile.

At this time the boss and the butcher-woman were putting the finishing touches to their display in the covered market, and giving last minute orders to the staff; there were few customers around as yet. As always when we were alone together, the butcher and me, we started the game, our game, our precious device for annihilating the world. The butcher was leaning on my till, right next to me. I did nothing, I sat up straight on my high stool. I listened, that's all.

And I knew that, in spite of myself, he could see my desire rise beneath his words, he knew the fascination his sweet-talking stratagem exerted.

'I bet you're already wet inside those little knickers of yours. Do you like me talking to you like this? Do you like getting off on nothing but words . . . I'd have to go on, forever . . . If I touched you, you see, it would be like my words . . . all over, gently, with my tongue . . . I'd take you in my arms, I'd do whatever I want with you, you'd be my doll, my little darling to caress . . . You would never want it to end . . .'

The butcher was tall and fat, with very white skin. As he spoke without pause he breathed lightly, his voice grew husky and dissolved into a whisper. I saw his face fill with pink patches; his lips glistened with moisture; the blue of his eyes lightened until they were no more than pale luminous spots.

In my half-conscious state I wondered if he were not about to come, dragging me along with him, if we were not about to let our pleasure flow in this stream of words; and the world was white like his overall, like the window and like the milk of men and cows, like the fat belly of the butcher, under which was hidden the thing which made him talk, talk into my neck as soon as we were alone together, and young and hot like an island in the middle of the cold meat.

'What I like more than anything is eating the pussies of little girls like you. Will you let me, eh, will you let me graze on you? I'll pull open your pretty pink lips so softly, first the big ones, then the small ones, I'll put the tip of my tongue in, then the whole tongue, and I'll lick you from your hole to your button, oh your lovely button, I'll suck you my darling you'll get wet you'll shine and you'll never stop coming in my mouth just as you want eh I'll eat your arse and your breasts your shoulders your arms your navel and the small of your back your thighs your legs your knees your toes I'll sit you on my nose I'll smother myself in your mound your head on my balls my huge cock in your cute little mouth let me my darling I'll come in your throat on your belly or on your eyes if you prefer the nights are so long I'll take you from the front from behind my little pussy it'll never end never end . . .'

He was now whispering in my ear, leaning right over me without touching, and neither of us knew anything any more—where we were, where the world was. We were transfixed by a breath become speech which emerged on its own, had its own life, a disembodied animal, just between his mouth and my ear.

The weather was getting hotter. It was the main topic of conversation. When the butcher came out of the freezer a customer would say, 'I bet it's nicer in there than out here?'

He would laugh in agreement. Sometimes, if he liked the woman, if she didn't look too unapproachable, he would hazard, 'Shall we try it then?' in as light a tone as possible, so as to distract attention from the glint in his eye.

His comment was not purely anodyne. It wasn't uncommon to see the boss and the butcher-woman come out of the freezer, ten minutes after going in, with buttons undone and hair dishevelled.

One day when the boss was away the butcher and the butcher-woman had locked themselves in the freezer. After a moment or two I had succumbed to the desire to open the door.

Between the rows of hanging carcasses of sheep and calves the butcher-woman was grabbing hold of two thick iron hooks above her head like someone keeping her balance on the tube or the bus. Her dress was pulled up and rolled around her waist exposing her thighs and her white stomach with her black tuft standing out in profile. The butcher was standing behind her, his trousers around his ankles, and his apron also twisted up around his belt, his flesh spilling out. They stopped fornicating when they saw me, but the butcher remained held in the butcher-woman's buxom behind.

Every time a customer mentioned the coolness of the freezer I saw that scene, the butcher-woman hanging like a carcass and the butcher pushing his excrescence into her in the middle of a forest of meat.

There was a constant flow of customers. The butcher no longer had time to talk. As he tossed the packets onto the scales he gave me winks, small signs.

As for the business with the butcher-woman, I had borne a grudge against him for several days, during which I had refused to let him whisper in my ear. So he began talking to me about his apprenticeship in the abattoirs. It was hard, very hard, it was a time he almost went mad, he told me. But he didn't take up the story, he quickly clammed up, his face clouded over.

Every day he brought up the abattoirs without being able to elaborate further. He became more and more gloomy.

Towards the end of the week, at half past one in the afternoon (the worst time of day because of tiredness, the effect of the aperitif and the wait for lunch to be served), he got into an argument with one of the assistants who had just come back from the market. They were exchanging curt remarks in loud voices, their heads raised and their muscles taut. The assistant hurled some insult, and with a broad sweep of the hand, as if brushing his opponent aside, he went into the freezer. The butcher was livid with rage, I had never seen him like that before. He grabbed a large knife from the stall and, his eyes blazing with anger, leapt into the room after the assistant.

I dashed across, grabbed him by the left hand, calling him by his first name to stop him closing the door behind him.

That was the first time I had touched him. He turned to face me, hesitated for a moment, then followed me back into the shop.

After that I had let him start his whispering again.

TERRY SOUTHERN

❦

FROM *The Magic Christian* [1996]

Out of the gray granite morass of Wall Street rises one building like a heron of fire, soaring up in blue-white astonishment—*Number 18 Wall*—a rocket of glass and blinding copper. It is the *Grand Investment Building,* perhaps the most contemporary business structure in our country, known in circles of high finance simply as *Grand's.*

Offices of *Grand's* are occupied by companies which deal in *mutual funds*—giant and fantastic corporations whose policies define the shape of nations.

August Guy Grand himself was a billionaire. He had 180 million cash deposit in New York banks, and this ready capital was of course but a part of his gross holdings.

In the beginning, Grand's associates, wealthy men themselves, saw nothing extraordinary about him; a reticent man of simple tastes, they thought, a man who had inherited most of his money and had preserved it through large safe investments in steel, rubber, and oil. What his associates managed to see in Grand was usually a reflection of their own dullness: a club member, a dinner guest, a possibility, a threat—a man whose holdings represented a prospect and a danger. But this was to do injustice to Grand's private life, because his private life was atypical. For one thing, he was the last of the big spenders; and for another, he had a very unusual attitude towards *people*—he spent about ten million a year in, as he expressed it himself, "*making it hot for them.*"

It was, as a matter of fact, Guy Grand who, working through his attorneys, had bought controlling interest in the three largest kennel clubs on the eastern seaboard last season; and in this way he had gained virtual dominance over, and responsibility for, the Dog Show that year at Madison Square Garden. His number-one *gérant,* or front man, for this operation was a Señor Hernandez Gonzales, a huge Mexican, who had long been known in dog-fancier circles as a breeder of blue-ribbon Chihuahuas. With Grand's backing, however; and over a quick six months, Gonzales became the celebrated owner of one of the finest kennels in the world, known now not simply for Chihuahuas, but for Pekinese, Pomeranians and many rare and strange breeds of the Orient.

It was evident that this season's show at the Garden was to be a gala one—a wealth of new honors had been posted, the prize-money packets substantially fattened, and competition was keener than ever. Bright young men and wealthy dowagers from all over were bringing forward their best and favorite pedigrees. Gonzales himself had promised a prize specimen of a fine old breed. A national picture magazine devoted its cover to the affair and a lengthy editorial in praise of this great American benignity, this love of animals—". . . in bright and telling contrast," the editorial said, "to certain naïve barbarities, *e.g.,* the Spanish bullfight."

Thus, when the day arrived, all was as it should be. The Garden was festively decked, the spectators in holiday reverence, the lights burning, the big cameras booming, and the participants dressed as for a Papal audience—though slightly ambivalent, between not wishing to get mussed or hairy, and yet wanting to pamper and coo over their animals.

Except for the notable absence of Señor Gonzales, things went smoothly, until the final competition began, that between "Best of Breed" for the coveted "Best in Show." And at this point, Gonzales did appear; he joined the throng of owners and beasts who mingled in the center of the Garden, where it was soon apparent his boast had not been idle—at the end of the big man's leash was an extraordinary dog; he was jet-black and almost the size of a full-grown Dane, with the most striking coat and carriage yet seen at the Garden show that season. The head was dressed somewhat in the manner of a circus-cut poodle, though much exaggerated, so that half the face of the animal was truly obscured.

Gonzales joined the crowd with a jaunty smile and flourish not inappropriate to one of his eminence. He hadn't been there a moment though before he and the dog were spotted by Mrs. Winthrop-Garde and her angry little spitz.

She came forward, herself not too unlike her charge, waddling aggressively, and she was immediately followed by several other women of similar stamp, along with Pekineses, Pomeranians, and ill-tempered miniature chows.

Gonzales bowed with winning old-world grace and caressed the ladies' hands.

"What a *perfect* love he is!" shrieked Mrs. Winthrop-Garde of the animal on Gonzales's leash, and turning to her own, "*Isn't* he, my darling? *Hmm? Hmm?* Isn't he, my precious sweet? And what*ever* is his *name?*" she cried to Gonzales when her own animal failed to respond, but yapped crossly instead.

"He is called . . . *Claw,*" said Gonzales with a certain soft drama which may have escaped Mrs. Winthrop-Garde, for she rushed on, heedless as ever.

"*Claude!* It's *too* delicious—the perfect darling! Say *hello* to Claude, Angelica! Say *hello* to Claude, my fur-flower!"

And as she pulled the angry little spitz forward, while it snapped and snorted and ran at the nose, an extraordinary thing happened—for what this Grand and Gonzales had somehow contrived, and for reasons never fathomed by the press, was to introduce in disguise to the Garden show that season not a dog at all, but some kind of terrible black panther or dyed jaguar—hungry he was too, and cross as a pickle—so that before the day was out, he had not only brought chaos into the formal proceedings, but had actually destroyed about half the "Best of Breed."

During the first hour or so, Gonzales, because of his respected position in that circle, was above reproach, and all of the incidents were considered as being accidental, though, of course, extremely unfortunate.

"Too much spirit," he kept explaining, frowning and shaking his head; and, as he and the beast stalked slowly about in the midst of the group, he would chide the monster-cat:

"Overtired from the trip, I suppose. Isn't that it, boy? *Hmm? Hmm?*"

So now occasionally above the yapping and whining, the crowd would bear a strange *swish!* and *swat!* as Gonzales and the fantastic beast moved on, flushing them one by one.

Finally one woman, new to the circle, who did not know how important Gonzales was, came back with an automatic pistol and tried to shoot the big cat. But she was so beside herself with righteous fury that she missed and was swiftly arrested.

Gonzales, though, apparently no fool himself, was quick to take this as a cue that his work was done, and he gradually retired, so that "Best in Show" was settled at last, between those not already eliminated.

Grand later penned a series of scathing articles about the affair: "Scandal of the Dog Show!" "Can This Happen Here?" "Is It Someone's Idea of a Joke?" etc., etc.

The bereft owners were wealthy and influential people, more than eager to go along with the demand for an inquiry. As quickly as witnesses were uncovered, however, they were bought off by Grand or his representatives, so that nothing really ever came of it in the end—though, granted, it did cost him a good bit to keep his own name clear.

JON LEE ANDERSON

❧

FROM *Che: A Revolutionary Life* [1997]

North of the Rio Grande, the forested land rises massively toward the sky, climbing away in blue mountain eddies toward the brown lunar scree of the Andean highlands in the far distance. Above the tree line, the great denuded hills and chilly plateaus give way to swooping ravines, dotted sparsely with rustic hamlets linked to one another by footpaths and the occasional dirt road. The inhabitants, mostly Indians and mestizos, live by tending pigs or cows, their corn patches and vegetable gardens forming geometric patterns on hillsides around their adobe houses. There is little foliage, and the natives can spot a stranger coming from miles away.

For two weeks Che's band climbed steadily upward, fording rivers, climbing cliffs, running once or twice into army patrols with tracker dogs. By now, the men were all showing the symptoms of breakdown of one sort or another. They squabbled over things such as who had eaten more food, accused one another of making insults, and, like children, came to tell Che their grievances and accusations. The most alarming symptom of all was displayed by "Antonio"—Olo Pantoja—who one day claimed to see five soldiers approaching; it turned out to be a hallucination. That night, Che made a worried note about the risk this troubling apparition of war "psychosis" might have on the morale of his men.

[. . .]

By October 7, the guerrillas were in a steep ravine near La Higuera, where a narrow natural passage leads down toward the Rio Grande. Their progress had been slow because Chino Chang, whose glasses were broken, was almost blind at night, held them back considerably. Still, Che was in a reasonably upbeat mood, beginning his diary entry that day by writing: "We completed the 11th month of our guerrilla operation without complications, in a bucolic mood."

At midday, they spotted an old woman grazing goats and seized her as a precaution. She said she knew nothing about soldiers—or anything else, for that matter. Che was skeptical and sent Inti, Aniceto, and Pablo with her to her squalid little farmhouse, where they saw she had a young dwarf daughter. They gave the woman fifty pesos and told her not to speak to anyone about their presence, although they did so, Che noted, "with little hope that she will keep her word."

There were seventeen of them left now. That night they set off down-hill again, under "a very small moon," walking through a narrow stream gully whose banks were sown with potato patches. At two in the morning they stopped because of Chang, who could not see well enough to walk farther. That night, Che listened to "an unusual" army report on the radio that said that army troops had encircled the guerrillas at a place between the "Acero" and "Oro" rivers. "The news seems diversionary," he observed. He wrote down their present altitude: "2,000 meters." It was the final entry in his diary.

Early the next morning, October 8, a company of freshly trained Bolivian Army Rangers led by a tall young army captain, Gary Prado Salmon, took up positions along the ridgeline above them. They had been alerted to the guerrillas' presence by a local peasant.

As daylight broke, the guerrillas spotted the soldiers on the bare ridges hemming them in on either side. They were trapped in a brushy gully called the Quebrada del Churo, about three hundred meters long and not more than fifty wide, in places much narrower than that. Their only possible escape was to fight their way out. Che ordered his men to take up positions, splitting them into three groups. Several tense hours passed. The battle began at 1:10 in the afternoon, when a couple of the guerrillas were detected by the soldiers as they moved around. As the soldiers opened up on the men below with mortar and machine-gun fire, the Bolivian Aniceto Reinaga was killed.

In the prolonged firefight that ensued, the guerrillas lost track of one another. Partially concealed behind a large rock in the middle of a potato patch, Che fired his M-2 carbine, but it was soon hit in the barrel by a bullet, rendering it useless. The magazine of his pistol had apparently already been lost; he was now unarmed. A second bullet hit him in the calf of his left leg; a third penetrated his beret. Helped by the Bolivian Simon Cuba, "Willy," he tried to climb up the bank of the gully in an attempt to escape. Some concealed soldiers watched them approach. When they were a few feet away, a short, sturdy highland Indian named Sergeant Bernardino Huanca broke through the brush and pointed his gun at them. He claimed later that Che told him: "Don't shoot. I am Che Guevara. I am worth more to you alive than dead."

[. . .]

At Lieutenant Colonel Ayoroa's request for volunteers, a man had already offered himself for the job, a tough-looking little sergeant named Mario Terán, and he waited expectantly outside. Rodríguez looked at him and saw that his face shone as if he had been drinking. Terán had been in the firefight with Che's band the day before and was eager to avenge the deaths of his three comrades who had died in the battle.

"I told him not to shoot Che in the face, but from the neck down," said Rodríguez, for Che's wounds had to appear as though they had been inflicted in battle. "I walked up the hill and began making notes. When I heard the shots I checked my watch. It was 1:10 P.M."

There are different versions, but according to legend, Che's last words, when Mario Terán came through the door to shoot him, were: "I know you've come to kill me. Shoot, coward, you are only going to kill a man." Terán hesitated, then pointed his semiautomatic rifle and pulled the trigger, hitting Che in the arms and legs. Then, as Che writhed on the ground, apparently biting one of his wrists in an effort to avoid crying out, Terán fired another burst. The fatal bullet entered Che's thorax, filling his lungs with blood.

On October 9, 1967, at the age of thirty-nine, Che Guevara was dead.
[. . .]
Slung onto the concrete washbasin of the laundry house of Vallegrande's Nuestro Señor de Malta Hospital, Che's body lay on view that evening and throughout the next day with his head propped up, his brown eyes remaining open. To prevent his decomposition, a doctor slit his throat and injected him with formaldehyde. As a procession of people including soldiers, curious locals, photographers, and reporters filed around the body, Che looked eerily alive. Among the hospital's nuns, the nurse who washed his body, and a number of Vallegrande women, the impression that Che Guevara bore an extraordinary resemblance to Jesus Christ quickly spread; they surreptitiously clipped off clumps of his hair and kept them for good luck.
[. . .]
By now the decision to deny Che a burial site had been made; his body, like those of his comrades who had died previously, would be "disappeared." To counter the initial reactions of disbelief coming out of Havana, General Alfredo Ovando Candia wanted to decapitate Che and preserve his head as evidence. Felix Rodríguez, who was still in Vallegrande when this was proposed, claims to have argued that this solution was "too barbaric," and suggested that they just sever a finger. Ovando Candia compromised: they would amputate Che's hands. On the night of October 10, two wax death masks were made of Che's face, and his fingerprints taken; his hands were sawn off and placed in jars of formaldehyde. Soon, a pair of Argentine police forensic experts arrived to compare the fingerprints with those on file for "Ernesto Guevara de la Serna" in Buenos Aires; the identification was positive.

In the early morning hours of October 11, Che's body was disposed of, as usual, by Lieutenant Colonel Andres Selich, with a couple of other officers acting as witnesses, including—according to him—Major Mario Vargas Salinas. It was dumped, according to Selich's widow, in a secret grave dug by a bulldozer somewhere in the brushy land near the Vallegrande airstrip, while another mass grave was dug nearby to bury six of his comrades.

Che's brother Roberto arrived in town later that morning, hoping to identify his brother and retrieve his remains, but it was too late. General Ovando Candia told him he was sorry, Che's body had been "cremated." It was only one of several versions regarding the fate of his remains that would circulate in coming days as the Bolivian generals contradicted one another, and the whereabouts of Che's body would remain an unsolved mystery for the next twenty-eight years.

WILL SELF

꧁꧂

FROM *Great Apes* [1997]

Dr Zack Busner, clinical psychologist, medical doctor, radical psychoanalyst, anti-psychiatrist, maverick anxiolytic drug researcher and former television personality, stood upright in front of the bathroom mirror teasing some crumbs from the thick fur under the line of his jaw. He'd had toast for his first break-fast that morning and, as usual, managed to get a fair amount of black cherry conserve into his coat instead of his stomach. He'd washed his fur thoroughly around the neck area—using the watercomb the Busners kept for just that pur-pose—but the crumbs obstinately refused to dissolve along with the jam. And the more he attempted to dig them out, the deeper into his fur they seemed to dig in.

No matter, he thought, turning his attention to dressing, Gambol can cope with it on the way into the hospital. Gambol, Busner's research assistant, was waved upon to groom his boss a great deal. Of course, so were all the junior doctors, nurses and auxiliary workers at Heath Hospital, whether attached to the psychiatric department or not. Nowadays the more senior medical staff—and sometimes even administrators—would cluster around Busner as he swung into the hospital and attempt to get their fingers in his fur. If they couldn't give him at least a cursory groom of deference, they would present to him and then scamper off about their business.

For Busner, while a nonconformist and even zany psychiatric practitio-ner in youth and middle age, had on the cusp of old age begun to acquire some-thing approaching respectability. The doctrinal excesses of the Quantity Theory of Insanity, with which he had been associated, fresh from his analytic training under the legendary Alkan, had long since been forgotten. The theory was now viewed—if chimps thought about it at all—as a piece of amusing wrongheaded-ness, a kind of socio-psychological version of Logical Positivism, or Marxism, or Freudianism. Obviously the predictions it had been designed to make had been disproved fulsomely, and yet, a second wave of apologists had sprung up to defend the theory, pointing out that the empirical verity of a hypothesis may not be the sole criterion on which to judge its significance.

Busner took the freshly ironed shirt from the hanger dangling on the back of the door and slipped it over his rounded shoulders. His fingers were still as nimble as ever. He fastened the buttons speedily, his thumbs managing to locate the knuckles of his index fingers to effect torsion, despite the arthritis that now plagued him. When he picked up his habitual mohair tie, looped it round his thick neck, knotted it, and folded down the collar, he was further reassured by the blur of motion in the mirror.

He left the collar unbuttoned and the tie knot slack—the better for Gambol to get at the crumbs. Meanwhile, one of his feet had, without any thought on his part, snatched a curry comb from the glass shelf underneath the sink, and he now found himself absent-mindedly combing his muzzle while squinting at his own reflected features.

Pronounced eyebrow ridges with a light coping of silver-grey hairs, deeply recessed nasal bridge, neat, almond-shaped nostrils, no bagging of the muzzle, just a series of wriggling lines scored at oblique angles across the smooth skin of his full and froggy top lip. His lips were as moon-crescented and thinly generous as when he was young.

Not bad for a chimp nearing fifty, he mused, fluffing up into a halo the long tufts of grey fur surrounding his balding pate. No sign of goitre or mange, no ulcers either. At this rate I might make it to sixty! He thrust out his broad chest and flexed his long arms. While it's true that in motion—which they almost always were—his features projected an impression of barely contained energy, in repose they slumped somewhat, slid into fleshly landslip, epidermal erosion. But Busner didn't notice this. Distinguished, that's what I am, he decided, and turned to remove a tweed jacket of uncommon tuftiness from a second hanger.

Busner's return to the popular media role that he had filled with such assurance—some might say bumptiousness—while a young male had been tempered by maturity. In the previous five years he had published three books* that had enormously augmented his reputation. While ostensibly collections of his patients' case histories, they had performed the unusual feat of making quite difficult themes and theories in the fields of psychology and neurology accessible to a wide audience. Further, this had not been achieved by in any way trivialising. Busner prided himself on not condescending to his readers.

The other noteworthy aspect of the books had been the dedication with which Busner had attached himself to his unusual patients. He had hit upon an observational and expository method that synthesised the objectivity and ra-

---

*The Chimp Who Mated an Armchair, 1986; Nestings, 1988; and A Primatologist Recounts, 1992. All published by Parallel Press, London and New York.

tionalism of his medical training at Edinburgh in the sixties, the imaginative flair and creative discipline imparted by his analytic training under the legendary Alkan*, and the existential phenomenology of his work at the Concept House he had run in Willesden during the seventies. His patients were thus both studied under clinical conditions and taken out into the wider world by Busner himself.

'The important thing,' Busner would sign his students and acolytes, 'is to achieve an inter-subjective "chup-chupp" approach, somehow to enter the "euch-euch" morbid consciousness of the patient and see the world with his eyes. It is no longer sufficient to adopt a hard physiological attitude to certain disorders, or to view them as motivationally based, arid therefore solely within the purlieus of "hooo" <pure> psychiatry . . .'

While this 'inter-subjective approach' had obvious and sound credentials, both intellectual and ethical, certain wags couldn't help noticing, and remarking upon, the bowdlerising tendencies of the practice. Like morbidly ebullient chimpanzee interest stories, Busner's case histories made great copy and highly entertaining television. In pursuit of his patients' distorted phenomenologies Busner would go waterskiing with paraplegics, to the opera with chronic epileptics, to acid-house raves with hebephrenics. It had even become somewhat *de rigeur* in publishing circles to have Busner and one of his protégés present at parties.

Thus chimps who barked involuntarily as they succumbed to the tics and spasms of Tourette's syndrome, or Parkinsonian chimps whose arms and legs undulated weirdly from the effects of L-dopa, or brain-damaged chimps whose gesticulatory sallies were imprisoned within the tape loop of acute amnesia, became a familiar social sight beside more conventionally behaved agents, authors and literary journalists, jostling for canapés and free drinks. 'It is,' Busner would sign to the little groups who congregated around him at such events, 'a practical demonstration of the "gru-nn" chimpunity of my approach to these disorders. By bringing these chimps into such settings'—and at this point he would usually have to break off and administer some emergency grooming to the chimp in question—'I am "chup-chupp" actively deconstructing the ideological categories that surround our notions of disease.'

Busner finished dressing and jumped up to pull the rear-view mirror down on its retractable arm from the ceiling. Is my anus clean? he mused, sending one exploratory hand round his broad back to grope in its folds and pleats of yellow-pink ischial skin, then bringing it up to his flared nostrils and waggling

*For a full discussion of Alkan's analytic method see his 'Implied Techniques in Psychoanalysis' (*British Journal of Ephemera*, March 1956).

lip. But despite the ghastly bout of the shits that had afflicted him when he got back from L'Escargot the previous evening, everything about his rear looked well sluiced. Gambol can go over it again on the way to the hospital, he decided, and straightening his jacket to ensure that the hem was above his magnificently effulgent arsehole, Busner snapped off the bathroom light, took a sprightly swing off the handhold at the side of the door, and bounded off down the corridor, his big balls swinging this way and that.

JEANETTE WINTERSON

❧

FROM *The Passion* [1997]

Our companion loosed her laces but kept her boots on, and seeing my surprise at forgoing this unexpected luxury said, 'My father was a boatman. Boatmen do not take off their boots.' We were silent, either out of respect for her customs or sheer exhaustion, but it was she who offered to tell us her story if we chose to listen.

'A fire and a tale,' said Patrick. 'Now all we need is a drop of something hot,' and he fathomed from the bottom of his unfathomable pockets another stoppered jar of evil spirit.

This was her story.

I have always been a gambler. It's a skill that comes naturally to me like thieving and loving. What I didn't know by instinct I picked up from working the Casino, from watching others play and learning what it is that people value and therefore what it is they will risk. I learned how to put a challenge in such a way as to make it irresistible. We gamble with the hope of winning, but it's the thought of what we might lose that excites us.

How you play is a temperamental thing; cards, dice, dominoes, jacks, such preferences are frills merely. All gamblers sweat. I come from the city of chances, where everything is possible but where everything has a price. In this city great fortunes are won and lost overnight. It has always been so. Ships that carry silk and spices sink, the servant betrays the master, the secret is out and the bell tolls another accidental death. But penniless adventurers have always been welcome here too, they are good luck and very often their good luck rubs off on themselves. Some who come on foot leave on horseback and others who trumpeted their estate beg on the Rialto. It has always been so.

The astute gambler always keeps something back, something to play with another time; a pocket watch, a hunting dog. But the Devil's gambler keeps back something precious, something to gamble with only once in a lifetime. Behind the secret panel he keeps it, the valuable, fabulous thing that no one suspects he has.

I knew a man like that; not a drunkard sniffing after every wager nor an addict stripping the clothes off his back rather than go home. A thoughtful man who they say had trade with gold and death. He lost heavily, as gamblers do; he won surprisingly, as gamblers do, but he never showed much emotion, never led me to suspect that much important was at stake. A hobbyist, I thought, dismissing him. You see, I like passion, I like to be among the desperate.

I was wrong to dismiss him. He was waiting for the wager that would seduce him into risking what he valued. He was a true gambler, he was prepared to risk the valuable, fabulous thing but not for a dog or a cock or the casual dice.

On a quiet evening, when the tables were half empty and the domino sets lay in their boxes, he was there, wandering, fluttering, drinking and flirting.

I was bored.

Then a man came into the room, not one of our regulars, not one any of us knew, and after a few half-hearted games of chance he spied this figure and engaged him in conversation. They talked for upwards of half an hour and so intently that we thought they must be old friends and lost our curiosity in the assumption of habit. But the rich man with his strangely bowed companion by his side asked leave to make an announcement, a most remarkable wager, and we cleared the central floor and let him speak.

It seemed that his companion, this stranger, had come from the wastes of the Levant, where exotic lizards breed and all is unusual. In his country, no man bothered with paltry fortunes at the gaming table, they played for higher stakes.

A life.

The wager was a life. The winner should take the life of the loser in whatsoever way he chose. However slowly he chose, with whatever instruments he chose. What was certain was that only one life would be spared.

Our rich friend was clearly excited. His eyes looked past the faces and tables of the gaming room into a space we could not inhabit; into the space of pain and loss. What could it matter to him that he might lose fortunes?

He had fortunes to lose.

What could it matter to him that he might lose mistresses?

There are women enough.

What would it matter to him that he might lose his life?

He had one life. He cherished it.

There were those that night who begged him not to go on with it, who saw a sinister aspect in this unknown old man, who were perhaps afraid of being made the same offer and of refusing.

What you risk reveals what you value.

These were the terms.

A game of three.

The first, the roulette, where only fate is queen.

The second, the cards, where skill has some part.

The third, the dominoes, where skill is paramount and chance is there in disguise.

Will she wear your colours?

This is the city of disguises.

The terms were agreed and strictly supervised. The winner was two out of three or in the event of some onlooker crying Nay! a tie, chosen at random, by the manager of the Casino.

The terms seemed fair. More than fair in this cheating world, but there were still some who felt uneasy about the unknown man, unassuming and unthreatening as he seemed.

If the Devil plays dice, will he come like this?

Will he come so quietly and whisper in our ear?

If he came as an angel of light, we should be immediately on our guard.

The word was given: Play on.

We drank throughout the first game, watching the red and black spin under our hands, watching the bright streak of metal dally with one number, then another, innocent of win or lose. At first it seemed as though our rich friend must win, but at the last moment the ball sprang out of its slot and spun again with that dwindling sickening sound that marks the last possible change.

The wheel came to rest.

It was the stranger whom fortune loved.

There was a moment's silence, we expected some sign, some worry on one part, some satisfaction on another, but with faces of wax, the two men got up and walked to the optimistic baize. The cards. No man knows what they may hold. A man must trust his hand.

Swift dealing. These were accustomed to the game.

They played for perhaps an hour and we drank. Drank to keep our lips wet, our lips that dried every time a card fell and the stranger seemed doomed to victory. There was an odd sense in the room that the stranger must not win, that for all our sakes he must lose. We willed our rich friend to weld his wits with his luck and he did.

At the cards, he won and they were even.

The two men met each other's gaze for a moment before they seated themselves in front of the dominoes and in each face was something of the other. Our rich friend had assumed a more calculating expression, while his challenger's face was more thoughtful, less wolfish than before.

It was clear from the start that they were evenly matched at this game too. They played deftly, judging the gaps and the numbers, making lightning calculations, baffling each other. We had stopped drinking. There was neither sound nor movement save the clicking of the dominoes on the marble table.

It was past midnight. I heard the water lapping at the stones below. I heard my saliva in my throat. I heard the dominoes clicking on the marble table.

There were no dominoes left. No gaps.

The stranger had won.

The two men stood up simultaneously, shook hands. Then the rich man placed his hands on the marble, and we saw they were shaking. Fine comfortable hands that were shaking. The stranger noticed and with a little smile suggested they complete the terms of their wager.

None of us spoke up, none of us tried to stop him. Did we want it to happen? Did we hope that one life might substitute for many?

I do not know our motives, I only know that we were silent.

This was the death: dismemberment piece by piece beginning with the hands.

The rich man nodded almost imperceptibly and, bowing to us, left in the company of the stranger. We heard nothing more, never saw either of them again, but one day, months later, when we had comforted ourselves that it was a joke, that they had parted at the corner, out of sight, given each other a fright, nothing more, we received a pair of hands, manicured and quite white, mounted on green baize in a glass case. Between the finger and thumb of the left was a roulette ball and between the finger and thumb of the right, a domino.

The manager hung the case on the wall and there it hangs today.

I have said that behind the secret panel lies a valuable, fabulous thing. We are not always conscious of it, not always aware of what it is we hide from prying eyes or that those prying eyes may sometimes be our own.

There was a night, eight years ago, when a hand that took me by surprise slid the secret panel and showed me what it was I kept to myself.

My heart is a reliable organ, how could it be my heart? My everyday, work-hard heart that laughed at life and gave nothing away. I have seen dolls from the east that fold in one upon the other, the one concealing the other and so I know that the heart may conceal itself.

It was a game of chance I entered into and my heart was the wager. Such games can only be played once.

Such games are better not played at all.

It was a woman I loved and you will admit that is not the usual thing. I knew her for only five months. We had nine nights together and I never saw her again. You will admit that is not the usual thing.

I have always preferred the cards to the dice so it should have come as no surprise to me to have drawn a wild card.

The Queen of spades.

She lived simply and elegantly and her husband was sometimes called away to examine a new rarity (he dealt in books and maps); he was called away soon after we met. For nine days and nights we stayed in her house, never opening the door, never looking out of the window.

We were naked and not ashamed.

And we were happy.

On the ninth day I was left alone for a while because she had certain household affairs to attend to before her husband's return. On that day the rain splashed against the windows and filled up the canals below, churning the rubbish that lies under the surface, the rubbish that feeds the rats and the exiles in their dark mazes. It was early in the New Year. She had told me she loved me. I never doubted her word because I could feel how true it was. When she touched me I knew I was loved and with a passion I had not felt before. Not in another and not in myself.

Love is a fashion these days and in this fashionable city we know how to make light of love and how to keep our hearts at bay. I thought of myself as a civilised woman and I found I was a savage. When I thought of losing her I wanted to drown both of us in some lonely place rather than feel myself a beast that has no friend.

On the ninth night we ate and drank as usual alone in the house, the servants dismissed. She liked to cook omelettes with herbs and these we ate with hot radishes she had got from a merchant. Occasionally our conversation faltered and I saw tomorrow in her eyes. Tomorrow when we would part and resume our life of strange meetings in unfamiliar quarters. There was a café we usually went to, full of students from Padua and artists seeking inspiration. She was not known there. Her friends could not find her out. Thus we had met and met too in hours that did not belong to us, until this gift of nine nights.

I did not meet her sadness; it was too heavy.

There is no sense in loving someone you can never wake up to except by chance.

The gambler is led on in the hope of a win, thrilled with the fear of losing and when he wins he believes his luck is there, that he will win again.

If nine nights were possible why not ten?

So it goes and the weeks pass waiting for the tenth night, waiting to win again and all the time losing bit by bit that valuable, fabulous thing that cannot be replaced.

Her husband dealt only in what was unique, he never bought a treasure someone else might have.

Would he buy my heart then and give it to her?

I had already wagered it for nine nights. In the morning when I left I did not say I would not see her again. I simply made no arrangement. She did not press me to do so, she had often said that as she got older she took what she could of life but expected little.

Then I was gone.

Every time I was tempted to go to her I went to the Casino instead and watched some fool humiliating himself at the tables. I could gamble on another night, reduce myself a little more, but after the tenth night would come the eleventh and the twelfth and so on into the silent space that is the pain of never having enough. The silent space full of starving children. She loved her husband.

I decided to marry.

There was a man who had wanted me for some time, a man I had refused, cursed. A man I despised. A rich man with fat fingers. He liked me to dress as a boy. I like to dress as a boy now and then. We had that in common.

He came to the Casino every night, playing for high stakes but not gambling with anything too precious. He was no fool. He clasped me with his terrible hands, with fingertips that had the feel of boils bursting, and asked me if I'd changed my mind about his offer. We could travel the world he said. Just the three of us. Him, me and my codpiece.

The city I come from is a changeable city. It is not always the same size. Streets appear and disappear overnight, new waterways force themselves over dry land. There are days when you cannot walk from one end to the other, so far is the journey, and there are days when a stroll will take you round your kingdom like a tin-pot Prince.

I had begun to feel that this city contained only two people who sensed each other and never met. Whenever I went out I hoped and dreaded to see the other. In the faces of strangers I saw one face and in the mirror I saw my own.

The world.

The world is surely wide enough to walk without fear.

We were married without ceremony and set off straight away to France, to Spain, to Constantinople even. He was as good as his word in that respect and I drank my coffee in a different place each month.

There was, in a certain city where the climate was fine, a young Jewish man who loved to drink his coffee at the pavement cafés and watch the world go by. He saw sailors and travellers and women with swans in their hair and all manner of fanciful distractions.

One day he saw a young woman flying past, her clothes flying out behind her.

She was beautiful and because he knew that beauty makes us good he asked her to stop awhile and share his coffee.

'I'm running away,' she said.

'Who are you running away from?'

'Myself.'

But she agreed to sit awhile because she was lonely.

His name was Salvadore.

They talked about the mountain ranges and the opera. They talked about animals with metal coats that can swim the length of a river without coming up for air. They talked about the valuable, fabulous thing that everyone has and keeps a secret. 'Here,' said Salvadore, 'look at this,' and he took out a box enamelled on the outside and softly lined on the inside and on the inside was his heart.

'Give me yours in exchange.'

But she couldn't because she was not travelling with her heart, it was beating in another place.

She thanked the young man and went back to her husband, whose hands crept over her body like crabs.

And the young man thought often of a beautiful woman on that sunny day when the wind had pushed out her earrings like fins.

We travelled for two years, then I stole his watch and what money he had on him and left him. I dressed as a boy to escape detection, and while he snored off his red wine and most of a goose I lost myself in the dark that has always been a friend.

I got odd jobs on ships and in grand houses, learned to speak five languages and did not see that city of destiny for another three years, then I caught a ship home on a whim and because I wanted my heart back. I should have known better than to risk my luck in the shrinking city. He soon found me out and his fury at being robbed and abandoned had not abated, even though he was living with another woman by then.

A friend of his, a sophisticated man, suggested a little wager for the two of us, a way of solving our differences. We were to play cards and if I won, I should have my freedom to come and go as I pleased and enough money to do so. If I lost, my husband should do with me as he pleased, though he was not to molest or murder me.

What choice had I?

At the time, I thought I played badly, but I later discovered by chance that the pack was fixed, that the wager had been fixed from the start. As I told you, my husband is no fool.

It was the Jack of hearts that caught me out.

When I lost, I thought he would force me home and that would be an end to it, but instead he kept me waiting three days and then sent a message for me to meet him.

He was with his friend when I arrived and an officer of high rank, a Frenchman whom I discovered to be General Murat.

This officer looked me up and down in my woman's clothes then asked me to change into my easy disguise. He was all admiration and, turning from me, withdrew a large bag from within his effects and placed it on the table between himself and my husband.

'This is the price we agreed then,' he said.

And my husband, his fingers trembling, counted it out.

He had sold me.

I was to join the army, to join the Generals for their pleasure.

It was, Murat assured me, quite an honour.

They didn't give me enough time to collect my heart, only my luggage, but I'm grateful to them for that; this is no place for a heart.

She was silent. Patrick and I, who had not uttered a word nor moved at all save to shield our scorching feet, felt unable to speak. It was she who broke the silence again.

'Pass me that evil spirit, a story deserves a reward.'

She seemed carefree and the shadows that had crossed her face throughout her story had lifted, but I felt my own just beginning.

She would never love me.

I had found her too late.

I wanted to ask her more about her watery city that is never the same, to see her eyes light up for love of something if not for love of me, but she was already spreading her furs and settling to sleep.

IVAN KLÍMA

❦

FROM *The Ultimate Intimacy* [1998]

Translated from the Czech by A. G. Brain

Matouš

Matouš leaves the courthouse. Even though he feels that the woman judge who has just released him fairly willingly from the shackles of marriage has removed his life's heaviest burden from him, he is overcome by nostalgia. He stops outside the front entrance. Although he won't admit it, he is waiting for Klára.

Finally Klára appears and notices him. She seems to hesitate for a moment, wondering whether to walk past him disdainfully as if he was of less interest than the window display of some boutique, but then she stops and says: 'Ciao then, you poor old devil. Enjoy yourself!'

She then permits Matouš to light her cigarette before walking away on high heels towards a Honda car in which some foreign devil is waiting for her. She climbs into the seat next to him and then drives out of Matouš's life, probably for good.

Matouš should feel relieved and light-headed at the prospect of a future of calm stretching out before him as well as the fulfilment of his destiny, but instead his legs become heavy.

He walks home, takes off his coat and stretches out on the bed. He lies there for a long time, several hours, gazing up at the ceiling and slowly drags himself through the thicket of hopeless contemplations. On the bedside table there is a jug of wine from the previous day, along with a loaf of bread going stale and a bowl of boiled rice with peanuts. There is no knife to hand so he simply breaks off lumps of bread and slowly chews them. There is also a pile of books by the bed. From time to time he picks up the topmost one and leafs through it for a while before tossing it to one side.

The ceiling is covered in cracks and the dirty threads of cobwebs which flutter in the draught that wafts into the room along with the screech of tram wheels and the din of lorries.

Faces flicker across the greyish surface of the ceiling. Some of them are savage and long forgotten, others are familiar: they are alive, more alive than all the faces of actors and non-actors that move across the television or cinema screens. Women whom he trusted or on whom he even showered love, while knowing they would leave him in the end, scowl and leer at him. He tries to ignore them and to ignore Klára who wantonly tumbles into bed with unknown men.

His thoughts turn to the nurse whom he now takes the liberty of calling Hana. He has already been twice to the church and listened to the confused litanies of her husband, whose aura has already totally disappeared, or possibly Matouš has not been able to concentrate enough to make it out. The time that Matouš was invited to lunch by the minister's wife, he actually had a conversation with the minister. He had felt an unconscious need to take issue with that follower of the resurrected Christ. Did the minister know that the Chinese, the world's most populated nation, had managed to get by without believing in a god and yet the people did not live any less morally than in those places where they acknowledged a god or gods? The minister was aware of this. In the East, he said, there was less individualism and people were more obedient to an order that had been established over centuries.

Did that mean that concepts of a god or gods and an immortal soul were simply products of our individualism, of our reluctance to countenance the extinction of our own selves?

The minister said that was not what he had in mind, although anxiety about the extinction of the self certainly played a role in our notions of God.

The minister was either incredibly conciliatory or was consumed with doubts of some kind. Either about himself or about God.

Matouš has only spoken to the minister's wife a couple of times since he promised her his poems, and he still hasn't taken them to her. He has been waiting for some more suitable moment: he has the feeling that his poems ought to crown his acquaintance with that woman, rather than be an opening gambit.

But on one occasion, when he was feeling particularly bad and Hana brought him his medicine for the second time, he had recited to her some of his poems and told her that she had been the inspiration for them.

Surely not—she replied in astonishment—how could I have?

Just by being you, he told her. There is something mysterious about you, something oriental and mystical.

That's all in your imagination, she commented.

No. My whole life was meaningless until I met you.

You sound delirious, she laughed in embarrassment, and even touched his forehead to see if he had a fever, but she took her hand away before he had time to press it to his forehead.

Now Matouš thinks about that good woman with particular intensity. He thinks about her not only because his solitariness was officially confirmed today, but also because he has an odd premonition that something bad has befallen Hana and that she might perhaps welcome Matouš's attention.

He ought to phone her and offer his help should she require it, but at this moment he lacks the will to do anything.

He who does, loses. All we hold we lose in the end.

Matouš falls asleep.

When he wakes up he can hear the boom of the ocean waves and the murmur of the crowd as they watch condemned prisoners being driven away to execution. Curiosity and indifference in the ant heap. Blazing fires.

Then his mother's voice intrudes upon him: Mattie, why aren't you eating? Stop complaining, Mattie, and pull yourself together, everything's going to be all right again. The touch of his mother's hand stroking his hair.

Matouš realizes that it is a long time since he visited either his mother's or his father's grave. That's bad. It is one's duty to pay respect to those who gave one life, and his mother was the only good woman he had met in his life. Then Matouš's thoughts stray once more to another woman, to Nurse Hana, and he realizes that he misses her; he misses her voice and her smile, he misses a mother's love.

At last he gets up, opens the refrigerator and finds in it a piece of dry salami and gobbles it down. Then he opens a can of goulash and with his fingers he fishes out pieces of meat from the unpleasantly smelling sauce before throwing the can into the pedal bin which emits a swarm of flies the moment he opens the lid.

He takes a shower and puts on a clean shirt.

For weeks now his poems have lain waiting on the table in a black binder. He has chosen almost two hundred of them, precisely one hundred and eighty-seven of them, in fact: the ones he feels sure are successful. He resists the temptation to open the binder and read at least the best ones once more—he knows them by heart anyway.

He lifts the receiver and hesitates for a moment before dialling the number of the manse. Luckily enough, the minister's wife answers the telephone.

He announces himself, but apparently she cannot recall his name, as she says: 'I expect you want to speak to my husband. I'm afraid he's in hospital.'

The nurse's voice is unusually sad.

'Anything serious?' he asks.

'A heart attack.'

'I hadn't heard. I'm sorry to hear it, Hana. And how is he?'

'Thank you. I think he has got over the worst of it.'

'I'm glad to hear it.' Nurse Hana is wrong, because she believes in some medical gadgetry and doesn't realize that her husband's life force is fading. She doesn't realize she will come into his wealth. It is unlikely she gives it a thought. He therefore says once more, 'I really am glad to hear it, you must have been very worried.'

'I expect you're calling about your poems,' the minister's wife recalls. 'You promised me them ages ago.'

'Only partly. I just had the feeling all of a sudden that something had happened to you, that something was troubling you and I ought to give you a ring.'

'Troubling me? Oh, yes, there's always something troubling one.' The minister's wife remains silent for a moment and he says: 'Everything will be all right again, you'll see.'

'Nothing will ever be the way it used to be,' says the minister's wife and Matouš makes out a quiet sob. Then that good woman forces herself to turn her thoughts from her own distress and ask him what his poems are about.

He says that it is impossible to say in a few words. They are attempts at capturing his moods, but he wouldn't like to bother her with them now, not unless his poems might bring her a little comfort.

Yes, that's something she would need at this moment. From the tone of her voice Matouš recognizes that Hana's thoughts are divorced from her words. None the less he tells her that poetry is there to console. Like music. Or meditation. Or prayer.

'If you like, and if you happen to be passing, you're welcome to drop by with them,' the minister's wife decides all of a sudden.

'Right away?'

'If you like. I have to visit my husband this afternoon.'

'Thank you, matron. I'll come in time to spend a little while with you. After all, you visited me when I was feeling low.'

Matouš is suddenly full of energy. He puts on his most expensive, pure silk tie—a golden Chinese dragon against a blue background—and carefully combs his thinning and already grizzled hair. Then he puts into his briefcase the black binder containing the one hundred and eighty-seven poems that will perhaps be published after all, just as he might eventually hope to receive some love or at least understanding. At the kiosk by the tram stop he buys three white carnations.

The minister's wife opens the door and thanks him for the flowers before inviting him in. She is pale and her eyes are red, either from lack of sleep or crying. If Matouš were to be taken to the hospital, or if he actually died there, who would weep for him?

Matouš asks after her husband's health once again. Hana is making coffee and in the process she gives him some of the details in a succinct and matter-of-fact way. Her husband is getting better; if things continue the way they have gone so far, he could be home in two weeks. He is being well looked after in the hospital and he is even in a side ward now, with a bedside telephone.

Matouš has the impression that her description of her husband is all a bit too professional, as if the sorrow in her face was related to something other than her husband's illness.

'So there's no point in upsetting yourself, Hana,' he says. 'In any case, you won't change fate by upsetting yourself.'

'Don't you think so? There are things I can't tell you, anyway.' The minister's wife pours the coffee into pink cups.

'All the more reason not to upset yourself,' Matouš repeats. 'We have to take life as it comes and realize that everything will pass away one day: pain and joy, and in the end ourselves too. Because what are we compared to the sky and the stars? Or even to a tree? At least within trees there is peace, whereas we just wriggle around in the throes of passion, rage, longing and betrayal.'

The matron sips her coffee. She looks away from him. Then she says: 'You're not like I thought you were.'

'In what way?'

'You're more serious.'

'We all have several faces. And we generally conceal the real one from other people.'

'I always thought there were people who didn't conceal anything.'

'And don't you think so any more?'

'I've never concealed anything,' she says, avoiding an answer.

'Everyone conceals something,' Matouš objects, 'we all have some secret or other.'

'All right. I've never done anything I would have to conceal.'

Matouš is now convinced that the source of her distress is not merely her husband's illness. Some duplicity or other has shaken her faith in human goodness. 'I'm sure that you would be incapable of harming anyone,' he says. 'I have never deceived anyone either.'

He looks at the woman opposite; there is still sorrow in her face, but also kindness. All of a sudden it is as if he was transported back whole decades: his mother is waiting for him with his lunch and asking how things were in school and he is starting to speak, complaining about his fellow pupils for mocking him or even beating him up. Matouš starts to take the minister's wife into his confidence. He doesn't speak about his travels, or about his real or imagined experiences in foreign parts, he speaks about himself, how he was deceived by women he loved, and most of all by the latest one, whom he took into his home and whom he divorced only yesterday.

Matouš starts to lament over his own goodness of heart and the ingratitude that has been his reward. He also talks about everything he had wanted to achieve in his life, but how he had managed almost none of it, because the world is not well disposed towards people like him, people who don't elbow their way through life, who lack both influence and property. The world is not wise—it respects strength, not decency and honesty. It's not interested in real values. People want to have a good time and live it up, regardless of what they destroy in the process.

The matron listens to him, the same way his mother used to. He has the feeling she agrees with him; subconsciously, Matouš is expecting this nice little lady, this good woman, to rise and come over to him, stroke his hair and say: Stop complaining, Mattie, and pull yourself together, everything's going to be all right again!

'You're not part of that world either,' Matouš goes on to say. 'That's why you are in low spirits. People like us ought to get together and live in mutual trust, so as to bear our burden more easily.'

Hana makes no response to his challenge, to his declaration. She looks at her watch and says, 'I'm sorry, but I have to dash to the hospital to see my husband.'

Matouš is taken aback. He starts to apologize for holding her up and heaping his own troubles on her when she has plenty of her own.

'Don't worry, I'm used to it. People often used to come to me like this; I am a minister's wife after all.'

Matouš suddenly collapses inside and can scarcely find the strength to get up. He doesn't even offer to accompany Hana to the hospital or take her there by taxi, seeing that he has delayed her.

No sooner does he reach the street than he realizes he has forgotten to give Hana his poems. Now he is unlikely ever to show them to her. In fact he is unlikely to show them to anyone at all. His poems will remain hidden like many other people's verses and, like many other people, he will end his days in loneliness.

FRANCISCO GOLDMAN

※

FROM *The Long Night of White Chickens* [1998]

Here is the other of Flor's most significant two letters, which arrived postmarked from Guatemala one month after her final visit to New York, almost four months before that final seventeenth of February, 1983. It was the next to last written communication I received from her, not counting her annual Los Quetzalitos Christmas card. It began with a "Dear Roger" and then just plunged in:

"Maybe you are never so involved with a lover, so full of a sense of dramatic discovery about your lover, as during the days when you are trying to work up the decisiveness to leave him. Sensing the end, you begin to pull away, and resent him all the more because he makes it so difficult for you to finalize the break. In a way, I have come to realize, you don't live *in* a small country so much as *with it,* in a way comparable to how you might find yourself sharing your life with a not necessarily complex but completely involving and painfully demanding person. You pick up habits, gestures, and deeper attitudes. One day this relationship can end, and you will go your own way, but what you've picked up might remain a part of you forever, and no one who doesn't know that country personally will recognize these traits in you at all. Thus, in New York, someone well might say, 'Why, how very French of you' or how German, Japanese, or Russian, but how many people there will ever say, 'Flor, how very Guatemalan of you,' when faced, for example, with my strangely caustic delight over a news story about a wealthy young Colombian bridegroom honeymooning in New York who, while his virgin bride prepared herself for the consummation of their marriage in the bathroom of their luxurious hotel suite, jumped up and down on the bed out of happiness and anticipation. Jumped up and down so much, you see, from so much happiness and anticipation, that he became dizzy, lost his balance, and fell through the window that he'd apparently pushed the bed up against so that they could bask in the drama of the imperial view during the consummation. Eighteen stories he plummeted, dressed only in his leopard-patterned bikini briefs, gold crucifix, and Cartier watch, to his death on Park Avenue.

"Many *guatemaltecos* had the chance to laugh or sigh with caustic or lamenting delight over that story when it was picked up from a North American wire service and prominently featured in the country's most popular paper. But that same day's *New York Times* made no mention of it. I didn't see the *New York Post,* of course, but I would guess that if they did report it they stressed the possible suicide or murder angle. Perhaps they would have discovered that the Colombian bridegroom came from a loutish drug cartel family and the bride from a distinguished one fallen on hard economic times and for that or perhaps other reasons would not have been as inclined as the Guatemalans to take at face value the bride's story of how as she prepared herself in the bathroom she could hear the bedsprings bouncing. Perhaps this is simply a question of cultural aesthetics or even morality, the type of story each culture prefers. I happen to know that the North American wire service report not only made no mention of the social standing of the newlyweds' respective families, they didn't mention what the groom was wearing as he plunged to his death either, nor what the bride heard as she prepared herself or said later. In fact, there was no mention of the bride's actual activities before the fatal free-fall at all. The wire service merely told that a young Colombian honeymooner had fallen to his death from the window of an elegant hotel in New York City, but an enterprising Guatemalan newspaperman had embellished those details in a way that his countrymen would especially appreciate. I am always surprised whenever a visiting foreigner expresses the opinion that we are a dour bunch with no sense of humor at all.

"So you can end up hating a small country just as you would a person. You cannot hate the United States, can you, with that sort of intensity without seeming a blind demagogue or extremist or plainly maladjusted— isn't the United States just too big, too full of situations and choices? (Needless to say, I have some not at all well-traveled Guatemalan friends who would disagree.) You live *in* the United States, amidst it, surrounded by it, and yet somehow always way off to the side with almost everyone else, spun out by a great centrifugal force, by that muscular, naked Idea of our Greatness holding the rest of us by the tail and spinning: the blur has become our nearsighted and *so* controversial focus. (Notice my slippery possessives: *my* Guate, *my* USA.) But isn't it true that certain abstractly peripatetic French philosophers count among our blessings particularly what so many prominent Latin American intellectuals denounce? Our theoretically blissful amnesia, our nation of Mr. Magoos driving through our neon Mojave of perpetually new *new.* Is that really the world I dispatch some of my quite historically prefaced orphans into? Is that more harmful than what the other side of the ocean offers them? Who am I to pass such judgments? But don't I remain here now because I trust myself to decide better than anyone else? Better to rely on the providential handshake and love springing to life in baby breath—charmed eyes than on eeny meeny miney mo, *cacara macara títere fue,* you to Sweden, you to Ohio, ho ho ho . . .?

"You cannot really love the United States with the same focused particularity and compassion you might feel towards a small country either. You would not ever sum up your understanding of the United States over a cup of coffee or two and then find yourself weeping over it. Directing a black bitter laugh at the United States, is this not like spitting into a rain cloud? Shouting *I love the USA* is not much more poignant than standing up and waving a big Stars and Stripes at a televised sporting event. *Triste*—this is much too flea sized a word to ever apply to the United States. Guatemala is bottomless grief in a demitasse.

"That's really all I've been trying to say.

"Listen, the city is so silent tonight, and a cool steady wind, like a minstral"—I guess that here Flor meant mistral, the steady wind that blows out of North Africa across the Mediterranean, unless she meant minstrel, or else an intentional evocation of both—"is fanning the leaves outside. If the wind is headed in the right direction, then it might carry into hearing range the roars and growls of the jaguars and lions in the zoo, which is less than a mile away. The jaguars from our jungles, mythological to the Maya, the lions from Africa. They wake up in their cramped cages roaring for their breakfasts of raw horse meat or in grief over their shattered dreams of jungle empires, and sometimes the wind will carry it here. Some of the children, when they hear it, talk of nothing else the next day. I more quietly share their enthrallment. But we take them frequently to the zoo, where we hear and see these animals up close. So it is this wind, liberating and blending the roars of Guatemalan jaguars and African lions into 'last night's' single enchanted *tigre,* that seems magical."

ROBERT OLEN BUTLER

❦

FROM *Mr. Spaceman* [2000]

I am Edna Bradshaw's husband, officially, by the customs of my home planet, and I am Edna Bradshaw's Spaceman Lover, by the customs of her former colleagues at Mary Lou's Southern Belle Beauty Nook in Bovary, Alabama. My hands are ready to initiate the actions that are most commonly associated with intimacy on this planet, given either role. But my cute-enough-to-eat Edna seems very tired and I choose instead to place her nearer to her dreams and, as intimacy is understood on my planet, even closer to me. Though on my planet we do not use the prophylactic of words with our voices. Be Safe, Be Sorry. I wave my hand and she sighs and drifts and I bring forth her voice to put inside me. I suggest a direction, gently, though this is not always effective: "Tell me about the sadness you feel at the pride in your sausage."

Edna looks about and then finds my eyes and the sounds begin, my own mouth moving in synchronicity. *The party went so well, don't you think? At least until the gun went off. It's not easy to cook for strangers, especially when they could be from all sorts of places other than Alabama. Sausage. Oh my. So much depends on sausage. You take a one-pound roll of sausage and there are so many things to consider. Spicy or mild, for instance, though if there's strangers with foreign tastes, you should always err on the conservative side. You choose the mild sausage, and if you're making it into sausage balls, Kraft American cheese. If they want a sharp cheese, then you can let them find that somewhere else along the table, if it's big enough, or for their next meal. If all they've got is what you're giving them and all you can give them is one thing, then better safe than sorry when it comes to spice.*

You need a good biscuit mix, and that's a choice right there, though I'm partial to Bisquick. And when you put all that together, you've got to have the stomach of a brain surgeon, I tell you. You can only do it with your hands. You try to make sausage and dry biscuit mix and grated cheese blend together—blend, you understand—it's like getting your daddy and your worthless ex-husband and your best friend at the hairdresser to lie down together naked in the town square of a Sunday afternoon. You got nothing to do but put your hands in it and they end up coated with grease.

This isn't what I'm trying to say, exactly. I am—well, let's face it—a little over forty years old, and I still don't know what happens when I start talking. Do you think I actually want to have a picture in my head of my own flesh-and-blood daddy and my gone-to-seed ex-husband and Ida Mae Pickett, who is the dearest girl in Bovary but maybe also the largest, lying buck naked in the grass under the statue of the South's Defenders? These are thoughts no human being should ought to have. But don't I also know that all three of them aren't near as hurtful to me there in the grass than if they're still talking to me in my head like they can do? Isn't that why when we tell things, they get bigger than life, all bent out of shape? So you can look at them and not have to take them so real?

How many mornings of my life was it just a frying pan and my daddy sitting in his undershirt with his chest hairs sticking out and his sausage patties frying there in front of me. Grease is grease. And so is sausage. Nothing bizarre about that. And my daddy talking in a long unstoppable sizzle of words about how I was too fat and too lazy and too much like my dead mama and too liberal in my thinking and did I get the brand of sausage without the monosodium glutamate this time, he wasn't having anything Chinese in his morning sausage, he was an American and proud of it. My daddy was a difficult man, but he wasn't ignorant. He knew how to read a label on a package and figure out what it meant. As far as I was concerned, if a thing was Chinese and made the flavor better—even of your country sausage—then it was okay. Even Tennessee Pride has that MSG in it, and they're still proud.

And if I just said to Daddy, "This is pure sausage, nothing but," he'd never know the difference anyway, from the taste, except it'd be good, and that's what he wanted. So sometimes I'd feed him the un-American sausage, making sure to throw out the label so he couldn't read it. To tell the truth, I'd rather lie to my daddy than disappoint him in the matter of his sausage. All his life long, he'd eat his breakfast one way. He'd cut the center right out of one of his patties and put it on the side and then eat all his eggs and his grits and his toast and all the other sausage, mixing them up together, wolfing them down, but he'd save that center bite for last. And it all came down to that. I couldn't help myself caring, being who I am. And it's been that way all my life. For a few years, my caring so bad about a thing like that shifted from my daddy to my husband. But he run away to Mobile in pursuit of I don't know what-all and I went back and lived with Daddy for a spell, till he got tired of me in general and he bought me and Eddie our mobile home out on the edge of town. Still, he done that on the condition that weekday mornings I'd continue to make his breakfast before I went in to work. Pretty much till my spaceman lover come into my life, I'd sit at the kitchen table where I grew up and wait till there was nothing left on my daddy's plate but that last bite of sausage and he'd slow way down and then at last he'd spear it with his fork and lift it up, like he was a Catholic which he wasn't, far from it, but if he was, he would've crossed himself right then, before putting it on his tongue, it was that important to him.

And the sad thing was, till I flew off into outer space for the first time, it was that important for me, too. My daddy'd taken everything else away, to feel good about. You know what I mean? I heard all those words he said. I knew I didn't have much to take pride in. Except that bite of sausage.

Weary now, and sad again, we stop speaking, my wife Edna Bradshaw and I. I am. I am apart. I wish to place my sixteen fingertips upon her. But her eyes droop shut, and I take her in my hands but I help her to slide down, her body sinking beneath the covers as if this were the sea and she were a pirate ship full of treasure.

ANTÓNIO LOBOS ANTUNES

※※

FROM *The Natural Order of Things* [2000]

Translated from the Portuguese by Richard Zenith

There are those who fly in the air and those who fly under the earth, although they're not yet dead, and I, daughter, belong to the latter group, having flown at a depth of a thousand feet with a lamp on my forehead, surrounded by blacks, in the tunnels of the Johannesburg mines, pushing ore-filled wagons along perspiring walls, and sometimes, while sitting on a rail eating canned food for lunch, I could hear the deceased floating—with their wedding clothes and endlessly sad flowers—far above me, almost next to the sun, separated from daylight only by their tombstones and crosses, the deceased who did not dare to descend as far as we did or to go up with us in the elevator which at day's end discharged us on the surface, still with picks in hand, coughing into our handkerchiefs, pulling goggles off our heads, and suddenly seeing not lamps, shadowy caverns, and sheets of dampness in the tunnels, but the trees and houses, with one room and a shower, of the neighborhood they'd built for us to sleep in and whose lanes were scoured by packs of dogs.

In Johannesburg, when I flew under the earth amid a flock of black men, each with a pickax and a light on his helmet, it initially seemed strange to me that the departed didn't take advantage of the elevator to return, in their wedding clothes and with spikenard in their arms, to the city where they were born, to sneak in through the kitchen door and peek into the pots on the stove. In Johannesburg it surprised me that they didn't want to go back to sleeping in their unmade beds or to working in the breweries or ceramicware factories, twirling their tuxes and bridal gowns amid co-workers who wouldn't even notice their smiles, until I understood, daughter, the dead people's fear that their families—already used to not having them, to missing them, to not being burdened by their final illnesses— would no longer receive them now that their money and furniture had been divvied up and the contents of their private letters divulged, the fear that the family would refuse to receive the censure of their silence, and perhaps it is because of this discretion, this reserve, this fear, that your mother won't leave her plot in Lourenço Marques to come and be here with us, with you, me, your aunt, and the sucker who pays our rent and groceries so that he can see the pans rattle on their nails when the trains of Alcântara rush by.

In Johannesburg, in 1936, I flew under the earth pulling gold out of the walls for fourteen hours a day, and on Sundays I took a break from being a bird, I sat in a chair in the canteen verandah, with a dozen bottles of beer to help me forget Monção, listening to the insects that buzzed in the grass and gazing at the clouds that arrived from the sea, while kids drummed on cans in the black encampment patrolled by policemen on horseback, and in my memory the Minho region was a terra-cotta Christmas manger, with its river that flowed through willowy slopes and separated me from Spain, with its tiny villages, the stone houses with jalousies and coats of arms shimmering in the sun, and oxen whose flanks sweltered in the August heat on fields that would soon be plowed, and the beer bottles were emptied, the African night snuffed out my childhood, and I rose from the chair, stumbling on the cans, stumbling on the policemen's horses, and stumbling on the encampment's refuse and stench as I sought the shack of a mixed-blooded Senegalese woman who was older than me

(back when people older than me existed),

a woman who cleaned offices at the mine's administration building and who received me on her mat surrounded by oil wicks, protecting me from homesickness for Monção, from thunderstorms, and from liver trouble with the palms of her hands.

I had been flying for ten years under the earth, far below the roots of mango trees and the fancy suits and shoes of the departed who hovered close to the sky of tombstones that kept me from ever seeing the stars, when a cousin of mine, a warehouse manager for customs in Mozambique, got me a job in Lourenço Marques as a longshoreman, loading and unloading crates of fruit, machine parts, broods of penguins, and midget prostitutes for the bars catering to colonists in the vicinity of the beach, where the gin-laced water made the fish tipsy. I never again flew under the earth in Johannesburg, but when I doze off in the living room after lunch, sometimes I still hear the dead who didn't dare rise to the surface.

I never again flew under the earth, because on a Sunday in November at a poor people's wake in a hovel on the island I met your mother, drinking vermouth next to a coffin in which the dead man's hands clasped a rose on top of his stomach while we smothered in our flannels, passing the bottle back and forth and talking while gazing, through the open door, at the baobabs that sprang from out of the low tide and at the flowers now hidden now unveiled by the waves, dripping dew from their stems. One week later I was married to the corpse's daughter, who spent all her time at the window, contemplating the Indian Ocean's trawlers and freighters and the whale that had gone off course and beached on the shore, where it was transforming into a structure of teeth and bones. She contemplated the trawlers and freighters day after day without talking to me, without talking to anyone, without answering questions, interested in nothing, forgetting to eat, to bathe, to comb her hair, to change her clothes, to sweep the house, forgetting you crying in your crib and your bottles scattered on the floor, and forgetting my needs as a man, until she was finally hauled off to an insane asylum on the northern edge of town, where the maniacs, wearing nightshirts, were tied to posts just like goats in the Minho region. I visited the asylum three or four times, on Fridays when returning home from the docks, and a nun led me to a basement where I found your mother staring through cracks in the wall at the sea, at the Indian Ocean's trawlers and freighters en route to Timor or Japan, staring at the sea in a cellar full of patients to whom attendants applied cupping glasses behind folding screens. She didn't ask about you or about me, she didn't complain about anything, didn't talk, didn't even veer her gaze when I stood right in front of her, and now that I'm old and death is gnawing my backbone and hardening my arteries, it occurs to me, when she comes to mind, that we all fly as best we can, however we can, I pushing mine cars through tunnels under Johannesburg, your mother in a nuthouse, drilling holes in the walls with her eyes to see the trawlers, you in the gillyflower cloud of your disease, and the clod who lives with us strolling in the backyard, disheveling the cabbages with the tip of his shoe and sniffing out the night with his idiotic smile.

We all fly however we can, or so I see it, I whose legs are so bad I don't even leave the apartment, I who expend miles of effort just to make the trip from my bedroom to the bathroom and back, I whom no friend, no godson, no former co-worker, and no cousin ever comes to visit, I who argue the whole blessed day with my sister to make sure I'm still breathing, to make sure I can still talk, to make sure I'm still alive, we all fly however we can, and perhaps your mother has kept on flying down in Africa since we left her to come to Lisbon, in the brouhaha of independence, perhaps she still flies among the freighters of the Indian Ocean, perhaps the civil war has spared the hospital on the northern edge of town where patients are tied to posts just like Minho goats, perhaps the whale's bones and teeth are still there on the beach,

the whale I sometimes dream about after supper, in front of the TV, imagining the waves of Lourenço Marques and the hovel on the island, imagining your grandfather, with his hands clasping a rose on top of his stomach, and us standing nearby, smothering in flannel, passing the bottle back and forth and talking while staring, through the open door, at the baobabs that sprang from out of the low tide, at women squatting under the palm trees, and at the vastness of the sunset, because as faces and voices collide on the screen and I hear you yelling in your room at the ninny who lives with us, I simultaneously dream of the baobabs, daughter, as I also dream of the willows in Monção,

as I also remember taking leave of your mother the day before I set sail for Lisbon, I remember taking a taxi through a plundered Lourenço Marques, looking out of the backseat window at the furniture on the streets and feeling completely indifferent, because I never liked Mozambique, I never liked all those blacks, the heat, the rain, I never liked the sudden fevers, the geckos, the snakes, or the silence following the storms, they could bomb wherever they liked, including the port, including my neighborhood, including my own possessions, and not one nerve would twitch with regret, because to hell with Mozambique, to hell with mango trees, to hell with the colonists, to hell with everything,

and so I walked into the hospital full of glee, thinking, Any day now Africa will be finished, hooray, any day now it'll vanish from the map with a bang, the nun with sandals came to get me at reception, I approached your mother, who had gotten thin and whose hair was starting to go white,

I approached your mother while repeating to myself, Any day now Africa will be finished, hooray, and the nun, speaking Spanish, scolded an old lady who had wet her bed, I heard the grenades downtown that were transforming Lourenço Marques into a scene of ruins, the old lady was wheezing with the aid of an oxygen bottle, I said to your mother, "I'm going to Portugal, Noemia," and she kept her eye on the wall, observing the trawlers with all of the interest that she never showed me,

I said, "I sold the house, Noemia, I'm taking our daughter with me," the old lady tensed her limbs, shook with a gasp, and became still, the nun unhooked the oxygen, another crazy woman, on all fours, tried to rip her mattress, and I said to your mother, "This is the last time I'll see you, Noemia,"

a cannonball whistled over the hospital, the ceiling light went out, and to myself I gloated, At last Mozambique will vanish into thin air, and meanwhile they'd already whisked the old lady out of the basement, and meanwhile the nun was scolding another madwoman who was shrieking, and neither your mother nor I was sorry to separate, she thinking only of the sea and I dying to get out of there, though I did reach out my arm to shake her hand or caress her shoulder, and I did think about giving her a kiss, it wouldn't be that hard, a measly kiss, we did after all live together for twelve years, and perhaps, daughter, she's still there in Africa, perhaps she's the one who now gets scolded for wetting her bed, perhaps she's the one they'll unhook from the oxygen, I didn't shake her hand, I didn't caress her shoulder, and I didn't kiss her, I walked to the exit without nostalgia, without regret, though I did, who knows why, turn around on the first step and look at your mother, staring at the wall with her usual intensity, counting up the trawlers on the wharf.

We all fly however we can, that's my theory, and I came back to Portugal to fly under the earth, but in the Minho there are no tunnels where one can push ore-filled wagons, there are no canteens, no neighborhoods for workers, no sounds of cans being drummed on Sundays, just small farms that grow onions, coriander, tomatoes, just water singing in the moss. Not in the Minho, not in Trás-os-Montes, not in Lisbon, and not in the Algarve, because there's no room in this country for flying under its statues and bridges, and yet, after a lot of searching, I did find in the Beira region an elevator to the earth's core, so I put on my helmet, pulled the lever, and was taken by rusty pulleys and cables down an unlit shaft, arriving at a platform where my steps echoed as in an empty theater. The light on my helmet revealed tools, spools of wire, pieces of track, and a mining car lying upside down in the lividness of an icy morning. At the mouth of the tunnels, wolframite rocks stubbornly waited for the shovel that would remove them, the walls were covered by the beards of lichens that thrive in soulless tunnels, and there was a second elevator, obstructed by a foreman, on which bundles and sacks were being loaded. Prevented from flying, I returned to the surface by the jogs and jolts of an ailing motor, unnerved by the cries of the bats that my helmet light frightened, and I stepped out onto an open land where olive trees leaned toward a churchless village with granite-paved alleys in between the buildings. The carcass of a small truck was decaying on a path, a partridge disappeared into the woods, the clouds were sailing to Spain, a boy grazed cattle among thistles, and a perfectly still kite flashed its aluminum wings. Walking downhill, I found a tavern where farmers got drunk without a word, a tavern with two casks and a blackboard where the wine debts were written in chalk, I bought a liter of brandy from the runty barman who was busy beating a mouse with his broom, I scrambled back up the slope and leaned against the truck's mudguard, at the entrance to the mine. The calves approached, asthmatically sweating, a tractor roared on the other side of the hill, and the kite suddenly swooped down on a group of startled chickens. I finished off the bottle, threw it into my bag, reached the door, put on my helmet, switched on the helmet light, jumped onto the elevator platform without a pick or any ropes at my waist, and vanished down the shaft, determined to fly as fly can under the earth.

DARCEY STEINKE

✄

FROM *Suicide Blonde* [2000]

Was it the bourbon or the dye fumes that made the pink walls quiver like vaginal lips? An acidy scent ribboned the pawed tub, fingered up the shower curtain. My vision was liquid and various as a lava lamp. In the mirror I saw the scar from the blackberry bramble that had caught my chin and scratched a hairline curve to my forehead. It was hardly noticeable, but left the impression that my face was cracked. Taking another sip of bourbon, I put on the plastic gloves and began parting my hair at the roots. As the dye snaked out there was a faint sucking sound, like soil pulling water, and I wondered: if I were brave enough to slit my wrists would I bother to dye my hair?

This is what happened: all day yesterday Bell had stared out the window, smoking cigarettes. There were his usual reasons—his father, no acting jobs, that he was getting ugly and old. Plus there was Kevin to moon over. He eyed the eggshell envelope of Kevin's wedding invitation and stared out the window for hours, his face vaguely twitching as he moved from one memory to the next. His melancholy made me think he was getting sick of living with me. And this, in turn, made me want to please him, to show him I was not one of his worries. So when he went walking I put on my black teddy and arranged myself on the futon. Looking at my breasts covered in lace flowers, I thought I seemed overly anxious, like a Danish or a little excitable dog. I looked desperate . . . using the one thing that would keep him near. It seemed manipulative, even if it was an attempt to jerk him from his melancholy. Men are never more appealing than when they brood.

Bell came in and walked to the foot of the bed. His eyes narrowed with lusty admiration for my forwardness. He lay over me and said, "I'm in charge now." But when he didn't release his weight I asked him if he was going to take off his clothes. "You seem to want me to," he said. I blushed and asked him if he felt bullied, told him now he knew how women felt. "You take off that," he said, stretching the lace of the teddy. I rolled it down and then adamantly pulled his shirt off. There was something hard in me that wanted him, no matter how awkward it was going to be. We kissed in a distracted way. Eventually, he turned his head, as if watching a bird move across the horizon. I saw dark continents under the paint of the walls beyond his profile.

"I'm bored," he said.

I sat up on the edge of the bed, then walked to the closet. Shifting the hanging clothes, I felt my hands already beginning to shake. I dressed and went into the kitchen. There was a taste of pennies in my mouth, a fierce nausea and tinny rawness, like the moment after you break a bone.

Bell sat in the dark at the painted table by the window. Occasionally the streetlight would show a wisp of cigarette smoke, his face dissected by crossing panes of light, his eyes clear and vacant like a cat's.

"I have to get more cigarettes," he said.

He didn't sound mean, just sullen. And I couldn't tell whether he was falling clunkily out of love with me, or if, as he claimed, it was just his usual reticence. Sometimes I suspected he was stunted, not capable of predictable human emotions. Last week he had laughed at a tourist couple separated by the BART train doors. I imagined a wire grid behind the skin of his forehead and a cold metallic look in his eyes. Of course it was only my imagination, but the sensation was terrifying, like finding out your lover is a killer.

Now he'd been gone twenty-four hours. For a while I had found his habit of floating off charming, but to appreciate this suddenly seemed masochistic. I didn't want to be one of those women addicted to indifference.

I peeled down my gloves and threw them gingerly, like used condoms, into the trash. The teddy incident was terrifying because it exacerbated the sensation that my feminine power was diminishing, trickling like drops of milk from a leaky pitcher. I wrapped my hair in a towel. The way I looked reminded me of some clichéd floundering female, so I took off my robe and lay across the couch, a better spot to watch shadows gather in the fleshy green fingers of the big jade plant. He'd inherited it from the last inhabitants of the apartment, because **it** wouldn't fit through the door when they moved. Near the plant was a cedar wall panel with a Japanese scene. Bell's boa hung on a hook beside his film stills; blurry body gestures from a super-8 film Bell made years ago. There were lots of little things: the blue glass lamp, the leopard with eyes that glowed, empty wine bottles, brass goblets, postcards of Europe from former lovers, candles and incense on a special table with a linen cloth, along with Bell's crucifixes, saints, Hindu gods, a GI Joe doll, obsidian voodoo beads, a dog's skull and an African mask of an antelope.

The window looked over Bush Street and toward the staggered roofs of Nob Hill, slanted like some Middle Eastern capital. The penthouse terraces had exotic French doors, miniature lemon trees and lacy wrought-iron furniture. On one there was a green fountain; another, on warm days, had a stand with a cockatiel. Above it all shone the neon Hotel Huntington sign, drenching our room with wavering green light.

My body was like a part of the room, a chair or a vase. I remembered the first time I saw my mother naked. She stood before a mirror, pulled at her hips, pressing her stomach, checking as I was now for signs of decay. The female body, I thought, has the capacity for such exquisiteness and such horror. I sat up to drink, but the bourbon spilled and trickled over my breasts, running all the way down to form a puddle in my navel.

Watching my body I had the sensation it was the same as Bell's. Images came fast: an expressive hand gesture, his smell—wet dirt and hand-rolled cigarettes—how his features were large and most beautiful when he was meditative, how in certain light his skin paled so that it looked blue, how he seemed at those times like a creature and I half expected to see wings appear on his shoulder blades.

In temperament Bell was not so much exotic as sophisticatedly adolescent. He had intellectualized youth's themes, perfected and lyricized them. And this core of exquisite longing was his excuse for brooding, for his erratic behavior, and the fuel for his philosophy of life's emptiness and the cult of pleasure. But Bell wasn't really immature, just trapped in some premature state, like a beetle whose back is all the more vivid because the last homogenizing stage to adulthood is never reached.

The clock ticked loud; it seemed to mock me with its pointy fingers and monotonous rhythyms. I took a swig from the bottle and realized I was drunk. My thoughts were jagged and I had the sensation that my life was exactly half over. It started with a tingle in the back of my skull that made me shiver, then spread over my head like a hood. But I've never felt any different. And I knew my memories, childhood or otherwise, were simply times I rose up into consciousness and was intensely myself. I heard the hum I always do when a memory is encasing itself and I recognized that sound as my particular and continual way of being alive.

My hair stunk up the whole apartment. I cracked the window and Bell's boa expanded with air. In the bathroom, the porcelain tub was cool to the touch. I adjusted the water, pulled the towel from my head and then got in, kneeling on all fours. My breasts swung down, reminding me of the utilitarian tits of mammals. And through the scope of cleavage I could see the hair between my thighs. The tiny black curls seemed scrawny, even obscene. Water beat on my hair. The bleach was strong. My face became prickly and warm and I realized that even though I was alone, I felt embarrassed. The acidic residue backed up, biting into my knees. *I am dyeing my hair to get Bell back,* I thought, *and because the whole world loves a blonde.* The bright light made the room stark, soap flecked into my eyes and I felt a rising frazzled sensation that always means I'm going to cry. The water ran clear down the drain. When I stood, my hair was steaming, tangled together in clumps like pale shiny snakes.

I moved, dripping through the dark apartment, to the window. The hotel sign blazing through the evening fog. Its aura occasionally flared out like a sunspot and I could feel the power spark into me through the thousand roots of my scalp, each one now flaunting a golden hair.

SHERMAN ALEXIE

❦

"The Toughest Indian in the World"
FROM *The Toughest Indian in the World* [2001]

Being a Spokane Indian, I only pick up Indian hitchhikers. I learned this particular ceremony from my father, a Coeur d'Alene, who always stopped for those twentieth-century aboriginal nomads who refused to believe the salmon were gone. I don't know what they believed in exactly, but they wore hope like a bright shirt.

My father never taught me about hope. Instead, he continually told me that our salmon—our hope—would never come back, and though such lessons may seem cruel, I know enough to cover my heart in any crowd of white people.

"They'll kill you if they get the chance," my father said. "Love you or hate you, white people will shoot you in the heart. Even after all these years, they'll still smell the salmon on you, the dead salmon, and that will make white people dangerous."

All of us, Indian and white, are haunted by salmon.

When I was a boy, I leaned over the edge of one dam or another—perhaps Long Lake or Little Falls or the great gray dragon known as the Grand Coulee—and watched the ghosts of the salmon rise from the water to the sky and become constellations.

For most Indians, stars are nothing more than white tombstones scattered across a dark graveyard.

But the Indian hitchhikers my father picked up refused to admit the existence of sky, let alone the possibility that salmon might be stars. They were common people who believed only in the thumb and the foot. My father envied those simple Indian hitchhikers. He wanted to change their minds about salmon; he wanted to break open their hearts and see the future in their blood. He loved them.

In 1975 or '76 or '77, driving along one highway or another, my father would point out a hitchhiker standing beside the road a mile or two in the distance.

"Indian," he said if it was an Indian, and he was never wrong, though I could never tell if the distant figure was male or female, let alone Indian or not.

If a distant figure happened to be white, my father would drive by without comment.

That was how I learned to be silent in the presence of white people.

The silence is not about hate or pain or fear. Indians just like to believe that white people will vanish, perhaps explode into smoke, if they are ignored enough times. Perhaps a thousand white families are still waiting for their sons and daughters to return home, and can't recognize them when they float back as morning fog.

"We better stop," my mother said from the passenger seat. She was one of those Spokane women who always wore a purple bandanna tied tightly around her head.

These days, her bandanna is usually red. There are reasons, motives, traditions behind the choice of color, but my mother keeps them secret.

"Make room," my father said to my siblings and me as we sat on the floor in the cavernous passenger area of our blue van. We sat on carpet samples because my father had torn out the seats in a sober rage not long after he bought the van from a crazy white man.

I have three brothers and three sisters now. Back then, I had four of each. I missed one of the funerals and cried myself sick during the other one.

"Make room," my father said again—he said everything twice—and only then did we scramble to make space for the Indian hitchhiker.

Of course, it was easy enough to make room for one hitchhiker, but Indians usually travel in packs. Once or twice, we picked up entire all-Indian basketball teams, along with their coaches, girlfriends, and cousins. Fifteen, twenty Indian strangers squeezed into the back of a blue van with nine wide-eyed Indian kids.

Back in those days, I loved the smell of Indians, and of Indian hitchhikers in particular. They were usually in some stage of drunkenness, often in need of soap and a towel, and always ready to sing.

Oh, the songs! Indian blues bellowed at the highest volumes. We called them "49s," those cross-cultural songs that combined Indian lyrics and rhythms with country-and-western and blues melodies. It seemed that every Indian knew all the lyrics to every Hank Williams song ever recorded. Hank was our Jesus, Patsy Cline was our Virgin Mary, and Freddy Fender, George Jones, Conway Twitty, Loretta Lynn, Tammy Wynette, Charley Pride, Ronnie Milsap, Tanya Tucker, Marty Robbins, Johnny Horton, Donna Fargo, and Charlie Rich were our disciples.

We all know that nostalgia is dangerous, but I remember those days with a clear conscience. Of course, we live in different days now, and there aren't as many Indian hitchhikers as there used to be.

Now, I drive my own car, a 1998 Toyota Camry, the best-selling automobile in the United States, and therefore the one most often stolen. *Consumer Reports* has named it the most reliable family sedan for sixteen years running, and I believe it.

In my Camry, I pick up three or four Indian hitchhikers a week. Mostly men. They're usually headed home, back to their reservations or somewhere close to their reservations. Indians hardly ever travel in a straight line, so a Crow Indian might hitchhike west when his reservation is back east in Montana. He has some people to see in Seattle, he might explain if I ever asked him. But I never ask Indians their reasons for hitchhiking. All that matters is this: They are Indians walking, raising their thumbs, and I am there to pick them up.

At the newspaper where I work, my fellow reporters think I'm crazy to pick up hitchhikers. They're all white and never stop to pick up anybody, let alone an Indian. After all, we're the ones who write the stories and headlines: HITCHHIKER KILLS HUSBAND AND WIFE, MISSING GIRL'S BODY FOUND, RAPIST STRIKES AGAIN. If I really tried, maybe I could explain to them why I pick up any Indian, but who wants to try? Instead, if they ask I just give them a smile and turn back to my computer. My coworkers smile back and laugh loudly. They're always laughing loudly at me, at one another, at themselves, at goofy typos in the newspapers, at the idea of hitchhikers.

I dated one of them for a few months. Cindy. She covered the local courts: speeding tickets and divorces, drunk driving and embezzlement. Cindy firmly believed in the who-what-where-when-why-and-how of journalism. In daily conversation, she talked like she was writing the lead of her latest story. Hell, she talked like that in bed.

"How does that feel?" I asked, quite possibly the only Indian man who has ever asked that question.

"I love it when you touch me there," she answered. "But it would help if you rubbed it about thirty percent lighter and with your thumb instead of your middle finger. And could you maybe turn the radio to a different station? KYZY would be good. I feel like soft jazz will work better for me right now. A minor chord, a C or G-flat, or something like that. Okay, honey?"

During lovemaking, I would get so exhausted by the size of her erotic vocabulary that I would fall asleep before my orgasm, continue pumping away as if I were awake, and then regain consciousness with a sudden start when I finally did come, more out of reflex than passion.

Don't get me wrong. Cindy is a good one, cute and smart, funny as hell, a good catch no matter how you define it, but she was also one of those white women who date only brown-skinned guys. Indians like me, black dudes, Mexicans, even a few Iranians. I started to feel like a trophy, or like one of those entries in a personal ad. I asked Cindy why she never dated pale boys.

"White guys bore me," she said. "All they want to talk about is their fathers."

"What do brown guys talk about?" I asked her.

"Their mothers," she said and laughed, then promptly left me for a public defender who was half Japanese and half African, a combination that left Cindy dizzy with the interracial possibilities.

Since Cindy, I haven't dated anyone. I live in my studio apartment with the ghosts of two dogs, Felix and Oscar, and a laptop computer stuffed with bad poems, the aborted halves of three novels, and some three-paragraph personality pieces I wrote for the newspaper.

I'm a features writer, and an Indian at that, so I get all the shit jobs. Not the dangerous shit jobs or the monotonous shit jobs. No. I get to write the articles designed to please the eye, ear, and heart. And there is no journalism more soul-endangering to write than journalism that aims to please.

So it was with reluctance that I climbed into my car last week and headed down Highway 2 to write some damn pleasant story about some damn pleasant people. Then I saw the Indian hitchhiker standing beside the road. He looked the way Indian hitchhikers usually look. Long, straggly black hair. Brown eyes and skin. Missing a couple of teeth. A bad complexion that used to be much worse. Crooked nose that had been broken more than once. Big, misshapen ears. A few whiskers masquerading as a mustache. Even before he climbed into my car I could tell he was tough. He had some serious muscles that threatened to rip through his blue jeans and denim jacket. When he was in the car, I could see his hands up close, and they told his whole story. His fingers were twisted into weird, permanent shapes, and his knuckles were covered with layers of scar tissue.

"Jeez," I said. "You're a fighter, enit?"

I threw in the "enit," a reservation colloquialism, because I wanted the fighter to know that I had grown up on the rez, in the woods, with every Indian in the world.

The hitchhiker looked down at his hands, flexed them into fists. I could tell it hurt him to do that.

"Yeah," he said. "I'm a fighter."

I pulled back onto the highway, looking over my shoulder to check my blind spot.

"What tribe are you?" I asked him, inverting the last two words in order to sound as aboriginal as possible.

"Lummi," he said. "What about you?"

"Spokane."

"I know some Spokanes. Haven't seen them in a long time."

He clutched his backpack in his lap like he didn't want to let it go for anything. He reached inside a pocket and pulled out a piece of deer jerky. I recognized it by the smell.

"Want some?" he asked.

Sure.

It had been a long time since I'd eaten jerky. The salt, the gamy taste. I felt as Indian as Indian gets, driving down the road in a fast car, chewing on jerky, talking to an indigenous fighter.

"Where you headed?" I asked.

"Home. Back to the rez."

I nodded my head as I passed a big truck. The driver gave us a smile as we went by. I tooted the horn.

"Big truck," said the fighter.

I haven't lived on my reservation for twelve years. But I live in Spokane, which is only an hour's drive from the rez. Still, I hardly ever go home. I don't know why not. I don't think about it much, I guess, but my mom and dad still live in the same house where I grew up. My brothers and sisters, too. The ghosts of my two dead siblings share an apartment in the converted high school. It's just a local call from Spokane to the rez, so I talk to all of them once or twice a week. Smoke signals courtesy of U.S. West Communications. Sometimes they call me up to talk about the stories they've seen that I've written for the newspaper. Pet pigs and support groups and science fairs. Once in a while, I used to fill in for the obituaries writer when she was sick. Then she died, and I had to write her obituary.

"How far are you going?" asked the fighter, meaning how much closer was he going to get to his reservation than he was now.

"Up to Wenatchee," I said. "I've got some people to interview there."

"Interview? What for?"

"I'm a reporter. I work for the newspaper."

"No," said the fighter, looking at me like I was stupid for thinking he was stupid. "I mean, what's the story about?"

"Oh, not much. There's two sets of twins who work for the fire department. Human-interest stuff, you know?"

"Two sets of twins, enit? That's weird."

He offered me more deer jerky, but I was too thirsty from the salty meat, so I offered him a Pepsi instead.

"Don't mind if I do," he said.

"They're in a cooler on the backseat," I said. "Grab me one, too."

He maneuvered his backpack carefully and found room enough to reach into the backseat for the soda pop. He opened my can first and handed it to me. A friendly gesture for a stranger. I took a big mouthful and hiccuped loudly.

"That always happens to me when I drink cold things," he said.

We sipped slowly after that. I kept my eyes on the road while he stared out the window into the wheat fields. We were quiet for many miles.

"Who do you fight?" I asked as we passed through another anonymous small town.

"Mostly Indians," he said. "Money fights, you know? I go from rez to rez, fighting the best they have. Winner takes all."

"Jeez, I never heard of that."

"Yeah, I guess it's illegal."

He rubbed his hands together. I could see fresh wounds.

"Man," I said. "Those fights must be rough."

The fighter stared out the window. I watched him for a little too long and almost drove off the road. Car horns sounded all around us.

"Jeez," the fighter said. "Close one, enit?"

"Close enough," I said.

He hugged his backpack more tightly, using it as a barrier between his chest and the dashboard. An Indian hitchhiker's version of a passenger-side air bag.

"Who'd you fight last?" I asked, trying to concentrate on the road.

"Some Flathead," he said. "In Arlee. He was supposed to be the toughest Indian in the world."

"Was he?"

"Nah, no way. Wasn't even close. Wasn't even tougher than me."

He told me how big the Flathead kid was, way over six feet tall and two hundred and some pounds. Big buck Indian. Had hands as big as this and arms as big as that. Had a chin like a damn buffalo. The fighter told me that he hit the Flathead kid harder than he ever hit anybody before.

"I hit him like he was a white man," the fighter said. "I hit him like he was two or three white men rolled into one."

But the Flathead kid would not go down, even though his face swelled up so bad that he looked like the Elephant Man. There were no referees, no judge, no bells to signal the end of the round. The winner was the Indian still standing. Punch after punch, man, and the kid would not go down.

"I was so tired after a while," said the fighter, "that I just took a step back and watched the kid. He stood there with his arms down, swaying from side to side like some toy, you know? Head bobbing on his neck like there was no bone at all. You couldn't even see his eyes no more. He was all messed up."

"What'd you do?" I asked.

"Ah, hell, I couldn't fight him no more. That kid was planning to die before he ever went down. So I just sat on the ground while they counted me out. Dumb Flathead kid didn't even know what was happening. I just sat on the ground while they raised his hand. While all the winners collected their money and all the losers cussed me out. I just sat there, man."

"Jeez," I said. "What happened next?"

"Not much. I sat there until everybody was gone. Then I stood up and decided to head for home. I'm tired of this shit. I just want to go home for a while. I got enough money to last me a long time. I'm a rich Indian, you hear? I'm a rich Indian."

The fighter finished his Pepsi, rolled down his window, and pitched the can out. I almost protested, but decided against it. I kept my empty can wedged between my legs.

"That's a hell of a story," I said.

"Ain't no story," he said. "It's what happened."

"Jeez," I said. "You would've been a warrior in the old days, enit? You would've been a killer. You would have stolen everybody's goddamn horses. That would've been you. You would've been it."

I was excited. I wanted the fighter to know how much I thought of him. He didn't even look at me.

"A killer," he said. "Sure."

We didn't talk much after that. I pulled into Wenatchee just before sundown, and the fighter seemed happy to be leaving me.

"Thanks for the ride, cousin," he said as he climbed out. Indians always call each other cousin, especially if they're strangers.

"Wait," I said.

He looked at me, waiting impatiently.

I wanted to know if he had a place to sleep that night. It was supposed to get cold. There was a mountain range between Wenatchee and his reservation.

Big mountains that were dormant volcanoes, but that could all blow up at any time. We wrote about it once in the newspaper. Things can change so quickly. So many emergencies and disasters that we can barely keep track. I wanted to tell him how much I cared about my job, even if I had to write about small-town firemen. I wanted to tell the fighter that I pick up all Indian hitchhikers, young and old, men and women, and get them a little closer to home, even if I can't get them all the way. I wanted to tell him that the night sky was a grave-yard. I wanted to know if he was the toughest Indian in the world.

"It's late," I finally said. "You can crash with me, if you want."

He studied my face and then looked down the long road toward his reservation.

"Okay," he said. "That sounds good."

We got a room at the Pony Soldier Motel, and both of us laughed at the irony of it all. Inside the room, in a generic watercolor hanging above the bed, the U.S. Cavalry was kicking the crap out of a band of renegade Indians.

"What tribe you think they are?" I asked the fighter.

"All of them," he said.

The fighter crashed on the floor while I curled up in the uncomfortable bed. I couldn't sleep for the longest time. I listened to the fighter talk in his sleep. I stared up at the water-stained ceiling. I don't know what time it was when I finally drifted off, and I don't know what time it was when the fighter got into bed with me. He was naked and his penis was hard. I felt it press against my back as he snuggled up close to me, reached inside my underwear, and took my penis in his hand. Neither of us said a word. He continued to stroke me as he rubbed himself against my back. That went on for a long time. I had never been that close to another man, but the fighter's callused fingers felt better than I would have imagined if I had ever allowed myself to imagine such things.

"This isn't working," he whispered. "I can't come."

Without thinking, I reached around and took the fighter's penis in my hand. He was surprisingly small.

"No," he said. "I want to be inside you."

"I don't know," I said. "I've never done this before."

"It's okay," he said. "I'll be careful. I have rubbers."

Without waiting for my answer, he released me and got up from the bed. I turned to look at him. He was beautiful and scarred. So much brown skin marked with bruises, badly healed wounds, and tattoos. His long black hair was unbraided and hung down to his thin waist. My slacks and dress shirt were folded and draped over the chair near the window. My shoes were sitting on the table. Blue light filled the room. The fighter bent down to his pack and searched for his condoms. For reasons I could not explain then and cannot explain now, I kicked off my underwear and rolled over on my stomach. I could not see him, but I could hear him breathing heavily as he found the condoms, tore open a package, and rolled one over his penis. He crawled onto the bed, between my legs, and slid a pillow beneath my belly.

"Are you ready?" he asked.

"I'm not gay," I said.

"Sure," he said as he pushed himself into me. He was small but it hurt more than I expected, and I knew that I would be sore for days afterward. But I wanted him to save me. He didn't say anything. He just pumped into me for a few minutes, came with a loud sigh, and then pulled out. I quickly rolled off the bed and went into the bathroom. I locked the door behind me and stood there in the dark. I smelled like salmon.

"Hey," the fighter said through the door. "Are you okay?"

"Yes," I said. "I'm fine."

A long silence.

"Hey," he said. "Would you mind if I slept in the bed with you?"

I had no answer to that.

"Listen," I said. "That Flathead boy you fought? You know, the one you really beat up? The one who wouldn't fall down?"

In my mind, I could see the fighter pummeling that boy. Punch after punch. The boy too beaten to fight back, but too strong to fall down.

"Yeah, what about him?" asked the fighter.

"What was his name?"

"His name?"

"Yeah, his name."

"Elmer something or other."

"Did he have an Indian name?"

"I have no idea. How the hell would I know that?"

I stood there in the dark for a long time. I was chilled. I wanted to get into bed and fall asleep.

"Hey," I said. "I think, I think maybe—well, I think you should leave now."

"Yeah," said the fighter, not surprised. I heard him softly singing as he dressed and stuffed all of his belongings into his pack. I wanted to know what he was singing, so I opened the bathroom door just as he was opening the door to leave. He stopped, looked at me, and smiled.

"Hey, tough guy," he said. "You were good."

The fighter walked out the door, left it open, and walked away. I stood in the doorway and watched him continue his walk down the highway, past the city limits. I watched him rise from earth to sky and become a new constellation. I closed the door and wondered what was going to happen next. Feeling uncomfortable and cold, I went back into the bathroom. I ran the shower with the hottest water possible. I stared at myself in the mirror. Steam quickly filled the room. I threw a few shadow punches. Feeling stronger, I stepped into the shower and searched my body for changes. A middle-aged man needs to look for tumors. I dried myself with a towel too small for the job. Then I crawled naked into bed. I wondered if I was a warrior in this life and if I had been a warrior in a previous life. Lonely and laughing, I fell asleep. I didn't dream at all, not one bit. Or perhaps I dreamed but remembered none of it. Instead, I woke early the next morning, before sunrise, and went out into the world. I walked past my car. I stepped onto the pavement, still warm from the previous day's sun. I started walking. In bare feet, I traveled upriver toward the place where I was born and will someday die. At that moment, if you had broken open my heart you could have looked inside and seen the thin white skeletons of one thousand salmon.

Acknowledgments

❧

Grove Press gratefully acknowledges the contributors and their representatives for granting permission to use the excerpts in this volume. All books were originally published by Grove Press on the dates provided in the text, except for the following:

The Monk, by Matthew G. Lewis, was originally published in 1796 (London: J. Bell).

"Must We Burn Sade?," by Simone de Beauvoir, was originally published in French in the December 1951 and January 1952 issues of *Les Temps Modernes*, under the title *"Faut-il brûler Sade?"*

Waiting for Godot, by Samuel Beckett, was originally published in French in 1952, under the title *En Attendant Godot* (Paris: Les Éditions de Minuit).

Molloy, by Samuel Beckett, was originally published in French in 1951, under the same title (Paris: Les Éditions de Minuit).

Notes and Counter Notes, by Eugène Ionesco, was originally published in French in 1962, under the title *Notes et contre-notes* (Paris: Librairie de Gallimard).

The Bald Soprano, by Eugène Ionesco, was originally published in French in 1954, in *Eugène Ionesco: Théâtre, Volume I* (Paris: Librairie de Gallimard).

The Theatre and Its Double, by Antonin Artaud, was originally published in French in 1938, in *Collection Métamorphoses* (Paris: Librairie de Gallimard).

In the Labyrinth, by Alain Robbe-Grillet, was originally published in French in 1959, under the title *Dans le labyrinthe* (Paris: Les Éditions de Minuit).

Moderato Cantabile, by Marguerite Duras, was originally published in French in 1958, under the same title (Paris: Les Éditions de Minuit).

Tropic of Cancer, by Henry Miller, was originally published in English in 1934, in an edition including the preface by Anaïs Nin (Paris: Obelisk).

Ficciones, by Jorge Luis Borges, was originally published in Spanish in 1956, under the same title (Buenos Aires: Emecé Editores).

My Life and Loves, by Frank Harris, was originally published in English in 1933 (Paris: Obelisk).

The Thief's Journal, by Jean Genet, was originally published in French in 1949, under the title *Journal du Voleur* (Paris: Librairie Gallimard).

The Homecoming, by Harold Pinter, was originally published in the United Kingdom in 1965 (London: Methuen & Co.).

Rosencrantz and Guildenstern Are Dead, by Tom Stoppard, was originally published in the United Kingdom in 1967 (London: Faber & Faber, Ltd.).

The Wretched of the Earth, by Frantz Fanon, was originally published in French in 1961, under the title *Les damnés de la terre* (Paris: François Maspero éditeur S.A.R.L.).

A Personal Matter, by Kenzaburo Oe, was originally published in Japanese in 1964, under the title *Kojinteki Na Taiken* (Tokyo: Shinchosa).

A Confederacy of Dunces, by John Kennedy Toole, was originally published in 1980 (Baton Rouge: Louisiana State University Press).

Kitchen, by Banana Yoshimoto, was originally published in Japanese in 1988, under the title *Kitchin* (Tokyo: Fukutake Publishing Co.).

The Magic of Blood, by Dagoberto Gilb, was originally published in 1993 (Santa Fe: University of New Mexico Press).

Airships, by Barry Hannah, was originally published in 1978 (New York: Alfred A. Knopf, Inc.).

The Painted Bird, by Jerzy Kosinski, was originally published in a second edition in 1976 (New York: Houghton Mifflin Company).

The Butcher, by Alina Reyes, was originally published in French in 1988, under the title *Le Boucher* (Paris: Éditions du Seuil).

The Magic Christian, by Terry Southern, was originally published in 1959 (London: Andre Deutsch Limited).

Great Apes, by Will Self, was originally published in 1997 (London: Bloomsbury Publishing).

The Passion, by Jeannette Winterson, was originally published in 1987 (London: Bloomsbury Publishing).

The Ultimate Intimacy, by Ivan Klíma, was originally published in Czech in 1996, under the title *Poslední stupeň důvernosti* (Prague: nakladatelství Hynek).

The Long Night of White Chickens, by Francisco Goldman, was originally published in 1992 (New York: Atlantic Monthly Press).

The Natural Order of Things, by Antonio Lobos Antunes, was originally published in Portuguese in 1992, under the title *A Ordem Natural das Coisas* (Lisbon: Publicações Dom Quixote).

Suicide Blonde, by Darcey Steinke, was originally published in 1992 (New York: Atlantic Monthly Press).

The Toughest Indian in the World, by Sherman Alexie, was originally published in 1999 (New York: Atlantic Monthly Press).